NEW

SHERLOCK
HOLMES

ADVENTURES

NEW

SHERLOCK
HOLMES

ADVENTURES

Edited by
Mike Ashley

CASTLE BOOKS

Originally published as

The Mammoth Book of New Sherlock Holmes Adventures

This edition published in 2004 by
CASTLE BOOKS ®
A division of Book Sales, Inc.
114 Northfield Avenue
Edison, NJ 08837

This edition published by arrangement with and permission of
Carroll & Graf Publishers, Inc.
161 William Street
New York, New York 10038

First published in the UK by Robinson Publishing 1997

First Carroll & Graf edition 1997

Collection and editorial material copyright © Mike Ashley 1997

Grateful acknowledgement is given to Dame Jean Conan Doyle for permission to use the Sherlock Holmes characters created by the late Sir Arthur Conan Doyle.

ISBN 0-7858-1880-4

Printed in the United States of America

CONTENTS

CONTENTS

CONTENTS

Foreword

Richard Lancelyn Green

One of the most famous opening paragraphs in a Sherlock Holmes story is that found in "Thor Bridge" (which was first published in the 1920s). Dr Watson says: "Somewhere in the vaults of the bank of Cox & Co., at Charing Cross, there is a travel-worn and battered tin dispatch-box with my name, John H. Watson, M.D., Late Indian Army, painted upon the lid. It is crammed with papers, nearly all of which are records of cases to illustrate the curious problems which Mr Sherlock Holmes had at various times to examine." Readers had already been offered tantalizing details of many unrecorded cases in preceding stories, but this confirmed that he had a "long row of year-books which fill a shelf, and there are the dispatch cases filled with documents". He rightly called it "a perfect quarry for the student, not only of crime, but of the social and official scandals of the late Victorian era". It is into these that the authors represented in the present volume have dipped.

The influence of Sherlock Holmes made itself felt within months of the publication of the first short stories in the *Strand Magazine.* There was plagiarism which achieved its apogee with Sexton Blake who had rooms in Baker Street, and there were rivals who knew they could succeed only by being different. The "Golden Age" of detective fiction was littered with a strange array of private inquiry agents who were fat, blind, Belgian or of the opposite sex. Yet for all their attempts at being different, they never entirely escaped the shadow of Sherlock Holmes. As Scotland Yard had discovered, his longest shots invariably hit their mark, and even when he was outwitted, as he was by Irene Adler, his reputation was enhanced.

It is the art of a great writer to leave the reader anxious for more, and Dr Watson was such a writer. He often erred on the side of discretion, and he intrigued the reader because of his less than perfect grasp of detail. Where his knowledge failed he resorted to imagination and was not unduly concerned when this led to contradictions and inconsistencies within the text. He introduced colour and variety and irrelevance, which added to the myth and gave the reader a picture which was sharp in its essentials, but blurred at the edges.

No reader has ever put down the stories believing that Watson had said the last word on the subject. For some there was an irresistible urge to parody the style and to play with the name of Sherlock Holmes (which lends itself well to mutations such as Shylock Bones, Sherluck Gnomes, Picklock Holes, or Sheerlecoq Omes). The parodies made fun of the contrasting characteristics of Holmes and Watson, between the infallible brain which could distinguish 144 types of cigarette ash or recognize clay and earth from the counties of England (something still denied to the most sophisticated computers of the late twentieth century) and the obtuseness of the all-admiring friend.

The greatest scope for other writers lay in the unrecorded, unfathomed and unfinished cases. When Watson made it known that Holmes had survived the struggle at the Reichenbach Falls, there were demands that he should furnish the public with details of the cases which he had already mentioned, and he proceeded to do so with "The Second Stain" (to which he had referred on two occasions). Even then there was an alternative literature provided by others, including major writers such as Bret Harte, and Mark Twain (who introduced Holmes into his late novel, *A Double-Barrelled Detective Story*).

The early apocryphal works did not profess to be part of the original 'canon', for the concept only developed after Ronald Knox had elevated the study of Sherlock Holmes to new and rarefied heights in 1911 with his famous satirical essay, "Studies in the Literature of Sherlock Holmes". This gave impetus to the serious study of the stories and raised the possibility that there was not one but two authors (as had been suggested in the writing of the *Odyssey*) or that Watson had described the early cases as they happened, but had invented the later ones to satisfy public demand. The new scholarship opened the way for others to take up their pens to continue the saga, while remaining faithful to their subject as had the story-tellers of old who created heroic deeds for Alexander the Great of which historians were previously unaware.

The apocryphal Sherlock Holmes story need not be a great detective story, but it has to be a convincing story of the great detective. The character is more important than the case. It is his method which appeals to the reader. It is the special relationship with Dr Watson, who holds up a mirror to nature and occasionally distorts the image to add glamour to the reflection. The additional stories should conform to the formula and yet should add variety. The purist might prefer the seemingly insignificant trifle that turns out to be important, and the humble and eccentric client often makes a better entrance at Baker Street than the representatives of the reigning houses of Europe or the emissaries of the Pope. The introduction of historical figures such as Oscar Wilde or Jack the Ripper is not always advisable as it could be said that they add an element of fiction to the self-contained world of Sherlock Holmes, and characters whose exploits have been documented by others sometimes have difficulty crossing the threshold at Baker Street. Watson could describe a case in which Sherlock Holmes outwitted Raffles, but it would not be the Raffles who is known to us through the writings of his friend, Bunny Manders. There again, there is no reason why Holmes's grandson should not ape his grandfather and form a working partnership with Dr Watson's granddaughter, but it is Dr Watson, and his work, who will always be most in demand. Whatever other cases remain in the battered dispatch box, readers are most anxious to have details of the cases which are known to them by name and which were solved by Sherlock Holmes.

This volume is exactly what is required. It contains an impressive array of cases which Watson mentioned and it has a scholarly status as it is arranged in chronological order with a connecting narrative which provides a biographical background. It is entertaining and informative, and is remarkable for the many distinguished writers who are among the contributors. It is a book which can be recommended and is in every sense a *magnum opus*.

Richard Lancelyn Green

ACKNOWLEDGEMENTS

Grateful acknowledgement is given to Dame Jean Conan Doyle for permission to use the Sherlock Holmes characters created by the late Sir Arthur Conan Doyle. My thanks also to Roger Johnson, Jon Lellenberg, Christopher Roden and R. Dixon Smith for their help and guidance during the preparation of this book, and to Richard Lancelyn Green for kindly providing the foreword. All of the stories in this volume are in copyright. The following acknowledgements are granted to the authors and their agents for permission to use their work.

"The Adventure of the Inertial Adjustor" © 1997 by Stephen Baxter. First publication, original to this anthology. Printed by permission of the author.

"The Adventure of the Amateur Mendicant Society" © 1996 by John Gregory Betancourt. This story has been revised. An earlier version appeared in *Resurrected Holmes*, edited by Marvin Kaye (New York: St Martin's Press, 1996). Printed by permission of the author.

"The Vanishing of the Atkinsons" © 1997 by Eric Brown. First publication, original to this anthology. Printed by permission of the author.

"The Adventure of the Fallen Star" © 1997 by Simon Clark. First publication, original to this anthology. Printed by permission of the author and the author's agent International Scripts Ltd.

"The Adventure of the Persecuted Painter" © 1997 by Basil Copper. First publication, original to this anthology. Printed by permission of the author.

"The Adventure of the Touch of God" © 1997 by Peter Crowther. First publication, original to this anthology. Printed by permission of the author.

"The Darlington Substitution Scandal" © 1997 by David Stuart Davies. First publication, original to this anthology. Printed by permission of the author.

"The Legacy of Rachel Howells" © 1994 by Michael Doyle.

Originally distributed privately in a limited edition for The Stormy Petrels of British Columbia, January 1994, and reprinted in *Canadian Holmes*, Autumn 1995. Reprinted by permission of the author.

"The Case of the Suicidal Lawyer" © 1997 by Martin Edwards. First publication, original to this anthology. Printed by permission of the author.

"The Adventure of the Bulgarian Diplomat" © 1997 by Zakaria Erzinçlioglu. First publication, original to this anthology. Printed by permission of the author.

"Foreword" © 1997 by Richard Lancelyn Green. First publication, original to this anthology. Printed by permission of the author.

"The Case of the Last Battle" © 1997 by L.B. Greenwood. First publication, original to this anthology. Printed by permission of the author.

"The Case of the Incumbent Invalid" © 1997 by Claire Griffen. First publication, original to this anthology. Printed by permission of the author.

"The Adventure of Vittoria the Circus Belle" © 1997 by Edward D. Hoch. First publication, original to this anthology. Printed by permission of the author.

"The Adventure of the Grace Chalice" © 1987 by Roger Johnson. Originally published in *The Sherlock Holmes Journal*, Winter 1987. Revised for publication in this anthology. Printed by permission of the author.

"The Adventure of the Suffering Ruler" © 1983 by H.R.F. Keating. First published in *John Creasey's Crime Collection 1983* edited by Herbert Harris (London: Victor Gollancz, 1983). Reprinted by permission of the author and the author's agent Peters, Fraser & Dunlop.

"The Repulsive Story of the Red Leech" © 1997 by David Langford. First publication, original to this anthology. Printed by permission of the author.

"The Enigma of the Warwickshire Vortex" © 1997 by F. Gwynplaine MacIntyre. First publication, original to this anthology. Printed by permission of the author.

"The Adventure of the Dorset Street Lodger" © 1997 by Michael Moorcock. First commercial publication, original to this anthology. Printed by permission of the author and the author's agent Curtis Brown Ltd.

"The Adventure of the Faithful Retainer" © 1997 by Amy Myers. First publication, original to this anthology. Printed by permission of the author and the author's agent, Dorian Literary Agency.

"The Mystery of the Addleton Curse" © 1997 by Barrie Roberts.

First publication, original to this anthology. Printed by permission of the author and the author's agent Laurence Pollinger Ltd.

"The Adventure of the Suspect Servant" © 1997 by Barbara Roden. First publication, original to this anthology. Printed by permission of the author.

"The Adventure of the Silver Buckle" © 1997 by Denis O. Smith. First publication, original to this anthology. Printed by permission of the author.

"The Case of the Sporting Squire" © 1997 by Guy N. Smith. First publication, original to this anthology. Printed by permission of the author.

"The Affray at the Kildare Street Club" © 1997 by Peter Tremayne. First publication, original to this anthology. Printed by permission of the author and the author's agent A.M. Heath & Co.

"The Adventure of the Parisian Gentleman" © 1997 by Robert Weinberg and Lois H. Gresh. First publication, original to this anthology. Printed by permission of the authors.

"The Bothersome Business of the Dutch Nativity" © 1997 by Derek Wilson. First publication, original to this anthology. Printed by permission of the author.

Introduction

THE LIFE AND ADVENTURES OF SHERLOCK HOLMES

For more years than I care to remember I have been researching the life of the first and best known of all private consulting detectives, Mr Sherlock Holmes. It has not been easy. Devotees of the Sherlock Holmes cases will know that his friend and colleague Dr John Watson kept an assiduous record of many of the cases after they first met in January 1881, but he was not involved in them all.

When Holmes was reflecting over his cases in the hours before his cataclysmic struggle with Professor Moriarty in "The Final Problem", he remarked to Watson that he had investigated over a thousand cases. That was in April 1891. In "The Adventure of the Solitary Cyclist" Watson comments that between 1894 and 1901 Holmes had been involved in every public case of any difficulty plus many hundreds of private cases. Watson goes on to say that "I have preserved very full notes of all these cases." Yet when you look at the standard omnibus volume of Sherlock Holmes you will find only fifty-six short stories and four novels, sixty cases in all. In writing up these cases Watson makes tantalizing passing references to others, such as the repulsive story of the red leech, or the singular adventures of the Grice Patersons on the island of Uffa, but though he kept notes of these stories he did not complete all of them as finished cases. Even then he refers to just short of a hundred cases, so that in total we know of only about 160 cases, which is likely to be less than a tenth of all of the cases Holmes investigated. How wonderful it would be to know about the others. That has been my life's work.

The obvious starting point was Watson's papers. He told us in "The Problem of Thor Bridge" that they were filed away in a despatch box stored in the vaults of the bank of Cox and Co., at Charing Cross. Imagine my horror when, many years ago, in attempting to gain access to these records I discovered two things. Firstly that Watson was clever and had stored only some of his records in that bank vault, and that others were hidden elsewhere. But more frustrating was that I had been pipped at the post. The

Cox Bank papers had already been collected by someone else and though he provided a name and identity for the purposes of the bank, I have never been able to trace him, and suspect that the identity he gave was false. Watson was fearful that his papers might be stolen. When he published the case of "The Veiled Lodger" in January 1927 he alerted the public to the fact that attempts had already been made to gain access to his papers and he gave a warning to one individual, whom he doesn't name, that facts would be revealed about him if he didn't desist. Occasionally stories purporting to be from these files have surfaced in books and magazines. Some may well be genuine, or at least give that appearance, but most are almost certainly false, written by those seeking to gain some reflected glory from the fame of Sherlock Holmes.

Over the years I have tracked down some of the original cases from papers at Scotland Yard, old newspaper files, and documents held in private archives. On rare moments I have stumbled across papers which almost certainly came from Watson's despatch box, but I fear that most of those records are hidden in one or more private collections, possibly not even in England, purchased, I dare say, for a phenomenal price.

The trail is complicated by many false avenues and windings. Not even Watson was helpful. Frequently in his published cases he disguised the names of individuals, for obvious reasons, and falsified dates and locations, so that when he recorded that Holmes was investigating such-and-such a case it was as likely that Holmes was somewhere else at that time involved in a very private affair. Watson did his job well in masking the trail, and it will probably never be fully uncovered.

However, the time has come for me to share the product of some of my research. It is far from complete, but for fear that something may happen to me or to my own papers, I thought it was right to place some of it in print. Perhaps the existence of this book may bring me into contact with others who have access to further papers. Who knows?

In this volume I have pieced together something of the investigations of Sherlock Holmes and have presented twenty-six new cases completed by fellow researchers who have helped me in my quest. I have endeavoured to show where these cases fit into Holmes's career and how they relate to the known cases. In an appendix at the end of this book I also provide a complete chronology of Holmes's life and known cases, including some of the other write-ups of his investigations where I believe there has been a genuine effort to get at the truth.

Let us begin our quest, therefore, and return to the early days of Sherlock Holmes.

Mike Ashley
May 1997

PART I: THE EARLY YEARS

There is precious little record of Holmes's early life. It is unusual that someone so famous could keep the details of his life so secret that it becomes necessary to think that it was deliberate. Holmes had little interest in the trivia of personal biography, so it is unlikely that he would have bothered to have disguised the trail. But others may certainly have done so in order to protect him, and thoughts turn immediately to his elder brother Mycroft Holmes who had considerable influence in government circles and could have easily pressed the right buttons in order to close whatever shutters were necessary.

We must therefore rely on what Watson himself tells us. In "His Last Bow", which takes place in August 1914, Watson refers to Holmes as "a tall, gaunt man of sixty". It is the only occasion where he mentions his age. We must be careful as he was describing Holmes in disguise as the Irish-American spy Altamont. Had Holmes aged himself or made himself look younger? We don't know. And did Watson mean precisely sixty, or was he in his sixtieth year – in other words fifty-nine? If we accept it at face value, and since no other clue is given as to Holmes's birthday, then we must conclude that Holmes was born in either 1853 or 1854, or at the latest in 1855. I prefer the earlier date because in "The Boscombe Valley Mystery" Holmes refers to himself as middle-aged which suggests forty-something. That story took place in 1889 or 1890 which would make Holmes's year of birth earlier than 1850, but middle-aged is an indeterminate phrase and we can assume that a birth year somewhere in the early 1850s is as close as we'll get. We may take some clue from the year in which Holmes retired, which was at the end of 1903. Did he do this on his fiftieth birthday? It would be an appropriate landmark.

Holmes came from a line of country squires but somewhere in his veins was the blood of the French artist Claude Vernet, from whose family Holmes also claimed descent. We do not know where Holmes was born, but his general dislike of the countryside suggests that he was raised somewhere remote, and as we shall see he certainly spent some of his youth in Ireland. This coupled with his reticence to discuss his childhood suggests that it might not have been happy, and we can imagine an almost reclusive child already intent upon his studies in logical deduction. Holmes was almost certainly educated at a private school before progressing to university.

It is at university that his abilities as a solver of puzzles came to the fore. Two of the recorded cases throw some light on Holmes's University days. "The Gloria Scott", Holmes tells us, was the first case in which he was engaged. He refers to the case again in "The Musgrave Ritual" saying that the Gloria Scott case "first turned my attention in the direction of the profession which has become my life's work." It is thus of some importance to date this investigation, but it is here that we first encounter Watson's masking of facts. We could put a rough dating on it on the assumption that Holmes went to university when he was about eighteen or nineteen, which would place it in the period 1868 to 1872, and he talks about it occurring after two years at university, or between 1870 and 1874. In "The Veiled Lodger" Watson tells us Holmes was in active practice for twenty-three years. Since he retired in 1903, counting back would bring us to 1880, but we must also deduct the years of the Great Hiatus between "The Final Problem" in April 1891 and Holmes's return in "The Empty House" in early 1894, a gap of three years. So he established himself as a consulting detective in 1877. We know from "The Musgrave Ritual" that Holmes set up his practice soon after university, so we can imagine he finished his university years around 1876. A span of university education from 1872 to 1876 therefore sounds realistic in the chronology and would place the Gloria Scott case in about 1874.

However, in the course of "The Gloria Scott" Holmes refers to events aboard the ship having taken place thirty years earlier in 1855, which would place the story in 1885. This has to be wrong, because Holmes and Watson met in 1881 by which time Holmes had been in practice for four years. Clearly there is some deliberate shifting of dates in this story, perhaps through Holmes's faulty record keeping (always possible, as he was not a great record-keeper of things he regarded as unimportant), or Watson's erroneous transcription of the case or, we should not forget, through Watson trying to hide the time of Holmes's university years.

In fact my own research has revealed two episodes that happened to Holmes while at university that have previously gone unrecorded. They reveal that Holmes's years at university were not without incident and it is not surprising that it has been difficult to tie him down, since he spent time at two universities. I am grateful to Peter Tremayne and Derek Wilson for their help in bringing the record of the episodes into their final form from scraps of evidence left by Watson. I have deliberately set the stories in reverse order of internal events because of the relative discovery of the episodes by Watson. The first happened during the period of Holmes's apparent death, whilst Watson learned of the second after Holmes's return. Here then, for the first time ever, are the earliest records of Sherlock Holmes.

THE BOTHERSOME BUSINESS OF THE DUTCH NATIVITY

Derek Wilson

The death of my dear friend, Sherlock Holmes, affected me more than a little and had I not had the demands of a growing medical practice and the care of a loving wife the loss which I, and indeed the nation, had suffered must have seriously undermined my constitution. For a long time I could scarcely bear it when my affairs took me to places where some of Holmes's greatest triumphs had been enacted or where together we had faced dangerous villains or petty scoundrels. As for Baker Street, I avoided it completely; always ordering cab drivers to proceed by some roundabout route when conveying me through that part of London.

Yet time, as has often been observed, is a healer. I shared that experience common to all bereaved people: the transformation of memories from dreams almost too painful to be endured into visitations of consolation. Increasingly I found myself turning over the leaves of my journals and the printed accounts of Sherlock Holmes's cases which I had been privileged to record. Much of the material I had garnered about my friend consisted of tantalizing scraps – hints about his earlier life and oblique references to cases of which I knew nothing. As the months passed more and more of my leisure time was spent in trying to arrange my memorabilia in some logical order so that I might obtain a grasp of the sweep of Holmes's life. I lost no opportunity of asking others who had known my friend for any details that might have eluded me and it was in this way that what I call the Bothersome Business of the Dutch Nativity came to my attention.

In the spring of 1893, my wife and I were invited to Oxford to spend a few days with the Hungerfords. Adrian Hungerford was a fellow of Grenville college and he and Augusta were distant relatives of Mary's. Despite Mary's insistence that I should enjoy meeting her cousins it was with no very great enthusiasm that I accompanied her from Paddington station on the short journey to England's most ancient centre of learning. As usual my beloved helpmeet was right. The Hungerfords were an intelligent and relaxed couple of middle years who gave us a welcome as warm as it was genuine.

It was on the second evening of our stay that Adrian Hungerford invited me to dine with him at his college. I enjoyed an excellent meal on the high table in Grenville's ancient hall over which I was able, with some effort, to hold up my end of an erudite conversation with the master and the dean. After dinner I retired with the dozen or so fellows to the senior combination room where, over the ritual of claret, port and cigars, discussion, somewhat to my relief, ran into less scholarly channels.

"Am I not right in thinking, Dr Watson, that you were at some time associated with that detective fellow . . . what was his name . . . Hutchings?" The speaker was a shrivelled little man enveloped in a rather gangrenous master's gown who had been earlier introduced to me as Blessingham.

"Holmes, Sherlock Holmes," Hungerford corrected before I had a chance to reply. "Watson helped him with several of his cases, isn't that so, John?" He turned to me with an apologetic smile. "You must forgive our isolationism, old man. We spend most of our time here behind a raised drawbridge protected from the more sensational doings of the outside world."

"Helped with several cases, did you say?" Blessingham, who was obviously hard of hearing, cupped a hand to his ear and leaned closer. "Well, you weren't here for his first case, were you?" He reached for the claret decanter, drained it into his glass and brandished it in the direction of a steward who hurried forward with a replacement.

"You refer, Sir, to the *Gloria Scott*, I assume," I said.

"Gloria who? Never heard of the woman." The old man gulped his wine. "No I mean the nonsense about that painting."

I was suddenly aware that other conversations had stopped and that all eyes had turned towards Blessingham. Several of them registered alarm.

Rather hastily the dean said, "Our guest doesn't want to hear about that lamentable incident."

By this time my curiosity was, of course, thoroughly aroused. "On the contrary," I said. "I am always eager to hear anything about my late friend."

The master made a flapping gesture with his hand. "It was nothing and best forgotten. Holmes was only with us for a short time."

"Holmes was here?" I asked with genuine surprise. "At Grenville? I had no idea . . ."

"Yes, 1872, I think . . . or was it '73? I know it was around the same time that Sternforth was up. He's making quite a name for himself

in Parliament now. Have you heard from him recently, Grenson?"
Skilfully, the master turned the talk to other matters.

It can be imagined that this unlocking and hasty refastening of
a hitherto unknown part of Holmes's early life stirred considerable
excitement within me. It was with difficulty that I contained all
the questions I was longing to ask about it. Not until the
following afternoon did I have the opportunity to interrogate
Hungerford on the matter. Mary and I were taking a stroll
through Christchurch Meadows with our host and hostess and
I contrived to urge Hungerford to a slightly faster pace so that
we might walk on ahead.

"What was that talk last night about Sherlock Holmes and a
painting?" I enquired. "It seemed to embarrass some of your
colleagues."

"A number of the older fellows are certainly still troubled by the
episode even after all these years," Hungerford mused, directing
his gaze along the river. "I must say that surprises me rather."

"But what was it *about?*" I almost shouted in my exasperation.
"Old Blessingham called it Holmes's first case yet I have never
heard of it."

Hungerford smiled at my impatience. "Well, Holmes was obviously an honourable man. The people over at New College enjoined
him to secrecy on the matter and he faithfully kept silence."

"But surely there's no need to maintain the mystery any longer,"
I urged.

"I suppose not. It was really nothing more than a storm in
an academic teacup; and yet in a closed little world like ours
such incidents do tend to assume greater importance than they
merit."

"Look, Hungerford," I said, "you can tell me the story. We doctors
are able to keep confidences, you know."

Thus prompted my distant cousin related the story which, with
a few emendations and name changes (made to honour my side of
the bargain) and with additional details furnished later by Holmes
himself, I can now set before the public.

It all began, as far as Holmes was concerned, at Paddington station.
It was the autumn of 1873 and he had just enrolled at Grenville
College after a year or two at Trinity in Dublin. On this particular
late afternoon he was returning to Oxford after a day spent in the
British Museum Reading Room. He had selected an empty, first-class
smoking compartment and was looking forward to a quiet journey in
the company of a recent dissertation on alkali poisons derived from
plants in the Americas. The train made its first clanking convulsion

preparatory to departure when a distraught figure appeared on the platform and grabbed the door handle. With a sigh of resignation Holmes leaped to his feet and helped a young man with a flapping topcoat into the compartment.

As Holmes slammed the door and the train gathered speed the stranger collapsed onto the seat opposite, spreading a pile of books and papers and other belongings out beside him. "Thank you, sir, thank you," he panted.

"Not at all. I perceive that you have had a particularly harassing afternoon." Holmes surveyed a young man in his late twenties of startlingly pale appearance. Even though flushed with exertion, his cheeks were as though drawn in pastels. His hair was the colour of white sand and the eyes that peered through thick-lensed spectacles were of the lightest blue. "It is always aggravating to mistake the time of one's train and then to have one's cab stuck in traffic – quite wretched."

The other man leaned forward, mouth open in astonishment. "You cannot possibly . . . Are you some kind of spirit who consorts with mediums?"

Now it was Holmes who was momentarily nonplussed. "Do you mean am I a medium who consorts with spirits?"

"That is what I asked, sir. If you are I must tell you straight out that I don't disapprove of such dabbling in forbidden waters . . . no, not at all."

Holmes laughed. "Then let me set your mind at rest. I am a student of very terrestrial sciences. There was nothing other-worldly about my observations. As to your mistake about train times, I simply perceived that your Bradshaw was out of date." He pointed to the bulky *Bradshaw's Railway Guide* which lay among the stranger's papers. "This particular train has been departing ten minutes earlier since the end of September."

"To be sure; to be sure," the other muttered, "but your reference to the traffic?"

"Even simpler, sir. It has been raining lightly for the past ten minutes yet only the upper part of your clothing is wet. Clearly you were obliged to leave the protection of your cab before reaching the station. That you did so in some haste is evidenced by the fact that, having paid the driver, you are still clutching your purse in your hand."

"Remarkable," said the stranger, sitting back in the seat. "You are obviously a very observant young man. May I know your name?"

"Sherlock Holmes, undergraduate of Grenville College, at your service, sir."

"Grenville, eh? Then we are close neighbours. I am . . ."

"William Spooner, fellow of New College. Please, do not register surprise, sir. You are one of the celebrities of Oxford." "The Spoo", as the young lecturer in Ancient History and Philosophy was known to undergraduates, had already acquired that reputation for eccentricity which was later to spread well beyond the confines of the university.

Spooner nodded mournfully. "Ah, yes, it's those *things* I say, isn't it? I can't help myself you know; they just pop out like habbits from a role."

After exchanging a few more courtesies each passenger settled to his own occupation for the journey. Holmes returned to his paper. Spooner spent a considerable time organizing his possessions into some semblance of order and arranging them on the overhead rack, then extracted a slim volume of Ovidian poetry from the pocket of his surtout, curled himself into the opposite corner and began to read with the page held close to his face. Yet neither was able to concentrate. Holmes was intrigued by the albino and was conscious that Spooner was taking no less interest in him. Several times the younger man glanced surreptitiously across the intervening space only to find that New College's most remarkable resident was staring fixedly at him. Once or twice Spooner opened his mouth as though he would speak but either the words would not come or he thought better of them. At last, however, he did break the silence.

"Mr Holmes, I apologize for disturbing you. I wonder, would you mind if I asked you to discuss a certain matter . . . delicate, bewildering?"

"If I can be of service, sir."

"It is not the sort of thing I would normally broach with someone upon such short acquaintance but you appear to be a singularly astute young man and it may be that Providence has brought us together."

Holmes waited with carefully suppressed amusement to hear what perplexing problem the eccentric don was about to share.

"I am convinced that the whole thing is an undergraduate prank. It may be that you have heard about it from the perpetrators."

"Heard about what, sir?"

Spooner squinted impatiently through his glasses. "Why the painting, of course – the Dutch *Nativity*. We've lost it permanently for three weeks."

"Perhaps, sir, if you were to start from the beginning?"

"Ah, yes, well Giddings, you see, our senior fellow, brilliant mind, Renaissance scholar, very gracious, not at all put out over the election."

The story which would have taken any normal narrator ten minutes or so to recite occupied Spooner for the remainder of the journey, involving, as it did, acrobatic leaps from thought to thought and perilous balancing on the high wire of tenuous connections. Holmes was amused as much by the effort of following the disjointed account as by the events to which it referred. Briefly, these were as follows:

Some eleven years previously there had been an election for the wardenship of New College. The contest had been between the then dean and the senior fellow, Dr Giddings. The fellowship had decided on the dean, for Giddings, though highly respected, was already well smitten in years and did not enjoy robust health. The old don had shown his regard for the college by warmly congratulating the warden elect and donating to the chapel a magnificent *Nativity* by Rembrandt. It was this painting which, in October 1873, had been stolen.

Holmes asked why the crime had not been reported to the police and received the reply that the fellows were disposed to regard it as an internal university matter. Over the past few months there had been a series of similar incidents in various colleges. Oriel's standard had been removed from its flagpole. A hanging candelabrum had been absconded from the hall at Merton. An ancient sundial had been prised from a quadrangle wall at Magdalen and, more recently someone had walked out of Radcliffe library with a rare incunabulum, deceiving the staff by leaving a superficial fake in its place. The New College authorities attributed these escapades to undergraduate high spirits and were persuing their own enquiries but to Holmes it was evident that Spooner and, probably, his colleagues were more exercised by their loss than they were prepared to admit.

Having heard his fellow passenger's tale, my friend could only express his condolences over New College's loss and regret that he knew nothing which could be of any help in the recovery of the painting. As a new arrival in Oxford he had yet to acquaint himself with the student grapevine, he explained, and, in any case, he was, himself, of a rather solitary and studious disposition.

Having arrived at Oxford the two travellers shared a cab into the city centre, where they parted company. Holmes resolved to put the New College painting from his mind but the curious elements of Spooner's narrative no less than the disjointed mode of its delivery declined to be easily banished. Thus he found himself next morning in the chapel of the nearby college gazing at a large area of empty stone wall. A small card pinned to a stall beneath the space read: 'THE NATIVITY OF OUR LORD by

REMBRANDT VAN RYN, 1661. This painting has been temporarily removed for restoration.'

Holmes climbed onto the wooden seat to inspect the wall more closely. Faint dust marks could be seen where the frame had touched the stonework and, using the span of his outstretched right hand, which he knew to be nine and a quarter inches in width, he measured the dimensions of the missing painting. It was as he was stretching upwards as far as he could reach to gauge the height of the absent masterpiece that he heard an outraged voice behind him.

"'Ere! What d'you think you're a-doing of?"

Calmly Sherlock Holmes stepped down and turned to confront an aged college servant whose faded black gown proclaimed him to be some sort of sexton or verger. "Are you in charge here?" he enquired.

"That I am and right tired of the antics of you young gentlemen. This is a house of God and not a place for your pranks. Now be off with you, before I call the dean."

"Oh, there's no need to disturb him," said Holmes casually. "I'm sure you can tell me all I need to know." He produced a half sovereign from his pocket. "I'm interested in your excellent painting and was very sorry not to be able to see it. Do you know where it has gone to be restored?"

The old man's tone changed at the sight of the gleaming coin. "Yes, sir," he said, holding out his hand for the unexpected gratuity. "I've got a note of the address in my vestry. If you'd care to step this way. I take it you're a student of art, sir."

"That's right," Holmes agreed.

"Well, I don't know as you'll learn much from that painting. Right dark and gloomy it is. You can't scarcely make out any of the figures in it. They say it's very valuable, but I wouldn't give it house room. If you wouldn't mind waiting there a moment, sir." He unlocked a small door and shuffled into a chamber scarcely larger than a broom cupboard. Seconds later he re-emerged bearing a card.

"Ah yes, Simkins and Streeter," Holmes said, nodding approvingly. "I know them well. They'll do a first class job. When did they take it?"

"It was three weeks ago."

"Was it Mr Simkins or Mr Streeter who called to supervise the removal?"

"That I couldn't say, sir. I wasn't here."

"You mean these people came from London and removed this valuable college treasure without your personal supervision?"

Holmes asked with an air of concerned astonishment. "That was not very courteous of them."

The verger visibly warmed to his visitor. "Well, that same thought did strike me, sir. Apparently it was all a rushed job. They was due to come in the afternoon but they never showed up. On the Thursday morning when I came in there was the picture gone. I was a bit worried, I don't mind telling you and I rushed straight to the dean. He set my mind at rest straight away. 'Not to worry, Tavistock,' he said. 'The restorers came for the painting quite late. It seems they'd had some trouble on the road with a lame horse and, by the time they'd changed it over they were running well behind time.'"

"So you never saw the men who collected it?"

"No, sir."

"It must have taken several people to remove the painting. It is large and heavy."

"That it is," the old man laughed. "Why, when old Dr Giddings presented the picture to the college it took six of us to put it up – an' all the time the dean – that's the former dean who's now warden – hopping and dancing around and shouting at us to be careful."

As they walked the length of the long nave Holmes asked, "You were saying you'd had some trouble with boisterous undergraduates."

"Gentlemen they call themselves!" the aged verger sniffed. "Sacrilegious and heathen hooligans I calls them. First week of term it was. I caught four of 'em in here, scrambling about over the stalls. One of them had a lamp and he was holding it up to that Dutch painting. I was afeared he'd set light to the thing. You can imagine, sir, when I saw you on the same spot it brought it all back. So you'll forgive me if I was a bit sharp with you."

"I quite understand," Holmes replied sympathetically. "Yours is a heavy responsibility. What happened to these rowdies?"

"I fetched Junkin, the senior porter, and a couple of his men. They were more than a match for a bunch of drunken undergraduates. We turfed them out and took their names and I reported them directly to the warden. What happened to them after that, I don't know. They've certainly not been back here."

"Do you remember any of their names?"

"Indeed I do, sir. They was all Magdalen men and their ringleader was the Hon. Hugh Mountcey, Lord Henley's son. You'd think the aristocracy would know better, wouldn't you, sir?"

They had arrived at the west door and the guardian of the chapel held it open. Holmes thanked his informant and passed into the narrow lane outside.

Back in his rooms Sherlock Holmes abandoned all pretence of pursuing his own studies. The mystery of the missing painting had quite taken hold of his reasoning faculties. He threw himself down on a sofa, lit a pipe and pondered the additional information gleaned from the verger. The *Nativity*, it appeared, had been scheduled for restoration, a fact which now enabled the fellows, temporarily, to conceal its abduction. It had also seemingly provided excellent cover for the thieves. As to the Magdalen men who had made a nuisance of themselves, that certainly suggested a connection with the earlier outrages perpetrated during the summer and autumn terms.

Clearly this motley assortment of stolen Oxfordiana had common features. Each item was treasured by the establishment which owned it. Abduction of each required audacity and daring. Its removal was designed to create embarrassment for its owners, who, for that reason, were unlikely to call in the police, thus risking scandal and popular ridicule.

Yet, Holmes mused, there were also disharmonies. The stolen objects differed greatly in quality, importance, and size. There seemed to be no pattern to the thefts. The removal of Oriel's flag had demanded mountaineering ability; Magdalen's sundial had been neatly prized from its surrounding stonework by someone well versed in the skills of the mason. Only a scholar with a knowledge of rare printed books could have created the forgery which had, briefly, deceived the Radcliffe library staff. Then there were the elements of difficulty and risk. With each escapade these had become greater. There was a considerable gulf between the nocturnal raid on Oriel to remove its standard and the carrying off of the New College painting. The former certainly had the air of a traditional student rag. The latter was a major crime and had called for elaborate and meticulous planning.

That brought one on to the issue of motive. What did the perpetrators want with this bizarre collection of objects? Three of the items had little monetary value. The incunabulum and the painting were, by contrast, highly prized artefacts which could only be disposed of through specialist underworld channels. Holmes dismissed the idea of student escapades. They were never malicious; they were simply tiresome displays of exhibitionism and high spirits. This series of thefts was different. It had caused distress and embarrassment to the colleges concerned. Had that been the intention?

Holmes knocked out his pipe in the hearth and consulted his pocket watch. There wanted a few minutes to two o'clock. It was time for another call. Donning a light top coat and extracting a cane from a wicker basket beside the sitting room door, he let himself out and ran lightly down the stone staircase.

Twenty minutes brisk walking through the city centre and out along the Banbury Road brought him to the edge of the city's suburbs. Here the substantial houses were well spaced out and overlooked fields and meadows running down to the Cherwell. Holmes found the one he was seeking almost at the end of the row. It was a large double-fronted villa approached by a short gravel drive. A pull upon the bell brought a manservant to the front door.

Holmes handed in his card. "I am an art enthusiast and an amateur collector, currently residing at Grenville College," he explained. "I must apologize for calling without an appointment, but I should deem it a great honour to be permitted to view Dr Gidding's collection."

The major domo admitted my friend to a spacious hall and asked him to wait. Within moments he returned, ushered the visitor into a well furnished library and announced him. Holmes looked around a room which, at first acquaintance seemed empty. Then he espied a bath chair, its back to him, facing a french window giving onto the garden.

"Over here, young man," a voice commanded from the conveyance.

Crossing a parquet floor scattered with Persian rugs, Holmes found himself confronted by a shrivelled figure almost completely bundled-up in a plaid rug. Gidding's greyish skin was drawn tight over his skull and a fringe of white hair protruded from beneath a velvet skull cap. However, if there was an air of quiet decay about the aged scholar this certainly did not extend to his bright, peering eyes or the mind behind them.

"Sherlock Holmes? Never heard of you, sir!" Giddings announced in a high-pitched voice.

"But I have heard of you, Dr Giddings, as has anyone with more than a passing interest in the history of art. Your studies on the northern Renaissance have greatly widened our understanding of the great masters of this side of the Alps."

"Huh!" the old man snorted. "I thought I'd been forgotten long ago."

Holmes affected a shocked tone. "By no means, sir. Quite the reverse. Some of the radical ideas which you advanced in the twenties and thirties are now taken for self-evident truth. As to your private collection . . ."

"I suppose that's what you're here to see; not me. Well come on then. You can work for the privilege. Push me. We go through that door over there."

Holmes grasped the handles of the invalid carriage and propelled it in the direction indicated. They passed through into a suite of three ground floor rooms interconnected by tall doors. The contents made Holmes gasp in amazement. Every surface from floor to ceiling was covered with paintings on canvas or panel. Scarcely a square inch of papered wall could be seen.

"This is truly remarkable," my friend exclaimed. "I had not prepared myself for such a treat."

"The work of a lifetime, young man. If you start now you might just be able to match it by the time you're eighty."

They made a leisurely tour of the private gallery and Giddings spoke with mounting enthusiasm and excitement about several items. Sherlock Holmes relaxed the aged don with flattery interspersed with pertinent comments and awaited the moment to broach the subject that had taken him thither.

At last he said, "I was devastated not to be able to see the Rembrandt you presented to your college. When I visited the chapel there was a notice saying that it had been sent for restoration but I heard a rumour . . ."

"Vandals!" The old man became suddenly animated.

"Then it's true, sir, that the painting has been stolen?" Holmes asked in shocked tones.

"They should have looked after it better. It's a priceless painting – magnificent example of the artist's best period. Now they've let some hooligans make off with it. It's probably mouldering in a fenland shed somewhere. It will be ruined! Lost!" Giddings subsided into a fit of coughing and pressed a large spotted handkerchief to his mouth.

"It must be very distressing to you, sir. I imagine the Rembrandt was the crowning item of your collection."

The old man nodded vigorously. "Yes, I bought it privately in The Hague a quarter of a century ago. It had impeccable provenance. It was quite a sacrifice to part with it but I thought it would make a suitable parting gift, to mark a lifetime of service to New College. They might not have appreciated me but at least they had something to remember me by. Now, however . . ." Giddings shrugged and seemed to shrink even further into his wrappings.

"You don't think the crime might be the work of professional thieves? The art world, as I understand is not without its share of unscrupulous men."

"Out of the question," the old man wheezed. "Too well known. Too difficult to sell."

Holmes propelled the chair towards the next door but stopped when Gidding's frame was convulsed by a fresh bout of violent coughing.

"Should I fetch your man?" Holmes enquired anxiously.

The invalid nodded by way of reply and my friend retraced his steps to the library where a tug on the bell pull quickly brought the servant. He conveyed his master back into the library. The old man had recovered from his fit but announced that he was rather tired and begged Holmes to excuse him. He invited the young student to return another day to conclude the tour. Holmes thanked his host volubly and withdrew.

His next call was upon Mr Spooner in his New College rooms. He informed the don that he had become intrigued by the theft and that, with Spooner's permission, he would like to follow up certain ideas which had occurred to him. He pressed the fellow for some details on certain points and asked him for a letter of introduction to Messrs Simkins and Streeter. Thus armed, Holmes travelled next day to London. A cab dropped him at the entrance of a narrow alley leading off Jermyn Street by way of which Holmes discovered a painted signboard and a flight of stairs which led to the restorers' second-floor premises. These consisted of a single, long room illumined by sunshine entering through large skylights. Easels and wide tables were scattered throughout the workshop and at these men in their shirtsleeves were working singly or in pairs upon an assortment of old paintings. On enquiring for the proprietors, Holmes managed to distract one of these craftsmen just long enough to elicit a nod in the direction of a partitioned-off cubicle at the far end of the room.

The man who stood behind a desk untidy with scattered papers to greet him as he stepped in through the open door was stocky and of middle years. He was, Holmes judged, a touch overdressed; his suit a shade flamboyant of cut; his diamond-fastened necktie slightly too bright of hue. "Henry Simkins at your service, sir," the man announced. "Whom have I the honour of addressing?"

Holmes handed over his card with Spooner's letter and carefully observed Simkin's reaction. The man displayed momentary alarm but quickly covered it up. "Well, Mr Holmes sit down, sit down do. I'll help you all I can, though I fear you've had a wasted journey, for Mr Spooner knows all there is to be known about this sad business."

Holmes dusted the proffered chair and sank down upon it. "I'm grateful to you for your time, Mr Simkins. There were just one or two details that Mr Spooner wanted me to check."

"Why then, fire away, Mr Holmes."

"When was it that you were invited by the warden and fellows of New College to carry out restoration work on their painting?"

"Well, now, that would be about the end of August. I can give you the exact date if you'll bear with me a moment." He swivelled his chair until he was facing an open roll-top desk against the back wall. From one drawer he lifted a bundle of papers tied with string, undid the knot and began to leaf through the sheets. To the precise-minded Holmes it seemed that the exploration would occupy more than "a moment" but within seconds Simkins uttered a little cry of triumph and flourished a sheet of embossed notepaper. "There we are, Mr Holmes," said he, laying it on the table before my friend.

Holmes quickly scanned the formal letter dated 25 August inviting Messrs Simkins and Streeter to examine Rembrandt's *Nativity of Our Lord* with a view to discussing possible restoration work. "You responded immediately, I presume," Holmes suggested.

"Yes, indeed, Mr Holmes." Simkins consulted a pocket diary. "We arranged for me to view the painting on Wednesday 10 September."

"Had you done work for New College, before?"

"No, sir, we had not previously enjoyed that privilege."

"Do you know who recommended you on this occasion?"

Simkins sat back in his chair, thumbs hooked into the pockets of his waistcoat. "Ah well, as to that, Mr Holmes, it might have been any one of a number of our satisfied clients. I'm proud to say that we are known to many connoisseurs, museum curators and inheritors of family collections. We have been of service to several of the nobility and gentry."

"Including Lord Henley?" Holmes ventured.

"Why yes, sir. Only last year we executed an important commission for his lordship."

"And Dr Giddings?"

"Him, too, sir. A wonderful connoisseur is Dr Giddings. He's been good enough to instruct us on several occasions."

"Were you acquainted with the Rembrandt before your visit to New College last month?"

"Only by reputation, sir."

"You had never seen it before?" Holmes asked in some surprise.

"Never."

"And you have been familiar with Dr Giddings's collection for . . . how long?"

"More than twenty years, I would say."

Holmes pondered that intelligence in silence for a few moments.

"And what was your impression of the painting when you did see it?"

For the first time the ebullient Simkins gave evidence of some discomfiture. "Why, to be truthful, Sir, I suppose I was a little disappointed."

"You thought it not a particularly good painting?"

The businessman's bushy eyebrows met in a frown. "Oh, no, Mr Holmes, nothing of that sort. I would not want you to think that I meant to cast any doubt upon the quality of the masterpiece. It was just that ... Well, I recall discussing that item many years ago with another client who had seen it in Holland and who waxed eloquent about it's warm, glowing colours. What I saw in Oxford was a painting that had been sorely mishandled at some stage of its life. It had upon it a thick, old discoloured varnish. What with that and its gloomy situation in the chapel it was very hard to make out details of the brushwork."

"So you concluded that it required a thorough cleaning and that you would only be able to comment upon the necessity of further restoration after that operation had been carried out."

"That's it precisely, Mr Holmes. We submitted an estimate for initial work. Naturally the warden and fellows needed time to consider our proposal. They responded," here he referred once more to the bundle taken from the roll-top desk, "on 1 October and we arranged to collect the painting a week later, on the eighth."

"But you did not do so?"

"No, on the morning of the eighth we received a telegram intimating that it was not, after all, convenient for us to call on that day and inviting us to make a new appointment."

"You had no reason to doubt the authenticity of this telegram?"

"None whatsoever."

"Tell me, Mr Simkins," Holmes ventured, "as someone who knows the world of pictures, dealers and collectors better than most, how hard do you think it would be to dispose of such a celebrated painting?"

"Very hard, indeed, I would say."

"But not impossible?"

Simkins pondered the question, head on one side. "There are collectors so obsessive that they are prepared to obtain by other means what they cannot fairly buy."

"And are there not international gangs operating to satisfy the cravings of such collectors?"

"Sadly, that is the case, Mr Holmes."

"And would you know how to make contact with just such a

gang?" Holmes asked the question in a casual, disarming tone and watched its effect on the other man.

Simkins's ample frame seemed to swell still further with indignation. "Mr Holmes, whatever are you suggesting?"

"Simply that someone in your position might well be approached, from time to time, by unscrupulous men – men requiring, perhaps, a convincing forgery or confirmation of a false attribution. I am sure that Simkins and Streeter would never knowingly be associated with such rogues but I would be surprised if you were not able to identify some of them."

"We know who to steer clear of, if that's what you're suggesting, young sir," Simkins admitted, only partially mollified.

"That and nothing else," Holmes said with a smile. "I wonder if I might trouble you for the names of some of these reprobates." As the other man firmly shook his head, he continued. "You see, someone deliberately deceived you and then passed off himself and his associates as representatives of Simkins and Streeter. That someone was highly professional. *Ergo*, I deduce that he is no stranger to the business of stealing and disposing of works of art."

"Well, sir, since you put it that way, there are a handful of men who might bear investigation. The police could do worse than question them – not, mind you, that I make any accusations." He found a scrap of paper among the confetti scattering before him and, taking up a pen from the holder, jotted down three names. "Well, Mr Holmes, I hope they may lead to the recovery of New College's *Nativity*, though I fear it has disappeared for many a long year."

Sherlock Holmes spent the return journey to Oxford recalling with total accuracy, every piece of information with a bearing on this case. It all pointed to one bizarre, though inescapable conclusion. Could it be proved, though? He resolved that prove it he would if it were humanly possible.

With that fixed intention he set out from Grenville after dark clad in tennis shoes, old trousers and shirt and carrying a hand lantern and a copy of *The Times*. He was gone for two hours and he returned in triumph. He had one more call to make and that would have to wait until the following evening.

The clock high on Grenville chapel's tower was chiming six as Holmes set out to walk the short distance to Magdalen College. When he reached Hugh Mountcey's apartments the outer door was open and there were sounds of conversation within. He tapped smartly and the portal was opened by a raffish, ginger-haired young man in evening dress and clutching a glass of champagne. "Yes?" he enquired languidly. Holmes proffered his card. The other held it up fastidiously. "I say, Huffy," he called out to someone inside, "do we know anyone by the name of Sherlock Holmes?" He uttered the name with an air of faint amusement. "No. Send him on his way," came the reply from within. "Be off with you, fellow," the sandy-haired man said, returning Holmes's card.

Before the door closed completely, Holmes handed over an envelope. "Please see that Mr Mountcey receives this."

Holmes stood on the landing and began counting. He had reached thirty-two when the door was re-opened by the same guardian. "Mr Mountcey says you'd better come in," he said.

"I rather thought he might," Holmes rejoined.

The chamber he now entered was opulently furnished. A table at one end was laid for four with sparkling silver and crystal and crisp knappery. Armchairs were drawn around the fire and in one the resident of this suite was sprawled. The Honourable Hugh Mountcey was a gangling, dark-haired young man, with a florid complexion. He held Holmes's letter by one corner between thumb and forefinger. "What's the meaning of this nonsense?" he demanded.

Holmes stood staring down at the aristocrat and recalled the verger of New College's disparaging comments on certain degenerate members of the upper class. "If it were nonsense you would scarcely have invited me in," he observed.

"Who the devil are you," Mountcey sneered.

"All that matters is that I know the truth about the New College Rembrandt. Apart from anything else I have identified your role in the business."

Mountcey's companion stepped across the room and grabbed Holmes by the sleeve. "Shall I teach this fellow some manners, Huffy?" he enquired. The next instant he was lying flat on his back holding a hand to his nose from which a trickle of blood was oozing.

Holmes rubbed the knuckles of his right hand. "I assure you that I have no interest in making life difficult for you. My only concern is to clear up this tiresome business of the missing painting so that I can resume my own studies. If you will be good enough to answer a few questions I will take my leave."

"And what do you intend doing with your information?"

"I shall place such items as are relevant before the authorities at New College."

"That might not suit my book at all. I certainly have no intention of informing on my friends."

"By friends I take it that you mean those responsible for the escapades at Oriel, Merton and here in Magdalen."

Mountcey nodded.

"I don't think it will be necessary for me to reveal their identity."

The dark-haired young man stared at Holmes for several seconds. Then a smile slowly suffused his features. He crumpled the letter he was still holding and tossed it into the fire. "No, Mr Holmes, you are a nobody and I am inclined to tell you to go to hell. Report whatever you like to the New College people. You have no proof. If it comes to a contest between you and those of us who count for rather more in this life it's pretty obvious who will end up being sent down, isn't it?" He waved his visitor towards the door and his friend held it open.

Holmes stood his ground. "But it isn't just you and your friends who are involved is it? It's your father and his associates."

Mountcey was caught off guard. "You can't possibly know . . ." he blurted out, leaping to his feet.

Holmes took a pencil and paper from his pocket, wrote a few words and passed the paper across to the Honourable Hugh.

"Damn!" Mountcey sank back onto the chair.

"So, sir, about those questions," said Holmes.

Sherlock Holmes called upon Mr Spooner shortly after eleven the following morning as the latter was returning from lecturing.

The don came up close and peered through his thick lenses. "Ah, Mr Grenville of Holmes, is it not? Come in, sir. Come in. Do sit down. I suggest you will find the seat in the window more than comfortable."

Holmes deposited himself upon the cushions in the window embrasure. "I have come to report the successful conclusion of my investigation," he announced. "About the theft of the painting from the chapel," he added as Spooner gazed vacantly into space.

"Ah, yes, excellent." The fellow's pallid features broke into a smile. "So you have discovered who was responsible. Was it Rembrandt?"

"No, sir." By now Holmes had discovered that the way to prevent Spooner's train of thought running into frequent sidings was to keep him concentrating hard on the matter in hand. "Perhaps it would be best if I explained, from the beginning, the sequence of events which led to the disappearance of the painting."

"Excellent idea, young man. Play the part of Chorus and leak your spines clearly."

Holmes began his explanation, hurrying on when his audience

showed signs of wishing to question or interrupt. "First, I must suggest to you that your reading of Dr Giddings's character owes more to charity than objective observation. I fear that the senior fellow was furious at being passed over for the wardenship and that that is why he gave his painting to New College."

"But, surely . . ."

Holmes scarcely paused for breath. "It was to be his revenge. You see, the painting was a fake, or more probably the work of an inferior artist touched up by the hand of an improver. I realized this when I spoke with Mr Simkins. He was puzzled because the painting which another of his clients had seen about the time Giddings bought it was 'vibrant' with 'warm, glowing colours' as he described it. Yet when Simkins, himself, viewed it in the chapel it was apparently obscured with ancient varnish. Now Giddings was the only one who could so have misused the picture and for only one reason: he realized, after adding it to his collection that it was not a work from the hand of the master. To avoid the humiliation of having to admit that he had been duped he had the picture varnished over, and waited for an opportunity to get rid of it. His exclusion from the wardenship provided the excellent chance to kill two birds with one stone. He disembarrassed himself of the fake Rembrandt and put one over on the fellows of New College. Giddings knew that, eventually, the painting would be cleaned and that, from beyond the grave, he would have his revenge.

"Then, long after the whole matter had been pushed to the back of his mind, he was alarmed to hear that the fellows had decided upon the immediate restoration of their Rembrandt. He knew Simkins and Streeter could not fail to discover the truth and that both his folly and his vendetta would be exposed. What could he possibly do to prevent the closing days of his life being lived under this double shame? Only the disappearance of the picture could save him but he could not encompass that. He would need accomplices. It was then that he bethought himself of his friend and fellow collector, Lord Henley."

"Lord Henley? Why on earth should that highly respected nobleman be a party to such a notorious escapade?"

"I confess that I, too, was puzzled on that score. Eventually I had to prize the truth from his son, Mr Mountcey."

"That young man is a scoundrel."

"Quite so, sir." Holmes rushed on. "It seems that not only did the two collectors share common interests, but Lord Henley owed a considerable debt of gratitude to Dr Giddings. A few years ago a crooked dealer attempted to implicate his lordship in a colossal art fraud. Had he been successful the scandal would have been terrible. Giddings was largely responsible for exposing the syndicate behind the imposture. Lord Henley now felt duty bound to assist his saviour. The two old friends planned the robbery together. Giddings found out through his college contacts the precise day on which Simkins and Streeter were to collect the painting. Then Lord Henley arranged for the fake telegram postponing the appointment and had one of his underworld contacts pose as the restorers' agent. Just in case anyone from the college who watched the removal became suspicious he arranged for the work to be done under cover of darkness when the chapel was almost certain to be empty."

"But what about the other thefts?"

"A fortuitous sequence of events that enabled the conspirators to muddy the water. Lord Henley's son was involved in a rather stupid society the object of which was to plan and execute ever more audacious 'japes', as they call them. The Oriel and Merton escapades were carried out by other members of the club and it was Mountcey and his friends who defaced the walls of Magdalen by removing the sundial. It seems that Lord Henley knew of these ridiculous revels and, being an over-indulgent parent, was not disposed to regard them seriously. It was he who put his son up to the fracas that took place early in the term. When Mountcey and his friends were caught examining the chapel painting the authorities connected this with the earlier misdemeanours, a suspicion that was reinforced when the picture went missing. Of course, Mountcey could not be proved to be implicated in the theft, so he was quite safe."

Spooner was frowning with concentration. "But, then, whose incunabulum stole the Radcliffe?"

"I am persuaded that it was Giddings himself who removed the book from the library. Mountcey gave me his word that he knew nothing of it. Such a reputed and infirm scholar as Dr Giddings was, of course, above suspicion, so it was the easiest thing in the world for him to leave with the precious artefact under the rug in his bath chair, having left the duplicate."

"Then the book and the painting are safe in Dr Giddings's house?"

"The book – yes. I am sure Dr Giddings would not harm it, nor intend to deprive the library of it for long. The painting, I suspect, is another matter." Holmes opened a portmanteau he had brought with him. He extracted a parcel roughly wrapped in newspaper and proceeded to unravel it.

Spooner leant forward to examine a blackened fragment of what had once been gilded wood and gesso and to which a fragment of charred canvas still adhered.

"The night before last," Holmes explained, "I paid a clandestine visit to Dr Giddings's garden. I found this on a bonfire in a corner of the grounds. The embers were still warm. Unless I am mistaken, that is all that remains of the fake Rembrandt – and just as well, perhaps."

"Whatever made you think of looking there?"

"When I called on Dr Giddings the previous day, he was obviously concerned about my interest in the Rembrandt. He tried to convince me that its theft was a student prank and he brought my visit to a sudden halt with what seemed to me rather a theatrical fit of coughing. I believe that was to prevent me looking inside the room where the painting was currently housed. I reasoned that he would want to be rid of the evidence very quickly after such a fright and there seemed to be only one easy way to do that."

Spooner removed his spectacles and polished them thoughtfully. "Mr Holmes," he said, "you are a remarkable young man. I predict that you will go far. May I ask you to put what you have just told me in writing? My colleagues will, I know, want to study it most carefully."

"I had anticipated that request," replied my friend, handing over a sealed envelope.

"How wise, Mr Solomon, how wise. The college is indebted to you. You will undoubtedly be hearing more from us. For the moment all I can do is personally grace my platitude on record." He shook Holmes warmly by the hand and escorted him to the door.

Sherlock Holmes reflected during the next few days on the immense pleasure and satisfaction this little enquiry had occasioned him. He had, at that time, no inkling that his vocation lay in the field of criminal detection but, as he later confessed to me, the bothersome business of the Dutch *Nativity*, was undoubtedly the case that opened up new possibilities to him.

All that lay in the future. One more immediate result manifested itself a few days later. Holmes received an unexpected invitation to dine with the Master of Grenville. He arrived at the lodge at the appointed time expecting to find himself one of a large party. To his surprise the only other guest was the Warden of New College. As soon as the three men had embarked on their meal the master introduced the subject of Holmes's recent investigations. The fellows of New College were very grateful to him for clearing the matter up but were anxious that none of the information he had gathered should go any further. Under the circumstances he felt sure that Holmes would appreciate that absolute secrecy must be a condition of his remaining in Oxford.

Holmes assured the dons that he would not contemplate breaking any confidences. What, he enquired would be happening to those involved in the series of outrages culminating in the theft of the painting? The warden replied, "Any action we might take could only embarrass several important people. Under the circumstances we think it best to draw a veil over all that has happened."

Holmes was stunned. "Forgive me, sir, if I mistake your meaning, but it seems to me that you are saying that truth weighs very lightly in the balance against personal reputation."

"That is a rather stark way of expressing it," the master suggested.

"But apparently accurate. Theft, forgery and deceit must go unpunished, even unremarked, because we must not make life awkward for members of the establishment. That is a philosophy I am surprised to hear advocated by men of learning and honest enquiry. I fear, gentlemen, that it is one to which I could never subscribe."

The subject was quickly changed but at the conclusion of the meal Sherlock Holmes returned to his chambers and immediately wrote a letter announcing his resignation from the college.

THE AFFRAY AT THE KILDARE STREET CLUB

Peter Tremayne

My narratives of the adventures of Mr Sherlock Holmes, the well-known consulting detective, have always attempted a modicum of discreetness. There is so much of both a personal and professional nature that Holmes confided in me which I have not passed on to posterity – much, I confess, at Holmes's personal request. Indeed, among Holmes's personal papers I had noticed several *aide memoirs* which would have expanded my sketches of his cases several times over. It is not often appreciated that while I indulged in my literary diversions, Holmes himself was possessed of a writing talent as demonstrated by over a score of works ranging from his *Practical Handbook of Bee Culture* to *The Book of Life: the science of observation and deduction.* But Holmes, to my knowledge, had made it a rule never to write about any of his specific cases.

It was therefore with some surprise that, one day during the spring of 1894, after the adventure I narrated as "The Empty House", I received from Holmes a small sheaf of handwritten papers with the exhortation that I read them in order that I might understand more fully Holmes's involvement with the man responsible for the death of the son of Lord Maynooth. Holmes, of course, did not want these details to be revealed to the public. I did acquire permission from him at a later date to the effect that they could be published after his death. In the meantime I have appended this brief foreword to be placed with the papers and handed both to my bankers and executors with the instruction that they may only be released one hundred years from this date.

It may, then, also be revealed a matter that I have always been sensitive about, in view of the prejudices of our age. Sherlock Holmes was one of the Holmes family of Galway, Ireland, and, like his brother Mycroft, was a graduate of Trinity College, Dublin, where his closest companion had been the poet Oscar Fingal O'Flahertie Wills Wilde, who even now, as I write, languishes in Reading Gaol. This is the principal reason why I have been reticent about acknowledging Holmes's background for it would serve no useful purpose if one fell foul of the bigotry and intolerance that arises out of such a revelation. Many good men and true, but with such backgrounds, have found themselves being shunned by their professions or found their businesses have been destroyed overnight.

This revelation will probably come as no surprise to those discerning readers who have followed Holmes's adventures. There have been clues enough of Holmes's origins. Holmes's greatest adversary, James Moriarty, was of a similar background. Most people will know that the Moriarty family are from Kerry, the very name being an Anglicization of the Irish name Ó Muircheartaigh meaning, interestingly enough, "expert navigator". Moriarty once held a chair of mathematics in Queen's University in Belfast. It was in Ireland that the enmity between Holmes and Moriarty first started. But that is a story which does not concern us.

If there were not clues enough, there was also Holmes's fascination with the Celtic languages, of which he was something of an expert. In my narrative "The Devil's Foot" I mentioned Holmes's study on *Chaldean Roots in the Ancient Cornish Language*. I did not mention that this work won high praise from such experts as the British Museum's Henry Jenner, the greatest living expert on the Cornish language. Holmes was able to demonstrate the close connection between the Cornish verb and the Irish verb systems.

The Holmes family were well known in Galway. Indeed, it was Holmes's uncle, Robert Holmes the famous Galway barrister and Queen's Counsel, whom the Irish have to thank for the organization of the Irish National School system for the poorer classes, for he was a member of the Duke of Leinster's seven-man education commission in the 1830s and 1840s responsible for many innovative ideas.

These few brief words will demonstrate, therefore, the significance of this *aide-mémoire*, which Holmes's passed to me in the spring of 1894.

My initial encounter with my second most dangerous adversary happened when I was lunching with my brother, Mycroft, in the Kildare Street Club, in Dublin, during the September of 1873. I was barely twenty years old at the time and thoughts of a possible career as a consulting detective had not yet formulated in my mind. In fact, my mind was fully occupied by the fact that I would momentarily be embarking for England where I had won a demyship at one of the Oxford Colleges with the grand sum of £95 per annum.

I had won the scholarship having spent my time at Trinity College, Dublin, in the study of chemistry and botany. My knowledge of chemistry owed much to a great Trinity scholar, Maxwell Simpson, whose lectures at the Park Street Medical School, advanced my knowledge of organic chemistry considerably. Simpson was the first man to synthesize succinic acid, a dibasic acid obtained by the dry distillation of amber. It was thanks to this great countryman of mine that I had produced a dissertation thought laudable enough to win me the scholarship to Oxford.

Indeed, I was not the only Trinity man to be awarded a demyship to Oxford that year. My friend, Wilde, a brilliant Classicist, a field for which I had no aptitude at all, was also to pursue his education there. Wilde continually berated me for my fascination with sensational literature and one day promised that he would write a horror story about a portrait that would chill even me.

My brother, Mycroft, who, like most of the Holmes family of Galway, was also a product of Trinity, had invited me to lunch at the Kildare Street Club. Mycroft, being seven years older than I, had already established his career in the Civil Service and was working in the fiscal department of the Chief Secretary for Ireland in Dublin Castle. He could, therefore, afford the £10 per annum which gave him access to the opulence of the red brick Gothic style headquarters of the Kildare Street Club.

The Club was the centre of masculine Ascendancy life in Ireland. Perhaps I should explain that these were the Anglo-Irish élite, descendants of those families which England had despatched to Ireland to rule the unruly natives. The Club was exclusive to members of the most important families in Ireland. No "Home Rulers", Catholics nor Dissenters were allowed in membership. The rule against Catholics was, however, "bent" in the case of The O'Conor Don, a direct descendant of the last High King of Ireland, and a few religious recalcitrants, such as the earls of Westmeath, Granard and Kenmare, whose loyalty to England had been proved to be impeccable. No army officer below the rank of major, nor below a Naval lieutenant-commander was allowed within its portals. And the only people allowed free use of its facilities were visiting members of the Royal Family, their equerries and the Viceroy himself.

My brother, Mycroft, basked and prospered in this colonial splendour but, I confess, it was not to my taste. I had only been accepted within this élite sanctuary as guest of Mycroft, who was known as a confident of the Chief Secretary and therefore regarded as having the ear of the Viceroy himself. I had only been persuaded to go because Mycroft wished to celebrate my demyship and see me off to Oxford in fraternal fashion. I did not want to disappoint him.

The dining room of the club was truly luxuriant. The club had the reputation of providing the best table in Dublin.

A solemn-faced waiter, more like an undertaker, led us through the splendidly furnished dining room to a table in a bay window overlooking St Stephen's Green for the club stood on the corner of Kildare Street and the green itself.

"An apéritif, gentlemen?" intoned the waiter in a sepulchral voice.

Mycroft took the opportunity to inform me that the cellar was of excellent quality, particularly the stock of champagne. I replied that I believed that I would commence with a glass of sherry and chose a Palo Cortaldo while Mycroft, extravagantly, insisted on a half bottle of Diamant Bleu.

He also insisted on a dozen oysters, which I observed cost an entire shilling a dozen, and were apparently sent daily from the club's own oyster bed near Galway. I settled for *pâté de foie gras* and we both agreed to indulge in a steak with a bottle of Bordeaux, a rich red St Estèphe from the Château MacCarthy.

In truth, Mycroft was more of a *gourmand* than a *gourmet.* He was physically lazy and already there was a corpulent aspect to his large frame. But he also had the Holmes's brow, the alert, steel-grey, deep set eyes and firmness of lips. He had an astute mind and was a formidable chess player.

After we had made our choice, we settled down and I was able to observe our fellow diners.

Among those who caught my immediate eye was a dark haired man who, doubtless, had been handsome in his youth. He was now in his mid thirties and his features were fleshy and gave him an air of dissoluteness and degeneracy. He carried himself with the air of a military man, even as he slouched at his table imbibing his wine, a little too freely I fear. His discerning brow was offset by the sensual jaw. I was aware of cruel blue eyes, drooping, cynical lids and an aggressive manner even while seated in repose. He was immaculately dressed in a smart dark coat and cravat with a diamond pin that announced expensive tastes.

His companion appeared less governed by the grape than he, preferring coffee to round off his luncheon. This second man was tall and thin, his forehead domed out in a white curve and his two eyes deeply sunken in his head. I would have placed him about the same age as his associate. He was clean-shaven, pale and ascetic looking. A greater contrast between two men, I could not imagine.

The scholarly man was talking earnestly and his military companion nodded from time to time, as if displeased at being disturbed in his contemplation of his wine glass. The other man, I saw, had rounded shoulders and his face protruded forward. I observed that his head oscillated from side to side in a curious reptilian fashion.

"Mycroft," I asked, after a while, "who is that curious pair?"

Mycroft glanced in the direction I had indicated.

"Oh, I would have thought you knew one of them – you being interested in science and such like."

I hid my impatience from my brother.

"I do not know, otherwise I would not have put forward the question."

"The elder is Professor Moriarty."

At once I was interested.

"Moriarty of Queen's University, in Belfast?" I demanded.

"The same Professor Moriarty," confirmed Mycroft smugly.

I had at least heard of Moriarty for he had the chair of mathematics at Queen's and written *The Dynamics of an Asteroid* which ascended to such rarefied heights of pure mathematics that no man in the scientific press was capable of criticizing it.

"And the man who loves his alcohol so much?" I pressed. "Who is he?"

Mycroft was disapproving of my observation.

"Dash it, Sherlock, where else may a man make free with his vices but in the shelter of his club?"

"There is one vice that he cannot well hide," I replied slyly. "That is his colossal male vanity. That black hair of his is no natural colour. The man dyes his hair. But, Mycroft, you have not answered my question. His name?"

"Colonel Sebastian Moran."

"I've never heard of him."

"He is one of the Morans of Connacht."

"A Catholic family?" For Ó Mórain, to give the name its correct Irish form, which meant "great", were a well-known Jacobite clan in Connacht.

"Hardly so," rebuked Mycroft. "His branch converted to the Anglican faith after the Williamite conquest. Sebastian Moran's father was Sir Augustus Moran CB, once British Minister to Persia. Young Moran went through Eton and Oxford. The family estate was near Derrynacleigh but I believe, after the colonel inherited, he lost it in a card game. He was a rather impecunious young man. Still, he was able to buy a commission in the Indian Army and served in the 1st Bengalore Pioneers. He has spent most of his career in India. I understand that he has quite a reputation as a big game hunter. The Bengal tiger mounted in the hall, as we came in, was one of his kills. The story is that he crawled down a drain after it when he had wounded it. That takes an iron nerve."

I frowned.

"Nerve, vanity and a fondness for drink and cards is sometimes an unenviable combination. They make a curious pair."

"I don't follow you?"

"I mean, a professor of mathematics and a dissolute army officer lunching together. What can they have in common?"

I allowed my attention to occupy the problem but a moment more. Even at this young age I had come to the conclusion that until one has facts it is worthless wasting time trying to hazard guesses.

My eye turned to the others in the dining room. Some I knew by sight and, one or two I had previously been introduced to in Mycroft's company. Among these diners was Lord Rosse, who had erected the largest reflecting telescope in the world at his home in Birr Castle. There was also the hard-drinking Viscount Massereene and Ferrard and the equally indulgent Lord Clonmell. There was great hilarity from another table where four young men were seated, voices raised in good-natured argument. I had little difficulty recognizing the Beresford brothers of Curraghmore, the elder of them being the Marquess of Waterford.

My eye eventually came to rest on a corner table where an elderly man with silver hair and round chubby red features was seated. He was well dressed and the waiters constantly hovered at his elbow to attend to his bidding like moths to a fly. He was obviously someone of importance.

I asked Mycroft to identify him.

"The Duke of Cloncury and Straffan," he said, naming one of the premier peers of Ireland.

I turned back to examine His Grace, whose ancestors had once controlled Ireland, with some curiosity. It was said that a word from Cloncury's grandfather could sway the vote in any debate in the old Irish Parliament, that was before the Union with England. As I was unashamedly scrutinizing him, His Grace was helped from his chair. He was, I judged, about seventy-something years of age, a short, stocky man but one who was fastidious in his toilet for his moustache was well cut and his hair neatly brushed so that not a silver strand of it was out of place.

He retrieved a small polished leather case, the size of a despatch-box, not more than twelve inches by six by four. It bore a crest in silver on it, and I presumed it to be Cloncury's own crest.

His Grace, clutching his case, made towards the door. At the same time, I saw Professor Moriarty push back his chair. Some sharp words were being exchanged between the professor and his lunching companion, Colonel Moran. The professor swung round and marched swiftly to the door almost colliding with the elderly duke at their portals. At the last moment, when collision seemed inevitable, the professor halted and allowed his Grace to move thorough the doors before him.

"Some argument has taken place between the professor and his companion," I observed aloud. "I wonder what the meaning of it is?"

Mycroft looked at me in disgust.

"Really, Sherlock, you always seem to be prying into other people's affairs. I would have thought you had enough on your plate preparing for your studies at Oxford."

Even at this time, I had become a close observer of people's behaviour and it is without any sense of shame that I record my surveillance into the lives of my fellow luncheon room occupants.

I returned my attention to the colonel who was sitting looking disgruntled at his wine glass. A waiter hovered near and made some suggestion but Moran swung with an angry retort, indicating the empty wine bottle on the table, and the waiter backed away. The colonel stood up, went through the motions of brushing the sleeves of his coat, and strode out of the dining room. I noticed that he would be returning for he had left his glass of wine unfinished. Sure enough, the waiter returned to the table with a half bottle of wine uncorked and placed it ready. The colonel, presumably having gone to make some ablutions, returned after some fifteen minutes and reseated himself. He seemed in a better mood for he was smiling to himself.

I was distracted to find that my brother was continuing to lecture me.

'I know you, Sherlock. You are an extremely lazy and undisciplined fellow. If a subject doesn't interest you, you just ignore it. It is a wonder that you have achieved this demyship, for I did not expect you to gain a degree at all."

I turned to my elder brother with a chuckle.

"Because we are brothers, Mycroft, we do not have to share the same concerns. Your problem is your love of good food and wine. You are an indulger, Mycroft, and physical inertia will cause the body to rebel one of these days."

I spoke with some conceit for during my time at Trinity I had taken several cups for swordsmanship, for boxing and was acknowledged a tolerable singlestick player.

"But you must consider what you will do with your career,

Sherlock. Our family have always been in government service, law or academic spheres. I fear you will fail your qualifications because of being so easily distracted by minutia . . ."

"But minutia is important in life . . ." I began.

At that moment we were interrupted by a disturbance at the door of the dining room.

The pale-faced waiter hurried into the room and made his way to where the elderly Duke of Cloncury and Straffan had been sitting. I watched in bemusement as the man first scrutinized the table carefully, then the top of the seats around the table and then, I have never witnessed such a thing before, the waiter actually went on his knees and examined under the table before, finally, his cadaverous features slightly reddened by his exertions, he hurried back to the door where the head waiter had now entered and stood with a troubled face.

There was a lot of shaking of heads and shrugs that passed between the two. The head waiter left the room.

As the waiter, who had conducted the search, was passing our table, I hailed the fellow much to Mycroft's astonished disapproval.

"Has His Grace mislaid something?" I queried.

The waiter, the same individual who had conducted us to our table when we entered, turned mournful eyes upon me. There was a glint of suspicion in them.

"Indeed, he has, sir. How did you know?"

"I observed that you were searching on and around the table where he had recently been seated. From that one deduces that he had lost something that he thought he had with him at that table."

The man's gaze fell in disappointment at the logic of my reply.

"What has he lost?" I pressed.

"His toilet case, sir."

Mycroft gave an ill-concealed guffaw.

"A toilet case? What is a man doing bringing a toilet case into a dining room?"

The waiter turned to Mycroft.

"His Grace is a very fastidious and eccentric person, Mister Holmes." The man evidently knew Mycroft by sight. "He carries the case with him always."

"A valuable item?" I hazarded.

"Not really, sir. At least, not financially so."

"Ah, you mean it has great sentimental value for the Duke?" I suggested.

"It was a gift which King William gave to one of His Grace's ancestors as a personal memento when the man saved his life during the battle at the Boyne. And now, gentlemen, if you have not seen the item . . ."

He went on his way.

Mycroft was passing his napkin over his mouth,

"Now how about a port or brandy in the hall?"

The lofty hall of the club, with its big game trophies and blazing fire and staircase of elaborately carved stonework, was where members gathered for their after luncheon drinks and cigars.

We rose and made our way out of the dining room. Our path led us by the table of Colonel Moran and as we passed by I noticed that the colonel's dark suit was ill-chosen for it showed up his dandruff. I grant you it is such small observations that sometimes irritate my fellows. But if one is prone to dandruff at least one should have the good sense to wear a light colour in which the tell-tale white powder and silver hairs would be less noticeable.

As we made our way into the hall we saw the elderly Duke of Cloncury and Straffan standing with the head waiter and a gentleman whom Mycroft informed me was the chairman of the directors of the club. His Grace was clearly distressed.

"It is priceless! A value beyond measure!" He was almost wailing.

"I cannot understand it, Your Grace. Are you sure that you had it with you in the dining room?"

"Young man," snapped the elderly duke, "do you accuse me of senility?"

The "young man", who was about fifty years of age, blanched, and took a step backward before the old man's baleful gaze.

"Not at all, Your Grace, not at all. Just tell me the facts again."

"After finishing my luncheon, I went into the wash room. I washed my hands and then brushed my hair. It is my custom to do so after luncheon. I took my silver hairbrush from my leather case, which I always carry with me. I remember clearly that I returned it to the case. I left the case on the wash stand and went into the toilet. I came out, washed my hands and then realized that the case was no longer there."

The head waiter was looking glum.

"I have already suggested to His Grace that the case might have been left in the dining room and sent one of the waiters to check. It was not there."

The old man bristled.

"Knew it would be a damned waste of time. Said so. I know where it went missing. I'd start interrogating your employees, sir. At once!"

The club chairman looked unhappy.

"Your Grace, please allow us time to search the premises before we start anything so drastic. Perhaps it has simply been mislaid . . .?"

"Mislaid!" The word was an explosion. "Dammit! Mislaid! Do you take me for a fool, sir? I demand that an interrogation of your employees begin at once. I suggest that you now send for the DMP!"

The mention of the Dublin Metropolitan Police had made the chairman slightly pale.

"Your Grace, the reflection on our reputation . . ."

"Damn your reputation, sir! What about my hair brush!" quivered the old man.

It was then I felt I should intervene.

"Excuse me, Your Grace," I began.

Rheumy blue eyes turned on me and assessed my youthful years.

"And who the devil are you, Sir?"

"My name is Holmes. I might be able to help you."

"You, you young jackanapes? What do you mean?"

I heard my brother "tut-tutting" anxiously in the background at my effrontery.

"With your permission, I think I might be in a position to recover the lost item."

Cloncury's eyes narrowed dangerously.

"Do you have it, you impudent whippersnapper?" he demanded. "By God, if you are responsible . . ."

Mycroft came to my help.

"Excuse me, Your Grace, this is my younger brother, Sherlock Holmes."

Cloncury glanced up and recognized Mycroft, knowing him to have the ear of the Viceroy. He looked slightly mollified.

"Why didn't he introduce himself properly then, hey? Very well, young Holmes, what do you mean by it?"

"With your permission, sir," I went on, unperturbed, "I would like to put a few questions to the chairman of the club."

The chairman began to flush in annoyance.

"Go ahead, then, Mister Holmes," instructed Cloncury. "I am sure that the chairman will be in favour of anything that stops the incursion of the police into this establishment."

It seemed that the chairman, albeit reluctantly, was in favour.

"Well, sir, if I remember correctly, the wash room is next to the cloak room, is it not?"

"Yes."

"Is the wash room attended?"

"It is not."

"And the cloak room? Is it attended at all times?"

"Of course it is."

"Your Grace, will you be so good as to show me where it was that you left your toilet box?"

We turned in a body, headed by the duke, and passed into the wash room. He pointed to one of the ornate marble wash basins at the far end of the room. It was one of a dozen such wash basins lining the entire left handside wall of the chamber which was fronted by a series of mirrors for the use of the members. The right handside wall was fitted with toilet cubicles in dark mahogany and brass fittings, except for a small area behind the main door. The marble tiled wall here was unimpeded by anything except for a small opening. It was about two feet square, framed in mahogany and with a hatch door.

I pointed to it.

"I presume that this hatch connects the wash room with the cloak room?"

"Naturally," barked the chairman. "Now what is all this about?"

I turned and led them out of the wash room into the cloakroom, where a uniformed attendant leapt from his chair, dropping a half-smoked cigarette into an ash tray and looking penitently from one to another of us.

"Can I help you gentlemen?" he stuttered.

"Yes, you can," I assured him. "You can bring me the garment that you are holding for Colonel Sebastian Moran. I think you will find that it is a heavy riding cloak or one of those new style long, loose coats which, I believe, is called an Ulster."

The attendant returned my gaze in bewildered fashion.

The chairman pushed forward.

"Good God, sir, what do you mean by it? Colonel Moran is a respected member of this club. Why are you presuming to ask for his coat?"

The Duke of Cloncury was looking at me with a frown of disapproval.

"You'd better have a good explanation, young Holmes," he muttered.

"I believe that you want the return of your toilet case?" I asked blandly.

"Gad, you know I do."

I turned to the attendant.

"Have you been on duty for the last half an hour?"

"That I have, sir."

"A short while ago Colonel Moran knocked on the hatch from

the wash room side and asked if you could pass him his coat for a moment. Is that correct?"

The man's jaw dropped in astonishment.

"It is, sir. He said he wanted to comb his hair and had left the toilet items in his coat. And the coat was, indeed, one of those new style Ulsters, sir."

"I believe the colonel then came around from the wash room, into the cloak room, in order to hand you back the coat?"

"That is exactly what he did, sir."

I turned and smiled at the astonished company, perhaps a little too superior in my attitude.

"How the hell did you know that?" growled the chairman.

"Now, my man," I said, ignoring him, but speaking again to the attendant. "Would you fetch Colonel Moran's Ulster?"

The attendant turned, picked down the garment and handed it to me in silence.

I took it and weighed it carefully with one hand before reaching into the inside lining. There were several large pockets there as was the fashion with such garments. The leather box was tucked neatly into one of them.

"How did you know?" gasped Cloncury seizing his precious box eagerly.

"Know? I merely deduce from facts, sir. If you will open the box and check the brush? I think you may find that in the brush are some strands of dark black hair. The colour of Colonel Moran's hair, which is easy to spot as it is dyed."

It took the duke but a moment to confirm that I was right.

"I think the colonel is someone given to seizing opportunity. A chance taker," I told them. "He followed His Grace into the wash room when His Grace had already entered the toilet. He saw the leather case there. He knew it had great sentimental value for His Grace. Perhaps he thought he might be able to blackmail Cloncury for its return, probably through an intermediary of course. He seized the opportunity, asking for his Ulster to be passed through the hatch in order to conceal the box in order to get it out of the club. He chanced that members would not be searched . . ."

"It would be unthinkable that a member of this club would be searched," muttered the chairman. "We are all gentlemen here!"

I chose not to comment.

"He could not carry the box out of the wash room into the cloak room without observation. When I saw the hatch I knew that he had only to ask for his coat to be passed through, place the box in his pocket unobserved, and the theft was complete."

"How did you know it was an Ulster or a riding cloak?" demanded his grace.

"He would have to be possessed of a heavy coat such as an Ulster or riding cloak with large enough interior pockets to conceal the box in."

"Why not pass the coat back through the hatch once he had hidden the box in the coat?" demanded Mycroft. "Why do you think that he came out of the wash room door, into the hall and then into the cloak room to return the cloak to the attendant?"

"Moran was cautious. Passing it back through the hatch might cause the attendant to feel the box and become suspicious, especially after Cloncury raised the alarm. So he carried it round and handed it to the attendant holding it upright by the collar. The extra weight would not be noticed. Is that correct?"

The attendant nodded confirmation.

"What made you think there would be hairs on the brush and that they would be his?" queried His Grace, staring dubiously at the black dyed hairs which were entangled on his silver-backed brush.

"Because Moran is a vain man and could not resist cocking a snoot at you, Your Grace, by brushing his own hair while you were within feet of him. It fits in with Moran's character, a demonstration of his nerve for any moment you might have opened the door and discovered him. Chance is his adrenaline."

"Holmes, this is amazing!" gasped Cloncury.

"It was another Trinity man who alerted me to the importance of careful observation," I informed him. "Jonathan Swift. He wrote that a stander-by may sometimes see more of the game than he who plays it." I could not resist turning to Mycroft and adding, *sotto voce*, "And Trinity almost refused to give Swift a degree because they thought he was too lazy and undisciplined!"

The chairman of the club signalled the uniformed club doorman and his assistant. They looked ex-military men.

"You will find Colonel Moran in the dining room," he instructed. "Ask him to join us immediately. If he will not comply, you have my permission to escort him here with as much force as you have cause to use."

The two men went off briskly about their task.

A moment later the colonel, whose appearance suggested that he had polished off the rest of the wine, was firmly propelled into our presence.

His red-rimmed eyes fell on his Ulster and on Cloncury holding his precious leather case. The man's face went white in spite of the alcoholic infused cheeks.

"By Gad, sir, you should be horsewhipped!" growled the Duke of Cloncury and Straffan menacingly.

"This is a fabrication!" bluffed Moran feebly. "Someone put the box in my inside coat pocket."

I could not forbear a grin of triumph.

"How did you know that it was the box which had been stolen? And how did you know it was found in your *inside* coat pocket, colonel?"

Moran knew the game was up.

"Moran," the chairman said heavily, "I shall try to persuade His Grace not to bring charges against you for the sake of the reputation of this club. If he agrees, it will be on the condition that you leave Ireland within the next twelve hours and never return. I will circulate your name in society so that no house will open its doors to you again. I will have you black-balled in every club in the land."

The Duke of Cloncury and Straffan gave the matter a moment's thought and then agreed to the conditions.

"I'd horsewhip the beggar, if it were me. Anyway. I think we all owe young Mister Sherlock Holmes our thanks in resolving this matter."

Moran glowered at me.

"So you tipped them off, you young interfering . . ." He made a sudden aggressive lunge at me.

Mycroft inserted his large frame between me and Moran. His fist impacted on the colonel's nose and Moran went sprawling back only to be neatly caught by the doorman and his assistant.

"Kindly escort Colonel Moran off the premises, gentlemen," ordered the chairman, "and you do not have to be gentle."

Moran twisted in their gasp to look back at me with little option but to control his foul temper.

"I have your measure, Sherlock Holmes," he glowered, seething with an inner rage, as they began to propel him towards the door. "You have not heard the last of me."

It was as Mycroft was sharing a cab in the direction of my rooms in Lower Baggott Street that he frowned and posed the question:

"But I cannot see how you could have identified Moran as the culprit in the first place?"

"It was elementary, Mycroft," I smiled. "When we left the luncheon room and passed behind Moran's chair, I saw that the colonel had dandruff on his shoulders. Now he had jet-black hair. But with the dandruff lay a number of silver strands. It meant nothing to me at the time for I was not aware of the facts. When I discovered that the missing case contained a hairbrush and comb, everything fell into place. The duke not only had silver hair but, I noticed, he also had dandruff to boot. By brushing his hair in such a foolhardy gesture, Moran had transferred the dandruff and silver hair to his own shoulders. It was easy to witness that Moran was a vain man. He would not have allowed dandruff and hair, if it had been his, to lay on his shoulders when he entered a public dining room. Indeed, I saw him rise from his table and go out, brushing himself as he did so. The sign of a fastidious man. He had, therefore, unknowingly picked it up during his short absence. Everything else was a matter of simple deduction."

As Moran had been thrown out of the Kildare Street Club, he had called out to me that I had not heard the last of him. Indeed, I had not. But I could not have conceived of how our paths would meet at that time nor of the sinister role Moran's friend, Professor Moriarty, would play in my life. While Moriarty became my most implacable foe, Colonel Sebastian Moran was certainly the second most dangerous man that I ever had to deal with.

PART II: THE 1880s

After Holmes left university he settled in rooms in Montague Street in London spending much of his time researching into those branches of science that were relevant to his new vocation, and gradually building a practice as the world's first consulting detective. It seems that not all of these early cases were successful or particularly interesting and although he referred Watson to several, including the Tarleton murders, the case of Vamberry the wine merchant, the adventure of the old Russian wife plus two particularly tempting ones – the singular affair of the aluminium crutch and the story of Ricoletti of the club-foot and his abominable wife – nothing sufficient on these cases has come to light to allow me to retell them. Records of them that I have seen, and which I mention in the appendix, I believe to be apocryphal. Holmes did tell Watson the story of "The Musgrave Ritual", which was his third case (and which we shall return to later), but he did not relate any others in detail. Without Watson as his amanuensis, and with Watson's papers stolen it has proven difficult to piece these years together. I have found some leads on the cases Holmes refers to as "Merridew of Abominable Memory" and "Mrs Farintosh and the Opal Tiara", but details of these must wait for another time.

It was when Holmes was searching for new rooms, in January 1881, that he and Watson met and came to share an apartment. At the outset, as related in "A Study in Scarlet", Watson was at a loss to know what Holmes did for a living, and was rather bemused at all the visitors who came to see him, including officers from Scotland Yard. It is clear that in these four years Holmes had established a strong reputation though he had not, at that stage, made much financial gain. That would come later.

After his own involvement in "A Study in Scarlet", Watson became increasingly drawn into Holmes's cases and recorded several that happened in the next couple of years: "The Resident Patient", "The Beryl Coronet" and the famous "The Speckled Band". At this stage, though, Watson was not fully into the habit of keeping methodical notes of the cases, because he had not yet pursued the idea of publishing them. At the start of "The Resident Patient" he talks about his "incoherent series of memoirs". However, by the time he came to write-up the case of "The Speckled Band" in 1888, five years after the events, he was clearly getting his notes in order, as he states so at the outset.

It means that for the first few years of their acquaintanceship, Watson's record of Holmes's cases is hit-and-miss, and he seems to have preserved only those that made a special mark on his memory because of their bizarre or unusual nature. It may not be that sinister, therefore, that so few of these *early cases survive and that, by 1884, we enter a relatively dark period when Holmes's activities are not well recorded. It may simply be that none of Holmes's cases were worth recording. Of course, the contrary could also be true. Since Holmes carefully vetted everything he let Watson publish we could deduce that he was involved in some very secret cases at this time. Some of the cases referred to in passing in later stories may date from this period, particularly those where Holmes began to move in higher circles in society, such as the help he gave to the King of Scandinavia and another time to Lord Backwater. These cases not only brought him prestige but were financially rewarding so that by the start of 1885 we find Holmes's practice on a firmer footing, and Watson keeping a better account of his cases.*

Thanks to the help of Claire Griffen, who came across some fragments of Watson's notes and related memorabilia that surfaced in an old book shop in South Australia, we have been able to piece together one of these cases that Holmes alluded to many years later. In "The Six Napoleons" he reminded Watson how the business of the Abernetty family came to his attention because of the depth that the parsley had sunk into the butter, an example of how not to overlook what may appear trifling detail. That case has puzzled Sherlockians for decades but at last we can report it in full.

THE CASE OF
THE INCUMBENT INVALID

Claire Griffen

Of all the adventures I shared with my friend Sherlock Holmes I cannot recall one other in which he was quite so ambivalent about its outcome than *the dreadful affair of the Abernettys*, nor one which he felt so reluctant to pursue, yet was driven to its tragic and macabre *dénouement.*

Because of his peculiar sensitivity regarding the role he played therein I have never chronicled the affair, but a chance remark recently while discussing with Inspector Lestrade the bizarre case of the Six Napoleons, and the fact that the main participants have long since been freed to seek new lives in South Australia, encourage me to believe he will tolerate my jotting down a few remembrances of the case.

The trivial remark of how far a sprig of parsley had sunk into melting butter on a hot day first seized his attention, but it was on a raw day in early January, 1885 when we first became embroiled in the question of Lady Abernetty's possible murder.

I was standing at our bow window gloomily surveying the prospect. Fog had shrouded the city in the earlier hours of the day and would probably return in the late afternoon, but at that hour a pale straggle of sunlight lit a street almost deserted but for the occasional cab and passerby ulstered and mufflered against the chill damp. Despite the warmth of the fire I could not resist a shiver.

"I'm sorry you feel you cannot afford to take the cure at Baden-Baden next spring," drawled my friend from his easy chair beside the hearth.

I confess he gave me rather a start. I had said nothing about my somewhat wistful ambition to pamper my indifferent health at the famous resort in the Black Forest.

Shortly before I met and took up residence with Holmes at Baker Street, I had returned from service in Afghanistan with the legacy of a jezail bullet and there were times, especially when I felt the London fog on my bones, that it throbbed remorselessly. I could more easily or cheaply take the cure at

Bath, but I had a fancy for Baden-Baden, not for its casino and race-course, but to stroll along the banks of the Oos where Brahms composed his Lichtenthal Symphony and Dostoevksy strolled under the ancient trees.

"My dear Watson," Holmes replied to my start of surprise, "you've been haunting travel agencies on your days off, your desk is littered with brochures and time-tables. I observed you studying the balance in your pass-book with a morose expression and you've been poor company ever since."

"I beg your pardon if I appear so. It's this dismal weather. Don't you find the fog depressing, Holmes?"

"Not I!" My companion's grey eyes sparkled. "I find it stimulating. I conjure up all manner of fiendish doings under its cover. By the way," he added, casually, "you will let me know when the carriage pulls up at our front door."

"Are we expecting someone?" My spirits lifted. Since I had resided with Holmes many interesting people had crossed the threshold of 221b Baker Street, some of whom had invited us into the most intriguing and dangerous adventures it had ever been my privilege to share and chronicle.

"A prospective client." Holmes took a note from inside his pocket and spread it open on his knee. "The hour mentioned is three. Ah, there strikes the clock."

"Anything of interest?" I enquired, eagerly.

"I fear not," sighed Holmes. "A domestic dispute, I fancy. Cases worthy of engaging my complete attention have been sparse in recent weeks."

I echoed his sigh. I had learned to dread these periods of inactivity when my friend lapsed into boredom and melancholy. I had discovered only recently his injudicious use of cocaine in such lapses, a regrettable weakness from which I seemed powerless to dissuade him.

"A carriage has just stopped at the kerb." I observed a rather large lady in furs and a rather small man in greatcoat and Homburg alight. "Could these be our visitors?"

"Ah, since you speak in the plural the lady must be accompanied. A Mrs Mabel Bertram, Watson, a widow she writes, so the gentleman is not her husband." He rose, gave his shoulders a twitch and stood with his back to the fire.

The knock on our door could almost be described as deferential. At my friend's nod, I admitted our visitors.

"Have I the honour to address Mr Sherlock Holmes, the famous detective?" enquired the gentleman, in a pleasant yet suave manner.

"I am Dr John Watson. This is Mr Sherlock Holmes. Won't you come in?"

The woman who advanced into the room was indeed Junoesque and stylishly dressed in a fur-trimmed coat of the colour that, I believe, was called cobalt blue, and a feathered hat perched somewhat coquettishly on Titian hair that owed more to the cosmetician than to nature. I perceived her to be a woman of fifty, whose features bore the remnants of a once-proud beauty.

Her companion was slim and dapper with dark lively eyes and a waxed moustache. He removed his Homburg to reveal a sleek, dark head.

"Mr Holmes, how kind of you to see me," greeted the lady, warmly. "I am Mabel Bertram. May I present Mr Aston Plush?"

Bows were exchanged and, standing well back, Holmes invited his visitors to take seats before the fire. Mr Plush preferred to stand with his back to the window so that he was almost in silhouette.

"Draw your chair closer to the fire, Mrs Bertram," coaxed my friend. "I observe you are shivering from the inclement weather."

"It is not the chill that makes me shiver, but the anxiety caused by my dilemma." She fixed her gaze imploringly on his face. "You are my last hope, Mr Holmes."

"Dear me!" After one swift scanning glance over her entire person, he leaned back in his armchair steepling his fingers against the shabby velvet front of his smoking-jacket and examining her face from eyes that were mere slits under his drowsy lids.

"You mentioned in your note you were concerned about the welfare of a relative. Pray go on."

"To be precise, my stepmother. I am the eldest daughter of Sir William Abernetty by his first marriage. Upon the death of my mother he married Miss Alice Pemberton, a lady some ten years older than myself. There was a daughter from this second marriage, Sabina, and a son born posthumously, Charles. You may be amazed at my concern for my stepmother when she has two children of her own, but being so close in age we have always been on the best of terms. Until recently."

"And what has happened to cause this rift?"

"Nothing!" burst out the lady. Restraining herself quickly, she went on. "Nothing that I can account for. There's been no quarrel, no exchange of harsh words, yet Charles and Sabina have informed me in the plainest of terms that she refuses to see me. I should add here that Lady Abernetty is an invalid. Neither my half-brother nor sister are married and both reside with their mother in Grosvenor Square."

Holmes raised his eyebrows ever so slightly. He had begun to look rather bored, but at the mention of the élite address he perked up a little. Nevertheless, he murmured, "I fail to see what assistance I can be. As you say, you are not the lady's daughter and can lay no claim to her affections. She may see you or not as she pleases. Her children are no doubt following her instructions."

"Hear me out, I implore you." Mabel Bertram laid aside her muff and clasped agitated hands. "I am not alone in being excluded from her door. My stepmother has suffered from an affliction of the lungs for many years and a doctor has been in constant attendance. Imagine my horror when I was informed by Dr Royce Miles that he no longer calls upon Lady Abernetty – at the request of her son Charles, and this after a professional attendance of many years." Her lower lip trembled. "Mr Holmes, I fear for my stepmother's life."

My friend frowned. "Have you reason to believe your brother and sister have anything but the most loving regard for their mother?"

Mabel Bertram coughed discreetly behind a lace-trimmed hand-kerchief. "My stepmother has many admirable qualities, Mr Holmes, but I think it fair to say that with her children she was something of a Tartar. There was never any question of either Charles or Sabina marrying. Her formidable manner drove away any suitors or lady friends. Alice much preferred to have them at her own beck and call. Son and daughter have always been expected to stay close to home and Alice has always kept a tight grip on the purse-strings. Now I hear Sabina's been seen gadding about in new gowns and Charles has joined the Footlights Amateur Dramatic Society."

"Dear me!" Holmes smiled in amusement.

"Mr Holmes, I fear my stepmother no longer has the power to influence her children."

"Would that be such a bad thing?" asked my friend, quietly. "Their indulgences seem innocent enough." He suddenly lifted a piercing gaze to her companion. "In what capacity do you accompany Mrs Bertram, Mr Aston Plush?"

The gentleman hesitated. "As Mrs Bertram's legal adviser and friend."

"You are a solicitor then?"

"Mr Plush handled my late husband's estate and before that his business affairs," intervened Mrs Bertram. "He has been kind enough to act for me in this matter."

"I have written several letters expressing Mrs Bertram's concern and requesting access to her stepmother. Beyond that my hands are tied. There is no legal way we can obtain admittance to the house on Grosvenor Square. Were we to force entry the

Abernettys would be quite within their rights to summon the police."

"I did enter the house through the servants' entrance on the first day I was refused admittance," confessed Mrs Bertram, with a slight blush.

"You did not tell me this . . ." began the lawyer in a vexed tone.

"My dear, it was a humiliating experience. I was actually ejected by the butler. Charles and Sabina reacted with quite uncharacteristic hostility. Perhaps because I had seen evidence of their neglect of their mother."

"Indeed, and what was that?" Holmes glanced at her keenly.

"It was Lady Abernetty's custom to have a roll with parsley butter for her breakfast every morning. The cook had obviously prepared the tray, but there was the butter still standing on the table at noon with the parsley quite sunk into the butter. Alice always demanded a well-run, fastidious kitchen . . ."

"And when did this visit take place?" interrupted Holmes.

"On the first day of August."

"And you have not seen Lady Abernetty since." He returned his attention to Aston Plush. "Did you receive any response to your correspondence?"

"Two letters, one from each of the children and each couched in similar terms, reiterating that their mother wished no further communication with Mrs Bertram. There was no cause for alarm concerning Lady Abernetty's health. Would Mrs Bertram please leave the matter as it stands?"

My friend returned his gaze to Mabel Bertram's face. "But you feel you cannot do so . . ."

The lady leaned forward. "I see I must confide in you my darkest fears. You may think me a fanciful, even hysterical woman, but I fear my stepmother has met with foul play. Only tell me this isn't so, Mr Holmes, and I will never intrude upon them again."

"Of course there is also the matter of the Power of Attorney," interjected Plush.

"Which has been given to the son?"

"Presumably."

My friend was silent for several minutes, his eyes closed, while the lady continued to gaze at him beseechingly. Behind Mrs Bertram's chair, Mr Aston Plush stirred uneasily.

When Sherlock Holmes reached a decision about taking a case he often moved quite abruptly. He did so now, springing briskly from his chair. "I will look into the matter for you."

"Oh, Mr Holmes, you will find me so grateful."

"And generous." Mr Plush had come forward to assist his client from her chair.

She flashed him a glance before she lowered her veil.

"Hopefully you will hear from me within the week. Watson, the door."

"How will you . . .?" she enquired timidly.

"My methods are my own. Good-day to you," he returned, brusquely.

I ushered out the pair and returned to find Holmes filling his pipe from a tobacco pouch he kept in an old Turkish slipper on the mantelpiece.

"Well, what did you make of that, Watson?" he asked, smiling.

"It seemed to me a tawdry affair. But, of course, the lady's anxiety was genuine."

My friend laughed softly. "One of your most endearing qualities, Watson, is your naivete about the good in people."

I must confess to feeling slightly nettled by my friend's cynicism. "How did she strike you?"

"Here we have a rather theatrical, still-handsome woman who knows how to deploy her charms. Did you notice which chair she took? With her back to the window, away from the daylight and where the firelight would soften and enhance her looks."

"She may not have wished to sully her dress with the rather obvious pipe-ash scattered on your chair," I retorted.

"Well done!" approved my friend. "And what did you make of the silent partner?"

"Mr Ashton Plush? I was surprised a lawyer should take such an interest in a domestic squabble."

"Indeed. I feel he has what is generally termed a vested interest. Did you mark where he stood, Watson?"

"Behind her chair, in a most protective manner."

"No, where his own face was in shadow and he could observe me observing her. He wanted to gauge my reaction to her story. There's more to this than meets the eye, Watson. A lady dressed in the height of fashion in the company of a man some ten years younger than herself. She evinces little sympathy for the plight of her siblings, yet a great deal of concern for her stepmother. What is her real concern? We might look into the father's background." He took down a red-covered reference book from the mantelpiece. "Ah, yes, Abernetty, Sir William, knighted for services to the crown. A son of impoverished country gentry. Made a fortune in the East by mysterious and possibly devious means. Returned to England in 1830 whereupon he married Clarissa, daughter of Sir Arthur Humphrey, and entered politics. Money opens many doors Watson, even one on Grosvenor Square. Wife died in 1848, one daughter Mabel. Married Miss Alice Fernberton 1850, died 1852. Aha, Watson! Made some bad investments in the East Indies, died with his fortune considerably reduced."

"What does that tell us, Holmes?"

"I'm not sure, but it should tell us something. What did you think of the story of the parsley sunk into the butter?"

"Almost ludicrous."

Holmes looked at me musingly. "Did you indeed? I hope to teach you the importance of trivialities. Do you have the time to join me on this adventure, Watson, if it is indeed to be an adventure? I doubt if I can promise you a baboon or a cheetah on this occasion."

"My dear Holmes, if you think I could possibly be of use." I still felt a thrill of pride at having my assistance requested as I had not yet shared as many exploits with my friend as I have to this date and it was all quite new and uncharted to my prosaic way of life.

Holmes smiled in one of his rare flashes of warmth. "Thank you. I shall as always value your company. And your medical expertise may be of value should we chance to meet the invalid. But at the moment I would greatly appreciate your going to your club. You may even choose to spend the night there to avoid the evening fog. I have to give this matter a great deal of thought and I can't predict how many pipes will bring me to a solution."

Being aware of his practice of using tobacco for a stimulus to his thought processes until the room was filled with an acrid pall of smoke, I was happy to oblige.

When I returned next day at noon I was met by an astonishing sight. My friend stood in our little sitting-room transformed into a Bohemian with flowing locks, a flourishing moustache, a hat with a curled brim, a dashing cape and yellow spotted silk bandana knotted at his throat.

"Come, Watson, we can't have you looking so dull. Break out your fancy duds." His eyes were dancing merrily in his long lean face.

Accustomed as I was becoming to my friend's disguises, I perceived some plan was afoot.

"I have nothing half so showy and shall be obliged to go as I am. Where are we going by the way?"

"I've work for you, Watson, if you're willing to undertake it."

"You know I'm always happy to oblige."

"Thank you. I want you to call upon your colleague, Dr Royce Miles. I understand he has rooms in Knightsbridge. I want you to enquire in your professional capacity about the health of Lady Abernetty. Say you have had an enquiry about her and seek a word of discreet advice. Take careful note of the interview, how the good doctor looks, what he has to say, any minor detail, you know my methods."

"And you, Holmes?"

"I'm off to join the Footlights Amateur Dramatic Society with the expectation of making the acquaintance of Charles Abernetty. You see before you Sebastian Flood, aspiring actor. These ladies and gentlemen of leisure and thesbian pursuits are meeting for rehearsal of their forthcoming production. We'll meet back here for supper and compare our findings."

I had removed my damp outer wear and was sitting before the fire in my dressing-gown reading *The Times* when Sherlock Holmes returned from his expedition. One glance at his face showed even under the disguise that he was in a brooding, taciturn mood.

"Not now," he said, in answer to my unspoken question. "I need to rid myself of these trappings and get a hot meal inside me before I can discuss the day's events. Will you ring for Mrs Hudson and advise her of our readiness for supper?"

After Mrs Hudson's excellent roast beef and Yorkshire pudding, he poured us both a whisky and soda and lit a cigar. For half an hour perhaps he sat in the darkened room, gazing meditatively into the fire. I knew him too well to break into his reverie.

The striking of the clock aroused him at last. "Let us have the lamp, Watson. I thought we might indulge in a game of whist before we go to bed."

"You astound me, Holmes."

"Do I? I won't when I inform you we've been invited for a hand tomorrow afternoon at Grosvenor Square. I need to freshen up my knowledge of the rules."

"I gather you've succeeded in making the acquaintance of Charles Abernetty."

"Indeed I have. He's quite the shining light of the Footlights Amateur Dramatic Society. A dapper little man, Watson, but somewhat nondescript in feature and colour which would I think give him the opportunity to play many roles. Quite theatrical in his approach to acting, but he has a few subtle nuances which are quite interesting."

"In personality or stage presentation?"

Holmes chuckled. "You always come straight to the point with these little pragmatisms of yours. Yes, where does one leave off and the other begin? After I had watched the rehearsal I begged to be introduced to him by the President of the Society, whose acquaintance I had previously made. I praised Mr Abernetty's performance extravagantly and he became quite enchanted with me with what seemed mingled vanity and a need for self-reassurance.

Such was the rapport we established he invited me to accompany him to Drury Lane one evening where an artist he greatly admires is presently performing.

"The subject of whist somehow crept into the conversation. When I said I played he immediately invited me for tomorrow afternoon. *Did I have a friend?* he asked. *Indeed I did,* said I. Then his sister Miss Sabina Abernetty would make a fourth."

"Well, you've got us over the doorstep. Well done, Holmes."

My companion shrugged his narrow shoulders. "I wonder if I *have* done well." He turned the conversation abruptly. "How did you fare with Dr Royce Miles?"

"I had feared he might be rather reticent about a former patient, but he was quite loquacious on the subject of Lady Abernetty. Glad to have her off his hands and wished me all the luck in the world. She is apparently one of those irascible patients all doctors dread to treat."

"And her ailment?"

"Congestion of the lungs which is placing quite a strain on the heart. Embarrassed left ventricle. Can't survive much longer, which will be a blessing for the children. She is, according to Miles, a cold woman who treats and has always treated her son and daughter like servants rather than loved children. Miles was full of praise for the care and attention they lavish on her."

"When neglect might carry her off sooner?"

"That's a harsh observation, Holmes."

"It's what Mrs Bertram says she fears."

"Miles was surprised at her apparent concern. She has made only one enquiry about her stepmother's health which was when she discovered the doctor had been dismissed. In his many visits to Grosvenor Square he never once saw her at the house."

"It's possible her visits didn't coincide with his. And what is the appearance of this Dr Royce Miles?"

"A bluff, somewhat florid man. Though I shouldn't venture such a remark about a fellow medico I fancy he likes his port."

"Which could be the reason for his dismissal."

"I'm sure he's competent enough." I hastened to the defence of my colleague.

My friend's only reply was a grunt.

"I must confess I'm baffled, Holmes. Do you believe Mrs Bertram's anxiety is genuine?"

"I believe Lady Abernetty's health is a subject of immense concern to quite a few people. The question is why."

"You surely give no credence to Mrs Bertram's suspicion that she's met with foul play. Having met Charles Abernetty . . ."

"Did I envisage him as capable of matricide, that vilest of crimes? Did Alice Abernetty, like Clytemnaestra, dream she had given birth to a serpent who suckled blood from her breast?" He threw away his mood with his cigar.

"Come, Watson, deal the cards."

The house in Mayfair, that most discreetly elegant of London districts was Georgian with a protective railing of iron spikes, double doors with flanking Doric pillars, large bay windows, a set of steps on the left leading down to the servants' entrance and mews leading to stable and coach-house.

"How much do you think this would fetch in realty?" murmured Sherlock Holmes. He had resumed his disguise of the previous day with luxuriant locks and moustache. "Sebastian Flood and John Watson," he announced to the elderly butler who answered the door. "I believe Mr Charles Abernetty is expecting us."

The small salon to which we were conducted had the furnishings of an earlier era with its marble Adam fireplace, its Chinese wall-paper and carpet and Chippendale furniture. Charles Abernetty greeted us enthusiastically. His sister, dressed in a dark cashmere gown, rose from a wing chair and glided across the floor to meet us. Her manner was more restrained, but no less welcoming. They were a singularly colourless pair, when one recalled the vivacity of their half-sister, both slight of build and with scarcely a year between them in age. They were so alike that the only differences between them were those determined by gender and a certain variance of personality. What soon became apparent was their deep affection for each other.

"You must forgive our old-fashioned furnishings," said Charles when introductions were exchanged. "This was how the rooms were originally when the house came into the family's possession, and Mother has always preferred it this way."

"Ah, you have a parent in residence," observed Holmes. "Will we have the pleasure of meeting Mrs Abernetty?"

"Our mother is an invalid and does not receive visitors," interposed Sabina. "The cold weather disagrees with her."

"Perhaps you would care to have my friend take a look at her." At their startled look he hurried on. "Watson here is a fully qualified medical practitioner. I'm sure that at any time he'd be happy to give you his professional opinion."

As I murmured acquiescence I saw Charles dart a look at his sister. She maintained an impeccable composure.

"Thank you, you're very kind, but we have our own family doctor who takes care of Mother's needs."

"Perhaps you might know him, Watson. What is his name?"

"Dr Halliwell," she replied, after a brief hesitation. She was beginning to look a trifle annoyed, as well she might, by Holmes's persistence.

"I'm sure he's a very good man," I said soothingly. "And pray don't apologize for your furnishings. This is a charming room."

"You are most fortunate," added my friend, in the irrepressible role he had adopted, "in owning this delightful residence in such an elite location. Its worth must be prodigious."

Charles flushed up to the eyes. "Mother would never consider selling up. It's quite impossible."

"I've offended you," said Holmes. "My candour runs away with my discretion at times. Ah, I see the cards are on the table. I enjoy nothing so well as a good game of whist with friends."

"Shall we play?" said Charles, eagerly, drawing out a chair.

As the game progressed companionably, I felt a sense of awe at the expertise in which Holmes sustained the bogus personality of Sebastian Flood. It was evident that Charles Abernetty admired him immensely and hung on his every word. It was equally apparent that Sabina Abernetty was reserving her judgement on their new acquaintance. She was pleasant, but decidedly cool.

At four o'clock she rose from the table and pulled on a bell-rope hanging beside the fire-place.

"Are you calling for tea, Sabie?" asked Charles. "That would be welcome."

Miss Abernetty's change of position had allowed her to see the fire had fallen low. "We must ask Minter to throw on more coal," she remarked.

"No need to bother Minter. He has enough work to do. I'll attend to the fire myself," responded her brother.

Another bell rang somewhere in the house. A look of vexation crossed Charles Abernetty's face. "There's Mother," he said, tersely.

"I'll go," said his sister, serenely. "It's time for her medicine."

"I suppose," remarked Holmes, idly, as he watched our host at his fireside task, "it requires quite a few servants to maintain a household of this magnitude." Charles did not appear to hear, but Holmes persisted. "It is admirable of Miss Abernetty to take the place of a nurse."

"It's how she wishes it," replied Charles. "While my sister is away, gentlemen, I think we have time for a glass of this very excellent port." He crossed to a decanter on the sideboard.

"Not an excellent port," observed Holmes, as he sipped appreciatively, "but a superb one."

Charles flushed with pleasure. "From my own cellar. I shall fetch you each a bottle."

"Nonsense. I'll go at once."

"For shame, to leave you alone," said Miss Abernetty a moment or two later. "Where is Charles? Minter is just about to bring in the tea."

"I believe your brother has gone down to the cellar."

A coal exploded from the fire onto the rug. Sabina started violently, seized the tongs and threw it back on the grate. She spent some little time examining the rug for signs of damage while my friend sat observing her.

Charles returned presently with a bottle under each arm. His demeanour had markedly changed. His face had a pale clammy look and his hands shook as he placed the bottles on the table.

"Why, Abernetty, you are ill!" exclaimed Holmes.

"Charles, come and sit down." His sister led him to the wing chair, turning a grave face to us over her shoulder. "My brother suffers from a morbid fear of confined spaces. You should have sent Minter, Charles."

"You're right, of course," Charles mopped his brow with his handkerchief, "but he does so hate to go there himself."

"Stuffy places, cellars," agreed Holmes. "I'm distressed that your kindness has caused you such discomfort."

"My dear fellow, think nothing of it. It's a foolish whimsy of mine and will soon pass."

After tea we took our departure with the promise to return the following Sunday afternoon for another hand. Once outside, the air of *bonhomie* Holmes had exhibited before the Abernettys fell away and his mood became thoughtful.

"Well, Holmes," said I, "we're no closer to solving the mystery, if there is one. It all seemed perfectly straightforward to me. Devoted children, really rather a sad pair. At least we know the mother exists."

"How do we know that, Watson?"

"Why, you heard it yourself. She rang for attention."

"A bell was rung from somewhere in the house, nothing more. But you are right, they are a sad pair. But there are undercurrents, Watson, that could be sinister. There were several incidents that pointed to this which you completely overlooked."

"I wish you'd explain them to me."

"By this time next week I will have uncovered their secret and I think it will be more evil than you can comprehend."

"If you say so. But I wish you weren't so jealous with your deductions."

I feel that Holmes's overweening vanity caused him to be mysterious in case he was proven wrong, or, in the instance of proving himself right, so that he could produce his solution with a flourish like a magician producing a rabbit out of a hat.

"There's far more to be unearthed before I can confide in you. But I do value your assistance."

"I don't seem to have contributed much," I replied somewhat ruefully.

"More than you know. Are you acquainted with Dr Halliwell?"

"No, but I can look him up in the Medical Register."

"Good man. There's a cab. Hail it, Watson. An early night for us, I think. There's work to be done tomorrow."

Holmes was up and about before I had stirred from my bed. When he returned at noon he made an even more astonishing figure in the rough clothes and hobnail boots of the British workman. His hat was worn on the back of his head, he wore a rakish scarf and had not shaved that morning.

"I've been out looking for work, Watson," he chuckled.

"Were you successful?"

"Not in Grosvenor Square."

"You tried the Abernettys' address?"

"I thought they might be in need of a coachman or groom. I went in through the mews. Quite deserted, Watson. No carriage, no horses, the coachman's house stood empty. Minter must have glimpsed me from the servants' quarters and came out. Sent me off with a flea in my ear. Curious, isn't it, that the only servant we've seen is the old butler? No maid, no footman, for all we know no boots."

"Mrs Bertram did mention the servants had been dismissed."

"Yes, I find that useful information."

"It simply means the Abernettys could no longer afford to keep them."

Holmes chuckled. "A great deal escapes your attention, Watson."

"One thing hasn't." I was standing at the window as I spoke. "The urchin who stands across the street watching our premises. He answers the description of the lad who came to our rooms earlier enquiring about me. He wasn't in need of my services so Mrs Hudson sent him off, but he's still hanging about. He must have seen you come in, Holmes."

My friend came to stand beside me. The youth leaning against a lamp-post wore a greatcoat two sizes too large for him and a cloth cap pulled down over his ears. Between his muffler and his cap nothing much could be seen of his face, but he occasionally darted glances up at our window.

"Things are moving fast and we must move with them," murmured Holmes. "Did you check the Register?"

"I'll do so straightway after lunch."

"I'm off to the Doctors' Commons after which we'll sacrifice that bottle of cognac on the sideboard as a gift for Mr Charles Abernetty to repay him for his kindness of yesterday."

When next we met Holmes's sallow cheeks bore the flush of a grim excitement.

"Well, what did you learn about Dr Halliwell? Are we able to contact him?"

"Only if we hold a seance. Been dead a year."

Holmes gave an odd little laugh. "I too have just spent an informative hour. Let me don my disguise, Watson, and we'll be away."

Miss Sabina Abernetty was not at home at Grosvenor Square, but Mr Charles Abernetty greeted us cordially although with some surprise.

"We were passing your door and hoped you would not mind us calling in with this little token of gratitude for your hospitality." He produced the bottle with a flourish.

Charles was suitably gratified and bade us sit in the small salon while he rang for tea.

"May we enquire about Mrs Abernetty's health?" Holmes was all solicitude.

Charles studied him in silence for several minutes before he spoke. "You know, I do believe Mother would like you as much as we do. Would you like to meet her?"

"Very much," declared Holmes.

"I'll go and see that all is in readiness. She's very vain despite her advancing years."

He left the room, shutting the door firmly behind him. I glanced quizzically at my friend, but he was frowning into the fire.

"Let's just give Mother half an hour, shall we?" Charles said on his return. "I warn you, you'll find her in a darkened room. She dislikes the light, even on a wintry day such as this. Invalids do have their little fancies, as the good doctor here will know."

Charles Abernetty's manner seemed both excited and nervous. He kept rubbing his hands together and smiling, not at his new acquaintances but inwardly as if silently congratulating himself.

"I can't think what's keeping Minter with the tea," he complained. "Shall we have cognac instead?"

"Please don't trouble yourself," said Holmes, hastily. "Tell me, have you quite recovered from your indisposition of yesterday."

Abernetty's smile faded. In fact, he looked annoyed at the reminder. "Quite. A trifling matter. Shall we go up to Mother? I'll just ring the bell to let her know we are coming."

He led the way up a balustraded staircase to the next floor and along an unlit carpeted passage. Away from the snug salon the air was chill, the passage gloomy and the carpet thin and worn under our feet.

"This is Mother's room," he said with his hand on the knob. "Do speak softly. She dislikes loud noises."

He flung open the door. "Mother, I've brought two gentlemen to see you."

The room was indeed dark, unlit by fire or lamp and with the curtains drawn. In a large old-fashioned fourposter bed lay the shadowy form of an elderly woman whose features could just be made out within the frill of a large nightcap. Her eyes were closed and we could hear her stertorous breathing.

"Oh, bother," said Charles, in vexation. "She's dropped off."

"*Charles, what are you doing?*" There was a piercing whisper from the passage behind us.

Sabina Abernetty had arrived home. The violence of the weather was evident in her pink cheeks and disordered hair. She had apparently just come in and discarded her coat and hat downstairs.

"Ah, Miss Abernetty, again a pleasure," drawled Holmes.

She ignored him and continued to address her brother indignantly. "You know how perverse Mother can be. She might have had one of her tirades."

"As it turns out, she's asleep," said Charles, sulkily.

"Which is as well. Do forgive my brother," she turned to us, summoning a smile. "He means well."

"No harm done. I'm sorry we missed the pleasure of meeting your mother," replied Holmes, cheerfully. "We must take our leave, but look forward with pleasure to our game on Sunday afternoon. Come, Watson."

Outside in the square we had to hold our hats against the blustering wind. We trudged in silence for several minutes.

"What did you make of that melodrama?" enquired Holmes, presently.

"Decidedly odd. But at least we know Lady Abernetty is alive and can set Mrs Bertram's fears at rest."

My companion snorted. "Did anything strike you about the sickroom?"

"I thought it uncommonly cold."

"It was as chill as a morgue. No fire, no steam kettle, both of which I'm sure would be recommended for a patient suffering from congestion of the lungs."

"Indeed. Are you suggesting neglect?"

"What else struck you? Come, man, you must have been in dozens of sickrooms. That slight odour common to all ..."

"... was missing. You're right, Holmes. Not even a whiff of carbolic. What does that imply?"

"I think we may receive a note from the Abernettys offering apologies for Sunday afternoon," was his only reply.

Holmes was not often confounded, but the next event produced that effect.

We were sitting beside the fire after supper that evening when we heard a light quick step on the stairs followed by a sharp rap on the outer door.

"Who could that be?" I asked, surprised.

"I suggest you open the door, Watson," replied Holmes in that slightly caustic tone he could adopt at times.

A woman stood in the doorway, shrouded in a long woollen cloak with a hood. Pushing past me, she advanced into the room, throwing back her hood to reveal the face of Sabina Abernetty.

Holmes rose from his chair and faced her. For the space of a minute they examined each other.

"So I've tracked you down, Mr Sherlock Holmes, the famous detective," she said, bitterly.

"I congratulate you." Holmes's voice was slightly uneven.

"Why have you donned disguise to make my brother's acquaintance? Why have you flattered and deceived him, and come to our home? I know the answer? You have been employed by that hateful woman, Mabel Bertram to pry into our affairs. What has she been telling you?"

"She's concerned for your mother's health, nothing more."

"Oh, there is a great deal more, Mr Holmes."

She checked her passionate outburst and fell silent. I took the opportunity to express a concern of my own.

"I trust you did not come alone through the night, Miss Abernetty."

"Minter is waiting in a hansom downstairs," she replied, curtly.

"Where is your brother?"

"At a meeting of his dramatic society." She turned fiercely on Holmes. "What will satisfy you? What will end this persecution?"

I was shocked at the violence of her words, but Holmes answered her promptly.

"Seeing Lady Abernetty is alive and in reasonable health."

"Very well. You shall meet her on Sunday afternoon." She crossed to the door, but turned on the threshold, her lip curling. "I despise you."

She drew up her hood and hurried down the stairs.

"There is a lady who does not bestow her contempt lightly." Holmes tried to laugh, but the tremor was still in his voice.

"A remarkable adversary," I observed.

"She is not my adversary," said Holmes, softly. "She is my enemy. Or rather I am hers." He crossed to the window. "Ah, there they go. Be a good fellow, Watson, and whistle me up a cab while I throw on my cap and Ulster. I have to go out for a short time."

"Would you like me to accompany you?"

"No, it's better that I go alone." Holmes looked shaken by the incident, but at the same time some grim determination had seized him and I knew better than to persist.

The following day he was restless and moody and spent hours scraping on his old violin until I felt compelled to protest.

"How does an evening at the theatre appeal to you?" Holmes became suddenly brisk. "Dan Leno's playing at Drury Lane. We'll dine out first."

I was surprised at his choice of entertainment since he usually preferred a violin recital at the Albert Hall.

As usual he read my thoughts. "Come, Watson, the most celebrated clog-dancer and dame of our time. The man's an artist, probably in his own field a genius."

Dan Leno was certainly in fine form that evening, performing acts of incredible physical ingenuity, and changing from persona to persona with an inimitable blend of Cockney humour and sentiment and a variety of wigs and gowns.

While the patrons about us rocked in their seats with laughter, Holmes sat silent, his fingers steepled across the front of his evening clothes, watching the performance under slumbrous lids. I had the impression, however, he was watching the little man's antics intently.

The following day, to my surprise, he dressed for his appointment with the Abernettys without his usual disguise.

"The game's up, Watson," he answered my look. "I think both parties are now aware of my identity and interest."

"Do you think we'll be introduced to the mother?"

"I have no doubt of it."

A pall of fog lay over London. The church bells sounded muffled and melancholy. It showed no signs of dissipating by early afternoon and I was amazed when Holmes suggested we stroll to Grosvenor Square.

"In this pea-souper? You must be mad, Holmes! Why on earth . . .?"

"I want to arrive at Grosvenor Square in a certain frame of mind and that only the fog can achieve. If you don't wish to accompany me by all means stay by your cosy fireside, but if you want to experience one of the strangest adventures you've ever put to paper, and I know how you like to jot down these little cases of ours, then put on your hat and greatcoat, your warmest muffler, take your stoutest stick and oh, yes, your service pistol."

"My pistol, Holmes? Surely you don't expect to encounter any danger from that pair?"

"It would be wise to prepare for any eventuality."

I found the next half-hour or so distinctly unpleasant. I flatter myself that I am not a nervous man or highly imaginative, but I seemed to feel the fog crawling on me like ghostly fingers. Lamp-posts stood out like beacons eagerly attained and reluctantly abandoned. The snickerings of leaves along the pavements seemed like the pattering of feet running up behind us. I was obliged to restrain myself from constantly glancing over my shoulder. A hansom looming at us suddenly like a phantom coach as we crossed Oxford Street gave me quite a start.

"Nearly there, Watson," chuckled Holmes.

"Mayfair seems almost deserted. Every sensible person is indoors."

Charles Abernetty evinced not the slightest surprise or curiosity at his new acquaintance's shorn hair and moustache. He greeted us with the same cordiality and drew us to the fire in the small salon.

"How damp your clothes are!" he exclaimed.

"We walked."

Charles blinked rapidly several times. "Through the fog? How extraordinary!"

"May we please see Lady Abernetty?" requested Holmes, rather tersely.

"Ah, here's Sabina. Sabie, the gentlemen would like to see Mother now."

"I'm afraid she's taking a nap, gentlemen. But rest assured, Mr Holmes, Dr Watson, you will meet her this afternoon."

Miss Abernetty's face was pale above a gown of maroon merino trimmed with velvet and lace, elegantly draped to a slight bustle.

Her manner towards my friend, although distant, was not overtly hostile.

"Shall we play a hand or two while we're waiting?" suggested Charles.

An expression of annoyance flitted over the detective's face, but he shrugged and sat down at the table. It was an uncomfortable game in a charged atmosphere. Only Charles seemed determined to make it companionable. I noticed that my friend observed Charles closely. Under the prevailing circumstances, the fellow seemed in unnaturally high spirits.

A knock at the door was followed by the appearance of the tall, gaunt butler.

"What is it, Minter?" asked Charles, peevishly. "I didn't ring for you."

"This just came for you by messenger, Sir." The butler presented a letter on a silver salver.

Charles excused himself and slit open the envelope. "It's from Randell Burke."

"One of my brother's thespian friends," explained Sabina.

"He's mislaid his script and wishes to borrow mine. Gentlemen, I'm afraid I shall have to step out for a minute."

"Oh, Charles, in this weather?" demurred his sister.

"It's only in Brook Street. A brisk walk will do me good. If our friends can walk from Baker Street I can manage a swift jaunt around the corner. It's a pity to spoil our game, but there is is."

Holmes crossed to the bay window and held aside the curtain. Presently we saw Abernetty hurrying past the spiked fence in greatcoat and muffler.

"May we see your mother now?" He turned to Miss Abernetty.

"I'll see if she's awake." She pulled the bell-rope. "Meanwhile, will you take tea?"

"Miss Abernetty, we both know this is not a social occasion, but strictly a business matter. Please allow me to see your mother at once."

"Mr Holmes," she came close to him and looked earnestly into his face, "please allow me to apologize for my words of Friday evening. My sister and I have not been on good terms for many years, but it still shocks me that she would hire a detective to spy on us. Are you aware of her motives?"

"I am not at liberty to discuss Mrs Bertram's motives," Holmes replied, coldly.

Minter re-appeared, pushing a tea-trolley. Holmes refused to partake and returned to the window. Feeling rather embarrassed, I joined Miss Abernetty in a cup of tea, but refused the seed-cake.

"Are you watching for Charles?" enquired Sabina, almost tran-quilly. "He shouldn't be long."

She lingered over her tea, making desultory small talk with me. Instead of becoming impatient, Holmes in his expression grew grimmer. When at last a bell sounded somewhere in the house there was a gleam of irony in his eyes.

"I think your mother is ready to receive us. Shall we go up?"

With the strain on my nerves occasioned by our eerie walk through the fog, I fancied the dim passage had a clammy feel as if the fog had seeped into the walls. Sabina moved softly, almost stealthily before us until she came to the door of the sickroom.

"Mother, I've brought some gentlemen to see you." She pushed open the door.

The shadowy figure in the four-poster bed hunched itself up on the pillows. Wisps of grey hair from under the frilled nightcap straggled over the forehead, eyes glared peevishly from a face grey with age and ill-health. Her hand came up from beside the bed, holding a walking-stick.

"What's this, you know my orders. I won't see anyone," she shrilled at us, querulously. "Go away, all of you. Get out of my sight."

"Mother, don't upset yourself," the daughter glided towards her, but was driven back by the flailing stick.

I will never forget the scene that followed; though I do not remember the words, the tone of the dreadful imprecations, the humiliating insults and cruelties that stripped the soul of our companion bare have never left me. I felt a deep shame at being, however obliquely, the cause of Miss Abernetty's discomfiture.

Throughout she was calm, but at last she turned to us and said in a low, tremulous voice. "Will that be all? Are you satisfied?"

Holmes turned abruptly and walked out of the room and I was fast on his heels. The strident voice followed us down the stairs. In the hall, Miss Abernetty faced us gravely. Her eyes looked large and dark in a face that had been drained of all its colour.

"Miss Abernetty, I owe you the profoundest of apologies and bid you good afternoon," said Holmes. "Minter, my Ulster."

The elderly butler was hovering by the front door.

"You are leaving," she said, quickly. "Won't you wait until my brother returns? Don't you also owe him an apology?"

"Pray convey to him my regrets. Come, Watson, we must go."

"At least allow me to send Minter down to the corner for a cab."

"Thank you, no, we will return as we came – on foot."

I smothered a groan as I struggled into my damp greatcoat and picked up my stick.

"That was an embarrassing exposure for Miss Abernetty," I observed, when we had regained the square. "I hope you're satisfied." I could not suppress the note of censure that crept into my tone.

Holmes gripped my arm. "Not another word."

We had reached the corner when he suddenly swung back. "Come, Watson, I want a word with Lady Abernetty."

"What! Have you gone mad, Holmes?"

"Not I. Not as mad as that poor raving invalid we've just left. Come on, Watson, the chase is on, this way through the mews and around to the coach-house. Ah, just as I thought!"

A candle was burning within, visible through a dingy window. My companion flung open the door. A figure in nightdress and frilled cap gave a startled cry.

"The game's up," Holmes said, grimly, "Mr Charles Abernetty."

Abernetty shrank back against the wall, his features contorted with fury under the grotesque make-up. "Damn you! I was brilliant. How could you possibly have found me out?"

"Indeed, you were comparable with the great Dan Leno. Let's say there were other factors that led to your unmasking."

Abernetty's eyes skimmed past Holmes to the doorway. "No, Sabie, don't!"

Sabina, equally as grim as Holmes, had materialized through the fog. She aimed a pistol at the detective's head.

"Do you feel quite so clever now, Mr Sherlock Holmes? Don't move, Dr Watson. Put your hand near your pocket and I'll put a bullet through your friend's head."

"Don't be foolish, Miss Abernetty," said Holmes, quietly. "You haven't yet committed murder."

Her face was a mask of cold, calculating fury. "There's no proof that you've been at Grosvenor Square. You didn't even hire a cab."

Holmes's hand moved swiftly to his lips. He blew three sharp blasts on his police whistle. "Inspector Lanner and his men will be here soon. Put away the pistol, Miss Abernetty. You'll only make things worse for yourself."

In her rage she fired at him. The expression on her face changed quickly to one of chagrin as the pistol misfired. I quickly brought up my stick, taking advantage of her confusion, and knocked the weapon from her grasp. Holmes kicked it out of sight as Inspector Lanner and two constables burst into the room.

"Good afternoon, Mr Holmes," the inspector nodded cheerfully at my friend. "How may I assist you?"

"I think if your men pry up the flagstones of the cellar floor and dig about a little you'll discover, as I suggested in our earlier conversation, the body of Alice Abernetty."

"Murdered?"

"No. I'm sure Lady Abernetty died of natural causes. Concealment of death and wrongful disposal of a body is the only crime here."

"I fear I shall not be the hero of this chronicle should you set it down on paper." Holmes stretched his slippers towards the fire and leaned his cheek pensively on his hand. "I have disinherited brother and sister for the sake of a greedy, already wealthy woman, who seeks to impress and snare a younger man with a fashionable address. The terms of Sir William Abernetty's will, now a matter of public record, gave me the answer. The house in Grosvenor Square only belonged to Lady Abernetty during her lifetime. On her death it passed to his eldest child Mabel from the first marriage. Charles and Sabina Abernetty were to be dispossessed. There was very little real money. They were, shall we say, in an unenviable position. There were many times, Watson, when I nearly abandoned the case, but I was drawn on to its fascinating and macabre conclusion."

"The law must be upheld, Holmes."

"Oh, yes, the law," he retorted, bitterly. "There are other laws, natural laws, that have been broken here."

Since our return he had fallen into a mood of black depression and I was worried that he might disappear into his room and seek solace in his unfortunate addiction to cocaine. I therefore attempted to distract him by laying before him the points of the case I did not yet fully understand.

"Who was the woman we saw in the sick-bed on our second visit?"

"That I suspect was Mrs Minter, the cook. However unwilling they may have been, the Minters were accomplices to all that occurred. They probably agreed to the conspiracy knowing they could find no other place at their time of life.

"Charles thought he was very clever with that little ruse, but it only served to convince me further that Lady Abernetty was dead. Of course, he wasn't aware of my identity then. But Miss Abernetty had already confirmed her suspicion of me. She was the youth watching our premises, Watson. When she burst into the sickroom later that day she was wearing a dress I had seen hanging up in the coach-house on my earlier visit as the groom in search of work. In their loveless, friendless childhood and youth they turned to a world of acting and make-believe. I'm quite sure Charles had his mother's character down accurately in that little display today. Can you imagine, Watson, their bleak, deprived existence, reviled by the one person who might be expected to give them affection. It makes my blood run cold to think of it." He leaned forward, his elbows hunched on his knees.

"What will become of them?"

"I can only hope the law will be kinder to them than I have been."

"Come, Holmes, you deal with yourself too harshly. Things would have gone much harder for Miss Abernetty if you had told the inspector she attempted your life. It was only pure luck that the pistol misfired."

"It was probably an old weapon that had belonged to her father and had been lying about in a drawer for years. She had every reason to hate me. By my interference I had brought their brief and pathetic idyll to an end. But they could not have carried on their deception indefinitely, not with that woman of remarkable perspicacity Mabel Bertram waiting in the wings."

"What was the significance of the parsley in the butter?"

"Ah, yes! Did you not hear Mrs Bertram remark that her stepmother invariably had a roll with parsley butter for her breakfast. I believe that the cook had been preparing her tray and the butter had been taken from the icebox. Meanwhile, Miss Abernetty had gone to the sickroom to tend her mother's needs and discovered she had died during the night.

"She acted quickly, Watson, and with great presence of mind. The servants were summarily dismissed and the plan put into action of burying the body under the flagstones in the cellar.

"In such a household, Watson, where the discipline is so rigid, so unyielding and the *presence* of the mistress, even one confined to a sick-room, so omnipotent, the butter in the natural course of events would have been returned to the icebox. The fact that the parsley had sunk so deep into the butter meant it had been left out for hours and other events, unnatural events, were taking place."

He reached inside his pocket and drew out a slip of paper. "This is the fee I require from Mrs Bertram."

"Holmes!"

"As she herself observed she intended to be *grateful* and Mr Aston Plush added the rider of *generous*. I have acquired for her a fashionable address and possibly a new husband. *You* shall have your little jaunt to Baden-Baden, Watson."

"That's exceedingly generous of you, Holmes," I stammered.

A smile warmed his austere features. "You deserve it, my dear fellow, after all I've put you through today. Even a solitary misanthropic chap like myself knows the value of true friendship."

THE ADVENTURE OF VITTORIA, THE CIRCUS BELLE

Edward D. Hoch

After "The Incumbent Invalid" there was a brief period when little came Holmes's way and he soon began to complain that his practice was "degenerating into an agency for recovering lost lead pencils and giving advice to young ladies from boarding-schools," an attitude which coloured his initial feelings about the case that became "The Adventure of the Copper Beeches". Despite the success of that case matters again went quiet and it is probably during this period that Holmes became more open in his use of cocaine for stimulation. Watson refers to it in "The Yellow Face", a case which arose in the spring of 1886 and which was one of Holmes's few recorded failures. Holmes was clearly in the doldrums during this period.

But matters soon began to improve. We find from the summer of 1886 cases begin to tumble one on top of another and Watson again found trouble keeping a record of them all. The American writer and scholar of crime, Edward D. Hoch, is renowned for his mystery stories, and he has occasionally turned a hand to writing stories featuring Sherlock Holmes. These are mostly of his own invention, but his interest in the circus caused him to stumble upon some records which helped us piece together the case later referred to by Watson about Vittoria, the Circus Belle.

My friend Mr Sherlock Holmes, upon looking through his fabled index of past cases, took occasion to remind me that I have never recorded the remarkable affair of Vittoria, the Circus Belle. My only excuse for this dereliction is that the summer of '86 had furnished us with a long series of interesting cases and somehow my notes for this one became buried among them. There was also an aspect of the case which was slightly embarrassing.

Certainly by that year Vittoria was known even to those who never attended a circus. In America during the year 1880 a rival of Barnum and the Ringling Brothers named Adam Forepaugh came up with a unique idea for promoting his tent show. Forepaugh was one of the circus world's most picturesque characters, forever coming up with new schemes. Inspired by America's first beauty contest held at a beach in Delaware, he sponsored a competition with a $10,000 prize for the country's most beautiful woman, resulting in the selection of Louise Montague as the winner. Forepaugh promptly hired her to ride in his circus parade and proclaimed her as "the $10,000 beauty".

It did not take long for a similar promotion campaign to take root in England. In 1882 the Rover Brothers, who imagined themselves to be our British version of the Ringlings, launched their own contest for the loveliest young woman in the country. The winner was Vittoria Costello, a young shopgirl who was immediately transformed into "Vittoria, the Circus Belle". When her likeness began to appear regularly on circus handbills and posters there was some grumbling about the similarity of her given name to that of Her Majesty, but it was the young woman's true name and she could not be prevented from using it.

This was all either Holmes or I knew about her when Mrs Hudson announced an unscheduled visitor – a veiled young woman – on a sunny morning in early August. "Show her up by all means!" Holmes instructed, putting down his pipe and rising to greet our visitor. "Clients who attempt to conceal their identity always intrigue me!"

After a few moments we were joined by the woman herself. She was tall and willowy, dressed in a black riding costume with hat and veil. I could barely distinguish her features through the double layer of netting. "Thank you for seeing me, Mr Holmes," she said. "Be assured it is a matter of utmost urgency that brings me here."

"Pray be seated, madam. This is my friend and associate, Dr Watson. We are at your service."

She took the chair opposite the door, as if fearful of someone who might be following her. "Mr Holmes, I believe my life to be in great danger."

"And why do you think that, Miss Costello?"

Her body jerked in surprise at his words. I admit I was surprised myself. "You know me?" she asked. "We have never met."

"Your veiling implies that your face would be known, and I note the unmistakable odor of tanbark about you, suggestive of a circus ring. No, no – it is not an unpleasant odor. It brings back memories of childhood. I believe there is even a bit of the bark itself clinging to your riding boot." My eyes were drawn to her boot, almost as large as my own, and to the trim calf that showed beneath her skirt. "Since the Rover Brothers Circus is the only one in the London area at the present time, and since Vittoria the Circus Belle rides in their parades, it seemed obvious to me that you were Vittoria Costello. Please continue with your story."

She lifted the veil, revealing a face of striking beauty. Her eyes, though troubled, still sparkled with youth and her hair had the shimmer of ravens' wings. The sketches on the circus posters hardly did her justice. "I had heard of your remarkable powers, Mr Holmes, but you astonish me. As you may know from the newspaper accounts, I was employed by Hatchard's bookshop on Piccadilly when friends persuaded me to enter the Rover Brothers' contest. I never thought I would win, and when I did I'll admit I was a bit reluctant to give up my old life and become Vittoria, the Circus Belle."

Holmes retrieved his pipe and studied her with piercing eyes. "I admit to knowing very little about circuses. Exactly what duties do you perform with the show?"

"When the Rovers hired me directly after the contest, they said I only had to ride a horse in the circus parade, and perhaps once around the ring at the beginning and end of the shows. Of course until recently circuses were mainly equestrian events, with a clown providing some acrobatic comedy and joking with the ringmaster between riding demonstrations. Now things are changing. P. T. Barnum in America has a tent that will hold twenty thousand spectators and has three rings, after the American custom. Astley's here in London has a permanent building with a large scenic stage for horses and other animals. The trapeze acts introduced by the French gymnast Leotard are becoming increasingly popular with many circuses. And they say the Hagenbecks will soon introduce a big cage for wild animal acts."

"You know a great deal about your profession," Holmes murmured.

"It may not be my profession much longer, Mr Holmes. You see, the Rover Brothers suggested last year that I develop some sort of talent to enhance my image, something besides my horsemanship. They even suggested I might try tightrope walking or snake handling. I was horrified by both suggestions. This spring they put me into a knife-throwing act with a Spaniard named Diaz." She showed us a slight scar on her left forearm. "This is what I received from it, and just during the rehearsal!"

"Is that what has brought you here?"

"Hardly! There is another young woman with the circus, an acrobat, who feels she should have the title of Circus Belle. Her name is Edith Everage. She has suggested several times that I leave my position and now I believe she is trying to kill me."

"Has there been an actual attempt on your life?"

"Two, in fact. A week ago yesterday, when the circus played at Stratford, a horse I was riding tried to throw me."

Holmes waved his hand. "A common enough occurrence."

"Someone had placed a burr beneath my saddle. When my weight pressed it into the animal's flesh he started to buck. Luckily there were people nearby to rescue me."

"And the other attempt?"

"Much more serious. Two days ago, shortly before the Monday afternoon performance in Oxford, the knife-thrower Diaz was poisoned. You may have seen it in the papers. The poison was in a water bottle I used between rides. I'm convinced it was meant for me."

"The knife-thrower died?"

"Yes. It was horrible!"

"Where is the circus playing now?"

"They're setting up in Reading for a performance tomorrow afternoon. A new tiger is arriving with its keeper tonight. I fear they might want me to perform with it and I'm afraid for my life, Mr Holmes."

"The two earlier incidents may have no relation to each other. Still, I have not attended a circus since my youth. What say, Watson? Shall we journey to Reading tomorrow for the big show?"

We caught a mid-morning train at Paddington station. The weather was warm for his usual traveling-cloak and he wore simple tweeds. As was his custom, Holmes read through several papers during the journey, expressing pleasure when he came upon an account of Diaz's death in Oxford. He had died from poisoning but no further details had been given by the Oxford police.

"Perhaps it was an accident," I ventured. "She may be worried about nothing."

"We shall see, Watson." He put down the last of the papers as the train was pulling into Reading Station. Off to the right we could see King's Meadow where a circus tent had been erected. Already carriages and strollers were heading in that direction, and there were children gathering at the animal enclosures.

The first thing we saw on alighting from the train was a large wall poster for the Rover Brothers Circus featuring Vittoria, the Circus Belle. A banner had been pasted across the bottom corner of the poster announcing a new wild animal act with a man-eating tiger, to be introduced that very afternoon. Having now seen Vittoria in person I was reminded again of how little the drawing revealed of her true charm and beauty. Holmes studied it for a moment before we continued to the street, where he hailed a carriage to take us the short distance to the circus grounds.

Vittoria had arranged that two admission tickets would be left for us at the box office. As we passed through the main gate I caught the odor of tanbark, so slight on our client but now bringing with it my own memories of childhood. "You're right, Holmes," I said. "There is a pleasant, nostalgic smell about a circus."

A small tent near the entrance bore a sign indicating it was the office of the Rover Brothers Circus, and Holmes made for it without hesitation. A slender dark-haired young man with a bushy mustache was at work inside, scanning the pages of a ledger. "Mr Rover, I presume?" Holmes addressed him.

The man looked up with a scowl. "Mr Charles Rover. Do you want me or Philip?"

"Either one will do. I am Sherlock Holmes and this is Dr Watson. One of your star performers, Vittoria, has invited us here to investigate the suspicious death of the Spanish knife-thrower known as Diaz."

Charles Rover grunted with something like distaste. "Nothing suspicious about it! An accident!"

"Vittoria believes he was poisoned and that the poison was meant for her."

"Who would want to kill that sweet child? She is the star of our show!"

"Then we have come here for nothing?" Holmes asked.

"It would seem so."

"Since we have made the journey from London, perhaps we could speak with some others – your brother Philip, if he's available, and one of the acrobats, Edith Everage."

Charles Rover consulted his pocket watch. "It's noon already. By one o'clock we will be preparing for the afternoon performance. See who you wish before one, then be gone."

"Where might we find Miss Everage?"

"In the main tent, rehearsing her act. We are introducing an Indian tiger into the show today, and the timing must be adjusted accordingly."

I followed Holmes as we left Rover and headed for the main tent. Along the way food venders were beginning to set up their wares and a pair of brightly painted clowns were inspecting each other's greasepaint. With the gates open, the trickle of arrivals was building to a steady flow, exploring the sideshows but not yet allowed into the main tent. Holmes and I ignored the signs and slipped through the closed tent flap.

In the big circus ring a half-dozen acrobats, clad in the tight-fitting garments developed by Leotard, were tumbling, somersaulting and cartwheeling. One was even swinging from a trapeze. When they came to rest for a moment, Holmes asked the nearest of the women, "Are you Miss Edith Everage."

"Edith!" she called out to one of the others, a brown-haired girl who appeared to be of school age. Her fine figure in the skin-tight garment made me blush as she walked up to us, though her face seemed too hardened for one so young.

"You want me?" she asked with a trace of London cockney in her voice.

Holmes introduced himself and came directly to the point. "We are investigating the recent attempts upon the life of Vittoria Costello, the so-called Circus Belle. Do you know anything about a riding accident?"

"The horse threw her. That wasn't an attempt on her life."

"She thought it was. And what about the poisoning of Diaz?"

Edith Everage shook her head. "They say that was an accident."

"Didn't he cut her once during his knife-throwing act?"

"Naw. They were thick as thieves."

"But you would like to replace her as the Circus Belle."

"I deserve it! I worked for the Rovers since I was fifteen. I'm even learning to do a trapeze act. They hired her with no experience at all, just because she won that bleedin' contest. And Mr Philip, he makes sure she treats him nice, if you get what I mean."

While they talked a cage had been wheeled into the ring. Though its bars were covered with canvas the growls emanating from inside left no doubt that the tiger had arrived. The trainer, armed with a whip, and a man in a frock coat accompanied the cage. Even at a distance I could recognize an older version of Charles Rover. Holmes must have had the same impression, for he asked her, "Is that Philip Rover?"

"It is," Edith acknowledged. "It's a wonder we ever see him, between Vittoria and that blonde doxy he brings on the road with him."

"Who would that be?"

"Milly Hogan. She was in a show at the Lyceum Theatre once and she considers herself above mere circus performers. She usually stays in his tent during the performance, but I saw them out playing with the new tiger this morning."

"All right," Philip Rover called to the acrobats. "Everyone out of the ring. We're going to start letting the crowd in soon. I want them to see nothing but that cage as they take their seats."

Edith hurried off with the others and Rover turned his attention to us. "You must be Sherlock Holmes. My brother told me you were in here, but for the life of me I can't imagine why. That Spaniard's death was an accident. The poison bottle had been prepared to dispose of an aging python. Diaz drank it by mistake."

"Your star, Vittoria, tells a different story. She fears for her life. Does she have any enemies here?"

"None," Philip Rover assured us.

"What about Edith Everage?"

"Everage? She's one of the acrobats, isn't she?"

"So I understand," Holmes told him. "Was she ever considered for billing as the Circus Belle?"

"Edith Everage? Certainly not! We ran a nationwide contest to choose a beautiful woman for the part. Vittoria was the winner. Edith was never considered."

"Yet there have been two attempts on Vittoria's life, possibly by Edith."

"Did you get these ideas from my brother?" Philip asked, anger beginning to show on his face. "I must tell you our Circus Belle is a popular woman with the younger men here."

"Including Charles?" Holmes studied the man with his piercing gray eyes, but before he could say anything else there came a shout from the direction of the tiger's cage.

Philip Rover turned and started toward one of the clowns who'd yelled. "What is it?" he barked.

The clown came running over, trying to keep his voice low. "Mr Rover, something's wrong! I just looked under the canvas and Vittoria's in there with the tiger. I think she's dead."

The minutes that followed were a nightmare. Pushing the great beast back with long poles, the handlers finally were able to unlock the cage and pull the body out of its grasp. As a physician it fell upon me to examine Vittoria's body when it was removed from the cage. I had no trouble pronouncing her dead, but the sight of that clawed, bloody face, with the dress virtually torn from her body, moved me to a great sadness. From her tiny feet to a gaping wound in her neck, there were claw marks everywhere.

Holmes watched it all in silence, and did not speak until I had finished my examination. "What do you think, Watson? Did the tiger kill her or not?"

It was not the first time I had found Holmes's reasoning a step ahead of my own. My eyes focused on the gaping neck wound. "His claws couldn't have made a wound like that and there seems to be no blood on his jaws or teeth."

"Exactly my thought! The woman was already dead when she was placed in the cage. It was covered with canvas and the killer expected it would not be found until show time." He turned to a pale Philip Rover. "Who had a key to this cage?"

"Only the animal's trainer. And I keep a spare one in my tent."

"Does your brother have one?"

"I don't think so."

Charles Rover joined us then, summoned by the ringmaster. "What happened here?" he asked.

"Someone killed Vittoria and put her body in the tiger's cage," his brother told him.

"My God! Should we cancel the afternoon performance?"

Philip Rover scoffed at the idea. "We have five hundred people out there already, with more arriving every minute. The show will go on, but get this tiger cage out of here. The police will want to examine it."

I could see something was troubling Holmes, beyond the traumatic fact of the crime itself. "Did you gentlemen carry any insurance on the life of Vittoria Costello?" he inquired.

Philip brushed aside the question. "We have enough other expenses. I know of no circus that insures its performers. Why would you ask that?"

"In a death where there has been facial injury, one has to be certain of identification. Fraud of some sort is always a possibility."

"Go and look at the body," Philip told his younger brother. "Assure Mr Holmes of its identity."

Charles returned after a moment, the blood drained from his face. "It's Vittoria," he assured us. "There's no doubt. The ringmaster identified her too."

Sherlock Holmes nodded. "Then we must go about finding her killer."

"The circus isn't hiring you," Philip stated quite clearly. "This is a job for the local police."

"Ah! But they did not do well in Oxford, did they? The death of the Spaniard is still unsolved."

"I told you about that," Philip insisted. "It was an accident. We have no money for you, Mr Holmes."

"I was hired by Vittoria Costello to protect her," he informed them. "Now I must find her killer."

"Hired?" the younger brother repeated. "How is this possible?"

"She came to my lodgings in Baker Street yesterday, and told me of the incident with the horse and the poisoning of Diaz in Oxford. She feared the killer would succeed on his third attempt." He repeated some of what she had told us.

"But this is untrue!" Philip insisted. "She fell off that horse, as she had done before. And I have already told you the Spaniard's poisoning was a simple accident on his part. The poison was meant for a sick python."

"Why would she lie?" Holmes asked. "It would seem her death is all the evidence we need that she told the truth."

But the Rovers were already hurrying away to meet the police.

A short time later, while the body was being removed through the big top's rear entrance, the spectators were finally allowed inside. There was a buzz of speculation among them. They had seen the police wagon draw up, and they knew something was amiss. Holmes and I took seats near the front of the grandstand, waiting for some sort of announcement. When it came it was vague and brief. The ringmaster held up his megaphone, a voice amplifier from America, and announced, "Welcome to the Rover Brothers Circus! Due to an unfortunate accident, Vittoria the Circus Belle will not appear at this performance. Settle back and enjoy the show!" There were some groans from the spectators.

First came the clowns, followed by the team of acrobats with some tumbling and trapeze acts. The middle portion of the show was devoted to the traditional equestrian performers. If Edith Everage had been responsible for Vittoria's death she showed no evidence of nervousness as she went through her acrobatics with split-second timing. Finally the tiger cage was wheeled back out to the center of the ring and an animal trainer brought out the magnificent tiger for all to see. There was no hint that the beast had been clawing at a woman's body only an hour or so earlier.

The performance ended with a fine equestrian display, the riders carrying flags representing Britain and its colonies. As the crowd headed for the exits I asked Holmes what we should do next. "There seems to be nothing more we can learn here," I said.

"You are correct that we have learned everything we need to, Watson. I direct your attention especially to the curious incident of the tiger in the morning."

"What curious incident? The tiger did nothing in the morning."

"That was the curious incident," said Holmes.

There was no way that the death of Vittoria could be hushed up or passed off as an accident. She had been killed and placed in that tiger cage. Both suicide and accident were out of the question. By the following morning the press had linked her murder with that of Diaz and the word was out that the famous consulting detective Mr Sherlock Holmes was on the case. The Rover Brothers Circus had been detained in Reading pending further investigation.

Holmes and I had taken a room for the night at the railroad hotel by the station. We had barely finished breakfast the following morning when Charles, the younger of the Rover Brothers, arrived to see us.

"I must speak with you about this terrible business," he said, pulling up a chair to join our table. "Philip and I want to hire you. He's had a complete change of heart on the matter."

Holmes smiled. "I already have a client. Vittoria Costello."

"I've found the dead aren't too prompt in paying their bills, Mr Holmes. We want this business wound up as quickly as possible."

"Very well," he replied. "Will this afternoon be soon enough?"

Charles Rover was taken aback. "Do you mean that you have solved the mystery already?"

"I believe so. Are you performing this afternoon?"

"Since the police are delaying our departure we have added a performance at two o'clock."

"Very good. Please hold tickets for Watson and myself."

When he had gone I turned to my friend in amazement. "You intend to reveal the killer this very day?"

"I need only one further piece of evidence and the case will be complete." He finished his tea and rose from the table. "Come, Watson! The game is afoot."

We arrived at King's Meadow shortly after one. The publicity had attracted a crowd but they were mainly adults. The expected audience of children had been kept away by fear of further violence. We could see why the Rover Brothers needed help. Once inside the gate Holmes surprised me by not heading toward the main tent. Instead he detoured to the smaller tents where the Rover Brothers stayed. Philip Rover was just emerging from his tent with a blonde young woman who seemed vaguely familiar. She wore a long green dress and gloves, more suited to a night at the theatre than an afternoon at the circus.

"Holmes!" Philip said, perhaps a bit startled by the encounter. "I want you to meet my friend Milly Hogan."

I remembered the Everage girl's description of her as Philip's blonde doxy who traveled with him but rarely attended the performances. Sherlock Holmes reached out as if to shake her hand, but at the last moment suddenly grabbed her left wrist instead.

"What is this?" she asked with a gasp of fright. Already he was pulling up the sleeve on her forearm, revealing a small scar, faint but visible. We had seen it before.

"I believe we meet again, Miss Hogan. You came to my rooms

in Baker Street on Tuesday posing as Vittoria Costello, as part of your plot to murder that young lady."

Both the Reading police and the Rover Brothers themselves demanded explanations, and Holmes was only too glad to supply them. We had adjourned to Philip's tent while Milly Hogan was being questioned elsewhere, and he began by describing her visit to us.

"The black wig was nothing to an actress, of course, nor was the assuming of Vittoria's character. If her plan went well we would never meet the real Vittoria so no comparisons would be made. Perhaps she had even intended to keep her face veiled until I guessed, wrongly, at her identity. As it was, both Watson and I noted how little she resembled the drawing on the posters, but we thought little of it. I believe the death of Diaz was indeed an accident, but it must have suggested the entire plan to her. She came to me two days later with her story of the previous attempts on Vittoria's life. Her whole point was to have me present the following day when the real Vittoria was killed, supposedly by the tiger the circus had just acquired."

I remembered his words of the previous evening. "You said the tiger did nothing in the morning, Holmes."

"And he did not. We established quickly enough that Vittoria was killed before being placed in the cage, but that still meant the murderer had to open the cage to do it. Opening the cage of a strange tiger, only just arrived with its trainer would be a highly dangerous undertaking. The fact that the tiger did nothing to attract attention meant that the person who opened the cage was no stranger to him. The trainer could be ruled out. He only just arrived the night before and would hardly have had a motive for killing Vittoria. But Edith Everage saw you, Philip, along with Milly, playing with the new tiger yesterday morning. That was probably no more than an hour or two before the murder. The tiger knew and remembered Milly."

"This whole thing is ridiculous!" Philip insisted. "The tiger cage was outside of our tents, in full view. How could Milly or anyone else have killed Vittoria and placed her body in there without being seen?"

"The cage may have been in full view, but it was covered with canvas. I would guess that Milly lured Vittoria out there to see the new tiger. Once under the canvas for a better look, Milly stabbed her in the throat before she could scream, then opened the cage and pushed her in. You told us, Philip, that you had an extra key to the cage in your tent."

"Why would she do it? What was her motive?"

"The Everage woman told me you were fond of both of them. Jealousy has led to more than one murder. Of course Milly planned to pin the crime on Everage, which is why she came to us impersonating Vittoria."

I asked a question now. "How did you know, Holmes? After all, you deduced our client was Vittoria and then canceled out your own deduction."

"I was deceived, Watson, until we pulled Vittoria's body from the tiger cage and I noticed her tiny feet. The woman who called on us in London had feet as big as yours, as you must have noticed. Foot sizes don't change overnight, so I knew it was a different woman. When Philip and Charles and others assured us the body was Vittoria's, that meant it was an impostor who'd visited us. I asked myself who it could have been, and the answer was obvious. The impostor had to be Vittoria's killer, or a close accomplice. We learned that the extra key to the tiger cage was kept in Philip's tent, where Milly Hogan also stayed. And we learned that Philip and Milly were playing with the new tiger yesterday morning. Milly had been an actress, performing at the Lyceum Theatre in London. And Milly had reason to be jealous of Vittoria. Such a motive made it unlikely that you were involved, Philip. If the two of you were close enough to plot a murder, she would have had no reason for jealousy in the first place. I also felt certain that if you had wanted to kill Vittoria you would have done it away from the circus grounds so as not to harm business. And surely you would not have insisted Diaz's death was accidental if you were party to a plot to link the two deaths as a double murder."

It was later, on the train back to London, after Milly Hogan had confessed, that I remarked to Holmes, "We never did meet Vittoria, the Circus Belle."

"No," he agreed. "But we met Milly Hogan twice, and in my profession I find a murderess more fascinating than a Circus Belle."

THE DARLINGTON SUBSTITUTION SCANDAL

David Stuart Davies

By late 1886 Holmes's caseload was increasing substantially, allowing him to be more selective in the work he took on, and this occasionally made him rather cavalier to those clients whom he felt were wasting his time. Some of these cases Watson did not write up, either because they seemed trivial or because Holmes wished to keep his clients' details confidential. Occasionally certain incidents were later remembered and one such case was "The Darlington Substitution Scandal" which Holmes refers to in "A Scandal in Bohemia". This case has been highly problematic to restore and even now the story may not be complete. Holmes was reminded of the case by his use of a fire alarm to unearth items of value, but it transpires it wasn't fire but a similar cause for alarm that helped Holmes resolve the matter.

Sherlock Holmes and I returned late one evening to our Baker Street rooms after spending some time in the realms of Wagner. My friend was still singing Siegfried's horn call even as we let ourselves in through the door of 221b. His recital was interrupted somewhat abruptly by the appearance of Mrs Hudson at the foot of the stairs. She was wearing a long grey dressing gown and appeared to be quite perturbed.

"You have a visitor, Mr Holmes," she whispered with a kind of desperate urgency. "He refuses to leave until he sees you. He is most insistent."

"Is he?" said Holmes, "Then we had better oblige the gentleman. Off to bed with you. Friend Watson and I will deal with the matter."

She gave an understanding nod, threw a brief smile in my direction and disappeared behind her door.

The visitor was a short, burly figure of some sixty years. He possessed a high, bald forehead, a shiny face and fierce blue eyes. He almost ran towards us as we entered our sitting room. "At last," he cried.

Holmes gave a gentle bow of the head in greeting as he flung off his coat and scarf. "Had his Lordship taken the courtesy to arrange an appointment he would not have had to wait over two hours to see me – the cigar butts in my ashtray indicate the length of time."

"You know me?"

"It is my business to know people. Even in this dim light it is not difficult to recognize the Queen's minister for foreign affairs, Lord Hector Darlington. Now, pray take a seat and tell me about the theft."

Lord Darlington dropped open-mouthed into the wicker chair. "Who has told you?"

Holmes gave a brief chuckle. "A brandy night cap for us all, eh, Watson?" he said, before replying to his Lordship's question. "You would not be here alone at this time of night if your errand concerned government business. Therefore, it is a private affair which brings you to my door. A *very* private affair if the official police are not to be involved. It is well known that you are an avid collector of priceless paintings and possess a very rich collection. It does not need Sherlock Holmes to deduce that the matter on which you wish to consult me concerns your paintings or more likely one of your paintings. The matter is urgent and so therefore it relates to loss rather than damage. Ah, thank you Watson." He retrieved a brandy from the tray and took a sip.

Lord Darlington shook his large head in disbelief. "By Jove, you are right, sir. If only you can unravel the mystery as easily as you have guessed at its nature, I will be in your eternal debt."

Holmes raised an admonishing finger. "I never guess. It is an impractical pastime. Now, if you would be so kind as to familiarize me with the facts of the matter, I may be able to shed some light on your particular darkness." So saying he sat back in his chair, both hands cradling the brandy glass, and closed his eyes.

Lord Darlington cleared his throat and began his narrative. "As you rightly stated, my passion in life is art and over the years I have built up what I believe is an enviable collection, one of the finest private galleries in Europe. It is not for their financial value that I treasure my canvases, you understand: it is for their beauty and power, their vivid interpretation of life."

"Quite," remarked Holmes dryly.

"Recently I took possession of a seventeenth-century painting by Louis de Granville, his 'Adoration of the Magi.' It is the most magnificent painting."

"Louis de Granville – didn't he die very young?" I said.

His Lordship gave me a brief smile. "Indeed. He died of

consumption at the age of twenty-seven. There are only thirty known canvases of his in existence and 'The Adoration' is regarded as his best. I was so fortunate to acquire this wonderful painting."

"Where did you obtain it?" asked Holmes

"For years it was deemed a lost masterpiece and then it turned up in a Paris auction house last spring. The bidding was fierce but I was determined to have it. One American bidder chased me all the way, but I managed to shake him off in the end."

"And now it has disappeared."

Lord Darlington's face crumpled at this reminder of his loss. "I use my gallery as some men use tobacco or alcohol. Sitting alone with my pictures I am able to relax and allow the stresses and strains of the day flow out of me. Today I was due to make a visit to see my counterpart in the French government but at the last moment the trip was called off, so instead of catching the night train to Paris, I went home. Both my wife and my son were out on various social engagements, so I took myself to my gallery for a few hours peace and relaxation. Imagine my horror when I pulled back the cord on my beloved de Granville to find that it was missing."

"The frame also?"

"Yes. There was no signs of forced entry and nothing else was disturbed. All my other pictures were there."

"How big is the painting?"

"It is about two foot by sixteen inches."

"Who has a key to the gallery besides yourself?"

"No one."

"No one?" I found myself repeating our visitor in surprise.

"My wife and son have no interest in my paintings and I welcome that. The gallery is my private domain."

"Who cleans and tidies the room?" asked Holmes languidly. It was clear that Lord Darlington's dilemma did not excite a great deal of interest within his breast.

"I do. It is a simple task. I perform it once a week."

"When did you last see the painting?"

"The previous evening. The charm of it is still so fresh for me that I rarely let a day go by when I don't spend some time with it. I know you may find it strange, gentlemen, but I was actually dreading my trip to France, knowing I would be deprived of my paintings for some days."

Sherlock Holmes drained his brandy glass and rose to his feet. "It is my experience that when the situation is so mysterious with no apparent clues, the solution must be quite simple. Do not lose sleep over it. I feel sure that we can recover your painting."

Our visitor beamed. "I do hope so."

"Watson and I will call around tomorrow morning to examine the scene of the crime and see if we can glean some suggestive facts."

"Won't you come now, gentlemen?"

Holmes yawned and stretched. "It is late, Lord Darlington. There is no danger in waiting for a new day before commencing our investigation. Shall we say at ten o'clock tomorrow morning? Watson will show you out."

When I returned, my friend was standing by the fireplace lighting up his pipe with a cinder from the grate clamped in the coal tongs. "You treated your new client in a rather cavalier fashion, Holmes," I said.

His head was momentarily enveloped in a cloud of grey smoke. When it cleared, I could see that he was smiling. "I object to being treated like a pet dog who will fetch and carry at the owner's whim. The privileged classes all too often forget the niceties of please and thank you. On this occasion it satisfied me to exercise my perogative to act when *I* saw fit." He threw himself down in his chair. "Besides, it is a straightforward matter and I'm sure that we shall clear it up within the next twenty-four hours."

In this instance, Sherlock Holmes was wrong. The disappearance of Lord Darlington's painting turned out to be far from a straightforward matter.

The following morning we arrived as arranged at Lord Darlington's Mayfair town house a few minutes after ten. We were shown into the drawing room where his lordship greeted us in a most jovial manner. His demeanour was quite different from that of the night before. He introduced us to his wife, Sarah, a small, blonde-haired woman of about the same age as her husband. She seemed nervous in our company and soon made an excuse to leave us to our "business".

"I am sorry to have troubled you last night, Mr Holmes," said his Lordship, "and it was remiss of me not to wire you this morning to save you a wasted journey. Nevertheless I am happy to pay whatever fees you deem appropriate for the services rendered."

"Indeed. Then the painting has reappeared."

"Yes. It is wonderful. I went into the gallery this morning and almost out of habit I pulled back the curtain and the de Granville was back in place as though it had never been missing."

"But it was missing yesterday," said my friend sternly, not sharing his client's glee.

"Yes, yes, it must have been, but that hardly matters now."

"I would beg to differ," snapped Holmes.

"You are sure that it is the genuine article?" I asked.

Lord Darlington looked puzzled for a moment. "Why, yes," he said slowly, with faltering conviction.

"What my friend is suggesting," said Holmes, "is that it is possible that the thief who stole the painting may well have replaced it with a very good copy, unaware that you knew of its disappearance. You were due to be in France when you discovered its loss, were you not?"

"Why, yes, but . . ."

"Come, come, Lord Darlington. There has been a theft. There must have been a reason for it. You cannot disregard the felony just because your painting has been returned to you."

Some of the sparkle left our client's eyes and he sat down on the sofa. "I suppose you are right. However, I am convinced that the picture resting in my gallery at this moment is the genuine article, but I will contact my friend Hillary Stallybrass, the art expert at the Royal Academy who verified the painting originally, to confirm my belief."

"You would be wise to . . ."

Holmes was cut short by the sudden entrance into the room of a tall young man with wavy blond hair and young, eager eyes. "Father, I must . . ." he cried and then on seeing us he faltered.

"Not now, Rupert. I am sure whatever it is you wish to see me about can wait."

The young man hesitated, uncertain whether to heed his father's injunction or proceed. His mouth tightened into a petulant grimace and he turned on his heel, leaving the room as swiftly as he had entered it.

"The impatience of youth," observed Lord Darlington mirthlessly.

"I should like to see your gallery," said Holmes as though the brusque interruption had not occurred.

With some reluctance Lord Darlington took us into his inner sanctum. It was a long chamber whose ceiling was studded with skylights, none of which, we were informed, could be opened. Down the two long walls were a number of red velvet curtains covering a series of paintings. In the centre of the room was a comfortable swivel chair and a table containing a tantalus and an ornate cigar box.

"May we see the de Granville?" asked Holmes.

Without replying, his Lordship pulled back the cord on one of the curtains to reveal the masterpiece. I have only a layman's appreciation of art, but even I could see that this was a work of great beauty and skill.

"It is magnificent," said Lord Darlington, almost caressing the frame.

"Indeed," said Holmes, examining the canvas closely with his lens. "Tell me, Lord Darlington, do you keep a dog?"

"A dog?" our client's mouth dropped open. "No. Why do you ask?"

Holmes shrugged. "It is no matter at the moment."

Lord Darlington seemed irritated at Holmes's vague response. He consulted his watch. "Gentlemen, I have an important appointment in the House at eleven-thirty . . ."

"Perhaps you could leave us in the capable hands of your wife. I should like to ascertain some details concerning the domestic arrangements."

"Very well, if you think it is important."

We were left in the hallway while our client arranged for his departure and informed his wife of our request. Holmes casually examined the calling cards in the tray. His face grew taut with excitement as he caught sight of one. He grinned. "Muddy waters grow clearer, my dear fellow," he said cheerily.

Once more we found ourselves in the drawing room. Lady Darlington had arranged coffee for us. She seemed to have lost her nervous edge and appeared composed and fully at ease, sitting on the edge of the sofa, hardly touching her drink.

"You do not share your husband's love of painting, Lady Darlington?"

"It is his passion. I could never match his devotion to art. He leads a difficult public life and his paintings afford him relief and a respite."

"You never visit the gallery?"

"Never."

"What about your son?"

"Rupert?" Her face softened at the mention of her son and a loving smile touched her lips. "He has a young man's interests, and old paintings form no part of those. Rupert and I are alike in that respect."

"He is a member of the Pandora Club."

Lady Darlington looked askance at Holmes. "He . . . he may be. I am not aware of all my son's leisure haunts."

"Or his acquaintances – like Lord Arthur Beacham, for example?"

"Lord Arthur, what of him?"

"He does not possess a very high reputation."

"Perhaps not in the circles in which you mix, Mr Holmes. You must not listen to the gossip of maids and gardeners. Lord Arthur is a pleasant gentleman, but only one of many among Rupert's associates. Now if you have no further questions . . ."

"Just one more, Lady Darlington. Who has a key to the gallery?"

"There is only one and it never leaves my husband's possession. He carries it on his watch chain."

"Thank you. Thank you very much."

As we were being shown out of the house by a dour and decrepit butler we encountered a florid-faced, rotund man on the doorstep. He gave Holmes a polite smile of recognition and shook his hand. Holmes leaned forward and whispered some words in his ear before we set off down the street.

"Let us walk back to Baker Street," said my friend vigorously, "I am in need of fresh air and exercise."

"By all means," I agreed, falling in step with him. "I gather that rather red-faced gentleman was Hillary Stallybrass come to verify the de Granville."

"Indeed, it was, and I passed on a little advice that may be beneficial to him and certainly to us. Time will tell on that account."

"What is all this business of Lord Arthur Beacham and the Pandora Club? Your remarks were rather pointed in that direction."

Holmes beamed. "They were, weren't they? Someone was rather careless in leaving his calling card on show in the hall. Contrary to Lady Darlington's opinion, Lord Arthur has rather a doubtful reputation: he is a dissolute fellow whose activities sometimes stray into the realms of criminality. And Scotland Yard have had their eye on the Pandora Club, Beacham's office of operations, for some time. It is the centre for a number of somewhat nefarious dealings."

"How naïve of Lady Darlington to consider him a suitable companion for her son."

"How naïve of you, Watson, to think so."

I ignored my friend's riddle. "Do you think Beacham is mixed up with the missing picture?"

"I do. I am not sure yet what he is up to and quite who else is involved, but I have my theory which I will put to the test later today."

After a simple lunch provided by Mrs Hudson, Holmes busied himself with some malodorous chemical experiments, while I caught up with correspondence and prepared some case notes ready for publication. As dusk was falling, he retired to his room, emerging some forty-five minutes later in disguise. He was attired in evening dress, but he had padded out his lithe shape so that he appeared quite plump. His face was flushed and a large moustache adorned his upper lip, while a monocle twinkled in his left eye. The touches of disguise were light, but at the same time they transformed the familiar figure who was my friend and fellow lodger into a totally different character.

"I am ready for a night at the Pandora Club," he announced, his own voice seeming unnatural emanating from this stranger standing in our rooms. "After all my admonishments to you about the cavalier manner in which you throw your wound pension away on the guesses of the turf, I shall be very careful not to lose too much."

"You do not require my services, then?"

"Later, m'boy, but tonight I need to act, or rather observe, alone."

At this moment, Billy arrived with a telegram. Holmes ripped it open with gusto. "Aha," he cried, reading the contents and then throwing the missive over to me. It was from Hillary Stallybrass. It read: "de Granville is genuine. Some of the other works are not."

It was at breakfast the following morning when I next saw Holmes. He emerged, without disguise, clad in a purple dressing gown and beaming brightly.

"I gather from that grin," said I, tapping the shell of my boiled egg, "that your excursion to the Pandora Club was fruitful."

"The process of deduction is catching," he grinned, joining me at the table and pouring himself a cup of coffee. "One day I must pen a monograph on the importance in the art of detection of developing a knowledge of international crime and criminals."

"Riddles at breakfast? Come now Holmes, speak your mind."

"Does the name Alfredo Fellini mean anything to you?"

I shook my head.

"You prove my point," my friend replied smugly. "Now I happen to know that he is the right hand man of Antonio Carreras, one of the biggest gangland chiefs in the New York area. Blackmail and extortion are his methods and he has grown fat on them. So much so that he has been able to build up quite an impressive art collection. So my friend Barnes at Pinkerton's informs me in his regular reports."

"Art collection?" I dabbed my chin with the napkin and, pushing my half-eaten egg away, gave Holmes my full attention.

"Yes. Now I observed Fellini last night at the Pandora Club where he spent a great deal of his time deep in conversation with a certain member of the Darlington household."

"His Lordship's son, Rupert."

"Precisely. And the conversation was animated, not to say acrimonious at times. And all the while that sly cove Lord Arthur Beacham hovered in the background like a concerned mother hen."

"What does it all mean, Holmes?"

"To use a painting metaphor, which in this case is somewhat appropriate, I have sketched the outlines of the composition but I still need more time to fill in the detail and work on the light and shade. However, it is clear that Rupert Darlington is involved in some underhand deal which involves the unscrupulous Beacham *and* one of the most dangerous criminals in America – a deal that involves the theft of the de Granville canvas."

"But the painting was returned unharmed."

"It had to be. That is Rupert Darlington's problem."

Holmes loved to throw enigmatic statements at me to catch my reaction. I had long since learned that no matter how I responded he would not impart any information he held until he thought it the appropriate moment to do so. I had no conception of what Rupert Darlington's problem might be but I knew that should I press my friend to explain this conceit he would in some manner refuse. Therefore I tried to take our conversation in another, more positive direction, only to find it blocked by further enigma.

"What is our next move?" I asked.

"We visit 'the dog man'," he replied with a grin.

Within the hour we were rattling in a hansom cab eastwards across the city. I had heard Holmes give the cabbie an address in Commercial Street near the Houndsditch Road, a rundown and unsavoury part of London. He sat back in the cab, his pale, gaunt features wrapped in thought.

"Who or what is 'the dog man' and what is the purpose of our visit? Since you requested my company on this journey it would seem sensible to let me know its purpose," I said tartly.

"Of course, my dear fellow," grinned my companion, patting my arm in an avuncular fashion, "what am I thinking of, keeping you in ignorance? Well now, 'the dog man' is my own soubriquet for Joshua Jones whose house is over-run with the beasts. His fondness for canines has driven both his wife and children from his door. He lavishes love and attention on the various mutts he takes in, far more than he does upon his own kith and kin. However he has a great artistic talent." Holmes leaned nearer to me, dropping his voice to a dramatic whisper. "He is one of the greatest copy artists of all time. Only the keenest of experts could tell the real 'Mona Lisa' from a Jones copy. I have used the fellow on a couple of occasions myself when fake works of art were required to help clear up a case. You see where he might fit into our mystery?"

"Not precisely."

"I suspected Jones was involved in the matter yesterday morning.

You may recall that when I examined the de Granville, I asked if Darlington kept a dog?"

"Yes. I do."

"That was because through my lens I observed several dog hairs adhering to the frame – hairs of at least three different breeds. It seemed quite clear to me that the painting had at some time recently been lodged in premises where several dogs had been able to brush past the canvas. Where else could this occur but in the home of Joshua Jones?"

"Because he was copying the canvas . . ."

Holmes nodded.

"I see that, but why then was the real painting returned and not the copy?"

"Ah, that is the crux of the matter and I wish to test my theory out on my friend Mr Joshua Jones."

Commercial Street was indeed an unpleasant location. The houses were shabby and down-at-heel with many having boarded windows. The cab pulled up at the end of the street and Holmes ordered the cabbie to wait for us. With some reluctance he agreed. We then made our way down this depressing thoroughfare. A group of ragged, ill-nourished children were playing a ball game in the street and ran around us with shrill cries, taking no notice of our presence, their scrawny bodies brushing against us.

"If this Jones fellow is such a succesful artist," I said, "why does he not live in a more salubrious neighbourhood?"

"I believe he has another house in town where his wife and two children reside but she has forbidden him to bring a single dog over the threshold, so he seems quite content to stay here for most of the time with his horde of hounds. Ah, this is the one."

We had reached number 23: a house as decrepit as the rest with a dark blue door and a rusty knocker. The curtains at the window were closed, shunning the daylight and the outside world. Holmes knocked loudly. As the sound echoed through the house it was greeted by a cacophony of wailing, yapping and barking cries as though a pack of hounds had been let loose.

"I trust these dogs are not dangerous" I said with some unease.

"I trust so too," replied Holmes, knocking loudly again and setting off a further fusillade of canine cries. Mingled with these came the sound of a human voice. Within moments the lock turned and the door creaked open a few inches; a beady eye and a beaky nose appeared at the crack.

"What do you want?" demanded the man.

"A little information, Joshua, if you please."

"Why it's Mr Holmes," came the voice again, this time softer and warmer in tone. "Give me a moment to settle my little 'uns down. I don't want any of them to get out. Dog meat's at a premium around here." So saying he shut the door and he could be heard shepherding his pack of dogs back into the recesses of the house.

After a while the door opened again, this time wide enough to reveal the occupant, who was a scrawny individual of around seventy years of age, or so his wild white hair, rheumy eyes and fine dry skin led me to believe. He was dressed in a pair of baggy trousers, a blue collarless shirt and a shapeless green paint-spattered cardigan.

"Come in gentlemen, come in."

Only two dogs appeared at their master's heels as he led us down a dingy corridor and into an equally dingy sitting room. The air was oppressive with the smell of hound. In a nearby room one could hear barking and yelping accompanied by the occasionally frantic scratching as some fretting dog attempted to burrow out.

Jones gave a throaty chuckle at the sound of the muted row. "The little 'uns don't like being separated from their daddy," he grinned, revealing a row of uneven brown teeth. With a casual wave of the hand he indicated we should take a seat on a dilapidated old sofa. "Well, Mr Holmes, what can I do for you?"

"I need information."

A thin veil of unease covered Jones's face. "Ah, well," he said slowly, "I am reticent in that department, as you well know. I cannot be giving away the secrets of my clients or, soon enough, I'd have no clients."

"I have no wish to compromise you, Jones," said Sherlock Holmes evenly. "Indeed, it is not fresh information I require, merely confirmation of my deductions, confirmation which will allow me to proceed further in my case."

Jones frowned. "What you're asking is something I cannot give you. I treat all who cross over my threshold, be it man or dog, with the same regard and assurance of discretion."

Holmes appeared unperturbed by Jones's intransigence. "I am glad to hear it," he said. "I have no intention of asking you to betray anyone's trust, even that of such a lowly character as Lord Arthur Beacham."

Jones blanched somewhat at the mention of this name and his eyes flickered erratically. "Then what do you want from me?" he asked, his voice lacking the earlier assertiveness.

"I wish to present a series of suppositions to you regarding my current investigation which concerns the theft of Lord Darlington's painting the 'Adoration of the Magi' by de Granville – a work I understand you know intimately. All I require from you is a slight inclination of the head if you believe that I am in the possession of the correct interpretation of events and a shake of the head if you perceive my suppositions to be incorrect. There is no need for verbal confirmation. This would help me tremendously in the same way I believe I have helped you in the past."

Jones, who was by now sitting opposite us on a wicker chair with one of the dogs perched on his lap, bent over and kissed the creature on the nose and ruffled its fur. "As you know, I never ask questions of my clients. However I cannot prevent you from expressing your views in my company, Mr Holmes," he said, as though he were addressing the dog.

"Indeed," agreed Holmes.

"And I may nod and shake my head as I feel fit. That is not to say that this will indicate definitely that I either agree or disagree with your statements."

"I understand perfectly. Now, sir, I happen to know that you have recently been asked to copy Louis de Granville's 'Adoration of the Magi' for a certain client."

Jones head remained in close proximity to the dog but it moved downwards in a virtually imperceptible nod.

"I believe your client to be Lord Arthur Beacham . . ." Holmes paused but Jones did not move.

"And I believe you have copied many paintings for him over the last six months or so."

Another gentle nod.

"The work was carried out over a day and a night and both paintings, the original and the copy, were returned to your client. He then returned the fake to the premises of the owner and sold the original to one of several unscrupulous collectors."

"I have no notion of what happens to the paintings when they leave these premises, Mr Holmes. I have no interest in the matter and would regard it as somewhat indiscreet to make enquiries."

"I can understand that. Such enquiries could lead you to learn information you would not wish to know."

For a moment a smile played on the old man's thin lips. He sat up, and looked Holmes in the eye and nodded.

Holmes continued: "I take it that you are able carry out pre-paratory work on most copies as their images are easily accessible in lithographic form."

"That is correct. I prepare what I call my skeleton work in advance. It speeds up the process and lessens the time the original work needs to be with me in my gallery."

"But in the case of the de Granville this was not possible, was it? Being a 'lost painting' there were no lithographs available, so you required a longer time with the original."

Another imperceptible nod.

"You are an excellent listener," cried Holmes enthusiastically, rising to his feet and pulling me with him. "Your silences have been most eloquent. My case is all but complete. I thank you."

"In expressing your gratitude please remember that I conveyed no information to you, nor confirmed any of your statements."

"Of course. The players in this sordid drama will condemn themselves without involvement from outside sources. Come, Watson, let us see if the cabbie has waited for us."

And so in this hurried manner we took our leave of "the dog man".

I was surprised at the speed by which this case came to its conclusion; and a very dark conclusion it was too. I would never have guessed that what began as as a fairly inconsequential affair concerning a missing painting would end in murder and a family's disgrace.

The cabbie had been as good as his word and was still waiting for us at the corner of the street. However an expression of relief crossed his ruddy features as he saw us returning. "Back to Baker Street is it?" he asked as we climbed aboard.

"No," responded Holmes, "Mayfair."

"This is a sad affair, Watson," said my friend, lighting a cigarette as he lounged back in the recesses of the cab. "The person who will be hurt most by its outcome is the only innocent player in the drama."

"Lady Darlington?"

He shook his head. "Her husband. His career is likely to crumble to dust if the facts become public. Lady Darlington is far from innocent."

"You cannot mean she was involved in the theft?"

"Think, Watson, think. There was only one key to the gallery. It was on Lord Darlington's watch chain. The only time he would not be wearing it would be at night when he was asleep. Then his wife, and only she, sleeping in the same room would have easy access to it. She is the only person who could have provided entry to the gallery. However improbable the circumstances, logic always provides certainties."

Lady Darlington was dismayed to see us and it was with a certain amount of ill grace that she bade us take a seat in the morning room. "I hope this will not take long, gentlemen. I have a series of pressing engagements today."

We had only just taken our seats when Holmes gave a sharp sigh of irritation and leapt to his feet. "I beg your pardon, Lady Darlington, my brain is addled today. I have just bethought me of a pressing matter that had slipped my mind. There is urgent need to send a telegram concerning another case of mine which is coming to fruition. If you will pardon me one moment, I will arrange for our cab-driver to deliver the message."

Before Lady Darlington had the opportunity to reply, Holmes had rushed from the room.

"What extraordinary behaviour," she observed, sitting stiffly upright, clutching her reticule.

"I am sure my friend will return shortly," I said, surprised as she was at at Holmes's sudden departure.

"I presume that you are not in a position to enlighten me as to the purpose of Mr Holmes's visit."

"Not precisely," I replied lamely. "But I am sure he will not be many minutes."

Her ladyship sighed heavily and I sat in embarrassed silence, awaiting Holmes's return. Thankfully, he was as good as his word and in less than five minutes he was sitting opposite our client's wife once more.

"Now, Mr Holmes, as you have already wasted some of my time, I beg you to be brief."

"My business here will take but a short time, but I thought it would be best if I consulted you first before I told your husband the truth behind the disappearing and reappearing painting and the roles that you and your son played in the mystery."

Lady Darlington gave a startled gasp. "I don't know what you mean."

"Oh yes you do," asserted my friend coldly. "The time for pretence and dissembling is over. You cannot go on protecting your son any longer."

"Mr Holmes, I will not tolerate any more of your nonsense. Would you please be kind enough to leave."

"I will leave, certainly, taking the key with me."

"The key?"

"I am afraid that I played a little trick on you just now. On leaving the room I did not go to instruct our waiting cabman as I intimated. Instead, I slipped upstairs to your son's room where it did not take me very long to discover the hiding place where he secreted the key." Holmes reached into his waistcoat pocket as though to retieve some small object. "The duplicate key that gains him access to your husband's gallery."

Lady Darlington's face turned white. "That is impossible," she cried in some agitation, snapping open her reticule.

"I agree," said Holmes, stepping forward and extracting a small golden key from her ladyship's bag. "I told you a tissue of lies in order for *you* to reveal the real hiding place of the duplicate key. It was a simple subterfuge engineered to reveal the truth."

At this, Lady Darlington broke down and sobbed uncontrollably. I was moved by her obvious distress and watched helplessly as her body shook with sorrow but Holmes remained stony-faced and waited until the lady had controlled herself enough to speak to him. "How much do you know," she asked at last, dabbing her watery eyes with her handkerchief.

"I know all. I know your son has built up a series of very large gambling debts at the Pandora Club. In an endeavour to keep these from your husband you helped pay for them at first, but when the amounts became too great for you to contend with, you aided and abetted your son in his scheme of replacing the paintings in Lord Darlington's gallery with fakes while your son's crony Lord Arthur Beacham sold the originals."

"The situation as you portray it is more damning than the real circumstances," said Lady Darlington, regaining some of her composure. "Rupert is the son of my first marriage and has never been accepted by Hector. He even denied him the common courtesies. Certainly Rupert was never shown any love by his step-father. I suppose in a reaction to this I lavished love upon him. I gave him liberties and freedoms that were perhaps inappropriate for such a headstrong youth. He lacked a father's controlling guidance. When he formed a friendship with Lord Arthur Beacham I was pleased at first. I believed that the influence of this older man would be good for him. Alas, I did not know what a scoundrel the fellow was. The truth only emerged when it was too late and Rupert was completely under his evil spell. Beacham led my son into reckless habits. Yes, there were the gambling debts which, despite my pleas to Rupert to abandon the game, grew and grew. I knew that if Hector found out he would disinherit him and cast him out of the house. What would become of the boy then? How could I let that happen?"

Lady Darlington paused for a moment as though she was waiting for an answer to her questions, although she avoided our glances. Holmes remained silent.

"When the amounts became too great to deal with out of my allowance, Rupert presented me with the plan regarding the paintings. It had been suggested by Beacham of course. He knew of a skilled painter who could copy the pictures so that only an expert could tell the difference and he also had contacts who could provide eager customers for the original canvases. Beacham, of course, demanded a large fee for his 'services'. To my eternal shame, I agreed, believing it would be only the one painting. One night when my husband was asleep, I took the gallery key from his chain and made a wax impression of it so that a copy could be made.

"The substitution of the first painting could not have been smoother. The exchange was carried out while my husband was away for two days on government business. Rupert took the picture early in the evening and returned the following morning with the forgery. My husband never suspected a thing. The apparent ease with which the plan had been carried out made Beacham bolder and greedier. He led my son into greater debt so that the substituition of another painting was needed. And so it became a regular process, every two months or so."

"Until the de Granville fiasco when your husband's trip to France was postponed and he returned earlier than expected."

"It was Beacham's idea to take the de Granville. He said it would bring the greatest fee yet, but the copier required more time since it was an unknown painting. As you know, my husband discovered the masterpiece missing . . ." Lady Darlington's eyes watered afresh and she dabbed them with her handkerchief.

"Both your son and Beacham knew it would be foolish to place the forgery where the original had hung now that its absence had been discovered. They were aware that your husband would, as a matter of course, call in an expert to verify that it was the original."

Lady Darlington nodded mutely.

"You have been a foolish woman, Lady Darlington. Although you may have acted with the best of intentions towards your son, you have allowed a situation to develop that cannot fail but to bring pain and disgrace to those two men whom you hold dear."

"I beg you not to tell my husband."

"Your husband is my client. He must be told. Besides, we are not dealing with a family squabble here. This matter concerns the theft of a series of master paintings. Two of the culprits are the son and wife of the owner, who is a minister of the crown. A scandal now is inevitable."

"I appreciate that the truth has now to come out. But I want to be the one to tell Hector. It is the least I can do to atone for my sins. Give me a day – twenty-four hours – to do this and also to try and persuade my son to give himself up to the authorities."

Holmes hesitated. He was somewhat moved by the woman's plight.

"Please be merciful," she begged.

My companion consulted his watch. "It is now approaching four o'clock. I will send a telegram to reach Lord Darlington in the morning, indicating that I shall call on him at four in the afternoon to convey information of the greatest moment."

"Bless you, Mr Holmes."

As events turned out, Holmes was never to make that visit. The following morning I was late down to breakfast and I found my friend slumped in his armchair perusing the paper. His face bore a grim expression.

"Violent delights have violent ends," he said, more to himself than me.

"Bad news?"

He shrugged. "Fate has entered the lists and we have effectively been relegated, old fellow." He waved the paper in my direction. "I refer to a report in here. Two bodies were washed up on the shingle below Tower Bridge late last night. They were bound and gagged and their brains had been blown out. They have been identified as Lord Arthur Beacham and Rupert Darlington, the son of the Minister for Foreign Affairs, Lord Hector Darlington."

"Great heavens what a tragedy. What happened?"

"It was no doubt the work of Alfredo Fellini and his cronies. Obviously Beacham, in his frustration regarding the de Granville painting, tried, foolishly, to pass the fake off as the original to the American. His treachery received the usual rough justice of the gangland courts. Rupert Darlington was seen as part of the conspiracy – which he may well have been. Ah, Watson, Scott had it aright: 'Oh what a tangled web we weave when we practise to deceive.'"

THE ADVENTURE OF THE SUSPECT SERVANT

Barbara Roden

The next case we stumbled over by sheer chance. Devotees of Sherlock Holmes will remember that Dr Watson met his future wife, Mary Morstan, when she sought Holmes's help in the case of "The Sign of Four". In introducing herself she reminded Holmes that he had once helped her employer, Mrs Cecil Forrester, to unravel "a little domestic complication." Holmes had to think for a while to remember and then recalled that the case "was a very simple one". It was so simple that Watson probably kept no record of it.

A few years ago that excellent scholar of ghost and mystery fiction, Barbara Roden, was undertaking research in a firm of insurers on another matter entirely, when she chanced upon some information about a certain Mr Forrester, and piece by piece she was able to rebuild "The Adventure of the Suspect Servant".

It is seldom that my friend, Mr Sherlock Holmes, has turned down an investigation which fell his way. There were times in our long association when his formidable brain was pre-occupied with a case of supreme importance, and such circumstances occasionally precluded the taking up of another, less pressing, matter. As a rule, however, it was his habit never to neglect an opportunity to exercise those powers of observation and deduction which it has been my privilege to observe and chronicle. No case was too small to engage his attention; and I have had cause to bless the advent of more than one client, whose misfortune, however trivial, lifted Holmes from out of the depression into which he was prone to sink when not occupied. If, in my chronicles, I have dwelt upon the macabre and the *outré*, it is because such cases, however unsatisfactory the outcome, have features which commend themselves to the reading public. I therefore set the following case before my readers as an example of an affair which was not as complex as some of my friend's other adventures, but which was no less pressing to those immediately concerned with it.

It was a morning in late October 1886, and London was enjoying a period of exceptionally fine weather known as St Luke's little summer. So warm was the day that I had flung open the windows of our sitting room, and was looking out over Baker Street and the bustling crowd contained therein. Holmes was perusing *The Times*, surrounded by the remnants of the *Chronicle*, *Standard*, *Telegraph* and *Post*, which lay in drifts around him.

I had been standing at the window for some minutes, watching the flow of the crowd, before I remarked casually, "We have a client, Holmes, so you might just tidy those papers."

My friend looked up, an expression of surprise upon his face. He cocked his head towards the door, rather in the manner of a hound listening for the view-halloa, then said, "I hear nothing, save Mrs Hudson downstairs. Yet you say we have a client?"

I chuckled, for I must confess that I enjoyed seeing my friend puzzled. He rose and joined me at the window, scanning the street for whoever had caught my eye. There was still no sound of footsteps upon the stair, and he looked at me quizzically.

"There," I said, gesturing to a woman who stood gazing into the window of a shop across from our door. "She is our client."

"And what leads you to that conclusion? Pray elucidate."

"When I see a lady," I began, emulating my friend's manner on such occasions, "alight from and dismiss a cab, I infer that she has some business to conduct which she anticipates will take more than a few minutes, or she would have kept the cab waiting. The fact that the cab stopped immediately outside our door shows that her business lies in our vicinity. When the lady then proceeds to pace the pavement opposite us, not once but four times, I deduce that she is deeply disturbed about something, and is endeavouring to reach a difficult decision. Although she has been gazing into the window of the bookbinder's shop opposite for the past few minutes, it is unlikely that anything there is causing her such consternation. What else, then, but a client for Mr Sherlock Holmes?"

"Your reasoning is certainly sound, Watson – ah, but here comes the lady herself, to silence all doubt."

She had indeed turned and, with an abruptness which signalled an end to indecision, crossed the road. We heard a ring of the bell and then a voice at the door, enquiring if Mr Holmes was at home, a signal which caused my friend to gather up the untidy papers and thrust them into his bedroom. He had exchanged his dressing-gown for a jacket when Mrs Hudson knocked at the door and announced, "Mrs Cecil Forrester."

The lady was middle-aged, yet her slim figure and graceful air gave her an air of youth that many a younger woman might have envied.

She was well and fashionably dressed in a navy-blue costume which combined elegance with restraint. Her features were attractive, yet drawn with worry and fatigue, and there were still traces of indecision marked upon her countenance. She looked from one of us to the other, and my friend stepped forward.

"Mrs Forrester, I am Sherlock Holmes, and this is my friend and colleague, Dr John Watson. Pray take a seat, and tell us what difficulty brings you here."

Our client took her seat in an armchair and Holmes sat opposite her. For a moment she remained silent, her eyes fixed on the rug and her hands twisting nervously in her lap. Then she took a deep breath, as one who steels herself for the worst, and looked up.

"Mr Holmes, I have come to you because I do not know what else to do, and there is no one else to whom I can turn. Over the past few weeks several items of value have disappeared from our home, and I need you to find the culprit."

"Surely the police would be . . .," began Holmes, but our client interrupted.

"The police have not the first idea as to the truth," she said with some anger. "My husband called them in at my urging, and all they have been able to do thus far is upset the staff and accuse my maid, Sarah, who I am sure knows nothing of the matter."

"Perhaps," said Holmes soothingly, "you might explain to us exactly what has occurred, so that we may form an opinion."

"Certainly, Mr Holmes." She paused for a moment, as if gathering her thoughts, and then launched into her tale.

"My husband is the assistant manager of Williams and Co., a firm of insurers in the City. He commands an excellent salary, and as I am not without some income of my own we live, quite comfortably, in a house in Camberwell. We were married twelve years ago, and all has gone smoothly with us until recently.

"My husband's business has increased a good deal in the past few months, and as they are short of staff at the moment Cecil has had to spend more time than usual in the City, so I have not seen him as much as I formerly did. It was two months ago that I first noticed something amiss. I was looking for a receipt in my husband's desk at home, and found that one of the drawers would not open properly. I managed to work it loose, and found that a box which had been placed at the back of it had jammed. I recognized the box as one which had contained a pair of gold and diamond cufflinks which I had given Cecil on his last birthday. The box was empty, and I thought that odd, as I knew Cecil wore the cufflinks on formal occasions only, and was hardly likely to wear them to work. I meant to ask him about them, but he was again late in arriving home. I had arranged to attend the theatre with friends and, as I was myself late in returning, the matter slipped my mind before I could mention it.

"Three weeks ago I noticed that a gold repeater watch he had inherited from his grandfather was missing from its case. I remembered, however, that it had not been striking properly, and Cecil said that he would have to have it cleaned and repaired. I naturally assumed that it was at the watchmaker's, and thought no more about it.

"It was last Wednesday when matters came to a head. I had planned to do some shopping in the afternoon, and then take tea with a friend, as it was the servants' half-day. I took a brooch out of my jewellery case before I left, and placed the case back in the drawer of my dressing-table. When I returned home and went to replace the brooch in the case, I noticed that the contents had been somewhat disturbed, and was horrified to find that a valuable emerald ring which had been in there had vanished. I searched the case and drawer thoroughly, thinking that perhaps it had fallen out, but could not find it anywhere. The ring has great sentimental value to me, as it belonged to my mother, and I was terribly distraught when Cecil arrived home.

"He saw at once that something was wrong, and went dreadfully pale when I told him about the ring. However, he did his best to console me, saying that he was sure I had merely misplaced it, and that it would come to light soon. It was then that a terrible thought struck me. I remembered the empty box where the cufflinks should have been, and the missing watch. Could there be some connection with my missing ring?

"I asked Cecil if he had taken the watch to be repaired, and he seemed very surprised that I should ask. His surprise gave me all the answer I needed, and I told him what I had found. It seemed obvious to me that a thief had been at work, and I urged Cecil to call in the police. A policeman came out to the house the next day, and we soon discovered that other items were missing, such as a tie-pin and a gold snuff-box."

Our client paused for breath. Holmes, who had been listening carefully to her tale, said, "Your husband has been working long hours for some time, you said. For how long, exactly?"

Mrs Forrester looked somewhat surprised at the question. "Really, Mr Holmes, I cannot see what that has to do with the matter."

"Nevertheless, Mrs Forrester, I repeat the question. The smallest matter may have a bearing upon the case."

"Well, it began in June, as far as I can remember."

"And has continued until the present time?"

"Yes."

"Have the hours remained unchanged?"

"No – no, he began working even later towards the end of August." Mrs Forrester had appeared puzzled by the line of questioning, but now understanding broke over her face. "I believe I see the reasoning behind your questions, Mr Holmes. You think that someone has been watching the house from outside, someone who has noted the long hours my husband works and knows when the house will be empty."

"Possibly," said my friend in a noncommittal voice. "I cannot theorize before I have all my data. The items that have gone missing thus far – cufflinks, a watch, a tie-pin, a snuff-box – all have belonged to your husband?"

"All except my ring, Mr Holmes."

"Quite so. Has anything else been missed?"

"No."

"Yet you must have many more items of value. Has none of your other jewellery vanished?"

"No, Mr Holmes. I am sure I would have noticed."

Holmes stretched in his chair. "Surely the official force found no difficulty in seeing to the bottom of this affair, for if you will pardon my saying so it hardly seems complex."

"Well, complex or no, Mr Holmes, the man accomplished little beyond turning our house upside-down before telling us that my maid, Sarah, was the most likely culprit, and that if he could search her belongings he was sure the missing items would be found."

"Upon what did he base this conclusion?"

"He had been told that Wednesday was the servants' half-day, and he checked on their actions during the afternoon. We employ four servants – a cook, a housekeeper, a governess, and Sarah. The cook had been visiting her family, and they all confirmed that she had been with them for the entire afternoon. Mrs Lodge, our housekeeper, had spent her afternoon with a friend, and again it was proved that she had been away from the house for the entire time. Mary, our governess, had been out with the twins, who were attending the birthday party of one of their young friends, and her whereabouts are above question. Poor Sarah, however, had been feeling rather poorly, and had spent the afternoon in her room, resting. Of course, she had no proof of this, and the policeman fixed on this point, as he could see no signs of anyone from outside forcing an entry into the house."

"That seems eminently reasonable, if a trifle mundane," said Holmes. "What makes you so positive that your maid is innocent?"

"Mr Holmes, Sarah has been with me for several years, and I know she would never do such a thing. The policeman thinks me foolish, I am sure, but I know that she is innocent, and I will not see her subjected to any indignities. The poor girl is very upset, and is terrified that she will lose her position, or worse."

"What, pray, is your husband's reaction?"

"Cecil does not want to see her prosecuted as a thief, and seems to feel that it will be difficult to prove the case against her conclusively. However, he seems convinced of Sarah's guilt, and is urging me to dismiss her. This I shall not do until I have proof one way or the other. That is why I have come to you for help."

I could not help but admire the woman for her compassion, and her staunch defence of her maid. My friend, however, merely shrugged and said, "The police case seems fairly clear. What exactly is it that you would have me do?"

"I would like you to come to the house and see what you can find. It is well known that you can see things which remain hidden to others. I am sure that you will find evidence which the police have overlooked or misconstrued. Please say you will help!"

Holmes thought for a moment, then said quietly, "Yes. I will help."

Our client gave a sigh of relief, and a smile erased some of the strain from her features. "Thank you, Mr Holmes. Will you come back to Camberwell with me now?"

"No," said Holmes. Noting her look of surprise and disappointment, he added, "I have a pressing engagement in an hour's time, but I shall be at your disposal after that. If you will leave your address with us, we shall be out to see you no later than three o'clock."

After our client had left, Holmes sat musing for some minutes, while I sat quietly, waiting. Much as I wished to know his thoughts, I refrained from interrupting his reverie, knowing his dislike of being disturbed. Finally he sprang from his chair and picked up his hat and stick.

"Off to your appointment?" I asked.

"Yes, Watson, and it is one to which you might be interested in accompanying me. I am off to see Mr Cecil Forrester, of the firm of Williams and Co."

"I was not aware that you had an appointment with him."

"Nor was I, until a few minutes ago, when I excused myself from accompanying Mrs Forrester. The truth is, Watson, that I wish to see Mr Forrester before examining the house."

We hailed a cab, and eventually found ourselves deposited in a small square off Threadneedle Street, in the shadow of the Royal Exchange. The office of Williams and Co. appeared to be prosperous, judging by the hum of activity which greeted us as we entered. Holmes explained to a clerk that we were there to see Mr Forrester on urgent business, and the emphasis placed on the word "urgent" caused the man to hurry off. He returned with the news that Mr Forrester would see us in a moment. Holmes, whose keen eye had been noting down details of the office, commented on the activity.

"We're no busier than usual," replied the clerk. "We did have another chap employed for a few months, to help us with some extra business, but we let him go three months ago. Ah, Mr Forrester will see you now."

We were ushered into his office, and the clerk left, closing the door behind him. Our client's husband was a man of about five- and forty, although his pale and somewhat haggard face made him seem older. He gazed at us in puzzlement.

"My clerk said you had urgent business with me, gentlemen, but I am afraid I cannot place your faces."

"Perhaps you can place our names," said my friend smoothly. "I am Sherlock Holmes, and this gentleman is my colleague, Dr Watson. We have been asked by Mrs Forrester to look into the matter of some missing jewellery."

Forrester's face went even more pale, and he sat down abruptly. "My wife came to you?" he asked in a hoarse voice.

"Yes," said Holmes, "and I informed her that I would call upon her at three o'clock this afternoon. Unless, that is, you would care to explain to me why you have secretly been taking your own possessions."

Forrester sprang from his chair and stood trembling behind his desk. He began to say something, but no words issued from his mouth. Then he sank back down and buried his face in his hands.

"It is all up," he said finally. "How much do you know?"

"I know most of what you did. You have been taking your own valuables one by one and either selling them or pawning them. When you had exhausted your own articles you took a ring from your wife's jewellery case, which brought everything to light. I should imagine that you would have preferred not to involve the police, but there really was no other way, and you must have counted on suspicion falling on a member of staff rather than the respectable head of the household. In this you were not disappointed, and you were prepared to see your wife's innocent maid accused and dismissed rather than admit your own culpability."

The man looked up, amazement struggling with the fear on his face. "How do you know this?" he whispered.

"Your wife said that all the missing items save the ring were yours, which was suggestive, as thieves are not usually selective in their choice. Then, too, there was the fact that the thefts occurred over a period of some weeks. If a servant was responsible, is it likely that she would take only one piece at a time, knowing that she could be discovered at any moment? No. Any thief would strike once, take all they could, and vanish. Your wife also mentioned that you had been working very long hours of late, and this change of habit was concurrent with the start of the thefts. It seemed likely that the cause of your late hours was not connected with work, but with something that required money. Am I correct?"

Forrester nodded. Now that the initial shock had passed, he seemed almost relieved, as if glad that his secret had been discovered. When at last he spoke he did so in a stronger voice than he had previously used.

"Yes. You are correct, Mr Holmes. I did take the items, which were pawned as soon as I had them. I took my own items first, as my wife was not as likely to miss them, and I could always invent a plausible story should she enquire. It was desperation which caused me to take the ring. But you are wrong about Sarah. I did not want to see the poor girl turned out with a thief's name, even though I suggested it. I hoped that the police would find no evidence and would drop the case."

"What caused this desperation?" I asked when he stopped. Forrester rose and gazed out the window behind him for a moment before replying, "Gambling."

He turned back to face us, and I was reminded of a prisoner in the dock making a confession. "I have been gambling at the track for some time now. At first it was done casually, but soon it became a mania, and I was caught tight in its grasp. Try as I might I could not break free, and I began to spend more and more time there. Soon I had heavy debts, and my salary was not enough. I continued betting, however, using the money from the pawned items in the gambler's forlorn hope that one stroke of good fortune would enable me to make good my losses. Soon the money was gone, however, and I needed more. I thought that with the money to be obtained from pawning my wife's ring I could win enough to pay my debts and redeem the pawned items. I was so desperate that I did not even think of what would happen should she discover its loss, for I could not see beyond my debts. I knew the house would be empty on Wednesday afternoon, so I returned and took the ring. I had no idea that Sarah was not feeling well, and had therefore not gone out. When the policeman indicated that he suspected her I was at first relieved, then appalled at what

I had done and what I had become. And now – now I do not know what to do."

He sat before us, a broken man. I felt a keen sympathy for him, having experienced some of his fascination for the turf. Well I knew what it could do to a man, for I had seen many ensnared by its coils and dragged down. I had escaped, but I knew many who had not. Still, it could be done, and I said so to Forrester.

"Escape?" he said, in a tired voice. "But how? What shall I do?"

"Tell your wife," said Holmes, who had been sitting quietly.

"My wife? But I cannot. The shame . . ."

"Is better than the ruin which will certainly come to you if you continue down this path. Come, Sir," he continued in a softer tone, "your wife is a compassionate woman. She came to us out of concern for her maid, and I am sure that if you are honest with her you shall have nothing to regret. Go to her now and explain everything, then tell Sarah that she has nothing to fear."

Holmes rose to go, but paused at the door. "I shall send a telegram, but please extend my regrets to your wife for not keeping our appointment. I am sure she will understand. Come, Watson."

THE ADVENTURE
OF THE AMATEUR
MENDICANT SOCIETY

John Gregory Betancourt

1887 was one of Holmes's busiest years. We know for certain of at least thirteen cases that year, and indications of several others. Watson refers to some of these at the start of "The Five Orange Pips" although, in his usual devious way, the case of "The Five Orange Pips" itself did not happen in that year but in 1889.

The year began with Holmes facing one of his most formidable opponents, the King of Blackmailers, Charles Augustus Milverton. It was followed by the case of "The Paradol Chamber", which I am still piecing together and hope to bring to you at a future date. After that Holmes was plunged into the major problems of the Netherland-Sumatra Company, which also resulted in the case enticingly referred to as "The Giant Rat of Sumatra", for which the world is not yet ready, and the daring schemes of Baron Maupertuis. It is of some significance, I believe, that all record of these cases has been extinguished and my researches and those of my colleagues have revealed nothing. I have no doubt that Watson was, in any case, concealing identities here, but I also have no doubt that these were amongst some of Holmes's most daring and important cases. His exertions upon them damaged his health to the extent that Watson ordered Holmes to join him on a few days vacation in Surrey to recuperate, whereupon Holmes promptly threw himself into the local case of "The Reigate Squires". The case acted like therapy and within days Holmes was reinvigorated and back in London.

One of the next cases that Holmes took on was "The Adventure of the Amateur Mendicant Society" which Watson delayed from writing down for several years. That delay meant that some of his earlier jottings about the case did not end up in his final papers stored in the despatch box and instead surfaced amongst some other papers found by bookdealer Robert Weinberg, whose own researches I shall return to later. Weinberg sold these papers to John Betancourt who has helped piece the case together.

As I have written previously, my first years sharing lodgings with Mr Sherlock Holmes were among the most interesting of my life. Of all his cases – both public and private – which took place during this period, there remains one in particular of which I have hesitated to write until this time. Despite an ingenious resolution – and to my mind a wholeheartedly satisfactory one – contrived by my friend, the bizarre nature of this affair has made me reluctant to place it before a general readership. However, I feel the time has come to lay forth the facts concerning Mr Oliver Pendleton-Smythe and the most unusual organization to which he belonged.

My notebook places our first meeting with Mr Pendleton-Smythe, if meeting it can be called, at Tuesday 24 April, 1887. We had just concluded a rather sensitive investigation (of which I am still not at liberty to write), and Holmes's great mind had begun to turn inexorably inward. I feared he might once more take up experimentation with opiates to satiate his need for constant mental stimulation.

So it was that I felt great relief when Mrs Hudson announced that a man – a very insistent man who refused to give his name – was at the door to see Mr Holmes.

"Dark overcoat, hat pulled low across his forehead, and carrying a black walking stick?" Holmes asked without looking up from his chair.

"Why, yes!" exclaimed Mrs Hudson. "How ever did you know?"

Holmes made a deprecating gesture. "He has been standing across the street staring up at our windows for more than an hour. Of course I noticed when I went to light my pipe, and I marked him again when I stood to get a book just a moment ago."

"What else do you know about him?" I asked, lowering my copy of the *Morning Post.*

"Merely that he is an army colonel recently retired from service in Africa. He is a man of no small means, although without formal title or estates."

"His stance," I mused, "would surely tell you that he a military man, and the wood of his walking stick might well indicate that he has seen service in Africa, as well might his clothes. But how could you deduce his rank when he's not in uniform?"

"The same way I know his name is Colonel Oliver Pendleton-Smythe," Holmes said.

I threw down the *Morning Post* with a snort of disgust. "Dash it all, you know the fellow!"

"Not true." Holmes nodded toward the newspaper. "You should pay more attention to the matters before you."

I glanced down at the *Morning Post*, which had fallen open to reveal a line drawing of a man in uniform. MISSING: COLONEL OLIVER PENDLETON-SMYTHE, said the headline. I stared at the picture, then up at Holmes's face.

"Will you see him, sir?" asked Mrs Hudson.

"Not tonight," said Holmes. "Tell Colonel Pendleton-Smythe – and do use his full name, although he will doubtlessly bluster and deny it – that I will see him at nine o'clock sharp tomorrow morning. Not one second sooner and not one second later. If he asks, tell him I am concluding another important case and cannot be disturbed." He returned his gaze to his book.

"Very good, sir," she said, and shaking her head she closed the door.

The second the latch clicked, Holmes leaped to his feet. Gathering up his coat and hat, he motioned for me to do likewise. "Make haste, Watson," he said. "We must follow the colonel back to his den!"

"Den?" I demanded. I threw on my own coat and accompanied him down the back stairs at breakneck pace. "What do you mean by 'den'?"

"Please!" Holmes put up one hand for silence and eased open the door. Pendleton-Smythe was striding briskly up Baker Street, swinging his walking stick angrily, as though it were a machete. We both slipped out and Holmes closed the door behind us. Then together we crossed the street and proceeded surreptitiously after the colonel. He seemed to be heading toward the river.

"What is this affair about?" I asked as I hurried after Holmes.

"Mr Pendleton-Smythe, had you bothered to read that article in the *Morning Post*, disappeared two days ago. Foul play was suspected. In the fireplace of his London home police inspectors found several scraps of paper, but little could be made out except one phrase: 'Amateur Mendicant Society.' What do you make of it?"

"A mendicant is a beggar, I believe."

"True!"

"But a whole society of amateur beggars? And for a retired army colonel to be involved in them! It boggles the mind."

"I suspect," said Holmes, "that modern views of beggary have colored your thoughts on this matter. Mendicants have been, at various times and in various cultures, both revered and despised. I suspect this is another name for the Secret Mendicant Society, a network of spies which is – or was, at any rate – quite real and much older than you realize. Its roots stretch back to the Roman Empire and as far abroad as Russia, India, and Egypt."

"You think it still exists, then?" I asked.

"I thought it had died out a generation ago in Europe, but it seems to have surfaced once more. I have heard hints in the last few years, Watson, that lead me to suspect it has become an instrument of evil."

"And Pendleton-Smythe . . ."

"Another Professor Moriarty, pulling the strings of this society for his own personal gain? Fortunately, no. He is, I believe, a pawn in a much larger game, although only a few squares on the board are yet visible to me. More than that I cannot say until I have questioned Pendleton-Smythe."

"What do these 'amateur mendicants' do? Are they beggars or not?"

"Quickly!" Holmes said, pulling me behind a stopped Hansom cab. "He's turning!"

Pendleton-Smythe had stopped before a small rooming house. As we peered out at him, he paused on the steps to look left then right, but did not see us. He entered the building and shut the door behind himself.

"Interesting," Holmes said. "But it confirms my theory."

"That he's a beggar?" I asked, feeling a little annoyed for all the rushing about. "If so, he is surely a well-lodged one."

"Pendleton-Smythe has gone into hiding out of fear for his life. Why else would a man who owns a house choose to rent a room in such shabby surroundings as these?"

"Are we to question him here, then?" I asked.

He paused, lips pursed, deep in thought. After a minute I cleared my throat.

"No, Watson," he said, turning back toward Baker Street. "I think that can wait until tomorrow. I have much to do first."

The next morning Holmes knocked loudly on my door until, bleary eyed, I called, "What is it, Holmes?"

"It's half past six," he said. "Mrs Hudson has the kettle on and breakfast will be ready at seven sharp."

"For heaven's sake," I said, sitting up. "Tell me, why have you awakened me so early?"

"We have an appointment!"

"Appointment?" I asked, still cloudy. I rose and opened the door. "Ah. Pendleton-Smythe and his amateur beggars, I assume. But that's not until nine o'clock sharp – you said so yourself!"

"Exactly!" He had a fevered look to his eye and I knew he'd been up most of the night working on the mysterious colonel's case – although what the actual nature of the case was, I still hadn't a clue. Yet Holmes seemed to place singular importance on it.

When I had shaved and dressed, I emerged to find an excellent repast set out for us by Mrs Hudson. Holmes had barely touched his plate. He was rummaging through stacks of old newspapers strewn across the floor and every flat surface of the room.

"Here it is!" he cried.

"What?" I asked, helping myself to tea, toast, and orange marmalade.

"A pattern is emerging," he said softly. "I believe I have all the pieces now. But how do they fit?"

"Explain it to me," I said.

He held up one hand. "Precisely what I intend to do, Watson. Your clarity of thought may be what I need right now." He cleared his throat. "In 1852, Oliver Pendleton-Smythe and six of his schoolmates were expelled from Eton. They were involved in some scandal, the nature of which I have yet to ascertain – official reports tend to be vague on that sort of matter."

"Rightfully so," I murmured.

"Young Pendleton-Smythe found himself shipped off to South Africa after six months of knocking about London, and there his career proved unexceptional. When at last he retired and returned to London, taking charge of his family's house, things seemed to go well for him. He announced his betrothal to Dame Edith Stuart, which you may also remember from the society pages."

"A step up for an army colonel," I commented.

"I suspect she may have been involved in the Eton scandal, but that is mere conjecture at this point," Holmes said. "Yes, to all appearances it is a step up for him. However, two weeks later he broke off the engagement, and the next day – three days ago, in fact – he disappeared."

"Until he showed up on our doorstep."

"Just so."

"Where does this Amateur Beggar Society fit in?" I asked.

"The Secret Mendicant Society, as it is more properly called, was part of a network of spies set up by the Emperor Constantine. The Roman Empire had more than its share of beggars, and Constantine realized they heard and saw more than anyone gave them credit for. Originally, noble-born members of the Society would dress as beggars and go forth to collect news and information, which then made its way back through the network to Constantine himself.

"The next few emperors made little use of Constantine's beggars, but oddly enough the Society seems to have established itself more strongly rather than collapsing, as one might have expected. It developed its own set of rites and rituals. One faction in India splintered off and became affiliated with the Thuggee, of whom you may be familiar."

"Indeed," I said, "I have heard of those devils."

Holmes nodded. "Sometime in the Middle Ages they seemed to disappear. However, in 1821 a condemned man mentioned them in his last statement. Since then I've found two other mentions of the Secret Mendicant Society, the first being a satirical cartoon from *Punch* dated 1832, which refers to them as a rival to the Free Masons as if everyone had heard of them, and the second being the scrap of paper found in Colonel Pendleton-Smythe's house."

"So where does the colonel fit in?"

"I was just getting to that," Holmes said. "Of the six chums expelled from Eton, I have been able to trace the movements of three. All three died in recent weeks under mysterious circumstances. What does this tell you?"

"That the colonel is next on the list to be killed?"

"Precisely, Watson. Or so it would seem."

"You have reason to believe otherwise?"

"Ha! You see right through me, Watson. It seems distinctly odd to me that this rash of murders should coincide with Pendleton-Smythe's return from Africa."

"Indeed, it does seem odd," I agreed. "But perhaps there are other circumstances at work here. You won't know that until you speak with the colonel himself." I looked at my watch. "It's only half an hour until our appointment."

"Time," said Holmes, "for us to be on our way."

I stared at him in bewildered consternation. "You'll have Pendleton-Smythe convinced you don't want to see him if you keep to this course!"

"Rather," he said, "I am endeavoring to make sure the meeting does take place. Your coat, Watson! We'll either meet him on the street on his way here – or if, as I suspect, he intends to skip our meeting since he was recognized yesterday, we will meet him at his rooming house!"

I grabbed my coat and hat and followed him once more out to the street.

We did not, of course, meet Pendleton-Smythe in the street; Holmes always did have a knack for second-guessing other people's actions. When we arrived at the rooming house, we found a stout gray-haired woman whom I took to be the landlady sweeping the steps.

"Excuse me," Holmes said briskly, "I wish to ask after one of your tenants – a military man with a slight limp, dark coat, dark hat. I have a letter he dropped last night and I wish to return it to him."

"You'd mean Mr Smith," she said. "Give it here, I'll hand it to him when he's up." She held out her hand.

"Is he in, then?" Holmes asked.

"Here now, who are you?" she said, regarding us both suspiciously and hefting her broom to bar our way.

I hastened to add, "This is Mr Sherlock Holmes, and we must speak to your Mr Smith. It's very urgent."

"Mr Holmes? Why didn't you say so, gents? 'Course I've heard of you, Mr Holmes. Who hasn't, round these parts? Come in, come in, I'm forgetting my manners." She lowered the broom and moved toward the front door. "I'm Mrs Nellie Coram, Sir, and I own this establishment. Mr Smith's room is on the second floor. I'll just pop up and see if he'll come down."

"If you don't mind," Holmes said, "I think we'd better come upstairs with you."

"Oh, is he a slippery one, then?" she said. "I thought he might be, but he paid me a fortnight's rent in advance, and I can't afford to be too nosy, business being what it is these days."

"He is not a criminal," Holmes said. "He is a client. But it is urgent that I speak with him immediately."

She laid a finger alongside her nose and gave him a broad wink, but said no more. She led us in at once, up a broad flight of steps to a well-scrubbed second floor hallway. She turned right, went down a narrow passage to a closed door, and there she knocked twice. A gruff whisper came in answer almost immediately: "Who is it?"

"Nellie Coram," the landlady said. "I have two visitors for you, Mr Smith."

The door opened a crack, and I saw a single piercing blue eye regard Holmes and me for a second. "Come in," said the voice, stronger now, and its owner moved back and opened the door for us.

Holmes and I went in. I looked around and saw a small but tidy room: bed, wash-stand, armoire, and a single straight-backed chair by the window. A copy of *The Times* lay open on the bed.

Pendleton-Smythe closed the door before Mrs Coram could join us, and I heard a muffled "Humph" from the other side and the sound of her footsteps as she returned to her tasks downstairs. The colonel himself was a man of medium height and strong build, with iron gray hair, blue eyes, and a small moustache. He wore dark blue trousers, a white pinstripe shirt, and a blue jacket. But it was the service revolver in his hand that most drew my attention. Pendleton-Smythe held it pointed straight at Holmes and me.

"What do you want?" he barked. "Who are you?"

Holmes, who had already taken in the room with a single glance, crossed to the window and parted the drapes. "Rather," he said, "I should ask what *you* want, Colonel. I am here to keep our appointment. I am Sherlock Holmes, and this is my colleague, Dr John Watson."

Holmes turned and stared at Pendleton-Smythe, and after a second the colonel lowered his revolver. His hands were shaking, I saw, and I steadied his arm for a second.

"I am glad to have you here, Mr Holmes," he said. Nervously he crossed to the bed and sat down, tossing the revolver beside him. He cradled his head in his hands, ran his fingers through his hair, and took a deep breath. "Truly, I am at my wit's end. I don't know if you can help me, but if any man in England can, it's you. Your presence here is proof enough of your remarkable abilities."

Holmes sat in the straight chair, steepled his fingers, crossed his legs, and said, "Begin at Eton, with your involvement in the Amateur Mendicant Society."

He started violently. "You know about that, too? How is it possible?"

"Then he's right," I said, "and the Amateur Mendicant Society *is* involved?"

"Yes – yes, damn them!"

"My methods are my own," Holmes said. "Please start at the beginning. Leave out no detail, no matter how small. I can assure you of our utmost discretion in this and all matters."

I sat on the bed beside the colonel. Suddenly he looked like a very tired, very old man. "You'll feel better," I told him. "They say confession is good for the soul."

He took a deep breath, then began.

"Everything started with one of my professors, Dr Jason Attenborough. He taught second-year Latin as well as classical history, and one day after class six of us stayed late to ask about the Secret Mendicant Society, which he had mentioned in passing in that afternoon's lecture. It was thrilling in its own way, the idea of spies among the ancient Romans, but we found it hard to believe any noble-born person could possibly pass as a beggar. Dr Attenborough said it was not only possible, it had happened for several centuries.

"Later, at a public house, almost as a dare, the six of us agreed to try it ourselves. It seemed like a rum lot of fun, and after a few rounds at the Slaughtered Lamb, we set out to give it a go.

"We went first to a rag merchant – he was closed, but we pounded on his door until he opened for us – and from him we purchased suitable disreputable clothing. Dressing ourselves as we imagined beggars might, we smeared soot on our faces and set out to see what news and pennies we could gather. It was a foolish sort of game, rather stupid really, and the prime foolishness came when we decided to visit Piccadilly Circus to see what sort of reception we got. We were pretty well potted by this time, you see, so anything sounded like fun.

"Suffice it to say, we terrorized several old women into giving us pennies and were promptly arrested for our trouble. The next day, after being ransomed home by disbelieving parents, we were summonsed to the Dean's office and informed that our activities had disgraced the school. In short, our presence was no longer desired. The news was devastating to us and our families.

"That's where things should have ended. We should have quietly bought our way into other schools, or vanished into military life, or simply retired to family businesses – there were many choices available. However, that night, as we gathered one last time in the Slaughtered Lamb, Dr Attenborough joined us. He was not consoling or apologetic. Rather, he was ebullient.

"He asked what we had learned as beggars – and we hadn't learned a thing, really – but as he led us through the lesson (for that's what it was to him), we could see that we had gone to the wrong section of the city, spoken to the wrong people, done all the wrong things. Beggars have their place in our society, as you know, and we had stepped outside their domain. That's where we had gone wrong.

"As he had done in his lecture hall, he inspired us that night with his speech. He persuaded us that we should go out again – and this time he went with us.

"Dressed once more as beggars, we ventured into the sordid, dark places near the docks, where such as we had never dared go at night. Using the Roman system as a model, he showed us what we had done wrong – and how we could do it right.

"We listened at the right windows. We lurked outside sailors' taverns and heard their coarse, drunken gossip. And suddenly we began to understand how the Secret Mendicant Society had worked so admirably well. Wine loosens men's tongues, and much could be gleaned from attentive listening. For who pays attention to shabby beggars, even among the dregs of our society?

"There were a dozen ship's captains who we could have turned in for smuggling, a handful of murders we could have solved, stolen cargoes that could have been recovered with just a word in the right ear at Scotland Yard.

"We did none of that. It was petty. But we were young and foolish, and Dr Attenborough did nothing but encourage us in our foolishness. Oh, he was a masterful speaker. He could convince you night was day and white was black, if he wanted to. And suddenly he wanted very much to have us working for him. We would be a new Secret Mendicant Society – or, as we chaps liked to call it, an Amateur Mendicant Society. Dabbling, yes, that was a gentleman's way. It was a game to us. As long as we pretended it was a schoolyard lark, it wasn't really a dirty deal.

"I regret to say I took full part in the Amateur Mendicant Society's spying over the following six months. I learned the truth from dishonest men, turned the information over to Dr Attenborough, and he pursued matters from there. What, exactly, he did with the information I can only guess – extortion, blackmail, possibly even worse. However, I do know that suddenly he had a lot of money, and he paid us handsomely for our work. He bought an abandoned warehouse and had a posh gentleman's club outfitted in the basement – though, of course, there were no servants, nobody who could break our secret circle. Later he leased the warehouse out for furniture storage.

"I was not the first to break the circle. Dickie Clarke was. He told me one evening that he had enlisted in the army. His father had used his influence to get him a commission, and he was off to India. 'I'm through with soiling my hands with this nonsense,' he told me. 'I've had enough. Come with me, Oliver. It's not too late.' I was shocked, and I refused – to my lasting shame.

"When Attenborough found out, he had an absolute fit – he threw things, screamed obscenities, smashed a whole set of dishes against the wall. Then and there I realized I had made a mistake. I had made a pact with a madman. I had to escape.

"The next day I too enlisted. I've been away for nineteen years – I never came back, not even on leave, for fear of what Dr Attenborough might do if he found out. He was that violent.

"I had stayed in touch with Dickie Clarke all through his campaigns and my own, and when he wrote from London to tell me Attenborough was dead, I thought it would be safe to return home. I planned to write my memoirs, you see.

"Only two weeks ago Dickie died. Murdered – I'm sure of it! And then I noticed people, strangers dressed as beggars, loitering near my house, watching me, noting my movements as I had once noted the movements of others. To escape, I simply walked out of my home one day, took a series of cabs until I was certain I hadn't been followed, and haven't been back since."

Sherlock Holmes nodded slowly when Pendleton-Smythe finished. "A most interesting story," he said. "But why would the Amateur Mendicant Society want you dead? Are you certain there isn't something more?"

He raised his head, back stiff. "Sir, I assure you, I have told you everything. As for why – isn't that obvious? Because I know too much. They killed old Dickie, and now they're going to kill me!"

"What of the four others from Eton? What happened to them?"

"The others?" He blinked. "I – I really don't know. I haven't heard from or spoken to any of them in years. I hope they had the good sense to get out and not come back. Heavens above, I certainly wish I hadn't!"

"Quite so," said Holmes. He rose. "Stay here, Colonel. I think you will be safe in Mrs Coram's care for the time being. I must look into a few matters, and then we will talk again."

"So you will take my case?" he asked eagerly.

"Most decidedly." Holmes inclined his head. "I'm certain I'll be able to help. One last thing. What was the address of the warehouse Attenborough owned?"

"Forty-two Kerin Street," he said.

As we headed back toward Baker Street, Holmes seemed in a particularly good mood, smiling and whistling bits of a violin concerto I'd heard him playing earlier that week.

"Well, what is it?" I finally demanded.

"Don't you see, Watson?" he said. "There can only be one answer. We have run into a classic case of two identical organizations colliding. It's nothing short of a trade war between rival groups of beggar-spies."

"You mean there's a real Secret Mendicant Society still at large?"

"The very thing!"

"How is it possible? How could they have survived all these years with nobody knowing about them?"

"Some people *can* keep secrets," he said.

"It's fantastic!"

"Grant me this conjecture. Imagine, if you will, that the real Secret Mendicant Society has just become aware of its rival, the Amateur Mendicant Society. They have thrived in the shadows for centuries. They have a network of informants in place. It's not hard to see how the two would come face to face eventually, as the Amateur Society expanded into the Secret Society's established territory. Of course, the Secret Mendicant Society could not possibly allow a rival to poach on their grounds. What could they possibly do but strike out in retaliation?"

"Attenborough and Clarke and the others . . ."

"Exactly! They have systematically eliminated the amateurs. I would imagine they are now in occupation of the secret club under the old furniture warehouse, where Attenborough's records would have been stored. And those records would have led them, inexorably, to the two Amateurs who got away – Dickie, who they killed at once, and our client, who they have not yet managed to assassinate."

"Ingenious," I said.

"But now Colonel Pendleton-Smythe is in more danger than he believes. He is the last link to the old Amateur Mendicant Society, so it should be a simple matter to –"

Holmes drew up short. Across the street from 221b Baker Street, on the front steps of another house, a raggedly dressed old man with a three-day growth of beard sat as if resting from a long walk.

"He's one of them," I said softly.

Holmes regarded me as though shocked by my revelation. "Watson, must you be so suspicious? Surely that poor unfortunate is catching his second wind. His presence is merest coincidence." I caught the amused gleam in his eye, though.

"I thought you didn't believe in coincidences," I said.

"Ye-es." He drew out the word, then turned and continued on toward our front door at a more leisurely pace. "Let us assume," he said, "that you are right. What shall we do with the devil? Run him off? Have him locked up by Lestrade?"

"That would surely tip our hand," I said. "Rather, let us try to misdirect him."

"You're learning, Watson, you're learning." We reached our house; he opened the door. "I trust you have a plan?"

"I was rather hoping you did," I admitted.

"As a matter of fact, I do," he said. "But I'm going to need your help . . ."

Two hours later, I stood in the drawing room shaking my head. The man before me – thick lips, stubbled chin, rat's nest of chestnut colored hair – bore not the slightest resemblance to my friend. His flare for the dramatic as well as a masterly skill for disguises would have borne him well in the theatre, I thought. I found the transformation remarkable.

"Are you sure this is wise?" I asked.

"Wise?" he said. "Decidedly not. But will it work? I profoundly hope so. Check the window, will you?"

I lifted the drape. "The beggar has gone."

"Oh, there are surely other watchers," he said. "They have turned to me as the logical one to whom Colonel Pendleton-Smythe would go for help." He studied his new features in a looking glass, adjusted one bushy eyebrow, then glanced over at me for approval.

"Your own brother wouldn't recognize you," I told him.

"Excellent." He folded up his makeup kit, then I followed him to the back door. He slipped out quietly while I began to count.

When I reached a hundred, I went out the front door, turned purposefully, and headed for the bank. I had no real business there; however, it was as good a destination as any for my purpose – which was to serve as a decoy while Holmes observed those who observed me.

I saw nothing to arouse my suspicions as I checked on my accounts, and in due course I returned to our lodgings in exactly the same professional manner. When Holmes did not at once show himself, I knew his plan had been successful; he was now trailing a member of the Secret Mendicant Society.

I had a leisurely tea, then set off to find Inspector Lestrade. He was, as usual, hard at work at his desk. I handed him a note from Sherlock Holmes, which said:

Lestrade,
Come at once to 42 Kerin Street with a dozen of your men. There is a murderer to be had as well as evidence of blackmail and other nefarious deeds.

Sherlock Holmes

Lestrade's eyes widened as he read the note, and a second later he was on his way out the door shouting for assistance.

I accompanied him, and by the time we reached 42 Kerin Street – a crumbling old brick warehouse – he had fifteen men as an entourage. They would have kicked the door in, but a raggedly dressed man with bushy eyebrows reached out and opened it for them: it wasn't so much as latched. Without a glance at the disguised Sherlock Holmes, Lestrade and his men rushed in.

Holmes and I strolled at a more leisurely pace back toward a busier street where we might catch a cab home. He began removing his makeup and slowly the man I knew emerged.

"How did it go?" I asked.

"There were a few tense moments," he said, "but I handled things sufficiently well, I believe."

"Tell me everything," I said.

"For your journals, perhaps?"

"Exactly so."

"Very well. As you headed down the street looking quite purposeful, an elderly gentleman out for a mid-day stroll suddenly altered his course after you. He was well dressed, not a beggar by appearance or demeanor, so I took this to mean he was now watching us. I overtook him, grasped him firmly by the arm, and identified myself to him.

"At once he cried out for assistance. Two elderly men – these dressed for business, not begging – rushed toward me from the sides. I had seen them, but not suspected them of being involved because of their advanced age.

"We tussled for a moment, and then I knocked the beggar down, threw off one of my opponents, and seized the other by his collar. I might have done him some injury had he not shouted that I was under arrest."

Holmes smiled faintly at my surprise.

"Arrest!" I cried, unable to contain myself. "How was this possible?"

"It made me pause, too," Holmes went on. "He might have been bluffing, but I knew I lacked a few key pieces of the puzzle, and this one seemed to fit. I told him, 'Very well, Sir, if you will call off your men and explain yourselves to my satisfaction, I shall gladly accompany you to police head-quarters.'

"When he nodded, I released him. He straightened his coat as his two fellows collected themselves. Frowning at me, he seemed to be thinking ahead. He had to be sixty-five or seventy years old, I decided.

"'I am pleased to make your acquaintance, Mr Holmes,' he finally said. 'I believe we may have business to discuss. But not at the police station.'

"'Exactly so,' I told him. 'Are you at liberty to speak for the whole Society, or must we report to your superiors?'

"'Come with me.' He dismissed the other two with a nod, turned, and led me to a quiet building on Harley Street. I had been there once before on business with the Foreign Office, but I showed no sign of surprise; indeed, this piece of the puzzle seemed to fit admirably well.

"He took me upstairs to see a rear admiral whose name I agreed not to divulge, and there the whole truth of the Secret Mendicant Society became apparent to me."

I said, "They no longer work for Rome. They work for us."

"Quite right, Watson," Holmes said. "This rear admiral took me into their confidence, since they have a file on me and know I can be trusted. The organization of the Secret Mendicant Society was once quite remarkable, though it seems near its end. Their membership is small and, as far as I can tell, consists largely of septuagenarians or older. The times have changed so much that beggary is dying out; modern spies have much more efficient means of political espionage . . . for that is the current goal of the Secret Mendicant Society."

"But what about the murders!" I exclaimed. "Surely not even the Foreign Office would –"

"Not only would they, they did. Politics is becoming less and less a gentleman's game, my dear Watson. For the security of our great country, nothing is above the law for them – laws that must govern the common man, such as you or I – or even poor Pendleton-Smythe."

"So there is nothing you can do to help the colonel," I said bitterly.

"The admiral and I rapidly reached an arrangement," Holmes said, "when I explained what I had done with you and Lestrade. With Scotland Yard about to close in on the headquarters of the Amateur Mendicant Society, there was nothing he could do but agree with me that the Amateurs must be exposed. The publicity surrounding them will camouflage the activities of the real Secret Mendicant Society and allow Pendleton-Smythe the luxury of living out the rest of his days in peace. He, for one, never for an instant suspected the Secret Mendicant Society actually existed. That is his salvation."

"But what of the new Amateur Mendicant Society? Surely they did not agree to surrender so blithely!"

"Indeed, they offered no objection, since with the exception of our client, they are all dead." Holmes paused a second. "After I left Harley Street, I proceeded at once to the warehouse. There I found the proper building, knocked twice sharply, and pushed my way inside when the door opened a crack by a man dressed as a beggar.

"'Here now –' he began. He pulled out a knife and pointed it at me. In earlier days he might have hurt or even killed me, but his reflexes had dulled with age. I caught his wrist, bent it back until he gave a moan of pain, and the knife fell to the floor with a clatter.

"'We have no time for that,' I told him. 'The police have been summoned. You have ten minutes to gather your organization's papers and vacate the building, or you will be captured and implicated in murder."

"'Who are you?' he demanded, rubbing his arm.

"'A friend. Now hurry!'

"He hesitated, looking to the two other men in the room: both were elderly, and both were dressed as gentlemen. They had been going over papers spread out on a table halfway across the room.

"'This must be Mr Sherlock Holmes,' one of them said.

"'True,' I said. 'You now have nine minutes.'

"Without another word, he began to gather up papers and stuff them into a case. His assistant did likewise.

"'Where are Attenborough's files?' I demanded.

"'In the back room,' he said. 'They were useless to us. Most deal with murder and blackmail.'

"'Do you object to the police obtaining them?'

"'No. You may do with them as you see fit.'

"'Thank you for the warning. It might have been embarrassing to be found here.'

"When they had gone, I checked the back room and found Attenborough's files. They seemed a complete record of his blackmail schemes. I also found Attenborough's body, tucked away behind a filing cabinet. He had clearly been dead for some months.

"'I arranged the body to look as though an accident had occurred – a bookcase had fallen on him – then came out just as you and Lestrade arrived. To the untrained eyes of Lestrade and his men, it will look as though Attenborough suffered an unfortunate accident.'"

"'What of Attenborough's files?' I asked. "Surely they will ruin what remains of Colonel Pendleton-Smythe's reputation."

"'That will be handled by the foreign office. Lestrade will uncover the records of the Amateur Mendicant Society, which reveal their wrongdoings in excruciating detail. Their specialty was blackmail and extortion, as we had surmised. The records will be doctored to include, I dare say, the full catalog of murders by Dr Attenborough, as he desperately tried to maintain control of a crumbling criminal empire. The newspapers will, I am certain, find much scandalous material in it – and the colonel will have little choice but to deny his participation and suppress that part of his memoirs, should he still choose to write them. All the Foreign Service wants, at this point, is to maintain the Secret Mendicant Society's anonymity while contributing whatever small gains it can to the war effort."

"It would seem, then," I said, "that everything has sorted itself out remarkably well. You're fortunate they didn't try to kill you," I commented.

"I believe the admiral considered it. However, I do make my own small contributions to the Foreign Office, as you well know. You might say we have friends in common."

"Your brother for one," I said.

"Just so," he said.

"Then we have reached a successful resolution to the case – after a fashion."

"After a fashion," Holmes agreed with a half smile. "After a fashion."

THE ADVENTURE OF THE SILVER BUCKLE

Denis O. Smith

*Holmes continued to throw himself into his cases as 1887 progressed
and they did not become any easier. There was the loss of the British
barque the* Sophy Anderson. *I have the details of this case but they
are not in a sufficient state yet to present to the reader, though they
again indicate the intensity of Holmes's involvement. Soon after this
he was involved in the case of the Davenoke family of Shoreswood Hall,
a long-unknown case which was identified by the renowned Holmesian
scholar Denis Smith, who also rescued the following story. After the
Shoreswood Hall case, Holmes investigated the death of Mrs Stewart
of Lauder. Although he resolved the murder to his own satisfaction
he was not able to find the conclusive evidence needed to convict
Sebastian Moran, whom Holmes was convinced was behind the plot.
This frustration caused both Holmes's spirit and energy to flag and
Watson again became concerned for his health. It was at this stage
that the case of the Grice Petersons on the island of Uffa, referred to
in "The Five Orange Pips" occurred. Its facts have been unearthed
by Denis Smith, who has produced other stories based on his research
which I list at the end of this book.*

It was in the late summer of '87 that the health of my friend,
Mr Sherlock Holmes, gave further cause for concern. The unre-
mitting hard work to which he invariably subjected himself allowed
little time for recuperation from the everyday infirmities which are
the lot of mankind, and from which even Holmes's iron constitution
was not immune. So long as he remained fit, all was well, but earlier
in the year he had reached a point of complete exhaustion from
which he had not properly recovered. Eventually it became clear to
all who knew him that unless he were removed from Baker Street,
and from the constant calls upon his time which were inescapable
while he remained there, he might never again fully recover his
health and strength.

By chance, I had at the time been reading Boswell's account of his journey with Dr Johnson through the Highlands of Scotland to the Herbrides, and had been fascinated by the remoteness of the places they had visited. Thus inspired, I ventured to suggest to my friend that we emulate the illustrious eighteenth-century men of letters. Holmes's only response was a laconic remark that our travels should be confined to dry land. Taking this to be the nearest to enthusiasm or agreement that I was likely to get, I went ahead at once with the necessary preparations, and, four days later, the sleeping car express from Euston deposited us early in the morning upon the wind-swept platform of Inverness station. From there, after some delay, a local train took us yet further northward and westward, until we reached a small halt, standing in lonely isolation in a silent and treeless glen, where a carriage waited to take us on the last stage of our journey.

It was a strange country we passed through that afternoon, a land of reed-girt lochs, and hard, bare rocks, which thrust through the thin soil like clenched fists. For many weary hours, our road twisted this way and that between these obstacles, until at length it dropped abruptly down a steep-sided valley, beside a sparkling waterfall, and brought us at last to the west coast, and the village of Kilbuie, nestling beneath towering hills on the northern shore of Loch Echil. There was a cheery, welcoming air about the little whitewashed cottages which clustered about the harbour, and the solid, granite-built Loch Echil Hotel, but I saw as we stepped down from our carriage that Holmes's face was pale and drawn, and it was clear that the journey had shaken him badly. It troubled me greatly to see so vital a man reduced to this state, and dearly I hoped that the fine invigorating country air would act quickly to restore his shattered health.

The Loch Echil Hotel was a pleasant, well-appointed establishment, sturdily built to withstand all that a Highland winter might hurl at it, and our rooms were cosy and comfortable. I had soon unpacked, and then, leaving Holmes resting in his room, I took a stroll to familiarize myself with our new surroundings. The weather was fine, and Loch Echil lay like a looking-glass between the hills. It was nearly a mile across at this point, but narrowed considerably to the east, where it extended for perhaps a further half-mile inland. To the west, just beyond the last building of the town, it widened out into a broad bay, where the water was broken by a great many little islands and rocks. I had brought my old field-glasses with me, and spent a pleasant hour on a bench by the water's edge, watching the fishing smacks out in the bay, where the shags and cormorants clustered upon the rocks, and the gulls circled high overhead.

The islands were largely featureless, low and bare, like an oddly stationary school of hump-backed whales, but on one, which was somewhat larger than the others, there appeared to be a dark, gaunt tower, rising high above the waves and rocks about it. Intrigued by this, I mentioned it to Murdoch MacLeod, the manager of the hotel, who was in the entrance-hall when I returned.

"That is the Island of Uffa," said he, "the home of Mr MacGlevin, or the MacGlevin, as he prefers to be known."

"You don't mean to tell me that anyone lives out there?" I said in surprise.

He nodded his head. "He's restored the old ruined castle on the island, and has part of it for a museum of antiquities, which is open to the public, and well worth a visit. Most of your fellow-guests in the hotel went over there yesterday. He has some very interesting and valuable pieces, including the famous MacGlevin Buckle, a very fine piece of Celtic workmanship, in solid silver. His one concern in life has been to establish a permanent home for his clan, but he's certainly picked a remote spot for it! He has a fine house in Edinburgh, but it's let for most of the year, as he prefers to hide up here. Apart from an old couple, kinsfolk of his, who help him to keep the place in order, he lives in splendid isolation, laird of all he surveys – such as it is!"

"He sounds something of an eccentric!"

"Aye, you could say that," MacLeod returned in a dry tone. "You may see him about, for he comes over occasionally in his little steam-launch, *Alba*, to pick up supplies. He's a great huge fellow with a ginger beard. If you meet him, you'll not mistake him!"

I could not have imagined then just how dramatic that meeting would be.

On the first floor of the hotel, immediately over the entrance, was a broad, airy drawing-room, illuminated by a row of tall windows, which commanded a magnificent view over the harbour, the loch, and the wilder sea out to the west. When the weather was poor, and Holmes did not feel up to venturing out of doors, we would often sit by these windows as the cloud-bank rolled down the steep hills across the loch, watching the little sailing-boats, their sails puffed out by the westerly wind, making their way up the huge expanse of water towards the harbour. Often, also, I watched anglers out on the loch in the hotel's distinctive little rowing-boats, and thought how pleasant it would be to be out there myself; but although I alluded to the idea once or twice, Holmes showed little inclination for such an excursion.

Our fellow-guests in the hotel were a singularly assorted group. There was, for instance, Doctor Oliphant, a balding, white-whiskered, elderly man, of a stooping, learned appearance. His voice was thin and reedy, which made him difficult to understand, but I gathered that he was something of an antiquary and archaeologist, from St Andrews, in Fife. Two sandy-haired young men I had judged to be brothers, so similar was their appearance, and this surmise proved correct when they introduced themselves as Angus and Fergus Johnstone, up from Paisley for the fishing. A soberly dressed and very reserved middle-aged couple, Mr and Mrs Hamish Morton, were from Glasgow, as was a very old woman, Mrs Baird Duthie, who wore widow's weeds, walked with a stick, and was almost stone deaf. It seemed unlikely that there would be much of common interest in such a group, but when the conversation of the talkative Johnstone brothers turned to angling, the quiet and withdrawn Mr Morton displayed an interest, and a discussion ensued between them on the merits of various kinds of fishing-tackle. Mrs Morton, not surprisingly, did not share in full measure her husband's interest in this subject, and I had the impression that she tolerated rather than approved of it. She herself, she informed me, had hoped to do some painting and sketching during their stay in Kilbuie, although the weather so far had limited her opportunities. This observation prompted Doctor Oliphant to some remark about mankind's perennial urge to artistic creation, whereupon he, she and I engaged in a lively debate on the subject. Holmes took little part in this or any other discussion, but sat back in his chair, his eye-lids languorously half-closed. I had ceased to follow the conversation at the other side of the room, between the rival fishermen, when Mrs Morton had begun to speak of her own interests, but I watched with some amusement as each of them in turn brought in his fishing equipment, unpacked it all upon the carpet, and argued its merits in the most serious tones.

I had, I confess, no great knowledge of the subject, but it seemed to me that they each spoke with the authority of an expert. Odd it was, then, that the very next day, all met with calamity whilst engaged in their sport. The Johnstone brothers returned shamefacedly to the hotel about tea-time. Angus Johnstone's rod had broken, and their fishing-lines had become entangled, and in the resulting confusion, Fergus had fallen overboard, and Angus had lost his reel in the water. Mr Morton's accident had been potentially the more serious, although, in the event, he too returned to the hotel chastened but unharmed. He had been out alone, fishing among the islands in the bay, his wife having remained behind to do some drawing by the harbour, when his boat had sprung a leak. Unable to stem the inrushing water, and with nothing with which to bale out, he had rowed with all speed for the shore, but his boat had disappeared beneath him before he had reached it, and he had had to swim

the remaining distance. Murdoch MacLeod was most distressed at
this account, and rung his hands in his misery.

"You must have feared for your life!" he declared in a tone of
great sympathy; but the other shook his head.

"I was nae worried," said he dismissively. "It was a matter of
only five-and-twenty feet before my feet touched solid ground. I
was more concerned about the walk home, I can tell ye! I came
ashore on the south side of the bay, ye see, so I've had to walk
the whole way round the loch to get back! My feet'll never be the
same again!"

"And you have lost all your equipment?" inquired MacLeod.

"Aye. All sunk wi'out trace."

"We will of course compensate you for your loss –"

"We can discuss it later," said Morton, turning on his heel. "For
now, all I'm interested in is a hot bath!"

"This season has been an unfortunate one for us," said MacLeod,
after Morton had left the room. "At this rate, we shall soon have
no-one wishing to stay here. Why, only two weeks ago, a young
lady from Peebles slipped and fell down the main staircase in odd
circumstances, and, just before your arrival, a Mrs Formartine from
Arbroath lost a valuable pearl brooch. Now this! I felt sure that all the
rowing-boats were sound. Thank goodness it was not more serious!"
He shook his head as he left the room.

"What an odd and unfortunate thing!" said I.

"Indeed," said Holmes, and I seemed to read in his face that
there was little point my raising again the idea of a fishing-trip.

It rained heavily that night, but the following morning dawned
bright and clear, and there was much discussion at breakfast-time of
plans for the day ahead. Several of the hotel-guests were to leave on
the Friday, and were thus keen to make the most of their last day in
Kilbuie. The Johnstone brothers, clearly undaunted by the previous
day's experience, intended, once they had replaced their lost and
damaged equipment, to spend their time fishing once more.

"We'll try among the islands today," remarked Angus Johnstone
as they were leaving. "Whatever happens, it canna be worse than
yesterday!"

To my surprise, the meek and frail-looking Doctor Oliphant also
announced that he would be taking a boat, his intention being
to visit Stalva Island, where, he said, there were the remains of
a Viking burial chamber. The Mortons hired a pony and trap
and set off with a picnic hamper and Mrs Morton's sketching
equipment, to visit the Falls of Druimar, a well-known beauty
spot, some dozen miles inland. The weather was fine and the
wind light, and Holmes and I passed a pleasant day in ambling

about the town and the harbour, and along the margin of the loch.

Despite MacLeod's worries for the welfare of his guests, there were no more accidents, and they all returned in good spirits, if a little late. I observed as Holmes and I went into dinner that evening that an extra table had been laid, but no-one arrived to claim it, and I saw MacLeod glance at the clock over the mantelpiece several times, and shake his head. It was clear that he was expecting someone, but how they might arrive, unless it were by private carriage all the way from Inverness, I could not imagine, for the coach which connected with the train had long since been and gone.

This little mystery was soon solved, however. As we were taking coffee in the drawing-room after our meal, the door was opened to admit two men, introduced to us as Alexander and Donald Grice Paterson, father and son respectively, who had, they informed us, arrived in their own little yacht which they had just moored in the harbour. Alexander Grice Paterson was a small, wiry man of about fifty, dark-haired and clean-shaven, with a shrewd, crafty, almost fox-like appearance. His son, Donald, was perhaps two-and-twenty, a little taller than his father, and sported a black moustache, but with the same dark, fox-like look to him. Plates of sandwiches and cheese were brought in for them, which they devoured hungrily, and, thus restored, they began to speak in excited tones. It was clear that they had recently had a very singular experience, which they were keen to share with their fellow-guests.

The older man was a senior partner in an Edinburgh legal firm, he informed us, into which his son had recently been admitted as a junior. Their speciality was commercial law, which could sometimes be a little dry, he admitted, even for those whose vocation it was.

"It's to remedy the dryness," he remarked with a crafty twinkle in his eye, in what was clearly a much-rehearsed witticism, "that each year we spend as long as possible on the water! In short, we have a little boat, a twenty-five-footer, the *Puffin*, which we sail about hither and thither for a week or two each year.

"In the past we've been blown all over the Firth of Clyde, back and forth from the Ayrshire coast to Kintyre. This year we thought we'd venture further afield, and plotted a course up the West Coast of Argyll and beyond. We've not had the best of wind, but we've done pretty well, all things considered, and two nights ago we slipped through the Sound of Sleat and moored for the night in Loch Alsh. Since then, we've not hurried, running in and out of bays and inlets, and exploring any nook of the coast which promised interest. We expected to arrive in Kilbuie this afternoon, but the wind has been unfavourable, and we've been beating this way and that for the last few miles. At last, earlier this evening, we turned into Echil Bay – and now we come to the most singular experience of my life! We knew when we first set off that we were sailing into unknown waters, to the land of myth and magic, but we never expected that we'd be the victims of Highland magic ourselves!"

He paused and took a large mouthful of the whisky and water which stood at his elbow, glancing round as he did so, as if to judge the effect of his words, for all the world like an advocate addressing a packed court-room. His opening remarks concluded, he now came to the crux of the matter.

"We steered a course between the islands, but the wind was not so much against us now, as almost non-existent, and our progress was slow. It was just as the sun was setting behind us, and the shadows were long ahead, that we noticed what appeared to be a ruined tower, on one of the larger islands. Donald consulted the charts, and was able to inform me that the island was Uffa, and that upon it were the ruins of an ancient religious establishment. This seemed too good an opportunity to pass up, and we determined to go ashore and explore.

"We moored the *Puffin* some thirty yards from the shore, and rowed the dinghy into a little natural harbour among the great jumbled rocks at the extreme western end of the island. By the time we had our feet on dry land, the light was fading fast, but there was a well-worn path through the heather, so we were confident of soon reaching the ruins. The path meandered steeply up and down, however, and after a few minutes, we had quite lost sight of the ruins, and it became apparent that to get from the west end of Uffa to the east, where the ruins were situated, was going to take us longer than we had expected. Still, as we had by this time gone some considerable distance, we thought, like Macbeth, that it were as well to go on as go back. A mistake, perhaps, but we were not to know." He paused. "Perhaps you could tell them what happened next, Donald," he said, turning to his son.

"It was fairly dark by then," the younger man continued after a moment. "We couldn't really see very much. There seemed to be paths everywhere, and we were just wondering if we'd taken the wrong one, when we came over the brow of a small hill and saw the ruins dead ahead of us. We'd thought the sky was dark, but the ruins were darker still, and showed up as a black silhouette. To the left stood the ruined tower, tall and stark, with a huddle of lower buildings surrounding it, to the right, some more disordered ruins; and then –" He broke off and swallowed before continuing.

"As we drew closer, picking our way carefully along the rocky path, there came all at once the sound of movement somewhere just ahead of us, and then a dark, crouching shape scuttled across the path not more than twenty feet away."

"The Black Pig!" cried Murdoch MacLeod.

"What?" cried the elder Grice Paterson in return.

"You are in superstitious country," said Doctor Oliphant. "There is a belief in these parts that the appearance of the Black Pig is an omen of evil."

"There are some," said MacLeod in a low tone, "who say that the Black Pig is the Evil One himself!"

Alexander Grice Paterson snorted. "Perhaps it is fortunate for us, then," he said, "that what we saw did not remotely resemble a pig. It was more like a man, crouching down."

"Aye," said his son. "Furtive and creeping, with his robes all draggling out behind him."

"I need hardly say that we were somewhat unnerved by this apparition," the elder Grice Paterson continued. "Then, as we stood there, rooted to the spot, a faint, wavering light sprang up in a window high in the tower. I think Donald must have cried out –"

"With all respect, Pa," his son interrupted, "I believe that you were the one doing the crying out."

"Well, well. Be that as it may, next moment an oblong of bright light appeared suddenly before us, as a door was flung open at the base of the tower, and a giant of a man with a great ginger beard stepped out, carrying a lantern.

"MacGlevin," said MacLeod softly, as Grice Paterson continued:

"'Who's there?' the giant's voice boomed out."

"Why, man," cried Angus Johnstone, laughing, "it sounds more like a Grimm's fairy tale every minute!"

"No doubt," returned Alexander Grice Paterson, appearing a little annoyed at this interruption, "but it did not strike us that way at the time. We stepped forward and introduced ourselves.

"'A strange time to come paying a visit,' the giant boomed back at us. I explained our situation, that we had had no idea that the island was inhabited.

"'On our map,' said I, 'this building is marked only as a ruin.'

"'Oh, is it?' replied he. 'Then your map, sir, is sadly in error – reprehensibly so – and I recommend that you buy yourself a new one! But, come! A MacGlevin does not turn even the meanest wretch from his door – no offence intended, Gentlemen! Pray step this way!'

"We followed him into his castle. He was most hospitable, I must say, and showed us into the clan museum that he has established there. 'I'll not light the lamps in here,' said he, 'for I ken you're in a hurry to be off, but take this lantern and have a look about, while I prepare something to warm you!' Shortly afterwards, we joined him before a blazing fire and drank his health, and five minutes later set off back to our boat, carrying the lantern he had lent us."

"Had you mentioned to him the creature you had seen earlier?" queried Holmes.

Grice Paterson shook his head. "I'd thought it best not to."

"Does he keep a dog?"

"No, and there are no sheep or other animals on the island, either."

"It's the Black Pig!" said Murdoch MacLeod again, in a tone of awe.

"One moment, *if* you please," said Grice Paterson. "Our story is not yet finished."

"Dear me!" cried Doctor Oliphant. "Yet more adventures?"

"Indeed! You have not yet heard the strangest episode. We eventually reached the western extremity of Uffa, although it was not easy finding our way in the pitch blackness, and the lantern was little help. There, where we had secured the dinghy, was –" He paused and looked about the room.

"Well?" queried Doctor Oliphant impatiently.

"Nothing."

"Nothing?"

"Not a thing. No sign whatever of our boat. Just the dark sea splashing over the black rocks. We could see the *Puffin* riding at anchor a little distance off, for we'd lit a lamp on her before we'd left, but we'd no way of reaching her. And I was as certain that the dinghy had been secured properly as I'd ever been certain of anything in my life."

"What did you do?" queried Fergus Johnstone.

"We had no choice but to trudge all the way back to MacGlevin's domain and throw ourselves on his mercy. He seemed none too pleased to see us again, but said he would row us round to the *Puffin* in his own skiff, which was moored in an inlet just below the castle. You continue, Donald."

"Just as we were rounding the western head of the island, approaching the *Puffin*, my father cried out. I looked where he pointed, and there was our little dinghy, neatly tucked in the inlet, just as we had left it. Of course, Mr MacGlevin was a wee bit upset at this, and expressed himself somewhat warmly. Even a whelk would realize, he said, that we had simply taken the wrong path and looked for our boat in the wrong place. His parting words to us as he rowed off, after setting us aboard our own dinghy, were that we should henceforth confine our inept navigational activities to the streets of Edinburgh."

"There it might have ended," continued the elder Grice Paterson: "as an embarrassing experience, but no more – although I was still convinced that the boat had not been there when we had looked for it before – but, as we were climbing from dinghy to yacht, Donald found something by his feet. Show them, my boy."

Donald Grice Paterson put his hand in his pocket, and pulled out a large, wooden-handled clasp-knife. He unfolded the blade, which was broad and strong-looking, with a curiously square end.

"It's not ours," said his father, "so how came it in the bottom of our boat?"

"May I see it?" said Holmes. He took the knife and examined it closely. "Made in Sheffield," he remarked; "which is hardly surprising information. The tip has been snapped off, which must have taken some considerable force."

The knife was passed around the room, amid much murmuring of interest, but no-one could make any useful suggestion regarding it.

"Someone has been playing tricks upon you," declared Doctor Oliphant.

"Someone – or some*thing*," said Murdoch MacLeod.

"A mischievous sprite," suggested Mrs Morton.

Sherlock Holmes offered no observation of his own, and later, when I queried his silence on the matter, he shook his head and smiled.

"My dear fellow," said he, "you must have observed in the past that an unresolved mystery possesses a charm and romance which its solution can rarely aspire to. It is for this reason that – unless it is likely to involve them in a personal loss – men often prefer mystery to enlightenment. I could have suggested at least seven possible explanations, but all of them were fairly prosaic, I'm afraid, and not really what the company was seeking!"

With that he retired for the night, and there the singular adventures of the Grice Patersons might have remained, but for the surprising sequel.

We were seated at breakfast the following morning when there came the sound of raised voices from the hallway outside. Moments later, the door was flung open, and, ignoring the protests of the manager, in strode a gigantic figure, whose tangled ginger hair and beard identified him instantly as MacGlevin, closely followed by a police constable. The Laird of Uffa's eyes passed quickly over the assembled diners, until they alighted upon the luckless Grice Patersons.

"There they are!" he roared. "There are the villains! Arrest those men at once, MacPherson!"

Like everyone else, Grice Paterson had been frozen into immobility by this sudden, amazing irruption, his egg-spoon poised half-way to his lips, but now he sprang to his feet.

"How dare you!" he cried angrily. "What is the meaning of this?"

"The meaning," returned MacGlevin in an equally heated voice, "is that you have abused my hospitality. I took you in out of the dark night, and you have returned this favour by treacherously stealing that which is most dear to my clan, the MacGlevin Buckle!"

"This is nonsense," snorted Grice Paterson. "I have stolen nothing. I have never in my life taken that which was not mine. Why, I have never even seen your wretched buckle!"

MacGlevin's face assumed a dark, angry hue, and the veins on his temples stood out like whipcord.

"How dare you refer to the heirloom of my family in those insulting terms!" he roared. "You despicable villain!"

How long this aggressive exchange might have continued, it is difficult to say. Certainly, MacGlevin appeared on the verge of imposing his huge physical presence on the little Edinburgh lawyer. But Constable MacPherson placed his considerable bulk between them, and managed to calm the atmosphere a little. "Gentlemen, gentlemen," he said, "let us discuss the matter like the civilized men we are!"

The facts of the matter were soon told. The Laird of Uffa had last seen his family's heirloom during the previous afternoon, when he had been re-arranging some of the exhibits in his museum. He had not entered the museum with Mr Grice Paterson and his son, but had given them a lantern and told them to look round by themselves if they wished. They had done so for two or three minutes before rejoining him for a hot toddy. Later he had entered the museum to fetch a book, and had found the buckle gone. It had not been protected from theft in any way, but had lain, uncovered, upon a velvet cushion, atop a small stand. No-one but the Grice Patersons had entered the house all day, and nor were there any signs of a forced entry. The case against the Edinburgh men seemed, then, on circumstantial evidence at least, to be conclusive, although, having conversed with them at length the previous evening, I could not really believe either of them to be guilty of so mean a crime. For their part, they declared that they had not observed the buckle the previous evening, having taken only a cursory glance around the museum.

The *impasse* was broken in a surprising manner. Sherlock Holmes

abruptly pushed back his chair from the breakfast-table and rose to
his feet. In a very few words, he introduced himself, and although
he had not then achieved the celebrity he was later to enjoy, the
name was recognized instantly by several of those there.

"I followed the Maupertuis case in the papers," said the policeman
with respect, but Holmes waved his hand dismissively.

"I think it would be as well to examine the scene of this crime
before any arrests are contemplated," said he, in a voice of quiet
authority. "It may well be that the circumstances there will decide
the question of guilt or innocence once and for all, and may also
suggest some other line of inquiry."

"Suggest fiddlesticks!" cried MacGlevin in contempt, but Constable MacPherson nodded his head.

"I canna arrest anybody merely on your say-so, Mr MacGlevin,"
said he. "This gentleman is correct. We must examine the scene.
You will favour us with your assistance, Mr Holmes?"

My friend assented, and MacPherson quickly made his arrangements. Holmes and he had a brief discussion, during which my
friend made several specific suggestions, the upshot being that
two of the local fishermen who were special constables were to
take charge of matters in Kilbuie in our absence, and the *Puffin*
was to be temporarily impounded. Then MacGlevin, MacPherson,
the elder Grice Paterson, Holmes and myself set off for the islands
in the steam launch, *Alba*.

The black tower of MacGlevin's abode loomed above us as we
approached Uffa, gaunt and solitary. Beyond it stretched the
length of the bleak and featureless island, its surface a mottled
dun colour. It was a strange and inhospitable place to make one's
home, and perhaps the most unlikely spot in which my friend had
ever investigated a crime. A hundred yards or so to the north were
further, smaller islands, the sea breaking in white foam over their
jagged rocks, and, perhaps two hundred yards to the south, the
nearest point on the mainland, an area of tumbled rocks and
tangled shrubs.

MacGlevin brought his little vessel alongside a small and rickety
wooden jetty, where his servant, a short, spry elderly man with
faded ginger hair, was waiting to take the rope, and we climbed
ashore. A steep little pathway brought us to the front door of
the building. The single tower, perhaps twenty feet square, rose
high above us, its little windows set in deep embrasures. At the
back of the tower was a long, low, single-storeyed wing, with a
shallow-pitched roof. To the left of the tower was a wide, flat
grassy area, with piles here and there of driftwood and sawn
logs, and at the other side of this open space stood the jumble

of lichen-blotched stones which was all that remained of the early Christian settlement.

We followed MacGlevin inside, and through to the museum, which occupied half of the single-storey wing, and which appeared as impregnable as a fortress. The walls were of stone, immensely thick, and hung all about with swords and shields, maps, paintings and tartans. High up along the left-hand wall was a row of windows, and in the sloping roof above was a series of small sky-lights, all of which had black iron bars across. The windows had all been fastened on the inside for the previous two days, the laird informed us, the sky-lights did not open at all, and there was no other door than the one through which we had entered, from the living-quarters of the house. Scattered about the room were several tables and cases containing exhibits, and in the middle stood a white-painted wooden pedestal, about a foot square and four feet high. Atop this was a red velvet cushion, depressed slightly in the middle. This was the usual resting-place of the MacGlevin Buckle, from which it had mysteriously disappeared.

Directing us to stand back, Holmes examined the cushion, the pedestal and the area round about with minute care, occasionally murmuring to himself. As he did so, there was a glint in his eye and an energy in his manner which it thrilled me to see. Like a weary hound who gets the scent of the chase in his nostrils, Holmes's keen, incisive nature had been kindled afresh by the task before him, and had quite thrown off the lassitude of former days. Grice Paterson caught my eye, raised his eyebrow questioningly, and seemed about to speak, but I shook my head and put my finger to my lips.

"The buckle was not fastened to the cushion in any way?" queried Holmes of MacGlevin. "No? But it appears that something was, for there is a little tear in the surface, as if something has been forcibly ripped from it." MacGlevin stepped forward to see, and declared that he had not noticed such a tear before.

Holmes was down on his hands and knees when he uttered a little cry of satisfaction as he picked something up from the floor, a couple of feet to the side of the pedestal. He continued his search for a while, without finding anything else, and presently he stood up and held out his hand. Upon the palm lay a tiny grey sphere of metal, little more than an eighth of an inch in diameter.

MacGlevin shook his head dismissively, and shrugged his shoulders. "It must have fallen from someone's pocket," he suggested. "I cannot see that it is of any significance. Why, any of my visitors might have dropped it!"

Holmes gave a little chuckle. "Really, Mr MacGlevin," said he; "if you wish your buckle to be returned to you, you would do well not to dismiss the evidence so quickly. This interesting little sphere –"

"Is a piece of lead shot of some kind," said Constable MacPherson in a thoughtful voice "and there's little opportunity for shooting rabbits in here, Mr MacGlevin!"

Holmes laughed. "There is no more to be seen here," said he. "Let us now examine the exterior of the building."

We followed him outside, and round to the back. Where the single-storey wing joined the rear wall of the tower at a right angle, there was a soft patch of muddy ground, to which Holmes devoted his attention.

"I reap the benefits of investigating a crime in such an unfrequented spot," said he, in good spirits. "There are some wonderfully clear prints here. Your shoe size, Mr Grice Paterson?"

"Seven."

"I thought as much. And your son's will be something similar. These prints are too large to be yours, and too small to be Mr MacGlevin's. Your servant, Mr MacGlevin?"

"Wattie? A tiny fellow, as you saw, with feet to match."

"Which eliminates him also, then. It rained heavily on Wednesday night, so these prints must have been made yesterday. You did not have any visitors?"

"I never open my house to visitors on a Thursday."

"Then these are the prints of the thief."

We all pressed forward to see. A clear impression of a right foot, the toe pointing into the angle of the building, was crossed by another, slightly deeper print of the same shoe, the toe pointing away from the wall.

"He has climbed the building here," said Holmes. "The deeper print was made when he jumped back down. Might this be where you saw your ghostly figure last night, Mr Grice Paterson?"

"It could very well have been," replied the lawyer. "It crossed the path from somewhere near here towards the ruins over there."

"What figure is this?" demanded MacGlevin.

"We thought we saw something," Grice Paterson returned, "but did not mention it lest you thought us foolish."

MacGlevin snorted, but made no comment.

While they were speaking, Holmes had been examining the wall closely. Presently his hand found a projecting stone some way above his head, and he managed to haul himself up. He quickly clambered over the gutter and onto the shallow-pitched roof of the museum wing, where he moved carefully along the slates, examining each skylight in turn.

"Oh, this is pointless!" said MacGlevin, who was becoming

impatient once more. "Even if someone did climb up there, the sky-lights don't open, the panes of glass are too small for anyone to pass through, and they're all barred on the inside, anyway."

"Nevertheless," Holmes called back in an agreeable tone, "someone has recently been tampering with this one. The lead strip round the edge has been bent back, the putty chipped away, and the nails . . . Ah!" He had been looking behind him, down the roof to the guttering. Now he carefully reached down and plucked from the gutter a small sliver of something metallic, which he held up between his finger and thumb and examined closely. "If you would be so good as to join me," he called to MacPherson, "I should be most obliged."

The sky had been growing darker for some time, and MacGlevin, Grice Paterson and I hurried for shelter as there came a sudden downpour of rain, leaving Holmes and MacPherson in conversation upon the roof. The shower soon blew over, and twenty minutes later, after a cup of tea, we went back out to find that the clouds had parted and the sun was shining. Holmes and MacPherson were nowhere to be seen, and we were wondering what had become of them, when there came a shout from below, and we turned to see a small rowing-boat approaching the little harbour below the castle, with Holmes and Macpherson in it. The policeman was pulling sturdily on the oars, while Homes sat in the stern, placidly smoking his pipe.

"We have just had a little run-round in the boat," he explained, as they stepped ashore.

"And?" said MacGlevin.

"The case is now complete."

We returned to Kilbuie to find the hotel in tumult. Luggage of all kinds was heaped up in confusion in the entrance-hall, so that we had to shuffle sideways to get past.

Doctor Oliphant ran up to us as we entered, his face a picture of agitation.

"What is the meaning of this?" he demanded of MacPherson in a shrill voice. "It is absolutely vital that I reach home this evening. I have an important lecture to deliver in Edinburgh tomorrow night, and I must have a day to prepare my notes. The coach is not here, and when I inquire why not, I am informed that it is held by order of the police!" His voice rose to a breathless cry. "This is an outrage! You have no right to detain a public coach! If it does not leave soon, we shall miss the connecting train!"

Murdoch MacLeod stepped forward, wringing his hands with anxiety.

"What *is going* on?" he queried in a hopeless voice. "Can you explain, Constable?"

"This is highly irregular," said Hamish Morton. "They tell us the coach cannot leave, but my wife and I must be back in Glasgow tonight, and Mrs Baird Duthie, too, is anxious to be away. Should we make our own arrangements?"

MacPherson pulled an enormous watch out of his pocket, and consulted it for a moment.

"You'll all get where you're going," he said shortly. "If you would just step through into the dining-room for a moment –"

The hotel servants were setting the tables for lunch, and looked up in surprise as we all filed in and arranged ourselves as best we could, here and there about the room. Old Mrs Baird Duthie was the last to shuffle in, Angus Johnstone supporting her elbow. His brother brought a chair forward for her and relieved her of her stick, and she sat down heavily. All eyes were on Sherlock Holmes, who stood patiently until everyone was settled, his hands behind his back.

"Now," said he at length. "A serious and ingenious crime has been committed. The famous MacGlevin Buckle has been stolen from the museum on the Island of Uffa. It must be returned to its rightful owner." He glanced at MacGlevin, who was standing with his arms folded by the doorway, a brooding expression on his face.

"It is, of course, most unfortunate," said Doctor Oliphant; "but what is it to us?"

"The buckle is in this hotel," returned Holmes. "Constable MacPherson and his deputed officers therefore propose to search the building until they find it."

There were loud groans about the room.

"Why, man, that could take days!" said Angus Johnstone.

"Let us make a start, then," said Homes. "beginning with *that.*" His long thin finger indicated the small leather and canvas satchel which hung from Mrs Morton's shoulder.

"But this contains only my painting and sketching things," said she, rising to her feet, the expression on her face a mixture of surprise and indignation.

"Will you open it, Madam, or shall I?" inquired MacPherson.

Reluctantly, she lowered the little bag to the floor, and began to unfasten the straps. "This is an absurd waste of time," said she, as she tipped the contents of the bag onto the carpet. I craned forward to see. There were numerous tubes of paint, several brushes and pencils tied up in a ribbon, a palette, a pad of paper, and a very dirty rag, stained with every colour of the rainbow.

"Kindly unfold that cloth," said Holmes.

"It is dirty," said she. "It is only the rag I wipe my paint-brushes on. I shall soil my gloves –"

Even as she was speaking, Holmes leaned quickly down and unfolded the screwed-up cloth. There in the middle of the multi-coloured wrapping, lay a large and ornate silver buckle. There were gasps all round the room, and, in that split second of quiet, Hamish Morton suddenly shot from his seat and bolted for the door. He had his hand on the door-knob, but MacGlevin, too, was quick, and grabbed him in a smothering embrace.

"You fool!" cried Mrs Morton to her husband, in a harsh voice. "'Let's leave Glasgow,' you said. 'Let's get away and lie low for a while'! But you just couldn't resist this, could you! And now see what you have done!"

It was startling to hear the violent tones of the woman's voice, and almost made my hair stand on end. Her husband, held tightly in the bear-like grip of the Laird of Uffa, made no response. Next instant, my blood ran cold, for with a quick, darting movement, her hand had dipped into her reticule and re-emerged gripping an evil-looking little revolver.

"Stand aside, all of you!" she said in a cold, clear voice, as she pointed the gun menacingly, from one person to another. "This pistol is loaded, and I am quite prepared to use it."

I saw Holmes catch the eye of Fergus Johnstone, then he spoke. "Mrs Morton," said he. For a fraction of a second, she turned her head, and in that instant, in a blur of movement, the gun was dashed from her hand. Fergus Johnstone, who had been standing a little to the side of her, had brought down the old lady's walking-stick on her wrist with a loud crack. Mrs Morton cried wildly with pain, and clutched her wrist, and Holmes stepped forward quickly and picked up the gun. In a minute MacPherson had whistled up his special constables and the prisoners had been taken away. Then MacGlevin stepped forward to where his precious heirloom still lay on the paint-smeared rag. With an air of reverence, he picked it up. As he did so, there came a further surprise, for there lying beneath it was an exquisite little silver clasp, set with creamy pearls.

"Mrs Formartine's brooch!" cried MacLeod, almost beside himself with joy.

Some two hours later, after lunch, we were all seated in the drawing-room of the hotel. The Mortons were safely under guard at the local police station, awaiting an escort to take them to Inverness. Doctor Oliphant and Mrs Baird Duthie had long since departed, and the Loch Echil Hotel had returned to an atmosphere of normality.

"I cannot thank you enough," said Alexander Grice Paterson to Holmes. "Without your intervention, I dread to think what might have become of us."

"I regret I was a little heated," said MacGlevin in a sheepish tone, holding out his hand to the man he had accused. "I just couldna' think how anyone could've taken it but you."

"That is all right," said the other, accepting MacGlevin's hand. "Let's forgive and forget. What I'd like to know is how you got to the bottom of the matter so quickly, Mr Holmes."

"It was not difficult. I will give you a full explanation when Constable . . . Ah! MacPherson! We were just speaking of you."

"Please excuse the delay, Gentlemen," said the policeman briskly. "I have had a busy time of it. I wired details of the Mortons down to Glasgow, and I have their reply here. We've landed bigger fish than we realized, Mr Holmes! They're fairly certain that the man calling himself Hamish Morton is in fact Charlie Henderson, wanted in connection with the Blythswood Square burglary, earlier this year –"

" – in which the thieves got away with works of art worth thousands," interjected Holmes, "and left the owner of the house seriously injured. I recall it very well."

"And the woman, who has used so many names in her career that it's hard to keep track of her, is wanted under the name of Mary Monteith, for a long series of frauds and forgeries. Apparently she has real artistic gifts, but she's used them only in the cause of crime. She's suspected of being behind some of the most brilliant art forgeries of the last dozen years."

"Well, I never!" ejaculated Grice Paterson. "But come, Mr Holmes, tell us how you got on to them."

"My interest was first aroused," said Holmes after a moment, "by Morton's report of his boating accident. He declared that all his fishing equipment had sunk without trace, yet when I had seen it the previous evening in this very room, I had observed, without giving it any special attention, that his rod was of the sort which is fitted with a large cork handle. It seemed unlikely that such a rod should have sunk. It might, of course, have become entangled with some other equipment, and been dragged down by it, but Morton merely said it had sunk. It seemed to me that he was lying, but I could not think why, unless he merely wished to swindle the hotel out of a few pounds by way of compensation. It was a petty matter, and I gave it little more thought.

"When we went out to Uffa, to investigate the theft, I had no pre-conceived ideas as to what had taken place there. For all I knew, the result of my examination might have been to confirm Mr Grice

Paterson's guilt. You did not look a very likely pair of thieves," he remarked, turning to the Grice Patersons with a chuckle; "but I have known many criminals in my time, and a good half of them did not appear capable of the crimes they had committed; so I preserved a professional detachment on the matter, and reserved my judgement.

"My examination of the museum revealed, as you saw, a small tear in the cushion upon which Mr MacGlevin's Buckle had been lying when last he saw it, which at once suggested to me that some hook, or other sharp device, had been used to lift the buckle. This in turn suggested, of course, that the thief had not been in a position to reach it with his hand. The obvious conclusion was that a line with a hook attached had been lowered from above, through one of the sky-lights. When I found on the floor a small piece of lead shot, such as fishermen use to weight their lines, this presumption became a certainty. The weight would help the line to drop straight, and give the thief more control over it. No doubt the piece of shot we found had become detached when the hook snagged the cushion and had to be forcibly yanked free.

"The next thing then, was to examine the exterior of the building. Here I was fortunate enough to find very clear indications of where the thief had climbed the wall. The fact that I could only just reach the only usable hand-hold – and I am a good six foot in height – indicated that the thief was not a small man, as also did the size of the footprints. These indications eliminated the Grice Patersons, as far as I was concerned.

"I then examined the sky-light which lay immediately above the stand on which the buckle had been displayed, and it was obvious at once that one of the panes of glass had been removed and later replaced. The lead around the glass had clearly been bent back, and then flattened again. That would have presented no problem, and nor would it have been difficult to chip away the putty with a knife. But there were also galvanized nails bent over beneath the lead to hold the pane firmly, which would have required a greater application of force. Was this, I wondered, how the knife-blade came to be broken? This conjecture was at once confirmed, for there in the gutter below me was a little shiny triangle – the missing tip of the blade.

"It seemed clear enough, then, what had happened. The thief had been at work when you chanced upon the scene, Mr Grice Paterson, and was evidently the figure you saw cross the path in the darkness. He would then have returned to his boat, but must have taken the wrong path in the darkness, and mistakenly set off in your boat, rather than his own. You came along shortly afterwards, found your boat missing, and returned to seek Mr MacGlevin's aid. The thief, meanwhile, must have realized his mistake, and so returned your boat, in which he had dropped his knife, found his own boat, and left the island for the second time.

"So much seemed clear. But who, then, was the thief? There seemed no way of knowing. It was then that I recalled Morton's reported accident, and his claim to have lost all his fishing tackle, about which I had had some doubt at the time. Now it struck me as possible that his boat had not sunk at all, but had been hidden in the bushes by the shore on the south side of the bay, together with his fishing equipment. If that were so, he would be able to use it when he wished to commit this crime, without the slightest suspicion attaching to him, even if the crime were discovered before he and his accomplice had left Kilbuie. MacPherson and I therefore rowed over to the mainland, which is no great distance at that point, and soon found what we were looking for – one of this hotel's distinctive little skiffs dragged up behind some rocks, with a disordered heap of fishing tackle within it.

"The case was therefore complete, and it remained only to locate the buckle. I was quite certain that the Mortons had it, but finding it might have taken some time. However, as you may recall, they had claimed on the day the crime was committed to have gone inland so that Mrs Morton might sketch – probably they did so, earlier in the day – and had therefore had the satchel containing the art materials with them. It seemed likely, then, that the stolen buckle had been secreted in there in the first place, and, if so, it seemed to me possible that it was still there, especially as Mrs Morton was demonstrating an unusual attachment to the bag. This surmise proved correct, and the rest you know. Mr MacGlevin has his heirloom restored to him, Mrs Formartine will soon have her brooch back – that was something of an unexpected bonus, I must confess – clearly Morton had been keeping his hand in – and two dangerous criminals are safely under lock and key."

"You make it sound so obvious and straightforward, Mr Holmes!" exclaimed MacGlevin in amazement. "I'm sure that if we had spent all day examining the museum, we should not have observed the little traces which you found, nor made anything of them if we had done!"

"Aye, it's a grand job of work all right," said MacPherson with feeling. "I may get my sergeant's stripes over this arrest. I don't know how I can ever thank you, Mr Holmes," he continued, extending his hand. "Without your help, I don't know that we should ever have caught those villains!"

"It is always a pleasure to assist the forces of law and order," returned my friend with a smile. "Now, Watson," he continued, turning to me: "the fresh air on Uffa has quite invigorated me! What say you to another expedition, this time to catch something a little smaller and tastier, for our supper?"

THE CASE OF
THE SPORTING SQUIRE

Guy N. Smith

*It was during 1887 that Watson obtained permission from Holmes
to seek formal publication for his account of their meeting and the
case known as "A Study in Scarlet". It's quite likely he finalized this
novel while on holiday in Scotland and submitted it to the publisher
Ward Lock via his agent Arthur Conan Doyle. Ward Lock published
it in their* Beeton's Christmas Annual *that December and that was
the first time that the general public came to learn of Sherlock Holmes.
It inevitably led to an upsurge in the number of requests Holmes
received and also, Holmes jokingly acknowledged, caused him to start
going about his business in disguise. More importantly, it meant that
Watson began to keep a better record of the cases. Flushed by the success
of this sale Watson now wrote up most of the cases that happened
over the following year from the end of 1887 and through 1888.
These include some of Holmes's best: "Silver Blaze", with the curious
incident of the dog in the night; "The Valley of Fear"; "The Greek
Interpreter" – which is remarkable in that not until now did Watson
apparently discover that Holmes had a brother, Mycroft, though we
know he was aware of him earlier; and "The Cardboard Box", in
which Holmes reveals his ability to deduce Watson's thoughts. Another
of the cases falling in this period was that of "The Sporting Squire",
one that Watson did not refer to but which came to light following the
investigations of that redoubtable author Guy N. Smith early in his
own career when undertaking research into the theory and practice of
gamekeeping.*

I have long learned to tolerate the varying moods of my colleague,
Sherlock Holmes. When a working fit was upon him, nothing could
exceed his energy; at other times he would lie on the sofa, scarcely
moving from morning to night, his eyes closed but I knew that he
did not sleep. He either contemplated some intricate problem or
else he was melancholic, but I knew better than to intrude upon
his thoughts for it would only evoke some brusque reply, for my

friend could be exceedingly rude when his private musings were disturbed.

It was in February 1888 that Holmes had reposed in such a fashion for three whole days, following upon a period when he had busied himself with his various files, scribbling on a notepad and occasionally muttering to himself. He had not eaten throughout this time, his only form of sustenance lying in that strong-smelling shag tobacco, a cloud of pipesmoke enshrouding him with the opaqueness of a November fog.

"Poison, Watson," his sudden emergence from that apparent somnial state caused me to start involuntarily, "is the device of more murderers who have escaped the gallows than any other weapon used. Poison is, in many cases, undetectable, only the symptoms of some being a guide to their identification. Often death occurs after the villain has returned to his normal routine and the victim is diagnosed as having died from natural causes. Doubtless you, yourself, have, on more than one occasion, been deceived by the guile of some insidious murderer who has later reaped the rewards of his vile deed."

"I would hate to think so, Holmes." I confess his words brought with them a pang of guilt, a momentary feeling that I had, in some instances, neglected my duty as a doctor.

"It is not a comforting thought but, undoubtedly, it has occurred." He regarded me with an unwavering stare. "Likewise, I, on rare occasions, have overlooked some vital clue that would have led to a conviction. None of us are infallible although, I hope, that over the past few days I have achieved something which will make those errors, where poison is concerned, something of a rarity."

"That is good news, indeed." I knew full well that he was about to confide in me the purpose of his recent writings and contemplations. I leaned forward expectantly.

"You will doubtless recall my original thesis on poisons," he became a silhouette behind a cloud of exhaled tobacco smoke, "in which I examined the varieties in some detail."

"Yes, yes," I had read it at his invitation some time ago. Some aspects of the paper did, indeed, throw new light on the subject.

"Well, I have revised and updated it, Watson. I would hope that from now on the prospective poisoner will think twice before administering some lethal dose to an unsuspecting victim."

"That is good news, Holmes." I have never doubted my friend's variable knowledge of botany, surpassed only by a profound understanding of chemistry.

"Cyanide, for example, works slowly if administered in small doses, produces symptoms of failing health which often deceives a well-meaning doctor right up to, and beyond, the point of death. Unless, of course, he perceives a faint smell of almonds on the doomed person's breath. Now, in total contrast . . ."

He was interrupted by the sound of footsteps on the stairs, followed by a knocking on the door which bespoke an urgency that transcended the routine delivery of a letter or telegram. My colleague was instantly alert for it was for such moments that he lived: the unexpected visitor, in a state of distress, ushered in by the long-suffering Mrs Hudson.

"A lady to see you, Mr Holmes," the landlady withdrew, closed the door behind her for she was accustomed to strange callers, day or night, and resolutely showed no surprise.

"Mr Holmes, please forgive this intrusion." Our visitor was an exceedingly attractive lady in her early twenties, long auburn hair falling about her shoulders, her expression one of acute anxiety.

"Pray, be seated, Miss . . ." Holmes, like myself, had already noticed that our caller wore no wedding ring.

"I am Gloria Morgan." She seated herself on the edge of the vacant chair, wrung her hands together in obvious anguish. "Mr Holmes . . . my father has murdered my mother, a vile deed which will go both undetected and unpunished unless . . ."

"Have you not informed the police, Miss Morgan?" Holmes stretched out his long legs. "Surely, that is the obvious course if you are so convinced that such a dastardly act has taken place?"

"It would be useless, Mr Holmes, for Doctor Lambeth is insistent that my mother died of lockjaw. But he is ageing, he retires shortly, and I do not think that he wishes to put himself in the embarrassing position of accusing a prominent member of the community of such a crime on slender evidence."

"Please start at the very beginning, Miss Morgan." Holmes reached the old slipper off the floor by his side and proceeded to stuff the blackened bowl of his pipe with fine cut dark tobacco. "I trust you have no objection to the smell of strong tobacco, Miss Morgan?"

"Not at all." She coughed slightly for the room was already thick with pipesmoke. "My father is Squire Royston Morgan of Winchcombe Hall in Hampshire."

"Ah, I recall the locality." Holmes leaned back, his fingertips pressed together, seemingly drowsy to anybody who was not familiar with his posture, but I knew that he listened intently. "Is that not in the proximity of Longparish, home of the legendary late Colonel Peter Hawker, undoubtedly one of the finest marksman which this country has ever produced, a veteran of the Crimean War who, upon being invalided out of the army, devoted the remainder of his life to the pursuit of fur and feather?"

"Indeed, it is," Gloria Morgan smiled wryly. "I curse him, too, even though he has been dead for half a century, for it is upon him that my father has modelled himself, although I would hope that Colonel Hawker's only shortcoming was his devotion to fishing and shooting."

"Hawker was surely the finest game shot of all time," Sherlock Holmes answered dreamily. "Not content with killing twenty-four snipe consecutively on one day, without missing a shot, he used to practise on bats around Longparish Hall at dusk, and, according to his books, with equal success."

"As my father does, especially when we have guests staying." There was no mistaking the contempt in her voice.

"I digress," Holmes said. "Please continue."

"As I have already said, my father has endeavoured to build his own reputation upon that of Colonel Hawker's. A fine shot, an excellent fly fisherman and a dashing horseman, understandably he has attracted the attention of other women. I would add, at this stage, that my parent's marriage has not been a happy one. One woman in particular, is a wealthy widow by the name of Eva Dann, who currently owns Longparish, the property most coveted by my father. There have, for some years, been whispered rumours of their relationship, and my mother has had to suffer the ignominy of it. For my sake, she clung to her marital status and rights, doubtless much to my father's chagrin.

"So, faced with the prospect of her remaining indefinitely at Winchcombe, and thereby depriving him of the opportunity to marry his mistress and acquire Longparish, he murdered her."

"Can you prove it?"

"Alas, no, but I have not a single doubt in my mind that he killed her."

"Then tell me everything you know, setting out your story as it happened, trying not to overlook the smallest detail, however irrelevant it may seem to you."

"My mother had resigned herself to living beneath the same room as my father, no matter how unpleasant that may have been. One of her interests was horticulture, and on fine days she would spend her time in the gardens. Her other love was literature. There is a small library in the Hall and, after dinner each evening, she would go there to read until she retired about ten o'clock. Lately, she took to locking herself in the library because, on those occasions when my father had been drinking heavily, he would go and vent his vile temper on her. Thus, by locking the door, she ensured herself of the tranquillity she required to immerse herself in her reading."

"And it was in the library where she met her untimely death?"

There was a gentleness in Sherlock Holmes's voice as he asked the question.

"Yes", Gloria Morgan stifled a sob. "The night before last. Dinner was an uneasy meal for my father was in an uncertain temper on account of having shot badly that day. Afterwards, my mother retired to the library as was her usual routine. I am not sure of my father's movements, possibly he went down to the gamekeeper's cottage to discuss with Randall the task of destroying a colony of moles which are currently rendering the lawns and borders an unsightly mess."

"And the gamekeeper?"

"Randall is a hateful man. He reminds me of the stoats and weasels which hang rotting and stinking on his vermin gibbet. He is the most hated man for miles around. Several cats and dogs, belonging to the villagers, have died in his traps and snares, or eaten the poison which he lays for foxes in the game preserves. The safety of his pheasants is paramount, the greater the slaughter on shooting days, the more prestigious his role becomes amongst the guests who shoot at Winchcombe."

"A decidedly unpleasant character, by all accounts," Holmes mused.

"Second only to my father. On the night in question I was somewhat later retiring than usual. As I passed the library about eleven o'clock, I noticed that a light still burned beneath the door. Fearing lest my mother might have fallen asleep in her chair, or perhaps become ill, I knocked on the door. After several knockings, and receiving no response, I hastened to summon Jenkins, the butler. Jenkins forced the door open and there . . . oh, Mr Holmes!"

I reached across and patted her hand. Bravely, Gloria Morgan pulled herself together, and continued her narrative. "It was clear at first glance that my mother was dead. That, in itself, was awful enough but nothing by comparison with the expression on her features and the way in which her body was twisted into an unnatural posture. Mr Holmes, there is no doubt that my mother died in indescribable agony, unable even to call for help."

"You then sent for the doctor?"

"Yes. Jenkins rode at once to the village to fetch Doctor Lambeth who arrived soon after."

"And your father?"

"My father did not return until after the doctor's arrival. His show of distress was so shallow that the most amateurish of stage actors could have improved considerably upon his pathetic performance. Doctor Lambeth examined my mother and diagnosed that she had died of lockjaw which seemed to satisfy my father."

"There would most certainly have been signs of the malady before death took place," I interposed. "A tetanus sufferer would have experienced pain long before the final convulsions."

"Precisely!" Holmes added. "Miss Morgan, did your mother appear unwell in any way during dinner?"

"No," Gloria Morgan dabbed at her eyes with a handkerchief, "but of late she has suffered a loss of appetite due, I presume, to her unhappy state of mind. She ate very little on the night in question, just picked at her food."

"And the remains of her meal?" There was a sharpness about my friend now which had been absent of late. It appeared that Miss Morgan's story had aroused his interest above the level of a routine investigation.

"Oh, I know what you're thinking, Mister Holmes," our visitor gave a hollow laugh. "The same thought crossed my mind, that some form of poison had been introduced into my mother's food. In my grief and anger I suggested that to both Doctor Lambeth and my father."

"And?"

"My father laughed cruelly. 'Very well', he said, leading us through to the dining room, 'just to prove to you how unfounded your stupid fears are, we will feed the remnants of your mother's meal to the dogs.' We followed him outside to the kennels where the dogs voraciously devoured those leftovers. The animals were still in excellent health when I left to catch the train to London this morning."

"I see." It was impossible even to guess what Sherlock Holmes was thinking as he lapsed into silence. I knew better than to enquire of him for he would reveal them when he was ready and not until.

Miss Morgan and I glanced at each other and there was no mistaking the anguish in her eyes. She had come here with a desperate plea for help and Sherlock Holmes was her only hope.

"Watson and I will travel down to Hampshire by the first available train in the morning." Holmes had made his decision and he knew, without asking, that I would accompany him. "It is important that I examine the scene of this untimely death without your father's knowledge, Miss Morgan. Can that be arranged?"

"Most certainly," There was sheer relief in her reply. "In spite of my mother's sudden death, my father has not seen fit to cancel a day's pheasant shooting tomorrow. He will be out in the fields and coverts with his guests from around ten in the morning until mid-afternoon."

"Admirable!" Holmes snapped his long thin fingers. "I would prefer you to return to Winchcombe this afternoon, Miss Morgan. I presume that your father has no idea that you have visited me."

"None, whatsoever. In fact, should he find out." I glimpsed a flicker of fear in her pale blue eyes. "I dread to think what he might do. As well as being one of the best shots in England, my father has a violent streak in him. This was evident only last winter when he and Randall caught a poacher in the Home Covert, an otherwise harmless villager who only sought a pheasant for his dinner. The man was in hospital for some weeks afterwards with broken bones. Had it not been for my father's position, as well as squire he is chief magistrate, then I fear that the local constabulary would have brought a charge of assault against him."

"Then we shall hope to conduct our investigations undetected." Sherlock Holmes smiled as he rose to his feet. "One final question, Miss Morgan, hurtful as it may be, your mother's body . . ."

"It lies in an ante room. The funeral has been arranged for the day after tomorrow."

"Excellent, Watson!" Holmes said when Gloria Morgan's receding footsteps had faded. "I shall be obliged for your professional opinion on the deceased in due course. Also, it might be advisable if you slipped your service revolver into your pocket. The man we are up against, as well as being of a violent temperament, is one of the best shots in England. We cannot afford to take any chances."

A shimmering of snow sparkled across the countryside as Holmes and I travelled down to Andover on the early morning train. My companion spoke little throughout the long journey and I knew that he was turning over in his mind everything that Miss Morgan had told us yesterday. Her story had a ring of truth to it, incredible though it seemed on reflection. Had her mother really been murdered or was it fanciful thinking by a distraught young lady? If it was murder, then how had Violet Morgan been killed within a locked room, and the act so disguised that her death had been diagnosed as from natural causes by an experienced GP? Was Doctor Lambeth in league with Royston Morgan? Was Randall, the gamekeeper, with his store of poisons with which to kill vermin and roaming domestic pets, involved? I had enough confidence in my companion to know that if there was foul play then he would unravel the truth. The weight of my service revolver in my overcoat pocket brought mixed feelings of comfort and unease. All too often when Holmes had instructed me to bring a pistol along we had had need of it. The man's intuition was astounding.

On our arrival at Andover, we hired a carriage, Holmes instructing the driver to take us to Winchcombe Hall but to remain at a safe distance and to await our return. It was early afternoon as we walked up the winding poplar-lined drive.

In the distance, where a long narrow wood snaked over the horizon, we heard the sound of gunfire. Occasionally, we glimpsed a whirring speck that was undoubtedly a pheasant bursting from cover, a bird that had survived the line of guns, gliding on downhill to land in a field of snow-covered turnips.

"At least our friend, the squire, will be kept busy for a while," Holmes remarked as we passed through a clump of rhododendrons and had our first view of the big house. I noticed that the extensive snow-covered lawns were severely disfigured by the workings of moles, something to which Miss Morgan had alluded on her visit to our rooms in Baker Street.

Winchcombe Hall was set in a large clearing amidst tall pines and mature shrubberies. It was clearly of Georgian origin, three-storeyed and with high chimneys. Undoubtedly, once it had been a magnificent country residence but now there was evidence of loose mortar and the west wall was badly damp-stained. Which was all the more reason for Royston Morgan wanting to acquire the wealth of an eligible widow, I decided, but kept my thoughts to myself for Holmes would not have thanked me for them. A number of carriages were parked at the rear; undoubtedly, Squire Morgan had a full compliment of sportsmen for today.

Even as we mounted the wide flight of steps, the front door opened and there stood Gloria Morgan, a long black dress accentuating her pallor. Yet in spite of her grief, her delight at seeing us was all too evident.

"Oh, Mr Holmes, Doctor Watson," she cried, "I can't tell you how grateful I am that you have come."

"Have there been any further developments?" My companion asked as we stepped into the marble-floored hallway.

"No." She shook her head. "Everything is still as it was when I left yesterday. My father is too preoccupied with his pheasant shooting to concern himself with a matter which he considers to be concluded. The library is through there." She indicated a door that was partly open. "My mother . . ." Her trembling finger pointed to a closed door at the rear of the hall.

"Perhaps, Watson," Holmes glanced meaningfully at myself, "you would be so kind as to take a swift professional look at the departed whilst Miss Morgan accompanies me into the library. I am curious to view a locked room where death can strike so swiftly. I will join you shortly."

I lifted the lid of the polished oaken coffin and looked down upon

Violet Morgan. Death, and the obvious agony that had accompanied it, had done its utmost to destroy her striking beauty. The soft lips were swollen and marked where she had bitten them, and even the passing of *rigor mortis* had not removed the grimace from her face. She screamed mutely up at me, for her final suffering had been terrible beyond belief.

I bent over and sniffed at her mouth but the only odour was that familiar smell of death. The palms of her hands were gouged where her fingernails had dug deep and the mortician had been unable to straighten out her fingers fully, it was as though they were afflicted with some deformity. I checked for any signs of an open wound, a cut or scratch, that might have allowed tetanus to enter her bloodstream, but there were none apart from those inflicted by herself.

Certainly the corpse bore some resemblance to the final sufferings of a victim of lockjaw but tetanus would not have struck so suddenly and without warning. Either Doctor Lambeth had never witnessed a case of lockjaw or he was taking advantage of an easy alternative. Or else he was determined to shield Squire Morgan at all costs. I was far from satisfied at what I had seen.

I heard the door open and Holmes joined me. He stood there looking down upon the corpse and I knew that his keen eyes missed nothing.

"Her suffering was terrible, indeed, Watson," he spoke in a low voice for fear that Gloria Morgan might overhear him.

"Yes, but it was not lockjaw," I asserted, "but surely some kind of poison that is undetectable."

"Many poisons leave little or no trace." He bent over the corpse. "You really must read my treatise on poisons, Watson. Ah!" His fingers lifted up one of Violet Morgan's clawed hands, moved it so that the fingertips were exposed to view. "You noticed that faint stain on the tip of the forefinger, Watson?"

"I did not regard it as being of any significance," I replied somewhat abruptly for I sensed that my companion was criticizing my professionalism.

"Let us return to the library." He straightened up. I followed him out into the hallway, feeling a little offended by his abruptness. Whatever the relevance of that discolouring of the deceased's fingertip, it clearly needed to be corroborated by an inspection of the scene of the crime. However, I knew better than to interrupt my colleague's train of thought.

In the library Holmes commenced a minute examination of the windows and the door.

"A beetle could have entered via the gap beneath the locked

door," he spoke without looking round, "but nothing larger than an insect. Miss Morgan informs me that her mother always kept the windows tightly shut, even in summer, as she had a phobia about night moths. But, on the night in question, the temperature would have been below freezing so no window would have been open, anyway." He moved across to a section of bookshelving, tilted his head slightly to one side to enable him to read the lettering on the spines of the volumes. "*Hawker's Diaries*, I perceive, and also that worthy man's *Instructions to Young Sportsmen*." He reached down the latter leather bound tome and flipped the pages. "Well read, I see."

"As I have already told you, my father virtually worships Hawker and everything that the man stood for," there was a note of mingled repugnance and annoyance in her tone at this seeming digression from Holmes's investigations. "My father's lifelong ambition was to acquire Longparish. The place would have been a virtual shrine for him, but I am afraid family finances have been dwindling for some time."

"And your father needed to acquire the necessary funds from other sources," Holmes remarked. "I see that there is a sizeable collection of medieval works. Also well read." He was examining another volume.

"My father was no lover of literature, Mr Holmes, he only read sporting books and those medieval works. Mostly reprints, as you will see, and some books appertaining to that period."

"Hmmm." Holmes's expression had changed, he was staring fixedly at the open pages of the volume in his hands. From where I stood I was just able to read the title on the spine, "*Herbs and Plants of the Thirteenth Century; Their Cultivation and Uses*" Holmes read intently, he seemed oblivious of our presence in the room.

"Mr Holmes," there was a new nervousness in Gloria Morgan's voice, "the day's shooting usually concludes towards mid-afternoon in order that the unscathed pheasants may go to roost in peace. The party will be returning shortly. I had not anticipated that your investigations would take so long."

"Tell me, Miss Morgan", Holmes appeared not to have heard her warning or else he chose to ignore it, "what was your mother's taste in reading?"

"English literature. She read and re-read her favourite authors."

Sherlock Holmes turned his attention back to the bookshelves, his gaze searching out that section which contained works of literature.

"Ah!" His exclamation was one of triumph as he reached down a book which protruded from one of the neat rows. "This is the one which your mother was reading at the moment of her untimely death, I perceive. It was returned to its rightful place, presumably by your butler when he tidied up the room, but, in his haste, he failed to replace it fully. Charles Dickens, I see, although I have not read his works myself."

"*Little Dorrit,*" Miss Morgan answered. "I know because she mentioned it at dinner that night. Also, the volume was lying beside her when we ... we found her. As you point out, Jenkins must have returned it to the shelves when he tidied up the room after Doctor Lambeth and the mortician had finished."

Sherlock Holmes carried the volume across to the mahogany reading table where he pored over it with an intensity which I had witnessed many times in the past.

"Your mother showed little respect for books." He was turning the pages delicately, almost as thought it was a sacrilege to touch them. From where I stood I could see that each leaf was creased in the top right hand corner as if it had been turned down to mark the reader's place.

"It was a habit which she developed in childhood, Mr Holmes, and never relinquished, that of turning each page with a wetted forefinger."

Holmes examined the pages with his lens, blew gently upon one. A faint puff of something white, it might have been dandruff from a previous reader's hair, was dislodged, fell to the floor and became indiscernible. A cloud of what I took to be some kind of ash floated down in its wake.

My colleague snapped the tome shut and, in a couple of strides, was at the window, staring out with an intensity which told me that he had spotted something which was relevant to our investigations.

"The moles," he snapped, "they have made a devil of a mess of the lawns and borders. What method is being used to halt their depredations?"

"My father has been attending to the matter himself." Gloria Morgan was visibly surprised by yet another digression. "I believe that he obtained some substance from Randall with which to kill the creatures. I recall him mentioning it to my mother a few days ago when she expressed concern at the damage done by the moles. Something which was put down the holes, I believe, although I did not take much interest at the time."

"Capital!" Holmes cried. "Everything fits at last, the final piece in the jigsaw has slotted into place."

"Mr Holmes!" Gloria Morgan's cry of alarm interrupted my companion's moment of exultation, and in the brief moment of silence which followed we heard the slamming of the front door, followed by heavy footfalls in the hallway. "Mr Holmes, it is too late, my father has returned!"

At that very moment the library door crashed back on its hinges and I was afforded my first view of Royston Morgan, the sporting squire of Winchcombe Hall. He stood there framed in the doorway, a giant of a fellow, well over six feet tall and surely all of sixteen stone in weight, seemingly even more immense clad in baggy plus-fours and a tweed shooting jacket which strained at the shoulder seams. Silver hair spilled from beneath a wide-brimmed floppy hat. His expression was one of escalating fury, wide cheeks darkly flushed, lips bared to reveal tusk-like teeth as he removed a long black cheroot from his cruel mouth.

But it was not just his size, the demoniac expression in his sunken eyes, nor his raging fury, which caused him to tremble in every limb, that had Miss Morgan cowering against the table. Rather it was the double-barrelled shotgun which he pointed in our direction as he demanded of his daughter in slurred stentorian tones, "Gloria, what is the meaning of this? Who are these gentlemen who have left their carriage down on the road and slunk up here like thieves intent on burgling us?"

"Father." I admired her for the way in which she regained her composure and spoke with a voice that had only the slightest tremor in it. "This is Mr Sherlock Holmes and his colleague, Doctor Watson."

"*Sherlock Holmes!*" The name was uttered in a whisper which embodied both shock and anger, accompanied by an intake of breath. His gaze fastened on my companion and those cheeks became darker still. "I have heard of you, Mr Holmes. Holmes, the meddler, Scotland Yard's errand boy! What brings you here? How dare you set foot in my house uninvited!"

"I invited Mr Holmes, Father", Gloria Morgan spoke coolly and looked even more radiant in her moment of defiance.

"Leave my house at once!" The gun barrels swung round and came to a halt, trained upon Holmes, "or I shall summon the local constabulary and have you arrested. Nobody sets foot in Winchcombe Hall except at my invitation!"

"I rather think that it will snow again before nightfall," Sherlock Holmes remarked as though he was totally unaware of the gun which threatened him.

"Get out!"

"Perhaps," Holmes continued, undeterred, "you would be good enough to summon your local constabulary, after all, Squire Morgan, so that I may present my recent findings to them. I am now able to reveal the manner in which you murdered your wife two nights ago."

Morgan might have been a statue, frozen into immobility, the gun extended, one-handed, forefinger curled around the front trigger. My own hand crept into the pocket of my overcoat, gripped the butt of my revolver, my thumb easing back the hammer slowly so that the cocking action would not click and reveal that I was armed. Indeed, I would have shot Royston Morgan through my pocket except that I feared that the impact of the striking bullet might cause the shotgun to detonate and blast Holmes at point blank range. That was the only reason why I did not shoot this fiend down in cold blood.

"This is preposterous!" Morgan's lips moved at last, his denial an unconvincing whine. "My dear wife died of lockjaw, caused, doubtless, by some wound whilst going about her horticultural interests."

"No." Holmes's gaze never wavered, not so much as a hint of fear did he show in the face of that scattergun. "There is no such wound upon your wife's body, my medical colleague has already checked and informs me, with authority, that she did not die from tetanus. Rather, she died from strychnine poisoning, which is both sudden and terrible, a tiny amount of the substance, which is odourless, proving fatal. You procured the poison from Randall, your gamekeeper, for the supposed purpose of poisoning moles but instead you used it to murder your unsuspecting wife."

"I . . . I used the strychine to poison the moles in the grounds." I was heartily relieved to see those gun barrels lowered and pointing to the floor.

"Some of it, perhaps." Sherlock Holmes gave a short laugh. "But it only required a minute quantity to bring about a terrible end for your wife and free you to marry into considerable wealth, thereby fulfilling your lifelong ambition of owning the Longparish estate. It was a foul and cunning plan, aided by the fact that an ageing medical practitioner would not even consider the possibility that the local squire might have committed murder."

"It's a lie, Mister Holmes, spawned by my daughter who has hated me since childhood, and who sees a means whereby to inherit Winchcombe Hall before her time."

"It is no lie, Squire Morgan, although certainly your own daughter had good reason to hate you. What better, you thought, than to have your wife die in a locked room, and the accusation of death by poisoning dispelled by feeding the remnants of her last meal to the dogs which showed not the slightest ill-effect."

"You can prove nothing, Mr Sherlock Holmes!"

"Indeed, I can." These were the moments which Sherlock Holmes enjoyed most, revealing his observations and deductions only when they were finalized beyond all possible doubt. "Your fascination for medieval herbs and potions led you to discover a means by which unsuspecting victims were poisoned five centuries or more ago. In the days of parchment and inflexible leaves, often readers wetted a finger to turn the pages. Your own wife had developed that same habit, and the idea occurred to you that if you adhered strychnine to the top right-hand corner of the pages of whatever book she happened to be reading at the time, then it was almost certain that the poison would be conveyed to her mouth. And so it was."

"Prove it!" Morgan growled but his tone now had an uncertainty in it. "You're guessing, bluffing."

"No." Sherlock Holmes shook his head, the smile still lingering on his lips. "Indeed, I can prove, beyond all doubt, that it was yourself who adhered strychnine to the pages of the book with moistened flour, rendering it virtually invisible against the whiteness of the paper. Having discovered which book your wife was reading, you carried out your filthy plan. Remnants of the strychnine would not, in itself, be enough to convict you. However, a small quantity of Burma cheroot ash was dislodged and showered on to the page in question whilst you were applying the poison. Some traces remain and I note, Squire Morgan, that you have a liking for that particular variety of strong cheroot. I am somewhat of an expert on the subject of tobacco ash, and I am able, at a glance, to differentiate between the various types."

Royston Morgan's previously florid features were now deathly pale. He was shaking, not from rage this time, but from fear because his dastardly deed had been exposed and he would undoubtedly go to the gallows. Cowardice prevailed, but my own concern was that his shaking finger might pull upon the trigger of his shotgun, or that he might blast us all in a desperate attempt to conceal his crime.

Fortunately, that was not to be. In one swift but ungainly movement, he turned, stumbled from the library, and the three of us stood listening to his shambling footsteps going back through the hall. We heard the outer door slam behind him.

I drew my revolver, and would have hastened after him, but Sherlock Holmes stayed me with an upraised hand.

"Let him go, Watson," said he.

For some moments I was bewildered for it was not in my companion's nature to allow a cold-blooded murderer to escape. I felt Gloria Morgan's hand upon my arm and I let her lean against me for surely the poor girl had suffered more than enough.

It was as we stood there, not knowing what Holmes intended, that we heard the simultaneous double blast of a shotgun from outside. We looked at one another, finally understanding, as the echoes rolled across the wintry landscape, slowly dying away.

"It is best that way," Sherlock Holmes demonstrated a rare tenderness in his nature as he squeezed Gloria Morgan's hand. "Nothing is to be gained by bringing the matter to the attention of the authorities. Your mother is now at peace, and her murderer has fittingly paid for his crime with his life. Far better, Miss Morgan, that you make a new life for yourself, unsoiled by a scandal that would follow you for the rest of your days."

Only now, with the passing of time, has Sherlock Holmes agreed to my request to record the facts concerning the case of Morgan the Poisoner, as he refers to it in his own files. I read in the *Daily Telegraph*, some months ago, that Miss Gloria Morgan, formerly of Winchcombe Hall in Hampshire, had married a wealthy mine owner from South Africa, and had subsequently emigrated to that country. Perhaps there she will find happiness at last, and be able to cast off those dark events of that cruel winter of '88.

THE VANISHING OF THE ATKINSONS

Eric Brown

It is more than likely that 1888 was also the year of "The Hound of the Baskervilles", perhaps Holmes's most famous case, and not a decade later as popularly recorded. Holmes was initially unable to venture to Dartmoor, and sent Watson in his stead. Holmes claimed he was involved in a blackmail case, which may be true, but it is also likely that he was being consulted over the Jack the Ripper murders. There have been many attempts to account for Holmes's involvement in that investigation, all of them, I believe, apocryphal. It is my belief that Holmes rapidly solved those murders to his own satisfaction and left Scotland Yard to bring the investigation to a conclusion, so that he could throw himself fully into the Baskerville problem.

Also at the time was the case of "The Sign of Four" in which Watson met and fell in love with Mary Morstan. They were married soon after, at the close of 1888. Watson moved out of the Baker Street apartments and also set himself up in a practice in Paddington. For a while Holmes continued his investigations on his own and it was not until March 1889 that the two were reunited in "A Scandal in Bohemia".

Watson only later came to learn of some of the cases that Holmes investigated on his own. Amongst them was the tragedy of the Atkinson brothers. Although Watson later wrote this up he never sought its publication. Some years ago a copy of this came to my attention and my colleague, Eric Brown, has made it suitable for publication.

I had not seen my friend Sherlock Holmes for some months, pressure of work on both our parts curtailing the niceties of social intercourse, and it was quite by chance that he happened to be in his chambers when I called upon him that evening.

"Watson!" Holmes declared as Mrs Hudson showed me into the room. "Take a seat, my friend. I trust the winter is not too inclement for you?"

I warmed my hands before the fire, and then accommodated myself in the proffered armchair. I made some comment or other to the effect that the winters were becoming even colder of late, which set my friend on the course of a lengthy speculation upon the subject of world meteorology, climatology, and allied topics.

I helped myself to a brandy and settled in for the evening.

By and by my friend recounted examples of severe weather he had encountered upon his many and divers travels. My interest quickened; it is the one regret of our friendship that Holmes rarely sees fit to avail me of the incidents that befell him during his sojourn to points east during the period I have termed, in my accounts of my friend's illustrious career, the Great Hiatus.

That night he was vague in the details of his travels, but at one point he did say: "Of course I had experience of the monsoon when I travelled from Tibet, south to Ceylon to revisit an old friend –"

I leaned forward, pouncing upon his use of the word "revisit". "Why, Holmes, do you mean to say that you visited the island before '94?"

My friend realized his mistake at once, and gestured with feigned unconcern. "A trifling affair at Trincomalee in '88 –"

"You actually worked on a case out there?" I expostulated. "But why haven't you mentioned this before?"

"An affair of little account and even less interest, Watson. And anyway, I was sworn to utmost secrecy by the Royal Ceylonese Tea Company. As I was saying, concerning the nature of the monsoon rains . . ."

Whereupon the affair at Trincomalee was dismissed by my friend in his desire to expound upon the subject of the Asiatic rains.

Towards midnight I took my leave and, during the course of the next few weeks, went about my business with hardly a thought for that evening's exchange.

I had quite forgotten about the affair when, one month later, I called upon my friend and found him at home. He showed me to the fire and urged to help myself to a snifter of brandy.

At length he gestured with a long, languid hand to a letter lying open on the table beside his chair.

"Do you recall that upon your last visit I mentioned a small affair at Trincomalee, Ceylon, and the injunction placed upon my mentioning the case by the Royal Ceylonese Tea Company?"

I sat up, quite excited. "Of course," said I. "But what of it?"

"It appears that the injunction no longer pertains, Watson," Holmes said casually. "Three weeks ago I received a letter from my friend out there, informing me that the Company has fallen

upon bad times and gone bankrupt – and so the last obstacle to
my telling of the tale is no more."

He proceeded to fill his pipe with tobacco from the battered
slipper he kept wedged down the side of his armchair. Soon we
were enveloped in a pungent blue fug; I took a sip of brandy and
made myself an audience, as I had on many an occasion before,
to my friend's oratorical skills.

"You recall the extraordinary case of the *Gloria Scott*, wherein I
was called to the aid of my university friend, Victor Trevor?"

"I most certainly do," I said. It had been one of the cases I had
written up during Holmes's long absence from these shores.

"For many years," he said, "I lost contact with Trevor. At length I
heard through a mutual friend that he had set sail for Ceylon, with
the idea of managing a tea plantation or some such. Whatever, I
heard no more . . . No more, that is, until the year of '88, when I
received a letter from my old friend, couched in such terms that
made it obvious he was in need of my assistance. Indeed, he almost
begged my presence on that far away island, and even went so far
as to include a return ticket on a cutter of the East India Line and
promise of payment for my troubles upon my arrival. He went on
to outline the details of a case that had baffled himself and his
employers, the Royal Ceylonese Tea Company, for a good three
months.

"Those details I found curious enough, and the pleas of my
friend sufficient to warrant a trip to those tropical latitudes. You
probably never missed me, my dear Watson, being too occupied
with other things at the time: it was shortly after your marriage that
I put my affairs in order, packed my bags and set sail aboard the
Eastern Empress. For the duration of the voyage I absorbed myself
in the analysis of the details of the case presented to me in Trevor's
somewhat hasty missive.

"The brothers Atkinson, Bruce and William, were neighbours
of Victor Trevor in Ceylon. They had left England some ten years
before, and set sail for the Far East with the intention of making
their fortunes. For a decade they worked for the Royal Ceylonese
Tea Company at various locations around the island, for the last two
years managing an estate of some one hundred native workers near
Trincomalee. They were by all accounts gentlemen of upstanding
and personable character, well liked by both the Ceylonese and the
expatriate community of fellow planters and other businessmen. My
friend Victor Trevor was a regular social visitor to the plantation; in
his own words the brothers were the salt of the earth". They never
married – a situation not uncommon among those of their chosen
vocation – and lived for their work. They had no enemies.

"Their disappearance was as sudden as it was mysterious. It occurred presumably in the early hours of 1 February: suffice to say, they were seen by their house-boy prior to turning in the night before, but in the morning they were gone. They did not appear for breakfast at six, nor show up to do their rounds of the plantation at seven. Their absence was reported to the Colonial Police at Trincomalee at nine o'clock that morning, and it was not until noon that my friend Trevor heard of their disappearance. He headed over to the plantation and arrived minutes before a Sergeant from the police. Together they searched the house, and found nothing to suggest anything amiss other than a broken gas lamp and an overturned table in the lounge room. The investigating officer suggested that these were suspicious, indicative of a struggle and foul play, but Trevor noted that the table had been positioned near an open window through which the wind disturbed a heavy curtain. It was conceivable that the wind had caused the damage.

"They searched the plantation, and even the neighbouring country, but found nothing and no one. They questioned the under-managers and local workers, who reported nothing suspicious or noteworthy. From that day, 1 February 1887, to the day Trevor penned the letter, the brothers Atkinson had neither been seen nor heard. It was as if they left the house that morning and vanished from the face of the earth.

"Of course, Trevor's account was selective and inconclusive – there was much that I wished to know of the affairs of the brothers before I might begin to give an opinion on the case. By the time the *Eastern Empress* docked at the port of Jaffna I was eager to set about my investigations.

"Victor Trevor met me on the quay, and we drove south in his trap to Trincomalee. The passage of time had done little to take the shine off the youth of my university friend, and for the duration of the journey we exchanged information concerning our exploits during the intervening years. I was to stay at the Atkinson's plantation itself, which Trevor was overseeing in the absence of the brothers. It was late by the time we arrived, and I had little time to question my friend as to the details of the case before he suggested that we turn in and discuss the reason for my presence in the morning.

"The miracle of dawn in those climes, Watson! I was up early the following morning to witness the rapid transformation from night to day from my verandah. One minute the land was clothed in darkness, the next a golden sunlight exposed the deep shadows of the valleys and the bright green expanse of the tea bushes. My friend was already risen, and we partook breakfast – excellent kippers and poached eggs – around the vast oak table of the dining room.

"'I see the brothers Atkinson were fond of a game of cards,' I observed, gesturing to the table-top. 'Bridge, if I am not mistaken.'

"'Your powers of deduction are as sharp as ever,' Trevor remarked. 'Recall how you amazed my father upon that first meeting? Now, an explanation, if you please.'

"'Simplicity itself: observe the marks of wear upon the polish of the table-top. Note the scuff mark where a hand would be picked up, and the two smaller indentations at either side of where the pack resides at the centre of the table, made when the pack would be lifted at the end of a hand.'

"'Remarkable.'

"'Further, three of the four players are right-handed, the fourth not so. This much is obvious from the slight groves in the patina of the polish, worn either to the right or left of the player. You are left-handed, Victor, and I deduce therefore that you were a frequent guest on bridge nights.'

"'Twice a week for the past two years, Holmes,' said he shaking his head.

"'I can tell, also, that penny bets were placed upon the outcome of the games. The scratches here and there attest to that.'

"At this my friend coloured. 'Why,' he blustered, 'you're right, Holmes. A little wager added interest to the contests.'

"'I am not a gambling man myself,' I said. 'I find that the scientific analysis of the pursuit results in the fact that one can never win, only break even, except when luck intervenes. And I have never been one to trust in the happy felicity of luck.'

"We finished our breakfast, and I asked then to be shown around the house, and expressed the desire to questions the Atkinsons' head house-boy and house-keeper.

"Victor showed me into the lounge, a spacious room affording a magnificent panorama across the sun-soaked terraces of the estate. Hanging above the fireplace was an oil painting of the brothers, tall, flaxen-haired men in the middle-thirties, posing with their rifles on either side of a prostrate tiger.

"'I have left everything in place, as found on the morning of the brothers' disappearance. Observe the table and gas-lamp.'

"As Trevor had mentioned in the letter, there were no suspicious circumstances to be drawn from the toppled table and lamp. A wind stirring the curtains through the open window might easily have occasioned the damage.

"'Were the doors locked upon the night of the disappearance?' I asked.

"'It is uncommon in these parts to take the precaution of locking doors. If we trust our staff, then we see no need . . .'

"We passed through the house from room to room, and I noticed nothing amiss or noteworthy as we did so. At length we stood upon the verandah and gazed out over the verdant hills of the estate. 'Tell me, Victor – were the brothers in the habit of taking hikes, or taking off on travels without notifying friends and staff?'

"'Most certainly not. They had the interests of the estate at heart. They were most conscientious in the running of the business. They would go nowhere without first notifying one of their managers. Twice a year they took a boat up to Madras to call on acquaintances for a week, at Christmas and again six months later at the end of June.'

"'So therefore their disappearance in February cannot have been simply a trip to Madras?'

"'Of course not! We checked this possibility at the shipping office in Trincomalee.'

"'Which company did the brothers use for their voyages to India?'

"'The Modras Line. They have offices in town.'

"'I might call upon them myself in the course of my investigation,' said I.

"The house-boy was summoned from the kitchen, and I questioned him upon the verandah. The 'house-boy' proved to be no boy at all, but a tiny, wizened Tamil in his fifties at least. He was polite and informative, but could shed no light on the mysterious vanishing of his employers. I ran the gamut of usual questions, from whether he noticed anything amiss on the night in question – he had not – to whether the brothers were liked and respected, which they were. Finally I asked: 'What, in your opinion, has become of Master Bruce and William?'

"At this his eyes filled with tears, and he murmured, 'I fear for their lives, Mr Holmes.'

"'You do, and why is this?'

"The little Tamil shook his head. 'Their spirits are abroad at night,' said he.

'I exchanged a glance with Trevor. 'They are? And what makes you so certain?'

"'Myself, I have not heard or seen them – but my kitchen boys report hearing their wails in the night from the hills around. Their spirits haunt the estate and will do so until their enemies are brought to justice.'

"I considered his words for some minutes, my thoughts entertaining dark possibilities in the bright sunlight of that equatorial country, whereupon I dismissed the house-boy and turned to Trevor.

"'And what, my friend do you make of that?'

"'Poppycock, Holmes! Superstition of the first water. There are no people on Earth more given to such flights of fancy than the natives of this island. They probably heard the trumpeting of an elephant and drew conclusions.'

"'Perhaps I might have a word with the house-keeper?'

"Trevor informed me that the girl employed by the brothers at the time of their disappearance was no longer in service here. 'She is pregnant, and shortly after the brothers' disappearance took ill. For the past three months she has been bed-ridden in a bungalow on the edge of the estate – the brothers hired a doctor in the early stages of her pregnancy, when she first showed signs of weakness. The doctor has attended her ever since. Later, if you wish, we might visit her and see what she can add to your investigations. Now, perhaps I could show you around the estate before the sun is at its height? I have my morning rounds to do anyway. If you would care to join me . . .'

"We took a trap along the rutted tracks excavated through the red soil of the estate. From time to time Trevor reigned the horse to a holt, climbed down and engaged native workers in long minutes' conversation. One hour before noon, with the sun beating down like some heavenly furnace, Trevor pulled up on the very perimeter of the estate, jumped down and strode through the knee-high bushes to address a worker bent over in inspection of the soil. While Trevor was thus occupied, and despite the fierce attention of the sun, I elected to leave the canopied shade of the trap and take a stroll.

"I inspected a number of tea plants, about which, over the course of my botanical investigations, I have come to know a little. At length I repaired to Trevor's side, interested in the involved conversation he was conducting with the worker. They were discussing the state and composition of the soil. At one point I interrupted. 'Might this account for the state of the plants in this area?' I enquired.

"'I didn't know you were a botanist too, Holmes,' said Trevor.

"'I've gleaned a passing knowledge of the science in my reading over the years,' said I. 'And these plants seem, if I am not mistaken, to be suffering from *Elsinoe thaea* – or mottle scab.'

"The manager nodded. 'And not only in this area, Mr Holmes. Fully half the estate is blighted.'

"Trevor swung his arm to indicate a broad swathe of land on the periphery of the plantation. 'The entire eastern sector will not produce this season,' said he. 'I closed down the whole area when I took charge in February, locked the outbuildings where the tea was stored for drying, and ensured that no-one approached these terraces, for fear of spreading the scab.'

"'Do you think that the Atkinsons were aware of the disease before they vanished?' I asked.

"Trevor considered the question before replying. 'It is possible, Holmes; indeed probable.' He was silent awhile.' Why?' he asked at length. 'Do you think that this might have some bearing on the case?'

"'It is too early to say,' I opined. 'But certainly it is a factor to be taken into consideration.'

"We had been joined, there upon the hillside, by a knot of curious native workers. They spoke rapidly in their own tongue, Sinhalese, upon which Trevor seemed to lose his temper and snap at them in their language. They fell immediately silent and appeared shame-faced.

"'What were they saying?' I asked.

"'Yet more superstitious claptrap,' Trevor said. 'They claim that six months ago, just after Bruce and William vanished, they heard the waiting of their spirits in this benighted sector. Complete rubbish, of course.'

"In due course we took our leave and drove east, towards the town of Trincomalee. 'The estate spreads over some five square miles,' Trevor informed me. 'The easternmost area, bordering the town, is where the locals have their abodes. The Atkinson's housekeeper is interned in the hospital bungalow.'

"Presently we came upon the hospital, but to grace the rude timber construct with such a title was optimistic in the extreme. It was little more than a shed occupied by four beds, only one of them taken. The doctor, an Indian in his eighties, showed us across to the girl, one Anya Amala. 'Two minutes only, sirs,' he said. 'The girl is most seriously weakened.'

"She was a small thing barely out of her teens, with a sheen of perspiration laid across her dusky brow. She eyed our approach with something like apprehension, and as I took a seat beside the bed I was at pains to put her at ease.

"'I wish only to ask a few simple questions,' I began. 'I will not detain you for long.'

"She glanced like a frightened animal from the doctor, to Trevor, and finally back to myself. She nodded, licking her lips nervously.

"'How long have you worked for the brothers?' I enquired.

"In a whisper so soft it was almost inaudible, she said, 'I have worked for William and Bruce almost two years, sir. They have been good and kind employers. I am most very upset when they disappear.'

"'Workers on the estate are of the opinion that the brothers are dead, Anya. What do you think on this matter?'

"She shook her head, and the movement dislodged tears which fell from her massive eyes and rolled down her brown cheeks. 'I . . . I – oh, I cannot imagine this terrible thing!'

"I patted her hand. 'There, there. We are doing all we can to resolve the situation.'

"The doctor gestured that the girl had had enough, and after thanking her for her time we took our leave.

"We returned to the house and had lunch in the shade of the verandah, after which I retired to my room and slept in the heat of the day. Dinner that night was a formal occasion attended by a few local planters and their wives. The case, of course, was the main topic of conversation, and a dozen wild and extravagant theories were proposed to explain the state of affairs.

"'It is quite obvious to me,' said one dowager, the wife of a retired planter, 'that the Atkinsons were facing a financial crisis and decided to abscond. They left like thieves in the night, and might at this very moment be enjoying the high life in Kuala Lumpur.'

"'Stuff and nonsense,' someone responded. 'All the boats from the island have been investigated. The brothers were upon none of them.'

"'But you do concede, do you not, that the brothers were capable of such duplicity?'

"An uneasy silence descended upon the gathered company. It is always unsettling to have suspicion pointed at erstwhile friends of hitherto impeccable reputation.

"Presently the conversation turned to matters colonial, and I excused myself and retired to my room.

"The following morning after breakfast I told Trevor that I wished to visit Trincomalee, and he arranged a trap and driver to transport me there.

"Trincomalee is a small town with stone-built, colonial buildings dominating the main street, and ruder constructions comprising the outskirts. I stepped down from the trap on the main street, which follows the length of the ridge for some hundred yards. I decided that my first port of call should be the Colonial Police headquarters, an imposing building difficult to miss. After negotiating the interminable bureaucracy that maintains in such institutions, I was finally shown into the office of one Sergeant Mortimer, the officer in charge of the Atkinson investigation.

"'Mr Holmes,' he said, rising from his desk to shake my hand. 'I heard that you were on the case. I must confess that I should be most grateful for any light you might shed on this dreadful matter I don't mind confessing that the affair has me baffled.' He dealt me a penetrating look. 'Might I ask how your investigations proceed?'

"I told him that I had been on the island just over one day, and that thus far I had learnt little. 'I would be pleased to hear your opinions on the case,' I said. 'There is a rumour doing the rounds that the Atkinsons' estate was falling, and rather than face the wrath of the owners, the brothers fled the country.'

"The Sergeant pursed his lips in contemplation. 'Well, the estate was not doing that well – that much I can attest. But to be perfectly honest I could not see the brothers' taking the cowards' way out and absconding. To cover that possibility, I had men posted at all the ports for two weeks following their disappearance.'

"'Have you in the course of your investigations looked into their financial situation?'

"'Of course. I made comprehensive enquiries at the local bank. They were overdrawn to the tune of some £1,000. The brothers . . . how can I put it? . . . the brothers were rather fond of an occasional flutter, shall we say?'

"'By that I take it that they played, and lost, at cards?'

"'So I have heard,' Seageant Mortimer said. 'But I enquired as to whether they had outstanding gambling debts, and so far as I could discover, such was not the case. The whole affair baffles me, Mr Holmes.'

"'Might they have been taken from the house and murdered by enemies?' I suggested.

"'If they had enemies,' the Sergeant said, 'then I might entertain the notion. But I knew the brothers well, and aside from their predilection towards gambling, they were as moral a pair as could be found. They did not have a detractor in the world.'

"We discussed the matter further, but I discovered no more details relevant to the affair, and in due course I thanked the Sergeant and took my leave.

"I decided to look in on the offices of the Madras Line, situated in a nearby weatherboard building. A harassed female clerk in a bright red sari barely glanced up at me as she busily copied out invoices. I introduced myself and stated my business. She was most brusque in her reply. 'The ledgers are piled over there,' she replied in the sing-song English of her people. 'Why don't you look for yourself?'

"I bit my tongue and began the arduous business of going through the records of tickets sold during the relevant period. Needless to say, I discovered nothing – as if, I told myself, the brothers would have booked tickets under their own names!

"I returned to the unfriendly clerk and requested to see the manager. The woman looked up and smiled at me. 'I am the manager, Mr Holmes,' said she.

"'In that case I would like to ask you a few questions, Madam.'

"For the next ten minutes I managed to extract answers from this impertinent soul – an operation as onerous as attempting to draw blood from a stone. For my pains, I learned that the brothers had not bought tickets from the Madras Line since the Christmas before, when they had taken their customary week's holiday with friends in India.

"I thanked the manager for her estimable courtesy and stepped out into the street.

"I was about to return to the waiting trap, with little accomplished, when I noticed across the street the boarded up windows of a building upon which a faded, painted sign advertised passenger ships to various destinations around the Indian sub-continent and Malaya.

"I entered the shop next door, a bicycle repair establishment, and asked how long the shipping office had been closed. The owner considered and duly answered that the business had gone into liquidation six months earlier.

"'Do you have any idea as to the whereabouts of its erstwhile manager?' I asked.

"'He is working as the deputy-manager at the Post Office,' I was told, and to these venerable premises I duly made my way.

"There, an ancient Tamil identified himself as the one-time proprietor of the shipping office. He proceeded to regale me with a catalogue of his mercantile misfortunes, until I could redirect his conversation towards more germane matters.

"'I would surely have recalled if either of the Atkinsons had bought a ticket,' he said, 'especially in light of subsequent events.'

"'As I suspected,' I murmured to myself. 'Thank you for your time.'

"'However,' he went on. 'I do recall an occasion when someone from the Atkinsons' estate purchased two one-way tickets for Calcutta. I thought nothing of it at the time, though since I have wondered if it were at all relevant . . .'

"'Can you describe this person?' I asked.

"He shook his head with an affect of great sadness. 'I am an old man, and my memory for faces fails me . . . However, I do recall that it was a young Sinhalese, and I wondered at the time now an estate worker might come by funds enough to purchase two such tickets.'

"'Can you recall the departure date of these tickets?' I asked.

"'Now let me think,' said the old man, rubbing his bristled chin. 'Perhaps, if my memory serves me, around the middle of February.'

"The middle of February, I mused: just two weeks after the disappearance of the brothers Atkinson.

"I thanked this veritable sage for his information and made my way to the waiting trap, confident that at last my enquiries were bearing fruit.

"More news awaited me upon my return to the estate. It was late afternoon and Trevor was seated upon the verandah with the first drink of the day at his elbow. 'Will you join me in a sundowner, Holmes?' said he. He despatched a boy with orders to fetch a second drink. 'And how went your inquiries?'

"'As well, if not better, than expected.' I told him about the tickets purchased by the worker from this very estate.

"'In that case the affair is solved!' Trevor cried. 'The brothers left upon the boat bound for Calcutta!'

"'I rather think not,' said I. 'You see, Sergeant Mortimer had men checking all the ships leaving the island for two weeks after their disappearance.'

"'Then what the deuce became of them?'

"We sat in silence for some minutes before Trevor recalled that he had news to impart. 'By the way, Holmes, you'll be glad to learn that the Anya girl gave birth at noon today. Mother and child fit and well. A little boy, so I'm told.'

"I lowered my drink. 'I would like to pay them another visit,' I said.

"Trevor stared at me. 'I didn't have you down as a sentimental type, Holmes!' he laughed.

"'I assure you that my interest is purely professional,' I said. 'I suggest that we make haste.'

"Trevor eyed me dubiously. 'Very well, Holmes. If you insist.'

"He called the boy to ready the trap, and five minutes later we were rolling down the hillside towards the hospital bungalow.

"I took the opportunity to broach a rather delicate issue. 'Trevor,' said I, as my friend manhandled the reins and we rounded a sharp bend. 'I learned today that the brothers were in debt, and moreover were rather partial to an occasional flutter.'

"I recalled my friend's reaction, the day before, when I observed that their card games involved the exchange of money. 'I put it to you that you played the brothers at cards for more than mere pennies.'

"Trevor stiffened. He would not even glance at me. 'You're right, Holmes. I should have known better than to hope you might not find out . . .'

"'How much did you win from them over the course of your encounters?'

"Trevor huffed and puffed for some time, before muttering, 'Some £500, all told.'

"'Very well. That is all I wished to know. You obviously had an agreement, and after all the game was conducted between gentlemen.'

"We continued the ride in uneasy silence. In due course we arrived at the hospital and hurried inside. The elderly doctor showed us to Anya's bed, beside which was a crib bearing the newborn baby.

"One glance at the infant was sufficient to confirm my suspicions. Beside me, Trevor gasped. 'Good God, man! I never thought . . .'

"The sleeping child had skin a tone lighter than his mother's, though that was not the clincher. The boy also possessed a fine head of luxuriant blond curls.

"From the bed, Anya was staring at us, tears falling from her massive eyes.

"'Bruce,' I asked her, 'or William?'

"It was some minutes before she could master her emotions and bring herself to reply. 'Young master William,' she said. 'We were in love. He promised that when our baby was born, we would go away, far from here, and start a new life together.'

"She broke down in another fit of tears, and I glanced at Trevor.

"'But does this have any bearing on their whereabouts?' he asked.

"'I think perhaps it might.' I turned to the young girl. 'I take it, Anya, that you conducted your affair with William elsewhere than the house?'

"She nodded, sobbing. At last she said, 'We met every second day, at six, at the bungalow on MacPherson's Hill.'

"'To MacPherson's Hill at once!' I said to Trevor.

"Anya grabbed my arm. 'William, Mr Holmes! Do you think . . .?'

"I feared the worst, but of course did not inform her. 'We can but hope and pray,' I told her without conviction.

"We lost no time and hurried from the hospital. Trevor drove us at breakneck speed across the estate, each passing minute taking us higher and higher into the green-clad hills.

"'I wish you'd tell me what you fear and suspect, Holmes!' he cried. 'I am almost beside myself with worry!'

"'I cannot be certain,' I told him, 'but I rather think that all is far from well.'

"We came upon a rise, and Trevor indicated a small timber bungalow situated a hundred yards further along the ridge. He whipped the horse to greater speed and seconds later we careered to a halt outside the bungalow. We jumped down and made our way into the building.

"I looked about the tiny sitting room, while Trevor reconnoitred the adjacent sleeping chamber. 'Holmes!' came the sudden cry.

"I hurried into the bedroom and beheld, placed upon the counterpane in the centre of the bed, a hastily scrawled note.

"I picked up the note and read it. 'Much as I supposed,' I said to myself, passing Trevor the paper.

He read aloud: 'My Dear Anya – make haste to Master Trevor with this note. Trevor – for Godsake help us! We were taken by bandits three mornings back. They hold us in the hills, demanding a ransom of some £500, to be left beside the well on Chatterjee Hill. If constables are present, they threaten to kill us. Trevor, I implore you – pay the ranson and we will reimburse you in due course. Please look after Anya until our release.'

"Signed, William and Bruce Atkinson.

"'But of course,' said I, 'the day after the brothers disappeared, Anya fell ill and could not make the usual rendezvous.'

"'Good God, man,' Trevor cried. 'What tragedy. They might lie dead with their throats cut as we speak. But what now? Do I go ahead and deliver the ransom?'

"'I rather think that it is too late in the day for that,' I said.

"'The kidnappers have despatched them already?'

"I refrained from answering him, but strode outside and climbed into the trap. Trevor rushed after me.

"I said, 'You mentioned yesterday that six months ago, shortly after the brothers disappeared, you locked the outbuildings on the eastern fringes of the estate –'

"'This I did. But I hardly see . . .'

"'Get your men to open every one and search them thoroughly. Time is of the essence.'

"We returned to the house, and Trevor ordered his men to do as I willed. He distributed keys, and we once again boarded the trap and made for the eastern sector.

"Fifteen minutes later we heard a cry from a native worker not 200 yards distant. He was standing with a crowd of other men outside the open double-doors of a storage shed. They stared into the dark interior, seemingly too fearful to enter.

"We hurried across and approached the shed, and the noisome

stench that assailed my nostrils confirmed my gravest fears. Covering our lower faces with 'kerchiefs, we cautiously entered the storage shed.

"Two bodies, dressed in tropical garb, were sprawled out across the floor. The heat of the shed had advanced their decay past the point of easy recognition. Trevor gagged and retched and hurried outside.

"'I swear,' he said at last, 'I swear to bring to justice the dogs responsible for this!'

"'Look no farther than the two men lying dead,' said I.

"'What!' he cried.

"'Trevor, my friend – *there were never any kidnappers*, except in the wily imaginings of the brothers' minds. This is indeed a tragic business.'

"'Do you mean to say . . .' he gestured at the corpses of his erstwhile friends, speechless.

"'They manufactured the whole sorry business, Trevor,' I said. 'They had gambling debts; their estate was failing . . . they took the cowards' way out and came up with this disastrous plan to extract from you the £5,000. Of course they would never have reimbursed you – they planned to take the money and leave behind them their debts and the failed estate, leave in disguise by the ship to Calcutta and start a new life with their criminal gains. Of course, they were thwarted by ill-luck: they were not to know that Anya would fall ill, or that you would happen by this shed and inadvertently lock them inside. These buildings are sturdy constructs; they had no hope of escape.'

"'Good God,' Trevor cried, stricken. 'Their cries! Those banshee wails reported by the workers . . .'

"'It was this detail that made me suspicious,' said I. 'I am a man of science, Trevor – I have no truck with ghosts and ghouls and such. Taken together with all the other small details of this case, the brothers' gambling debts, the failing estate, the tickets booked for Calcutta, and Anya's unforeseen illness . . . I began to see what tragedy might have occurred.'

"I left him pondering these terrible circumstances and made my way to the trap. At length Trevor hurried after me. 'But one thing puzzles me,' said he. 'You said that two tickets were booked for Calcutta – and yet Anya says that William promised that together they would head for India to start a new life . . .'

"I paused in the process of climbing into the trap, and stared Trevor directly in the eye.

"'There are two scenarios we can deduce from the facts as we know them,' I said. 'One, that William would indeed honour his professed love for Anya: once they had picked up the ransom money, Bruce would leave the island by some other means, and William would spirit Anya off to India –'

"'And the other?'

"'The other,' I said, 'is that William and Bruce were not the gentlemen you assumed; that they booked tickets for the two of them and planned to leave Anya here while they escaped with your £5,000.'

"'And which", asked Trevor, 'do you suppose is the truth?'

"I made a hopeless gesture. 'I would like to think, for Anya's peace of mind, that William intended to take her with him . . .'

"Trevor stared into the heavens, his countenance racked by anguish. 'Whichever,' said he, 'the company cannot have the truth of the matter spread far and wide! Why, the scandal . . . You must promise me, Holmes, that your lips are sealed.'

"'My friend,' said I, 'you have my assurance that I will breathe a word of the matter to no one.'"

Mr Sherlock Holmes paused to refill his pipe. "There the matter ended," said he. "And, but for this letter, the details of the case might never have been known."

"What did Trevor tell the company?"

Holmes inclined his aquiline head. "I advised him to destroy the spurious ransom note, and concoct a tale whereby the brothers went one morning to check the storage shed, were bitten by a snake or somesuch, and succumbed before they might summon help. Their bodies were accidentally locked in the shed and thus the tragedy went undiscovered for six long months."

"And what became of Anya?" I enquired.

"Ever the romantic, Watson!" Holmes smiled at me. "When I returned in '94, Anya was working for Trevor on his estate, and her son was a fit and healthy six year old. I even, you will be astonished to learn, left a certain sum in trust to go towards the upbringing and education of the boy."

His eyes twinkled at me as he reached for the bottle.

"Would you care for another brandy, Watson?" he asked.

THE ADVENTURE OF THE FALLEN STAR

Simon Clark

Holmes was never comfortable in the company of women. There is no evidence that he spent any social time with Watson and his wife after their marriage except for the very occasional call forced upon him by business. Only once did Holmes meet a woman whom he believed was his intellectual equal, and that was Irene Adler, whose case is recounted in "A Scandal in Bohemia".

It was after this case that Watson became closely involved with Holmes again, suggesting that either the gloss of his marriage had started to dull, or that Mary Morstan was remarkably understanding. For a period Holmes was involved in a number of small cases many of which he felt were important but lacked interest. Some were clearly bizarre. He refers to the Dundas separation case in which the husband had developed the habit of hurling his false teeth at his wife after every meal. None of these cases appear to have been written up, either because Watson was not around or Holmes rapidly lost interest in them. All that is, except one, "The Adventure of the Fallen Star". This began as one of those minor cases, which Holmes almost overlooked when he became wrapped up in "A Case of Identity", but soon after events unravelled themselves which presented Holmes a singularly unusual case. Its facts were unearthed by Simon Clark.

"My dear fellow, you are puzzled; admit it," demanded Sherlock Holmes, as we sat side-by-side in the four-wheeler being briskly driven through the maelstrom of foot, hoof and wheel that is the Strand on a Friday noon.

"Indeed I am, Holmes." I held up the stone, no larger than a grape, that he'd not two moments before handed to me. "You pass me a little pebble and ask me what I make of it."

"Yes."

"Well, I confess I make nothing of it." I smiled and shook my head. "Nothing at all."

"Ha! That's because although you look, you do not observe. Remember, Watson: detail, detail, detail."

"It has, I take it, a bearing on a case you are currently investigating?"

"Only partly. But he's a curious fellow, isn't he?"

"The stone?"

"Yes, the stone, lying there in the palm of your gloved hand." Holmes, in a playful mood, gave a devil of grin. "Come on, play the game, Watson. Read the stone. See its appearance, the markings upon its surface. Feel its weight. Gauge its constitution. If it pleases you, describe to me any clairvoyant vibration that may emanate from its stony heart."

"You are teasing me, Holmes."

"I am. Yes."

I raised a questioning eyebrow.

"Forgive me please, Doctor; I am teasing you, for the case I have taken is, if I'm not mistaken, nothing more than a tease, a practical joke, a whimsical prank."

"Then I am all in the dark."

"Ha! But soon all will be clear as day."

"What possessed you to accept such a case?"

"Normally, I wouldn't have glanced at it twice. However, I am acquainted with the gentleman involved."

"A friend?"

"Ah, I would describe you as my sole friend, Watson. This gentleman, although I have never yet met him in person, was of considerable service in the past when he furnished me with invaluable information on the constitution of certain metals, which enabled me to lay to rest the matter of the golden bullet murders in King's Lynne. In short, I owe him one small favour. By Jove! Look at that, London becomes busier by the day. Within a decade the city will become so congested the only sure transport will be by Shanks's pony!"

"Then at least our slow passage northwards to Hampstead will give you sufficient time to tell me the facts of the case before we reach the home of your client."

"Indeed it will. First, Watson, the stone! Pray focus your attention upon it. Read it as if it were the page from a book." With that my friend placed the tips of his long fingers together, closed his eyes; only the slight wrinkling of his forehead beneath the brim of his shiny top hat betraying he would listen closely to my every word.

I listed everything of significance I could discern from the stone. "Weight: let me see. An ounce, perhaps. Size: no larger than a grape. Shape: pear shaped. Colour: um, silvery. Odour: none.

Appearance: smooth as glass; subjected to intense heat, I would surmise."

"Where is it from?" asked Holmes without opening his eyes.

"A furnace I should suppose, before that I dare not say."

"Ha!" Holmes opened his penetrating eyes.

"You know where the stone originated?"

"Indeed. It came from the depths of the universe. The scorched appearance of the stone was caused by its headlong rush through our world's atmosphere. The speed being so great that the very air rubbing against the surface produced such tremendous temperatures those surfaces did in fact melt, hence the ablated base of the stone."

"Good Lord, then it is an aerolite?"

"Spot on, Watson. Yes, an aerolite, more commonly known as a shooting star or meteorite. Above us, in the heavens, are countless millions of stone fragments, whirling silently through the cold depths of space. Occasionally one falls to Earth. One might look up on a clear night and see the fiery trail one of these fragments makes. Only rarely do they reach the surface of the Earth."

I looked at our stony visitor from the heavens with more interest. "Then it's valuable?"

"Pooh, pooh, not in the least. A few shillings."

"But you say it has a bearing on the case?"

"Again I can only repeat partly. I brought it along as an introduction to the facts. This stone itself, I purchased along with a trunkful of other mineral samples many years ago." He took the stone from me, held it between the finger and thumb of his gloved hand, his face in profile to me, his striking aquiline features just inches from the stone as his heavy-lidded eyes gazed dreamily upon it. "Imagine though, Watson if you will. This slight chip of stone, so insignificant in appearance, has drifted between the stars for many millions of years. By chance it struck this world, where it whistled groundward in a fiery streak of light. Imagine if the stone were large enough for you and I to ride upon it as it flew high above continents and oceans. At night the lights of our great cities would shine like the dust of diamonds sprinkled upon black velvet. In those cities people live their lives – real people, Doctor! – not mere ciphers. There, sons of kings and paupers might lay awake at night vexed by worries, fears, jealousies. And in those cities housing million upon million of human souls there are enough men and women intent on crimes great and small to dizzy even the greatest statistician. Imagine if you will, Watson, our world revolving beneath you, like a classroom globe. And with every tick of the watch there are a thousand thefts; with every tock of the clock a dozen murders. Ha!" He tossed the stone into the air, deftly caught it in the palm of his hand, then slipped it into his waistcoat pocket. "So, Watson, why am I sitting here in a carriage, on this day in flaming June, sizzling like a Dover sole upon its griddle, engaged on such a trifling matter?"

"The acquaintance? A favour you mentioned?"

"Of course. The case is so slight we should have the solution long before we take afternoon tea, but this gentlemen is much troubled by the case. Inordinately so. And I dare say that you, being a medical man, are consulted by a great number of people with many a cough, coryza and pimple who, clearly to you, are not particularly ill but seek reassurance from a man with the power to allay their worries."

"Ah, this case . . ."

"Oh forgive me, Watson, please. You must know the facts. My acquaintance, by correspondence only, is one Professor Charles Hardcastle of Hampstead. He wrote to me a few days ago beseeching me to call on him as he feared his house was being periodically entered by an individual who, in the words of the professor, 'intends to visit an iniquitous injury upon the household.'"

"Then you are looking for a common burglar?"

"Perhaps."

"So it is a matter for the police?"

"Perhaps not."

"But something was stolen?"

"Stolen? No. Borrowed."

"Borrowed?"

"Barely, the facts are these, Watson. Professor Charles Hardcastle lives in a large house in Hampstead. It stands, he tells me, in expansive grounds. Living with him in the house are his wife and son, whom is ten years of age. Also residing there are the domestic staff. The professor specializes in metallurgical sciences and has long since being interested in aerolites which are often composed of metals such as iron and nickel. These are of particular significance to him because they are not of this Earth and he hopes to discover within them metals with singular properties. The man is forty years of age, modest, hard-working, financially secure and not given to any outrageous vices. Last Monday the professor worked late into the night in his laboratory, which is housed in a purpose-built annex that adjoins his home; there he conducted certain chemical tests on aerolites. The aerolites are locked in glass-fronted cabinets. The largest stone, which is no larger than a plum, occupies pride of place in the centre of one of these cabinets. At ten to midnight, with his experiment complete, he retired to bed, locking the stones into their cabinets, then carefully locking the door of the laboratory behind him. The laboratory can be accessed from the rear courtyard through twin stout doors which are bolted from within, and through a door which leads directly into the main house. Have you followed me so far?"

"It is very clear."

"If you remember Monday's was a hot, dry night. Professor Hardcastle, mindful of his wife's concerns that he doesn't neglect his stomach, took a little supper of milk and biscuits. Then he made his way to bed. Only then did he remember he'd left his pince-nez spectacles in the laboratory, and as he is quite short-sighted he returned to the laboratory to retrieve them. He unlocked the door that leads from the house to the laboratory and entered. As he picked the pince-nez from the bench he noticed that one of his glass-fronted cases lay open. And upon placing the pince-nez on his nose he immediately saw that the largest aerolite had been taken."

"There had been a forced entry?"

Holmes shook his head. "The door he had entered by was locked. So were the twin doors to the courtyard: locked and securely bolted. The windows all locked, too."

"An oversight then. He left the door to the house unlocked?"

"He's most particular to ensure it is locked. The laboratory contains many poisons and powerful acids. He states quite clearly in his letters it is his great fear that his son might find his way into the laboratory and injure himself playing with test-tubes and so forth. Therefore, he's most scrupulous in keeping the door locked."

"So that is the mystery?" I said.

He sighed, disappointed. "A very slight one, I'm afraid."

"That an intruder stole an aerolite, shooting star, call it what you will? And that he left no clue as to his entry?"

"But there the mystery thickens."

"Yes, you remarked the object wasn't stolen, merely borrowed?"

"Correct. The stone vanished on the Monday night between Professor Hardcastle locking the laboratory then returning to it to retrieve his pince-nez which, he gauges, to be an interval of forty minutes."

"When did the stone reappear?"

"It reappeared on the Wednesday morning on the son's bedside table."

I looked at Holmes in surprise then chortled. "Then it is a childish prank. The son took the stone. Carelessly he allowed it to be discovered."

Holmes smiled. "We shall see."

The carriage left the overheated chaos of central London behind. The air became fresher, although the carriage slower, as it climbed the steep hills toward Hampstead. The canyons of town houses and commercial premises gave way to the widely spaced villas and the great expanse of Heath that rolled away beneath a clear blue sky. The clip and clop of the horse became less frequent, too, as it toiled up that particularly steep lane that soars upward beside the prominent elevation of The Spaniard's Inn. Not more than a hundred yards beyond the inn Holmes directed the cabbie to make a sharp right turn into a driveway leading to a large redbrick villa. A single-storey annex of fresher red brick abutted one flank of the house.

The moment the four-wheeler entered the driveway the garden bushes parted and a man leapt from them. He roared with the ferocity of a lion. In his hand he carried a bunch of twigs which he shook at us with extraordinary ferocity.

"It is time!" bellowed the man. "*It is time!*"

I recoiled in shock. "Good heavens, the man is going to attack us."

He shouted repeatedly, "It is time! Dear God! It is time!"

"Take care, Holmes," I said as my friend ordered the driver to halt while simultaneously throwing open the door of the carriage. "The man is clearly dangerous."

"On the contrary, Watson. You'd rarely find highwaymen and footpads dressed in carpet slippers and well pressed trousers. This must be Professor Hardcastle. Oh. My good man, do be careful."

Professor Hardcastle ran forward, stumbling as he did so to his knees. He was panting. A look of such horror in his face that it aroused my immediate pity.

The man gasped, his face a vivid red beneath his blond hair. "It is time. It is time . . ."

He struggled unsteadily to his feet and held out his trembling hand. Clutched in his fingers were the fresh green sprigs of some plant. "Mr Holmes . . . it is Mr Holmes, isn't it . . . of course, it must." He struggled to master his breathing. Then more calmly he fixed us with a glittering gaze. "You see?" he said, looking from one to the other. "It's time." He repeated the sentence in a whisper, "It is time."

Holmes glanced at the plant, then to me. "Ah, I see. The professor is referring to *thyme*. He holds sprigs of the herb, thyme. And clearly he's had a dreadful shock. If you would be so good to lend a hand, Watson, we'll get the gentleman to his home, where perhaps brandy should help his poor nerves."

The brandy did indeed soothe the man's nerves. Once he'd dressed in a manner he deemed fully respectable, and we were seated in the morning room, he told Sherlock Holmes and I his story. At least he endeavoured to, for he was still in a state of shock. His hand trembled terribly. "Mr Holmes. Dr Watson. Dear sirs, I must apologize for my extraordinary behaviour earlier . . . but I've never experienced such a shock to my senses before . . . I was at my wit's end. I thought my only hope was to seize the scoundrel and strangle the life out him there and then in the garden. Oh! Mercy! But if only that were not impossible . . . *impossible!*"

Holmes said soothingly, "Professor Hardcastle. Take your good time, sir. But please tell me exactly what did happen this morning. Speak freely before Dr Watson here. I explained in my note to you he would attend this case with me."

"Of course. Of course." He breathed deeply to steady his rattled nerves. "I wrote to you concerning the missing aerolite and how it reappeared in my son's room. At the time I was alarmed, but after what happened this morning, I confess, I am terrified. For today, as I climbed the stairs to dress for our meeting, I was met by one of the maids who had been making up my son's bed. 'Excuse me, Professor,' she said to me. 'I found these on your son's bedside table.'"

"The aerolite once more?"

"Yes."

"And the sprigs of thyme?"

"Yes, arranged so the stone rested within like an egg inside a bird's nest. The moment I saw the stone and the thyme I don't believe I could have experienced a greater shock if I had been struck by lightning. Well, sirs . . . at that very instant I ran from the house dressed in nothing but trousers, waistcoat and carpet slippers. I'd been in my son's bedroom not ten minutes before so I knew the devil had only just placed the stone on the table."

"The devil?"

"Yes the devil, the demon . . . whatever damned title he must bear, because I tell you this, Mr Holmes, the man who left the aerolite and the thyme leaves in my son's room has been dead these last five years."

Sherlock Holmes smoked a small cigar as he spoke to a now less distraught Professor Hardcastle who sat in the armchair, the pince-nez upon his nose, his fingers tightly knitted, troubled thumbs pressing against each other. I sat upon a claret-coloured sofa, and, from time to time, made notes with pencil and paper.

For a moment, Holmes stood meditatively before the fireplace, which was vast enough to roast a whole side of mutton. Lost in thought, he smoked the cigar, blowing out jets of blue smoke, that were caught, even on this still summer's day, by the updraft flowing up the flue, and carried the tobacco smoke away up the huge gullet of the chimney. "Now, professor. A few questions first before we discuss your suggestion that the aerolite and the thyme where left in your son's bedroom by a deadman."

"Ask what you will, Mr Holmes."

"Exactly who was in the house at the time the aerolite made its second reappearance?"

"The domestic staff only. Mrs Hardcastle is calling on her mother in Chelsea. My son is at school."

"Day school then, he does not board?"

"No."

"Your son took the stone from your laboratory, plucked a few strands of thyme from the Heath, then left them so arranged bird's nest fashion for a prank."

"No."

"Why so certain? Boys of that age thrive on mischief."

"Edward is a perfectly healthy boy, capable of pranks and japes like the next."

"But?"

"But he didn't leave the stone."

"When we first saw you, you were crying out, 'It is thyme, it is thyme.'"

"Yes."

"Then it was the appearance of that particular herb that troubled you so?"

"Yes."

"And the appearance of the herb, alongside that piece of stone, has special significance for you?"

"Indeed." Professor Hardcastle sighed, perhaps in the same manner a person who has seen the portents of doom and destruction manifesting in frightful sharp relief about him. From his pocket he brought out a stone as large and as dark as a damson plum and placed it on a copy of *The Times* newspaper that lay upon a table. "This is the aerolite referred to in my letter. It is of little monetary value. In my collection it bears the name 'The Rye Stone', simply because that's where I found it all of three and twenty years ago. Then I was a boy of seventeen, yet already I had my life mapped out. I intended to make science my vocation, convinced as I was that mankind needed metals of ever-increasing strength for our machines, bridges and railways. At that time in Rye was a very famous and well respected astronomer, a one Dr Columbine, not a medical man you understand, but a man of science. He was the author of many books and papers. Astronomers from all over the world would travel just to speak with him. His lectures always delivered capacity audiences. I attended one such lecture in Rye and was entranced by the man's genius and his vision of the universe. He was a small man with red hair and fiery side whiskers. Indeed he was very small – dwarfish, you might say. Boys would taunt him in the street, all of which he took with good humour, I might add. Small and fiery is how I remember him. He spoke to the audience with that same fiery passion. His eyes would flash like lamps. I immediately enrolled in Rye's astronomical society of which he was its most illustrious member. By degrees I contrived to speak with him: I outlined my own ambitions. He listened carefully, then spoke enthusiastically, exhorting me not to rely on the preconceived ideas found in textbooks. And it was Dr Columbine who revealed to me that the Earth is inundated daily by seemingly heaven-sent pieces of metal ore from the depths of the universe. And couldn't these starborne metals hold the key to our producing new, improved alloys that might revolutionize our industries? Assiduously I began collecting aerolites, accumulating a splendid array of specimens. Then one June night as we worked at his observatory we witnessed the fall of such a shooting star. In high excitement we saw it drop to Earth just beyond the town. You might imagine our excited calls as we two, Dr Columbine in frock coat and hat, myself in blazer and cap, climbed over fences like jubilant school boys, as we sallied forth to find the stone."

"You say there were just the two of you?" said Holmes.

"Yes. We found the stone where it had fallen into a clump of wild thyme. It had struck the plants with sufficient force to bruise the leaves releasing the aroma of the herb into the warm evening air."

"I see."

"Briefly, to bring the story up to date," continued Professor Hardcastle, "I moved on to university and my studies. And Dr Columbine continued his work in astronomy. But that's when the tragedy occurred."

"Tragedy?"

"Yes. Some malady laid Dr Columbine down. I don't know its nature. But, with hindsight, it clearly resulted in some creeping destruction of the brain. It wasn't immediately apparent at the time but the public lectures became yet more fiery, and the man's ideas became even more astonishing. He embarked upon a plan to build the world's largest telescope, which would be constructed upon the peak of Mount Snowdon in Wales where the cleaner air at that altitude is far more conducive to astronomical observation. And with this telescope, of absolutely gargantuan proportions, he would be able to divine what lay at the innermost heart of our universe."

"Then the man may have been visionary, not ill in his mind?"

"At first we believed this was the case. That it was his vibrant genius alone that drove him to anger when his plans didn't quickly reach fruition. But then it became apparent to all that he was indeed ill. Ill psychologically. The years passed, yet not a month would go by without his former acquaintances receiving increasingly vicious letters demanding that we sponsor his scheme – with every penny we possessed if need be! Rumours circulated that Dr Columbine threatened eminent scientists with violence if they did not pledge to fund this impossibly large refracting telescope. Indeed, five years ago I received a letter from him, stating categorically that because I had not myself pledged financial support for this instrument he would see to it that he destroyed what I loved most in the world, because I and my fellow men of science had destroyed what he, Dr Columbine, loved most in his world, his dream to build the telescope."

"The man was clearly mad," I observed.

"Indeed."

Holmes said crisply, "You say you received this threatening letter five years ago. How did you respond?"

"Until that time I'd ignored all his earlier letters demanding sponsorship. On that occasion I reported the matter to the police."

"And?"

"They attempted to locate Dr Columbine, but by that time, yet unknown to me and my brethren, the man was penniless and all but resided in the gin shops of Whitechapel."

"The police failed to find him?"

"On the contrary, three months later a corpse was pulled from the Thames. It had been in the water so long its identity could only be discerned by the laundry label in the coat, giving the owner's name; oh! and there was also an inscribed pocket watch."

"Which, I take it," said Holmes blowing out a cloud of cigar smoke above his head, "gave every indication that the poor wretch found drowned in the Thames was none other than Dr Columbine?"

"Quite. The police were satisfied as to the identity of the body, which was later buried in a pauper's grave in Greenwich."

"And the threatening letters ceased to arrive. And no one saw hide nor hair of Dr Columbine?"

"Naturally, the man was dead."

"So the police surmised."

"Yes. What doubt could there be?"

"Every doubt. There's a gardener trimming your hedge wearing a pair of your boots. If he turned up in the Thames wearing those boots, and unrecognizable by any other evidence might not the police surmise that man was you, Professor?"

"Yes ... well of course, such a mistake might be made ... but ... good heavens how do you know the man is wearing a pair of my boots?"

Professor Hardcastle, eyes wide with astonishment behind the lenses of the pince-nez, turned to stare out of the window at the gardener, a man of around fifty years, who was scrupulously trimming privet just half a dozen yards beyond the window.

"Your gardener," continued Holmes, fingers lightly pressed together, "is recently married to a good woman of a character similar to his own, that is both are hard working and anxious to please. Both love each other dearly. Moreover, the man wears a pair of boots once owned by yourself."

Hardcastle squinted through his pince-nez at the boots. "Why? Yes. Yes. Those are – were my old boots. My wife, rather than throwing them out, would have seen that they were offered to Clarkson. And, yes, I found the man very eager to please, indeed anxious to give satisfaction for his wages, but how could you know that?"

Holmes smiled. "Gardeners don't wear such expensive boots while they work. If he could have afforded such a pair he would have saved them for 'Sunday best.' Also from the way the man hobbles quite painfully, they are far too small for him. Indeed they would, sir, fit someone with your size feet. A size seven."

"Ah, size eight."

"I think you'll find a trifle smaller. Nevertheless, the boots you gave him are too small, but rather than appearing ungrateful he makes a point of wearing them when you will notice."

"That is why he's wearing the boots so near the window?"

"Indeed so, and vigorously trimming a hedge that visibly requires no trimming. But he's keen to create a good impression. I dare say you'll find his more comfortable workboots concealed behind some nearby bush which he will change into once he's demonstrated his gratitude to you."

"And recently married?"

"Have you seen many a gardener with clothes so clean and trousers so carefully pressed? The wife is eager to please, too. And, he, in love with his wife, is so closely shaven that he has nicked his face four, five times. Now!" Holmes briskly rose from the chair and paced the room. As he did so, he appraised, with those two keen eyes of his, certain areas of the carpet, and paid particular attention to the crystal wine decanters on the table. Holmes continued, "My example of the gardener and his wearing another man's boots disposes, I believe, with the apparently insoluble problem of Dr Columbine returning from the dead to plague you. Evidently, another man wore his coat and possessed his watch when he unfortunately fell in the Thames. Either stolen or purchased from the Doctor."

"Then Columbine is alive?"

"Yes." Holmes picked the aerolite from the table and held it between forefinger and thumb. "That is, if he were the only man to know that you found The Rye Stone in a patch of thyme?"

"Yes, he was . . . its place of landing is irrelevant to my experiments. I never once mentioned it to another living soul."

"But not irrelevant to this case. As you realized, most powerfully, when you saw the sprigs of thyme and the stone together. That little conjunction of herb and stone was nothing less than a message to you, sir, from Dr Columbine, which states plainly: Professor Hardcastle, I am alive. I have not forgotten my threat. I have the ability to come and go into your home at will. Now I am merely biding my time before I strike."

"My son?"

"Specifically, your son. He will murder your son in his bed within forty-eight hours."

The man's face turned white as paper. "Oh, heavens, what a horrible prediction. How can you know that?"

"I will return tomorrow morning whereupon. I will explain everything?"

"But my son is under a sentence of death. What you've told me is unspeakably cruel."

"But necessary. When I return to tomorrow I will do my utmost to save your son – but we are dealing not just with a madman, but a man who is uncommonly intelligent."

"Please don't go."

"I must make some very necessary preparations. But first please pass me the sprig of thyme from the table. Thank you, Professor."

For a moment we sat there, I upon the sofa, the professor perched unhappily on the edge of the armchair, his wide eyes watching Holmes's every move.

Holmes, took the sprig of herb to the window where the light was brightest. He gazed at the stem, then the leaves of the plant, in the peculiar introspective fashion which was characteristic of him. "It is *Thymus serpyllum*, more commonly known as wild thyme, a mat-forming undershrub, prevalent in dry grassy places, particularly

heaths; its flowers possessing rounded heads of a reddish-purple."
He lifted the plant to his nostrils. "Quite aromatic." He looked
closely at the plant's stalk. "Evidently the plant is Dr Columbine's
calling card; he intended it to be so. But let us see if . . . ah, yes!"
said he in a tone suggesting a puzzle solved. "Let us see if the plant
tells us a little more than Columbine intended." Taking one of his
own calling cards from his pocket, Holmes placed it face down on
a small table by the window. Then quickly drawing a Swiss Army
knife from his trouser pocket he opened a glittering blade and
gently scraped one of the plant's small leaves.

"Mr Holmes, what is it?" asked the professor, anxiously. "What
have you found?"

"Just one moment, sir."

"You mentioned the plant occurs on heathland. Then the
madman must have plucked it from Hampstead Heath which is
across the road from my home."

"Ah, not necessarily, Professor. The plant is yielding a clue to
as its origins."

From what I could see, tiny particles had fallen from the leaf
when scraped, which peppered the white calling card with black.
Holmes peering at these most closely, carefully drew the flat of his
penknife blade from left to right across the card.

"In fact," said Holmes crisply. "The plant was taken from alongside
the railway track that leads into King's Cross station, which is served
by The Great Western Railway company."

"But how . . . I don't understand." The professor shook his head
bemused.

"Professor, you will of course know that locomotives eject not
only soot and smoke from the their funnels, but small fragments
of unburnt coal. English coal is hard and does not leave any
appreciable mark on paper; Welsh coal, however, is quite different.
It is very soft and leaves a rich mark when drawn across paper –
as richly dark as an artist's charcoal. Here, I see many grit-like
particles of coal adhering to the leaves of this plant. This tells
me it was plucked close to a railway line. The coal is indeed
Welsh – please note the black marks it has left on my calling
card. Therefore, I conclude the plant was picked close to the
broad gauge track which serves King's Cross station. The Great
Western Railway company being the only company to exclusively
use Welsh coal to power its locomotives. I'd conclude, therefore,
that the unfortunate Dr Columbine lives the life of a vagrant close
by the aforementioned railway track."

"Yes," said the professor a trifle dazed. "But what course of action
do we take now? How can we find the man?"

Instead of immediately replying, Holmes held up his hand for a moment, which caused both the Professor and I to lean forward expectantly, sensing Holmes had seen something of great relevance within the room. I tried to follow that razor sharp gaze; however, I discerned nothing amiss. Holmes continued briskly: "Leave that to me, Professor. I will alert my contacts and they will search every gin shop, ale house and railway arch until the man is found. Dwarfish, you say, with bushy red hair and sideburns?"

"Yes."

"Come, Watson. There's no time to lose."

The professor was clearly anguished at being abandoned there to the mercy of the madman for yet another night. "But what if he returns tonight?"

"He will not?"

"You can be so sure?"

"Yes."

"How?"

"Explanations must wait until tomorrow."

I'd begun to rise from the sofa when I witnessed a most peculiar thing.

Holmes advanced to the door, as if eager to make his exit. Yet after opening the door to the hallway he abruptly turned *volte face* and then recrossed the room. Swiftly, silently he picked up *The Times* newspaper which had been lying on the table, and opened it noiselessly.

The professor from his chair, and I from the sofa, watched in utter bewilderment as Holmes quickly fanned the newspaper so as to separate the pages into a billowing white cloud of loose leaves.

My bewilderment turned to astonishment as Holmes produced a box of safety matches from his pocket, deftly struck one, then applied the brilliantly flaring match head to the corner of the newspaper.

The dry paper caught instantly.

With a look of triumph Holmes flung the burning newspaper into the firegrate where, instantly, the still substantial updraft of air drew the flames, smoke, fiery pages and all up into the cavernous throat of the chimney back.

Professor Hardcastle gaped in astonishment, his hands clutching the arms of his chair so fiercely they shook.

He must have thought my friend quite mad.

Indeed, I, too, began to suspect that world famous brain had begun to suffer the ill-effects of the furiously hot June day, when all of a sudden I heard a terrific scraping and thumping sound.

Not one moment later an object looking very much like a bundle of rags fell heavily from the chimney and into the grating in a splash of sparks and ashes from the still burning newspaper.

Hardly believing my two eyes I witnessed a pair of filthy arms erupt from the rag bundle. Before I could exclaim, an equally filthy pair of hands grasped Sherlock Holmes by the wrists.

"Professor!" called Holmes, wrestling the creature emerging from the rags. "Now is the time to test your gardener's loyalty. We need his strong arms in here – *now!*"

Recovering from my astonishment, I rushed to my friend's assistance as he endeavoured to draw forth from the fireplace a hissing, spitting demon of a creature, that kicked wildly with a pair of bare feet, its toes quite ink black with soot.

"Careful, Watson! He has a razor!"

Holmes, bracing his foot against the iron fire grating, gripped the two filthy wrists and pulled hard, taking care so the barber's razor clutched in one evil looking hand did not pare his own flesh.

With a furious roar a head appeared from the flaps of cloth.

Beneath a shock of red hair was a white face set with two eyes that burned with the ferocity of lamps.

The creature was more ape than man; nevertheless, I grabbed hold of the madman's collar and Holmes and I together hauled him from the fireplace. All the time he hissed and spat in a way that aroused in me equal portions of amazement and horror.

"Watson, grab the fellow's wrist. Hold it . . . tightly, man. He'll take off our heads with that razor. There . . . hold him. Tsk! Careful, this creature bites. Now where is . . . ah, there he is! Good man!"

The gardener had appeared at the professor's command, and doing as he was bade, held the madman in his own two powerful arms as Holmes and I bound the madman at the feet and wrists with the curtain cords.

There at our feet, writhing, spitting, straining at the chords, his face distorting into fantastical grimaces, lay a tiny man – almost a dwarf of a man – with fiery red hair.

Holmes straightened, mastering his respiration. "This is . . . Dr Columbine."

"Yes . . ." Professor Hardcastle had not yet recovered from his shock. "Yes . . . And the man was concealed inside the chimney breast all the while?"

"Indeed he was, Sir, and listening to every conversation within the room. Now, please ask your gardener to summon the police. Oh, Professor, perhaps you would be so kind to allow Clarkson to change back into his own boots, those on his feet are pinching his toes terribly."

Once the police had taken the madman, straitjacketed and cursing, away, Holmes lit a cigarette and explained: "We know the poor demented Dr Columbine was hell bent on exacting his revenge upon you, Professor. Sadistically, he felt the need to prolong the torture before doing away with your son. So he contrived to hide himself away inside your house, then appear to come and go almost as if he could assume a cloak of invisibility. Accordingly, he'd place such obvious clues as the meteorite and the thyme inside your son's bedroom. You might imagine the madman lying within the chimney breast, laughing silently to himself as he listened to you and your wife's anxious conversations concerning the invisible intruder in this room. He would feast on your fears with nothing less than a vampiric intensity."

"But how the dickens did he climb into the chimney, and remain concealed there for so long? Why did he not starve or die of thirst?"

"Gaining access to the house itself is child's play. The catches on the windows can be slipped with even a table knife. Once inside the house – ah! – that's when the peculiar obsessive mind of the madman comes into play. He desired more than to cause physical harm to your family, he wanted to be here to savour every expression of your discomfort and fear. So he hit upon the plan of hiding himself away in that very chimney breast. Which is not as outlandish as it first appears. It is summer, no fires, therefore, are lit in the grate. The chimney itself is quite clean of soot, you Professor, having had the chimney swept in the late spring as is the practice of households throughout the land. And perhaps you, yourself, will have witnessed in the past the chimney sweep sending his lad up inside the chimney to ensure it is thoroughly swept. Indeed, there are footholds and handholds inside the chimney flue to assist the child's climb." Holmes sniffed. "Though the practice of sending children up inside chimneys was, I might add, a thoroughly inhumane affair. Nevertheless, it demonstrates that if the chimney is large enough for a child to enter via the fireplace, it is also large enough to accommodate the dwarfish body of Doctor Columbine. See?" Holmes crouching by the fireplace, pointed up inside the chimney flue. "Up there he made himself a pretty little nest. On the ledges within the chimney are his supplies – water bottle, bread, biscuit, dried fruit. You'll notice he didn't chose any aromatic foods, the odours of which might have aroused your suspicions, Professor." Holmes, lifted a small cloth bag from the hearth which had tumbled down with the madman. "Ah, and inside here we find a pair of clean pumps that he'd don on leaving the chimney breast to enable him to move not only quietly around the house, but to do so without leaving any sooty footprints upon the carpets. Before ascending to his hiding place once more he will have removed these, then climbed barefoot into the chimney." Holmes dropped the bag onto the hearth. "Gentlemen, you'll notice, also, he was able to devise something akin to a hammock, rigged from lines and blankets, where he would curl himself up quite comfortably to eavesdrop on you and your good wife's frightened conversations." Holmes stood up and briskly brush a speckling of soot from the palms of his hands. "So, Dr Columbine lay snug, and quite safe from discovery in the very heart of your home. After all, who would ever think to regularly examine the interior of their chimney breast?"

"Yes," said Hardcastle. "I see how he did it – and why. But how in heaven's name did you know the devil was concealed inside the chimney?"

Holmes walked slowly up and down the room. "As in science, the solution to a crime often arrives inexplicably in a flash of inspiration, what the scientific or criminal investigator must then do is extract the hard evidence to substantiate what betting men call a hunch."

The professor's eyes widened behind the pince-nez. "You mean you guessed immediately?"

"Let us say I explored, imaginatively, areas within a house that a man of very small stature might conceal himself, yet be able to eavesdrop, and learn what evil affect his machinations are having on the family. Of course, then I proceeded to seek clues. The man must eat and drink. No doubt he slipped out at night to steal small enough amounts that would not be noticeable from your larder. The man had become fond of drink." Holmes gave a wave of a hand that took in the decanters on a table. "You'll see a dirty thumbprint on the crystal stopper. I saw, also, fine speckles of soot upon the fireplace that escaped the attentions of your chimney sweep, and that were dislodged by Columbine's entrance and egress to and from the chimney."

"But you deduced from the thyme leaves that they'd been plucked from alongside the King's Cross line?"

"Ah! My final test. The deduction was entirely spurious. There are no coal particles. The black particles upon the card are nothing more than common London soot. Moreover, you should have noticed the Great Western Railway is served not by King's Cross station, but by Paddington station. Our viciously intelligent madman would have known that. And I realized that although our man could conceal himself inside the chimney, and not reveal his position by remaining silent, unmoving as a statue, even he had to breathe. And the more heavily he breathed, the more he moved within the chimney breast, even if it was nothing beyond a more pronounced rising and falling of his breast. Therefore, my patently absurd deduction wrongly linking the Great Western company with King's Cross station was deliberate. In short, you can imagine the man curled tightly there in the throat of the chimney, eyes blazing in the darkness, clutching his stomach and laughing silently over the supposedly great criminologist Sherlock Holmes's foolish errors; this caused a more pronounced movement of his body; enough to dislodge a single bread crumb from his clothing, or from the hammock arrangement, which I observed fall down into the hearth. Ergo: within the chimney breast was a living, breathing creature!"

"Then it is over?" asked Professor, hardly daring to believe it so. "My boy is safe?"

"Quite safe." Holmes picked up The Rye Stone. "Here is your aerolite, Professor; your very own fallen star. For countless aeons it drifted through space only to happen by chance to fall to Earth in a streak of fire. It did not will itself to engage in such a spectacular and dramatic display; it happened by pure chance, gentlemen. Such a pure chance, perhaps as a microbe in our water supply, or perhaps minuscule defect at birth brought the fiery genius of Dr Columbine crashing down into such a vile state of madness. He was no lucid criminal. He did not will his evil, any more than the stone willed itself to fall to Earth in a fiery and dramatic display of flame and thunder. It is impudent of me to suggest such a thing; however, perhaps you and your brethren, Professor, might consider creating some modest trust fund to enable your once illustrious teacher to live out his final days in a sanatorium where he can dream harmlessly of what astronomical wonders might lie in the depths of our universe. Now, Watson, if you concur, lunch at the Spaniard!"

PART III: THE 1890s

After "The Adventure of the Fallen Star", Watson seems to have assiduously recorded a number of cases that followed on quite quickly: "The Stockbroker's Clerk", "The Man With the Twisted Lip" – a case which was considerably more than a three-pipe problem, "Colonel Warburton's Madness" – one of the lost cases, and "The Engineer's Thumb". These and others during this busy period are listed in the appendix. Amongst them are the well-known cases of "The Boscombe Valley Mystery" and "The Red-Headed League" plus a few cases which are probably apocryphal though they have the ring of authenticity about them, including "The Adventure of the Megatherium Thefts" and "The Adventure of the First-Class Carriage".

By the start of 1891, however, Holmes had placed himself firmly on the trail of James Moriarty, the most dangerous man in London, whom he planned to confront once and for all. This led to the case of "The Final Problem" ending with the presumed death of Sherlock Holmes as he and Moriarty plunged into the Reichenbach Falls.

There follows the period known as the Great Hiatus, when Holmes travelled in disguise throughout Europe and Asia. He refers to some of these travels in "The Empty House", but it is difficult to know which of the many curious cases recorded on the continent during this period really marked the involvement of Sherlock Holmes. It is a period worthy of a separate book, and one that I hope to produce at some future date. But here we concern ourselves primarily with Holmes's investigations with Watson. Watson, believing Holmes to be dead, had spent the time finalizing and preparing for publication several of his records of Holmes's cases, and these appeared in The Strand Magazine *between 1891 and 1893. They made the name of Sherlock Holmes a household word. Unfortunately, Watson's wife died towards the end of 1893, so it was a rather sad Watson who was shocked and dazed at the sudden reappearance of Sherlock Holmes at the end of March 1894. (Subsequent investigations reveal that this event happened in February and, once again, Watson disguised the date.)*

After "The Empty House", and the entrapment of Sebastian Moran, Holmes felt sufficiently confident to resume his investigations. Watson, now alone, was delighted to resume his old rôle with Holmes, and from 1894 till Holmes's retirement ten years later, the two seemed inseparable. This was the high period of Holmes's career with a catalogue of remarkable cases. Immediately following "The Empty House" came "The Second Stain", "Wisteria Lodge" and "The Norwood Builder", plus the unrecorded case of the steamship Friesland, *which nearly cost them both their lives. That autumn Holmes had to move out from 221b Baker Street to allow for some refurbishment and redecoration and he and Watson briefly took lodgings at Dorset Street. There they became involved in a strange little case which was unearthed by the indefatigable Michael Moorcock who found them amongst the papers of a distant relative who had evidently been an acquaintance of Dr Watson.*

THE ADVENTURE OF
THE DORSET STREET LODGER

Michael Moorcock

It was one of those singularly hot Septembers, when the whole of
London seemed to wilt from over-exposure to the sun, like some
vast Arctic sea-beast foundering upon a tropical beach and doomed
to die of unnatural exposure. Where Rome or even Paris might
have shimmered and lazed, London merely gasped.

Our windows wide open to the noisy staleness of the air and our
blinds drawn against the glaring light, we lay in a kind of torpor,
Holmes stretched upon the sofa while I dozed in my easy chair and
recalled my years in India, when such heat had been normal and
our accommodation rather better equipped to cope with it. I had
been looking forward to some fly fishing in the Yorkshire Dales but
meanwhile, a patient of mine began to experience a difficult and
potentially dangerous confinement so I could not in conscience go
far from London. However, we had both planned to be elsewhere
at this time and had confused the estimable Mrs Hudson, who had
expected Holmes himself to be gone.

Languidly, Holmes dropped to the floor the note he had
been reading. There was a hint of irritation in his voice when
he spoke.

"It seems, Watson, that we are about to be evicted from our
quarters. I had hoped this would not happen while you were
staying."

My friend's fondness for the dramatic statement was familiar
to me, so I hardly blinked when I asked: "Evicted, Holmes?"
I understood that his rent was, as usual, paid in advance for
the year.

"Temporarily only, Watson. You will recall that we had both
intended to be absent from London at about this time, until
circumstances dictated otherwise. On that initial understanding,
Mrs Hudson commissioned Messrs Peach, Peach, Peach and
Praisegod to refurbish and decorate 221b. This is our notice.
They begin work next week and would be obliged if we would
vacate the premises since minor structural work is involved. We

are to be homeless for a fortnight, old friend. We must find new accommodations, Watson, but they must not be too far from here. You have your delicate patient and I have my work. I must have access to my flies and my microscope."

I am not a man to take readily to change. I had already suffered several setbacks to my plans and the news, combined with the heat, shortened my temper a little. "Every criminal in London will be trying to take advantage of the situation," I said. "What if a Peach or Praisegod were in the pay of some new Moriarty?"

"Faithful Watson! That Reichenback affair made a deep impression. It is the one deception for which I feel thorough remorse. Rest assured, dear friend. Moriarty is no more and there is never likely to be another criminal mind like his. I agree, however, that we should be able to keep an eye on things here. There are no hotels in the area fit for human habitation. And no friends or relatives nearby to put us up." It was almost touching to see that master of deduction fall into deep thought and begin to cogitate our domestic problem with the same attention he would give to one of his most difficult cases. It was this power of concentration, devoted to any matter in hand, which had first impressed me with his unique talents. At last he snapped his fingers, grinning like a Barbary ape, his deep-set eyes blazing with intelligence and self-mockery . . . "I have it, Watson. We shall, of course, ask Mrs Hudson if she has a neighbour who rents rooms!"

"An excellent idea, Holmes!" I was amused by my friend's almost innocent pleasure in discovering, if not a solution to our dilemma, the best person to provide a solution for us!

Recovered from my poor temper, I rose to my feet and pulled the bellrope.

Within moments our housekeeper, Mrs Hudson, was at the door and standing before us.

"I must say I am very sorry for the misunderstanding, sir," she said to me. "But patients is patients, I suppose, and your Scottish trout will have to wait a bit until you have a chance to catch them. But as for you, Mr Holmes, it seems to me that hassassination or no hassassination, you could still do with a nice seaside holiday. My sister in Hove would look after you as thoroughly as if you were here in London."

"I do not doubt it, Mrs Hudson. However, the assassination of one's host is inclined to cast a pall over the notion of vacations and while Prince Ulrich was no more than an acquaintance and the circumstances of his death all too clear, I feel obliged to give the matter a certain amount of consideration. It is useful to me to have my various analytical instruments to hand. Which brings us to a problem I am incapable of solving – if not Hove, Mrs Hudson, where? Watson and I need bed and board and it must be close by."

Clearly the good woman disapproved of Holmes's unhealthy habits but despaired of converting him to her cause.

She frowned to express her lack of satisfaction with his reply and then spoke a little reluctantly. "There's my sister-in-law's over in Dorset Street, sir. Number Two, sir. I will admit that her cookery is a little too Frenchified for my taste, but it's a nice, clean, comfortable house with a pretty garden at the back and she has already made the offer."

"And she is a discreet woman, is she Mrs Hudson, like yourself?"

"As a church, sir. My late husband used to say of his sister that she could hold a secret better than the Pope's confessor."

"Very well, Mrs Hudson. It is settled! We shall decant for Dorset Street next Friday, enabling your workman to come in on Monday. I will arrange for certain papers and effects to be moved over and the rest shall be secure, I am sure, beneath a good covering. Well, Watson, what do you say? You shall have your vacation, but it will be a little closer to home that you planned and with rather poorer fishing!"

My friend was in such positive spirits that it was impossible for me to retain my mood and indeed events began to move so rapidly from that point on, that any minor inconvenience was soon forgotten.

Our removal to number 2, Dorset Street, went as smoothly as could be expected and we were soon in residence. Holmes's untidiness, such a natural part of the man, soon gave the impression that our new chambers had been occupied by him for at least a century. Our private rooms had views of a garden which might have been transported from Sussex and our front parlour looked out onto the street, where, at the corner, it was possible to observe customers coming and going from the opulent pawn-brokers, often on their way to the Wheatsheaf Tavern, whose "well-aired beds" we had rejected in favour of Mrs Ackroyd's somewhat luxurious appointments. A further pleasing aspect of the house was the blooming wisteria vine, of some age, which crept up the front of the building and further added to the countrified aspect. I suspect some of our comforts were not standard to all her lodgers. The good lady, of solid Lancashire stock, was clearly delighted at what she called "the honour" of looking after us and we both agreed we had never experienced better attention. She had pleasant, broad features and a practical, no nonsense manner to her which suited us both. While I would never have said so to either woman, her cooking was rather a pleasant change from Mrs Hudson's good, plain fare.

And so we settled in. Because my patient was experiencing a difficult progress towards motherhood, it was important that I could be easily reached, but I chose to spend the rest of my time as if I really were enjoying a vacation. Indeed, Holmes himself shared something of my determination, and we had several pleasant evenings together, visiting the theatres and music halls for which London is justly famed. While I had developed an interest in the modern problem plays of Ibsen and Pinero, Holmes still favoured the atmosphere of the Empire and the Hippodrome, while Gilbert and Sullivan at the Savoy was his idea of perfection. Many a night I have sat beside him, often in the box which he preferred, glancing at his rapt features and wondering how an intellect so high could take such pleasure in low comedy and Cockney character-songs.

The sunny atmosphere of 2 Dorset Street actually seemed to lift my friend's spirits and give him a slightly boyish air which made me remark one day that he must have discovered the "waters of life", he was so rejuvenated. He looked at me a little oddly when I said this and told me to remind him to mention the discoveries he had made in Tibet, where he had spent much time after "dying" during his struggle with Professor Moriarty. He agreed, however, that this change was doing him good. He was able to continue his researches when he felt like it, but did not feel obliged to remain at home. He even insisted that we visit the kinema together, but the heat of the building in which it was housed, coupled with the natural odours emanating from our fellow customers, drove us into the fresh air before the show was over. Holmes showed little real interest in the invention. He was inclined to recognize progress only where it touched directly upon his own profession. He told me that he believed the kinema had no relevance to criminology, unless it could be used in the reconstruction of an offence and thus help lead to the capture of a perpetrator.

We were returning in the early evening to our temporary lodgings, having watched the kinema show at Madame Tussaud's in Marylebone Road, when Holmes became suddenly alert, pointing his stick ahead of him and saying in that urgent murmur I knew so well, "What do you make of this fellow, Watson? The one with the brand new top hat, the red whiskers and a borrowed morning coat who recently arrived from the United States but has just returned from the north-western suburbs where he made an assignation he might now be regretting?"

I chuckled at this. "Come off it, Holmes!" I declared. "I can see a chap in a topper lugging a heavy bag, but how you could say he was from the United States and so on, I have no idea. I believe you're making it up, old man."

"Certainly not, my dear Watson! Surely you have noticed that the morning coat is actually beginning to part on the back seam and is therefore too small for the wearer. The most likely explanation is that he borrowed a coat for the purpose of making a particular visit. The hat is obviously purchased recently for the same reason while the man's boots have the "gaucho" heel characteristic of the South Western United States, a style found only in that region and adapted, of course, from a Spanish riding boot. I have made a study of human heels, Watson, as well as of human souls!"

We kept an even distance behind the subject of our discussion. The traffic along Baker Street was at its heaviest, full of noisy carriages, snorting horses, yelling drivers and all of London's varied humanity pressing its way homeward, desperate to find some means of cooling its collective body. Our "quarry" had periodically to stop and put down his bag, occasionally changing hands before continuing.

"But why do you say he arrived recently? And has been visiting north-west London?" I asked.

"That, Watson, is elementary. If you think for a moment, it will come clear to you that our friend is wealthy enough to afford the best in hats and Gladstone bags, yet wears a morning coat too small for him. It suggests he came with little luggage, or perhaps his luggage was stolen, and had no time to visit a tailor. Or he went to one of the ready-made places and took the nearest fit. Thus, the new bag, also, which he no doubt bought to carry the object he has just acquired. That he did not realize how heavy it was is clear and I am sure if he were not staying nearby, he would have hired a cab for himself. He could well be regretting his acquisition. Perhaps it was something very costly, but not exactly what he was expecting to get . . . He certainly did not realize how awkward it would be to carry, especially in this weather. That suggests to me that he believed he could walk from Baker Street Underground Railway station, which in turn suggests he has been visiting north west London, which is the chiefly served from Baker Street."

It was rarely that I questioned my friend's judgements, but privately I found this one too fanciful. I was a little surprised, therefore, when I saw the top-hatted gentleman turn left into Dorset Street and disappear. Holmes immediately increased his pace. "Quickly, Watson! I believe I know where he's going."

Rounding the corner, we were just in time to see the American arrive at the door of Number 2 Dorset Street, and put a latch-key to the lock!

"Well, Watson," said Holmes in some triumph. "Shall we attempt to verify my analysis?" Whereupon he strode up to our fellow lodger, raised his hat and offered to help him with the bag.

The man reacted rather dramatically, falling backwards against the railings and almost knocking his own hat over his eyes. He glared at Holmes, panting, and then with a wordless growl, pushed on into the front hall, lugging the heavy Gladstone behind him and slamming the door in my friend's face. Holmes lifted his eyebrows in an expression of baffled amusement. "No doubt the efforts with the bag have put the gentleman in poor temper, Watson!"

Once within, we were in time to see the man, hat still precariously on his head, heaving his bag up the stairs. The thing had come undone and I caught a glimpse of silver, the gleam of gold, the representation, I thought, of a tiny human hand. When he recognized us he stopped in some confusion, then murmured in a dramatic tone:

"Be warned, gentleman. I possess a revolver and I know how to use it."

Holmes accepted this news gravely and informed the man that while he understood an exchange of pistol fire to be something in the nature of an introductory courtesy in Texas, in England it was still considered unnecessary to support one's cause by letting off guns in the house. This I found a little like hypocrisy from one given to target practice in the parlour!

However, our fellow lodger looked suitably embarrassed and began to recover himself. "Forgive me, gentlemen," he said. "I am a stranger here and I must admit I'm rather confused as to who my friends and enemies are. I have been warned to be careful. How did you get in?"

"With a key, as you did, my dear sir. Doctor Watson and myself are guests here for a few weeks."

"Doctor Watson!" The man's voice established him immediately as an American. The drawling brogue identified him as a South Westerner and I trusted Holmes's ear enough to believe that he must be Texan.

"I am he." I was mystified by his evident enthusiasm but illuminated when he turned his attention to my companion.

"Then you must be Mr Sherlock Holmes! Oh, my good sir, forgive me my bad manners! I am a great admirer, gentlemen. I have followed all your cases. You are, in part, the reason I took rooms near Baker Street. Unfortunately, when I called at your house yesterday, I found it occupied by contractors who could not tell me where you were. Time being short, I was forced to act on my own account. And I fear I have not been too successful! I had no idea that you were lodging in this very building!"

"Our landlady," said Holmes dryly, "is renowned for her discretion. I doubt if her pet cat has heard our names in this house."

The American was about thirty-five years old, his skin turned dark by the sun, with a shock of red hair, a full red moustache and a heavy jaw. If it were not for his intelligent green eyes and delicate hands, I might have mistaken him for an Irish prize fighter. "I'm James Macklesworth, sir, of Galveston, Texas. I'm in the import/export business over there. We ship upriver all the way to Austin, our State Capital, and have a good reputation for honest trading. My grandfather fought to establish our Republic and was the first to take a steam-boat up the Colorado to trade with Port Sabatini and the river-towns." In the manner of Americans, he offered us a resume of his background, life and times, even as we shook hands. It is a custom necessary in those wild and still largely unsettled regions of the United States.

Holmes was cordial, as if scenting a mystery to his taste, and invited the Texan to join us in an hour, when, over a whiskey and soda, we could discuss his business in comfort.

Mr Macklesworth accepted with alacrity and promised that he would bring with him the contents of his bag and a full explanation of his recent behaviour.

Before James Macklesworth arrived, I asked Holmes if he had any impression of the man. I saw him as an honest enough fellow, perhaps a business man who had got in too deep and wanted Sherlock Holmes to help him out. If that were all he required of my friend, I was certain Holmes would refuse the case. On the other hand, there was every chance that this was an unusual affair.

Holmes said that he found the man interesting and, he believed, honest. But he could not be sure, as yet, if he were the dupe of some clever villain or acting out of character. "For my guess is there is definitely a crime involved here, Watson, and I would guess a pretty devilish one. You have no doubt heard of the Fellini Perseus."

"Who has not? It is said to be Fellini's finest work – cast of solid silver and chased with gold. It represents Perseus with the head of Medusa, which itself is made of sapphires, emeralds, rubies and pearls."

"Your memory as always is excellent, Watson. For many years it was the prize in the collection of Sir Geoffrey Macklesworth, son of the famous Iron Master said to be the richest man in England. Sir Geoffrey, I gather, died one of the poorest. He was fond of art but did not understand money. This made him, I understand, prey to many kinds of social vampires! In his younger years he was involved with the aesthetic movement, a friend of Whistler's and Wilde's. In fact Wilde was, for a while, a good friend to him, attempting to dissuade him from some of his more spectacular blue and white excesses!"

"Macklesworth!" I exclaimed.

"Exactly, Watson." Holmes paused to light his pipe, staring down into the street where the daily business of London continued its familiar and unspectacular round. "The thing was stolen about ten years ago. A daring robbery which I, at the time, ascribed to Moriarty. There was every indication it had been spirited from the country and sold abroad. Yet I recognized it – or else a very fine copy – in that bag James Macklesworth was carrying up the stairs. He would have read of the affair, I'm sure, especially considering his name. Therefore he must have known the Fellini statue was stolen. Yet clearly he went somewhere today and returned here with it. Why? He's no thief, Watson, I'd stake my life on it."

"Let us hope he intends to illuminate us," I said as a knock came at our door.

Mr James Mackelsworth was a changed man. Bathed and dressed in his own clothes, he appeared far more confident and at ease. His suit was of a kind favoured in his part of the world, with a distinctly Spanish cut to it, and he wore a flowing tie beneath the wings of a wide-collared soft shirt, a dark red waistcoat and pointed oxblood boots. He looked every inch the romantic frontiersman.

He began by apologizing for his costume. He had not realized, he said, until he arrived in London yesterday, that his dress was unusual and remarkable in England. We both assured him that his sartorial appearance was in no way offensive to us. Indeed, we found it attractive.

"But it marks me pretty well for who I am, is that not so, gentlemen?"

We agreed that in Oxford Street there would not be a great many people dressed in his fashion.

"That's why I bought the English clothes," he said. "I wanted to fit in and not be noticed. The top hat was too big and the morning coat was too small. The trousers were the only thing the right size. The bag was the largest of its shape I could find."

"So, suitably attired, as you thought, you took the Metropolitan Railway this morning to –?"

"To Willesden, Mr Holmes. Hey! How did you know that? Have you been following me all day?"

"Certainly not, Mr Macklesworth. And in Willesden you took possession of the Fellini Perseus did you not?"

"You know everything ahead of me telling it, Mr Holmes! I need speak no more. Your reputation is thoroughly deserved, sir. If I were not a rational man, I would believe you possessed of psychic powers!"

"Simple deductions, Mr Macklesworth. One develops a skill, you know. But it might take a longer acquaintance for me to deduce how you came to cross some six thousand miles of land and sea to arrive in London, go straight to Willesden and come away with one of the finest pieces of Renaissance silver the world has ever seen. All in a day, too."

"I can assure you, Mr Holmes, that such adventuring is not familiar to me. Until a few months ago I was the owner of a successful shipping and wholesaling business. My wife died several years ago and I never remarried. My children are all grown now and married, living far from Texas. I was a little lonely, I suppose, but reasonably content. That all changed, as you have guessed, when the Fellini Perseus came into my life."

"You received word of it in Texas, Mr Macklesworth?"

"Well, sir, it's an odd thing. Embarrassing, too. But I guess I'm going to have to be square with you and come out with it. The gentleman from whom the Perseus was stolen was a cousin of mine. We'd corresponded a little. In the course of that correspondence he revealed a secret which has now become a burden to me. I was his only living male relative, you see, and he had family business to do. There was another cousin, he thought in New Orleans, but he had yet to be found. Well, gentlemen, the long and the short of it was that I swore on my honour to carry out Sir Geoffrey's instructions in the event of something happening to him or to the Fellini Perseus. His instructions led me to take a train for New York and from New York the *Arcadia* for London. I arrived yesterday afternoon."

"So you came all this way, Mr Mackleworth, on a matter of honour?" I was somewhat impressed.

"You could say so, sir. We set high store by family loyalty in my part of the world. Sir Geoffrey's estate, as you know, went to pay his debts. But that part of my trip has to do with a private matter. My reason for seeking you out was connected with it. I believe Sir Geoffrey was murdered, Mr Holmes. Someone was blackmailing him and he spoke of 'financial commitments'. His letters increasingly showed his anxiety and were often rather rambling accounts of his fears that there should be nothing left for his heirs. I told him he had no direct heirs and he might as well reconcile himself to that. He did not seem to take in what I said. He begged me to help him. And he begged me to be discreet. I promised. One of the last letters I had from him told me that if I ever heard news of his death, I must immediately sail for England and upon arriving take a good sized bag to 18 Dahlia Gardens, Willesden Green, North West London, and supply proof of my identity, whereupon I would take responsibility for the object most precious to the Mackelsworths. Whereupon I must return to Galveston with all possible speed. Moreover I must swear to keep the object identified with the family name forever.

"This I swore and only a couple of months later I read in the Galveston paper the news of the robbery. Not long after, there followed an account of poor Sir Geoffrey's suicide. There was nothing else I could do, Mr Holmes, but follow his instructions, as I had sworn I would. However I became convinced that Sir Geoffrey had scarcely been in his right mind at the end. I suspected he feared nothing less than murder. He spoke of people who would go to any lengths to possess the Fellini Silver. He did not care that the rest of his estate was mortgaged to the hilt or that he would die, effectively, a pauper. The Silver was of overweening importance. That is why I suspect the robbery and his murder are connected."

"But the verdict was suicide," I said. "A note was found. The coroner was satisfied."

"The note was covered in blood was it not?" Holmes murmured from where he sat lounging back in his chair, his finger tips together upon his chin.

"I gather that was the case, Mr Holmes. But since no foul play was suspected, no investigation was made."

"I see. Pray continue, Mr Mackelsworth."

"Well, gentlemen, I've little to add. All I have is a nagging suspicion that something is wrong. I do not wish to be party to a crime, nor to hold back information of use to the police, but I am honour-bound to fulfil my pledge to my cousin. I came to you not necessarily to ask you to solve a crime, but to put my mind at rest if no crime were committed."

"A crime has already been committed, if Sir Geoffrey announced a burglary that did not happen. But it is not much of one, I'd agree. What did you want of us in particular, Mr Mackelsworth?"

"I was hoping you or Dr Watson might accompany me to the address – for a variety of obvious reasons. I am a law-abiding man, Mr Holmes and wish to remain so. There again, considerations of honour . . ."

"Quite so," interrupted Holmes. "Now, Mr Mackelsworth, tell us what you found at 18 Dahlia Gardens, Willesden!"

"Well, it was a rather dingy house of a kind I'm completely

unfamiliar with. All crowded along a little road about a quarter of a mile from the station. Not at all what I'd expected. Number 18 was dingier than the rest – a poor sort of a place altogether, with peeling paint, an overgrown yard, bulging garbage cans and all the kind of thing you expect to see in East Side New York, not in a suburb of London.

"All this notwithstanding, I found the dirty knocker and hammered upon the door until it was opened by a surprisingly attractive woman of what I should describe as the octoroon persuasion. A large woman, too, with long but surprisingly well-manicured hands. Indeed, she was impeccable in her appearance, in distinct contrast to her surroundings. She was expecting me. Her name was Mrs Gallibasta. I knew the name at once. Sir Geoffrey had often spoken of her, in terms of considerable affection and trust. She had been, she told me, Sir Geoffrey's housekeeper. He had enjoined her, before he died, to perform this last loyal deed for him. She handed me a note he had written to that effect. Here it is, Mr Holmes."

He reached across and gave it to my friend who studied it carefully. "You recognize the writing, of course?"

The American was in no doubt. "It is in the flowing, slightly erratic, masculine hand I recognize. As you can see, the note says that I must accept the family heirloom from Mrs Gallibasta and, in all secrecy, transport it to America, where it must remain in my charge until such time as the other "missing" Mackelsworth cousin was found. If he had male heirs, it must be passed on to one of them at my discretion. If no male heir can be found, it should be passed on to one of my daughters – I have no living sons on condition that they add the Mackelsworth name to their own. I understand, Mr Holmes, that to some extent I am betraying my trust. But I know so little of English society and customs. I have a strong sense of family and did not know I was related to such an illustrious line until Sir Geoffrey wrote and told me. Although we only corresponded, I feel obliged to carry out his last wishes. However, I am not so foolish as to believe I know exactly what I am doing and require guidance. I want to assure myself that no foul play has been involved and I know that, of all the men in England, you will not betray my secret."

"I am flattered by your presumption, Mr Macklesworth. Pray, could you tell me the date of the last letter you received from Sir Geoffrey?"

"It was undated, but I remember the post mark. It was the fifteenth day of June of this year."

"I see. And the date of Sir Geoffrey's death?"

"The thirteenth. I supposed him to have posted the letter before his death but it was not collected until afterward."

"A reasonable assumption. And you are very familiar, you say, with Sir Geoffrey's hand-writing."

"We corresponded for several years, Mr Holmes. The hand is identical. No forger, no matter how clever, could manage those idiosyncracies, those unpredictable lapses into barely readable words. But usually his hand was a fine, bold, idiosyncratic one. It was not a forgery, Mr Holmes. And neither was the note he left with his housekeeper."

"But you never met Sir Geoffrey?"

"Sadly, no. He spoke sometimes of coming out to ranch in Texas, but I believe other concerns took up his attention.

"Indeed, I knew him slightly some years ago, when we belonged to the same club. An artistic type, fond of Japanese prints and Scottish furniture. An affable, absent-minded fellow, rather retiring. Of a markedly gentle disposition. Too good for this world, as we used to say."

"When would that have been, Mr Holmes?" Our visitor leaned forward, showing considerable curiosity.

"Oh, about twenty years ago, when I was just starting in practice. I was able to provide some evidence in a case concerning a young friend of his who had got himself into trouble. He was gracious enough to believe I had been able to turn a good man back to a better path. I recall that he frequently showed genuine concern for the fate of his fellow creatures. He remained a confirmed bachelor, I understand. I was sorry to hear of the robbery. And then the poor man killed himself. I was a little surprised, but no foul play was suspected and I was involved in some rather difficult problems at the time. A kindly sort of old-fashioned gentleman. The patron of many a destitute young artist. It was art, I gather, which largely reduced his fortune."

"He did not speak much of art to me, Mr Holmes. I fear he had changed considerably over the intervening years. The man I knew became increasingly nervous and given to what seemed somewhat irrational anxieties. It was to quell these anxieties that I agreed to carry out his request. I was, after all, the last of the Mackelsworths and obliged to accept certain responsibilities. I was honoured, Mr Holmes, by the responsibility, but disturbed by what was asked of me."

"You are clearly a man of profound common sense, Mr Mackelsworth, as well as a man of honour. I sympathize entirely with your predicament. You were right to come to us and we shall do all we can to help!"

The relief of the American's face was considerable. "Thank you, Mr Holmes. Thank you, Doctor Watson. I feel I can now act with some coherence."

"Sir Geoffrey had already mentioned his housekeeper, I take it?"

"He had sir, in nothing less than glowing terms. She had come to him about five years ago and had worked hard to try to put his affairs in order. If it were not for her, he said, he would have faced the bankruptcy court earlier. Indeed, he spoke so warmly of her that I will admit to the passing thought that – well, sir, that they were . . ."

"I take your meaning, Mr Mackelsworth. It might also explain why your cousin never married. No doubt the class differences were insurmountable, if what we suspect were the case."

"I have no wish to impune the name of my relative, Mr Holmes."

"But we must look realistically at the problem, I think." Holmes gestured with his long hand. "I wonder if we might be permitted to see the statue you picked up today?"

"Certainly, sir. I fear the newspaper in which it was wrapped has come loose here and there –"

"Which is how I recognized the Fellini workmanship," said Holmes, his face becoming almost rapturous as the extraordinary figure was revealed. He reached to run his fingers over musculature which might have been living flesh in miniature, it was so perfect. The silver itself was vibrant with some inner energy and the gold chasing, the precious stones, all served to give the most wonderful impression of Perseus, a bloody sword in one hand, his shield on his arm, holding up the snake-crowned head which glared at us through sapphire eyes and threatened to turn us to stone!

"It is obvious why Sir Geoffrey, whose taste was so refined, would have wished this to remain in the family," I said. "Now I understand why he became so obsessed towards the end. Yet I would have thought he might have willed it to a museum – or made a bequest – rather than go to such elaborate lengths to preserve it. It's something which the public deserves to see."

"I agree with you completely, sir. That is why I intend to have a special display room built for it in Galveston. But until that time, I was warned by both Sir Geoffrey and by Mrs Gallibasta, that news of its existence would bring immense problems – not so much from the police as from the other thieves who covet what is, perhaps, the world's finest single example of Florentine Renaissance silver. It must be worth thousands!

"I intend to insure it for a million dollars, when I get home," volunteered the Texan.

"Perhaps you would entrust the sculpture with us for the night and until tomorrow evening?" Holmes asked our visitor.

"Well, sir, as you know I am supposed to take the *Arcadia* back to New York. She sails tomorrow evening from Tilbury. She's one of the few steamers of her class leaving from London. If I delay, I shall have to go back via Liverpool."

"But you are prepared to do so, if necessary?"

"I cannot leave without the Silver, Mr Holmes. Therefore, while it remains in your possession, I shall have to stay." John Mackelsworth offered us a brief smile and the suggestion of a wink. "Besides, I have to say that the mystery of my cousin's death is of rather more concern than the mystery of his last wishes."

"Excellent, Mr Mackelsworth. I see we are of like mind. It will be a pleasure to put whatever talents I possess at your disposal. Sir Geoffrey resided, as I recall, in Oxfordshire."

"About ten miles from Oxford itself, he said. Near a pleasant little market town called Witney. The house is known as Cogges Old Manor and it was once the centre of a good-sized estate, including a working farm. But the land was sold and now only the house and grounds remain. They, too, of course, are up for sale by my cousin's creditors. Mrs Gallibasta said that she did not believe it would be long before someone bought the place. The nearest hamlet is High Cogges. The nearest railway station is at South Leigh, about a mile distant. I know the place as if it were my own, Mr Holmes, Sir Geoffrey's descriptions were so vivid."

"Indeed! Did you, by the by, contact him originally?"

"No, sir! Sir Geoffrey had an interest in heraldry and lineage. In attempting to trace the descendants of Sir Robert Mackelsworth, our mutual great-grandfather, he came across my name and wrote to me. Until that time I had no idea I was so closely related to the English aristocracy! For a while Sir Geoffrey spoke of my inheriting the title – but I am a convinced republican. We don't go much for titles and such in Texas – not unless they are earned!"

"You told him you were not interested in inheriting the title?"

"I had no wish to inherit anything, sir." John Mackelworth rose to leave. "I merely enjoyed the correspondence. I became concerned when his letters grew increasingly more anxious and rambling and he began to speak of suicide."

"Yet still you suspect murder?"

"I do, sir. Put it down to an instinct for the truth – or an overwrought imagination. It is up to you!"

"I suspect it is the former, Mr Mackelsworth. I shall see you here again tomorrow evening. Until then, goodnight."

We shook hands.

"Goodnight, gentlemen. I shall sleep easy tonight, for the first time in months." And with that our Texan visitor departed.

"What do you make of it, Watson?" Holmes asked, as he reached for his long-stemmed clay pipe and filled it with tobacco from the slipper he had brought with him. "Do you think our Mr Mackelsworth is 'the real article' as his compatriots would say?"

"I was very favourably impressed, Holmes. But I do believe he has been duped into involving himself in an adventure which, if he obeyed his own honest instincts, he would never have considered. I do not believe that Sir Geoffrey was everything he claimed to be. Perhaps he was when you knew him, Holmes, but since then he has clearly degenerated. He keeps an octoroon mistress, gets heavily into debt and then plans to steal his own treasure in order to preserve it from creditors. He involves our decent Texan friend, conjuring up family ties and knowing how important such things are to Southerners. Then, I surmise, he conspires with his housekeeper to fake his own death."

"And gives his treasure up to his cousin"? Why would he do that, Watson?"

"He's using Mackelsworth to transport it to America, where he plans to sell it."

"Because he doesn't want to be identified with it, or caught with it. Whereas Mr Mackelsworth is so manifestly innocent he is the perfect one to carry the Silver to Galveston. Well, Watson, it's not a bad theory and I suspect much of it is relevant."

"But you know something else?"

"Just a feeling, really. I believe that Sir Geoffrey is dead. I read the coroner's report. He blew his brains out, Watson. That was why there was so much blood on the suicide note. If he planned a crime, he did not live to complete it."

"So the housekeeper decided to continue with the plan?"

"There's only one flaw there, Watson. Sir Geoffrey appears to have anticipated his own suicide and left instructions with her. Mr Mackelsworth identified the handwriting. I read the note myself. Mr Macklesworth has corresponded with Sir Geoffrey for years. He confirmed that the note was was clearly Sir Geoffrey's."

"So the housekeeper is also innocent. We must look for a third party."

"We must take an expedition into the countryside, Watson." Holmes was already consulting his Bradshaw's. "There's a train from Paddington in the morning which will involve a change at Oxford and will get us to South Leigh before lunch. Can your patient resist the lure of motherhood for another day or so, Watson?"

"Happily there's every indication that she is determined to enjoy
an elephantine confinement."

"Good, then tomorrow we shall please Mrs Hudson by sampling
the fresh air and simple fare of the English countryside."

And with that my friend, who was in high spirits at the prospect
of setting that fine mind to something worthy of it, sat back in his
chair, took a deep draft of his pipe, and closed his eyes.

We could not have picked a better day for our expedition. While
still warm, the air had a balmy quality to it and even before we
had reached Oxford we could smell the delicious richness of an
early English autumn. Everywhere the corn had been harvested
and the hedgerows were full of colour. Thatch and slate slid past
our window which looked out to what was best in an England whose
people had built to the natural roll of the land and planted with
an instinctive eye for beauty as well as practicality. This was what I
had missed in Afghanistan and what Holmes had missed in Tibet,
when he had learned so many things at the feet of the High Lama
himself. Nothing ever compensated, in my opinion, for the wealth
and variety of the typical English country landscape.

In no time we were at South Leigh station and able to hire
a pony-cart with which to drive ourselves up the road to High
Cogges. We made our way through winding lanes, between tall
hedges, enjoying the sultry tranquillity of a day whose silence was
broken only by the sound of bird-song and the occasional lowing
of a cow.

We drove through the hamlet, which was served by a Norman
church and a grocer's shop which also acted as the local post
office. High Cogges itself was reached by a rough lane, little
more than a farm track leading past some picturesque farm
cottages with thatched roofs, which seemed to have been there
since the beginning of time and were thickly covered with roses
and honeysuckle, a rather vulgar modern house whose owner had
made a number of hideous additions in the popular taste of the
day, a farmhouse and outbuildings of the warm, local stone which
seemed to have grown from out of the landscape as naturally as
the spinney and orchard behind it, and then we had arrived at the
locked gates of Cogges Old Manor which bore an air of neglect.
It seemed to me that it had been many years since the place had
been properly cared for.

True to form, my friend began exploring and had soon discovered
a gap in a wall through which we could squeeze in order to explore
the grounds. These were little more than a good-sized lawn, some
shrubberies and dilapidated greenhouses, an abandoned stables,

various other sheds, and a workshop which was in surprisingly neat order. This, Holmes told me, was where Sir Geoffrey had died. It had been thoroughly cleaned. He had placed his gun in a vice and shot himself through the mouth. At the inquest, his housekeeper, who had clearly been devoted to him, had spoken of his money worries, his fears that he had dishonoured the family name. The scrawled note had been soaked in blood and only partially legible, but it was clearly his.

"There was no hint of foul play, you see, Watson. Everyone knew that Sir Geoffrey led the Bohemian life until he settled here. He had squandered the family fortune, largely on artists and their work. No doubt some of his many modern canvasses would become valuable, at least to someone, but at present the artists he had patronized had yet to realize any material value. I have the impression that half the denizens of the Café Royal depended on the Mackelsworth millions until they finally dried up. I also believe that Sir Geoffrey was either distracted in his last years, or depressed. Possibly both. I think we must make an effort to interview Mrs Gallibasta. First, however, let's visit the post office – the source of all wisdom in these little communities."

The post office-general store was a converted thatched cottage, with a white picket fence and a display of early September flowers which would not have been out of place in a painting. Within the cool shade of the shop, full of every possible item a local person might require, from books to boiled sweets, we were greeted by the proprietress whose name over her doorway we had already noted.

Mrs Beck was a plump, pink woman in plain prints and a starched pinafore, with humorous eyes and a slight pursing of the mouth which suggested a conflict between a natural warmth and a slightly censorious temperament. Indeed, this is exactly what we discovered. She had known both Sir Geoffrey and Mrs Gallibasta. She had been on good terms with a number of the servants, she said, although one by one they had left and had not been replaced.

"There was talk, gentlemen, that the poor gentleman was next to destitute and couldn't afford new servants. But he was never behind with the wages and those who worked for him were loyal enough. Especially his housekeeper. She had an odd, distant sort of air, but there's no question she looked after him well and since his prospects were already known, she didn't seem to be hanging around waiting for his money."

"Yet you were not fond of the woman?" murmured Holmes, his eyes studying an advertisement for toffee.

"I will admit that I found her a little strange, sir. She was a foreign woman, Spanish I think. It wasn't her gypsy looks that bothered me, but I never could get on with her. She was always very polite and pleasant in her conversation. I saw her almost every day, too – though never in church. She'd come in here to pick up whatever small necessities they needed. She always paid cash and never asked for credit. Though I had no love for her, it seemed that she was supporting Sir Geoffrey, not the other way around. Some said she had a temper to her and that once she had taken a rake to an under-footman, but I saw no evidence of it. She'd spend a few minutes chatting with me, sometimes purchase a newspaper, collect whatever mail there was and walk back up the lane to the manor. Rain or shine, sir, she'd be here. A big, healthy woman she was. She'd joke about what a handful it all was, him and the estate, but she didn't seem to mind. I only knew one odd thing about her. When she was sick, no matter how sick she became, she always refused a doctor. She had a blind terror of the medical profession, sir. The very suggestion of calling Doctor Shapiro would send her into screaming insistence that she needed no 'sawbones'. Otherwise, she was what Sir Geoffrey needed, him being so gentle and strange and with his head in the clouds. He was like that since a boy."

"But given to irrational fears and notions, I gather?"

"Not so far as I ever observed, sir. He never seemed to change. She was the funny one. Though he stayed at the house for the past several years and I only saw him occasionally. But when I did he was his usual sunny self."

"That's most interesting, Mrs Beck. I am grateful to you. I think I will have a quarter-pound of your best bullseyes, if you please. Oh, I forgot to ask. Do you remember Sir Geoffrey receiving any letters from America?"

"Oh, yes, sir. Frequently. He looked forward to them, she said. I remember the envelope and the stamps. It was almost his only regular correspondent."

"And Sir Geoffrey sent his replies from here?"

"I wouldn't know that, sir. The mail's collected from a pillar-box near the station. You'll see it, if you're going back that way."

"Mrs Gallibasta, I believe, has left the neighbourhood."

"Not two weeks since, sir. My son carried her boxes to the station for her. She took all her things. He mentioned how heavy her luggage was. He said if he hadn't attended Sir Geoffrey's service at St James's himself he'd have thought she had him in her trunk. If you'll pardon the levity, sir."

"I am greatly obliged to you, Mrs Beck." The detective lifted his hat and bowed. I recognized Holmes's brisk, excited mood. He was on a trail now and had scented some form of quarry. As we left, he murmured: "I must go round to 22lb as soon as we get back and look in my early files."

As I drove the dog-cart back to the station, Holmes scarcely spoke a further word. He was lost in thought all the way back to London. I was used to my friend's moods and habits and was content to let that brilliant mind exercise itself while I gave myself up to the world's concerns in the morning's *Telegraph.*

Mr Macklesworth joined us for tea that afternoon. Mrs Ackroyd had outdone herself with smoked salmon and cucumber sandwiches, small savouries, scones and cakes. The tea was my favourite Darjeeling, whose delicate flavour is best appreciated at that time in the afternoon, and even Holmes remarked that we might be guests at Sinclair's or the Grosvenor.

Our ritual was overseen by the splendid Fellini Silver which, perhaps to catch the best of the light, Holmes had placed in our sitting-room window, looking out to the street. It was as if we ate our tea in the presence of an angel. Mr Mackelsworth balanced his plate on his knee wearing an expression of delight. "I have heard of this ceremony, gentlemen, but never expected to be taking part in a High Tea with Mr Sherlock Holmes and Doctor Watson!"

"Indeed, you are doing no such thing, sir," Holmes said gently. "It is a common misconception, I gather, among our American cousins that High- and Afternoon- tea are the same thing. They are very different meals, taken at quite different times. High Tea was in my day only eaten at certain seats of learning, and was a hot, early supper. The same kind of supper, served in a nursery, has of late been known as High Tea. Afternoon-tea, which consists of a conventional cold sandwich selection, sometimes with scones, clotted cream and strawberry jam, is eaten by adults, generally at four o'clock. High Tea, by and large, is eaten by children at six o'clock. The sausage was always very evident at such meals when I was young." Holmes appeared to shudder subtly.

"I stand corrected and instructed, sir," said the Texan jovially, and waved a delicate sandwich by way of emphasis. Whereupon all three of us broke into laughter – Holmes at his own pedantry and Mr Macklesworth almost by way of relief from the weighty matters on his mind.

"Did you discover any clues to the mystery in High Cogges?" our guest wished to know.

"Oh, indeed, Mr Macklesworth," said Holmes, "I have one or two things to verify, but think the case is solved." He chuckled again, this time at the expression of delighted astonishment on the American's face.

"Solved, Mr Holmes?"

"Solved, Mr Macklesworth, but not proven. Doctor Watson, as usual, contributed greatly to my deductions. It was you, Watson, who suggested the motive for involving this gentleman in what, I believe, was a frightful and utterly cold-blooded crime."

"So I was right, Mr Holmes! Sir Geoffrey was murdered!"

"Murdered or driven to self-murder, Mr Macklesworth, it is scarcely material."

"You know the culprit, sir?

"I believe I do. Pray, Mr Mackleworth," now Holmes pulled a piece of yellowed paper from an inner pocket, "would you look at this? I took it from my files on the way here and apologize for its somewhat dusty condition."

Frowning slightly, the Texan accepted the folded paper and then scratched his head in some puzzlement, reading aloud. "My dear Holmes, Thank you so much for your generous assistance in the recent business concerning my young painter friend . . . Needless to say, I remain permanently in your debt. Yours very sincerely . . ." He looked up in some confusion. "The notepaper is unfamiliar to me, Mr Holmes. Doubtless the Athenaeum is one of your clubs. But the signature is false."

"I had an idea you might determine that, sir," said Holmes, taking the paper from our guest. Far from being discommoded by the information, he seemed satisfied by it. I wondered how far back the roots of this crime were to be found. "Now, before I explain further, I feel a need to demonstrate something. I wonder if you would be good enough to write a note to Mrs Gallibasta in Willesden. I would like you to tell her that you have changed your mind about returning to the United States and have decided to live in England for a time. Meanwhile, you intend to place the Fellini Silver in a bank vault until you go back to the United States, whereupon you are considering taking legal advice as to what to do with the statue."

"If I did that, Mr Holmes, I would not be honouring my vow to my cousin. And I would be telling a lie to a lady."

"Believe me, Mr Mackelsworth if I assure you, with all emphasis, that you will not be breaking a promise to your cousin and you will not be telling a lie to a lady. Indeed, you will be doing Sir Geoffrey Mackelsworth and, I hope, both our great nations, an important service if you follow my instructions."

"Very well, Mr Holmes," said Macklesworth, firming his jaw and adopting a serious expression, "if that's your word, I'm ready to go along with whatever you ask."

"Good man, Mackelsworth!" Sherlock Holmes's lips were drawn back a little from his teeth, rather like a wolf which sees its prey finally become vulnerable. "By the by, have you ever heard in your country of a creature known as 'Little Peter' or sometimes 'French Pete'?"

"Certainly I have. He was a popular subject in the sensational press and remains so to this day. He operated out of New Orleans about a decade ago. Jean 'Petit Pierre' Fromental. An entertainer of some sort. He was part Arcadian and, some said, part Cree. A powerful, handsome man. He was famous for a series of particularly vicious murders of well-known dignitaries in the private rooms of those establishments for which Picayune is famous. A woman accomplice was also involved. She was said to have lured the men to their deaths. Fromental was captured eventually but the woman was never arrested. Some believe it was she who helped him escape when he did. As I remember, Mr Holmes, Fromental was never caught. Was there not some evidence that he, in turn, had been murdered by a woman? Do you think Fromental and Sir Geoffrey were both victims of the same murderess?"

"In a sense, Mr Mackelsworth. As I said, I am reluctant to give you my whole theory until I have put some of it to the test. But none of this is the work of a woman, that I can assure you. Will you do as I say?"

"Count on me, Mr Holmes. I will compose the telegram now."

When Mr Macklesworth had left our rooms, I turned to Holmes, hoping for a little further illumination, but he was nursing his solution to him as if it were a favourite child. The expression on his face was extremely irritating to me. "Come, Holmes, this won't do! You say I helped solve the problem, yet you'll give me no hint as to the solution. Mrs Gallibasta is not the murderess, yet you say a murder is most likely involved. My theory – that Sir Geoffrey had the Silver spirited away and then killed himself so that he would not be committing a crime, as he would if he had been bankrupted – seems to confirm this. His handwriting has identified him as the author of letters claiming Mr Macklesworth as a relative – Macklesworth had nothing to do with that – and then suddenly you speak of some Louisiana desperado known as 'Little Pierre', who seems to be your main suspect until Mr Macklesworth revealed that he was dead."

"I agree with you, Watson, that it seems very confusing. I hope for illumination tonight. Do you have your revolver with you, old friend?"

"I am not in the habit of carrying a gun about, Holmes."

At this, Sherlock Holmes crossed the room and produced a large shoe-box which he had also brought from 22lb that afternoon. From it he produced two modern Webley revolvers and a box of ammunition. "We may need these to defend our lives, Watson. We are dealing with a master criminal intelligence. An intelligence both patient and calculating, who has planned this crime over many years and now believes there is some chance of being thwarted."

"You think Mrs Gallibasta is in league with him and will warn him when the telegram arrives?"

"Let us just say, Watson, that we must expect a visitor tonight. That is why the Fellini Silver stands in our window, to be recognized by anyone who is familiar with it."

I told my friend that at my age and station I was losing patience for this kind of charade, but reluctantly I agreed to position myself where he instructed and, taking a firm grip on my revolver, settled down for the night.

The night was almost as sultry as the day and I was beginning to wish that I had availed myself of lighter clothing and a glass of water when I heard a strange, scraping noise from somewhere in the street and risked a glance down from where I stood behind the curtain. I was astonished to see a figure, careless of any observer, yet fully visible in the yellow light of the lamps, climbing rapidly up the wisteria vine!

Within seconds the man – for man it was, and a gigantic individual, at that – had slipped a knife from his belt and was opening the catch on the window in which the Fellini Silver still sat. It was all I could do to hold my position. I feared the fellow would grasp the statue and take it out with him. But then common sense told me that, unless he planned to lower it from the window, he must come in and attempt to leave by the stairs.

The audacious burglar remained careless of onlookers, as if his goal so filled his mind that he was oblivious to all other considerations. I caught a glimpse of his features in the lamp-light. He had thick, wavy hair tied back in a bandanna, a couple of day's stubble on his chin and dark, almost negroid skin I guessed at once that he was a relative of Mrs Gallibasta.

Then he had snapped back the catch of the window and I heard his breath hissing from his lips as he raised the sash and slipped inside.

The next moment Holmes emerged from his hiding place and levelled the revolver at the man who turned with the blazing eyes of a trapped beast, knife in hand, seeking escape.

"There is a loaded revolver levelled at your head, man," said

Holmes evenly, "and you would be wise to drop that knife and give yourself up!"

With a wordless snarl, the intruder flung himself towards the Silver, placing it between himself and our guns. "Shoot if you dare!" he cried. "You will be destroying more than my unworthy life! You will be destroying everything you have conspired to preserve! I underestimated you, Macklesworth. I thought you were an easy dupe – dazzled by the notion of being related to a knight of the realm, with whom you had an intimate correspondence! I worked for years to discover everything I could about you. You seemed perfect. You were willing to do anything, so long as it was described as a matter of family honour. Oh, how I planned! How I held myself in check! How patient I was. How noble in all my deeds! All so that I would one day own not merely that fool Geoffrey's money, but also his most prized treasure! I had his love – but I wanted everything else besides!"

It was then I realized suddenly what Holmes had been telling me. I almost gasped aloud as I understood the truth of the situation!

At that moment I saw a flash of silver and heard the sickening sound of steel entering flesh. Holmes fell back, his pistol dropping from his hand and with a cry of rage I discharged my own revolver, careless of Fellini or his art, in my belief that my friend was once again to be taken from me – this time before my eyes.

I saw Jean-Pierre Fromental, alias Linda Gallibasta, fall backwards, arms raised, and crash through the window by which he had entered. With a terrible cry he staggered, flailed at the air, then fell into an appalling silence.

At that moment, the door burst open and in came John Mackelsworth, closely followed by our old friend Inspector Lestrade, Mrs Beck and one or two other tenants of 2 Dorset Street.

"It's all right, Watson," I heard Holmes say, a little faintly. "Only a flesh wound. It was foolish of me not to think he could throw a Bowie-knife! Get down there, Lestrade, and see what you can do. I'd hoped to take him alive. It could be the only way we'll be able to locate the money he has been stealing from his benefactor over all these years. Good night to you, Mr Mackelesworth. I had hoped to convince you of my solution, but I had not expected to suffer quite so much injury in the performance." His smile was faint and his eyes were flooded with pain.

Luckily, I was able to reach my friend before he collapsed upon my arm and allowed me to lead him to a chair, where I took a look at the wound. The knife had stuck in his shoulder and, as Holmes knew, had done no permanent damage, but I did not envy him the discomfort he was suffering.

Poor Macklesworth was completely stunned. His entire notion of things had been turned topsy-turvy and he was having difficulty taking everything in. After dressing Holmes's wound, I told Macklesworth to sit down while I fetched everyone a brandy. Both the American and myself were bursting to learn everything Holmes had deduced, but contained ourselves until my friend would be in better health. Now that the initial shock was over, however, he was in high spirits and greatly amused by our expressions.

"Your explanation was ingenious, Watson, and touched on the truth, but I fear it was not the answer. If you will kindly look in my inside jacket pocket, you will find two pieces of paper there. Would you be good enough to draw them out so that we might all see them?"

I did as my friend instructed. One piece contained the last letter Sir Geoffrey had written to John Macklesworth and, ostensibly, left with Mrs Gallibasta. The other, far older, contained the letter John Macklesworth had read out earlier that day. Although there was a slight similarity to the handwriting, they were clearly by different authors.

"You said this was the forgery," said Holmes, holding up the letter in his left hand, "but unfortunately it was not. It is probably the only example of Sir Geoffrey's handwriting you have ever seen, Mr Mackelsworth."

"You mean he dictated everything to his – to that devil?"

"I doubt, Mr Macklesworth, that your namesake had ever heard of your existence."

"He could not write to a man he had never heard of, Mr Holmes!"

"Your correspondence, my dear sir, was not with Sir Geoffrey at all, but with the man who lies on the pavement down there. His name, as Doctor Watson has already deduced, is Jean-Pierre Fromental. No doubt he fled to England after the Picayune murders and got in with the Bohemian crowd surrounding Lord Alfred Douglas and others, eventually finding exactly the kind of dupe he was looking for. It is possible he kept his persona of Linda Gallibasta all along. Certainly that would explain why he became so terrified at the thought of being examined by a doctor – you'll recall the postmistresses words. It is hard to know if he was permanently dressing as a woman – that, after all, is how he had lured his Louisiana victims to their deaths – and whether Sir Geoffrey knew much about him, but clearly he made himself invaluable to his employer and was able, bit by bit, to salt away the remains of the Mackelsworth fortune. But what he really craved, was the Fellini Silver, and that was when he determined the course of action which led to his calculating deception of you, Mr Mackelsworth. He needed a namesake living not far from New Orleans. As an added insurance he invented another cousin. By the simple device of writing to you on Sir Geoffrey's stationery he built up an entire series of lies, each of which had the appearance of verifying the other. Because, as Linda Gallibasta, he always collected the mail, Sir Geoffrey was never once aware of the deception."

It was John Macklesworth's turn to sit down suddenly as realization dawned. "Good heavens, Mr Holmes. Now I understand!"

"Fromental wanted the Fellini Silver. He became obsessed with the notion of owning it. But he knew that if he stole it there was little chance of his ever getting it out of the country. He needed a dupe. That dupe was you, Mr Macklesworth. I regret that you are probably not a cousin of the murdered man. Neither did Sir Geoffrey fear for his Silver. He appears quite reconciled to his poverty and had long since assured that the Fellini Silver would remain in trust for his family or the public forever. In respect of the Silver he was sheltered from all debt by a special covenant with Parliament. There was never a danger of the piece going to his creditors. There was, of course, no way, in those circumstances, that Fromental could get the Silver for himself. He had to engineer first a burglary – and then a murder, which looked like a consequence of that burglary. The suicide note was a forgery, but hard to decipher. His plan was to use your honesty and decency, Mr Macklesworth, to carry the Silver through to America. Then he planned to obtain it from you by any means he found necessary."

Macklesworth shuddered. "I am very glad I found you, Mr Holmes. If I had not, by coincidence, chosen rooms in Dorset Street, I would even now be conspiring to further that villain's ends!"

"As, it seems, did Sir Geoffrey. For years he trusted Fromental. He appears to have doted on him, indeed. He was blind to the fact that his estate was being stripped of its remaining assets. He put everything down to his own bad judgement and thanked Fromental for helping him! Fromental had no difficulty, of course, in murdering Sir Geoffrey when the time came. It must have been hideously simple. That suicide note was the only forgery, as such, in the case, gentlemen. Unless, of course, you count the murderer himself."

Once again, the world had been made a safer and saner place by the astonishing deductive powers of my friend Sherlock Holmes.

Postscript

And that was the end of the Dorset Street affair. The Fellini Silver was taken by the Victoria and Albert Museum who, for some years, kept it in the special "Macklesworth" Wing before it was transferred, by agreement, to the Sir John Soane Museum. There the Macklesworth name lives on. John Macklesworth returned to America a poorer and wiser man. Fromental died in hospital, without revealing the whereabouts of his stolen fortune, but happily a bank book was found at Willesden and the money was distributed amongst Sir Geoffrey's creditors, so that the house did not have to be sold. It is now in the possession of a genuine Macklesworth cousin. Life soon settled back to normal and it was with some regret that we eventually left Dorset Street to take up residence again at 221b. I have occasion, even today, to pass that pleasant house and recall with a certain nostalgia the few days when it had been the focus of an extraordinary adventure.

At the start of "The Adventure of the Golden Pince-Nez," which took place in November 1894, Watson refers to his three massive manuscript volumes covering the cases of 1894, and he lists five other cases in addition to the six that had already happened in the first half of the year. Four of those cases tumbled one on top of each other during October and early November, and I present them here without interruption. I must thank the individuals who helped reconstruct these cases.

Barrie Roberts, the tireless delver into matters Sherlockian, spent many years tracking down the clues that allowed him to rebuild the case of the Addleton tragedy. Robert Weinberg is an American bookdealer, collector and writer who has a remarkable talent for finding obscure papers and records. He acquired a batch of notes some years ago and amongst these were early scribblings by Watson on a number of incidental cases, which he later wrote up but did not publish. One of these was the case of Huret the Boulevard assassin, which Mr Weinberg was able to complete with the assistance of Lois Gresh. Stephen Baxter, is a well-known science-fiction writer. His investigations into the early life of H.G. Wells identified the clues that allowed us to reconstruct the forgotten "Adventure of the Inertial Adjustor". Alert readers will find a passing reference to a red leech suggesting that this story may be the one Watson refers to under that name although, as we shall see, there is another story by that title. Finally Peter Crowther, who hails from Yorkshire, had some remarkable luck only recently in some research he was undertaking for a book on angels, when he came across some old records which enabled him to piece together the case of Crosby the Banker.

THE MYSTERY OF THE ADDLETON CURSE

Barrie Roberts

It is to the very great credit of my friend Mr Sherlock Holmes that his willingness to enter into an enquiry was never motivated by financial considerations. Indeed, I saw him often reject the possibility of large fees in cases which did not arouse his interest and at least as often

I witnessed his involvement for no fee in matters which stimulated his curiosity and offered him the opportunity to pit his logical processes against some complicated pattern of events.

I have remarked elsewhere that 1894 was a busy year for Holmes, my notes of cases filling three large volumes, yet even in that year he took up an enquiry from which he had no hope of profit.

We sat at breakfast one morning that autumn, reading our way slowly through the many daily papers to which Holmes subscribed.

"Did you not say", he asked suddenly, "that your friend Stamford was treating Sir Andrew Lewis?"

"Yes", I said, "Stamford told me that he had had to call in Sir William Greedon and even that eminent gentleman was baffled by the symptoms."

"Really!" said Holmes. "Do you recall what they were?"

I cast my mind back to the conversation I had had with Stamford over a game of billiards a couple of weeks previously.

"Apparently Sir Andrew was the victim of a general debility with lesions of the skin, headaches, fainting spells, loss of hair, attacks of vomiting. In addition the poor fellow's mind seems to have been affected – he believed he was the victim of a curse."

"And what did Stamford believe it was?"

"He admitted to me that he hadn't the least notion. Greedon believed it was some obscure tropical disease that Sir Andrew picked up during his work abroad. Apparently Lewis's son died in his twenties of something similar, though it took him more swiftly. Greedon thought that they had both been infected abroad and that the son, having caught the disease as a child, was more vulnerable. Why do you ask?"

"Because", Holmes replied, "the combination of Stamford and Sir William Greedon has failed to save Lewis. His obituary appears this morning," and he passed me his newspaper.

The article recited the dead man's academic honours and titles, described some of his more famous archaeological explorations and listed the many museums which displayed items that he had discovered. It referred to the controversy which had clouded his career and caused him to withdraw from public life in recent years.

"Good Heavens!" I exclaimed as I drew towards the end of the article, "Perhaps he was the victim of a curse."

"Why do you say so?" asked Holmes, raising one eyebrow.

"Because it is suggested here," I said, "Listen," and I read him the relevant passage:

The accusation concerned his conduct during the excavation of an allegedly cursed barrow at Addleton, and must have been the more painful for coming at the time of his son's death. Sir Andrew made no defence against his attacker, save to state that he acted honourably at Addleton. Fellow archaeologists were unanimous in decrying the attack, but Sir Andrew evidently felt it very deeply, for he took no further part in any excavation, confining himself to writing a definitive series of papers and presenting occasional lectures. The shadow which he at least, perceived as clouding his career now followed by his death from a condition which has defeated the best medical brains in Britain might perhaps encourage the villagers of Addleton to believe that their barrow was truly cursed. Sir Andrew leaves one unmarried daughter.

"What do you make of that?" I asked. "What was the accusation against him?"

"That", said Holmes, emphatically, "is journalism of a kind that one would hope not to find in an allegedly responsible paper. As to the accusation against Lewis, it was brought by his assistant on the Addleton excavation, one Edgar. He published a letter which raised what he claimed was a mysterious difference between the curious decorations on a sealed container found in the barrow and its contents which, though valuable, were in no way unusual. He contrived to imply, without saying so, that a valuable item had been removed from the container overnight, after it had been discovered and before it had been taken from the excavation."

"As you have read," he continued, "the academic world was outraged and supported Lewis to a man. Edgar's own career certainly suffered. He was well thought of until the Addleton affair but is now, I believe, a lecturer at a suburban institute." We returned to our newspapers. Holmes was now into the more popular papers, which he read closely for their reports of crimes and accounts of Police Court proceedings. As he finished one he passed it to me and I was turning to the racing page when a heading caught my eye:

THE ADDLETON CURSE
DEATH OF EMINENT ARCHAEOLOGIST

I started the article out of idle curiosity, but as I read on I became more engrossed.

"Stamford should read this," I said, when I had done.

"Really," said Holmes, in a voice that suggested a total lack of interest.

"Yes," I persisted. "Do you know what it says here?"

My friend sighed and laid down the *Police Gazette.* "No doubt you are going to tell me, eh Watson?"

"This article", I said, "states that the Addleton barrow had been the subject of evil legends as long as anyone can recall. It stood on Addleton Moor, surrounded by many smaller burial mounds. It seems that light falls of snow never covered it and even in the hardest winter the snow always melted on that barrow first. The locals called it the "Black Barrow" because the grass would not grow on it."

"Watson," interrupted Holmes, "the grave on which the snow melts soonest and where the grass will not grow is a commonplace of rural legend. Half the country churchyards in Britain claim such a grave."

"I know," I said, "but that's not the interesting part. They say here that after Sir Andrew Lewis opened the barrow the village of Addleton was struck by a strange disease. It's symptoms were similar to Sir Andrew's but it was not always fatal. Since then the area has suffered many stillborn children and numbers of deformities. The villagers insist that it resulted from Lewis tampering with the Black Barrow. What do you say to that Holmes?"

He looked thoughtful for a moment. "Sadly, that is not the most reliable of our public prints, but if its report is true then the matter is a singular one. What is your medical opinion, Watson?"

"Perhaps Greedon was right. Maybe Sir Andrew picked up something peculiar during his years in Egypt and passed it on to the people at Addleton. Maybe it's hereditary. Lewis's son died of it. It could be that his father acquired the infection before his son's birth. Perhaps it's one of those unpleasant diseases that can lie dormant for years and then become active."

"Perhaps so," he said. "Watson, be a good fellow and pass me my writing case will you?"

He busied himself with a letter and I believed that the Addleton affair had passed from his mind until he reverted to it at breakfast a couple of days later.

"Do you recall our conversation about the death of Sir Andrew Lewis?" he asked.

"Certainly," I replied.

Holmes lifted a letter from beside his plate. "The press accounts of the affair excited my curiosity," he said, "to the extent that I dropped a line to the County Officer of Health."

"Did you indeed? And what does he have to say?"

Holmes referred to the letter. "While deploring any attempt to suggest that a curse is at work, he confirms that, in the year following

Sir Andrew's excavation of the Black Barrow, the village of Addleton suffered a number of deaths from what appeared to be an obscure form of anaemia and a number of stillbirths and deformed births. He suggests that there is no connection between these misfortunes and the archaeological expedition and that the source of the problem may be some effect of the local water supply."

"And what do you believe?" I asked.

"My disbelief in curses is only matched by my disbelief in coincidences. Those who have most occasion to be concerned – the people of Addleton – associate their tragedies with Sir Andrew's excavation. They may be wrong in believing that one is the cause of the other, but that does not mean that there is not a link between the two phenomena. As to the water supply, Addleton stands in a valley surrounded by hills of limestone. In such areas the water is famously pure. One recalls that the villages of south Derbyshire hold ceremonies every summer to celebrate the purity of their limestone streams which, they believe, saved them from the Great Plague."

"And have you any alternative explanation?" I enquired.

"It is far too early for that," he replied. "It would be a serious error to attempt an explanation when we have so little data. Our next effort must be to acquire further information so that the full pattern of these curious events reveals itself."

It was the afternoon of the following day when he enquired, "Have you any engagement this evening, Watson?" When I replied in the negative he said "I thought we might take in this evening's lecture at the Aldridge Institute. Mr Edgar, of Addleton fame, is lecturing on 'The Stones and the Stars', apparently a dissertation on Sir Norman Lockyer's theory that ancient religious monuments were constructed in relation to the movements of heavenly bodies."

The Institute turned out to be in a remote part of south London and Mr Edgar's lecture was not well attended. Nevertheless it was an interesting evening. Edgar was a man of about forty, with the long hair of a scholar and owlish spectacles that imparted a solemn aspect to his face though his lecture revealed a ready wit. His lantern slides, from photographs which he himself had taken, were not only informative but in some cases strikingly attractive. I recall particularly a picture of the great trilithon at Stonehenge lit from behind by the rising sun of midwinter. His arguments in favour of Lockyer's theory, though complex, were lucidly explained for a lay audience and convincing.

As the small audience trickled out at the lecture's end Holmes rose and approached Edgar who was giving some instruction to the lantern operator.

"We have enjoyed your talk," said Holmes,

"Thankyou, gentlemen," said the lecturer, "but I hope you are not journalists."

"Why should you think so?" asked Holmes.

"Because I have received a deal of attention from that profession since the death of Sir Andrew Lewis, and I have nothing to say to the press."

"You may be assured that we are not journalists," said my friend. "I am Sherlock Holmes, and this is my colleague, Dr Watson."

The lecturer's eyes widened behind his round spectacles. "The consulting detective!" he exclaimed, "What, may I ask, is your interest in archaeology?"

"You may have read", said Holmes, "my papers on 'Logical Deductions from Strata' and 'Early English Charters as a Guide to the Keltic Principalities', though they were not published under my own name, but it is not those that bring us here. I would welcome your assistance in my enquiries into the death of Sir Andrew Lewis."

"The death of Sir Andrew!" repeated Edgar. "Surely it is not thought that . . ."

Holmes raised a hand. "No, Mr Edgar. This is not a matter of murder. Sir Andrew, so far as anyone can tell, died naturally, but the manner of his death bears a strange similarity to the deaths and sicknesses that struck Addleton after the opening of the 'Black Barrow'."

"You believe in the so-called Curse of Addleton, then?" asked Edgar.

"Certainly not," said Holmes, "but I have reliable information that the village has suffered a strange disease since the excavation and it would be in the interest of Addleton's people to determine the cause."

"I know nothing of medicine, Mr Holmes. How can I help you?"

"Simply by telling me what you recall of the excavation at Addleton Moor," said Holmes.

The archaeologist began packing his lantern-slides away in their long wooden cases, while he spoke.

"It was a favourite project of Sir Andrew's," he began. "As a student he had been on Addleton Moor and seen that snow did not lie on the Black Barrow and grass did not grow upon it. He did not, of course, believe in the Curse, but he did believe that there was something unique about that barrow."

"So we went up there, that summer ten years ago, to see what we could find. The weather was fair and Addleton is a pretty village, but I tell you Mr Holmes, before we'd been there long I could have believed in the curse."

"Why was that?" asked Holmes.

Edgar indicated his slides. "One of my functions", he said, "was to take photographs for Sir Andrew. I had no difficulty taking pictures of the Moor, of the other tumuli upon it or anything except the Black Barrow. On the first day I took a group of all the party standing by the barrow. It did not come out. I thought it to be merely a faulty plate, as all my other pictures that day were successful, but, as the excavation progressed, I found that every single plate of the barrow failed."

"In what way?" asked Holmes.

"They were all fogged, Mr Holmes. Every one. I could have a bright, sunny day, an exposure timed to the second, and the picture would come out looking as if it had been taken in a London pea-souper."

"Have you any idea of the cause?" Holmes enquired.

"None whatever. It went on for days and then it ended as mysteriously as it began."

"It ended!" exclaimed Holmes.

"Oh yes," said Edgar. "I have pictures of the barrow. Suddenly the fogging was gone and everything was all right. I never knew what caused it."

"You hinted," said Holmes, "that there were other difficulties."

"There were indeed," said Edgar. "In the early stages Sir Andrew and several other members of the party became ill."

"With what?" I asked.

"Nothing the village doctor could put a name to. There was sickness and itchiness. At first we tended to blame the beds or the food at the inns, but they were two different pubs at opposite ends of Addleton. Then people started saying it was some disease of the local cows or sheep, but that was madness, just the irritability of fellows who were not up to par. Then that passed off, just like my photographic problem."

"And was there anything else?" said Holmes.

"There were Sir Andrew's personal problems. His son arrived from London. He was in the army, you know, and the young idiot had got himself cashiered for debt. His father was furious at the disgrace and there was his son bothering him for money. He was a wretched nuisance, hanging about the inn where his father stayed and, when Sir Andrew wouldn't give him his time, he'd turn up at the digging and hang about pestering his father. It was all very distracting for Sir Andrew."

He paused. "Then he fell ill," he said. "Not like the rest of us, something really serious. We were just finishing up and Sir Andrew had come back to London, leaving his son sick in Addleton. He sent the best doctors up from London, but they did no good. The lad was dead in weeks. Do you wonder that I said it was easy to believe in the Curse?"

"No," agreed Holmes, "and when you returned there was the row in the papers."

"I hope you do not blame me," said Edgar, sharply, "though I blame myself for the timing of it. But I thought about it for weeks before I wrote my letter. I could not believe my own thoughts, but in the end, in all conscience, I had to say what I thought, and it appeared just as Sir Andrew's son died. I felt wretched, attacking at such a time a man I had admired and looked up to. It was all pointless, anyway. There was a wave of sympathy for him, the profession closed ranks and nobody gave any serious attention to what I was saying. They say I destroyed his profession." He gave a mirthless laugh and waved a hand around him. "It didn't exactly do mine much good."

"What was it about?" I ventured, for I had not completely understood Holmes's remarks on this aspect of the matter.

"Have you seen the Addleton casket?" Edgar asked. "It was in the Barnard Museum, though they withdrew it from display when the row started, to avoid attracting vulgar sensation-seekers."

I shook my head and he continued.

"It was at the heart of the barrow, at ground level. Now usually you find a small stone chamber with ashes, or pots with ashes, bits of burned bones, a few funeral artefacts, that kind of thing. When we reached the bottom and uncovered the top of the casket we were delighted. We knew we'd found something utterly unique. We had come to the usual box of stone slabs and, when we removed the top slab, there was this magnificent casket. It was oval, made in bronze, with silver and enamelled decoration all over it, the finest work of its kind I've ever seen."

He paused and his eyes turned beyond us. "There was just Sir Andrew and myself that evening. The sickness was at its height and the other fellows had gone down from the Moor at tea-time, but sick or not you couldn't keep Sir Andrew from his work. I stayed on with him because I didn't like the idea of him up on the Moor alone. It's a creepy sort of place, you know."

"Well, it was late, almost dark when we uncovered the casket. We went to lift it, but it was infernally heavy and in the end Sir Andrew said to cover it up and leave it, let the other fellows see it *in situ* in the morning. Before we put the slab back I recall crouching in the pit with a lantern, for it was twilight, peering at the decorations on that wonderful thing and trying to make sense of them, and when I did I shuddered."

He shuddered slightly again at the recollection.

"Why was that?" asked Holmes.

"Death," said the archaeologist. "That splendid casket was covered in symbols of death. I have never seen anything like it, Mr Holmes. Those old peoples were like us, they believed in rebirth. If there are decorations connected with their burials they are always signs of life, sun wheels, spirals, plants, animals, but this was completely different. It was covered in skulls and bones."

"And what did that suggest to you?" asked Holmes.

"I was excited. I believed that the casket would contain something remarkable, something that its creators regarded as of great importance. Because we could not lift it, Sir Andrew and I covered it up and went down from the Moor. We knew no villager would venture onto Addleton Moor after twilight. It was dark when we got back to our lodgings, and the other fellows had turned in, but I could scarcely sleep for wondering what lay in that bronze box."

"Next morning we returned to the excavation and carefully lifted the container and opened it. As soon as the lid was removed we knew why it had been heavy and I knew that it had been tampered with. Apart from being constructed from very thick bronze, the casket had been lined with a layer of lead. Now lead, as you may know, can decay into a powdery, ash-like form, and parts of the lining had done so. Pieces crumbled away as we lifted it, and fell into the box, and, while the rest of them gazed at the contents, I became aware that those dusty fragments of lead had been disturbed by human fingers. The marks were clear."

"I could not understand it. We were the first, or so it seemed, who had looked into that casket since it was placed under the barrow, but then I looked at the contents."

"What were they?" I asked.

"You might have seen those, too, in the Barnard Museum," he said. "A pair of fine bronze mirrors, brooches, beads, knives, cups, a strange quartz pebble mounted in a bronze holder, knives and the usual bone fragments and ashes contained in two handsome pottery urns. A very satisfactory find, or so my colleagues thought it, but they were wrong."

"Why was that?" enquired Holmes.

"Because there was nothing there that had not been seen in other excavations, nothing at all to justify those sinister decorations on the outside of the container, and thereby I knew that something had been removed."

He drew a deep breath. "Only Sir Andrew and I had even known of the casket's existence overnight, but someone had opened it, disturbed the leaden lining and removed something, and that someone could only have been Sir Andrew."

He closed a slide-box with a snap. "As I said, we came away, Sir Andrew distracted by his son's illness and the necessity to leave him at Addleton and I appalled by the looting of our excavation by the man who had been my friend and mentor. The rest you know."

"There is really only one more question," said my friend.

"Which of Addleton's inns was Sir Andrew's lodging?"

Edgar stared at us blankly for a moment. "The Goat and Boots," he said shortly and turned away.

The next morning found Holmes and me on the doorstep of the late Sir Andrew's home. Like Edgar, the butler was disposed to believe we were journalists and drive us away, but my friend's card gained us an introduction to Sir Andrew's daughter.

She received us in the morning room. Lady Cynthia was a tall, fair, young woman, on whom sombre black sat well.

"Mr Holmes, Doctor", she said. "My father would have welcomed the opportunity to meet you. He read your accounts, Doctor, of Mr Holmes's cases, with great pleasure and approved of your application of logic."

"It is kind of you to say so," said Holmes, "and I could have wished to meet in happier circumstances, but it is about your father that we have called."

"About my father?" she queried. "Surely you do not believe that there is anything suspicious about his death? Sir William Greedon believed the cause to be an old infection from his Egyptian explorations, similar to that which carried off my poor brother."

"You must not assume that my involvement indicates a crime, Lady Cynthia. The press has linked Sir Andrew's death with the so-called Curse of Addleton . . ."

"That is mere vulgar sensationalism," she interrupted. "We experienced the same nonsense at the time of Anthony's death."

Holmes nodded, sympathetically. "Nevertheless," he said, "I have reliable information that Addleton has suffered some strange infection since Sir Andrew opened the Black Barrow."

"Surely you do not believe in the Curse, Mr Holmes!"

"No madam, not for one moment, but I have often observed that what the superstitious or the lazy-minded call supernatural or coincidental is, in fact, the occurrence of two striking events which have a common cause or share a connection. I believe that such may be the case here."

"If it will prevent deaths such as my brother's and my father's," said Lady Cynthia, "then of course I will assist your enquiries. How can I help you?"

"You might tell me what it was that occupied Sir Andrew's mind in his last days, Lady Cynthia."

An expression of pain passed across her features. "When he first fell sick," she began, "he became anxious to write up his paper on Addleton. He had never published it, you know, because of the row with Edgar. But he never completed it, for he would fall into strange excitements and sudden obsessions."

"And what form did they take?" asked Holmes.

"He began to blame himself for my brother's death. When his own health was already failing, he insisted on travelling alone to Addleton, saying that he must ask Tony's forgiveness. I pleaded to travel with him, if he must go, but he said that he must go alone."

She gazed at the handsome portrait of her father which hung above the fireplace.

"After that his health deteriorated rapidly. While he was not yet confined to his bed he sat in his workshop, scribbling endlessly."

"Do you have any of his scribblings?" asked Holmes.

"No, Mr Holmes. I looked at them after his death and they were unconnected nonsense. I destroyed them."

"Might we see his workshop?" asked my friend.

"By all means," she replied and rose from her chair. We followed her to the rear of the house, where she led us into a long room, lit by three tall windows that overlooked an attractive garden. Its walls were lined with bookshelves and down the middle ran a long, solid table, littered with tools and scraps of various materials. In one corner stood a writing desk.

"This was always my father's working place," said Lady Cynthia. "Please feel free to make any examination that you wish. If you will join me in the morning room when you have done, I shall arrange some tea," and she withdrew.

Sherlock Holmes looked about him. "I think you had better take the books," he said.

"How do you mean?" I queried.

"Examine the bookshelves, Watson, for anything which occurs to you as out of the ordinary."

"But I am not sure that I know what an eminent archaeologist would ordinarily read," I protested.

He ignored me and began to pace around the big central table. I turned to the bookshelves and attempted the task that Holmes had set me. There were shelf upon shelf of archaeological journals, some in foreign languages, there were works on history, legend and folklore, but nothing that struck me as anomalous. Eventually I turned back to Holmes who was looking at some objects at one corner of the bench.

"He seems to have nothing here but professional reading," I observed.

"Very well," said Holmes. "Then we must make what we can of his work-bench," and he passed to me a small dark pad.

"Moleskin," I said, as soon as my fingers touched it, "A piece of moleskin folded over and stitched into a – a pin-cushion perhaps?"

"Moleskin," confirmed my friend, "but not a pin-cushion, I think. Smell it, Watson."

I lifted the little pad and my nostrils wrinkled. "Faugh!" I exclaimed, "it reeks of rancid tallow."

"Precisely," said Holmes, "and what about this?"

He picked up from the bench a curious wooden object and I took it from him. It was about eighteen inches long and rounded at one end to form a handle such as one would find on many tools, but above the handle it widened out, one side being flat and the other curved. The opposite end from the handle was cut quite flat. It was evidently a manufactured object and had been stained, though the curved and flat surfaces bore signs of impact.

"I've never seen anything like it," I said. "Are you sure it is complete?"

"Oh, it is quite complete," said Holmes, "and exactly what I expected to see. Now, I think it only remains to examine the writing desk."

The desk yielded little. The pigeon-holes had been cleared and there were two note-pads on the desk from which the upper sheets had been removed.

"Nothing here, Holmes," I said.

"I do not know," he replied, and slipping his lens from his pocket began an examination of the blank note pads. "Have you a cigarette, Watson?" he asked, suddenly.

I took out my case and opened it. "I see," said Holmes, "that the horses have not lived up to your expectations. You are reduced to cheap Virginias. Still, they will suffice," and he took one and lit it.

After a few vigorous puffs he leaned over the desk and tapped his ash onto one of the note-pads, rubbing it into the paper with his forefinger. After a moment he smiled.

"See," he said, lifting the pad, "the ash has darkened the paper, except where it has been compressed by the weight of a pencil on the sheet above. Now, what have we here?"

He held the paper to the light. "We have some decipherable words, Watson, and they seem to be 'poor Tony's death'. Now, what will the second pad reveal?"

Soon he had applied his process to the second pad and examined it. "'Lead? Lead? Lead?'" he read from it, "Each time with a question mark. That seems to be all on this one."

He crumpled the two ash-stained sheets into his coat pocket and straightened up. "I think," he said, "we should take our farewells of Lady Cynthia."

While we took tea with Lady Cynthia, Holmes assured her that he expected to unravel the mystery of her father's death and would communicate with her when his researches were complete. I, however, had been growing more mystified at each of my friend's moves and, in the cab back to Baker Street, I said so.

"Watson, Watson," he said, shaking his head. "It was you who drew my attention to this pretty little puzzle. Since then I have merely pursued a completely logical investigation into the mystery and have been able to acquire certain data which will, I firmly believe, lead me to a successful conclusion. You should know my methods well by now. Surely you have some inkling?"

I shook my head.

"Then consider these important facts," he said, striking them off on his fingers as he announced them. "Firstly, the people of Addleton believe the Black Barrow to be accursed because grass does not grow and snow does not lie upon it; secondly, the County Medical Officer confirms that a strange disease struck the village after the opening of the barrow; thirdly, Mr Edgar believes, with good reason, that something was removed from the barrow illicitly. Does none of that assist you?"

I had to admit that it did not, and he shook his head again in wonderment, but offered no further explanation.

"What will be your next move?" I asked, seeking some indication that might help me.

"I should have thought," he said, "that that also would have been obvious to you. We must go to Addleton and view the *locus in quo*, indeed the scene of the crime."

"But I thought you believed there was no crime here!" I exclaimed.

"I set out," said Holmes, "to solve a medical mystery, but we have stumbled across crime on our path. There has been a crime, Watson. One with very far-reaching consequences."

The next afternoon found us in Addleton, a stone-built village which consisted largely of one long street with an inn at either end, huddled deep beneath the great square bulk of Addleton

Moor. Once we had settled our baggage at the Goat and Boots Holmes sought out the village's only doctor. Doctor Leary was an affable Irishman in his forties, who welcomed us into his surgery.

"And what," he asked, when we had introduced ourselves, "brings a famous consulting detective all the way from London to Addleton? We have no murders here, Mr Holmes, and apart from a bit of head-thumping among the quarrymen on pay nights we have no other kind of crime."

"But you have a mystery," said Holmes.

"A mystery? Ah, surely a man of reason and logic like yourself is not looking into the Curse of the Black Barrow?"

"Certainly not," said Holmes. "I am, however, looking into events which have led the popular press to allege that the Curse is real, namely the death of Anthony Lewis, the deaths, sicknesses, stillbirths and deformed births that have occurred here, and the recent death in London of Sir Andrew Lewis. Would you deny that they create a curious pattern?"

"There certainly seems to be a connection though, like you, I reject the supernatural explanation," said Dr Leary. He groped in his pocket for his pipe and lit it. When it was well alight he continued.

"I came here, you know, fresh from Medical School. I thought I'd found a nice pitch", he said. "A pretty village, a bracing climate, clean water, nice people and nothing much to worry me or them except old age and quarry accidents. And so it was for the first few years, then they opened the Black Barrow, and if it wasn't cursed then it certainly deserves to be so."

"What did you make of the sickness that affected the excavators?" Holmes asked.

"Very little, I admit. It was not serious and it might have had a number of causes. They were sweating away up on the Moor in the summer sun, some of them young fellas who were more used to a pen than a pick. I thought it could be a touch of the sun and I treated it as such."

"And young Lewis?" said my friend.

"That, of course, was different. At the time I made no connection with the archaeologists. He came to me first with burns on his hands. I thought he had picked up something too hot with both hands. He said that he had not, that he had red patches appear on his hands for no reason and then open up like burns. I treated him with salves and wondered if it was some foreign skin disease, for he told me he had been abroad as a child."

The doctor puffed at his pipe, reflectively. "Then it got worse. He had fainting fits, headaches, nausea – soon he was too weak to leave his bed. His father sent the best of Harley Street to help me, but they were helpless. We could only watch him fade away."

"And how did the sickness spread?" enquired Holmes.

"Very quickly," said Leary. "Though it was never as fierce as in young Lewis. The next was the boot boy at the Goat. He died some weeks after the young man. It seems he had been in the habit of slipping into Lewis's room in his spare time and listening to tales of soldiering and the silly lad must have caught his death from Lewis. Then there was old McSwiney. He was a retired peeler who spent all his time in the Goat. He was old enough to go at any time if he hadn't pickled himself in alcohol, but he'd never had much in the way of sickness until the end. He had the vomiting and that, but not the burns, but it was clear it was the same thing."

"That was when I called in the County Officer of Health. We went over everything, the food and drink at the Goat, the water, the bedding, everything. There was nothing to find, the place was as clean as a whistle."

"Your Medical Officer seems to think the disease is water-borne," said Holmes.

"Rubbish!" said Leary. "He says that because he can't think of anything else. We have deep limestone wells here. I've had the water under a microscope, Mr Holmes. There's nothing in it except a few extra salts that people pay for in fancy spas."

"And what do you make of it, Dr Leary?"

"I've racked my brains for ten years," he said. "I know no more about that disease now than I did then, except one thing. As well as the deaths we had a few cases that were milder. When the deaths and the sickness stopped we thought it had gone, but then there came the births you have heard about. I didn't see how it could have been the same thing, but now I'm sure it was."

"And what made you so sure?" asked Holmes.

"Geography," said Leary. "Lewis died in the 'Goat' the boot boy died in the 'Goat', McSwiney drank in the 'Goat', those who had the sickness drank in the 'Goat', though not so much as McSwiney, Lord save him. When the stillbirths and the deformities occurred I saw the same pattern. They were all at that end of the village, close to the 'Goat'. And I'll tell you one more thing. All of the women were already pregnant when Lewis died."

He knocked out his pipe on the fender. Holmes steepled his fingers in front of his face for a moment, then looked up at the Irishman. "Is it over?" he asked.

"Oh yes. It's over – for now. But we don't know what it is or how it came here. I can't tell my people that it won't happen again."

"I hope," said Holmes, "that I can give you that assurance in the

very near future. Is there anything else at all that you believe may
help us?"

Leary laughed. "They say there's a bright side to everything. You
won't have seen it in the papers, for they only deal in bad news,
but we did have two miraculous cures at the same time."

"What were they?" said Holmes.

"One was Mary Cummins, the daughter of the landlord at the
'Goat'. She was seventeen at the time, a sweet, pretty thing, but
she started with blinding headaches, dizziness, fainting. This was
before the barrow was opened, when there was no thought of a
new sickness. Nothing I could do for her made any difference.
Soon she had spells when her mind wandered. I began to wonder
about a tumour on the brain, but do you know that while others
were sickening she suddenly got well? She lost all her symptoms
and she's as right as rain to this day.

The other was old Mrs Henty, next door to the pub. Her
daughter-in-law was the mother of one of the deformed babies,
but Mrs Henty had a persistent eczema on both forearms. She'd
had it all her life, she told me, but it vanished in days."

"Astonishing," said Holmes. "Now, Doctor, we have taken up
enough of your time. I assure you again, that I believe I am well
on the track of this thing and will let you know my conclusions."

We dined that night at our inn and had the good fortune to
be waited upon by the same Mary Cummins that Dr Leary had
mentioned to us. Whatever her difficulties of ten years ago, she was
now a buxom, raven-haired countrywoman in her middle twenties,
vigorous and witty.

After dinner we established ourselves beside the fire in the back
parlour, where Mary brought us our drinks.

"Miss Cummins," said Holmes, "may I ask if you know why
Dr Watson and I are in Addleton?"

She smiled. "'Tis no business of mine," she said, "but I hear tell
you've come about the Black Barrow."

"Perhaps you would sit with us for a moment," he suggested.
"You are right that we are investigating the singular disease that
affected the village when the barrow was opened."

She took a chair and he continued. "I believe that, so far from
being one of the sick, you actually recovered from an illness at
that time. Would it embarrass you to tell us about it?"

"Not at all, sir," she replied. "I had been ill for nearly two years
and getting worse all the time. First it was giddy spells, then faints,
then cruel headaches and sometimes I seemed to lose my wits
altogether. Dr Leary tried all sorts but it kept getting worse. He
said I should have to have an operation on my head and I was

rare frightened, but then, so fast as it came, it was gone, and as true as I'm sitting here I've never known a day's sickness since."

"Remarkable," said Holmes. "And to what do you attribute your cure?"

"Well, they say as all the sickness came out of that old barrow, and if it did, I say as my cure came out too."

Holmes eyed her, thoughtfully. "You remember young Mr Lewis?" he asked.

"Indeed I do," she said. "Poor young man. He was all in trouble with his father and then to die like that."

"Did you know him well?"

She blushed prettily. "Well, sir, when he was well he would make up to me. No more than was proper, though. And I daresay I was younger then and looked after him a bit special because of it."

"Did he ever show you, or tell you, what he had in his possession?" asked Holmes.

"How did you know about that?" she asked. "He said as no one knew he had it and I must keep his secret."

"You need not fear my knowing, Mary," said Holmes. "May I ask what it was?"

"Well, I had gone to his room one day, to tidy up, you know, and he came in. Now father's always been very strict about me not lingering in guests rooms when they're there, so I made to go, but Mr Lewis said, 'Let me show you something.' He pulled his trunk out from under his bed and he took out a great old pot, a big round earthenware pot with a lid. 'What's that?' I said, and he smiled and said, 'That's the strangest thing in the world. It'll be the making of me,' then he took my hand and put it on the pot and it was warm outside, like a brick that's been in the oven."

"I pulled my hand away, but he turned the lamp down and says 'Look at this, Mary.' He lifted the lid off that pot and there was a beautiful blue light came out of it, all shimmering like water. It took my breath away, I tell you. 'Whatever's in there?' I said, and he smiled again and said 'My fortune, Mary. No matter what my father may do,' and he closed the lid again."

"And what did you think it was?" enquired my friend.

"To tell the truth, I thought it was magic. I've never seen the like before or since." She got up from her chair. "I'll tell you something else, Mr Holmes, that I've never told nobody – sometimes I think it was what he had in that funny old pot that cured my brain. Now that's daft, isn't it?"

"You may very well be right, Mary," said Holmes. "If we might ask one more favour – is Mr Lewis's old room occupied?"

"No, sir," she said. "Did you wish to change?"

"Not at all," said Holmes, "but I would like a glimpse of that room."

She offered to take us up at once, and led us to a room at the end of the main landing. Holmes stood in the middle of the little, low-ceilinged bedroom, then stepped to the casement. "You can see the Moor from here," he observed, "and whose is that cottage next door?"

"That's old Mrs Henty's," said Mary. "She had a cure too. All her skin trouble went. Poor Mr Lewis, and little Georgie the boot boy and old McSwiney, they all went and all them others was sick, but Mrs Henty and me we seemed to get the good side. Funny, isn't it?"

"It is certainly strange," said Holmes, and led the way out of the room.

Holmes was down early in the morning, at the breakfast table before I joined him. He was in high good humour, though a cold snap in the night had brought a sprinkling of snow to Addleton.

"What next?" I asked him, having virtually abandoned any attempt to understand his enquiries.

"I told you, Watson. We have come here to view the *locus in quo*, and once the village photographer arrives, we shall pay a visit to this ill-famed barrow."

We had finished our breakfast when Mary informed us that Mr Swain, the village photographer, awaited us in the parlour. He greeted us cheerfully and offered the opinion that it would be pretty on the Moor in the snow.

We took the inn's pony-trap and, loading Mr Swain's equipment, set out for the Moor. Although the top of Addleton Moor lies at about 1,100 feet above sea level, a decent track winds up from the village at one corner and, even with a slight covering of snow, we had no difficulty in reaching the top.

On the exposed top the snow lay thicker, a blanket of white that glittered in the morning sun. All around us hummocks in the snow revealed the presence of burial mounds, each casting a pale lilac shadow in the white. Holmes stood up in the trap and gazed around him.

"Ah! There it is!" he exclaimed, and pointed.

Ahead of us and to our left a dark mark broke the whiteness and, as we moved towards it, we could see that it was another tumulus, bare both of snow and vegetation, exposing raw earth.

"Have you ever photographed the Black Barrow before?" Holmes asked the photographer.

"No, sir. That would be a wasted plate. Nobody hereabouts would pay for a picture of that thing," he replied with some vehemence.

We drew to a halt close to the Black Barrow and Mr Swain set up his camera under Holmes's directions. I walked around the mound, finding it nothing more than a heap of compacted soil, unrelieved by any blade of grass. Its lower edge was ringed with flat stones and, looking closely at its surface, it was possible to see where Sir Andrew's men had cut their trench through its centre. Apart from its nakedness, there was nothing to distinguish it from any of the forty or fifty mounds round about. One did not have to be superstitious to find something disturbing in that patch of dead, dark, soil.

I stepped aside while Mr Swain exposed half a dozen plates and then we were back in the trap and returning to the village.

Holmes was still in good spirits over luncheon, so that I queried his mood. "I have every right to be cheerful, Watson. This morning's excursion gave me the final piece of evidence. Nature has assisted my enquiry, though I made assurance doubly sure and asked Mr Swain for his photographs."

Mr Swain joined us over coffee, rather nervous and apologetic. "I do not know what has happened, Mr Holmes," he said. "The general views of the Moor are crystal clear, as they should have been with this morning's light, but all four plates of the barrow are spoiled. Look," he said and laid the box of plates on the table.

Holmes took each plate in turn and held it up to the window, passing each to me when he had done with it. Two were fine panoramas of the snowclad Moor but each of the others was just a swirl of fog.

"But this is exactly what Edgar said happened to his plates!" I exclaimed.

"Precisely," declared Holmes, "and thereby our case is closed. I am deeply grateful to you, Mr Swain."

The confused photographer took the money that Holmes offered, thanked him and left rapidly, as though he feared my friend would change his mind.

When the coffee was done Holmes drew out his watch. "We might", he said, "catch the mid-afternoon express to London. Would you be so kind as to ask the boy for our bags and the reckoning?"

On the way back to London Holmes discoursed wittily on anarchists and poisoners, on underworld argot and a dozen different topics, but I heard him with only half an ear for my mind was churning in its attempts to make sense of what Sherlock Holmes evidently regarded as a successful enquiry. At length I could stand it no longer.

"Holmes!" I exclaimed, "I have never been so completely at a loss to understand one of your enquiries. What in Heaven's name has this all been about?"

He laughed. "Do you recall", he said, "that when we had not known each other long you took issue with me over my proposition that, by logical deduction, it should be possible to infer the existence of an ocean from a single grain of sand?"

"Well, yes," I said, "but I was not then so familiar with your remarkable methods."

"I fear," he said, "that you are not yet familiar with them. I have been engaged in one of the most enjoyable enquiries that I can recall, enjoyable because I have had to infer the existence of something which I have never seen and to construct the pattern of its movements and assess its influence by pure reason."

"You have left me a long way behind," I grumbled.

"Consider the patterns, Watson," he said.

"The patterns on the casket?" I asked. "What of them?"

"No, Watson," he sighed. "The patterns of the evidence as it unfolded." He leaned forward.

"Let us begin at the beginning. The newspapers told us that snow would not lie and grass would not grow upon the Black Barrow. I admit I took that for folklore or exaggeration, but you heard Edgar say that it was the case. What did that suggest to you?"

I confessed to no idea at all.

"Watson!" he expostulated. "You have been in mining districts; you have seen heaps of coal waste on which grass will not grow nor the snow lie."

"But that is caused by fires smouldering within the heaps," I said. "Ordinary soil does not smoulder, Holmes."

"No indeed, Watson, but that analogy led me to believe that something within the barrow might be emitting some influence or emanation that warmed its surface yet discouraged growth."

"Such as what?" I asked.

"I admit that, at first, I could see no solution along that line, but then I recalled pitchblende."

"Pitchblende?" I echoed, "What on earth is that?"

"It is an ore, of uranium, found in several places. For centuries German miners have been aware of it and afraid of it, for they knew that it could cause burns and sickness. Now, you will recall my telling you of my experiments in coal-tar derivatives at the Montpelier laboratories in France, earlier this year?"

"Certainly."

"Among my colleagues there was a French scientist, Jacques Curie, a specialist in electro-magnetism. He introduced me to a remarkable group of people who have theories about that substance. One was a Monsieur Becquerel, another was Curie's own brother, Pierre, and another was Pierre's assistant and fiancee, a determined and intelligent young Polish lady called Marie Sklodovska. All of them believe that pitchblende emits some influence that can affect its surroundings."

"Good Heavens!" I said. "This sounds more like witch-craft than science."

"I assure you that they are all very fine scientists, Watson, and it occurred to me to proceed on the basis that they are right and that pitchblende, or something like it, had been hidden in that barrow when it was first set up."

He paused. "That would neatly explain our first few facts, but what of the disease? Well, Mr Edgar gave us the answer to that, with his clear proof that the bronze casket had been rifled in the night. Edgar's spoiled photographs were also the proof that something was in the barrow that spoiled his plates. He failed to realize it, but the later success of his photography was also the proof that something had been removed from the mound. He was sadly wrong about Sir Andrew's guilt. It was, of course, the younger Lewis. No doubt, as Edgar described, he waited at the inn for his father's return, and Sir Andrew, fresh from his discovery, would certainly have mentioned it to his son. And so Anthony Lewis robbed the Black Barrow that night as a revenge on his father for refusing to meet his debts, and by so doing he brought about his own death."

"By Jove!" I said, "I begin to see. Everyone who came near was affected in some degree, but he slept with it beneath his bed," and I shuddered at the thought of the luckless youth asleep while the malign emanations that Holmes had described seeped into him hour by hour.

"Exactly, Watson. I told you that we had stumbled upon a crime in our enquiries, but it brought with it its own fearful sentence. Sadly, the presence of that baleful urn at the 'Goat and Boots' was also responsible for the deaths and other effects in the village, though I suppose we should rejoice at the good fortune of Mrs Henty and young Mary. Evidently the influence of the substance is not entirely malign and, if my friends on the Continent, can refine and control it, it may yet prove a blessing."

"If it can destroy a malignant tumour it will be an enormous blessing," I said. "But how came Sir Andrew to die of its effects and why does the snow still not lie on the Black Barrow? Is there more of the stuff still in there?"

Holmes shook his head. "Sir Andrew would have realized his son's crime when he saw what was in the dead man's trunk, and to spare his dead son further shame he hid the urn. Somewhere secure, apparently, for it took ten years for the influence to affect him. When it did he will have realized the significance of the unique decoration on the outer casket. It was a warning that nobody heeded. He could not leave that deadly urn to destroy others. His notes prove that he connected it with his son's death and also suggested to me the remedy that he devised. The bolster confirmed it."

"Bolster?" I said, "Where was there a bolster?"

"A wooden implement, Watson, known as a bolster or lead-dresser, used by plumbers for knocking sheet lead into shape, as a moleskin pad impregnated with tallow is used to wipe the joints of leaden pipes and containers. Sir Andrew evidently recalled the leaden lining of the bronze casket and reasoned, perhaps, that it had some inhibiting influence on the ore's emanations. This morning's visit and Mr Swain's photographs confirmed my deduction. Sir Andrew's last visit to Addleton may have been to stand at his son's grave, but it was also to return the stolen urn to the Black Barrow. He was quite right. No one will re-open that mound, the locals keep away and there will never be a road or railway or houses on the Moor. Its poisonous influence is as harmless there as if it was at the bottom of the ocean."

"I admit that it all makes sense," I said, "but it still seems very theoretical to me."

"Theoretical!" he snorted. "The pieces of my puzzle have been the words of witnesses who had no cause to lie. All I have added is the unproven, but entirely reasonable, theory of a number of eminent scientists. In the absence of data, Watson, it is permissible to theorize in directions which do not conflict with such data as does exist. It seems that my application of their theory has provided Curie and his friends with further data. In connection with which, Watson, I must ask you not to add this case to your published stories if only because publication might prematurely disclose the reasoning of my French friends and rob them of their just triumph in due course. But I must really write and tell Curie this singular tale."

I confess that I had no intention of publishing an account of the Addleton affair. I could not fault Holmes's reasoning, but I could not quell a suspicion that it was all rather too logical and was not capable of proof.

Holmes wrote to Lady Cynthia and to Dr Leary, assuring them that the Addleton disease would never occur again and also to Edgar, explaining his understandable error. That fair-minded man wrote at once to the papers saying that, in the light of new information, he wholeheartedly and entirely withdrew any implication he had made against Sir Andrew Lewis.

Twenty-five years have elapsed since the Addleton tragedy and science has moved on. I owe my friend an apology for doubting him and I make it here. It was less than two years after Holmes had explained his reasoning to me that Becquerel established the existence of an emission from uranium ore which affected photographic plates. Miss Sklodovska, or Madame Curie as she is now widely known, realized that pitchblende contained something that emitted "Becquerel rays" more strongly than uranium and, thereby, discovered radium, the medicinal use of which has saved countless lives. The Curies and Becquerel have richly deserved their Nobel prizes for their efforts in turning a freak of nature to the advantage of mankind, and it seems to me that my friend Sherlock Holmes deserves recognition for having made what must surely have been the earliest practical application of their theories.

As to the deadly aspects of "Becquerel rays", they are now well understood by scientists. Now we know their dangers and, unlike our primitive forefathers, we do not have to fear that they will ever be carelessly unleashed upon the world.

THE ADVENTURE OF THE PARISIAN GENTLEMAN

Robert Weinberg & Lois H. Gresh

1

More than once in my chronicles detailing the amazing deductions of Sherlock Holmes have I commented on my friend's irritating lack of modesty. Though hating publicity of any sort, Holmes was justifiably proud of his work as a consulting detective. Never a humble man, he could be at times insufferably smug. However, when it came to morality, Sherlock Holmes never let vanity sway his sense of what was right. Never was this fact more clearly demonstrated than in the episode of the Parisian Gentleman.

It was a quiet evening in early October, 1894. A thick blanket of fog covered Baker Street. The evening edition contained little of interest and I relaxed, half-dozing, on the sofa. Holmes stood in front of the fire, smoking his pipe, a thoughtful expression on his face. From time to time, he glanced to the window. It was quite clear he was expecting a visitor.

"Are we due for some company tonight, my dear Holmes?" I asked, wondering what manner of trouble would soon be knocking at our door. "Something odd in the paper? Or, perhaps a difficult problem for the Yard?"

"Neither, Watson," declared Holmes, his eyes gleaming with amusement. "Our client comes from abroad. Start thinking about your wardrobe for a trip to the Continent. Tomorrow, we set off for Paris."

"What?" I said, astonished. "Obviously, Holmes, you've already had discussions with this new patron."

"Not at all," said Holmes. "I have never spoken to the gentleman."

"His letter then," I continued. "He mentioned details in his correspondence with you."

"Nothing of the sort," said Holmes. He dug out a folded piece of stationary from his jacket pocket and handed it to me. "See for yourself."

The paper was from the French Embassy. Scribbled in bold

handwriting were the words, *9 PM at your quarters. Utmost urgency. Privacy Required.* The note was signed, *Girac.*

"Who is this Girac?" I asked, shaking my head in bewilderment. I knew better than to question Holmes's deductions. Though how these few words signalled a journey to Paris was a mystery to me. "Do you know him?"

"Only by reputation," said Holmes. There were footsteps on the stairs leading to our rooms. My friend stepped to the door. "A member of the French Sûreté, he is quite famous for his problem-solving abilities. Some call him, I am told, the French Sherlock Holmes."

A brisk knock indicated the arrival of our guest. "Inspector Girac," said Holmes, as he ushered the Frenchman into our parlor. "I am Sherlock Holmes. And this is my friend and associate, Dr Watson."

"A pleasure, gentlemen," said Girac in a smooth, deep voice without the least trace of an accent. He was a tall, heavyset man with clean-shaven features, a thick mop of black hair, and dark, observant eyes. His gaze never rested, moving quickly from one point to another in our apartment. "Please excuse the lateness of the hour, but I needed to see you as soon as possible and embassy business kept me occupied until now."

"Please be seated," said Holmes, waving Girac to an empty chair. My friend strolled back to his place in front of the fire as the Frenchman sat down. "You are here, of course, concerning a new problem involving the Dreyfus case."

"*Mon Dieu!*" exclaimed Girac, his eyes bulging in shock. "Can it be there is a spy in the Embassy? My mission is quite secret. Other than the President himself, no one knows why I'm in England." The Frenchman shook his head in dismay. "We are undone."

"Surely, Holmes," I said, equally startled, "This revelation is magic."

"Nonsense," said Holmes. "Merely an elementary exercise in logical thinking, Watson. You should know by now that superstition is no match for basic deduction."

My friend held out the note he had shown me a few minutes earlier. He assumed the pose of a university professor, about to lecture his students. "Receiving this letter in the morning, I instantly knew important events were brewing. Why would Inspector Girac, famous in his own country as a detective and investigator, need to visit me? Only a case of the highest national interest, requiring he use every available resource, would force the Inspector to seek the skills of an outsider. But why me, a foreigner, instead of another member of the Sûreté? The answer had to be that Monsieur Girac harbored suspicions about his comrades. As you well know, Watson, police organizations are normally a tightly knit group. Such apprehensions can only be the result of national turmoil. While I do not regularly follow French politics, I am not blind to news of the world. It was therefore quite apparent to me that Girac's visit concerned the notorious Dreyfus spy case."

I nodded, immediately recognizing the truth in what Holmes said. The infamous crime had rocked France, unleashing long simmering hatreds. After Dreyfus's conviction for treason, powerful factions in the Army and Church had unleashed blistering verbal attacks on the Jewish population of France. The virulent race baiting had turned brother against brother, friend against friend. The whole country trembled on the brink of revolution. Once Holmes explained his reasoning, the inexplicable became transparent. "But, you mentioned a trip, Holmes?"

Holmes turned and his piercing eyes stared at the French police official. "Monsieur Girac's note demanded privacy, Watson. He wanted to meet at night, in secret. Not normal conduct for a member of the Sûreté. Besides, though his mission involved the Dreyfus Affair, that matter had already been settled in military court. The officer was pronounced guilty and sentenced.

"He has been sent to Devil's Island to serve the rest of his life in hard labor. Despite some doubts to the validity of the charges, the case is closed."

Holmes paused dramatically. The theater had lost a great thespian when my friend chose to become a detective. "Whatever aspect of the case Monsieur Girac wants me to investigate, it is definitely not a minor matter. Since the government refuses to conduct further investigations into the Dreyfus Case, the Inspector's business must concern possible repercussions from the affair. Since he does not trust his colleagues among the Sûreté, it seems logical he requires our assistance in their stead. Such investigations are best conducted at the scene of the crime. Girac comes from Paris, so I assume we are to travel there to pursue our case."

Girac, his features pale, nodded. "I need for you to return with me to Paris immediately, Mr Holmes. I dare not trust any of my assistants. No one knows who has been corrupted by this scandal. Treason walks at the highest levels of the government and the military. Disaster approaches and only with your help can I prevent it from happening."

"Pray tell," said Holmes, raising his pipe to his lips, "what is the nature of the catastrophe?"

"*Assassination*," whispered Girac, his tone low, as if afraid of being overheard. "I have from reliable sources that a group of Jewish anarchists have hired Jacques Huret, the Boulevard Assassin, to murder the new President of the Republic in retaliation for Dreyfus's imprisonment. I am resolved not to let that event take place."

"With the assassination of President Sadi Carnot just months ago," said Holmes, thoughtfully, "a second murder could quite possibly plunge France into civil war. I find it difficult to believe a group of Jewish intellectuals would embark on such a risky venture. Are you sure that they are the ones who hired Huret?"

"Who else has a motive?" declared Girac. He waved a hand in the air, dismissing Holmes's doubts. "The villains behind the crime are unimportant at present. What matters is the deed itself. In the past five years, Huret has been responsible for the deaths of nearly a dozen men. The few clues we've found indicate that he's a man of wealth and breeding. We don't know why such a man would be a killer, as he certainly doesn't need money."

"Perhaps," I said, choosing my words carefully, "he kills to prove his mental superiority over his peers."

Holmes shook his head. "For the true intellectual, such games are unnecessary. This flaw in Huret's character will be his downfall."

"Let us hope so," said Guret. "The man is a master of disguise. No one knows his features or his methods. He strikes like a snake then disappears without ever being seen. Only his victims serve as evidence of his skill.

"You are famous as a solver of crimes, Mr Holmes. However, the challenge faced here is much greater. Can you, without clues or evidence, prevent a murder from taking place? Can you stop Huret, Parisian man-about-town and professional murderer, from crippling my country?"

My friend's eyes glistened with excitement. He lived for such moments. "Your assessment of the difficulty of the case is correct, Inspector. Preventing a crime verges on the impossible. Outguessing a dedicated assassin requires genius. The criminal can pick his time, his spot, and his method of execution. There are too many variables to prepare for every possibility. And, from what little I have read about Huret, he is the best of the breed. In the past, he has proven unstoppable. But," and there was more than a hint of arrogance in my friend's voice, "never before has he been confronted by Sherlock Holmes."

2

The next morning, Holmes and I set off for Paris. It was a dull, uneventful trip. For secrecy's sake, we traveled on our own, without Girac. Holmes remained deep in thought the entire journey, his eyes closed in concentration. Knowing better than to disturb, I kept myself busy by reading the accounts of Huret's previous crimes left with us by Inspector Girac.

The more I read, the worse I felt. Holmes had faced many challenges in his illustrious career, but never before had he faced a criminal without a face. Huret was no street Apache roaming the back alleys of Paris. The assassin was a gentleman rogue who mocked the police over their inability to stop him.

Though he was responsible for nearly a dozen murders, Huret remained a complete enigma to the Sûreté. He could be anyone, a fact gleefully picked up by the newspapers who dubbed Huret "The Boulevard Assassin". As the journalists had it, the murderer could be the gentleman walking the boulevard at your side. He could be your neighbor or your best friend. He could be anyone.

In one instance, Huret disguised himself as an Earl's footman. Having killed the real servant, Huret took his place, and several days later, murdered the nobleman on the way to the opera. Clearly, Huret's disguise had been so masterful that he completely fooled the Earl, a man who had employed the footman for twenty years.

Perhaps worse, on another occasion, Huret assumed the identity of a chef in one of Paris' leading clubs. In a private room, an elderly Viscount and his three sons were dining. Huret cooked an elaborate dinner – red mullet with Cardinal sauce, turtle soup, oyster pâtés, fish, sweetbreads, stewed beef, fruit, chocolate creams: ten full courses in all. Huret was seen by the owner of the club and the servants who waited on the diners; all were convinced that Huret was the chef they'd known for the past sixteen years. By the time the servants left the kitchen with the desserts and sherry, Huret was long gone. But the sherry killed all four men.

The only fact known about Huret was that he was a man of tremendous vanity. He delighted in baiting the police. After each crime, he sent a letter to the leading newspapers claiming responsibility for the assassination. According to his statements, he wanted no innocent bystander blamed for his deed. Oftentimes, Huret mentioned sharing a drink with his victim shortly before their death. In his closing, the assassin never failed to state that after posting his letter he would raise a glass of champagne, paid by his ill-gotten gains, in a farewell toast to his victim, then down it with a dish of currant pudding.

That audacious act of knavery elucidated Holmes's only remark on the crimes during our entire trip. We were in a cab speeding to the house Girac had arranged for our use while in Paris. "You noticed, Watson, that Huret in each of his letters never once fails to describe his farewell toast," said Holmes, breaking long hours of silence.

"He might be a gentleman in station, Holmes," I replied, "but he is a rogue at heart. The insufferable gall of the man, Holmes!"

"Actually, I thought his posts were quite clever," said Holmes, who then proceeded not to say another word.

Girac met us personally at the house located only a short distance from the Chamber of Deputies. That he came alone was yet another indication of his mistrust of those in his own office.

"I have done exactly as you requested, Mr Holmes," said Girac as soon as we were alone. "I informed several members of the Chamber of Deputies that the President, at my urging, has agreed to take a much-needed vacation in the country. They accepted my story that this constant bickering over the Dreyfus affair has him weary of Paris. Though I refused to reveal the exact location of his hideaway, I did mention a secure villa in the south of France, guarded round the clock by my most trusted assistants."

"Good work," said Holmes. "The trap is set."

Girac grimaced. "You suspect one of the ministers is involved in the plot? Or several?"

"Perhaps, perhaps not," said Holmes mysteriously. "However. I feel confident that news of Casimir-Perier's trip will soon reach Huret. Aware of his limitations, he will try to strike before the scheduled journey."

Holmes made no mention of what those limitations might be, and as Girac said nothing, I felt it best to remain silent. Lighting his pipe, Holmes deeply inhaled the smoke. "You have the President's itinerary for the next few days with you?"

"Of course," said Girac. "He is scheduled for a full round of meetings tomorrow. In the evening, he travels to his club for an informal dinner with the Belgian ambassador. Afterwards, he plans to attend a reception for a few close friends at their embassy. The next day, he consults with the Minister of Finance. That night, he is scheduled to attend the opera. The following morning, his supposed vacation begins."

"The opera," I declared, "that is where Huret will strike. What better location for the rogue. A huge crowd, plenty of noise. A meeting place for the Boulevard set. The perfect place for an assassination attempt."

"You have the mind of a policeman, Watson," said Holmes, drawing in another puff of smoke.

He nodded to Girac. "I'm sure the Doctor would enjoy dinner at the President's club, Girac. Why not arrange for him to accompany you while you keep watch tomorrow evening?"

"But what of you, Holmes?" I asked.

"I shall be nearby, Watson," replied Holmes, the smoke curling about his head like a mask.

Upon rising the next morning, I discovered Holmes was already gone – on errands, according to Girac – but that he would meet us in the evening. Though he rarely discussed his far travels after his final duel with Professor Moriarity, I knew that Holmes had spent considerable time in Paris. Much of that period was spent investigating the curious affair of the Opera Ghost. My friend knew every twist and turn of the fabled Paris Opera House. I felt certain he was visiting old haunts and making preparations to deal with a new phantom.

I spent most of the day with Girac, reviewing his plans for protecting the President. The Inspector's greatest challenge was to make sure that his men always remained in the background, not noticeable. News of a plot to assassinate Casimir-Perier could be almost as damaging to the state of the nation as the act itself. The President was surrounded by police, but all in disguise, and all at a distance. It was a difficult assignment, but Girac handled it with a cool head and keen mind. I could find no fault in his preparations.

Dinner was at nine, and Girac and I arrived by carriage shortly before it was scheduled to begin. There was no sign of Holmes and I was beginning to worry. Huret had killed a dozen men. Holmes was quite capable of defending himself in a brawl, but what chance did he have against a professional assassin?

The dining room of the club was a small, intimate chamber, with no more than a dozen tables. The rich and powerful of France took supper here and Girac delighted in pointing out those politicians he distrusted, whose number encompassed nearly everyone in the room. In the background, a string quartet played soft music.

The food was excellent, though not the hearty English fare I preferred. Wine flowed freely and after long hours of worry, I relaxed. A half-dozen of Girac's best men, dressed as gentlemen of leisure, were scattered throughout the dining room. Another three inspectors assisted the waiters.

We were just starting our quail when one of Girac's men approached the table. Bending over, he consulted for a moment in low tones with the Inspector. The color drained from Girac's face.

"Please, excuse me for a moment, Doctor Watson," said Girac, getting to his feet. "There has been a disturbance outside. Some sort of scuffle involving the coachman. I will return in an instant. Please pay close attention to our . . . clients."

I nodded, feeling perfectly safe in the dining room with the President surrounded by nearly a dozen police officers. Still, I worried where Holmes might be.

Girac had been gone for less than a minute when, without warning, a series of extremely loud pistol shots rang out in the courtyard fronting the club. Instantly, all through the room, men leapt to their feet and quickly converged on the President and his guest. The other patrons of the club, not knowing what was happening and seeing the stampede, started shouting. For a few seconds, panic reigned unchecked.

"Quickly," said one of the officers, his authoritative voice rising over the pandemonium, "guard the entrance. Allow no one other than Inspector Girac. I will escort the President through the kitchen to safety."

"That, sir, I regret to inform you," said the violinist, stepping apart from the Chamber Quartet and placing a hand on the policeman's right arm, "will not be possible."

Angrily, the officer tried to shake himself free. But the musician refused to let go. "Who the devil do you think you are, giving orders to a member of the Sûreté?" the officer demanded, his voice shrill.

"I am Sherlock Holmes," said the violinist. "And you sir, despite your protests to the contrary, are not a police officer. Instead, I believe I have the pleasure of addressing Huret, the notorious Boulevard Assassin."

3

"You are insane," declared the officer, shaking himself free of Holmes's grip. "You are jeopardizing the life of the President with your mad accusations."

Inspector Girac returned to the dining room and stared at the officer, as if trying to determine who he was. He shook his head, puzzled. "You look like Edward Ronet, but . . ."

The officer laughed. He was tall and handsome, with soft brown eyes, smooth brows, and a delicate mouth. His hair was a spray of blond curls peeking from beneath his officer's cap. "I *am* Edward Ronet. I've been in your employ, sir, for most of my life, as was my father before me."

Holmes removed his own cap, then peeled off a wig of long dark curls. "You are not the only master of disguise in this room," he said, with a slight smile. "Accept your fate, Huret. Your bluff is undone."

My friend glanced at the Inspector. "Any problems with the street Apaches outside."

"They were nothing," said Girac, shrugging. "Just a minor disturbance."

"As I thought," said Holmes. "Such working class hoodlums posed no threat to the safety of Monsieur Casimir-Perier. They're after nothing but a rowdy good time. A small but important part of Huret's scheme."

Inspector Girac stared at the false officer. "An excellent disguise, but not good enough. Ronet has a small scar beneath his left eye. You, sir, do not."

Girac gestured to his men. "Escort the President and the Ambassador to their carriage. They are overdue at the Embassy. Keep close watch, though I suspect there is nothing more to fear."

Girac returned his gaze to Huret. "Take this one to the prison. Lock him in solitary, and guard him well. I've waited a long time to meet Monsieur Huret. We have a great deal to discuss. I am sure our conversations will be most interesting. But, before we speak, I personally want to inform the newspapers that he will no longer be writing them letters."

"Brag all you like," snarled Huret, as the police dragged him off. "It doesn't matter. You have no evidence, no proof. I have powerful friends. You will never see me stand trial."

Holmes' features were grim as the officers dragged Huret from the dining room. "He's a very dangerous man, Girac. To many people."

"I will make sure he is guarded day and night, Mr Holmes," declared the Inspector. The room had emptied and we stood alone in its center. "The President, I am sure, will want to thank you personally for saving his life. A brilliant piece of detection."

Holmes waved a hand in the air, as if dismissing the compliment. "Elementary, Girac. Huret's letters to the newspapers aroused my immediate suspicion. No truly professional criminal brags of his crimes without reason. Best to keep their misdeeds secret. Since Huret never failed to write about each murder, I sensed that the communications served some purpose. The common thread in all of them was his mention of a champagne toast to his victim. I therefore reasoned that Huret was trying to establish his status as a gentleman of leisure."

"The papers dubbed him the Boulevard Assassin, Holmes," I declared. "So he succeeded in convincing them of his stature."

"Exactly, Watson. And what gentleman would ever stoop so

low as to associate with the working class? Definitely not a Boulevardier."

"So our assassin assumed the identities of common laborers to commit his crimes?" asked Girac.

"Exactly," said Holmes. "Along with his champagne toast, he always mentioned a bit of currant pudding in his letters. What gentleman eats pudding, Inspector? That is a meal for the poor."

"But surely, Holmes," I said, "why would Huret give himself away, while at the same time, pushing his image as a Boulevardier?"

Holmes reached into his violin case for his pipe. "You gave me that answer, Watson, when you remarked that Huret killed to prove his mental superiority over his peers. And I told you that such vanity would be Huret's downfall. Some of us have no need to play such games. Huret simply wasn't smart enough."

"The scoundrel!" exclaimed Girac. "To think he could pull this off, pretending to be one of my men –"

"A rogue, as Doctor Watson described him," said Holmes, "but nonetheless a clever one. Who better to commit a crime than an assassin disguised as a police officer? They can go where others cannot, are ignored by the general public, and are considered above suspicion. And, except to a perceptive few, one policeman looks like every other."

"An assassin who disguised himself as a member of the police force," I declared, amazed. "What audacity."

"Tonight?" asked Girac.

"With no guarantee when the President would return to Paris, Huret had to strike before Casimir-Periot left. His employers, whomever they may be, I am sure wanted immediate results. Thus, he was forced to choose between the opera or the club.

"The crowds of people at the opera, I suspect, would have made it impossible for him to reach the President. Besides, with the police thinking him a gentleman, they would naturally assume he would prefer to act in such surroundings. That belief was, of course, mistaken. Huret's success relied on deceit and disguise. In the confines of a private club, his chance of success was much greater. I planned a trap, using the President as bait, and Huret stepped into my web.

"His plan was simple and effective. An attack by street thugs on the President's carriage draws you, Girac, away from the dining room. Then, the same thugs fire their pistols into the air, creating a disturbance inside the club. In the ensuing confusion, Huret enters from the kitchen, in police uniform. By sheer force of will, he commands your men to guard the front door – from a menace that does not exist – while he escorts the President to safety. Once out of sight, he stabs the President and walks away, mentally composing his letter to the newspapers."

"He would have made a fool of me and my men, Mr Holmes," said Girac. "I owe you a debt that cannot be paid."

"I will take that into account when I send you my bill, Inspector," replied Holmes, solemnly.

4

We returned to London the next day, arriving back in the city to be confronted by several challenging problems that kept Holmes busy for the next few months. Our brief visit to Paris was almost forgotten until we received two final reminders of the case.

The first was a terse note from Girac. "Huret killed while trying to escape."

"As the assassin predicted, Watson," said Holmes, his face set in grim lines, "his case never went to trial. Though I doubt he realized he was forecasting his own murder. Huret knew too many secrets to be allowed to testify."

The second came by messenger from the French Embassy. Enclosed in a box was an autograph letter of thanks from the French President and the Order of the Legion of Honour. It was one of many awards given to Holmes by foreign governments, most of which decorated our quarters in Baker Street. Holmes stared at the letter and the medal for quite some time. Then, he looked me right in the eye, the container resting on his knees.

"I am not a fool, Watson, placated by trinkets and certificates. A secret cabal of Jewish anarchists did not hire Huret. He was engaged by the French military, who hoped that killing the President would create even greater problems for the liberals and Jews in their country. The President's own supporters and political allies wanted him dead, a martyr to their cause. The President's life meant nothing to them. I suspect if he is wise, he will resign shortly.

"As for Captain Dreyfus, my readings about the affair as well as our pursuit and capture of Huret have convinced me that the Captain was completely innocent of all charges. He was made a scapegoat by his superiors because of his religious beliefs. Girac came to us not because he didn't trust his men, but because he didn't trust his government. As he stated, the corruption was everywhere. Many of the most important politicians and officials in France knew the truth but did nothing."

With a sigh, Holmes dropped the container holding the autograph letter and the medal into a drawer of his desk. "When Dreyfus is a free man, I will post these awards Watson. Until then, they will remain untouched."

For twelve long years, the medal and the letter stayed sealed in that drawer, even after Holmes moved to Sussex. Sherlock Holmes was a man of his word. And, for all of his vanity, he was a man of honor.

THE ADVENTURE OF THE INERTIAL ADJUSTOR

Stephen Baxter

Our visitor was perhaps twenty-eight: a short, broad-shouldered young man, a little prone to fat, the voice high and thin, and he moved with a bright, bird-like bounce. His face, under thinning hair, was pale – perhaps he was consumptive – and his blue eyes were striking, wide and dreaming. He could hardly have presented a greater contrast, physically and in his manner, to my friend Holmes. And yet his conversation sparked with Holmes's, as if their two minds were poles of some huge electrical battery.

This visitor had presented Holmes with a set of rather grainy photographs, taken with one of the New York Kodaks which are so popular. Holmes was inspecting these with his lens. The visitor, with some malicious glee, was challenging Holmes to deduce, from the evidence of each photograph, the elements of some unusual situation, after the manner of a parlour game. Holmes had just finished with a blurred image of some withered white flowers. I studied this for myself, and could see little untoward about the flowers, although I could not immediately place their natural order – perhaps it was the genus *Malva* – for instance, the shape of the gynoecium, clearly visible, was rather unusual. Holmes appeared rather irritated by this harmless image, and had passed on to the next, while his young visitor was grinning. "I'm not surprised he made nothing of it. The apparatus of a classic hoaxer!" he told me.

Holmes passed me the next print. "See here, Watson. What can you make of that?"

This appeared more promising – and, I observed, the visitor was somewhat more serious about it. At first glance it seemed to me an undistinguished portrait of a commonplace luncheon party – although it was set in unusual surroundings, the table and guests being all but engulfed by bulky electrical equipment, wires and cylinders and coils and cones, and in the background I could make out the fittings of a workshop: a steam lathe, metal turners, acetylene welding equipment, a sheet-metal stamp and the like. I ventured, "I observe that our visitor this evening was a guest at the lunch. I do not know these others –"

"They are the Brimicombes, of Wiltshire," said the visitor. "My hosts that day: two brothers, Ralph and Tarquin. Ralph is an old college friend of mine. The brothers work together – or did so – on mechanical and electrical inventions."

"It was a sunny day," I said. "I see a splash of light here on the tablecloth, just behind the dish containing this handsome sausage."

"Yes," said Holmes with tolerant patience, "but what of the sausage itself?"

I looked again. The sausage sat on its own plate, the centrepiece of the meal. "It is a succulent specimen. Is it German?"

Holmes sighed. "Watson, that is no sausage, German or otherwise. It is evidently a prank, of dubious taste, served on their guests by these Brimicombes."

The visitor laughed. "You have it, Mr Holmes. You should have seen our faces when that giant concoction crawled off its plate and across the tablecloth!"

"A man of your profession should recognize the beast, Watson. It is an aquatic annelid, of the suctorial order *Hirudinea*, employed for the extraction of blood –"

"Great Heaven," I cried, "it is a giant leech!"

"You cannot see the colour in the Kodak," said the visitor, "but you should know it was a bright red: as red as blood itself."

"But how can this be, Holmes? Is it some freak of nature?"

"Of nature – or Man's science," Holmes mused. "Consider the influences acting on that wretched leech. It is drawn towards flatness by the force of the gravity of the Earth; that much we know. And its collapse to a pancake is resisted only by its internal strength. But it is hard to believe a creature as gross as this specimen would even be able to sustain its own form. Why, then, has it evolved such a magnitude? What gives it the strength to hold itself up, to move?" He eyed his visitor sharply. "Or perhaps we should ask, *what is reducing the force which drags it down?*"

The visitor clapped his hands in delight. "You have it, sir!"

Holmes handed back the photograph. "Indeed. And perhaps you might care to set out the particulars of the case."

Confused, I asked, "Are you so sure you have a case at all, Holmes?"

"Oh, yes," he said gravely. "For did our visitor not speak of the work of these Brimicombe brothers in the past tense? Evidently something has disturbed the equilibrium of their fraternal lives; and you would not be here, sir, if that were not something serious."

"Indeed," was the reply, and now the visitor was solemn. "There could be nothing more serious, in fact: my visit here was motivated by the death of the elder brother, Ralph, in unusual circumstances – circumstances deriving from the more obscure corners of the physical sciences!"

I asked, "Is it murder?"

"The local coroner does not think so. I, however, am unsure. There are puzzling features – inconsistencies – and so I have come to you, Mr Holmes – I am a journalist and author, not a detective."

I smiled. "In fact, sir, I already know your occupation."

He seemed surprised. "Forgive me. We have not been introduced."

"No introduction is necessary, nor was any deep deduction on my part. Your portrait has been as common enough this year."

He looked flattered. "You know my work?"

"As it has been featured in the *Pall Mall Budget*, *The National Observer* and elsewhere. I am a great admirer of your scientific romances." I extended my hand. "It is good to meet you, Mr Wells!"

Holmes agreed to travel with Wells to the Brimicombe home, near Chippenham, and he prevailed on me to accompany him, despite my reluctance to leave London, so close was I to my bereavement. But Holmes persisted, kindly. "You know how few of my cases involve the deeper mysteries of science, Watson. Perhaps this will be a suitable candidate for your casebook! It will be quite like old times." And so it was, the very next day, that I found myself with my valise clambering aboard the ten-fifteen from Paddington Station. We had the carriage to ourselves, Holmes, Wells and I. Holmes wrapped himself in his grey travelling-cloak and stretched out his long legs on the cushioned seat, as Wells, in his thin, piping voice, set out the full details of the case for us.

"I have known Ralph Brimicombe since we both attended the Normal School of Science in the 'eighties," he began, "and I remained in friendly contact with him until his recent death. He was a rather dream-like, remote figure – oddly impractical in the details of everyday life – to the extent that I was somewhat surprised when he married, when still a student at the Normal School. But his mind always sparked with creative energy. His subjects at the School were Astronomy, Astrophysics – all that sort of thing – along with Electricity and Magnetism. Even as a student he began to develop intriguing ideas about the coupling, as he put it, between electricity and gravity. Our theories of gravity were long due for an overhaul, he claimed. And perhaps there could even be practical applications. He was a delight to debate with! – you can imagine how I found him a soul-mate."

Holmes asked, "A coupling?"

"Gravity, as you know, is that force which imbues our bodies with weight. Ralph became convinced that the gravity of a large mass such as the Earth could be mitigated by a suitable arrangement of large currents and magnetic fluxes. Mitigated, or reduced."

"Reduced?" I said. "But if that were true, the commercial possibilities would be enormous. Think of it, Holmes. If one could reduce the weight of freight goods, for example –"

"Oh, to hang with commerce and freight!" Wells exclaimed. "Doctor Watson, Ralph Brimicombe claimed to have found a way to have removed the influence of gravity altogether. Without gravity, one could fly! He even claimed to have built a small capsule, and flown himself – alone, mind you, and without witnesses – all the way to the moon. He showed me injuries which he said were due to an exhaustion of his food and water, an exposure to the Rays of Space, and burns from the lunar Vacuum. And he gave me a small vial, of what he claimed was moon dust, as 'proof' of his journey. I have it about me." He patted his pockets.

Holmes raised a thin eyebrow. "And did you believe these claims?"

Wells hesitated. "Perhaps I wished to. But not entirely. Ralph was never above exaggerating his achievements, so impatient was he for acceptance and prestige.

"But I run ahead of my account. Ralph, for all his ability, could only scrape through the examinations at the Normal School, so distracted did he become by his gravitational obsession. After that, no respectable institution would take him on, and no journal would publish the revised theories and partial experimental results he claimed." Wells sighed. "Perhaps Ralph's greatest tragedy was the untimely death of his father, some months after he left the Normal School. The father had made a fortune in the Transvaal, and had retired to Chippenham, only to die of recurrent malaria. He left everything, with few tiresome legal complications, to his two sons: Ralph, and the younger Tarquin. This sudden legacy made Ralph a rich man. No longer did he need to convince peers of the value of his work. Now, he could plough a lone furrow, wherever it might take him.

"Ralph returned to Wiltshire, and devoted himself to his studies. He privately published his results which – while of great interest to students of the esoteric like myself – were roundly and rudely rejected by other scientists."

"And what of Tarquin?" Holmes asked.

"I knew Tarquin a little. I never much liked him," Wells said. "He was quite a contrast to Ralph. Full of vanity and self-regard, and not nearly so intelligent, though he has some smattering of an education, and, as I understand it, a crude grasp of his brother's accomplishments. Tarquin squandered his own inheritance in trying to follow his father's footsteps in Southern Africa, failed roundly, and came home pursued by debtors. Eventually his brother took him on as a species of senior assistant. Tarquin acquired equipment for Ralph's experiments, arranged apparatus and so forth. But even in this he proved less than competent, and Ralph was forced to demote him, effectively, to work as subordinate to Ralph's own engineer, a stolid local chap called Bryson."

I remarked, "It looked as if your lunch party took place in the midst of Ralph's apparatus."

"Yes." Wells smiled. "He was fond of such spectaculars. And I must describe the purpose of that apparatus to you, for it will be of significance to your investigation.

"I have mentioned Ralph's attempts – partially successful, he claimed – to nullify gravity. But this proved possible only over a small volume. To extend his abilities – to build greater ships which might carry teams of men across the Void of Space – Ralph pursued studies of more subtle aspects of the gravitational phenomenon, notably the Equivalence between Inertial and Gravitational Mass. You see –"

I held up my hands. "I cannot speak for Holmes, but I am already baffled, Mr Wells. I know nothing of gravity, save for its slow dragging at the lower spines and arches of my patients."

"Let me explain by analogy. Mr Holmes, can I trouble you for some coins? A sovereign and a farthing should do – there. Thank you." He held the two coins over the carriage floor. "Look here, Watson. The sovereign is considerably heavier than the farthing."

"That is clear enough."

"If I release these coins simultaneously they will fall to the floor."

"Of course."

"But which will arrive first? – the farthing, or the sovereign?"

Holmes looked amused. I felt that embarrassed frustration which sometimes comes over me when I cannot follow some elaborated chain of reasoning. And yet, the case seemed simple enough. "The sovereign," I said. "Disregarding the resistance of the air, as the heavier of the two –"

Wells released the coins. They fell side by side, and struck the carriage floor together.

"I am no expert in Gravitational Mechanics," Holmes chided me, "but I do remember my Galileo, Watson."

Wells retrieved the coins. "It is all to do with various Laws of Newton. Under gravity, all objects fall at the same rate, regardless of their mass. Think of it this way, Watson: if you were in a lift, and the cable snapped, you and the lift would fall together. You would feel as if you were floating, inside the lift car."

"Briefly," I said, "until the shaft floor was reached."

"Indeed. It was precisely this effect which Ralph strove to study. In the luncheon chamber I showed you, with an apparatus of coils and cones and loops, he managed to create a region of space in which – as Ralph showed us with a series of demonstrations and tricks – thanks to the adjustment of the gravity field with electrical energy, heavier objects did indeed fall more rapidly than the lighter! This was the 'Inertial Adjustor', as Ralph called it. It sounds a trivial feat – and is much less spectacular than shooting a capsule at the moon – but it is nonetheless quite remarkable. If true."

"But you doubt it," Holmes said. "In fact, you employed the word 'tricks'."

Wells sighed. "Dear old Ralph. I do not think he lied deliberately. But his optimism and energy for his own work would sometimes cloud his critical judgement. And yet the acceptance of his theories and devices – particularly his Inertial Adjustor – were central to his life, his very mental state."

"So central, in fact, that they led to his death."

"Indeed," said Wells. "For it was in that very chamber, within the Inertial Adjustor itself, that Ralph Brimicombe died – or was killed!"

It was after three o'clock when at last we reached Chippenham. We took a trap to the Brimicombe residence, a well-appointed affair of the Regency period which had been rather allowed to run to seed.

Holmes stepped from the trap and sniffed the air. He walked to the verge of the gravel drive and inspected the lawn grass, which I noticed was discoloured here and there by small brown circles, samples of which Holmes disturbed gently with the toecap of his boot.

A young man came out to meet us: tall and blond, his eyes a vacuous grey. He greeted Wells rather contemptuously – "If it isn't Bertie Wells!" – and introduced himself as Tarquin Brimicombe. We were escorted into the house and introduced to various others of the household. Jane, the widow of Ralph, was a tall, willowy woman who was younger than I expected, and her eyes were puffy as if from habitual crying; and Jack Bryson, Ralph's trusted engineer, bald of head and square of shoulder, appeared puzzled and ill at ease.

Holmes smiled at the widow with the sudden kind warmth perceived in him only by those who know him well, and which made my own heart rise, for I sympathized all too well with this lady's loss of her spouse. "Madam," said Holmes. "My very deepest sympathies."

"Thank you."

"And how is your labrador? Is she still ill?"

She looked confused. "Convalescing, I think. But how did you know?"

He inclined his head. "The patches on the lawn are clear evidence of a canine – and a bitch at that, for it is well known that a bitch will empty her bladder in a single spot, so depositing enough material to damage the grass, whereas a dog will release small quantities of liquid to mark his territory. I have a monograph in draft on the excretory habits of other domestic and urban wildlife. And as to her breed, the golden hairs adhering to your lower skirt are evidence enough of that, Mrs Brimicombe, as well as to your affection for the animal."

"Oh! But you knew of her illness?"

Holmes smiled sadly. "If she were well, I should expect her to come bounding out with you to challenge three such rough strangers as ourselves."

Wells clucked admiringly.

Jane Brimicombe waved a hand rather vaguely. "The illness is baffling to the vets. Sheba has some difficulty standing, and her bones are oddly brittle and prone to breaking. She was involved in experiments of Ralph's, you see, and –"

"I know," said Holmes.

"You do? But how?"

But Holmes did not answer. Instead he drew me aside. "Watson, I'd be grateful if you'd take a sample of the droppings from the wretched animal. Perform some kind of assay."

"Looking for what?"

"My dear fellow, if I told you that I might prejudice your results."

"And how am I supposed to achieve it? I am no vet, Holmes, still less a chemist. And we are a long way from town."

"I am sure you will find a way." Now he turned back to Mrs Brimicombe, and with deft skill, began to draw her out on the subject of her husband's demise.

"It was early morning. I was in the kitchen. Mr Bryson had just come in, having completed an hour's work already." She avoided the eyes of the engineer Bryson, I observed, and the soubriquet "Mr Bryson" did not come naturally to her lips. "We would often eat together, though Mr Bryson was always busy and in a rush. For breakfast he would eat one fried egg and a slice of toast."

"Egg?" asked Holmes. "What egg?"

"From the small coop we keep at the back of the house," Mrs Brimicombe said.

Holmes asked, "And how was the egg that day?"

Mrs Brimicombe dropped her gaze. "Mr Bryson remarked on its fine flavour. I recall Tarquin – Mr Brimicombe – brought them in from the coop, fresh that morning."

"Really?" Holmes turned an appraising eye on the brother, Tarquin. "Sir, are you in the habit of visiting the hen-house?"

Tarquin blustered. "I should say not – I used to help Millie with the eggs as a boy – it was a fine morning – can't a fellow act on impulse once in a while?"

Wells was growing impatient. "Look here, Holmes, why are you so interested in this business of a breakfast egg? Isn't it rather trivial? And can't you see it's causing the lady distress?"

I knew my friend well enough to understand that nothing is truly trivial – there was surely some pattern to his close questioning which none of us could discern – but Mrs Brimicombe was, indeed, becoming agitated, and so Holmes dropped his interrogation of her and allowed Tarquin to lead us through to the drawing room, where he provided sherry. "I have to say I did not invite Mr Wells here," he said. "At first I regarded his interest and his insistence on coming here as an intrusion into my family's grief. But my view has changed, as I have meditated on the recent tragic events. Now that you are here I am glad, Mr Holmes. I need your help."

"Why so?"

"Ralph's life was not lost. Mr Holmes, it was stolen. After the coroner's report, the police are not interested. I was not sure who to approach, and –"

Holmes held up his hands. "Tell me exactly what you mean."

His pale blue eyes were fixed on Holmes. "Ralph's death was no accident."

"Who was present in the Inertial Adjustor chamber at the time of the incident?"

"Only two of us. Myself and Bryson, my brother's engineer."

"Then," I said doggedly, "you are accusing Bryson –"

"– of murder. That is right, doctor. Jack Bryson killed Ralph."

Holmes is always impatient to visit the scene of a crime, and Wells was clearly enjoying the whole affair hugely; and so we agreed to accompany Tarquin at once to the Inertial Adjustor chamber, the site of Ralph Brimicombe's death.

We had a walk of a hundred yards or so across the grounds to an out-building. By now it was late afternoon. I took deep breaths of wood-scented air, trying to clear my head after the fumes of the train. I could hear the clucking of chickens, evidently from the hen coop Mrs Brimicombe had mentioned.

I was startled when an insect no less than six inches long scuttled across my path, disturbed by my passage. At first I thought it must be a cockroach, but on closer observation, to my astonishment, it proved to be an ant. It ran with a blur of legs towards an anthill – a gigantic affair, towering over the lower trees like an eroded monument.

"Good Lord, Holmes," I said. "Did you observe that? What was it, do you think, some tropical species?"

He shook his head. "Ralph Brimicombe was no collector of bugs. Given the pattern of events here I have expected some such apparition."

"You expected it? But how?"

"Surely that repulsive red leech of Wells's was enough of a clue. But in any event – all in good time, my dear friend."

We reached a laboratory, of crude but functional construction, and I ran my eyes for the first time over the gruesome details of the Inertial Adjustor itself. The main chamber was fifty feet tall; and it was dominated by the stupendous wreck of a vehicle. This latter had been a cone some fifteen feet in length and perhaps as broad, but it was without wheels, sails or runners: for its purpose, Tarquin told us in all seriousness, had been to fly, freed of gravity by Ralph's invention, into Space! To simulate to its occupant some of the stresses and impacts to be expected during a flight, the vessel had been suspended in midair, at the heart of the Inertial Adjustor itself, by a series of cables and gimbals.

Now the cables dangled uselessly. The ship, after an evident fall, had gouged a crater a few inches deep in the floor; it looked as if a great hammer had pounded into the concrete. And it was inside this capsule, this aluminium dream of flight in Space, that Ralph Brimicombe had fallen to his death.

Around the massive wreck were arrayed the elements of the Inertial Adjustor apparatus: coils and armatures, cones of paper and iron, filamented glass tubes, the poles of immense permanent magnets, great shadowy shapes which reached up and out of my vision, the whole far beyond my comprehension. There were besides some more mundane elements: drafting tables laden with dusty blueprints, lathes and vices and tools, chains for heavy lifting suspended from the ceiling.

I observed, however, that the fall of the vehicle had done a pretty damage to the equipment in that chamber, surely rendering it inoperative.

My eye was caught by a series of small glass-walled cages, beside a dissecting table. There was a series of leeches in stoppered jars, none of them as big as the specimen in Wells's photograph, but all so large they were indeed unable even to sustain their characteristic tubular forms; they lay against the thick glass at the bottom of their jars, in evident distress. Among the higher animals imprisoned here there were mice, but of an unusual morphology, with remarkably long and spindly limbs. Some of the mice, indeed, had trouble supporting their own weight. I remarked on this to Holmes, but he made no comment.

Holmes, Wells and I stepped over the crater's cracked lip and walked around the wrinkled aluminium of the capsule's hull. The fall had been, I judged, no more that ten feet – a drop that seemed barely enough to injure, let alone kill a man – but it had been sufficient to compress the ship's entire structure by perhaps a third of its length.

"How terrible," Wells said. "It was in this very spot – suspended under the glittering hull of Brimicombe's moon ship itself – that he bade us dine."

"Then perhaps you have had a lucky escape," said Holmes grimly.

"The workmen have cut the capsule open." Tarquin indicated a square rent in the wall, a shadowed interior beyond. "The body was removed after the police and the coroner studied the scene. Do you want to look in there? Then I will show you where Bryson and I were working."

"In a minute," said Holmes, and he studied the corpse of the fantastic ship with his usual bewildering keenness. He said, "What sort of man was Ralph? I see evidence of his technical abilities, but what was it like to know him – to be related, to work with him?"

"Among those he worked with, Ralph stood out." Tarquin's face was open and seemed untainted by envy. "When we were children, Ralph was always the leader. And so it remained as we entered adult life."

Wells remarked, "I never knew if you liked him."

Tarquin's eyes narrowed. "I cannot answer that, Bertie. We were brothers. I worked for him. I suppose I loved him. But we were also rivals, throughout life, as are most brothers."

Holmes asked bluntly, "Do you stand to benefit from his death?"

Tarquin Brimicombe said, "No. My father's legacy will not be transferred to me. Ralph made out his own will, leaving his assets to his wife; and there is no love lost between the two of us. You may check with the family solicitors – and with Jane – to verify these claims. If you are looking for a murder motive, Mr Holmes, you must dig deeper. I will not resent it."

"Oh, I shall," muttered Holmes. "And Ralph Brimicombe is beyond resenting anything. Come. Let us look in the capsule."

We stepped over the shattered concrete to the entrance cut in the capsule wall. A small lamp had been set up, filling the interior with a sombre glow. I knew that the body – what was left of it – had been taken away for burial, but the craft had not been cleaned out. I dropped my eyes to the floor, expecting – what? a dramatic splash of blood? – but there were only a few irregular stains on the burst upholstery of the aviator's couch, where Ralph had been seated at the moment of his extinguishing. There was surprisingly little damage to the equipment and instrumentation, the dials and switches and levers evidently meant to control the craft; much of it had simply been crushed longways where it stood.

But there was a smell, reminiscent to me of the hospitals of my military service.

I withdrew my head. "I am not sure what I expected," I murmured. "More – carnage, I suppose."

Tarquin frowned thoughtfully; then he extended his index finger and pointed upwards.

I looked up.

It was as if a dozen bags of rust brown paint had been hurled into the air. The upper walls and ceiling of the ship, the instruments, dials and switches that encrusted the metal, even the cabin's one small window: all were liberally coated with dried blood.

"Good Lord," said Wells, and his face blanched. "How did that get up there?"

Tarquin said, "The coroner concluded the vessel must have rolled over as it fell, thus spreading my brother's blood through its interior."

As we moved on, Wells muttered to me, "Such a size of ship, rolling over in ten feet? It hardly seems likely!"

I agreed with the young author. But Holmes would make no remark.

Tarquin took us to a gantry which crossed the chamber above the wrecked ship. We stood a few inches from a bank of cables, many of which showed necking, shearing and cracking; they had clearly snapped under extreme pressure. But one cable – a fat, orange-painted rope as thick as my arm – had a clean, gleaming termination. At my feet was a gas cutting kit, and a set of protector goggles. It seemed absurdly obvious, like a puzzle set by a child, that a load-bearing cable had been cut by this torch!

Tarquin said, "Not all the cables supported the weight of the ship. Some carried power, air for the passenger, and so forth."

Holmes said, "You say you were both working up here, on this gantry, when the accident occurred? Both you and Bryson?"

"Yes. We were doing some maintenance. We were the only people in the chamber – apart from Ralph, of course. He was inside the vessel itself, performing calculations there."

Holmes asked, "And the Inertial Adjustor was in operation at the time?"

"It was."

I pointed to the fat orange cable. "Was that the main support?" He nodded. "Although I did not know that at the time."

"And it has been cut with this torch?"

"That is right," he said evenly. He leaned against the gantry rail, arms folded. "The flame sliced clean through, like ice under a hot tap. When the big one went the others started to stretch and snap. And soon the ship fell."

"And Bryson was using the torch? Is that what you are saying?"

"Oh, no." He looked mildly surprised at Wells's question. "I was doing the cutting. I was working it under Bryson's supervision."

I demanded, "But if you were working the torch, how can you accuse Bryson of murder?"

"Because he is responsible. Do not you see? He told me specifically to cut the orange cable. I followed his instructions, not knowing that it was supporting the capsule."

"You said you are trained to know every detail of the ship, inside and out."

"The ship itself, yes, doctor. Not the details of this chamber, however. But Bryson knew."

Wells remarked, "But it must have taken minutes to cut through that cable. Look at its thickness! Did Bryson not see what you were doing and stop you?"

"Bryson was not here," Tarquin said coldly. "As you have heard, he was taking breakfast with my sister-in-law, as was their wont. You see, gentlemen," he went on, a controlled anger entering his voice, "I was just a tool Bryson used to achieve his ends. As innocent as that torch at your feet."

Wells stared at the torch, the ripped cables. "Tarquin, your brother knew Bryson for years. He relied on him utterly. Why would Bryson do such a thing?"

He straightened up, brushing dust from his jacket. "You must ask him that," he said.

The next step was obvious to us all: we must confront the accused.

And so we returned to the drawing room of the main house, and confronted the wretched Bryson. He stood on the carpet, his broad, strong hands dangling useless at his side, his overalls oil-stained and bulging with tools. He was, on Wells's testimony, solid, unimaginative, able – and utterly reliable. I could not avoid a sense of embarrassment as Holmes summarized to Bryson the accusation levelled against him.

Jack Bryson hung his head and ran his palm over his scalp. "So you think I killed him," he said, sounding resigned. "That is that, then. Are you going to call in the police?"

"Slow down." Holmes held his hands up. "To begin with, I do not know what possible reason you could have for wanting to harm Ralph Brimicombe."

"It was Jane," he said suddenly.

Wells frowned. "Brimicombe's wife? What about her?"

"She and I –" He hesitated. "I may as well tell you straight; you will find out anyway. I do not know if you would call it an affair. I am a good bit older than she is – but still – Ralph was so distant, you know, so wrapped up in his work. And Jane –"

"– is a woman of warmth and devotion," Holmes said gently.

Bryson said, "I knew Jane a long time. The closeness – the opportunity. Well. So there is your motive, Mr Holmes. I am the lover who slew the cuckolded husband. And my opportunity for murder is without question."

I found it painful to watch his face. There was no bitterness there, no pride: only a sour resignation.

Wells turned to Holmes. "So," he said, "the case is resolved. Are you disappointed, Holmes?"

For answer he filled and lit his pipe. "Resolved?" he said softly. "I think not."

Bryson looked confused. "Sir?"

"Do not be so fast to damn yourself, man. You are a suspect. But that does not make you a murderer: in my eyes, in the eyes of the law, or in the eyes of God."

"And will the courts accept that? I am resigned, Mr Holmes: resigned to my fate. Let it be."

To that dignified acceptance, even Holmes had nothing to say.

Holmes ordered Bryson to take us through the same grisly inspection tour as Tarquin. Soon we were walking around the wreck once more. Unlike Tarquin, Bryson had not seen this place since the day of the accident; his distress was clear as he picked his way through the remnants of the support cables. He said: "The fall took a long time, even after the main support was severed. The noise of the shearing cables went on and on, and there was not a thing I could do about it. I ran out for help, before the end. And when we heard Ralph had been killed –" Now he turned his crumpled face to Holmes's. "No matter who you call guilty in the end, Mr Holmes, I am the killer. I know that. This is my domain; Ralph Brimicombe's life was in my hands while he was in this room, and I failed –"

"Stop it, man," Holmes said sharply. "This self-destructive blame is hardly helpful. For now, we should concentrate on the facts of the case."

Holmes took Bryson to the entrance cut in the capsule. With obvious reluctance the engineer picked his way to the crude doorway. The light inside cast his trembling cheeks in sharp relief. I saw how he looked around the walls of the cabin, at the remnants of the couch on the floor. Then he stood straight and looked at Holmes, puzzled. "Has it been cleaned?"

Holmes pointed upwards.

Bryson pushed his neck through the doorway once more and looked up at the ceiling of the capsule. When he saw the human remains scattered there he gasped and stumbled back.

Holmes said gently, "Watson, would you –"

I took Bryson's arm, meaning to care for him, but he protested: "I am all right. It was just the shock."

"One question," Holmes said. "Tell me how the cable was cut."

"Tarquin was working the torch," he began. "Under my direction. The job was simple; all he had to do was snip out a faulty section of an oxygen line."

"Are you saying Ralph's death was an accident?"

"Oh, no," Bryson said firmly. "It was quite deliberate." He seemed to be challenging us to disbelieve him.

"Tell me the whole truth," said Holmes.

"I was not watching Tarquin's every move. I had given Tarquin his instructions and had left to take breakfast before progressing to another item of work."

"What exactly did you tell him to do?"

He considered, his eyes closing. "I pointed to the oxygen line, explained what it was, and showed him what he had to do. The air line is a purple-coded cable about a thumb's-width thick."

"Whereas the support cables –"

"are all orange coded, about so thick." He made a circle with his thumbs and middle fingers. "It is hard – impossible – to confuse the two."

"Did you not see what he was doing?"

"I was at breakfast with Mrs Brimicombe when it happened. I expected to be back, however."

"Why were you not?"

He shrugged. "My breakfast egg took rather longer to cook than usual. I remember the housekeeper's apology."

Wells tutted. "Those wretched eggs again!"

"At any event," Bryson said, "I was only gone a few minutes. But by the time I returned Tarquin had sliced clean through the main support. Then the shearing began."

"So you clearly identified the gas line to Tarquin."

"I told you. I pointed to it."

"And there is no way he could have mixed it up with the support cable?"

He raised his eyebrows. "What do you think?"

I scratched my head. "Is it possible he caught the support somehow with the torch, as he was working on the gas feed?"

He laughed; it was a brief, ugly sound. "Hardly, doctor. The support is about four feet from the air line. He had to turn round, and stretch, and keep the torch there, to do what he did. We can go up to the gantry and see if you like." He seemed to lose his confidence. "Look, Mr Holmes, I do not expect you to believe me. I know I am only an engineer, and Tarquin was Ralph's brother."

"Bryson –"

"But there is no doubt in my mind. Tarquin quite deliberately cut through that support, and ended his brother's life."

There we left our enquiries for the day.

I fulfilled Holmes's request regarding the dog Sheba. On a cursory inspection I found the poor animal's limbs to be spindly and crooked from so many breaks. I collected a sample of her urine and delivered it to the Chippenham general hospital, where an old medical school friend of mine arranged for a series of simple assays. He had the results within the hour, which I tucked into my pocket.

I rejoined my companions, who had retired to the "Little George" hostelry in Chippenham for the evening. They had been made welcome by a broad-bellied, white-aproned barman, had dined well on bread and cheese, and were enjoying the local ale (though Holmes contented himself with his pipe), and talking nineteen to the dozen the while.

"It is nevertheless quite a mystery," said Wells, around a mouthful of bread. "Has there even been a murder? Or could it all be simply some ghastly, misunderstood accident?"

"I think we can rule that out," said Holmes. "The fact that there are such conflicts between the accounts of the two men is enough to tell us that something is very wrong."

"One of them – presumably the murderer – is lying. But which one? Let us follow it through. Their accounts of the crucial few seconds, when the cable was cut, are ninety per cent identical; they both agree that Bryson had issued an instruction to Tarquin, who had then turned and cut through the support. The difference is that Bryson says he had quite clearly told Tarquin to cut through the air line. But Tarquin says he was instructed, just as clearly, to slice through what turned out to be the support.

"It is like a pretty problem in geometry," went on Wells. "The two versions are symmetrical, like mirror images. But which is the original and which the false copy? What about motive, then? Could Tarquin's envy of his brother – plain for all to see – have driven him to murder? But there is no financial reward for him. And then there is the engineer. Bryson was driven to his dalliance with Jane Brimicombe by the tenderness of his character. How can such tenderness chime with a capability for scheming murder? So, once again, we have symmetry. Each man has a motive –"

Holmes puffed contentedly at his pipe as Wells rattled on in this fashion. He said at last, "Speculations about the mental state of suspects are rarely so fruitful as concentration on the salient facts of the case."

I put in, "I'm sure the peculiar circumstances of the death had something to do with the nature of the Inertial Adjustor itself, though I fail to understand how."

Holmes nodded approvingly. "Good, Watson."

"But," said Wells, "we don't even know if the Adjustor ever operated, or if it was another of Ralph's vain boasts – a flight of fancy, like his trip to the Moon! I still have that vial of Moon dust about me somewhere –"

"You yourself had lunch in the chamber," Holmes said.

"I did. And Ralph performed little demonstrations of the principal. For instance: he dropped a handful of gravel, and we watched as the heaviest fragments were snatched most rapidly to Earth's bosom, contrary to Galileo's famous experiment. But I saw nothing which could not be replicated by a competent conjurer."

"And what of the mice?"

Wells frowned.

"They were rather odd, Mr Wells," I said.

"We can imagine the effect of the distorted gravity of that chamber on generations of insects and animals," Holmes said. "A mouse, for instance, being small, would need the lightest of limbs to support its reduced weight."

Wells saw it. "And they would evolve in that direction, according to the principles of Darwin – of course! Succeeding generations would develop attenuated limbs. Insects like your ant, Watson, could grow to a large size. But larger animals would be dragged more strongly to the ground. A horse, for example, might need legs as thick as an elephant's to support its weight."

"You have it," said Holmes. "But I doubt if there was time, or resource, for Ralph to study more than a generation or two of the higher animals. There was only his wife's unlucky labrador to use as test subject. And when Watson opens the envelope in his pocket, he will find the assay of the urine samples from that animal to display excessive levels of calcium."

That startled me. I retrieved and opened the envelope, and was not surprised – I know the man! – to find the results just as Holmes had predicted.

"The calcium is from the bones of the animal," Holmes said. "Trapped by Ralph in a region in which it needed to support less weight, the bitch's musculature and bone structure must have become progressively weaker, with bone calcium being washed out in urine. The same phenomenon is observed in patients suffering excessive bed rest, and I saw certain indications of the syndrome in those discoloured patches of lawn."

"Then the means of his death," Wells said, "must indeed be related to Ralph Brimicombe's successful modification of gravity itself."

"Certainly," said Holmes. "And similarly related are the motive behind the crime, and the opportunity."

Wells grew excited. "You've solved it, Holmes? What a remarkable man you are!"

"For the morrow," Holmes said. "For now, let us enjoy the hospitality of the landlord, and each other's company. I too enjoyed your *Time Machine*, Wells."

He seemed flattered. "Thank you."

"Especially your depiction of the crumbling of our foolish civilization. Although I am not convinced you had thought it through far enough. Our degradation, when it comes, will surely be more dramatic and complete."

"Oh, indeed? Then let me set you a challenge, Mr Holmes. What if I were to transport you, through time, to some remote future – as remote as the era of the great lizards – let us say, tens of millions of years. How would you deduce the former existence of mankind?"

My friend rested his legs comfortably on a stool and tamped his pipe,. "A pretty question. We must remember first that everything humans construct will revert to simpler chemicals over time. One must only inspect the decay of the Egyptian pyramids to see that, and they are young compared to the geologic epochs you evoke. None of our concrete or steel or glass will last even a million years."

"But," said Wells, "perhaps some human remains might be preserved in volcanic ash, as at Pompeii and Herculaneum. These remains might have artifacts in close proximity, such as jewellery or surgical tools. And geologists of the future will surely find a layer of ash and lead and zinc to mark the presence of our once-noble civilization –"

But Holmes did not agree –

And on they talked, H.G. Wells and Sherlock Holmes together, in a thickening haze of tobacco smoke and beer fumes, until my own poor head was spinning with the concepts they juggled.

The next morning, we made once more for the Brimicombe home. Holmes asked for Tarquin.

The younger Brimicombe entered the drawing room, sat comfortably and crossed his legs.

Holmes regarded him, equally at his ease. "This case has reminded me of a truism I personally find easy to forget: how little people truly understand of the world around us. You demonstrated this, Watson, with your failure to predict the correct fall of my sovereign and farthing, even though it is but an example of a process you must observe a hundred times a day. And yet it takes a man of genius – a Galileo – to be the first to perform a clear and decisive experiment in such a matter. You are no genius, Mr Brimicombe, and still less so is the engineer, Bryson. And yet you studied your brother's work; your grasp of the theory is the greater, and your understanding of the behaviour of objects inside the Inertial Adjustor is bound to be wider than poor Bryson's."

Ralph stared at Holmes, the fingers of one hand trembling slightly.

Holmes rested his hands behind his head. "After all, it was a drop of only ten feet or so. Even Watson here could survive a fall like that – perhaps with bruises and broken bones. But it was not Ralph's fall that killed him, was it? Tarquin, what was the mass of the capsule?"

"About ten tons."

"Perhaps a hundred times Ralph's mass. And so – in the peculiar conditions of the Inertial Adjustor – *it fell to the floor a hundred times faster than Ralph.*"

And then, in a flash, I saw it all. Unlike my friendly lift cabin of Wells's analogy, the capsule would drive rapidly to the floor, engulfing Ralph. My unwelcome imagination ran away with the point: I saw the complex ceiling of the capsule smashing into Ralph's staring face, a fraction of a second before the careening metal hit his body and he burst like a balloon . . .

Tarquin buried his eyes in the palm of his hand. "I live with the image. Why are you telling me this?"

For answer, Holmes turned to Wells. "Mr Wells, let us test your own powers of observation. What is the single most startling aspect of the case?"

He frowned. "When we first visited the Inertial Adjustor chamber with Tarquin, I recall looking into the capsule, and scanning the floor and couch for signs of Ralph's death."

"But," Holmes said, "the evidence of Ralph's demise – bizarre, grotesque – were fixed to the ceiling not the floor."

"Yes. Tarquin told me to look up – just as later, now I think on it, you, Mr Holmes, had to tell the engineer Bryson to raise his head, and his face twisted in horror." He studied Holmes. "So, a breaking of the symmetry at last. Tarquin knew where to look; Bryson did not. What does that tell us?"

Holmes said, "By looking down, by seeking traces of Ralph on the couch, the floor, we demonstrated we had not understood what had happened to Ralph. We had to be shown – as had Bryson! If Bryson had sought to murder Ralph he would have chosen some other method. Only someone who has studied the properties of a gravity field changed by the Inertial Adjustor would know immediately how cutting that cable would kill Ralph."

Tarquin sat very still, eyes covered. "Someone like me, you mean?"

Wells said, "Is that an admission, Tarquin?"

Tarquin lifted his face to Holmes, looking thoughtful. "You do not have any proof. And there is a counter-argument. Bryson could have stopped me, before I cut through the cable. The fact that he did not is evidence of his guilt!"

"But he was not there," Holmes said evenly. "As you arranged."

Tarquin guffawed. "He was taking breakfast with my sister-in-law! How could I arrange such a thing?"

"There is the matter of Bryson's breakfast egg, which took unusually long to cook," Holmes said.

"Your egg again, Holmes!" Wells cried.

"On that morning," said Holmes, "and that morning alone, you, Mr Brimicombe, collected fresh eggs from the coop. I checked with the housekeeper. The eggs used for breakfast here are customarily a day or more old. As you surely learned as a child fond of the hens, Tarquin, a fresh egg takes appreciably longer to cook than one that is a day or more old. A fresh egg has a volume of clear albumen solution trapped in layers of dense egg white around the yolk. These layers make the egg sit up in the frying pan. After some days the albumen layers degenerate, and the more watery egg will flatten out, and is more easily cooked."

Wells gasped. "My word, Holmes. Is there no limit to your intelligence?"

"Oh," said Brimicombe, "but this is –"

"Mr Brimicombe," Holmes said steadily, "you are not a habitual criminal. When I call in the police they will find all the proof any court in the land could require. Do you doubt that?"

Tarquin Brimicombe considered for a while, and then said: "Perhaps not." He gave Holmes a grin, like a good loser on the playing field. "Maybe I tried to be too clever; I thought I was home clear anyway, but when I knew you were coming I decided to bluff you over Bryson to be sure. I knew about his involvement with Jane; I knew he would have a motive for you to pick up –"

"And so you tried to implicate an innocent man." I could see Holmes's cool anger building.

Wells said, "So it is resolved. Tell me one thing. Tarquin. If not for your brother's money, why?"

He showed surprise. "Do you not know, Bertie? The first aviator will be the most famous man in history. I wanted to be that man, to fly Ralph's craft into the air, perhaps even to other worlds."

"But," Wells said, "Ralph claimed to have flown already all the way to the moon and back."

Tarquin dismissed this with a gesture. "Nobody believed that. I could have been first. But my brother would never have allowed it."

"And so," said Wells bitterly, "you destroyed your brother – and his work – rather than allow him precedence."

There was a touch of pride in Tarquin's voice. "At least I can say I gave my destiny my best shot, Bertie Wells. Can you say the same?"

The formalities of Tarquin Brimicombe's arrest and charging were concluded rapidly, and the three of us, without regret, took the train for London. The journey was rather strained; Wells, having enjoyed the hunt, now seemed embittered by the unravelling of the Brimicombe affair. He said, "It is a tragedy that the equipment is so smashed up, that Ralph's note-taking was so poor, that his brother – murderer or not – is such a dullard. It will not prove possible to restore Ralph's work, I fear."

Holmes mused, "But the true tragedy here is that of a scientist who sacrificed his humanity – the love of his wife – for knowledge."

Wells grew angry. "Really. And what of you, Mr Holmes, and your dry quest for fact, fact, fact? What have you sacrificed?"

"I do not judge," Holmes said easily. "I merely observe."

"At any rate," said Wells, "it may be many years before humans truly fly to the moon – oh, I am reminded." He dug into a coat pocket and pulled out a small, stoppered vial. It contained a quantity of grey-black dust, like charcoal. "I found it. Here is the 'moon dust' which Ralph gave me, the last element of his hoax." He opened the bottle and shook a thimbleful of dust into the palms of Holmes and myself.

I poked at the grains. They were sharp-edged. The dust had a peculiar smell: "Like wood smoke," I opined.

"Or wet ash," Wells suggested. "Or gunpowder!"

Holmes frowned thoughtfully. "I suppose the soil of the moon, never having been exposed to air, would react with the oxygen in our atmosphere. The iron contained therein – it would be like a slow burning –"

Wells collected the dust from us. He seemed angry and bitter. "Let us give up this foolishness. What a waste this all is. How many advances of the intellect have been betrayed by the weakness of the human heart? Oh, perhaps I might make a romance of this – but that is all that is left! Here! Have done with you!" And with an impetuous gesture he opened the carriage window and shook out the vial, scattering dust along the track. Holmes raised an elegant hand, as if to stop him, but he was too late. The dust was soon gone, and Wells discarded the bottle itself.

For the rest of the journey to Paddington, Holmes was strangely thoughtful, and said little.

THE ADVENTURE OF THE TOUCH OF GOD

Peter Crowther

It was with a mixture of trepidation and eager anticipation that, on a cold and dank November evening, having just arrived back at our rooms in Baker Street from a day-long symposium on glandular deterioration, I greeted Sherlock Holmes's announcement that we were to journey to Harrogate.

Despite being some 200 or more miles from the capital's bustling familiarity and drudgery (two indistinguishable sides of the same tarnished coin), the trip clearly promised a return to matters of detection. For though Holmes complemented news of our impending departure with the promise of bracing Yorkshire air to clean clogged and jaded tubes – of both a bronchial and a cerebral nature – I suspected an ulterior motive.

That is not to say that my good friend was not given to displays of impetuosity. Indeed, he had proven to me on many occasions that he was the very soul of immediacy. It was as though he were cognizant of his own mortality. Sometimes, I even thought that he was frightened of idleness, though he was not a man prone to fear or cowardice. Rather it was, or so it seemed, the prospect of inaction that presented the most serious affront to his sense of being. Action, or "the game" as he liked to regard the often heinous crimes whose unravelling he was frequently called upon to master, was what he was here to do. It was for this singular reason that I so welcomed the prospect.

For myself, however, the approach was entirely different. Somewhat in contradiction to the cautious and even begrudging excitement I have already mentioned, it was my custom to regard the prospect of further nefarious activities with some apprehension. On the occasion in question, this feeling was particularly pronounced.

"Might I at least remove my topcoat?" I enquired.

"No time for that, old fellow," Holmes blustered. "We are to leave within the hour. Here." He held out to me a single sheet of paper and the envelope in which it had arrived.

Affixing my reading spectacles, I glanced at the letter and its careful and practised copperplate hand. "Read it aloud, old fellow," Holmes proclaimed with a pride that suggested he himself as the missive's author.

"'My Dear Mr Sherlock Holmes,' it begins," I said. "'Please forgive the brevity of this note and its undoubted intrusion on your privacy but I am in dire need of advice and assistance on a matter of grave importance.'"

"'Grave importance'," Holmes said, turning his back to the fire crackling in the grate. "Capital!" He glanced across at me and waved a dismissive hand. "Do continue, Watson."

I returned my attention to the letter.

"'A situation has arisen,'" I resumed, "'here in Harrogate which, I feel, requires a level of experience and a depth of knowledge that I am in all honesty quite unqualified to provide, despite some thirty years with the Force.'"

"Force?" I enquired of Holmes. "The sender is a policeman?"

"Read on, read on," Holmes instructed, and he walked to the window and stared into the street.

I returned to the letter. "'We are plagued with a villain the likes of what I have never encountered,'" I read, "'a madman in whose wake we now have three deaths and little or no explanation as to the reason behind them. It would be not proper for me to outline the manner of these inhuman atrocities in this letter but I feel sure that they will be of sufficient interest to warrant your visiting us at your earliest availability.'"

The letter closed with the writer's assurance that, in the event of our accepting his invitation, rooms would be arranged for us on our behalf at a nearby hostelry, and at no cost to ourselves. It was signed Gerald John Makinson, Inspector of the North Yorkshire Police.

"What do you say to that, Watson?" Holmes said, warming himself against the fire, his back arched like that of a cat.

I did not know quite what to make of it, save that the Inspector's grasp of the King's English was somewhat lacking and I told my friend as much. "For that matter," I added, "who is this Makinson fellow?"

"I was introduced to him by our very own Lestrade, last June as I recall. The fellow was down in London to attend a series of presentations on the increasing use of behavioural science in law enforcement. His address was most enlightening."

"Apparently the meeting made something of an impression," I observed.

"And one beside that of simple grammatical impropriety," said Holmes. He stepped away from the fire and rubbed his hands gleefully before removing his watch from a pocket in his waistcoat. He glanced at the timepiece. "Almost five and twenty past seven, Watson." He returned the watch and smiled, his eyes narrowing. "There is a milk train which leaves King's Cross station at four minutes past ten o'clock. It is my intention that we be on it."

I was about to protest, fully realizing that it would be to no avail, when Holmes turned around and strode purposefully from the room. "Might I rely on you to pack some suitable clothes, old fellow?" he requested over his shoulder. "And please do bear in mind that Yorkshire is not a county renowned for the clemency of its weather, particularly at this time of the year." With that, he slammed his bedroom door.

I glanced down at the single sheet of paper in my hand. It never ceased to amaze me at how little it took to propel my friend to levels of great excitement, and at how quickly those levels could be so attained. It was a trait that was at once both enviable and despairing to behold, for these high moods when he was absorbed in a case were countered by depths of depression when he was not. It was at times such as this that Sherlock Holmes reminded me not so much of a sleuth as of a young schoolboy, so pure were his beliefs and motivations.

I set to preparing overnight bags for the two of us, including sufficient clothes for a few days' stay, and, when Holmes reappeared, we left our rooms and, without further conversation, ventured out into the cold evening.

We boarded the train at five minutes to ten o'clock and made our way immediately to our sleeping compartments. At the prescribed time, the train departed King's Cross and headed for Yorkshire. As the gently rocking motion of the carriage lulled me towards sleep, I watched the dark countryside pass by the window, noting somewhat ominously that the fog was growing seemingly thicker with each yard we travelled northwards.

We arrived in Leeds at a little after a quarter past six on the following morning.

I had had a reasonable enough night's sleep, the rocking of the carriage keeping me quite comforted. Holmes, however, appeared not to have fared so well and, when I first saw him in the corridor, he looked pale and drawn, his eyes pouched and discoloured. He was fully dressed and clearly ready to disembark and begin the next stage of our journey.

"Sleep well, old fellow?" he enquired in a tone that suggested the answer was less important than the fact that, in his opinion, he had been waiting too long to pose it.

"I did indeed," I replied. "And you?"

He gave a slight grimace and adjusted his gloves. "As you know, I dislike periods of enforced inaction. Periods during which there is little to demand my attention." He clapped his hands together and his face beamed beneath his ear-flapped travelling-cap. "However, we are but some fifteen miles from our destination. There is a train leaving on the half-hour." With that, he lifted his bag and walked along the corridor to the door.

Harrogate is a delightful town, a criss-cross of busy streets and thoroughfares surrounded by an interlocking grid of cultivated grassland called "The Two Hundred Acres" or, more commonly, "The Stray", which we had seen in all of its early-morning, mist-enshrouded finery as we approached the station.

A brisk walk ensued and we arrived at the police station as a distant clock chimed ten, to be greeted by a tall, burly, uniformed sergeant whose face displayed a florid expression and the most singularly inquisitive eyes.

"Now then, gentlemen," he boomed, "and what can we be doing for you this fine morning?"

It transpired that my friend had telegraphed Inspector Gerald John Makinson the previous afternoon, informing him of our intended arrival time. "So you're Mr Sherlock Holmes, then?" the officer enquired.

Holmes set down his bag on the station steps, removed the glove from his right hand and held it out. "I am he," he said.

The officer gave, I thought, a somewhat forced smile and shook the proffered hand once. "And you must be Mr Watson," he said turning to me.

"I am, indeed, *Doctor* Watson," I said, accepting the hand. The shake was as brusque as his manner.

"I'm Sergeant Hewitt. Come on inside," he said, lifting both of our overnight bags. "There's a fresh pot of tea made and it'll take but a minute to do you some toast. Inspector Makinson will be along presently. Perhaps you'd be kind enough to wait in here, gentlemen," he said, ushering us into a small, square room ringed by chairs around a circular table. He rested our bags on one of the chairs and proceeded to help us off with our coats and hats, which he then placed on a hatstand next to a blazing fire. "Tea'll be along in a minute. Will you be having toast?"

"That would be most welcome," Holmes said.

"Right then, toast it –" The sound of a door banging outside interrupted him and he turned to see who had just entered. "Ah," he said, turning back to us, "Inspector Makinson has arrived. I'll be back presently."

Hewitt stepped back to permit entrance to a short gentleman

with quite the most bristling moustache I have ever seen. The man removed his bowler and nodded to the officer who backed out and closed the door gently behind him. "Good morning, gentlemen," he said offering his hand which, ungloved, was freezing cold to the touch. "Gerald Makinson."

We made our introductions and took seats by the fire.

"Mr Holmes, it's a great pleasure to meet you again, sir," Makinson began as he rubbed his hands together vigorously in front of the flames, "though we might've hoped for more pleasant circumstances."

"While Patience may well be a card game from which I have derived some considerable pleasure," Holmes responded with a thin smile, "it is not, I fear, my strongest suit. I wonder if you might give us some indication of your situation. If I am not mistaken there had been further developments in the case even as we were travelling here from London."

"Quite so, quite so. Well, it's like this, gentlemen.

"Almost two weeks ago – the second of November, to be precise – the body of Terence Wetherall, one of the town's most prominent landlords, was discovered by one of his tenants. Murdered."

The Inspector imbued the last word with an almost absurd theatrical flourish and I had to stifle a smile, thankfully unobserved.

"What was the manner of his death?" Holmes enquired.

"He'd been strangled. No instrument was found but the nature of the marks around his neck suggests some kind of rope or string. We found traces of coarse hair in the wound. But the worst thing was the man's heart had been removed."

"Good Lord!" I ventured.

"Quite, Doctor Watson, his chest had been slit open and the unfortunate organ torn out. It was a messy affair, I can tell you," he added. "There was no indication of careful surgical procedure – we've had a local surgeon examine the wound and it appears that the heart was just pulled out. His chest looked like a pack of wild dogs had been at it . . ."

"Suspects?"

The Inspector shook his head. "Mr Wetherall was extremely well-liked as far as we can make out. His wife – sorry: widow – knew of no reason why anyone would wish him harm. And certainly she knows of no one who would conceivably wish to defile his body in such a way."

"I wonder if we might see the body," I said.

"Of course, Doctor. You can see them all."

I glanced across at Holmes who tented his fingers in front of his face and carefully studied the tips. "Do continue, Inspector."

At that moment, Sergeant Hewitt reappeared with a tray containing a teapot, three cups and saucers, a small jug of milk, a large plate of buttered toast, a small phial of marmalade and one of honey, and three side plates. It was a meal which, despite its simplicity, was a sight for weary eyes. We set to pouring tea and helping ourselves to the toast, and Inspector Makinson resumed his story.

"A few days later, 7 November, a farmer was brutally slain in the nearby village of Hampsthwaite. Shotgun-blasted in the back of the head, point blank range. He'd gone outside to check his livestock – something he did every evening at the same time – and the killer must've been waiting."

The Inspector took a sip of tea and returned the cup to his saucer.

"And, once again, the heart of the unfortunate victim had been removed, though this time the damage to the body was less.

"The third slaying was last week, the eleventh, and this was maybe the most heinous of them all. A young woman, Gertrude Ridge, a schoolteacher in the town, was reported missing on the morning of the tenth when she didn't appear at school. She was discovered on the embankment by the side of the railway line . . . or, should I say, *some* of her was discovered."

Holmes leaned forward. "*Some*, you say?"

The Inspector nodded gravely and reached for his cup of tea. "Only the torso was found – it was identified by her clothes. Both legs, both arms and the unfortunate girl's head were missing."

"But her heart?" I said.

"Her torso was intact, Doctor Watson. And we've since found both legs, the head and one of the arms."

"Where were these limbs found, Inspector?" Holmes enquired.

"A little way along the embankment, in the bushes."

"Were they close together?"

Inspector Makinson frowned. "Yes, yes I believe they were."

"And the embankment has been thoroughly searched?"

"In both directions, and with a toothcomb, Mr Holmes. The other arm wasn't there."

Holmes lifted his coffee and stared into the swirling liquid. "And now you have another murder, I take it."

Makinson nodded and twirled his moustache. "Yes, a fourth body was reported in the early hours of this morning to a Bobby on the beat. Down a small alleyway alongside the market buildings in the town square. Another shotgun blast, this time in the face at point blank range. Took most of his head with it, it did. We identified the corpse from what we found in his pockets.

William Fitzhue Crosby, the manager of our local branch of Daleside Bank."

"And the man's heart?" I enquired.

"Ripped out like the first two."

"Who reported the body?" asked Holmes.

"An old cleaner woman for the market buildings. She lives there all the time. She heard the shot, looked out of her windows and saw the body."

I watched my friend drain his cup and return it to the tray before him. He settled back into his seat and glanced first at me and then at the Inspector.

"Tell me, Inspector," he said at last. "How much disturbance had there been around the teacher's body?"

Gerald Makinson frowned. "Disturbance?"

I recognized a touch of impatience in the way my friend waved his hand. "Blood, Inspector. How much blood was there on the ground?"

"Very little, Mr Holmes. But our doctor tells me that once the heart was removed there wouldn't be much blood loss. The girl's clothes were soaked, mind you."

Holmes nodded. "Were there any traces of blood on the grass leading to and from the severed limbs?"

Makinson shook his head. "None as we could find," he said dolefully.

Holmes considered this before asking, "And what signs were about the body of the banker?"

"Again, very little. We put it down again to –"

"to the removal of the heart."

"Yes," Inspector Makinson agreed.

"Quite so." Holmes nodded slowly and then closed his eyes. "And why would anyone want to steal a heart? Or, more significantly, three hearts plus an assortment of severed limbs and a head? For that matter, why would they leave the young woman's heart in place?"

"It's like I say," said the Inspector, "it's a puzzle and no denying . . . which is, I might add, why I called upon your services. And those of the good doctor," he added with a peremptory nod in my direction.

"And we are both delighted that you did so, Inspector," said Holmes. "But what if," he continued, leaning forward suddenly in his chair, "the murderer simply forgot to take the girl's heart."

"*Forgot* it!" I was so astounded by the seeming preposterous nature of my friend's suggestion that I almost choked on a mouthful of toast. "Why ever would he do that when that was his entire objective?"

"But *was* it his objective, old fellow?" said Holmes.

"What are you saying, Mr Holmes?"

"Just this: suppose the removal of the hearts was simply to cover up some other reason for the murders?"

"I cannot imagine any reason for murder which is so despicable that the murderer would want to cover it up with the removal of a heart," I observed.

"No, perhaps not, Watson. Not a *despicable* reason, I agree. But perhaps a reason that might lead us to his identity."

While Inspector Makinson and I considered this, my friend continued.

"Inspector, did your men find any traces of blood or tissue . . . perhaps even bone fragments . . . on the wall which took the shotgun blast?"

Inspector Makinson's eyes widened. "Why, I don't believe we did."

"Quite, Inspector. That fact and the fact that was little or no evidence of blood around the body, despite the removal of the heart, means that the murder was committed somewhere else and the body carried to the alleyway.

"I sense a confusion of red herrings," Holmes continued.

"Red herrings?"

"Quite so, Watson," Holmes said as he got to his feet. "But before we go any further, I think we should see the bodies."

Without further ado, Inspector Makinson led us out of the room, along a series of corridors and then down a long staircase.

Finally, we arrived at a large oaken door inlaid with sheets of metal and an iron bar manacled through two support frames. The door opened onto a narrow corridor through whose windows we got our first glimpse of the unfortunate victims.

The entrance to the "resting" room was at the far end of the corridor and, as we walked along, I could not help but stare at the series of cots covered over with bottle-green sheets, and at the unmistakable human shapes beneath.

The room itself smelled of death, the familiar aroma – to me, at least – of putrefying flesh, a mixed scent of ruined fruit and stale milk. There is something about dead bodies which causes the living to speak in hushed tones in their presence. Indeed, it was several months of concentrated autopsy work before even I myself could overcome the need to affect some kind of reverence. But a dead body is not a person. This knowledge, too, comes only with practice and repeated exposure.

Makinson walked across to the first cot and crouched down to read the label tied to the support. "This one, Mr Holmes, is –"

"Could we have them in the order they were murdered, Inspector?" Holmes boomed. "And I don't think there's any need to whisper. Nothing we say in here will be any revelation to the victims."

Makinson stood up, ran a finger across his moustache and coughed loudly. He walked across to the second cot, studied the label and then crossed to the third. "This," he announced in grand tones, "is Mr Wetherall."

I followed Holmes across to the cot and watched as Makinson pulled back the sheet.

Decomposition was well underway, despite the cool temperature of the room.

I could see that the man had been in his mid forties although the sunken eyes and hollowing cheeks were giving him a countenance of someone considerably older. A wide ligature around the neck had discoloured to a dull brown shade.

"What do you make of that, Watson?" Holmes said, pointing to the man's chest.

The wound was extensive, apparently caused by a series of slashes into the flesh, some of which extended vertically from the collarbone almost to the waist while others crossed the sternum either horizontally or diagonally. "These wounds were presumably made to expose the heart," I concluded, "but it looks like a frenzied attack. Considering that the man would have been dead when these were committed, I can only conclude that the murderer was in a terrible hurry. See here, several sections of flesh appear to have been hacked out."

Holmes stepped in front of Makinson, who shuffled to one side, and bent over the body. "Did you find these pieces of flesh, Inspector?"

"No. But we had noticed they was missing. We presumed that the killer took them with the heart."

"By mistake or in haste, you mean?" I shook my head. "That does not make sense. The flesh is entirely separate to the heart. Once exposed – as these wounds would surely have done easily – the heart would be encased within the sternum. You can see where he broke the lower ribs to get at it. Once he had the heart, it would be unlikely that he would take a large piece of flesh with it."

"Then why would he take it?" said Holmes. He turned to the Inspector who started to shrug. "Let us look at the next one, Inspector, the farmer, I believe."

We moved back to the second cot and Makinson pulled back the sheet.

This man had been much older, possibly sixty. The Inspector had been right. The damage to the chest was markedly less than that on the first victim, a simple cross-cut over the sternum and two vertical wounds, each less than a foot in length, which enabled the flesh to be pulled back to expose the heart. "It almost seems to be the work of a different person," I observed. "It's certainly not the work of a professional, however, despite its relative neatness. Perhaps he had more time. Or perhaps he was simply not so nervous."

I pulled the head to one side and looked at the damage at the back. The neck appeared to be almost completely destroyed right up to the hairline. The base of the skull was exposed and fragmented. Bending over, I could see that the wound extended down onto the shoulders.

"I wonder if we might turn him over," I said.

Both Makinson and Holmes stepped forward and, between the three of us, we managed to twist the body onto its side.

The shotgun blast had indeed been concentrated on his lower neck and upper back, right between the shoulder blades. The flesh there had been pulverized exposing portions of the spine and lower shoulder blades, themselves showing some fragmentation.

I bent closer. "That's interesting . . ."

"What's that, old fellow? Found something?"

"Perhaps, perhaps not," I said. "But there does seem to be some indication of another wound."

Holmes and Makinson moved alongside me and looked where I was pointing. Just to the left of the start of the ruination caused by the shotgun blast, a tiny piece of skin appeared to have been removed. That piece of skin could, of course, have been merely the tip of a much larger piece and I mentioned this fact. "One has to consider it as cart tracks disappearing momentarily into a puddle from which they re-emerge on the other side," I said. "The puddle in this case is the shotgun wound."

"Are you suggesting that something was done to him before the shot was administered?" asked Makinson.

I looked back at the top of the wound, where it met the hairline, and lifted the shreds of loose skin and matted hair. It was as I suspected. The base of the skull was badly depressed, suggesting a hard blow from a solid object.

"He appears to have been struck from behind," I said. "And with a blunt instrument. See, the skin is not broken. The fracture of the skull suggests that such a blow would certainly have rendered the man immediately unconscious and, very probably, would have resulted in his death by haemorrhage. I would need to open up the brain pan to confirm that," I added, "but I would expect to find evidence of subdural haematoma plus bruising on the frontal lobes due to contra-coup."

Holmes was smiling. "Capital, Watson, capital." He strode to the window overlooking the corridor and spread his hands on the shelf. "Before we go any further, let us make one or two assumptions." He turned around and checked them off on the fingers of his left hand.

"The killer murders his first victim by strangulation," Holmes announced. "Then he sets about removing the victim's heart, a process during which a piece of flesh disappears. The means by which the chest is opened up suggests fear or haste ... it also, at least initially, makes the disappearance of the piece of flesh seemingly unimportant. I suspect neither fear nor haste played any part in these killings. Rather, it is the work of a severely deranged mind and one that is exceedingly cunning."

He held up a second finger. "The killer strikes again. This time the method of slaying is inconclusive. Initial investigations suggest the cause of death to be a shotgun blast to the back but we now have evidence of a blow to the base of the skull. Which, not unnaturally, prompts the question why should he kill his victim twice? We also have suggested evidence which points to some kind of incision or skin removal immediately below the wound. The wound also extends, almost, to the site of the blow to the skull ... as though, perhaps, the murderer were wanting to conceal both of those events.

"Certainly if, as we believe, the strike to the head rendered the victim unconscious at best, then it would have been a relatively simple matter to go about the removal of the heart without the need of further violence. This therefore suggests a further motive for the use of the shotgun, the second red herring."

"Second?" said Makinson.

"Indeed, Inspector. The first one is the removal of the hearts, though quite what such an intrusion could possibly disguise I have, as yet, no opinion. Equally, the reason for the missing flesh or the partial incision is still unclear."

We moved across to the third cot, pulling back the sheet to expose a grisly collection. The young woman's head was propped between the legs while the arm lay before it like some kind of gift and all were set out on the torso as if to resemble a construction puzzle. I lifted first the arm, turning it over in my hands, and then the legs, performing a similar study. There seemed nothing to give any clue for such a crime. I laid the limbs at the foot of the cot and turned my attention to the head.

The woman appeared to have been in her middle twenties. I

lifted the head carefully, some hidden and forgotten part of me half expecting the eyes to open and regard me with a cruel disdain, and turned it around. There was a similar depressed fracture to that suffered by the farmer and I was sure, simply by the pulpy feel of the bone around the occipital region, that death would have been instantaneous. I set the head down with the limbs and moved to the torso.

The limbs had clearly been removed by chopping as opposed to sawing and one of the shoulders showed signs of mis-hits, with some cosmetic damage to the edge of the right clavicle. One could only give thanks that the poor girl had been dead when the madman went about his business.

I turned to face Holmes and shook my head. "Nothing here," I said.

"Nothing save for the fact that the arm is missing," Holmes pointed out. "There is clearly some significance in that fact and the fact that the heart has not been removed."

"Why's that, then?" said the Inspector.

"Elementary, my dear Makinson," said Holmes, clearly pleased to be asked to explain his deduction. "I suspect that the killer simply forgot about the heart, being so concerned with his plan to remove all the limbs and then discard those he did not need. If your men have been as thorough in their investigations around the scene of the slaying as you say – and I have no reason to doubt that such is the case – then the killer must surely have taken the arm with him."

"You mean that he was prepared to chop off everything just to get one of her arms?"

Holmes nodded. "Otherwise, why did he not leave all of the limbs together? For that matter, why remove them and then leave them?"

"Why indeed?" I agreed.

"Let us consider the final body," said Holmes.

The face of William Fitzhue Crosby no longer existed. Where once had been skin and, undoubtedly, normal characteristics such as a nose, two eyes and two lips, now lay only devastation, a brown mass resembling a flattened mud pie into which a playful child had inserted a series of holes.

The sheer ruination of that face spoke of a hell on Earth, a creature conceived in the mind of Bosch – though whether such a description might not be more aptly levelled at the perpetrator of such carnage is debatable.

"Look at the rear of the head, Watson," said Holmes.

I turned the head to one side and felt the skull: the same fracture was there and I said as much.

"Inspector," said Holmes, "did you know Mr Crosby personally? By that I mean, were he still alive, would you recognize him on the street?"

"I'm not sure as I would, Mr Holmes," said Makinson, frowning. "I don't as doubt that him and me has passed each other by on occasion but –"

Holmes strode purposefully from the cot to the door. "We've finished here, I believe. Come Watson, we have enquiries to make."

"Enquiries?" I pulled the sheet up over Crosby's face.

"We must speak with the relatives of the victims." He walked from the room, pulling his Meerschaum from his pocket. "The game is most definitely afoot. Though, if I am correct, then that in itself poses a further puzzle."

I had grown used to if not tolerant of such enigmatic statements, though I had long since recognized the futility of pressing for more information. All would become clear in good time.

In the early evening we gathered once more at the police station, a full and somewhat depressing day behind us.

The November air in Harrogate was cold but "bracing", to use the Inspector's vernacular. For Sherlock Holmes and myself, however, grown used to the relative mildness of southern climes, the coldness permeated our very bones. To such a degree was this invasion that, even standing before a roaring fire in the Inspector's office, it was all I could do to keep from shivering.

Holmes himself, however, seemed now impervious to the chill as he sat contemplating, staring into the dancing flames.

It had been a productive day.

Due to the fact that William Crosby had no relatives in the town, having moved to Yorkshire from Bristol some eight years earlier, we were forced to call in at the branch of Daleside Bank, on the Parliament Street hill leading to Ripon, there to interview staff as to the possibility of someone having some reason to murder their manager. A tight-faced man named Mr Cardew, enduring rather than enjoying his early middle age, maintained the stoic calm and almost clinical immobility that I have discovered to be the province of bankers and their ilk over the years. They seem a singularly cheerless breed.

When pressed, first by Holmes and subsequently by Inspector Makinson, Mr Cardew visited the large safe at the rear of the premises to see if the money deposited the previous evening was still in place and accounted for. Throughout the exercise, I watched Holmes who viewed the procedure with a thinly disguised disinterest. Rather he seemed to be anxious, as if needing to ask something of Cardew.

Whether my friend would have got around to phrasing his question to such a degree of correctness in his own mind that he would have committed it to speech I will never know for we chanced upon a portrait photograph of William Fitzhue Crosby hanging from the wall outside his office.

The photographer had gone to some considerable trouble to make the finished photograph as acceptable as possible – presumably to Mr Crosby – using shadows and turning his subject into profile in order, clearly, to minimize the effect of the banker's disfigurement. But, alas, it had been to little avail.

In the photograph, Crosby's eyes spoke volumes about his attitude to the dark stain which, we subsequently discovered from Mr Cardew, ran from his left temple and down across his cheek to his chin. Those were eyes that barely hid a gross discomfort, hardened around the corners with something akin to outright hatred.

Cardew explained that, in the flesh, as it were, Crosby's stain was a deep magenta. The banker had grown his sideburns in an attempt to hide at least some of it but the effect had been that the sideburn on the left side had been wiry and white.

Believing that the answer to the puzzle involved a killer so mortally offended by such a mark that he would go to great lengths to remove it, we proceeded from the Daleside Bank to the school at which Gertrude Ridge had been, until recently, a teacher, having decided that it might not be necessary to trouble the young woman's grieving parents. On the way, Holmes seemed particularly thoughtful.

The story at the school was similar. Miss Ridge had had a large birthmark on the back of her right hand, stretching up over her wrist to an undetermined point above. Her colleagues at the school had been unable to comment as to how far that might be, Miss Ridge never deeming to appear at school in anything less than a long-sleeved blouse or dress, and even then one with the most ornate ruffled cuffs.

Diana Wetherall and Jean Woodward, widows of, respectively, the deceased landlord and the Hampsthwaite farmer, said that their husbands had suffered similar markings, Terence Wetherall's being a small circular stain about the size of a saucer, situated just to the left of centre of his chest, while Raymond Woodward's disfigurement had stretched across the back of his neck and down between his shoulder blades.

It was I who, eventually, back at the police station, voiced what had been Holmes's concern all along. "We now most probably know the reason for the killings," I said, "but how on earth did the killer know of Wetherall's and Woodward's marks? They were covered at all times when they were not at home."

Makinson frowned and considered this.

Holmes, meanwhile, said, "You say we know why the killer committed the acts, Watson. But do we *really* know?"

"Why, of course we do," I ventured. "The chap is mortally offended by what are, in his eyes, such abominations and he feels it his rigorous duty to remove them from sight. He came up with the idea of removing hearts simply to mislead us hence, on one occasion, even forgetting to remove the young woman's."

Holmes nodded. "I think you are *almost* correct, old fellow," he said, in a gentle tone that was anything but patronizing. "However, you have neglected to take into account the fact that the killer first stuns his victims and only then obliterates nature's handiwork. My point is," he continued, "the killer *needs* to stun his victim without interference with the mark."

"Whatever for, Mr Holmes?" enquired Makinson.

Holmes looked across at the Inspector and gave a thin smile that was devoid of any sense of pleasure. "In order to remove them, Inspector."

"*Remove* them?" I said. The suggestion seemed preposterous.

"Indeed, Watson. Let us adapt the facts as we know them to my proposition.

"Wetherall, the landlord, was stunned or killed by a blow to the head. The killer then stripped his victim to the waist and skilfully removed the birthmark from his chest. Then, in order to conceal his action, he proceeded to open up the chest in such a heavy-handed manner that the disappearance of the piece of skin which once bore the mark would not be so noticeable. He concealed the opening of the chest with the removal of the heart.

"The farmer was next. Again, the blow to the head was the all-important immobilizing factor. Once that had been effected, the killer could concentrate on removing the mark from the victim's neck and back before training a shotgun on the exposed area and destroying all signs. However, the blast failed to cover up all signs of his work, as you noticed, Watson. The removal of Woodward's heart tied his murder into the first death quite neatly."

Holmes cleared his throat.

"Then came the teacher. With her it was more complicated. The position of Miss Ridge's mark – on her arm – was such that a blast to the affected area, once he had removed the skin bearing the mark, could not be the killing factor. Similarly, the removal of the heart would not conceal the removal of the mark. Thus he decided upon the method of removing her limbs, still tying the murder into the first two deaths by peripheral association, only later to discard the three limbs for which he had no use. The final limb, the young woman's right arm, he discarded far from the scene of the crime and only then when he had removed the affected area. You mentioned earlier that he had forgotten to remove the heart: the fact was that he did not consider it necessary.

"With the banker he returns to the earlier method. A blow to the head, a common element throughout, then the careful removal of the facial skin bearing the mark, and then the shotgun blast to the face, destroying once again the evidence of his real reason for the murder. The removal of the heart ties the crime to the first two and, arguably, to the case of Miss Ridge."

Holmes stretched towards the fire and warmed his hands. "I read the reports from your forensics people, Inspector," Holmes continued. "I was interested to discover that, while there were traces of linen and wool fibre in the farmer's wound, there were no traces of skin except at the very extremities of the blasted area, confirming that, perhaps, a portion had been removed prior to the blast. And as for the banker, Mr Crosby, the gun shot damage to the wall bore no traces of skin or tissue. This indicates that the killing shot and the invasion which preceded it were done at some other location, with a second shot being fired directly at the wall."

"But what other place might that be, Mr Holmes?" Makinson enquired.

"Wherever Mr Crosby went after leaving the bank might give us a clue," Holmes retorted. "I saw from your report, Inspector, that Crosby's apartment showed no signs of anyone being there since the morning: the fire was burnt down and breakfast things were in the sink. It is my opinion that wherever Mr Crosby went early that evening is where he encountered his killer."

"Good lord," I said. I glanced across at Makinson and saw that he looked as queasy as I felt.

"But why would he want these . . . these marks in the first place? What does he do with them?"

Holmes turned to me. "Watson, perhaps you would be kind enough to explain the causation of a so-called birthmark?"

"Well," I said, "nobody actually knows why they are caused.

"They are most common in newborn babies, often called the 'stork's beak' mark because they occur on the forehead between the eyebrows and on the nape of the neck . . . as though a stork had had the child's head in its beak. These are transient phenomena that disappear as the baby grows. A popular but incorrect theory is that they are caused by the caul, the inner membrane enclosing the foetus, adhering itself to the child and becoming enmeshed into the child's own skin as it develops in the womb. Such marks are also sometimes referred to as 'God's fingerprints', and to many they signify good fortune."

Makinson snorted loudly. "Doesn't seem much like good fortune to me," he said, "carrying a big red mark on your face all your life."

"As I said, Inspector, these marks usually disappear as the child grows older. The ones that stay are called port wine stains or strawberry naevi, due to their colouring. The technical name is cutaneous haemangiomata, which refers to an abnormally large collection of blood vessels in the skin ... an over production, if you will. These are most commonly on the face – the case of Crosby the banker is typical – although they can occur anywhere on the body.

"The port wine stains stay throughout life, although they do lose some of the intense colouring in later years; the strawberry naevi do not usually persist."

Holmes nodded. "Let us imagine that our killer believes the old tale that such signs *are* the harbingers of good fortune," he said. "It might follow that such a fellow could conceivably feel that to own more of these would be to improve the quality of his life. Someone, perhaps, whose life has not been particularly fortunate."

"You said 'more' of these," I said.

"Yes, I did. I would expect the killer to be equally marked and to have been told, perhaps by his mother, that such a marking meant that he had been touched by God. The fact that his life did not reflect such fortune caused him to think that further marks were needed to change his luck."

I looked across at Makinson. The Inspector seemed unconvinced. "That's as well as maybe, Mr Holmes," he said, "but how does the killer identify his victims? Apart from the teacher and the banker, these marks was covered over all the time they was on public show."

"Perhaps not *all* the time, Inspector," said Holmes, his eyes flashing wide. "Tell me, do you have a municipal swimming bath in the town?"

Makinson shook his head. "No, nearest swimming bath is in Leeds."

Holmes smiled, and this time the smile did have traces of pleasure. "Watson," he said, unable to keep the excitement from his voice. "For what is Harrogate renowned?"

"Renowned? Harrogate?" I searched my brain for some clue as to what my friend had in mind. "Other than a cold wind that would not be out of place at the North Pole, I cannot imagine," I said at last.

"The water, Watson!"

"Water?" I still failed to grasp the significance.

"Harrogate is a spa town, famed for the so-called medicinal and curative properties of its water, taken from natural springs. Is that right, Inspector?"

"Why, yes it is, Mr Holmes," said the Inspector.

"And you have in the town a bath which enables people to bathe their bodies in these waters?"

"A Turkish bath and such, yes," said Makinson. "I've never been, myself, of course, but I believe as how they're popular with some people." He paused. "Run by a queer sort of fellow, they are," he added.

Holmes leapt to his feet. "Queer, you say? With a birthmark?"

Makinson shook his head. "No, no birthmark – at least none as is visible."

Holmes visibly shrank in size, the excitement evaporating almost as quickly as it had appeared. "Then why queer?"

"Well, he's . . ." Makinson seemed to be having trouble describing the fellow and I was about to prompt him when he added, "he's sort of big on one side and smaller on the other."

"That's it, Holmes!" I shouted. "Is one half of his body visibly larger than the other, Inspector? Is that what you're saying?"

"Yes, his head is mis-shaped and one arm is longer than the other. His leg is longer on that side, too, and he walks with a limp because of it." The Inspector shook his head at the thought. "Strange fellow and no denying."

I turned to Holmes. "Hemi hypertrophy," I said. "Caused by an underlying brain haemangioma, beneath a port wine stain; it means an increased blood flow through the mark results in a disproportionate growth on one side of the body. He's our man," I said, "I'd bet my pension on it!"

"What is the name of this fellow?" Holmes enquired of the Inspector.

"His name is Garnett, as I recall, Frank Garnett. The spa baths stay open until ten o'clock in the evening," the Inspector said. He removed his watch from his waistcoat pocket and flipped open the casing. "Five and twenty to nine," he said.

Holmes sprang for the door, grabbing his hat, scarf and coat on the way. "Come, Watson, Inspector ... there's no time to lose."

Minutes later we were on our way by carriage, driven by a hard-faced Sergeant Hewitt through a blustery, moonless night.

The Pump Rooms in Harrogate are situated down Parliament Street and on the left towards the Valley Gardens, a scenic spot favoured in the daylight and early summer evenings by young couples and nannies walking their charges. When we arrived, Holmes leapt from the carriage and burst through the doors.

A matronly woman wearing a pince-nez and seated behind a desk in the foyer got to her feet, her hand to her throat.

"My apologies for our entrance, madam," Holmes began, "but I am with Inspector Makinson, here, and Sergeant Hewitt of the Harrogate police, and my colleague Doctor Watson, and we are on a matter of grave importance. Tell me, if you can," he said, "the whereabouts of your colleague, Mr Frank Garnett."

"Why, Frank's in the shower room," she said. "Whatever do you need *him* for?"

"No time to explain," said the Inspector. "Which way's the shower room?"

The woman pointed towards a double door to the right of the foyer. "Is it about his accident?"

"Accident?" I said.

"He's hurt himself. Bandages all over the place."

Makinson frowned and led the way.

Through the doors we were on a long corridor from the end of which we could hear the unmistakable sound of water running.

"You and Mr Watson stay back, Mr Holmes," Makinson barked. "Jim, you stick with me. But go gently now," he added, "we don't want this fellow to get away."

Holmes reluctantly stepped back to allow Sergeant Hewitt to take the lead with the Inspector. We reached the end of the corridor and stood before a door bearing the sign SHOWERS. Makinson leaned his head against the door and listened. A faint whistling could be heard with the running water.

Makinson took hold of the handle. "Right, Jim?"

Sergeant Hewitt nodded.

"Right, gentlemen?"

Holmes nodded.

The Inspector turned the handle and rushed into the room.

Some fifty yards away from us was what seemed to be a tall man, standing in profile, brandishing a broom which he was using to

sweep water across the floor and into an empty communal bath
beside him. At the sound of our entrance, he turned to face
us and I saw immediately that the other side of his body was
noticeably smaller. His right wrist was tightly bandaged and
one side of his face was covered in gauze, held in place by
sticky tape. A further bandage was wrapped about his neck like
a scarf.

"We need to talk to you, Mr Garnett," Inspector Makinson
said.

Garnett hefted the broom and threw it in our direction. Then
he glanced across to the wall for an instant, as though considering something, before turning quickly and heading towards
a door at the rear of the room. He moved awkwardly and
within but two or three steps he listed to one side, like a
ship encountering stormy seas, and plunged head first into
the empty bath. There was a single strangulated cry followed
by a crash.

We ran across to the bath-side and looked over.

Garnett lay some seven or eight feet directly beneath us, on his
back, one leg doubled up beneath him and his arms spread-eagled
as though he were relaxing on his bed. A pool of blood was spreading
beneath his head.

Without a second thought, I sat on the edge of the bath and
lowered myself down until I was standing alongside Garnett.
He had lifted one hand and was pulling back the bandage
on his wrist. With a gasp of horror, I watched a piece of
shrivelled flesh fall from beneath the bandage onto the bath
floor. His eyelids flickering, Garnett then proceeded to undo
the buttons of his shirt, beneath which I could see a further
bandage.

I knelt down and took hold of the hand, feeling for a pulse. It
was there but only weak and fluttery. Garnett's lips were already
turning blue.

He pulled the hand free and, in one movement, tore the bandage
from his face. Crosby's stained cheek flesh lifted with it for a second
and then slid down to cover Garnett's mouth.

"How is he, Doctor Watson?" Makinson asked softly.

I shook my head and watched as Garnett took the grisly trophy
from his mouth and clasped it tightly. He began rubbing it feverishly
between thumb and forefinger.

"Make me well again," he muttered hoarsely. "Make me well
again . . ."

"Shall I get an ambulance, sir?" Sergeant Hewitt asked.

I looked up at him and shook my head.

Makinson had clambered down to join us, watching as I undid the tape affixing the bandage to Garnett's chest. I had no doubt what we would find beneath that bandage and no doubt what lay beneath the one about his neck.

"Why did you do it, Frank?" Makinson said softly, kneeling by the man's head.

Garnett muttered something seemingly in response.

I had now exposed Garnett's chest and, as I expected, the skin which he had removed from Terence Wetherall. But beneath even that was a further mark, a port wine stain of such volume and intensity that, despite what the man had done, my heart went out to him. Garnett's own birthmark was clearly malignant, its surface covered by clusters of small pustules many of which had burst open and were weeping a pungent gelatinous liquid.

Makinson leaned closer to Garnett's face, his ear against the man's mouth. "I can't hear you, Frank."

Garnett whispered again and then settled back against the floor, still.

The Inspector knelt up and whispered, "Who?" but there was no response. He got to his feet. "He's gone, poor devil."

"What did he say?" I asked.

"He said she told him as how it'd get better . . . that he'd been touched by the Almighty and how he mustn't complain." Makinson shook his head. "But he said it hadn't got better, it had got worse. He asked me to forgive him. That was the last thing he said."

"Who's 'she'?" asked Sergeant Hewitt.

Makinson shrugged. "He didn't say. Someone who cared for him, I expect."

As I clambered out of the bath, Holmes was standing by the wall holding in his hands a walking stick bearing an elaborately carved head for its handle.

"That must've been what he was thinking about," said Sergeant Hewitt. "When he seemed to hesitate."

"He needed it to walk," Holmes said. He handed the stick to the policeman, running his slender fingers across the handsome features of the heavy ivory handle. "But I think he used it for other things, too, Sergeant," he said. Then he turned around and walked back towards the foyer.

When I got outside, Sherlock Holmes was standing on the steps staring into the wind.

"He thought he had been touched by God, Watson," he said as I walked up beside him. "But the truth was God had turned his back on him. In fact, God had turned his back on them all."

I did not know what to say.

Then Holmes turned to me and smiled, though it was without any trace of humour. "I find God does that far too often these days," he said. Then he thrust his hands into his coat pockets and walked alone towards the waiting carriage.

THE ADVENTURE OF THE PERSECUTED PAINTER

Basil Copper

1

Watson recorded 1895 as the year in which Holmes was on top form. The earliest case he recorded for that year was "The Three Students" which took place at the end of March. Earlier that month, however, Holmes and Watson found themselves in Dorset in "The Adventure of the Persecuted Painter". Watson may have written this case up and lost it along with his other papers, but thankfully descendants of the residents in the local village remembered the story vividly. I am most grateful to that fine scholar of Sherlock Holmes and his successor Solar Pons, Mr Basil Copper, for investigating the case and restoring it for the first time in over a century.

It was a dreary evening in early March when I returned to our familiar rooms in Baker Street. I was soaked to the skin for it had been raining earlier and I could not find a cab, and the dark clouds and louring skies promised a further downpour. As I opened the door to our welcoming sitting room, which was in semi-darkness, a familiar voice broke the silence.

"Come in, my dear Watson. Mrs Hudson will be up with a hot meal in a few minutes, as I had already observed you from the window, my poor fellow."

"Very good of you, Holmes," I mumbled. "I will just get into some dry things and rejoin you."

"It must have been very damp down Hackney way," my friend observed with a dry chuckle.

"How could you possibly know that, Holmes?" I said in some surprise.

He burst into a throaty laugh.

"Because you inadvertently left your engagement pad on the table yonder."

When I returned to the sitting room the lamps were alight and the apartment transformed, with the motherly figure of Mrs Hudson, our amiable landlady, bustling about laying the table, the covered dishes on which were giving off an agreeable aroma.

"Ah, shepherd's pie!" said Holmes, rubbing his thin hands together and drawing up his chair.

"You have really excelled yourself this evening, Mrs Hudson."

"Very kind of you to say so, sir."

She paused at the door, an anxious expression on her face.

"Did your visitor come back, Mr Holmes?"

"Visitor, Mrs Hudson?"

"Yes, sir. I was just going out, you see, and he said he would not bother you now. He said he would be back between six-thirty and seven-thirty, if that was convenient. I hope I have done right."

"Certainly, Mrs Hudson."

Holmes glanced at the clock over the mantel.

"It is only six o'clock now so we have plenty of time to do justice to your excellent meal. What sort of person would you say?"

"A foreign-looking gentleman, Mr Holmes. About forty, with a huge beard. He wore a plaid cape, a wide-brimmed hat and carried a shabby-looking holdall."

I paused with a portion of shepherd's pie halfway to my mouth.

"Why, you would make an admirable detective yourself, Mrs Hudson."

Our good landlady flushed.

"Kind of you to say so, sir. Shall I show him up as soon as he arrives, Mr Holmes?"

"If you please."

Holmes was silent as we made inroads into the excellent fare and it had just turned seven when he produced his pipe and pouch and sat himself back in his chair by the fire.

"A foreign gentleman with a beard and a shabby case, Holmes," I said at length, after the débris of our meal had been cleared and the room had resumed its normal aspect.

"Perhaps, Watson. But he may be an Englishman with a very mundane problem. It is unwise to speculate without sufficient data on which to base a prognosis."

"As you say, Holmes," I replied and sat down opposite him and immersed myself in the latest edition of *The Lancet.* It was just half-past seven and we had closed the curtains against the sheeting rain when there came a hesitant tap at the sitting room door. The apparition which presented itself was indeed bizarre and Mrs Hudson's matter of fact description had not prepared me for such a sight.

He was of great height, and his dark beard, turning slightly grey at the edges, now flecked with rain, hung down over his plaid cloak like a mat. His eyes were a brilliant blue beneath cavernous brows and his eyebrows, in contrast to the beard, were jet-black, which enhanced the piercing glance he gave to Holmes and myself. I had no time to take in anything else for I was now on my feet to extend a welcome. He stood just inside the door, water dripping from his clothing on to the carpet, looking owlishly from myself to Holmes, who had also risen from his chair.

"Mr Holmes? Dr Watson?" he said hesitantly in a deep bass voice.

"This is he," I said, performing the introductions.

He gave an embarrassed look to both of us.

"I must apologize for this intrusion, gentlemen. Aristide Smedhurst at your service. Artist and writer, for my pains. I would not have bothered you, Mr Holmes, but I am in the most terrible trouble."

"This is the sole purpose of this agency – to assist," said Holmes, extending a thin hand to our strange guest.

"Watson, would you be so kind? I think, under the circumstances, a stiff whisky would not come amiss."

"Of course, Holmes," I said, hastening to the sideboard.

"That is most gracious of you, gentlemen," said Smedhurst, allowing himself to be led to a comfortable chair by the fire.

As I handed him the whisky glass his face came forward into the light and I saw that he had an unnatural pallor on his cheeks.

"Thank you, Dr Watson."

He gulped the fiery liquid gratefully and then, seeing Holmes's sharp eyes upon him, gave an apologetic shrug.

"Forgive me, Mr Holmes, but if you had been through what I have experienced, it would be enough to shake even your iron nerve."

"Indeed," said Holmes in reassuring tones. "Pray do not apologize, my dear Mr Smedhurst. I observed when you first entered that your cape and trousers were covered in mud, as though you had fallen heavily. You have come all the way from Dorset today, I presume, so the matter must be serious."

Our strange visitor gazed at Holmes open-mouthed.

"I did indeed have a nasty fall in my anxiety to catch my train. But how on earth could you know I came from Dorset?"

My old friend got up to light a spill for his pipe from the fire.

"There was nothing extraordinary about my surmise, I can assure you. Watson and I attended your exhibition at the Royal Academy last summer. Those extraordinary oils, water colours and pencil sketches of those weird landscapes remained long in my memory . . ."

"Why, of course, Holmes . . ." I broke in.

"And the exhibition catalogue, if I am not mistaken, gave your address in Dorset and said that you habitually worked in that fascinating part of the world," Holmes went on smoothly. "But you have a problem, obviously."

"Yes, Mr Holmes. I thought Dorset was fascinating at first," went on Smedhurst bitterly. "But no longer after my experiences of the past two years."

"But you called earlier and then went away. Why was that?"

A haunted look passed across the bearded man's face.

"I thought I was followed here," he mumbled, draining his glass. He eagerly accepted the replenishment I offered him.

"You are among friends, Mr Smedhurst," Holmes went on. "Pray take your time. You are staying in town, of course."

"At the Clarence, yes."

"An admirable establishment. Which means you are not pressed for time this evening?"

"No, sir."

The haggard look was back on our visitor's face.

"For God's sake, Mr Holmes, help me!. This ghastly thing has appeared again. Both my sanity and my life are at stake!"

2

There was a long silence in the room, broken only by the distant clatter of a passing hansom. Holmes waited until our visitor had regained his calm and then gently asked him to continue. Draining the contents of his second glass of whisky with one fierce gulp, Smedhurst plunged straight into his story.

"I had grown tired of London, Mr Holmes, and felt the need of country air. There was also a young lady with whom I had formed an attachment. We had met at one of my exhibitions and I had escorted her to several functions in London. She lived at Parvise Magna, a small village in Dorset, so when I went down I searched for a suitable dwelling in the area. I soon found what I wanted. It was an ancient cottage and needed a lot of repair but stood in its own land about a mile from the village. It had belonged to an old man, Jabez Crawley, who had let it go to rack and ruin, and who had died the previous year. However, I negotiated a fair price with a local lawyer who had handled Crawley's affairs, and moved in. At first, all went well and when my renovations had been completed I was extremely happy."

Here Smedhurst paused and flushed slightly. Holmes leaned forward in his chair, a gentle smile softening his austere features.

"You had come to an understanding with this young lady."

"Exactly so, Mr Holmes. A Miss Eveline Reynolds, a very charming person."

"I can well imagine, Mr Smedhurst," I put in.

Holmes's smile widened.

"Ah, there is your romantic streak again, Watson."

"Well, Mr Holmes," our visitor continued, "as I have indicated things went admirably. I had my studio on the first floor of the cottage and was turning out good work. Eveline – Miss Reynolds, that is – was a frequent visitor to the cottage and I also visited her home. She is an orphan and lives with an elderly aunt, the latter making me welcome enough. The first indication that something was wrong occurred a few months after my taking up residence. I returned home from a visit to Eveline one evening to find the premises in some disarray. Things had been moved from their familiar places, there were muddy boot-marks on the stairs, and some canvases in the studio had been disturbed."

"In other words a search had been made," said Holmes, a gleam of interest in his eyes.

"Exactly, sir. To say I was extremely annoyed, let alone alarmed and dismayed, would not adequately describe my feelings. I lit every lamp in the place and made a thorough search but found nothing."

"The front door had been securely locked?"

"Certainly, Mr Holmes. I would never leave my home in that lonely place without first making all secure."

"Perhaps your domestic help . . ." I put in.

Smedhurst shook his head.

"I have a woman who comes in twice a week to do some cleaning and cooking but she arrives only when I am there."

"No one else has a key?" said Holmes.

"Not that I am aware of, Mr Holmes. There is only one key, an enormous thing more suited to the Bastille. The lawyer explained that the old man was terrified of being robbed and insisted on one key only and had a special lock fitted."

"And the back door?"

"Firmly locked and bolted."

"Nothing was stolen?"

"I made a thorough inventory but nothing was missing, so far as I could make out."

"Did Miss Reynold have a key?"

Again the vehement shake of the head.

"I offered to have one made for her but she did not wish it. We both felt it might compromise her."

"Quite so," I put in.

Holmes got up to knock out his pipe in the fender, his face alive with interest.

"Hmm. This is intriguing. There is more, of course?"

"Much more, Mr Holmes, but I will be as concise as possible. The next thing that happened was strange noises around the house. Heavy footsteps as though someone were on the prowl. Then the front door latch would be tried. That was the most frightening thing of all, Mr Holmes. In a lonely cottage, late at night, all sorts of thoughts pass through one's head."

"Quite so."

"And then there were ghostly tappings at the window. I can tell you, Mr Holmes, that by that time my nerves were considerably on edge. These things continued for some months. In the interim Miss Reynolds and I had become engaged to be married."

I was about to offer my congratulations when I was arrested by the warning look on Holmes's face.

"You told your fiancée nothing about these unnerving incidents?"

"Certainly not."

"You did not investigate these happenings?"

"I did, Mr Holmes. I have a very powerful hand lantern and I lit that and went outside. But I left the front door open, so that the light spilled across the garden, and I never moved more than three yards from the door."

"You were very wise, Mr Smedhurst. Someone was evidently attempting to lure you from your home."

Smedhurst turned white and caught his breath with a little gasp.

"I had not thought of that, Mr Holmes. This happened on several occasions, but I could never find anyone though there were occasional traces of boots in the mud when the weather was wet. Thank God, all these activities stopped when spring came."

"Obviously, Mr Smedhurst. The person who was trying to frighten you could not carry out his activities during light spring and summer evenings."

"But what is the point of all this, Mr Holmes?"

"Hopefully, we shall see in due course," said my companion.

"Well, with the cessation of these manifestations, I regained my spirits somewhat and Miss Reynolds and I formally announced our engagement. In the meantime I visited the lawyer and in a roundabout way asked whether the former occupier of the cottage, Jabez Crawley, had ever mentioned anything out of the way there."

"And what was this gentleman's reaction?"

"Oh, he simply asked me a few questions about faulty drains, draught and damp and so forth and then queried whether I wished to sell the cottage."

Holmes clasped his thin fingers before him and sat studying my client's troubled face in silence for a long moment.

"Last winter the things began again," said Smedhurst. "Only it was worse this time. Not only weird noises, footsteps and tappings but one evening a fortnight ago a ghastly face like crumpled parchment appeared at the parlour window. I had left the curtains drawn back and you may remember the severe weather in February, so that there was a rime of frost on the panes. I caught a glimpse only for a moment but it turned my soul sick inside. A hideous white idiot face like a dwarf. I sat slumped for what must have been an hour without stirring outside. Nothing else happened or I should not have been able to answer for my sanity."

"You may well say so. But you have other troubles also, Mr Smedhurst."

The bearded man looked startled.

"I have heard that you can work miracles, Mr Holmes, and that you can almost see into people's minds."

Holmes gave a short laugh.

"Hardly, Mr Smedhurst. But I know a deeply troubled man when I see one. There is something beyond all this business, is there not? Something connected with Miss Reynolds?"

Smedhurst half-started from his chair and gave a strangled cry.

"You are right, Mr Holmes. There has been a growing estrangement because of all this. She wanted to know why I had changed but I did not want to involve her ..."

He broke off and buried his head in his hands.

"Now I hear that she has taken up with a young man who has come to live in the village ..."

Holmes put his finger to his lips and then laid his hand on our visitor's shoulder.

"All may yet come right, Mr Smedhurst. Do not despair."

"I have not told you the worst, Mr Holmes. Last night someone tried to shoot me as I stood outside my cottage door. It was dusk and the shot missed me by inches. I have never been so frightened in my life."

"Perhaps a poacher with a shotgun ..." I began.

Smedhurst stood up abruptly, trying to control the trembling that shook his frame.

"No, Dr Watson. I know a rifle shot when I hear one. That bullet was meant for me!"

"Why did you not call in the police, Mr Smedhurst?"

"We have only a sleepy village constable, Mr Holmes, and I had no evidence."

Holmes was on his feet now.

"Is there an inn in this Parvise Magna of yours?"

"Yes, Mr Holmes, the 'George and Dragon'."

"Good. If you will telegraph for rooms we will accompany you to Dorset in the morning. I take it you would wish to come, Watson?"

"By all means, Holmes. I will just warn my locum that I may be away for several days."

"Admirable! Your revolver, Watson, and a packet of cartridges in your luggage, if you please. We have no time to lose!"

3

It was a bitterly cold day with a fine drizzle when we left London the following morning and after several changes we found ourselves on the Somerset and Dorset Railway, in a small and uncomfortable carriage which seemed to be carrying us into a bleak and inhospitable landscape. We had the compartment to ourselves and our client, evidently exhausted from his trials of past days, sat huddled in deep sleep in a far corner. Holmes sat smoking furiously next to me, the fragrant emissions from his pipe seeming to emulate the black smoke our funny little engine was shovelling over its shoulder as we wound our interminable way into the gathering dusk.

"Well, what do you make of it, Watson?"

I shrugged.

"Pointless, Holmes. An old cottage ransacked, ghostly manifestations and then a murderous attack."

"But it adds up to a definite pattern, my dear fellow."

"If Mr Smedhurst has the only key to the cottage, how could a marauder gain entrance without breaking a window or something of that sort?"

"Ah, you have taken that point, have you. There must obviously be another. Or someone must have manufactured one."

"But for what purpose, Holmes?"

"That remains to be seen," said he, his sharp, feral face alive with interest.

"What I cannot understand," I went on, "is why, if someone has a key, they have not been back."

Holmes gave a dry chuckle.

"That is simple enough. He has satisfied himself that the object of his search will not be easily discernible. He may wait for the owner himself to discover it."

"Or scare him away."

Holmes nodded approvingly.

"Excellent, Watson. You have hit the nail on the head."

And he said not another word until we had reached our destination. This proved to be a somewhat ramshackle halt with a plank platform and I thought I had seldom seen a more desolate spot. Several oil lanterns beneath the station canopy were already alight and cast grotesque shadows as they swayed to and fro in the rising wind. But a closed carriage, which Smedhurst had already ordered from the hotel, was waiting and once our client had shaken off the torpor which had overtaken him on the train, he quickly took charge of the situation and we were speedily rocking through the approaching dusk to our journey's end.

I was surprised to find that Parvise Magna was not really a village but a small town composed of a broad main street, long lines of stone-built cottages and larger houses; no less than two inns; an ancient church; and a covered market.

"Things are looking up, Holmes," I said, as the cheering lights of our substantial hostelry, The George and Dragon, came into view.

It was indeed a comfortable-looking inn, with blazing log fires, and when we had quickly registered and deposited our baggage with the manager, Holmes looked inquiringly at our client.

"There should be an hour or so of daylight left. Would that be sufficient time for me to visit your cottage?"

"Oh, indeed, Mr Holmes. It would take only twenty minutes to get there, providing we can retain the carriage."

After a brief word with the manager Smedhurst led the way round to a side yard where the equipage was still waiting, and then we were driving swiftly out of the town and up into the winding fastnesses of the blunt-nosed hills. Presently we stopped at a place where an oak finger-post pointed up the hillside.

"I think we can walk back," said Holmes, giving the driver a half guinea for his trouble, much to that worthy's surprise and gratitude.

"It will give us an appetite for dinner," Holmes added.

We followed Smedhurst up a broad, zig-zag path, just wide enough for a horse and cart, that eventually wound between large boulders. It was an eerie and desolate place and I should not have cared to have spent one night there, let alone made it my permanent abode. I whispered as much to Holmes and he gave me a wry smile. There was still light enough in the sky to see our way and in a short while we came to a large stone cottage set back in a rustic enclosure that might once have been a garden.

Our client then produced a massive, wrought iron key which, as he had said, might well have served for the entrance to the Bastille, and unlocked the stout iron-studded front door. Holmes and I stood on the flagstone surround until Smedhurst had lit lamps within. The parlour was a huge room, with an ancient stone fireplace surmounted by a bressumer beam. The furniture was comfortable enough but the stone-flagged floor gave it a dank atmosphere, though Holmes seemed oblivious to such things. He went quickly to the large windows which fronted the room.

"This is where you saw the apparition, Mr Smedhurst?"

The tall man gulped.

"That is so, Mr Holmes. The nearest one."

I waited while my companion examined the glass carefully. Then he went outside and I could hear his staccato footsteps going up and down. When he reappeared, his face was absorbed and serious.

"Then the flagstone surround which appears to run round the entire house would not have shown any footprints."

"That is so, Mr Holmes."

"Let us just examine the rest of your abode."

Smedhurst lit lamp after lamp as we toured the ground floor, which consisted of a simple toilet; a corridor; a store room; and a kitchen, which was primitively equipped. We went up a creaky wooden staircase to the first floor, where there were three bedrooms and a huge apartment with northern lights equipped as a studio, and canvases stacked against the walls. Holmes went over to stare at a grotesque charcoal sketch of distorted trees and bleak moorland, set all aslant by the near-genius of the artist.

"Presumably this room is the reason you bought the house?"

"That is so, Mr Holmes."

"Very well."

My companion suddenly became very alert.

"We just have time to see outside before the light completely fails."

He led the way downstairs at a rapid pace, Smedhurst and myself having difficulty in keeping up with him. We rejoined him on the paved area in front of the cottage.

"So your phantom made off in this direction?"

He pointed in front of us to where the paving gave out into a narrow path which wound among bushes. Again the haunted look passed across Smedhurst's face and he went back and carefully re-locked the front door.

"Yes, Mr Holmes."

"Let us just see where this leads."

By the yellow light of the lantern which the artist carried and which cast bizarre shadows before us, we traversed the path and presently came out on a cleared space which appeared to be floored with some hard substance difficult to make out in the dim light.

"Ah!"

Holmes drew in his breath with a sibilant hiss, as a vast black pit composed itself before us.

"A quarry, I presume?"

"Yes, Mr Holmes. I know little of such matters but I understand it was where they cut Purbeck stone with which they built houses hereabouts. It has not been in use this fifty years. It is not within my land, of course. My boundary ends just beyond the paved area and is marked by a post. I have not bothered to have a fence erected."

"Quite so."

Holmes was craning forward, looking intently into the forbidding depths before us.

"This place looks decidedly dangerous."

"Yes. It is over a hundred feet deep. A sheer drop, as you can see."

"But an ideal spot into which your phantom might have disappeared."

Smedhurst gave me a startled look in the yellow light of the lantern he carried. There was a leprous glow on the far horizon and I was in a sombre mood as our small procession made its way back to the cottage. Smedhurst unlocked the front door and extended his hand in farewell.

"Will you not join us for dinner and stay the night at the hotel?" I said.

He shook his head.

"I do not care to be about after dark in these parts, gentlemen. But I will join you at the 'George' tomorrow."

"About midday," Holmes replied. "I have a few calls to make in the morning. Until then."

As we walked away we could hear the grating of the lock and the ponderous shooting of bolts at the great front door. At that moment I would not have changed places with our client for anything in the world.

"What a grim place, Holmes," I said as we walked swiftly back through the gloom toward the faint glow that indicated the welcoming streets of Parvise Magna.

"Ah, I see you lack the artistic temperament, Watson," said Holmes.

Our footsteps echoed unnaturally on the uneven, rocky surface of the path and dark clouds obscured the moon, only a few faint stars starting out on the horizon.

"I much prefer 221b, Holmes," said I.

My companion chuckled, a long chain of sparks from his pipe, which he had lit on his way down from the cottage, making fiery little stipples on his lean, aquiline features.

"I certainly agree there, my dear fellow."

4

The next morning I was up early but Holmes was earlier still for I found him at breakfast in the cheerful, beamed dining room, where a few sickly rays of sun glanced in at the windows. When we had finished our repast, Holmes jumped up swiftly and made for the door, hardly leaving me time to collect my overcoat from the rack and follow somewhat protestingly in his rear.

"We have very little time, Watson," he said as I caught up with him in the surprisingly busy street.

"Firstly, we must just pay a call upon Mr Amos Hardcastle, the lawyer and see what he has to say about this matter."

We had only some 300 or 400 yards to go and when we neared the brass plate which indicated that gentleman's office, Holmes took me aside and pretended to study the contents of a saddlery shop window.

"Leave the talking to me, my dear fellow. My name will be Robinson for the purpose of this business."

I had scarcely time to take this in before Holmes led the way up a dusty staircase to where a stout wooden door repeated the legend on the brass plate outside. A distant clock was just striking the hour of nine but the office was already astir and Holmes opened the door without further ado and I followed him in.

An elderly woman with grey hair rose from her desk in the dingy outer office and welcomed us with a wry smile. When Holmes had introduced himself as Robinson and explained that he would not keep Mr Hardcastle more than ten minutes, she nodded and crossed to an inner door, tapping before entering. There was a muffled colloquy from behind the panels and then the door was opened again. The solicitor was a man of heavy build and late middle age, who wore a snuff-stained waistcoat and gold pince-nez. His white hair fell in an untidy quiff over his forehead but his manner was cheerful enough and he asked Holmes and myself to sit down opposite his battered desk.

The room, which was lit by two large and dusty windows, was

piled high with papers on the far side while the area behind Hardcastle's desk was stacked with labelled tin boxes from floor to ceiling. Holmes, in his persona as Robinson said that Smedhurst was thinking of selling his cottage and that he, Robinson, was thinking of buying it. He had come down with myself to view the property but had found that Smedhurst had apparently gone away for several days. He wondered if the lawyer had a key to the house so that we could have a look at it.

A cautious, professional look immediately settled on the lawyer's face.

"Dear me, Mr Robinson, this is the first I have heard of it. Have you any written authority for what you say? This is merely a formality you understand, my dear sir, but I'm sure you realize . . ."

"Certainly."

I was even more astonished when Holmes produced a crumpled letter from the pocket of his ulster and passed it across to Smedhurst's solicitor. He scanned it cursorily through his pince-nez, biting his lip as he did so.

"All seems in order, Mr Robinson," he said as he handed it back.

He turned to the massed japanned boxes behind him and went down them rapidly. He took one up from the end of the piles and rattled it as though he expected to find something unpleasant inside it.

"Here we are."

He put it down on his desk, brushing the dust from the top of the box with a frayed sleeve. He opened it and went through a pile of yellowing papers. After sifting about for what seemed like an interminable time, he shook his head.

"I am so sorry to disappoint you, Mr Robinson, but I have nothing here. If I remember rightly my late client was a very retiring sort of person and inordinately frightened of burglars, though what he could have had of value up there was beyond me."

He chuckled rustily.

"Some years ago he had the front door lock changed. It came with a massive single key, which he always retained on him. I have no doubt Mr Smedhurst has it still. My regrets, gentlemen."

Holmes rose with alacrity and extended his hand to the lawyer.

"It was just a possibility. I am sorry to have disturbed you."

"Not at all, not at all."

He waved us out with a smile and as soon as we had regained the street I turned to Holmes.

"Where on earth did you get that letter?"

My companion smiled.

"Forged it, my dear fellow. I thought it might come in useful. I have a passable talent in that direction which has served its purpose from time to time. Now we must interview the young lady, which might be a more delicate matter and then I shall warn Smedhurst to make preparations for his departure."

"Departure, Holmes?" I said as we walked rapidly down the busy street. "I am all at sea."

"It is not the first time, old fellow," said he with a wry smile. "But hopefully all will be made plain in due course."

We walked several hundred yards and then turned at right-angles down a small alley, lined with pleasant old stone-built cottages. He stopped at the third on the right and opened a wrought-iron gate which gave on to a minuscule garden, where withered plants struggled for existence at this time of year. A motherly-looking lady in her early sixties opened the front door to his knock. She looked surprised, as well she might have.

"We wish to see Miss Eveline Reynolds on a most important matter. Please do not be alarmed, dear lady. A short interview will be greatly to her benefit."

The cloud gathering on her face disappeared immediately.

"Please come in. My niece is in the next room sewing. Whom shall I say . . .?"

Holmes leaned forward and whispered something in her ear. I saw a surprising change come over her face.

"I am sure she will be pleased to see you in view of what you have just told me."

She ushered us into a charmingly furnished oak-beamed parlour where a slim, golden-haired girl of some twenty-eight years was sitting at a sewing frame. She got up suddenly as we entered and looked enquiringly at her aunt.

"Please don't be alarmed, dear. These are friends of Mr Smedhurst."

"Ah!"

The girl could not suppress the exclamation that rose to her lips. The aunt had silently withdrawn and Miss Reynolds came forward to shake hands formally, beckoning us into easy chairs near the welcoming fire.

"You have news of Aristide? I have been so worried about him . . ."

There was such a pleading look on her face that I saw a dramatic change in Holmes himself.

"This is an extremely difficult matter, Miss Reynolds. But I am afraid we are forgetting our manners. I am Sherlock Holmes and this is my friend and colleague Dr Watson. I have asked your aunt not to reveal our identities and I would ask you to do the same."

He held up his hand as the girl started forward in her chair.

"Please let me continue. Mr Smedhurst is in some great difficulty and he has called upon me to help him. Am I to take it that your engagement has been broken off?"

The girl bit her lip.

"It is nothing of my doing, Mr Holmes. He has changed over the last year or so and become evasive. He no longer confides in me. He has taken to drinking rather heavily and now he has grown that ridiculous-looking beard!"

Little red spots of anger were starting out on her cheeks.

"Forgive me again, my dear young lady, but Mr Smedhurst appears to think that you have transferred your affections elsewhere."

The girl stared at Holmes in astonishment and then burst out laughing.

"You must mean Mr Jacob Ashton. He is a young Australian who came to the village a long while back. He is a surveyor by profession. My aunt and I occasionally lunch or dine at The George and Dragon and we made his acquaintance there. He is in practice here, but we are friends, nothing more."

"Ah, that is good news indeed, Miss Reynolds," said Holmes, rising abruptly from his chair. "I cannot confide in you at the moment but you may be sure that all will yet be well between you."

"Ah, if only I could believe you, Mr Holmes!"

"You may. And I might add that he was thinking only of you in his present troubles and did not wish you involved."

The girl shook hands with us warmly, and after Holmes had again asked her not to reveal his identity, we left the house with its occupants more cheerful than when we had arrived.

"Now Mr Smedhurst, Watson. I must prime him as to his role in our little drama. Ah, there is our man himself!"

He had just noticed our client's reflection in a shop window and, turning, we saw that he was making for The George and Dragon. We followed as quickly as possible, catching him at the entrance, where Holmes had a muffled conversation, before following him into the crowded restaurant. A waiter hurried forward as we sat down to order our meal when Smedhurst gave an exclamation and said, "Why, there is young Ashton at the table yonder."

Holmes leaned forward and put his hand gently on our client's shoulder.

"You have no need to worry. Miss Reynolds and Ashton are merely friends."

With a muffled apology he rose from the table and I was astonished to see him make straight for the surveyor, who was lunching alone at a side table. He bent over, presumably to introduce himself and then beckoned me across.

"Please forgive this intrusion, Mr Ashton, but I understand you are a surveyor. Myself and my friend Mr Watson are hoping to buy a cottage down here and have found exactly what we require. Mr Smedhurst, who is lunching with us, as you have perhaps noticed, is anxious to sell and we wondered whether you would be kind enough to undertake the survey."

Ashton, who was a pleasant-looking man of about thirty with black curly hair, seemed embarrassed, I thought.

"Certainly, Mr Robinson," he stammered. "But this is the first I have heard of it. Miss Reynolds did not mention it."

"It was a sudden decision," said Holmes smoothly. "Mr Smedhurst is going to London for a few days this evening, but is leaving the key of the cottage with us. I have the address of your office. And now, I have interrupted your lunch long enough."

Ashton got up to shake hands with the pair of us.

"Honoured, my dear sir," he said with a smile. My hours are from nine-thirty a.m. until six p.m., unless I am out on survey. I look forward to seeing you soon."

"I cannot see, Holmes . . ." I began as we regained our table.

"I seem to have heard you say that before, Watson," said my companion with a disarming smile. "I think the oxtail soup and then the steak will do admirably in my case."

And he talked of nothing but trivial matters until the meal was over.

5

"Now, you understand the procedures I have outlined to you, Mr Smedhurst," said Holmes as we regained the street.

Our client nodded.

"I will leave Parvise Magna this afternoon, in daylight, with my luggage and make sure my departure is noted in the town, both by pony and trap and by train. I will give out that I am going to London for a week to see an aunt and make myself conspicuous on the platform. I will stay away for three nights. I will leave the cottage key behind a big boulder about thirty feet from the front door. You cannot miss it, Mr Holmes. There is a fissure at the back and I will place it there, well concealed."

"Excellent, Mr Smedhurst. Now there is just one thing more."

"What is that, Mr Holmes?"

My companion gave him a thin smile.

"Shave off your beard. Miss Reynolds does not like it."

I spent part of the afternoon reading in the smoking room of The George and Dragon, while Holmes was away on some errand of his own. Presently he rejoined me and we both noted with satisfaction the departure of Smedhurst as his pony and trap clattered down the main street on its way to the station. As gas lamps began to be lit in the street outside Holmes rose from his deep leather chair, his whole being tense and animated.

"I think you might fetch your revolver, old fellow. We may need it before the night is out. I have some provisions in my greatcoat pocket so we shall not go hungry."

"In that case I will bring my whisky flask," said I.

A quarter of an hour later we left the hotel and made our way inconspicuously through side streets, as though taking an innocuous afternoon stroll. Though there was still an hour or so of daylight the sky was dark and sombre as we cleared the outskirts of Parvise Magna and a pallid mist was rising from the drenched fields which skirted the rounded hills. We were both silent as we continued our walk and presently Holmes turned aside to avoid approaching our client's cottage from the front. When we could just see the roof of the property through the bare branches of leafless trees, we diverged from the path and in a few moments found ourselves on the overgrown track that led to the quarry. It was a grim place at that late time of day and we both paused as though possessed of the same impulse, and gazed down over the hundred foot drop.

"An awful spot, Holmes."

"Indeed, Watson. But I think there is a more agreeable approach yonder."

He pointed forward and I then saw what appeared to be a white thread which turned out to be a shelving part of the quarry that led downward in gentle slopes. Our feet gritted on the loose shale and after we had descended about halfway my companion gave a sharp exclamation.

He led the way across the face of the quarry to where a dark hole gaped. It was obviously man-made and had perhaps provided shelter for the quarrymen in years gone by. I followed him in and saw that the cavern was about ten feet across and some twenty feet deep. There was a narrow shelf of rock on the left-hand side, about five feet in.

"Hulloa", I said. "Here is a candle, Holmes."

I bent closer.

"And recently used, I should say, judging by the spent matches which are perfectly dry and not wet as they would be had they been there a long time."

Holmes came to look over my shoulder.

"You are constantly improving, my dear fellow. You are not far out."

He went back into the rear of the cave which the failing daylight still penetrated.

"Someone has made a fire," I said, as he stirred the blackened ashes on the rough floor with his boot. "A tramp has been living here, perhaps."

"Perhaps, Watson," he said, as though his thoughts were far away.

Then he stooped to pick up a small slip of cardboard from the remains of the fire. I went across to see what he had found. I made out the faint white lettering on a blue background: CARROLL AND CO.

"What does it mean, Holmes?"

"I do not yet know," he said reflectively. "Time will tell. I think I have seen enough here to confirm my tentative theories. In the meantime we must get back to the cottage before it is completely dark."

And he led the way up the quarry at a swift pace. He put his finger to his lips as we drew close to our destination and bending down behind the large boulder our client had indicated, he brought out the massive wrought-iron key. It was the work of a moment to open the cottage door and re-lock it from the other side. The key turned smoothly so it was obvious why Smedhurst's mysterious intruder had been able to gain entry so easily.

"Could we have a light, Holmes?" I whispered.

"There is a dark lantern on the table yonder, which I observed on our previous visit. I think we might risk it for a few minutes to enable us to settle down. If he is coming at all tonight our man will not move until long after dark. I have baited the trap. Now let us just see what comes to the net."

I could not repress a shudder at these words, and I felt something of the terror that Smedhurst had experienced in that lonely place. But the comforting feel of my revolver in my overcoat did much to reassure me. I lit the lantern, shielding the match with my hand, and when we had deposited our sandwiches and made ourselves comfortable in two wing chairs, I closed the shutter of the lantern so that only a thin line of luminescence broke the darkness. I placed it beneath the table where it could not be seen from the windows, and after loading my pistol and securing the safety catch I placed it and my whisky flask near at hand as the light slowly faded.

What can I say of that dreary vigil? That the dark cloud of horror which seemed to hang about the cottage that night will remain with me until my dying day. Combined with the melancholy screeching of distant owls, it merely emphasized the sombreness of our night watch. Holmes seemed impervious to all this for he sat immobile in his chair, for I could see his calm face in the dim light that still filtered through the parlour windows. Presently we ate the sandwiches and fortified with draughts of whisky from my flask, I became more alert. Several hours must have passed when I became aware that Holmes had stirred in his chair.

"I think the moment is approaching. Your pistol, Watson, if you please."

Then I heard what his keen ears had already caught. A very faint, furtive scraping on the rocky path that led to the cottage. I had the pistol in my hand now and eased off the safety catch. The clouds had lifted momentarily and pale moonlight outlined the casement bars. By its spectral glow I suddenly saw a ghastly, crumpled face appear in the nearest frame and I almost cried aloud. But Holmes's hand was on my arm and I waited with racing heart.

Then there was a metallic click and a key inserted from outside began to turn the lock. I was about to whisper to my companion when the door was suddenly flung wide and cold, damp air flowed into the room. We were both on our feet now. I vaguely glimpsed two figures in the doorway and then Holmes had thrown the shutter of the dark lantern back and its light flooded in, dispelling the gloom and revealing a dark-clad figure and behind him, the hideous thing that had appeared at the window. A dreadful cry of alarm and dismay, the pounding of feet back down the path and then the horrible creature had turned the other way.

"Quickly, Watson! Time is of the essence! I recognized the second man but we must identify the other."

We were racing down the tangled pathway now, stumbling over the rocky surface but the white-faced creature was quicker still. I discharged my pistol into the air and our quarry dodged aside and redoubled its efforts. Then we were in thick bushes and I fired again. The flash and the explosion were followed by the most appalling cry. When we rounded the next corner I could see by the light of the lantern which Holmes still carried, that the thing had misjudged the distance on the blind bend and had fallen straight down into the quarry.

"It cannot have survived that fall, Holmes," I said.

He shook his head.

"It was not your fault, old fellow. But we must hasten down in case he needs medical aid."

A few minutes later we had scrambled to ground level and cautiously approached the motionless thing with the smashed body that told my trained eye that he had died instantly. I gently turned him over while Holmes held the lantern. When he removed the hideous carnival mask we found ourselves looking into the bloodied face of young Ashton, the surveyor, whose expression bore all the elements of shock and surprise that one often finds in cases of violent death.

6

Holmes's hammering at the knocker of the substantial Georgian house at the edge of the town, presently brought a tousled housekeeper holding a candle in a trembling hand to a ground-floor window.

"I must see your master at once!" said Holmes. "I know he has just returned home so do not tell me that he cannot be disturbed. It is a matter of life and death!"

The door was unbolted at once and we slipped inside.

"Do not be alarmed, my good woman," said Holmes gently. "Despite the hour, our errand is a vital one. I see by the muddy footprints on the parquet that your master has only recently returned. Pray tell him to come downstairs or we shall have to go up to him."

The housekeeper nodded, the fright slowly fading from her face.

"I will not be a moment, gentlemen. Just let me light this lamp on the hall table."

We sat down on two spindly chairs to wait, listening to the mumbled conversation going on above. The man who staggered down the stairs to meet us was a completely changed apparition to the smooth professional we had previously met.

"You may leave us, Mrs Hobbs," he said through trembling lips.

He looked from one to the other of us while anger and despair fought for mastery in his features.

"What is the meaning of this intrusion in the middle of the night, Mr Robinson?"

"My name is Sherlock Holmes," said my companion sternly. "Your friend is dead. We must have the truth or you are a lost man!"

Amos Hardcastle's face was ashen. He mumbled incoherently and I thought he was going to have a stroke. I put my hand under his arm to help him down the last few treads and he almost fell into the chair I had just vacated. He looked round blankly, as though in a daze.

"Jabez Crawley's nephew dead? And you are the detective, Sherlock Holmes."

"Tell us the truth, Mr Hardcastle," said Holmes, a smile of triumph on his face. "Or shall I tell the story for you."

Something like anger flared momentarily in the lawyer's eyes.

"My client . . ." he began but Holmes cut him short.

"Must I repeat; your client is dead. He tried to kill Mr Smedhurst. That makes you an accessory."

The lawyer's face turned even whiter if that were possible.

"I knew nothing of that," he whispered. "Did you kill him?"

This to me. I shook my head.

"No. He fell over the edge of the quarry."

"I will have you disbarred for unprofessional conduct and you will stand trial for criminal conspiracy and accessory to attempted murder," said Holmes sternly. "It was unfortunate for you that I recognized you by the light of the lantern."

"I beg you, Mr Holmes!"

"The time is long past for begging. Let me just try to reconstruct your dishonest sequence of events. I am sure you will correct me if I am wrong."

Holmes sat down in a chair opposite the crushed figure of the lawyer and eyed him grimly.

"Let us just suppose that old Jabez Crawley did not leave a proper will. Just a scribbled note or two, leaving the cottage to his nephew in Australia, his only surviving relative. And supposing he had hinted that there was something valuable hidden there, without indicating its whereabouts. Money perhaps, bonds or the deeds to properties. There were two keys to the cottage. There had to be or you and the nephew could never have gone there and made searches while Mr Smedhurst was out. But that is to run ahead. Am I correct so far?"

The old man nodded sullenly. He looked like a cornered rat with his hair awry and his muddy clothes.

"You wrote to the nephew in Australia at his last known address. You got no reply, I presume?"

"No, sir. More than eight months had passed and I surmised that young Ashton had either died or moved to some other country."

Holmes smiled thinly.

"You had many fruitless searches at the cottage in the interim – without result. So you sold it to Mr Smedhurst and pocketed the proceeds. You are a pretty scoundrel, even for a provincial lawyer."

Hardcastle flushed but said nothing, his haunted eyes shifting first to Holmes and then on to me.

"After a long interval you got a reply from the nephew. Your letter had gone astray or been delayed. All this is fairly elementary."

"I think it quite remarkable, Holmes," I interjected. "I had no idea . . ."

"Later, old fellow," he interrupted. "So young Ashton made his way here and you gave him all the information at your disposal without, of course, telling him that he was the rightful owner of the cottage and that you had yourself sold it and kept the money."

One look at the lawyer's face told me that once again my companion had arrived at the right conclusion.

"You worked out a plan of campaign. The nephew would try and sow a little discord between Smedhurst and his fiancée, in the most subtle way, of course, at the same time keeping an eye on Smedhurst's activities. Then the pair of you invented the series of ghostly happenings. When you drew a blank there and further searches threw no light on old Crawley's secret, you resorted to stronger measures, with the apparition at the window and then, finally, a short while ago, the attempt at murder."

The old man wrung his hands.

"I can assure you, Mr Holmes . . ."

"Well, that is a matter between you and the police," said Holmes curtly. "We must inform them about the body in the quarry and the circumstances first thing in the morning, Watson. It is almost dawn, anyway."

"Of course, Holmes."

I glanced at my pocket watch and saw that it was almost four a.m. I felt a sudden weariness following the events of the night.

"What about the cave in the quarry?" I asked.

"That was as clear as crystal, Watson. When carrying out his dangerous masquerade, Ashton needed a refuge and an opportunity for a ghostly disappearance. He found the place near the cottage which suited his purposes admirably. When he had made his escape and was sure no one had followed, he lit the candle and tidied his clothing. Perhaps he cleaned his shoes if they were coated with mud."

"But the fire, Holmes?"

He gave a thin smile.

"Why, simply to burn that huge papier-mâché carnival mask, Watson. The fragment of label unburned, reading CARROLL AND CO. showed that the mask had been bought from a well-known Soho emporium specializing in such things. Obviously, Ashton had bought a number of them."

"Yes, but how would he take them to the cottage, Holmes?"

"Why, probably in a large paper bag. No one would take any notice when he passed through the town in broad daylight. The early hours were another matter. He could not risk taking that mask through the town to his house at dead of night in case he were seen; he might even have been stopped and questioned by the local constable. Hence the fire. Correct, Mr Hardcastle?"

"You are a devil, Mr Holmes," was the man's broken reply. "But you are correct in every detail."

We left the shattered figure of Hardcastle huddled on the chair and walked back toward the centre of the town.

"How did you come to suspect Ashton?" I said.

"There was the irony, Watson. It could have been anyone in Parvise Magna. But then the idea grew in my mind. Ashton was young and personable; he had come from Australia; soon after the ghostly manifestations had appeared; and he had attached himself to Smedhurst's fiancée."

"Remarkable, Holmes."

"You do me too much credit, my dear fellow."

"I wonder what the secret of the cottage is?" I said.

He shrugged.

"Only time will tell. Otherwise, a very obvious affair".

7

And so it proved. Some weeks later I came to the breakfast table to find Holmes smiling broadly. He passed a cheque across to me and my eyes widened as I read the amount above Smedhurst's signature.

"Our artist has struck lucky at last, Watson," he said. "His letter is full of news. He has shaved off his beard and is reunited with his fiancée."

"Excellent, Holmes."

"And there is more. Just glance at these two newspaper cuttings."

The first related to the preliminary police court proceedings against Hardcastle, which Holmes and I had attended, and his subsequent striking off the legal rolls. The opening of the inquest on Ashton, which we were also required to attend had been held *in camera* due to the involvement of Hardcastle in these proceedings also, and had been adjourned *sine die.* Therefore there had been no reports of these proceedings in the Dorset or national newspapers. During the inquest a high-ranking police officer had informed Holmes that a sporting rifle with one spent cartridge in the breech had been found at Ashton's home, together with a number of carnival masks.

The second cutting was even more sensational than the first. It was a lurid tale of an artist who had discovered £20,000 in golden guineas in a series of tin boxes beneath the oak flooring of his studio. There was no mention of Holmes, as I had expected, and the report merely concluded with the information that the discovery had been made by a carpenter carrying out work for Smedhurst.

"And here is something for you, Watson."

Holmes passed across a small buff envelope. That too was from Smedhurst and was an invitation to his wedding celebrations a month hence. I glanced up at Holmes's own invitation on the mantelpiece.

"Will you be joining me, Holmes?"

My companion gave me an enigmatic smile.

"I think not, Watson. Marriage is a very uncertain and risky business. But you may give the bride and groom my best wishes and a suitable gift from Garrard's if you will."

And he reached out for his violin.

Eighteen ninety-five also saw the recorded cases of "The Solitary Cyclist", "Black Peter" and "The Bruce-Partington Plans", as well as several unrecorded cases, amongst them that of Wilson, the notorious canary trainer and the sudden death of Cardinal Tosca. There have been many attempts at recounting the episode of the notorious canary trainer and I am suspicious of all of them. And since there was no Cardinal Tosca, I have as yet not been able to identify what case Watson was referring to.

1896 is something of a mystery year. There are very few recorded cases until the autumn, and there is some dispute as to whether "The Disappearance of Lady Frances Carfax" belongs in 1895, 1896 or 1897, but it is certainly one of these three. I favour 1896 if only because I suspect Watson was giving us a clue as to Holmes's whereabouts that year. Holmes could not, originally, investigate the Carfax mystery because he was involved in the case of old Abrahams, who was in mortal fear of his life. In fact Holmes believes, perhaps with a degree of wry delight, that he should not leave the country because Scotland Yard needed him. No matter how puckish a comment this may have been, it is likely that Holmes was involved in a major investigation for Scotland Yard, and that possibly it had taken him abroad at some time. The Yard's files are blank on this, and the year remains a mystery. There is doubtless a further clue at the start of "The Veiled Lodger", one of the cases which took place at the end of 1896, where Watson refers to attempts that had been made in senior circles to gain access to Watson's files and papers. He drops a hint that if any more of this happens then the case of "the politician, the lighthouse and the trained cormorant" would be revealed. Despite playful attempts by some to reveal this story, its facts have remained a mystery.

Nevertheless by the close of 1896 Holmes was clearly back in circulation. Watson records the case of "The Sussex Vampire" in addition to "The Veiled Lodger", and my researches have unearthed three other cases.

"The Adventure of the Suffering Ruler" perhaps indicates that Holmes's recent pursuits had put a significant strain upon his deductive skills. H.R.F. Keating, that renowned author of crime stories had, I believe, a certain pleasure in bringing this story back from the dead.

In "The Repulsive Story of the Red Leech" we have what is evidently a second episode that relates to this title, as Watson's earlier reference to it suggested it happened in 1894, and the incident in "The Inertial Adjustor" seems to support that statement. David Langford's computer skills tracked down clues via the Internet which first alerted us to the facts in this case which he has now brought together for the first time.

Roger Johnson, another formidable Sherlockian, spent much time investigating the case of Henry Staunton, and has now completed it in "The Adventure of the Grace Chalice".

THE ADVENTURE OF THE SUFFERING RULER

H. R. F. Keating

It was in the early autumn of 1896 that, returning one day from visiting by train a patient in Hertfordshire and being thus in the vicinity of Baker Street, I decided to call on Sherlock Holmes, whom I had not seen for several weeks. I found him, to my dismay, in a sad state. Although it was by now late afternoon he was still in his dressing-gown lounging upon the sofa in our old sitting room, his violin lying on the floor beside him and the air musty with cold tobacco smoke from the neglected pipe left carelessly upon the sofa arm. I glanced at once to the mantelpiece where there lay always that neat morocco case which contained the syringe. It was in its customary place, but, when under pretence of examining the familiar bullet-marked letters "VR" on the wall above, I stepped closer, I saw that it lay upon the envelope of a letter postmarked only two days earlier.

"Well, Holmes," I said, jovially as I could, "I see that your bullet holes of yore are still here."

"It would be strange indeed, Watson, had they disappeared," my old friend answered, with somewhat more fire than he had earlier greeted me.

He laughed then in a melancholy enough fashion.

"Yet I could wish that they had vanished between one night and the next morning," he added. "It would at least provide my mind with some matter to work upon."

My spirits sank at the words. Holmes had always needed stimulation, and if no problem was there to arouse his mind a seven per cent solution of cocaine awaited.

"But have you no case on hand?" I asked.

"Some trifling affairs," Holmes replied. "A commission for the Shah of Persia, a little question of missing securities in Pittsburgh.

Nothing to engage my full attention. But, you, my dear Watson, how is it that you have been visiting a patient in Hertfordshire?"

I turned to my old friend in astonishment. I had said nothing of the reason for my being in the vicinity.

"Oh, come, doctor," he said. "Do I have to explain to you once again the simple signs that tell me such things? Why, they are written on your person as clearly as if you carried a newspaper billboard proclaiming them."

"I dare say they may be, Holmes. But beyond the fact that Baker Street station serves that particular county and that I nowadays visit you chiefly when I chance to be in the locality, I cannot see how this time you can know so much of my business."

"And yet the moment you removed your gloves the characteristic pungent odour of iodoform was heavy in the air, indicating beyond doubt that your excursion had been on a professional matter. While your boots are dust-covered to the very tops, which surely means that you travelled for some little time on a country lane."

I glanced down at my boots. The evidence was all too plain to see.

"Well, yes," I admitted. "I did receive this morning a request to visit a gentleman living near Rickmansworth whose condition was causing him anxiety. An unhealed lesion on the abdomen complicated by brain fever, but I have high hopes of a good recovery."

"My dear Watson, under your care who can doubt of that? But I am surprised to hear that your practice now extends to the remote Hertfordshire countryside."

I smiled.

"No, no. I assure you none other of my patients necessitates any journey longer than one performed easily in a hansom."

"And yet you have just been down to Hertfordshire?"

"Yes. I was called on this morning by the manservant of a certain Mr Smith, a trusted fellow, I gathered, though of European origin. He told me that his master had instructed him to seek out a London doctor and to request a visit as soon as possible. Apparently, Mr Smith has a somewhat morbid fear of any of his close neighbours knowing that he is ill and so prefers a physician from a distance, even if the visit means a considerably greater financial outlay."

"You were well remunerated then?"

"I think I may say, handsomely so."

"I am not surprised to hear it."

"No, there, Holmes, you are at fault. My services were not asked for because of any particular reputation I may have. In fact, the manservant happened to be in my neighbourhood upon some other errand and, so I understand, simply saw my brass plate and rang at my door."

Holmes raised himself upon one elbow on the sofa. His eyes seemed to me to shine now with a healthier light.

"You misunderstand me, Watson. You had already indicated that your services were called upon more or less by chance. But what I was saying was that the size of your fee did not surprise me, since it is clearly evident that you were required for a quality quite other than your medical attainments."

"Indeed?" I answered, a little nettled I must confess. "And what quality had you in mind?"

"Why, distance, my dear fellow. The distance between medical adviser and patient, and the complete discretion that follows from that."

"I am by no means sure that I understand."

"No? Yet the matter is simple enough. A person living in a remote country house, a gentleman for whom monetary considerations have little weight, sends a trusted servant to obtain the immediate services of a London doctor, of any London doctor more or less, and you expect me to be surprised that you received a fee altogether out of the ordinary?"

"Well, Holmes," I replied, "I will not disguise that my remuneration was perhaps excessive. But my patient evidently is a wealthy man and one prey to nervous fears. He trusts, too, to receive my continuing attentions from week to week. The situation does not strike me as being very much out of the ordinary."

"No, Watson? But I tell you that it is out of the ordinary. The man you attended this afternoon is no ordinary man, you may take my word for that."

"Well, if you say so, Holmes, if you say so," I replied.

Yet I could not but think that for once my old friend had read too much into the circumstances, and I quickly sought for some other subject of conversation, being much relieved when Holmes too seemed disinclined to pursue a matter in which he might be thought to have me at a disadvantage. The remainder of the visit passed pleasantly enough, and I had the satisfaction of leaving Holmes looking a good deal more brisk and cheerful than he had done upon my arrival.

I went down to Hertfordshire again a week later and found my patient already much better for the treatment I had prescribed. I was hopeful enough, indeed, to feel that another two or three weeks of the same regimen, which included plenty of rest and a light diet, would see the illness through.

It was just as I stepped back from the bed after concluding my examination, however, that out of the corner of my eye I detected a sharp movement just outside the window. I was so surprised, since there was no balcony outside, that something of my alarm must have communicated itself to my patient who at once demanded, with the full querulousness of his indisposition, what it was that I had seen.

"I thought I saw a man out there, a glimpse of a face, dark brown and wrinkled," I answered without premeditation, so disturbed was I by an aura of malignancy I had been aware of even from my brief sight of that visage.

But I quickly sought to counteract any anxiety I might have aroused in my already nervous patient.

"Yet it can hardly have been a man," I said. "It was more likely a bird perching momentarily in the ivy."

"No, no," Mr Smith said, in sharp command. "A face, A burglar. I always knew this house was unsafe. After him doctor, after him. Lay him by the heels. Catch him. Catch him."

I thought it best at least to make pretence of obeying the peremptory order. There would be little hope of calming my patient unless I made an excursion into the garden.

I hurried out of the room and down the stairs, calling to the manservant, who, I had gathered, was the sole other occupant of the house. But he evidently must have been in the kitchens or elsewhere out of hearing since I had no reply. I ran straight out of the front door and looked about me. At once, down at the far side of the garden, I detected a movement behind a still leaf-clad beech hedge. I set out at a run.

Holmes had been right, I thought, as swiftly and silently I crossed a large, damp-sodden lawn. My patient must be a man of mystery if he was being spied upon by daylight in this daring fashion. His cries of alarm over a burglary must, then, be false. No ordinary burglar, surely, would seek to enter a house by broad daylight.

My quarry had by now gone slinking along the far side of the beech hedge to a point where I lost sight of him behind a dense rhododendron shrubbery. But I was running on a course to cut him off, and I made no doubt that before long I would have the rogue by the collar.

Indeed, as soon as I had rounded the dense clump of rhododendrons, I saw a small wicket gate in the hedge ahead with the figure of the man who had been spying on my patient only just beyond. He appeared from his garb to be a gypsy. In a moment I was through the gate, and in another moment I had him by the arm.

"Now, you villain," I cried. "We shall have the truth of it."

But even before the man had had time to turn in my grasp I heard from behind me the sound of sudden, wild, grim, evil laughter. I looked back. Peering at the two of us from the shelter of the rhododendrons was that same brown, wrinkled face I had glimpsed looking in at my patient's window. I loosened my grip on the gipsy, swung about and once more set out in pursuit.

This time I did not have so far to go. No sooner had I reached the other side of the shrubbery than I came face to face with my man. But he was my man no longer. He wore the same nondescript clothes that I had caught sight of among the brittle rhododendron leaves and his face was still brown-coloured. But that look of hectic evil in it had vanished clear away and in its place were the familiar features of my friend, Sherlock Holmes.

"I am sorry, Watson, to have put you to the trouble of two chases in one afternoon," he said. "But I had to draw you away from that fellow before revealing myself."

"Holmes," I cried. "Then it was you at the window up there?"

"It was, doctor. I knew that it was imperative that I myself should take a good look at this mysterious patient of yours, and so I took the liberty of following you, knowing that this was your day for visiting the case. But you were a little too quick for me in the end, my dear fellow, and I had to beat a more hurried retreat than I altogether cared to."

"Yes, but all the same, Holmes," I said. "You cannot have had any good reason to suppose that it was necessary to spy upon my patient in that manner."

"No good reason, doctor? Why, I should have thought the third finger of his right hand was reason enough, were there no other."

"The third finger of his right hand?"

"Why, yes, my dear fellow. Surely you are not going to tell me that you noticed nothing about that? Come, I was at that window for little more than three or four minutes and I had grasped its significance long before you turned and saw me."

"Now that I think about it," I replied, "my patient does wear a finger-stall on the third finger of his right hand. Some trifling injury, I suppose. It certainly could in no way contribute to his condition."

"I never suggested that it did, doctor. I am sure you know your business better than that. Trust me, then, to know mine."

"But does his concealing that finger have some significance?" I asked.

"Of course it does. Tell me, what does a man customarily wear upon his third finger?"

"A ring, I suppose. But that would not be upon the right hand, surely?"

"Yes, Watson, a ring. You have arrived at the point with your customary perspicacity. But why should a man wish to conceal a particular ring? Tell me that."

"Holmes, I cannot. I simply cannot."

"Because the ring has a particular meaning. And who is it who would wear a ring of that nature? Why, a monarch, of course. I tell you that man in bed there is a king, and he is hiding for some good reason. There can scarcely be any doubt about that."

To my mind, there was at least room for a measure of disagreement with this conclusion. Smith was perhaps a name that anyone wishing to live anonymously might take, but certainly my patient had shown not the least trace of a foreign accent, as he was surely likely to do if he were the ruler of one of the lesser European states whose appearance, especially since he wore a full beard, might be unknown to me. Yet he did have a manservant of European origin, though here again this was not an altogether uncommon circumstance for a single English gentleman who might be something of a traveller. I would have liked to put all these doubts and queries to my friend, but from the moment that he had told me what he had deduced from my patient's concealed finger he lapsed into one of those moods of silence well familiar to me, and for the whole of our journey back to London he uttered scarcely a word, little more than to say to me at the station in Hertfordshire that he had a number of telegrams which he needed urgently to despatch.

I was curious enough, however, to find an opportunity of visiting Baker Street again next day. But, though I found Holmes fully dressed and a great deal more alert than on my last visit, I was unable to obtain from him any hint about the direction of his inquiries. All he would do was to talk, with that vivacity of spirit which he could display whenever the mood took him, about a bewildering variety of subjects, the paintings of the Belgian artist, Ensor, the amorous adventures of Madame Sand, the activities of the Russian nihilists, the gravity of the political situation in Illyria. None was a matter on which I felt myself particularly informed, yet on each Holmes, it seemed, had a fund of knowledge. At length I went back to my medical round not one whit better able to decide whether my Hertfordshire patient was no more than the nervous Englishman, Mr Smith, whom he seemed to be, or in truth some foreign potentate sheltering under that pseudonym in the safety of the Queen's peace.

The following morning, however, I received a telegram from

Holmes requesting me to meet him at his bank in Oxford Street at noon "in re the hidden finger." I was, you can be sure, at the appointed place at the appointed hour, and indeed a good few minutes beforehand.

Holmes arrived exactly to time.

"Now, my good fellow," he said, "if you will do me the kindness of walking a few yards along the street with me, I think I can promise you a sight that will answer a good many of the questions which I have no doubt have been buzzing in your head these past few days."

In silence we made our way together, along the busy street. I could not refrain from glancing to left and right at the passers-by, at the cabs, carriages and vans in the roadway and at the glittering shopfronts in an endeavour to see what it was that Holmes wished to show me. But my efforts were in vain. Nothing that I saw roused the least spark in my mind.

Then abruptly Holmes grasped my arm. I came to a halt.

"Well?" my companion demanded.

"My dear fellow, I am not at all clear what it is to which you are directing my attention."

Holmes gave a sigh of frank exasperation.

"The window, Watson. The shop window directly before you." I looked at the window. It was that of a photographer's establishment, the whole crowded with numerous likenesses of persons both known and unknown.

"Well?" Holmes demanded yet more impatiently.

"It is one of these photographs you wish me to see?" I asked.

"It is, Watson, it is."

I looked at them again, actors and actresses, the beauties of the day, well-known political figures.

"No," I said, "I cannot see any particular reason for singling out one of these pictures above any of the others. Is that what you wish me to do?"

"Watson, look. In the second row, the third from the left."

"The Count Palatine of Illyria," I read on the card below the portrait which Holmes had indicated.

"Yes, yes. And you see nothing there?"

Once more I gave the photograph my full attention.

"Nothing," I answered at last.

"Not the very clear likeness between the ruler of that troubled state and a certain Mr Smith at present recovering from illness in Hertfordshire?"

I examined the portrait anew.

"Yes," I agreed eventually. "There is a likeness. The beards have a good deal in common, and perhaps the general cast of the countenances."

"Exactly."

From an inner pocket Holmes now drew a newspaper cutting. "*The Times*," he said. "Of yesterday's date. Read it carefully."

I read, and when I had done so looked up again at Holmes in bewilderment.

"But this is a report of the Count Palatine appearing on the balcony of his palace and being greeted with enthusiasm by a vast crowd," I said. "So, Holmes, how can this man in the photograph be my patient down in Hertfordshire but two days ago?"

"Come, Watson, the explanation is childishly simple."

I felt a little aggrieved and spoke more sharply than I might have done in reply.

"It seems to me, I must say, that the sole explanation is merely that my patient and the Count Palatine of Illyria are not one and the same person."

"Nonsense, Watson. The likeness is clear beyond doubt, and nor is the explanation in any way obscure. It is perfectly plain that the man glimpsed at a distance by the crowd in Illyria is a double for the Count Palatine. The situation there, you know, is decidedly grave. There is the most dangerous unrest. If it were widely known that the Count was not at the helm in his country, the republican element would undoubtedly make an attempt to seize power, an attempt, let me tell you, that would in all likelihood be successful. However, you and I know that the Count is seriously ill and is living in Hertfordshire, under your excellent care, my dear Watson. So the solution is obvious. With the connivance of his close circle the Count has arranged for a substitute to make occasional public appearances in his stead in circumstances under which he will not easily be identified."

"Yes, I suppose you must be right, Holmes," I said. "It certainly seems a complex and extraordinary business though. Yet your account does appear to connect all the various elements."

"It connects them indeed," Holmes replied. "But I think for the time being we can assure ourselves that all is well. Do me the kindness, however, doctor, to let me know as soon as there is any question of the Count becoming fit enough to resume his full powers."

It was, in fact, no later than the following week that I was able to give Holmes the reassuring news he had asked for. I had found my patient very far along the road to recovery, and though, not wishing to let him know that Holmes had penetrated his secret, I had not said to him that quite soon he would be ready to travel, I had left his bedside with that thought in my mind. In consequence I went from the station at Baker Street on my return directly to our old rooms.

"He is distinctly better then?" Holmes asked me.

"Very much so, I am happy to say. The lassitude that originally gave me cause for anxiety has almost completely passed away."

"Bad. Very bad, Watson."

"But surely, Holmes . . ."

"No, Watson, I tell you if the Count's enemies should gain any inkling of the fact that he is likely to be able to return to Illyria in the near future, they will stop at nothing to make sure that he never crosses the Channel."

"But, Holmes, how can they know that he is not in Illyria? You yourself showed me that extract from *The Times*."

"I dare say, Watson. Yet an illusion of that sort cannot be kept up indefinitely. No doubt the conspirators watch every appearance the supposed Count makes upon the Palace balcony. At any time some small error on the part of the substitute may give the game away. Very possibly that error has been already made and suspicions have been aroused. Remember that I myself was not the only spy you caught down in Hertfordshire a fortnight ago."

"The gipsy, Holmes? But I thought he was no more after all than a passing gipsy."

"Quite possibly he was, Watson. Yet did it not strike you as curious that the fellow was skulking in the grounds of the house?"

"Well, I had supposed that he had in fact never penetrated the garden itself."

"Indeed, Watson? Then it is perhaps as well that I have taken an interest in the matter. We should not wish the Count Palatine to fail to reach his homeland in safety. You have said nothing of his rapid recovery to anybody but myself?"

"Of course not, Holmes. Of course not."

Yet just one week later as, making what I hoped might be my last visit into Hertfordshire, I approached my mysterious patient's residence I was reminded with sudden shame that I had in fact spoken about his recovery outside the house the previous week when I had been talking to the manservant who had driven me back to the station in the dog-cart, and I recalled too that I had spoken in tones deliberately loud and clear so as to make sure that I was understood by this foreigner. I was debating with myself whether those words of mine could perhaps have been overheard then by some lurker, when my eye was caught by just such a person within some fifty yards of the gate of the house itself, an individual who seemed by his dress to be a seaman. But what was a seaman doing here in Hertfordshire, so far from the sea?

I decided that it was my duty now at least to deliver an oblique warning to the Count Palatine's faithful manservant, even though I still did not wish to disclose that I knew through Holmes whom he served. I succeeded, I hope, in giving him some general advice about the dangers of burglars in the neighbourhood, advice which I hoped would alert him without betraying what Holmes and I alone knew. I was relieved, too, when my patient, having declared his intention of visiting a Continental spa now that he felt so much better, asked if his servant could collect from me a supply of a nerve tonic I had prescribed sufficient to last him for a number of weeks. I gladly arranged for the man to come to me next day for the purpose, thinking that I could in this way get the latest tidings before the Count Palatine – if indeed this were the Count Palatine – left our shores.

My anxieties over the lurking seaman I had noticed by the house gate proved fully justified when the manservant called on me the day afterwards. He reported that he had encountered this very fellow in the garden at dusk the night before, and that he had given him a thorough beating before chasing him from the premises. I decided it would be as well to visit Holmes and report on the favourable turn to the situation. It ought, I believed, to assuage any fears he might have. Instead therefore of returning home to lunch I called in at my club, which lies between my house and Baker Street, to take some refreshment there.

It was while I was hastily consuming a boiled fowl and half a bottle of Montrachet that the place next to me at the table was taken by an old acquaintance, Maltravers Bressingham, the big-game hunter. I enquired whether he had been in Africa.

"Why, no, my dear fellow," he replied. "I have been shooting nearer home. In Illyria, in fact. There is excellent sport to be had in the wild boar forests there, you know."

"Indeed?" I answered. "And were you not disturbed by the state of the country? I understand the situation there is somewhat turbulent."

"Turbulent?" Bressingham said, in tones of considerable surprise. "My dear fellow, I assure you that there are positively no signs of unrest at all. I spent a week in the capital, you know, and society there is as calm and as full of enjoyment as one could wish."

"Is it indeed?" I said. "I believed otherwise, but it must be that I have been misinformed."

Sadly puzzled, I left the club and took a hansom for Baker Street.

I found Holmes in bed. I was more dismayed at this than I can easily say. A fortnight before, when I had first called on him after a period of some weeks, he had been lying on the sitting room sofa certainly and in a condition I did not at all like to see. But his state now seemed a good deal more grave. Was that indomitable spirit at last to succumb totally to the sapping weakness which lay for ever ready to emerge when there was nothing to engage the powers of his unique mind? Was the world to be deprived of his services because it held nothing that seemed to him a worthy challenge?

"Holmes, my dear fellow," I said. "What symptoms affect you? Confide in me, pray, as a medical man."

In response I got at first no more than a deep groan. But I persisted, and at length Holmes answered, with a touch of asperity in his voice which I was not wholly displeased to hear.

"Nothing is wrong, Watson. Nothing. This is the merest passing indisposition. I do not require your professional services."

"Very well, my dear fellow. Then let me tell you of events down in Hertfordshire. I trust they will bring you not a little comfort."

But even as I spoke those words, my heart failed me. Certainly I had what had seemed glad tidings from Hertfordshire. But my news was of the foiling of an apparent attempt on the Count Palatine of Illyria, a ruler whom I had believed, on Holmes's authority, to be needed urgently in a country prey to severe unrest. Yet I had heard not half an hour before from an eye-witness of impeccable antecedents that there was no unrest whatsoever in Illyria, and if that were so was not the whole of Holmes's view of the situation a matter for doubt?

Yet I had broached the subject and must continue.

"I happened on my final visit to our friend, Mr Smith, the day before yesterday to notice lurking near the gates of the house a person dressed as a seaman," I said.

Holmes in answer gave a groan yet louder than any before. It caused me to pause a little before continuing once more, in an altogether less assured manner.

"I considered it my duty, Holmes, to warn Mr Smith's manservant of the presence of that individual, and to hint in general terms that the fellow might be some sort of burglar intent on the premises."

Another deep groan greeted this information. Yet more falteringly I resumed.

"This morning, my dear chap, the manservant called to collect from me a quantity of nerve tonic that I had prepared for his master, and he told me that he had surprised just such a mysterious seaman in the grounds of the house last evening and that he had —"

Here my hesitant account abruptly concluded. Holmes had given vent to yet another appalling groan, and I was able to see, too, that he was holding his body under the bedclothes in an altogether unnaturally stiff position.

A silence fell. In the quiet of the bedroom I could hear distinctly the buzzing of a bluebottle fly beating itself hopelessly against the window panes. At last I spoke again.

"Holmes. My dear old friend. Holmes. Tell me, am I right in my guess? Holmes, are you suffering from the effects of a thorough thrashing?"

Another silence. Once more I became aware of the useless buzzings of the fly upon the pane. Then Holmes answered.

"Yes, Watson, it is as you supposed."

"But, my dear fellow, this is truly appalling. My action in warning that manservant resulted in your suffering injury. Can you forgive me?"

"The injury I can forgive," Holmes answered. "The insult I suffered at the hands of that fellow I can forgive you, Watson, as I can forgive the man his unwitting action. But those who were its cause I cannot forgive. They are dangerous men, my friend, and at all costs they must be prevented from wreaking the harm they intend."

I could not in the light of that answer bring myself to question in the least whether the men to whom Holmes had pointed existed, however keenly I recalled Maltravers Bressingham's assertion that all was quiet in Illyria.

"Holmes," I asked instead, "have you then some plan to act against these people?"

"I would be sadly failing in my duty, Watson, had I not taken the most stringent precautions on behalf of the Count Palatine, and I hope you have never found me lacking in that."

"Indeed I have not."

"Very well then. During the hours of daylight I think we need not fear too much. They are hardly likely to make an attempt that might easily be thwarted by a handful of honest English passers-by. And in any case I have telegraphed the Hertfordshire police and given them a proper warning. But it is tonight, Watson, that I fear."

"The Count's last night in England, Holmes, if indeed . . ."

I bit back the qualifying phrase it had been on the tip of my tongue to add. Common sense dictated that the terrible situation Holmes foresaw was one that could not occur. Yet on many occasions before I had doubted him and he had in the outcome been proved abundantly right. So now I held my peace.

Holmes with difficulty raised himself up in the bed.

"Watson," he said, "tonight as never before I shall require your active assistance. We must both keep watch. There is no other course open to me. But I fear I myself will be but a poor bruised champion should the affair come to blows. Will you assist me then? Will you bring that old Service revolver of yours and fight once more on the side of justice?"

"I will, Holmes, I will."

What else could I have said?

The hour of dusk that autumn evening found us taking up our watch in Hertfordshire in that same thick rhododendron shrubbery where Holmes had hidden in the disguise of an old, wrinkled, brown-faced fellow at the beginning of this singular adventure. But where he had from deep within that leafy place of concealment looked out at the mellow brightness of afternoon, we now needed to step only a foot or two in among the bushes to be quite concealed and we looked out at a scene soon bathed in serene moonlight.

All was quiet. No feet trod the path beyond the beech hedge. In the garden no bird hopped to and fro, no insect buzzed. Up at the house, which beneath the light of the full moon we had under perfect observation, two lighted windows only showed how things lay, one high up from behind the drawn curtains of the bedroom where I had visited my mysterious patient, another low down, coming from the partly sunken windows of the kitchen where doubtless the manservant was preparing the light evening repast I myself had recommended.

Making myself as comfortable as I could and feeling with some pleasure the heavy weight of the revolver in my pocket, I set myself to endure a long vigil. By my side Holmes moved from time to time, less able than on other such occasions in the past to keep perfectly still, sore as were his limbs from the cudgel wielded, with mistaken honesty, by that European manservant now busy at the stove.

Our watch, however, was to be much shorter than I had expected. Scarcely half an hour had passed when, with complete unexpectedness, the quiet of the night was broken by a sharp voice from behind us.

"Stay where you are. One move and I would shoot."

The voice I recognized in an instant from the strength of its foreign accent. It was that of Mr Smith's loyal servant. Taking care not to give him cause to let loose a blast from the gun I was certain he must be aiming at our backs, I spoke up as calmly as I could.

"I am afraid that not for the first time your zeal has betrayed you," I said. "Perhaps you will recognize my voice, as I have recognized yours. I am Dr Watson, your master's medical attendant. I am here with my friend, Mr Sherlock Holmes, of whom perhaps you have heard."

"It is the doctor?"

Behind me, as I remained still as a statue, I heard the crunching of the dried leaves underfoot and a moment later the manservant's face was thrust into mine.

"Yes," he said, "it is you. Good. I was keeping guard because of the many rogues there are about here, and I saw in the bushes a movement. I did not like. But it is you and your friend only. That is good."

"You did well," Holmes said to him. "I am happy to think that the Count has another alert watcher over him besides ourselves."

"The Count?" said the servant. "What Count is this?"

"Why, man, your master. There is no need for pretence between the three of us. Dr Watson and I are well aware that the man up in the house there is no Mr Smith, but none other than the Count Palatine of Illyria."

Holmes's voice had dropped as he pronounced the name, but his secrecy was greeted in an altogether astonishing manner. The formerly gruff manservant broke into rich and noisy laughter.

"Mr Smith, my Mr Smith the Count Palatine of Illyria?" he choked out at last. "Why, though my master has travelled much, and though I began to serve him while he was in Austria, he has never so much as set foot in Illyria. Of that I can assure you, gentlemen, and as to being the Count Palatine . . ."

Again the manservant's laughter overcame him, ringing loudly into the night air.

I do not know what Holmes would have done to silence the fellow, or what attitude he would have taken to this brazen assertion. For at that moment another voice made itself heard, a voice somewhat faint and quavering coming from up beside the house.

"What is this? What is going on there? Josef, is that you?"

It was my patient, certainly recovered from his nervous indisposition enough to venture out to see why there was such a hullabaloo in his grounds.

"Sir, it is the doctor and, sir, a friend of his, a friend with a most curious belief."

At the sound of his servant's reassuring voice my patient began to cross the lawn towards us. As he approached, Sherlock Holmes stepped from the shrubbery and went to meet him, his figure tall and commanding in the silvery moonlight. The two men came together in the full middle of the lawn.

"Good evening," Holmes's voice rang clear. "Whom have I the honour of addressing?"

As he spoke he thrust out a hand in greeting. My patient extended his own in reply. But then, with a movement as rapid as that of a striking snake, Holmes, instead of taking the offered hand and clasping it, seized its third finger, covered as always with its leather finger-stall, and jerked the protective sheath clean away.

There in the bright moonlight I saw for the first time the finger that had hitherto always been concealed from me. It wore no heavy royal signet ring, as indeed was unlikely on a finger of the right hand. It was instead curiously withered, a sight that to anyone other than a medical man might have been considered a little repulsive.

"You are not the Count Palatine of Illyria?" Holmes stammered then, more disconcerted than I had ever seen him in the whole of our long friendship.

"The Count Palatine of Illyria?" Mr Smith replied. "I assure you, my dear sir, I am far from being such a person. Whatever put a notion like that into your head?"

It was not until the last train of the day returning us to London was at the outskirts of the city that Holmes spoke to me.

"How often have I told you, Watson," he said, "that one must take into account all the factors relevant to a particular situation before making an assessment? A good many dozen times, I should say. So it was all the more reprehensible of me deliberately to have imported a factor into the Hertfordshire business that was the product, not of the simple truth, but of my own over-willing imagination. My dear fellow, I must tell you that there were no reports of unrest in Illyria."

"I knew it, Holmes. I had found out quite by chance."

"And you said nothing?"

"I trusted you, as I have trusted you always."

"And as, until now, I hope I have been worthy of your trust. But inaction has always been the curse of me, my dear fellow. It was the lack of stimulus that drove me to deceit now. You were right about your patient from the start. He never was other than a man with a not unusual nervousness of disposition. You were right, Watson, and I was wrong."

I heard the words. But I wished then, as I wish again now with all the fervour at my command, that they had never been uttered, that they had never needed to be uttered.

THE REPULSIVE STORY OF THE RED LEECH

David Langford

"Our client, Watson, would seem somewhat overwrought," remarked Sherlock Holmes without lowering his copy of *The Times*.

We were alone, but I had grown accustomed to the little puzzles which my friend was amused to propound. A glance at the window showed nothing but grey rain over Baker Street. I listened with care, and presently was pleased to say: "Aha! Someone is pacing outside the door. Not heavily, for I cannot discern the footsteps, but quite rapidly – as indicated by the regular sound from that floorboard with its very providential creak."

Holmes cast aside his newspaper and smiled. "Capital! But let us not confuse providence with forethought. That board has been carefully sprung in imitation of the device which in the Orient is known as a nightingale floor. More than once I have found its warning useful."

As I privately abandoned my notion of having the loose plank nailed down and silenced, there was a timid knock at the door.

"Come in," cried Holmes, and in a moment we had our first sight of young Martin Traill. He was robust of build but pale of feature, and advanced with a certain hesitation.

"You wish, I take it, to consult me," said Holmes pleasantly.

"Indeed so, sir, if you are the celebrated Dr Watson."

A flash of displeasure crossed Holmes's face as he effected the necessary introductions; and then, I thought, he smiled to himself at his own vanity.

Traill said to me: "I should, perhaps, address you in private."

"My colleague is privy to all my affairs," I assured him, suppressing a smile of my own.

"Very well. I dared to approach you, Dr Watson, since certain accounts which you have published show that you are not unacquainted with *outré* matters."

"Meretricious and over-sensationalized accounts," murmured Holmes under his breath.

I professed my readiness to listen to any tale, be it never so bizarre, and – not without what I fancied to be a flicker of evasiveness in his eyes – Martin Traill began.

"If I were a storyteller I would call myself hag-ridden . . . harried by spirits. The facts are less dramatic, but, to me, perhaps more disturbing. I should explain that I am the heir to the very substantial estate of my late father, Sir Maximilian Traill, whose will makes me master of the entire fortune upon attaining the age of twenty-five. That birthday is months past: yet here I am, still living like a remittance-man on a monthly allowance, because I cannot sign a simple piece of paper."

"A legal document that confirms you in your inheritance?" I hazarded.

"Exactly so."

"Come, come," said Holmes, reaching for a quire of foolscap and a pencil, "we must see this phenomenon. Pray write your name here, and Watson and I will stand guard against ghosts."

Traill smiled a little sadly. "You scoff. I wish to God that I could scoff too. *This* is not a document that my hand refuses to touch: see!" And, though the fingers trembled a little, he signed his name bold and clear: Martin Maximilian Traill.

"I perceive," said Holmes, "that you have no banking account."

"No indeed; our man of business pays over my allowance in gold. But – good heavens – how can you know this?"

"Yours is a strong schoolboy signature, not yet worn down by repeated use in the world, such as the signing of many cheques. After ten thousand prescriptions, Watson's scrawl is quite indecipherable in all that follows the W. But we digress."

Traill nervously rubbed the back of his right hand as he went on. "The devil of it is that Selina . . . that my elder sister talks to spirits."

I fancied that I took his point a trifle more quickly than the severely rational Holmes. "Séances?" I said. "Mischief in dark rooms with floating tambourines, and the dead supposedly called back to this sphere to talk twaddle? It is a folly which several of my older female patients share."

"Then I need not weary you with details. Suffice it to say that Selina suffers from a mild monomania about the ingratitude of her young brother – that is, myself. Unfortunately she has never married. When I assume formal control of our father's fortune, her stipulated income from the estate will cease. Naturally I shall reinstate and even increase the allowance . . . but she is distrustful. And the spirits encourage her distrust."

"Spirits!" snapped Holmes. "Professor Challenger's recent monograph has quite exploded the claims of spirit mediums. You mean to say that some astral voice has whispered to this foolish woman that her brother plans to leave her destitute?"

"Not precisely, sir. On the occasion when I was present – for sisters must be humoured – the device employed was a ouija board. You may know the procedure. All those present place a finger on the planchette, and its movements spell out messages. Nonsense as a rule, but I remember Selina's air of grim satisfaction as that sentence slowly emerged: BEWARE AN UNGENEROUS BROTHER. And then, the words that came horribly back to mind on my twenty-fifth birthday: FEAR NOT. THE HAND THAT MOVES AGAINST ITS OWN KIN SHALL SUFFER FIRE FROM HEAVEN.

"And my hand did suffer, Dr Watson. When I took up the pen to sign that paper in the solicitor's office, it burnt like fire as though in my very bones!"

I found myself at a loss. "The pen was hot?"

"No, no: it was a quill pen, a mere goose feather. Our family lawyer Mr Jarman is a trifle old-fashioned in such matters. I do not know what to think. I have made the attempt three times since, and my hand will not sign the document. Jarman is so infernally kind and sympathetic to my infirmity, but I can imagine what he thinks. Could some kind of mesmerism be in operation against me? What of the odic force? Some men of science even give credence to the spirit world –"

"Pardon me," said Holmes, "but with my colleague's permission I would like to administer two simple medical tests. First, a trivial exercise in mental acuity. This lodging is 221b Baker Street, and it is the seventeenth of the month. How rapidly, Mr Traill, can you divide 221 by seventeen?"

As I marvelled and Traill took up the pencil to calculate, Holmes darted to his cupboard of chemical apparatus, returning with a heavy stone pestle and mortar. In the latter he had placed a small mirror about three inches square. Looking at Traill's paper, he said: "Excellent. Quite correct. Now, a test of muscular reactions – kindly shatter this glass *now*."

Traill performed the feat handily enough, with one sharp tap of the pestle, and stared in puzzlement. It resembled no medical procedure that I knew.

Holmes resumed his seat, rubbing his hands in satisfaction. "As I thought. You are not in the slightest superstitious, Mr Traill; I guessed as much from the tone in which you spoke of spirits. A mathematical result of thirteen does not make you flinch, nor did you hesitate before breaking a mirror. You are masking your real concern. Why do you consult a doctor? Because you fear madness."

With a sob, Traill buried his face in his hands. I stepped to the gasogene and spirit-case, and mixed him a stiff brandy-and-soda with Holmes's nodded approval. In another minute our client had composed himself, and said wryly: "I see that I have fallen among mind-readers."

"My methods, alas, are more prosaic," said Holmes. "Inference is a surer tool than wizardry. I now infer that there is some special circumstance you have yet to reveal to us, for I recall no history of insanity in the family of Sir Maximilian Traill."

"You are troubled and overwrought," I put in, "but speaking as a doctor I see no sign of madness."

"Thank you, Dr Watson. I will begin again, and tell you of the red leech.

"My lodgings are in Highgate and – since the allowance from my father's estate frees me from the need to seek employment – I have fallen into the habit of walking on Hampstead Heath each morning, in search of inspiration for the verses by which I hope one day to be known. (*The Yellow Book* was good enough to publish one of my triolets.) Some friends used to chaff me for being a fixed landmark at luncheon-time, when I generally enjoyed a meal of sandwiches and a bottle of Bass in the vicinity of the Highgate Ponds." Traill shuddered. "Never again! I remember the day quite vividly: it was a warm Tuesday, perhaps six months ago . . ."

"Prior to your twenty-fifth birthday?" asked Holmes sharply.

"Why, yes. I sat on the grass in a reverie, idly watching someone's great black retriever splash in and out of the water. I was thinking of foolish things . . . my sister's maggot of distrust, and the structure of the sestina, and *The Pickwick Papers* – you will remember Mr Pickwick's investigations of tittlebats and the origin of the Hampstead Ponds which lie across the heath. My thoughts were very far away from the heath. Perhaps I even dozed. Then I felt a hideous pain!"

"On the back of your right hand?" said Holmes.

"Ah, you have seen me rub it when troubled."

"Already my methods are transparent to you," Holmes remarked with pretended chagrin.

I leaned across to look. "There is a mark resembling a scald, or possibly an acid-burn."

"It was the red leech, doctor. You will surely have heard of it. A repulsive, revolting creature. The thing must have crept on me from the long grass; it clung to my hand, its fangs – or whatever such vermin possess – fixed in me."

"I know of no such leech," I protested.

"Perhaps it is a matter which does not concern a general

practitioner," said Traill with a hint of reproach. He plucked a folded piece of paper from his wallet, and handed it to me; it was a newspaper clipping. I read aloud: "Today a warning was issued to London dwellers. Specimens of *Sanguisuga rufa*, the highly poisonous red leech of Formosa, have been observed in certain parkland areas of North London. The creature is believed to have escaped from the private collection of a naturalist and explorer. A representative of the Royal Zoological Society warned that the red leech should be strictly avoided if seen, for its bite injects toxins with long-lasting effects, which may include delusions, delirium or even insanity. The leech is characteristically some three to four inches in length, and is readily distinguished by its crimson hue."

"Most instructive," said Holmes dreamily.

Traill continued: "The horror was unspeakable. The leech clung to my hand, biting with a burning pain, rendering me too horrified to move. I was lucky that a doctor was passing by, who recognized the awful thing! He plucked it from my flesh with a gloved hand and threw it aside into the undergrowth. And then, straight away, on the grass of Hampstead Heath, this Dr James unpacked his surgical instruments from his black bag and cut the mouth-parts of the horrid beast out of my hand, while I averted my gaze and struggled not to cry out. 'A narrow escape young fellow,' he said to me. 'If my eye had not been caught by the press report' – and here he handed me the scrap of paper which you hold – 'it might have gone badly for you. There is something in Providence after all.' I thanked Dr James profusely, and at my insistence he charged me a guinea. Although he had dressed the tiny wound carefully, it was painful and slow to heal.

"And now you know why I fear madness. My mind seems unclouded, but my senses betray me – the leech-bitten hand burns like fire when I try to move against my sister's wishes, as though her infernal spirits were real after all."

"Quite so," said Holmes, regarding him with intense satisfaction through half-closed eyes. "Your case, Mr Traill, presents some extraordinarily interesting and gratifying features. Would you recognize Dr James if you met him again?"

"Certainly: his great black beard and tinted glasses were most distinctive."

This seemed to cause Holmes some private merriment. "Excellent! Yet you now consult the estimable but unfamiliar Watson, rather than the provenly knowledgeable James."

"I confess that in my over-excitement I must have misheard the address Dr James gave to me. There is no such house-number at the street in Hampstead where I sought him."

"Better still. The time has come to summon a cab, Watson! We can easily reach the Highgate Ponds before twilight."

"But to what purpose?" I cried. "After six months the creature will be long gone, or dead and rotted."

"Well, we may still amuse ourselves by catching tittlebats – as Mr Pickwick chose to call sticklebacks. The correct naming of creatures is so important, is it not?"

All through the long four-wheeler cab ride I struggled to make sense of this, while Holmes would talk of nothing but music.

In the bleak grey of late afternoon, Hampstead Heath was at its most desolate. A thin, cold rain continued to fall. The three of us trudged through wet grass on our fool's errand.

"I must ask you for a supreme effort of memory, Mr Traill," declared Holmes as the ponds came into view. "You must cast your mind back to that Tuesday in the spring. Remember the pattern of trees you saw as you sat on the ground; remember the dog that pranced in the water. We must know the exact place, to within a few feet."

Traill roamed around dubiously. "It all looks different at this time of year," he muttered. "Perhaps near here."

"Squat on your heels to obtain the same perspective as when you sat," suggested Holmes. After a few such reluctant experiments, our client indicated that he was as close as memory would take him.

"Then that patch of hawthorn must be our goal – the leech's last known domicile," Holmes observed. "Note, Watson, that this picnic-spot is several yards from the beaten path. The good Dr James must have been quite long-sighted, to see and recognize that leech."

"He might easily have been taking a short cut across the grass," I replied.

"Again the voice of reason pours cold water on my fanciful deductions!" said Holmes cheerfully. As he spoke, he methodically prodded the hawthorn bushes with his walking-stick, and turned over the sodden mass of fallen leaves beneath. He seemed oblivious to the chill drizzle, now made worse by a steadily rising wind from the east. A quarter of an hour went miserably past.

Then – "A long shot, Watson, a very long shot!" cried my friend, and pounced. From a pocket of his cape he had produced a pair of steel forceps, and from another a large pill-box. Now something red glistened in the forceps' grip, and in a trice the thing was safely boxed. Traill, who had given an involuntary cry, backed away a step or two with an expression of revulsion.

"*Another* of the vile creatures?"

"I fancy it is the same," Holmes murmured. And not a word more would he utter until we were installed in a convenient public house which supplied us with smoking-hot whisky toddies. "It is villainy, Mr Traill," he said then. "One final test remains. I experimented not long ago with a certain apparatus, without fully comprehending its possibilities in scientific detection . . ."

It was late night in Baker Street, and the gas-mantles burnt fitfully. A smell of ozone tinged the air, mingled with a more familiar chemical reek. Holmes, as he linked up an extensive battery of wet cells, expounded with fanciful enthusiasm on the alternating-current electrical transmission proposals of one Mr Nikola Tesla in the Americas, and of how in the early years of the new century he fully expected electric lighting to be plumbed into our lodgings, like the present gas-pipes. I smiled at his eagerness.

At length the preparations were complete. "You must refrain from touching any part of the equipment," Holmes now warned. "The electrical potential which drives this cathode-ray tube is dangerously high. Do you recognize the device, Watson? The evacuated glass, the tungsten target electrode within? It has already been employed in the United States, in connection with your own line of work."

The tangle of glassware, the trailing wires and the eerie glow from the tube made up an effect wholly unfamiliar to me, reminiscent perhaps of some new scientific romance by Mr H.G. Wells. It was only very gingerly that young Traill placed his right hand where Holmes directed.

"I have seen something a little like this before," he mused. "Old Wilfrid Jarman's brother dabbles in electrical experiments. He vexed Selina once with a tedious demonstration of a model dynamo."

"Healing rays?" I asked. "Earlier in the day we spoke of Mesmerism, which according to my recollection was a charlatan's ploy to heal by what he called animal magnetism. Has electrical science made this real at last?"

"Not precisely, Watson. The apparatus of Herr Doktor Röntgen does not heal, but lights the way for the healer. In years to come, I fancy it will be remembered as the greatest scientific discovery of the present decade."

"But I see nothing happening."

"That is what you may expect when there is nothing to see. – No, Mr Traill, I must entreat you to remain quite still. The rays of Röntgen, which he has named for algebra's unknown quantity X, do not impinge on the human eye. That faint glow which you may discern is not the true glow, but secondary fluorescence in the glass."

I pondered this, while Holmes kept a wary eye on his pocket-watch. "Very well," he said at last. "You may lift your hand now, but have a care . . ." And he took up the mysterious sealed envelope on which Traill's hand had rested. "What the eye cannot see, a photographic plate can still record. I must retreat to the darkroom and – lift the veil of the spirits. Kindly entertain our guest, Watson."

Traill and I stared at each other, lost in a mental darkness deeper than that of any photographic darkroom. Infuriatingly, I knew that to Holmes this night-shrouded terrain of crime was brilliantly lit by the invisible rays of his deductive power.

Nor was I much the wiser when morning came. Holmes, dancing-eyed and evasive, had bundled Traill into a homeward-bound hansom and directed him to return to Baker Street after breakfast, when the case would be resolved. Then he had settled into his favourite chair with his pipe and a pound of the vilest shag tobacco: I found him in the identical position when I arose from sleep.

Over breakfast, he unbent a trifle. "Well, Watson, what do you make of our case?"

"Very little . . . I had thought," I ventured, "that you would dissect or analyse the leech itself and perhaps identify its toxins."

"The naked eye sufficed." He pulled the red thing from his dressing-gown pocket and tossed it casually on to my plate of kippers, causing me to recoil in horror. "As you may readily discern for yourself, it has been artfully made from rubber."

"Good heavens!" I studied the ugly worm more closely, and was struck by a thought. "Holmes, you suspected this artificial leech from the outset, or the excursion to Hampstead Heath would have been futile. What gave you the clue? And has Traill deceived us – are we the butts of some youthful jest?"

Holmes smiled languidly. "In a moment you will be telling me how obvious and elementary was the reasoning that led me to distrust that repulsive object. Look again at the newspaper cutting."

I took it from his hand and examined it once more, to no avail.

"Setting aside the fact that the type fount does not correspond to that of any British newspaper known to me (the work of a jobbing printer, no doubt) . . . setting aside the extreme unlikelihood that such a striking report should have escaped my eye and failed to be pasted into our own celebrated index volume . . . may I direct your attention to this red leech's scientific name?"

"*Sanguisuga rufa*," I repeated. "Which I should say means something like 'red bloodsucker'."

"You are no taxonomer, Watson, but you are a doctor – or, as some country folk still call the profession, a leech. Can you bring to mind the Latin name for the leech once used in medicine?"

"*Hirudo medicinalis*, of course. Oh! That is strange . . ."

"In fact, *Sanguisuga* is not a scientific class name. It is poetic. It was used of leeches by Pliny. Our villain, who may or may not be 'Dr James', knows his Latin but not – if I may so phrase it – his leechcraft."

I said: "How obvious and elem . . . that is, ingeniously reasoned!"

Holmes inclined his head ironically. "Here is our client at the door. Good morning, Mr Traill! Dr Watson has just been explaining with great erudition that your red leech is a fake – a rubber toy. And now the chase leads us to Theobald's Road, to the law office of Jarman, Fittlewell and Coggs, where today you will at last claim your inheritance. Watson, that excellent revolver of yours might well be of use."

"My reconstruction," said Holmes as our cab rattled through a dismal London fog, "is a trifle grisly. There you were, Mr Traill, arguably somewhat drowsy from the compounded effects of warm weather, literary reveries and a bottle of Bass. Your habit of picnicking near the Highgate Ponds is well known to your friends – even, I dare say, your sister?"

"That is so. In fact, Selina has publicly twitted me more than once for what she calls my shiftless habits."

"Thus the miscreant 'Dr James', whose appearance is a transparent disguise but whose true surname I fancy I know, had little difficulty in locating you. It was easy for him to approach you stealthily from behind and drop or place this little monstrosity upon the back of your hand as you sprawled on the grass." He displayed the leech once more.

"The thing still revolts me," Traill muttered.

"Its underside seems to have been coated with dark treacle: that would provide a convincingly unpleasant-looking and adhesive slime. But in addition, the 'mouth' section was dipped in some corrosive like oil of vitriol – see how it is eaten away? That was what you felt."

Again Traill convulsively massaged the back of his hand. "But, Mr Holmes, what was the purpose of this horrid trick? It strikes me that your investigations have made matters worse! Before, I could blame my hand's infirmity on the leech poison. Now you have eliminated that possibility and left me with nothing but madness."

"Not at all. You will be pleased to hear that the apparatus

of Röntgen pronounces you sane. We have eliminated the impossible story of the leech. There remains another, highly improbable explanation, which we will shortly confirm as true. By the way, may I assume that either Wilfrid Jarman or his brother was present on the occasion when that planchette spelt out such a disquieting message?"

"Yes, Basil was there. The brother."

"The brother who dabbles in electrical devices. I wonder if he applied his ingenuity to enlivening those séances. In any case, according to my researches, it is far from difficult for a determined hand to influence the oracle of the ouija board. But here we are! Watson, I am sure you have change for the cabman."

Jarman, Fittlewell and Coggs, solicitors and commissioners of oaths, occupied a fourth-floor set of offices. Without a great deal of ado we were shown into the large, dim room where Wilfrid Jarman awaited. He was a plump and kindly looking man in late middle age, whose baldness and pince-nez spectacles were slightly reminiscent of Mr Pickwick. A frowsty legal atmosphere exuded from numerous shelves of books bound in dull brown calf. Holmes's nostrils widened like a hound's as he keenly sniffed the air. I unobtrusively followed suit, and thought to detect a trace of not unfamiliar chemical whiff.

Jarman was greeting our client, saying, "I am most pleased, Martin, that you feel equal at last to your little ordeal. So many people take fright at a simple affidavit or conveyance! But you must introduce your friends."

The formalities over, Jarman indicated the bulky document that lay on his desk. "A tiresome necessity," he said with a shrug. "Believe me, my dear boy, I would readily dispense with it – but we lawyers must live by the law, or where would we be?"

The question being unanswerable, Traill muttered something suitably meaningless.

"*Look!*" cried Holmes suddenly. "That face at the window! We are being spied upon!"

Our heads jerked around to the large office window, which showed only the dim and fog-shrouded skyline across Theobald's Road. The solicitor even took a ponderous step or two towards the window, before turning back and stating acidly: "Mr Holmes, we are on the fourth floor. And expert cat-burglars do not commonly risk their necks for legal paperwork."

Holmes made some feeble apology and mentioned trouble with his nerves. I recognized the signs of a ruse, and on reflection thought that – out of the corner of my eye – I had seen his hand dart to the broad desktop. But all seemed unchanged.

"Let us deal with the business at hand," said Jarman, placing a finger on the thick paper where the signature was to go.

Traill took up the quill pen and dipped it in ink. He hesitated. His trembling hand moved forward, back, and then resolutely forward again. The air seemed suddenly charged with menace. From behind the desk Jarman smiled indulgently, and seemed to shift his weight a little to one side. For an instant I thought I felt, rather than heard, a faint sourceless whining.

Simultaneously, Traill snatched his hand back with a cry, and there was an explosion of blinding, dazzling light from the desk. Jarman's thick voice uttered an oath. I clapped my hand to my revolver, but the room was blotted out by coruscating after-images. White smoke swirled. Slowly some shreds of vision returned.

"'Tis sport," Sherlock Holmes quoted, "to have the engineer hoist with his own petard."

"I felt my hand burning again," said Traill. "But that great flash was not my nerves, nor spirits either."

The fat solicitor's hand seemed burnt as well, from the flare; he cursed in a low, filthy undertone.

Holmes said briskly, "Forgive my theatricality. It seemed a useful notion to slip a flat packet of magnesium flash powder, appropriately fused, underneath that interesting document. Mr Jarman's office may appear old-fashioned, but it conceals some thoroughly modern equipment – specifically, a high-frequency Tesla coil within the desk, which is activated when Mr Jarman chooses to step on a particular floorboard. Within a limited area, its rapidly fluctuating electromagnetic field has the effect of heating metals to a painful temperature. This heat detonated my little flash charge."

"Metal?" said Traill, now still more puzzled. "I wear no rings."

"True enough. But your right hand contains a steel needle, inserted there by the false Dr James under the pretext of removing the poisoned mouth-parts of the red leech."

I was thunderstruck as I realized the fiendish ingenuity of the plot. Even the quill pen was part of the design, for a steel nib would instantly have given the game away. And of course that faint smell in the air was the sulphuric-acid reek of hidden wet-cell batteries. Meanwhile, Jarman uttered a forced laugh. He appeared to be sweating profusely. "What a farrago of nonsense! Such a thing would be impossible to prove."

"On the contrary, I have photographed it by means of X-radiation." Holmes drew something from one of his capacious pockets. "This shadowgraph shows the bone structure of Mr Traill's right hand. Bone, being less pervious to the rays than flesh, appears as nearly white. Here is the solid white of the needle, lying between the metacarpal bones."

Traill shuddered again.

"No doubt we will find that Mr Jarman cannot account for his time on that Tuesday six months ago when you had your famous adventure on Hampstead Heath . . . ah, Mr Jarman, you are smiling. Therefore you have an alibi, and the deed was done by your good brother Basil, who likes to experiment with electricity. What, no smile now?"

I had belatedly trained my revolver on Jarman.

"What was the purpose of this terrible charade?" asked Traill.

"It is possible," said Holmes gently, "that you are no longer heir to a great estate. If the assets or a large part of them have somehow slipped through the fingers of Jarman, Fittlewell and Coggs, then it naturally became necessary to delay – by fair means or foul – your legal acquisition of Sir Maximilian's fortune. We shall find out when, as Mr Jarman very nearly put it, those who lived by the law shall perish by the law."

"Mr Sherlock Holmes, you are an officious meddler," stated Jarman, gazing intently at my friend. "And you over-reach. Your remarks are slanderous, sir. A true accounting of the estate's affairs lies here upon my desk, and will show no defalcation: perhaps you would care to glance through the record?" The lawyer tapped his scorched index finger upon the book in question, a heavy ledger with a tarnished brass clasp that lay askew upon a mound of papers near the desk's far edge. "Within, all your questions are answered."

For half a minute, Holmes's right hand had lain concealed within the folds of his bulky Inverness cape. Now he reached forward to the ledger, but did not flick open the clasp as I had anticipated. Instead he swiftly lifted the entire tome clear of the papers, and two oddities were made manifest. First, from the underside of the book's brass clasp there trailed a long, springy, shining copper wire which vanished into the artfully disarrayed papers. Second, Holmes's hand was seen to be sheathed in a heavy, rubber glove.

"How many volts, Mr Jarman?" he enquired pleasantly. "Hundreds? Thousands? I presume this jest was ultimately intended for Mr Traill, whose death would have bought you yet more time. My admiration for your ingenuity increases."

WIlfrid Jarman's composure was broken at last, and with an inarticulate cry of rage he stepped to one side, reaching into a drawer. Even as I realized that his hand now held an old-fashioned pistol, he had dextrously placed himself so that Holmes lay in my line of fire. I flung myself uselessly forward, to see Jarman aiming at point-blank range while Holmes flung the ledger in what seemed a futile shielding gesture. Blue-white sparks flew. The pistol's flash and bang echoed with dread authority in the musty room. Then a heavy body fell to the floor. There was a long silence.

"I suspect that our friend did not finish pulling the trigger," said Holmes, whose austere face was now very pale. "His infernal electricity exploded the shell in the breech, even as it struck him dead. Gun-barrels, as well as copper wires and brass clasps, are excellent conductors of electrical current. – Watson, I must trouble you to bind up my shoulder. The bullet did not go entirely astray." He bent over to scrutinize the corpse more closely. "As he truly said, that ledger contained the answer to all questions. The *rictus* of his features is characteristic of electrically-induced spasms and convulsions. Best not to look, Mr Traill. Some things are even less pleasant to gaze upon than the red leech."

Some time afterward, at the trial which concluded with the sentencing of the co-conspirator Basil Jarman to a long term of hard labour, we learned that almost half of the Traill estate still remained. Thus our client continued his life of idle literary dabbling, while his blameless sister Selina presumably receives a sufficient allowance to fritter away on psychic mediums.

Besides his own substantial fee, Holmes somehow contrived to retain a small souvenir of the case. To this day, our untidy mantelpiece in 221b Baker Street boasts a matchbox best not opened by the unwary, for its coiled rubber occupant is repulsive to the eye. The box is labelled in Holmes's own neat hand: *Sanguisuga rufa spuriosa.* I have my doubts about the Latin.

THE ADVENTURE OF THE GRACE CHALICE

Roger Johnson

"Watson," said Mr Sherlock Holmes from the bow-window, where he had stood for the past half-hour, gazing moodily down into the street, "if I mistake not, we have a client."

I was more than pleased to hear the excitement in his voice. Holmes had been restlessly unemployed for nearly a week, and neither his temper nor mine had been helped by the dull, leaden skies of March with their intermittent showers, which caused my old wound to ache abominably.

"A prosperous man," he continued. "Purposeful and not without self-esteem. Ah, he has paid off the cab and is approaching our door. Let us hope that he brings something of interest." He turned away from the window, and at that moment we heard a determined ring upon the front-door bell. Within a minute our good landlady had shown into the room a plump man with heavy jowls and thick grey hair.

"Gentlemen," said our visitor, as the door closed softly behind Mrs Hudson, "my name is Henry Staunton, and I am the victim of a most audacious theft!"

"Indeed?" replied Holmes, calmly. "Pray take the basket-chair, Mr Staunton. Your name is, of course, familiar to me as that of a connoisseur of *objets d'art*. Has some item from your collection been stolen?"

"It has, sir. It has! I shall come straight to the point, for I dislike circumlocution, as, I am sure, do you. Besides, I wish to have the matter settled without even the least delay. You must know, then, that I recently acquired from old Sir Cedric Grace the celebrated golden cup known as the Grace Chalice. I may say that it cost me a very considerable sum – a pretty penny, sir! But I do not grudge it, for the chalice is unique, quite unique.

"Now, before depositing it with my bankers, I determined to retain the chalice at my house for a short while, so that I might study it thoroughly. I live at The Elms at Hampstead, a very desirable residence, near the Heath and somewhat away from the main thoroughfare. Ahem! I kept the chalice in a safe in my study, securely built into the wall, and hidden behind a looking-glass. You may imagine my distress – my utter distress, sir – when, this very morning I discovered the safe unlocked and the chalice gone!

"I am a man who values his privacy, Mr Holmes, and I have no desire to admit the official police to my property. Instead, I am resolved to rely upon your skill and discretion in the matter." He made a little flourish with his hand, and I remembered my friend's assessment of him as a man not lacking in self-importance.

Holmes himself sat quietly, his eyes closed and his long legs stretched out before him. "That is very good of you, Mr Staunton," he replied blandly. "You will appreciate, however, that I must have all the details, however trivial they may seem."

"Of course, sir, of course. Well, my maid, Robinson, called me at seven o'clock this morning, rather earlier than usual, and she was in a most agitated state. Rather than trust to her somewhat incoherent account, I went myself directly to my study, where I found that the safe door stood open and that the study window was broken. Here, plainly, the miscreant had gained entrance, inserting his hand through the broken pane and unlocking the casement. I observed also a double line of footsteps running across the bare, damp earth from the high garden wall, and returning thither."

This case presents some curious features," remarked Sherlock Holmes, glancing intently at our client. "Are we to understand that your study overlooks bare ground?"

Staunton permitted himself a pained chuckle. "No doubt it seems odd to you, sir," said he, "but the matter is simply explained: the ground has been prepared for the laying of a new lawn, and the turves have not yet been laid. A fortunate thing, as I am sure you will agree, sir! Most fortunate, for now we have the clearest clues to the thief's means of entrance and egress. Naturally, I have left strict instructions that the footsteps are to be left untouched."

"Naturally," agreed Sherlock Holmes. "Very well, Mr Staunton. I think that we had better come at once and investigate the scene of the crime. Watson, will you call a cab?"

On the short journey to Hampstead, we learned that our client was a bachelor, living quietly with the immediate household of a maid, a cook and a single manservant. He kept no dog, for he disliked the creatures, and his only recreation was to play cards twice a week – for money, he admitted with candour – with a cousin, a retired gunsmith named George Cresswell, who lived at Mill Hill. Under Holmes's determined questioning, he further confessed that although none of his servants knew of his remarkable purchase he had mentioned it to his cousin. "But you may dismiss any suspicion of George," said he, "for he remarked only that I ought to deposit the cup in a bank-vault as soon as possible. Besides, sir, my cousin would have no cause to steal from me. I should tell you that as a result of our card-playing I am in his debt for a tidy sum."

At The Elms, which struck me as a large house to be run by a staff of only three, we were first shown the windows of the upper rooms where the servants slept and then led to the far side of the building, where the crime had been committed. It was plain that if the burglar were sufficiently quiet the servants need have heard nothing. Staunton himself admitted to being a very heavy sleeper.

Holmes made a minute examination of the very clear footsteps that ran, just as we had been told, directly from the high garden wall to the study window and back. The damp earth had preserved the impressions wonderfully, and since no one had had occasion to trespass upon this smooth, bare patch there were no other prints to be seen.

"Our burglar could hardly have left plainer traces if he had intended to," remarked Holmes to me. "There are two very singular features here, however. For instance, it would appear that our man let himself down from the wall with commendable delicacy, for there is no indication that he jumped, and we look in vain for the marks of a ladder. Hum – size ten boots, new or recently soled. A long stride. Just so! Mr Staunton, describe your cousin, if you please."

Our client looked up hastily from a self-conscious glance at his own small feet. "Really, sir!" said he. "I fail to . . . Oh, very well! George Cresswell is a large and strong man, quite as tall as yourself, Mr Holmes. He is fifty-four years of age, with thick hair, still dark brown, a heavy brown moustache and – er – somewhat faded blue eyes. And – oh, dear! Yes, I do believe that he takes a size ten in boots."

"Quite so," replied my friend. "Now, let us turn our attention to the study. Ha! This window has been broken in a most professional manner, with the noise muffled by a sheet of strong paper smeared with treacle. Well, well. And what shall we find in the room itself?"

The furniture of the study, itself of much interest, held an eclectic accumulation of antiques, witness to Henry Staunton's abiding pursuit. On the thick carpet were muddy patches leading from the window to the opposite wall, where the door of the safe stood open, just as our client had described it. There was little to be learned from the safe, even by such an expert as Sherlock Holmes. We could descry faint smears that might have been made by gloved fingers, and the lock was quite undamaged, indicating that it had been opened with a key. To my friend's questions, Mr Staunton admitted reluctantly that George Cresswell might have had the opportunity within the past few weeks to take an impression of the safe key. Plainly the thought distressed him, for he seemed truly fond of his cousin, but it was clear to me that the evidence grew ever stronger against the retired gunsmith.

Shortly afterwards, Holmes and I left The Elms, with assurances of that we should certainly pursue the case. My friend was manifestly unsatisfied with his investigation so far, and I in my turn recalled an earlier remark of his that had puzzled me. "You suggested," said I, "that there was yet another odd feature about the footsteps in the garden. What was it?"

He looked at me in his singular, introspective fashion. "You did not notice it? Why, it was simply that at no point did the steps returning from the house overlap those made in going to the house."

While I pondered up this, he continued, "My next move must be to call upon Mr George Cresswell – I have his address – and I think that I shall go alone. Time may be of importance now."

I returned to Baker Street to find our old friend Mr Lestrade of Scotland Yard waiting in our sitting room, positively bursting with news. "It's the Freeling case, Doctor," he explained. "You'll remember that the man escaped from Chelmsford Prison a couple of weeks ago? Well, we think that we've found him. I put it like that because the man we have is very dead and savagely mutilated."

I recalled the case well. Esme Freeling was a smooth, elegant and dangerous man who preyed upon the weak. He was a proven card-sharp, a known blackmailer and a suspected murderer. Holmes had been responsible in part for his arrest and incarceration, and would certainly wish to know of this strange and brutal conclusion to a wicked career.

"It's not a nice thing, Dr Watson," said Lestrade. "The man's face has been quite burned off with acid. Horrible, it is. He was killed by a savage blow to the head, and then . . . Well, there's not enough of his face left to identify him, but all the rest fits. He's a big man, muscles well developed from rowing, thick brown hair. We found him, of all places, in Highgate Cemetery, behind one of the tombs. But here's an odd thing, now – every single label had been removed from his clothes! Well, perhaps he was going about incognito, but it seems he couldn't escape his fate."

Declaring that he would wait until Holmes returned, Lestrade accepted a cigar from me, and we sat in companionable silence until Holmes entered the room, grim-faced, with the news that

George Cresswell had not been seen for nearly two days. "Our client wished to keep this matter confidential," he remarked, "but it seems that we shall have to call in the police after all."

Upon hearing Lestrade's information, he shrugged his thin shoulders and said, "Then let us go and see the last of the Freeling case."

I had seen many unpleasant sights during my time as an Army Surgeon, but nothing quite as grisly as that which lay on a white marble slab in the mortuary at Highgate. Yet to Sherlock Holmes this hideous and pitiful object was not the mutilated shell of a fellow man but merely an object of professional study. Gently he raised the dead head and carefully scrutinized the great bruises at the base of the skull. Then, after a brief glance at the raw wound that had once been a human face, he turned his attention to the muscular arms. He ran his sensitive fingers over them and, taking the hands in his own, he closed the fists.

"Feel those forearm muscles, Watson," he commanded. "Their condition should be of interest to a medical man."

The muscle of the right forearm indicated considerable strength, consistent with what we knew of Esme Freeling, but that of the left astounded me. It stood out like an egg, and was by far the most highly developed I had ever seen.

"Good heavens!" I exclaimed. "This man must have been left-handed and immensely strong."

"Freeling was strong, sir," said Lestrade, in response to my friend's questioning glance, "but there's nothing in the files about his being left-handed. Besides, his only sport was rowing, and that would tend to develop both arms equally. Are we to take it, Mr Holmes, that this is *not* Esme Freeling?"

"Just so," replied Holmes. "I know of only one activity that can cause such muscular development in a man. The muscle swells like that through years of taking the recoil of a rifle. You know little of this as yet, Lestrade, but Watson is informed. Look at the man, Doctor! Look at his tall stature, his thick brown hair, his large feet. Imagine the moustache and the pale blue eyes, and now tell me who he is."

"Why," said I, "surely this can only be the retired gunsmith, George Cresswell!"

"Precisely. We have encountered a singularly brutal and fortunately unsuccessful attempt on the part of a very wicked man to disguise the identity of his victim. Lestrade, I must ask you to restrain your natural impatience until later this evening, for I have to make a few further enquiries. Then, I think I can promise that you shall have your murderer."

My own impatience must have been quite as great as the police detective's, and how either of us contrived to bear the waiting I cannot say. Holmes had left us directly, and did not return to our lodgings until the evening was far advanced, but the expression upon his face was one of satisfaction. The three of us proceeded immediately to Hampstead, where we were joined by two uniformed constables from the local Police Station.

Henry Staunton was not pleased to see our companions, but his demeanour changed upon hearing Holmes's bleak announcement of the disappearance of Mr George Cresswell. This fact, said my friend, meant that the theft of the Grace Chalice must inevitably become a matter for the police.

"Dear me," observed our client, sententiously. "Such a wicked crime – wicked, sir! Who would have thought it?"

"Who indeed?" replied Sherlock Holmes. "Murder is a very wicked crime, Mr Staunton. And when you add to that the attempt to defraud the insurance company . . ."

Staunton's face had turned very pale, and his fleshy features seemed to sag. "Really, sir, I – I fail to understand you!" he blustered.

"Oh, it won't do, you know. Really it won't. Mr Lestrade here has a warrant, and we intend to search this house until we find the Grace Chalice – Hold him, gentlemen!"

Staunton, his face twisted with inexpressible malice, had sprung for the door, but in a flash the two constables were upon him. He put up a considerable struggle, but at last I heard the satisfying click of handcuffs.

"I told you," said Holmes later, when the precious cup had been retrieved from its hiding-place beneath a flagstone in the cellar of The Elms, "that I had some more enquiries to make this afternoon. Well, I discovered, as I had suspected, that our client had gambled heavily upon the Stock Exchange in recent years and, not to mince words, he was now over head and ears in debt. This, of course, was in addition to the large sum that he owed to his easy-going cousin. His plan, clearly, was to stage this false robbery, collect the insurance money, and then to sell the chalice. His cousin was murdered to provide a scapegoat for the crime, and to ensure that the gambling debt need not be paid. The escape from prison of Esme Freeling was merely a fortunate coincidence. There was more to the murder, however, for Henry Staunton hated his cousin as only a mean man can hate a generous and contented one.

"As you may have surmised, Watson, it was the supposed burglar's footsteps that first suggested to me that all was not right. They appeared to lead from the garden wall, but there was no evidence that anyone had ever come over that wall. More important was the singular fact that the outgoing steps did not overtread those incoming. The two lines of prints were close but quite separate. Now, what burglar would ever tread so artistically? There could be but one explanation: the footsteps did not, in fact, lead from the wall to the study and back, but from the study to the wall and back. In all probability, then, our client himself was responsible for this mummery, and had he not stepped too carefully the fact of an inside job would have been plain to the meanest intelligence. For the rest, he wore boots – new ones, you will recall – fully three sizes too large for him, and strode out manfully to give the impression of a taller man. We may eventually find the boots, but I fear that they have been destroyed."

On this point, however, Holmes was wrong. It is a matter of record that the boots were discovered, carelessly discarded, in the attic of The Elms, and proved to fit exactly those damning footsteps in the garden. This was the final link in the chain of evidence that took Henry Staunton to an unmourned death on a cold morning at Pentonville Prison.

THE CASE OF
THE FAITHFUL RETAINER

Amy Myers

Watson secured publication of several cases that happened in 1897, including "The Abbey Grange", "The Red Circle", "The Devil's Foot" – the case that nearly saw the end of Sherlock Holmes – "The Dancing Men" and "The Missing Three-Quarter". There were certainly other cases during the year, but the only one that we have been able to date conclusively is "The Case of the Faithful Retainer". We have been fortunate that this case survived amongst the papers of the family of M. Auguste Didier, the master-chef whose investigations Amy Myers has been reconstructing. I am indebted to her for allowing me access to these papers.

"You are correct, my dear Watson. The hour may indeed have come when it is in the interests of our great nation that your readers should be permitted to know the full truth behind my indisposition of 'ninety-seven'."

As so often in the past, my old friend had correctly broken into my thoughts. "How could you know –" I began. But why should I be amazed that his powers of observation and deduction remained undimmed, infrequently though circumstances had permitted me to visit Mr Sherlock Holmes, during his years of retirement on the Sussex downs? We were taking our ease in his pleasant farm garden, on a summer day in 1911, and I had been studying the grave news reported in my newspaper.

Holmes shrugged. "You are absorbed in *The Times* report of this Agadir crisis. I noted your frown, and the fact that you read the report several times; hence my conclusion that you consider that the sending of the gunboat to Morocco demonstrates that a certain great European nation is once more flexing its muscles, and casting its shadow over the peace not only of Europe but of the British Empire itself, was simplicity itself. It was then but a small step to deduce from your unconscious glance towards me that in your opinion the unfortunate case of the faithful retainer should now be made known to the world. I agree, but masked, I must insist, in suitable anonymity."

"Of course, Holmes," I replied stiffly, somewhat offended that my old friend could imply I had so little delicacy as to reveal the identities of those involved in the services to the nation that had led to Holmes being offered a knighthood in June 1902, the coronation month (had not illness postponed the celebration) of our late and gracious monarch, Edward the Peacemaker. For reasons that must perforce remain undisclosed, these services had been rendered some years earlier, in the spring and early summer of '97, at a time when the world supposed Holmes to have been ill, a fiction at which I have hitherto been obliged, from the highest of motives, to connive. His iron constitution, I wrote – truthfully – showed some symptoms of giving way. It did not in fact do so.

On a chilly day late in February 1897 Holmes and I were lunching in the Baker Street rooms, when a telegram arrived. This was hardly an unusual occurrence, but my engagement with Mrs Hudson's mutton chop ceased immediately when Holmes's face was suddenly transformed, flushed and with a glitter in his eyes, followed by an expression of extreme thoughtfulness. He handed the telegram to me, his brows drawn into two dark lines. It read: "*Come at once. My club Mycroft.*"

"When Brother Mycroft commands, and during the hour of luncheon at that, we may be sure that weighty matters are afoot, Watson."

"Shall I accompany you, Holmes?"

"Why, certainly. We leave immediately. Mrs Hudson will no doubt forgive our abandonment of her excellent treacle pudding. I smell danger in its place, though of a form which I trust should have no need of your pistol."

Within the half hour we were being ushered into a private room of the Diogenes Club in Pall Mall, one of the few places where speaking was permitted in this club of most unclubable gentlemen. There we found not only Mycroft awaiting us, but three other most distinguished visitors. The remains of a hasty luncheon suggested they had been foregathered some time. One of the visitors we recognized instantly and indeed Holmes had undertaken cases for him on former occasions. If anything were needed to convince us of the seriousness of the circumstances that called us here, it was the presence of the elderly Lord Bellinger, once more Premier of Britain. The second was Sir George Lewis, solicitor in delicate matters to the highest in the land. He too was no stranger to Holmes, though my presence brought a swift frown to his face which was only removed by a nod from Lord

Bellinger. The third, a keen-eyed tall man of about thirty-five, was introduced to us as Mr Robert Mannering, a name familiar to us as Lord Bellinger's Adviser on European Affairs. He had inherited the mantle, though not yet the high office, of the late Trelawney Hope, Lord Bellinger's Secretary for European Affairs at the time of the Adventure of the Second Stain. Holmes' brother Mycroft sat in the midst of the group, a huge and ungainly spider in the centre of the web of Government diplomacy and intrigue.

"I had not thought we should yet again have need of your services, Mr Holmes," the Premier began. "Your brother informs us you are exceptionally busy at the moment."

"That is so."

"We have to ask you to lay all else aside, save that which we are about to ask you to undertake."

"That is scarcely feasible, Lord Bellinger." Holmes was taken aback at this request. "There is the interesting case of the Vanishing Pedlar, and the affair of the Ten Black Pillowcases."

"Insignificant trifles, Sherlock," Mycroft rumbled.

From no one but his brother would Sherlock Holmes have accepted this without considerable demur.

"Well, well, that may be debated on a future occasion."

"Let me explain, Mr Holmes. I act on behalf of a –" Sir George coughed slightly as though he were unwilling even to commit himself so far, "– a noble client of the highest station, who is concerned on behalf of his mother, a – um – lady of venerable years," Lord Bellinger and Mr Mannering's eyes were momentarily averted from us, "who is held in highest public esteem and affection and who has no knowledge whatsoever of the events that I am about to relate to you. Nor must she ever have. That is mandatory. His mother – let us call her Lady X –"

"If you insist," Holmes agreed in a bored voice.

"Lady X," Sir George continued hurriedly, "is mistress of an exceptionally large household in London and several country residences. She was widowed early after a most happy marriage, and though blessed with a large and loving family, inevitably as each in turn chose matrimony she came more and more to rely in her private life on a large group of retainers, and one in particular, a loyal and faithful servant who was her personal attendant and confidant to a degree that aroused the disquiet of some of her advisers, though he was an honest enough fellow."

"To the point, Sir George. I believe this loyal and faithful retainer of yours to be dead these fourteen years," Holmes said, displaying some impatience.

Sir George bowed his head in slight amusement, despite his

obvious anxiety. "As always you are correct, Mr Holmes. He died in one of Lady X's larger country residences and afterwards his effects were naturally returned to his family in Scotland. He left no will, and her ladyship made the request of his appointed executor that such correspondence as had passed between them, on matters concerning the estate and so forth – should be extracted and returned to her. This was done, or so it was believed."

"Believed?"

"We have reason to believe that one letter never reached the security of Lady X's archives. The librarian keeps the correspondence under lock and key, not to mention his own coded system. He is positive it has not been touched since it entered his possession. I need hardly say he himself is above suspicion. Yet this morning, Mr Holmes, I received an unsigned letter informing me that the writer had in his possession a letter from Lady X to her retainer and was prepared to part with it for a suitable sum."

"On a matter concerning the estate?" Holmes queried politely.

Sir George hesitated, and Robert Mannering after a nod from Lord Bellinger replied for him. "We must rely on your complete discretion, Mr Holmes, Mr Watson."

"You may be assured of it," my friend replied coldly.

"This letter, a copy of which was enclosed, was written during the retainer's last illness, which was a highly infectious one precluding any visits by Lady X to his bedside. It was a letter of warmth, full of affection and gratitude for the years of devoted service and friendship that he had given her."

"Come, come, Mr Mannering. We trifle."

"By an enemy," Robert Mannering continued steadily, "that letter, assuming it to be no forgery, might be capable of grievous misinterpretation by those who seek an opportunity for mischief."

"If that is the case," I said eagerly, "why has nothing been heard of it for fourteen years?"

"Good, Watson," Holmes cried. "However, an event is to take place this summer which must surely rank above all others in placing Lady X at the forefront of world attention. At such a time the letter, if it fell into the wrong hands, might well be used to devastating effect."

"To ruin her reputation?"

"Worse, Watson. To besmirch not only England, but the Empire itself, if I am not mistaken. Why else should the Premier's Adviser on European Affairs be with us today?"

"You are not mistaken, Mr Holmes." Lord Bellinger spoke gravely. "We must buy that letter back."

"Pray let me see the copy, and the letter to you, Sir George."

After a moment's hesitation, Sir George handed both to him. "It will tell you nothing. It came by hand from an unknown messenger."

"Nothing in itself inevitably conveys information," Holmes remarked, scanning the contents. Both were penned in a bold black copperplate, and the letter to Sir George was brief: "The writer is prepared to part with the original of the enclosed letter for a sum to be arranged. The crest will prove its provenance. The personal columns of the daily newspapers will convey my next instruction."

"They are written by hand," Holmes observed to his brother.

Mycroft chuckled. "I can supply names, Sherlock."

I was bewildered at this exchange, and indeed I was only now appreciating the gravity of the whole affair. Holmes did not pursue the subject.

"We would ask you to carry out the negotiation on our behalf, Mr Holmes," Sir George said.

"I believe my services may be required for more than mere barter," Holmes replied quietly, "or Mycroft alone would be handling this affair."

"Why, Holmes?" I was startled, but the expression on Lord Bellinger's face confirmed it.

"Ten years ago this month, Watson, there was another occasion of equal importance to Lady X yet nothing was heard of this letter then. Does that not suggest that the writer of the letter is no ordinary sneaksman, but plays for large stakes and to whom, since time appears no object, the game is of more importance than the outcome? A dangerous opponent, Watson. Ten years ago – correct me if I err, Mr Mannering – the leader of the European power who now casts envious eyes on Britain's prosperity, had not yet succeeded his father on the throne, and moreover his country had a great and wise Chancellor to guide it. Today, however, the son rules alone, and through jealousy, his relations with England are currently so bad that he would stop at nothing to mar the additional prestige that this summer will undoubtedly bring to Lady X and the British Empire."

"I fear you are right, Mr Holmes," Robert Mannering said heavily, "and that this affair will by no means be a straightforward financial transaction."

"What then?" I asked, as no one spoke.

"There will be other bidders, Watson," Holmes replied. "It remains to be seen whether we shall be permitted to be one of them."

"But Sir George's letter –"

"The game, Watson, the game."

Readers of my chronicles may recall the name which was now to be mentioned, and whose dramatic introduction to my friend I stated that I might some day recount. I am now able to do so, for Sir George said briskly: "All the more reason that the world must not know that you are involved, Mr Holmes. I have already taken the liberty of arranging for you to visit Dr Moore Agar of Harley Street who will issue instructions to you to surrender all your cases and take a complete rest, lest you suffer a breakdown of health. The newspapers will be informed of this. Dr Agar is well accustomed to such confidential work on our behalf."

Holmes, who prided himself, despite his addiction to the notorious drug, on his strong constitution, reluctantly concurred.

In order to maintain the fiction we hailed a cab even for the short distance from Harley Street to our Baker Street rooms. No sooner had we entered than he flew to his index of biographies. After a mere ten minutes he exclaimed, "I have it. The chief player in our game, Watson."

"Who is he, Holmes?"

"What man would play such a game for its own sake? I sought a woman. You may have wondered what I found informative about the handwriting. Why, nothing, save that its use told me that the writer did not fear discovery. It followed that we dealt with no common criminal but with someone well acquainted with the highest circles in the land and who gambled that the identity of the thief would be nothing compared with the need to recover the letter. It also follows that the thief is unlikely to be British with a social position to be maintained at all costs. The Baroness Pilski is most certainly our thief." He brandished the heavy volume in the air. "A redoubtable lady, Watson, deserving of our respect. Her late husband fled to England after the failed uprising of the Poles in 'sixty-three and, of an émigré family herself, she married him in 'seventy-nine at the age of twenty-three. For some years a lady-in-waiting to Lady X, she resigned the position ten years ago and has since employed her skills to wreak damage to whom and where she chose. You may recall I crossed swords with the lady in the curious incident of the Limping Jarvy."

"Cannot Lestrade arrest her?"

"Tut, tut, our friend will be prepared for such a move. It is the letter we seek, Watson. No, we must wait upon events."

We did not have long to do so. Three days later, at breakfast, Holmes, deep in his study of *The Times*, startled me with a glad cry. "By Jove, I have it!" His long forefinger pointed to a notice in the personal column.

"The butler is a reptile who sleeps in the shadows until summoned by Zeus," I read. "A cipher, Holmes?"

"I think not, Watson. Until summoned bears no hint of the cipher about it. The butler of course refers to our faithful retainer, Zeus the Thunderer to *The Times*, and the reptile – well, that is surely obvious." He had sprung to his feet and seized a timetable from the shelves.

"The Reptile House of the Zoological Gardens." I rose eagerly, ready to depart at once.

"Pray resume your seat, my dear fellow. See, our express train departs at eleven forty-five and that is time enough for you to consume Mrs Hudson's excellent muffin in its entirety."

"But where are we going?"

"Why, to Cornwall."

He would say no more, and shortly before midnight we were established in a tolerably comfortable inn after a drive from the small country railway station of St Erth. On our way I had glanced at a signpost, dimly lit by the cab's lamp: "The Lizard".

"The reptile, of course," I exclaimed.

"It is always 'of course' *after* my explanations, Watson, never before, I note."

It was unusual for my friend to speak so sharply and a measure of the anxiety that preyed upon him.

Next day we found ourselves a small cottage on a grassy headland near Poldhu Bay, in order to further the fiction of complete rest for my friend. Rest? I have seldom known my friend so restless during the weeks that followed. As day followed day, and bluebells replaced the primroses, daffodils and violets in the tall grassy banks that bordered the quiet lanes, and still nothing appeared in the newspaper, I became concerned once more about his health. The ancient Cornish language, as I recounted in an earlier chronicle, did indeed arrest his attention at this time, convinced as he became that it was rooted in the Chaldean, but it could not sufficiently occupy that great mind. Had it not been for the horrible affair of the Devil's Foot which so unexpectedly cropped up in the nearby hamlet of Tredannick Wollas, I should indeed have prescribed the rest Dr Agar had supposedly ordered. After the case was solved, however, he relapsed into the same silent preoccupation, with such feverish eyes that made me wonder if the Devil's Foot root we had both imbibed in his quest for experimentation had not had lasting effects.

However I awoke one morning to a grey spring day, promising yet more of that soft and gentle rain with which Cornwall is so plentifully endowed, and Sherlock Holmes was standing by my bedside. Gone were the signs of feverishness, replaced now with the vital strength I had come to know so well.

"If ever I am presumptuous enough to place my services at the disposal of the nation, Watson, pray remind me of the faithful retainer. We return to London today, and by heaven I trust we are not too late." He spoke gravely.

"For what reason, Holmes?" I struggled from my bed.

"Why, to study the Chaldean language, my dear fellow." But the words were kindly spoken, not with the mocking sharpness of the last few weeks.

In a jolting restaurant carriage on the Great Western Railway I ventured to press for an explanation of our sudden departure. Even *The Times* had remained unread today.

"Come, Watson, surely with this excellent sole before us you can adopt Mr Auguste Didier's methods, even if mine remain unfathomable to you?"

"Isn't he that cook fellow at Plum's Club for Gentlemen who solved one or two cases?"

"Indeed he is. I was curious enough to pay him a visit in 'ninety-six after the remarkable affair at Plum's. I cannot approve all his methods, since he will have it that detection is not purely a science, whereas I maintain that it is entirely a process of logical deduction. He holds that cookery is akin to detection in the assembling of ingredients and their selection, and fashioning into a palatable dish requires a measure of creativity. I doubt if Mrs Hudson would agree. However, consider, Watson, the ingredients in the puzzle before us."

"The letter, the Baroness –"

"And other bidders, Watson. That is deduction, not creativity. We may also deduce that the Baroness would assume that this affair is too important for my services not to be called upon. It follows, if the Baroness acknowledges this, then so do the other bidders. I have been an ass, Watson." His bantering tone returned to its former anxiety.

"I assumed," he continued, "that the message which sent us scurrying so precipitately to Cornwall was from the Baroness. It was not. It was placed in order to throw me off the scent, no doubt by another bidder, and it succeeded."

"But nothing has appeared in *The Times*."

Holmes replied sombrely: "How do we know the summons will be in *The Times*? The original instruction stated merely the daily newspapers. Fortunately Mrs Hudson is under instructions to throw nothing away in any circumstances. Let us trust that two months' supply of the London newspapers from the *Daily Graphic* to the

Financial Times awaits us in Baker Street. By God, Watson, if I have thrown our chance away –' He broke off, rare emotion consuming him.

"Who might such a bidder be?" I asked quietly.

"You will recall the matter of the Bruce Partington Plans in 'ninety-five; Mycroft informed me there were few who would handle so important an affair. The only contenders worth considering were Adolph Meyer, Louis La Rothière and Hugo Oberstein. The villainous Oberstein now resides in prison, and thus we are left with La Rothière and Adolph Meyer."

"Meyer must surely be our man," I exclaimed.

"For once I agree, Watson. He still resides in London at 13 Great George Street, Westminster. La Rothière has been known to me for some years, and I believe we may dismiss him. I have made it my business, however, since 'ninety-five, to find out what I can of Adolph Meyer. The gentleman is plump, portly, a friendly soul, with a passion for music though his execrable taste runs more to Mr John Philip Sousa than to the classical. He favours the tuba, not the violin. Inside that affable shell, however, beats the heart of as evil a man as ever lived. He is unofficial agent to the Baron von Holbach. The name means nothing to you, Watson? I am hardly surprised. He does not seek the limelight, but his Machiavellian hand was behind Bismarck's dismissal, the Kruger telegram, and countless other intrigues. He has the ear of the Kaiser, whereas the Chancellor himself remains unheard. He is no friend to England, and Meyer is his tool. Watson, if I could choose my enemy, send me one that wears the *face* of evil."

"And you are convinced he is involved in this affair?"

"Yes. He now knows me well enough to fear my powers – though how can I call them powers when my wits have deserted me? Two months in Cornwall, and the Empire at risk!"

He remained plunged in gloom until the train steamed into Paddington station. I shall long remember his long figure hunched at my side as if to spur the cab the faster to Baker Street. On entering the familiar rooms, he did not even wait to remove his ulster (for although it was May, the cool night air had been chilly) and despite the late hour plunged towards the tidy but huge piles of newspaper carefully stacked by Mrs Hudson.

Seldom have I felt more useless. No sooner had I read and absolved a newspaper of containing anything to do with our current problem than Holmes would seize it from me to ensure I had missed nothing. After three hours I could endure no more and retreated to my bed for what remained of the night. I left Holmes surrounded by newspapers, now in untidy heaps all around him, and occasionally scribbling a note on a pad. When I awoke in the morning, he was still where I had last seen him, red-eyed but still alert.

"I have it, Watson." He pushed the pad towards me.

I stared at his work in horror. It consisted merely of childish doodles; circles, squares, dots, crosses, and pin men and women.

"Holmes, my dear fellow, what is this?"

"Hah!" he cried, as he saw the expression on my face. "You believe I have over-indulged in the syringe! No, my dear fellow. See, this may be the saving of us." He thrust a copy of the *Daily Mail* before my eyes, stabbing with his finger at a message on the front page personal column. The issue was dated 9 March.

"The circle contains a stop," I read. "A cipher, Holmes?" I tried once more.

"You think of nothing save cryptograms, Watson. No, no, this explains why we may yet be in time. There is nothing more until the messages resumed early this month." He placed a second sheet before me.

"Turpin has a dog," I read. Against it, in Holmes's neat handwriting, was written: "issue of 6 May." Underneath were more senseless jumbles of words. "Cupid strikes the right fox four times"; that was the issue of Monday, the 10th. Thursday the 13th bore the legend: "The smiling cook bears a cross". Friday the 14th: "The pinman and the pageboy take nine paces", and yesterday's, the 18th, the day of our return: "The circle has a cross."

"Surely you are mistaken, Holmes? I have passed over many such messages in the personal columns. Why pick upon these?"

"My dear fellow, have you no eyes?" He thrust under my nose the sheet of doodles to which I have already referred. "We await only the *time* of our rendezvous. The date we have."

He paced the room in a state of combined exhilaration and disquiet, ignoring my request for further enlightenment. "Thank God we are in time."

"You speak in riddles, Holmes."

"Cannot you see," one finger impatiently jabbed at the doodles. "Well, well, perhaps you cannot. *Argot*, my dear Watson, is a language even more worth studying than the Chaldean, and of more practical use. Consider what profession our Baroness follows."

"Lady-in-waiting?"

"*Burglar*, Watson. She has joined the underworld, what more natural than that she should amuse herself with burglar's *argot*? How often have you passed a garden fence with such childish scrawls chalked upon it? Frequently no doubt, and thought nothing of it. Yet such scrawls are the living language of two groups of outsiders in our world, burglars and tramps. Each has their own code – yes, Watson, your code at last, but these marks are the code of the illiterate. Since prehistoric times, drawings in simple form have portrayed messages left for those that come after. A burglar or a tramp goes about his trade with the same dedication as Mr Didier for his. Where the latter collects ingredients, our lawless and vagrant friends deal in information: which servants have been squared, for example."

"Ah! The cook bears a cross."

"You excel yourself, Watson," Holmes murmured. "Similarly they convey how many live in the house, whether there are dogs, how many servants, the best means of access; tramps have a similar code, more concerned with what their brethren might expect from the house. Here before us is all we need to know."

"Turpin?" I enquired.

"An exception, but simple enough. An acquaintance with the Dover Road should tell you that Turpin is associated with The Old Bull coaching inn on the summit of Shooter's Hill in Kent. Hence the reference to a dog. The old Old Bull no longer exists, but a new hostelry of the same name stands there."

"The meeting is there?"

"No, Watson, no. 'Cupid strikes the right fox four times'." He pointed to the doodle of an arrow with the figure 4 written by it. "At the foot of Shooter's Hill stood the old Fox in the Hill public house, conveniently close to the gallows to whet the lips of the onlookers. Both are now vanished, but again a new public house stands close to the old. The hill is lined with villas and I have little doubt that the fourth on the right from The Bull is our place of rendezvous and that therein works a cook who will no longer qualify for the title of faithful retainer. She has been squared, and the gentleman and male retainer of the household step out at nine o'clock, we are informed."

"And the day, Holmes?" I was by amazed at the depth of my friend's knowledge of the underworld.

"'The circle has a cross'. A tramp sign conveying that the householder is religious. A little more obscure, but let us take the religious connection. We lack a date and Ascension Day is tomorrow, Thursday the 20th."

"Suppose it implies Whitsun?"

"Would the gentleman of the house then leave it at nine o'clock? He would be in church or at breakfast. No, no, it is tomorrow, and surely today the last piece of the jigsaw must fall into our hands."

At this moment Mrs Hudson brought in the daily newspapers and with an eager cry Holmes sprang across the room to receive them from her hands. Mrs Hudson cast one look at the state of the room, then wisely departed without comment.

"I have it! See here, Watson. The cross gains a leg." In triumph he added it in pictorial form to his list. "Eleven o'clock."

"Should we not ask Lestrade to seek out the Baroness?"

"And lose the only hope we have of recovering the letter? No, Watson, we shall attend this auction sale. We are permitted to bid any sum, but I have other plans – I recommend you bring your pistol."

His pipe then claimed his attention, and it was not until the cab was taking us to Charing Cross station that I was able to ask Holmes why the Baroness had gone to so much trouble to disguise the rendezvous.

He answered readily enough. "Because I know our good friend Lestrade is hot on the track of both the Baroness and Meyer, though he has orders not to take them up. Why else did the first message, 'The circle contains a stop' appear? It conveys: 'Danger of being quodded'. The Baroness feared arrest and that is what gave us our second chance, Watson, the delay between the messages. There must be no question of failure now."

We descended from the London, Chatham and South-Eastern Railway train at half-past ten at Blackheath station, whence it was but a short drive up from the village to the wild heathland and the Dover Road, and then to Shooter's Hill. All conversation had ceased, and one might well have imagined us as Scarlet Pimpernels in a desperate race to Dover. Indeed, our own mission was of even more importance. Our driver halted at an old mounting block near the summit of the hill and no sooner was he paid than Holmes was striding eagerly down the hill back towards London, ignoring the dust thrown up by passing vans and carriages. A milk cart swayed dangerously near, its measuring cans almost catching my friend, and its driver grinning infuriatingly. The air was sweet and fragrant after the smoke of London, and in the villa gardens late tulips, giving way to the blue and purples of May, made a pretty sight after the grimy and blackened buildings bordering the streets of London.

However, we had no time to linger over such pleasures. Already Holmes was striding up the path that led to the tradesmen's door of a sizeable villa. I struggled to keep abreast of him, but by the time I reached the door he was already rapping upon it for the second time. When no answer came, he thrust it open, having found it unlocked. I patted the pistol in my pocket for reassurance, as I followed him in. There was something about the place I did not like. Perhaps it was its silence, its grey coldness. We walked into a surprisingly large and airy kitchen, and the sensation of an empty house intensified.

"We are somewhat early," I commented, merely for the sake of breaking the silence to counter my unease.

"Hush." Sherlock Holmes walked through into the main house, and hard on his footsteps, I came to the parlour door. This too was open.

The house was empty of life indeed, but the appalling sight that met our eyes told us that life had not long fled from it. My hand was at my pistol even as my eyes took in the terrible scene before us. Sprawled on the Persian rug before the hearth was a woman's body, clad in black bombazine, and its sightless, staring eyes turned horribly towards us; blood covered the carpet and was splattered on the walls. There was no weapon to be seen, only a profusion of blood to suggest a stab wound in the chest. But there was worse. By the window overlooking the rear garden lay the body of another woman. This one was of a somewhat younger woman, perhaps forty, old for the mob cap and print gown she wore. The maid had died in the same appalling way as her mistress, whom I presumed to be the cook-housekeeper. I hurried to confirm what I knew must be the case, that there would be no pulse to be found in either.

"Is there life, Watson?"

"In neither, Holmes," I replied quietly, rising to my feet after a brief examination of both bodies. "What devilry is this? To stab the housekeeper *and* the maid?"

He made an impatient gesture. "You see, but you do not observe, Watson. This may well be the housekeeper, but that is no serving maid. What maid could afford such kid boots, or keep her hands in such fine condition? See the nails – and this." Gently he removed the cap and long, well-cared for auburn tresses tumbled from it. "No maid's face either, Watson. It is that of an adventuress who has lived by her wits these last few years and now died by another's. The Baroness did not deserve such a fate, of that I am sure. The maid's outfit was doubtless to give her anonymity until she could be sure of the identities of any bidders."

"And the letter?"

Holmes shrugged. "We can search, but we will not find. You will have noticed my silence on the way here. I had reasoned that the cross with the leg indicated eleven o'clock, since nine o'clock, with the leg on the other side, would hardly have been practical with the man of the household leaving at that precise hour, a deduction which the Baroness was fully capable of appreciating I would surely make. We were meant to arrive too late, Watson."

"She would hardly have connived at her own murder, Holmes," I protested.

"The game was planned to a different end, Watson. Had Meyer

not been the evil monster he is, I have little doubt we should have arrived, only to have the cook hand us a note from the Baroness mocking us for our tardiness. As it is –" He broke off, as the door opened behind us.

"Good morning, Mr Holmes, Dr Watson." Lestrade's eyes went to the bodies. "A pretty pickle," he remarked after a moment.

"Meyer has preceded us both, Lestrade. I have no doubt that a certain rotund milkman I observed on his cart was he."

"Shall I set my men after him, Mr Holmes? We can hold him and search his house."

"And he will have the letter safely stowed elsewhere. He must hand it to his European masters."

"Every port will be watched. Even callers to the Legation."

"Good, good," Holmes muttered absently.

"Suppose he sends it to von Holbach by mail or smuggles it by boat?" I asked.

"Such a prize is too valuable for that," Holmes replied. "No, he will hand it over personally."

"Then it won't be in Germany," Lestrade declared stoutly. "And we'll be watching lest von Holbach comes here, and hold him."

"On no account do so, Lestrade. Von Holbach is known to us, an agent who would then doubtless be sent would not be. Let the game continue."

The days then weeks passed, while Holmes fretted. The newspapers carried a short paragraph about an unfortunate stockbroker who had returned to find his home full of police constables, and his cook together with a total stranger, who was as yet unidentified, lying murdered on his floor.

As June opened, a heightened sense of excitement swept through London as it prepared for Her Majesty Queen Victoria's Diamond Jubilee on the 22nd of the month. Carpenters were already at work on a huge stand in Whitehall, another in the churchyard of St Martin's Church, and a colossal one by St Paul's churchyard. Large sums were being demanded of the visitors now flocking into London from all quarters of the globe, for space at windows. From the eleventh of the month when the official programme was published, the sole topic of conversation wherever one walked or dined was Jubilee Day. Everywhere, that is, save in our Baker Street rooms, where my friend paced in silence save for a few days when he disappeared, and, I suspected, disguised as a beggar or postman, tramped the streets of London in search of his prey.

Even Mrs Hudson's patience wore thin, as the air became thick with smoke, and meal after meal was returned uneaten. Pursuing the fiction of his illness, he avoided going out save in disguise, keeping the curtains drawn much of the time.

Of Adolph Meyer there was no sign whatsoever. Lestrade swore he had not left the country, but he was not to be found in London. His servants professed not to know his whereabouts. A watch on the Legation ensured he had not sought sanctuary there. Towards the end of the week of the 13th, decorations began to blossom all over the city, transforming grey stone into a veritable bower of flowers and coloured flags. Favours sprouted in buttonholes and hats, and bicycles and carriages streamed with red, white and blue.

Returning to Baker Street late on Saturday the 19th, I found to my relief that Sherlock Holmes was at last disposed to talk. "Sir George visited me today. Watson, he has come."

"Who, Holmes?"

"Von Holbach himself. He lodges at the Legation. He has no official invitation, of course, for his master's regrettable severing of friendly relations between his nation and ours at Cowes in 'ninety-five means that not only can he not cross the Channel, but his *eminence grise* is not officially welcomed here either."

"Then when Meyer goes to deliver the letter, we have him."

"He would be arrested before he pulled the bellrope. No, he will seek some other means." Holmes picked up his violin and I knew we were in for another long spell of waiting, though the sands of time were running out fast.

My friend's violin droned on that evening and again on the Sunday morning, the usual sign of great pressure bearing upon him. The hot, stifling air around us in the darkened rooms bore insupportably in upon me. "Holmes," I cried, "at least play some recognizable tune."

A screech from the fiddle. "Tune, Watson?" my friend replied icily. "What could my poor violin choose to please you? "God save the Queen" might be appropriate. Or a Sousa march? The Ride of the – Watson!" he exclaimed, "I have not been using the wits God granted me." In a moment, the violin lay disregarded on the table as his eyes took on the gleam with which I was so familiar.

"I grow dangerously near that practice of which our friend Mr Didier might approve, but I have always distrusted, that of assuming an end as yet unsupported *entirely* by fact. We have very little time left to us. Logical deduction is our only hope. *The Times* of yesterday, if you please, Watson, and the Jubilee programme you so kindly purchased for Mrs Hudson."

When I returned from my errand, having promised to return the booklet to her possession, he snatched the programme from my grasp, and after a few moments' perusal cried: "Come Watson, you will need your best straw hat, your smartest cane, and that unfortunate blazer you purchased for boating."

"Where are we bound, Holmes?" I asked eagerly, relieved beyond measure that at last we were taking action. "Shall I have need of my pistol?"

"To take a solitary turn round St James' Park, Watson?" he jested. "I trust not. Though you go alone, the ducks are not thought to be a hazard."

My hopes fell. I was in no need of a constitutional walk, but of a resolution of this affair. However, he was in no mood to bandy words; he was set upon my taking this walk.

"Very well, Holmes," I agreed, albeit reluctantly.

"Good old Watson. And after your stroll, I recommend to your earnest attention the concert advertised to begin at the St James's Park bandstand at noon."

"Concert, Holmes? Good heavens, how can I think of music at such a time as this?"

"What more obvious place for us to meet, my dear fellow?"

Relieved that Sherlock Holmes had indeed some plan in mind, I took a cab to the Birdcage Walk entrance to the park and had it not been for the urgency of the dark situation in which we were placed, would have enjoyed my stroll in this delightful park, now crowded with Jubilee visitors. Children bowled hoops in and out of the promenaders round the lake, sweethearts floated in a blissful world of their own, flowers spread a carpet of colour before my eyes, and as I crossed the bridge the sun chose to appear. The weather had been capricious for some time, but nothing could dim the enthusiasm of these crowds.

I obediently took my seat at the bandstand, towards the back of the rows of seats as befitted my cavalier holiday appearance. A travelling ice-cream vendor wheeling his bicycle passed by, as I looked anxiously for Sherlock Holmes. There was no sign of him. The front rows were filled with those of high social standing, amongst whom the ticket-seller was now moving, a rough-looking fellow despite his peaked cap and crumpled navy uniform. The German band, usually resident in Broadstairs in Kent, was already preparing to play by the time the ticket collector reached me; I handed over the sixpence demanded of me, my thoughts elsewhere.

"The game is afoot, Watson."

The hoarse whisper as the ticket collector bent down to retrieve a fallen coin startled me. But why should I have been surprised to see Sherlock Holmes himself, presently the most unremarkable ticket collector the Royal Parks had ever boasted? He passed on, exchanging a few gallant remarks with the young lady next to me, which made me wonder if my friend had not courted more young ladies than he acknowledged, whether in pursuance of his profession or otherwise.

Of course. A brass band concert. Holmes was expecting Meyer himself to be in the audience, and for von Holbach to join him. But when? The concert proceeded without incident, though I was scarcely in a mood now to appreciate it. A rousing selection of Gilbert and Sullivan choruses concluded the concert, and the audience rose for the National Anthem, sung with deep feeling and solemnity on this opening day to the week's festivities. I was in great anxiety. Holmes had vanished, the band was packing its instruments, and the audience was drifting away. *Now* was the time and yet I could see no one amongst the groups of lingering spectators to answer Holmes's description of Meyer.

At last I spotted Holmes, on the platform, and hurried as unobtrusively as I could to be at hand. He was busy helping the band with their instruments and the music stands, no doubt to gain a vantage point over the audience. A few people had mounted the bandstand to congratulate the players, and I watched an insignificant man in mackintosh and Homburg hat approach the tuba player to shake his hand, though a less musical instrument I have yet to hear.

"Watson!"

Holmes's shout sent me running for the steps to his aid, as unbelievably he hurled himself between the two men. Amid the general alarm, the tuba player recovered his balance and aimed a vicious blow to Holmes's body sending him staggering back. I caught a glimpse of the most malevolent eyes I have ever seen, and then he was pinioned, by myself and, I recognized with relief, Lestrade. I had not recognized him, in his guise as ice-cream vendor. His whistle was even now summoning his constables.

"Herr Meyer, we meet again. I trust you enjoyed the sea air at Broadstairs." Holmes addressed the handcuffed Meyer. "And now the letter, if you please."

"Too late," he cried in triumph.

Horrified, I remembered the other man. There was no sign of him.

"Holmes, von Holbach has gone," I groaned, blaming myself.

"That is only to be expected, Watson. He is a diplomat."

"You are remarkably cool, Mr Holmes," Lestrade said. "I take it this letter is of little importance then?"

"On the contrary, it is perhaps the most vital instrument for the maintenance of peace in Europe since the Treaty of London guaranteeing Belgium's neutrality in "thirty-nine."

An evil smile came to Meyer's lips as he saw Holmes examining the music stand. "The peace is lost, Holmes," he chuckled, as Lestrade finished a fruitless search of his pockets, hat and shoes.

"Do not be so sure, Meyer," my friend said quietly, his lean figure bending down to pick up Meyer's tuba.

It was from there, deep and safe within the confines of the bell, that he plucked a sheet of paper. I caught a brief glimpse of a familiar and illustrious crest before Holmes whisked it from our sight. "It is Sunday, Watson. But somehow I think Sir George will forgive us if two informally dressed visitors call upon him at his home."

Jubilee Day promised little sunshine as Holmes and I took our places in the seats reserved for us at a window in Whitehall. The grey old road, however, was ablaze with colour, both from the decorations and the scarlet coats of the soldiers lining the route.

"You have not explained, Holmes, how it was you picked upon the very place where the fateful meeting was to take place."

"A matter of deduction, my dear fellow. Meyer could not be found in London. Constabularies the country over had been instructed to watch for him. Useless. He could not appear there or in London in his own guise."

"But he made no attempt to disguise his heavy beard and figure."

"The best disguise is in the eye of the observer, not the face of the quarry. You saw a tuba player; I saw what I expected. Meyer simply absorbed himself into the part of the bandsman."

"Excellent, Holmes."

"Not at all. Once one recalled the man's passion, it was merely a question of scanning the programme for suitable venues. I have listened to many execrable brass bands in the course of the last week. For a violin player it was torment."

Fortunately the sudden noise from the crowd distracted his attention from my involuntary smile.

As the Colonial troops began to pass the sun shone out at last, and "Queen's weather" blessed us for the rest of that memorable day. After the Colonial contingent came the advance guard of the Royal procession. The mass of colour, scarlet, gold, purple and emerald, was followed by an open carriage drawn by eight cream-coloured horses. In it, sat a small figure, clad in black, with touches of grey, quite still under a white sunshade. Gone now was any desire to feast the eye on dazzling colour; for a moment the crowd was silent, even the sound of the horses' hooves could be heard. The carriage had no escort; nothing could come between Her Majesty and her people. Then the roars of the spectators rose to the sky.

Holmes's eyes followed the carriage as it made its way along Whitehall." I am told that when in due course circumstances permit, I may expect a knighthood."

"Holmes, my dear fellow, that is no more than you deserve," I replied warmly.

"You are mistaken, Watson. I shall, should a knighthood be offered, be obliged to refuse it."

"*Refuse*, Holmes?" I was astounded." Surely such an honour can be nothing but welcome."

He brushed this aside with a smile. "You know my methods, Watson. I would consider the majority of my cases more suitable to be worthy of such an honour than this present affair. As an exercise in the pure logic of deduction it has proved disappointingly simple."

"Simple, Holmes?" I rebutted this argument energetically. "With such an enemy, and so much at stake?"

"Yet the game so narrowly won." We watched as the carriage finally disappeared from our view. "No, Watson, they may keep their honours, and I shall continue to remain Their present and future Majesties' most loyal and faithful retainer, Mr Sherlock Holmes."

By 1898 the number of Holmes's recorded cases seemed to be running down. This does not necessarily mean that Holmes was investigating any less, but that Watson was not recording them so avidly. We know that Holmes was often critical of Watson's accounts, sometimes mercilessly so, and he was also very strict over what Watson could publish. The cases towards the end of the century, therefore, were almost certainly more secretive, but also perhaps of less interest in terms of unusual incident. The only ones that Watson did publish were "The Retired Colourman", which overlapped with the unpublished case of the two Coptic patriarchs, and "The Six Napoleons". It is almost certain that during this period Holmes also investigated the disappearance of the cutter Alicia and the fate of Isadora Persano. I have the papers about that last case but there remain some unresolved details which make it as yet unready for publication.

PART IV:
THE FINAL YEARS

THE CASE OF
THE SUICIDAL LAWYER

Martin Edwards

The change in the century did not diminish Holmes's caseload. Within a week or two of the death of Queen Victoria, Holmes was heavily involved in at least three cases. The first was the Abergavenny Murders. Martin Edwards, a writer who is also a solicitor, was allowed access to old files in the archives of the Director of Public Prosecutions, which enabled him to reconstruct the case. At the same time circumstances arose which allowed Sherlock Holmes to revisit one of his very earliest cases, "The Musgrave Ritual". After considerable research Michael Doyle, who is not related to Watson's agent, or so he tells me, was able to piece together this strange coda, which at last settled matters after over twenty-five years in "The Legacy of Rachel Howells". It also resolves a mystery noted by Conan Doyle himself in his later writings.

"You have arrived just in time, Watson," Holmes said as I returned to 221b Baker Street after a stroll one crisp February morning. There was a twinkle in his eye as he added, "I am expecting a visit from that rarest of creatures – a lawyer who is prepared to put his hand in his own pocket, rather than that of one of his clients, to pay for my professional services."

"Wonders never cease, Holmes!" I said lightly. "The circumstances which bring him here must be remarkable indeed."

My friend gave a dry chuckle. "They possess certain features which are of interest. It seems that Mr Matthew Dowling took a young man into his firm believing him to be a Dr Jekyll, but now has reason to fear that he may also be in partnership with a Mr Hyde."

I was delighted to see Holmes in a genial humour. For several months he had been engaged on a series of cases of the utmost consequence and of late his temper had begun to suffer. I regarded this as a warning sign that he might again be putting his health at risk. Some of his investigations had to be conducted in circumstances of the greatest secrecy and it must suffice to say that on one occasion during this period the destiny of a throne depended upon his personal intervention. Other cases excited the attention of the Press and general public throughout the land and I may in due course put them into print. These included the business of the Lincoln seamstress and her extraordinary pets and the conundrum which I have referred to in my notebook as the case of the melancholy wicket-keeper.

The strange features of those puzzles, coupled with the undeniable pleasure Holmes experienced in seeking to succeed, through the rigorous application of logic, where extensive police work had failed, at least meant that he had no need of artificial stimulation. I feared above all that he might resort again to cocaine if boredom threatened. For all that, I was concerned that the nervous energy he had expended would once again take its toll. He was himself aware of the punishing effect on his constitution of the long hours he had been working and in recent weeks a couple of chance remarks had suggested that he was beginning to contemplate retirement. Much as I relished our collaborations, my first concern was his well-being and the eagerness with which I anticipated his response to a fresh challenge was therefore matched by the silent hope that it would not tax him beyond endurance.

"So your new client has a junior partner who leads a double life?" I asked.

"Of sorts. Perhaps you would like to read what the solicitor has to say?"

He tossed me a letter bearing the previous day's date and a private address in Doughty Street.

Dear Mr Sherlock Holmes, – I am aware of the considerable esteem in which you are held as a consulting detective and my cousin Mr Tobias Wrigley speaks highly of your work in connection with Madame Montalambert's affidavit. I should therefore like to consult you personally in a matter of the utmost sensitivity. It concerns not a client of my firm, but rather Mr John Abergavenny, whom I invited to become my junior partner a little less than twelve months ago. I took him in, believing that he was a competent, likeable and trustworthy young fellow who would adhere to the same high standards which I have always set for myself. Yet his personality has suddenly undergone a grotesque and inexplicable transformation. He has become an incompetent and a debauchee. He has also threatened to commit suicide. I have taxed him on these matters, but his response has been wholly unacceptable. I have no wish to be unfair to him, but I cannot permit conduct which may damage the firm whose reputation I have laboured these past thirty years to establish, especially as we act for clients in the most sensitive transactions. I am left contemplating the need to dissolve our partnership, but before taking such a drastic step, I should be most grateful for your professional opinion. If it is convenient, I would propose to call upon you at ten o'clock tomorrow morning. I understand from Mr Wrigley that you charge at a fixed rate and for the avoidance of doubt I should make it clear that for a first consultation, I would regard the fees you agreed with Mr Wrigley as entirely reasonable.

Yours faithfully
MAXWELL DOWLING

I thought for a moment before saying, "You deduce that he is a solicitor rather than, say, a stockbroker or other professional man, because that is Wrigley's line?"

"Not that alone. The prolixity of Mr Dowling's literary style suggests to me that he learned the law in the days when legal draughtsmen were paid by the word. It is a fussy letter, yet it makes the salient points. There is, too, the phraseology that he employs which I would associate with a lawyer rather than, say, a financier or a medical man. He cannot be a barrister, however, since members of the Bar do not practise in partnership. Above all, though, I would refer you to the obvious fact that this letter appears to have been composed by a man who is genuinely troubled by a mystery which he wishes to resolve with all due speed."

"Hence the early appointment?"

"Precisely. You will note, however, that he takes care to specify with some precision the terms upon which he proposes to contract for my services. Think of all those others who have anxiously sought my assistance over the years. Who else but a lawyer would take such trouble? I do not accuse Dowling of possessing an especially mercenary turn of mind. I would rather say simply that the habits of a lifetime are seldom abandoned, even *in extremis*. Depend upon it, my boy, this new client is a solicitor. But there is a ring at the bell. We shall soon have an opportunity to test the accuracy or otherwise of the inferences I have drawn."

We heard a measured tread upon the stairs and within moments Mr Maxwell Dowling was ushered into our room. He was a man of about sixty, small, neat and anxious in manner. He wore a hat, gaiters, black trousers and pince-nez attached by a long ribbon to the lapel of his frock-coat. He studied us both through the glasses before giving a bow which seemed to denote satisfaction with what he observed.

"It is good to meet you, Mr Holmes. Thank you for being prepared to see me at short notice. I must admit I have not myself read the accounts of your exploits penned by your faithful chronicler here, Dr Watson. Young Abergavenny has yet to persuade me of the appeal of sensational literature. But as I mentioned in my letter, I have heard from my cousin that you are intrigued by the bizarre, and the matter which brings me here is nothing if not that."

"If we are agreed that I am to charge you by the hour for my services," Holmes said, with a touch of mischief, "perhaps it would prudent for you to explain the details without more ado."

"Ah yes. Forgive me, my dear wife has been known to complain that I am a trifle long-winded." Dowling coughed. "Ahem. The further and better particulars. Certainly. I should first say, Mr Holmes, that I am solicitor with a small office in Essex Street. For the past three decades I have been a sole practitioner acting for a number of – if I say so myself – most distinguished clients. But during the past eighteen months or so, my wife has been encouraging me to think of the future. As a result, I began to look around for a partner, someone who might come into the business with a view in the long term to buying out my share of it."

Our visitor paused and I had the distinct impression that he was about to confide in us at some length concerning the financial anxieties faced by a man in such a position. Holmes was no doubt of the same mind, for he said briskly, "And so you took in this Mr John Abergavenny?"

"Yes, he had been working for a firm in Holborn with which I have regular dealings. He seemed a splendid fellow, an ideal choice. Hard-working and capable, a thoroughly decent young man. Above all, there was no question as to his integrity. He seemed to be a man I could trust and that, of course, was a matter of the most fundamental importance. He was the first to admit that he was not in the same league as his gifted elder brother, but he made it clear that he was determined not to be wholly over-shadowed."

"His brother?" Holmes asked.

"Hugh Abergavenny. The name may be familiar to you."

My friend raised his eyebrows. "Indeed. He was a lawyer, too, as I recall."

"You are correct, although he practised at the Bar rather than as a solicitor. I have seen him more than once in court and I can assure you he had a rare gift for winning over a jury, even in cases where he was appearing on behalf of the most undeserving wretch. It was a sad loss to the legal profession when he decided to devote his time to writing rather than to his career. A mistake, if I may say so, which Dr Watson here has been wise not to make."

"I could not claim," I said hastily, "to possess a fraction of the imaginative powers of Hugh Abergavenny. I must have read all of his books, although I think I am right in saying he has published nothing for some years. I regarded his early novels as splendid thrillers, reminiscent in some respects of Le Fanu and Wilkie Collins."

"As I said earlier, I cannot claim to share your enthusiasm for writing of that kind, but I would readily acknowledge that it is remarkable that he should have prospered in two such distinct fields. For John, on the other hand, success has not come so easily. Yet what he may lack in natural talent, he has always compensated for with persistence."

Holmes nodded. "That counts for a good deal in the law."

"Assuredly, Mr Holmes. When we first met, John confessed to me that he had long nourished a burning desire to emulate his brother as a writer of thrilling tales, but I sought to convince him that his future lay in enjoying the security that a partnership in a sound legal practice can provide. Certainly, after he joined my firm he did not mention his literary ambitions again and I thought I had been able to concentrate his mind on the creative possibilities which exist within the law of real property."

"So until the recent sequence of events mentioned in your note, you had no reason to regret your choice of partner?"

"None whatsoever."

"What has happened to cause you to change your mind?"

"I began to notice that John seemed constantly to be tired. His eyes looked red and sore, his manner in the morning was often sleepy. It was as if he had been up all night. Thereafter it came to my notice that he had made a number of errors in his work. There was a problem with a conveyancing transaction, a relatively simple point to which he had failed to attend. Another client complained of a mistake in a bill of costs which caused me considerable embarrassment – to say nothing of a not insignificant sum of money. More in sorrow than in anger, I took John to task about these unfortunate events. He promptly accepted that he had been at fault and assured me that there would be no recurrence."

"Did he give any reason for the difficulties that had occurred?"

"With hindsight, I recognize that he was vague. He referred to a minor health problem which had caused him trouble in sleeping and said he had obtained more suitable medication from his doctor. I have to admit that I did not regard his answers as entirely plausible, but I was hopeful that I had made my point and that there would be no need to pursue the complaints any further."

"Yet in the event you were disappointed?"

"Indeed, Mr Holmes, and I find the latest developments both shocking and perturbing. First, my outdoor clerk Bevington told me in confidence that he had been crossing Lincoln's Inn Fields late one night when he saw John Abergavenny approaching. He was in the company of a woman who appeared not – shall we say? – to be a suitable companion for a respectable young solicitor." Dowling winced. "John was talking loudly and as he passed Bevington, he hailed him with an atrociously rude remark before bursting into a fit of wild laughter. My clerk is a teetotaller and he was shocked both by John's behaviour and the fact that he stank of drink. Naturally embarrassed, Bevington hurried straight home. He has been with me for upwards of twenty years and was most reluctant, I am satisfied, to inform me of the unfortunate occurrence. He felt, however, that it was his duty to do so in the interest of the firm and I assured him that he was right."

Holmes placed his finger-tips together and looked at the ceiling. "Does your partner have a weakness for the fair sex?"

"On the contrary. I have always regarded him as a decent fellow. He is engaged to be married to a delightful young lady whose father is a diplomat. She is at present in India with him and is not due to return for another six weeks. I always understood John to be devoted to her and her alone."

"Did you speak to him about Bevington's story?"

"Immediately. This time his reaction was a prompt and outraged denial. He said he was deeply hurt by what I had said. Bevington was a blind old fool who must have been mistaken. Frankly, I would have accepted his word but for two things. First, Bevington may be old, but he is neither blind nor a fool. Second, Hugh Abergavenny himself came to see me the following day."

Holmes leaned forward. "What did he have to say?"

"Like Bevington, he was plainly unhappy about having to speak to me, but believed he had no proper alternative. I had not met him previously. I gather that the two men are not close and Hugh told me that he was aware that John had, in his younger days, felt that he was living in the shadow of his brother's achievements. In such circumstances, jealousy is perhaps inevitable."

"I might take issue with you there," Holmes interrupted. "I have myself a gifted elder brother and have always looked on him as my mentor. Let it pass, though. What did the famous novelist have to say?"

"He said that he had been anxious for some time to improve his relations with John. Apparently he had promised this to their mother some time before her death two or three years ago and his failure to do so has been on his conscience ever since. He was aware of John's enthusiasm for writing and had tried to give him help and encouragement, but to no avail. I understand that he had kindly offered to read the manuscript of a work over which John had been labouring, in the hope that he might be able to persuade his own literary agent to take it on. Regrettably, the story proved to be a clumsily executed penny dreadful. When the brothers met again, Hugh tried to be constructive in his comments, but realized that John was sorely distressed by them. Apparently John had continued to cherish the belief that he might one day publish a book of his own and he went so far as to say that, if Hugh's judgement was sound, he had no reason to go on living. He added that he had half a mind to kill himself."

Dowling shook his head and sighed. "Emotion has no place in the law, Mr Holmes. I was saddened to hear that my partner could have responded so wildly. Once again it cast doubt on his judgment."

"As an experienced solicitor," Holmes pointed out, "you will appreciate that it is far from uncommon for words to be uttered in the heat of the moment which the speaker soon has cause to regret. I assume, however, that since Hugh Abergavenny mentioned his brother's remarks to you, he was of the opinion that they should be taken seriously."

"You are right, Mr Holmes. Hugh explained that over the years his brother had been prey to bouts of depression and that his chosen remedy, the bottle, invariably exacerbated the problem. He was especially concerned because John had been drinking before he arrived that evening and was evidently far from sober. Moreover, he made a specific threat, saying, 'If that's what you really think, I may as well chuck myself into the Thames and have done with it all.' With that, he turned on his heel and left. Hugh's anxiety was such that he followed John at a safe distance. While his brother called at a local tavern, he waited outside for upwards of an hour. Eventually, John was thrown out by the landlord and Hugh was able to call a cab and ensure that his brother was taken home safely."

"Did he arrive at the office as usual the next morning?"

"Yes, he had an appointment in court. Again, I noticed that he was rather bleary-eyed. He conceded that he had been to see his brother and had perhaps had more to drink that was strictly wise."

"Did you inform him that you had spoken to Hugh Abergavenny?"

"No. I should explain that Hugh said he felt that I was the one man left whose opinion John would respect. In view of their disagreement, he felt that he had little opportunity to exert any influence for the good, but he remained deeply troubled. He implored me not to disclose our conversation to John, but to keep a close eye on him, lest he might seek to do harm to himself."

"And did you?"

"To the best of my ability, Mr Holmes. Despite all that has occurred, I do retain a warm regard for the young man and I am appalled by the prospect that he may do himself harm."

Dowling closed his eyes for a few seconds before continuing. "The rest of that day passed without incident, but at the end of the next afternoon I had an even more perturbing visitation. One of the ushers from the Law Courts, a decent fellow by the name of Stewart, came to see me. He said that the previous evening he had been approaching Blackfriars Bridge when he saw a man with an unsteady gait trying to climb up on the parapet. As Stewart drew nearer, he recognized the figure as John Abergavenny. Alarmed, he called out John's name and asked what he thought he was doing. John spun round, seemed to recognize Stewart and then uttered a series of foul blasphemies before clambering down from the bridge. He broke into a run and, although the erratic course he took suggested to Stewart that he was far from sober, he managed to make good his escape. It was at that point that I decided to consult you, Mr Holmes. This morning my first task was to confront John and put to him the report I had received from Stewart. He denied it hotly. Even if I was prepared to believe that Bevington might have mistaken someone else for John, I could not accept that Stewart had made the same error. I was shocked that John should lie to me. For the first time we quarrelled openly and voices were raised."

Dowling paused and wiped a bead of perspiration from his forehead. It was clear that he was in a state of some distress. "It cannot go on like this, Mr Holmes. I see little alternative but to end our partnership. I cannot bear dishonesty and John has badly let me down. Yet if my act were to push him into carrying out his threat to commit suicide, I would find it hard indeed to live with myself. I welcome any guidance that you feel able to give."

"The explanation for your partner's conduct may be straight-forward. Drink can corrupt a man more quickly than any other vice." Holmes glanced briefly at me as he spoke and I guessed that his own occasional lapses were passing through his mind. "Yet I fancy that the problem may be more complex than it appears at first blush."

"Have you been able to form an opinion upon the basis of the information I have provided to you?"

Holmes shook his head. "With no disrespect to you, I sense that I have yet to be presented with a complete picture of events. I need to make further enquiries."

"By all means, Mr Holmes, but where would you wish to start?"

"Perhaps by speaking to your man Bevington, as well as to John Abergavenny himself."

Dowling flushed. "Certainly you may talk to my clerk. As for John, perhaps you would bear in mind the need to be circumspect. Although my intentions are entirely honourable, I would not wish him to think that I had recruited you to spy on him."

"You need have no fear. I shall be discreet. If it is convenient, perhaps Dr Watson and I can accompany you back to your office in the hope of determining where the truth lies."

A cab took us to Essex Street. Sombre skies contributed to the air of mourning which hung over London. Barely two weeks had passed since the death of the Queen and the sense of grief among her subjects was still as palpable as a dockland fog. Our journey passed almost wholly in silence. I realized that Holmes was turning over in his mind the facts that the solicitor had placed before him and seeking to draw the different threads into a pattern that satisfied him. For my own part, the conclusion seemed obvious enough. John Abergavenny was suffering a mental breakdown. It was a case for a doctor rather than a detective.

The firm of Dowling and Company occupied the ground floor of a building close to the Embankment end of the street and after we had spent a couple of minutes warming ourselves in front of the fire in Dowling's room, the solicitor returned accompanied by his clerk.

"Please would you repeat to the two gentlemen here the facts that you reported to me the day before last concerning your encounter with Mr Abergavenny in Lincoln's Inn."

"But Mr Dowling –"

"Bevington," the solicitor said gently. "You and I have known each other for a long time, have we not? I realize that you are unwilling to be a teller of tales and your attitude does you credit.

I simply ask you to bear with me. I will leave you with these two gentlemen for a few minutes and I know that you will be as frank with them as you were with me."

Thus entreated, Bevington gave us his account. It did not differ in any material respect from Dowling's summation. The old clerk was stooped and short-sighted, but after listening to him for a few minutes, I was convinced that the report he had made to his principal was tainted neither by malice nor by a mistake as to the identity of the man who had been carousing with the street-walker. Bevington was, I felt sure, not blessed with an imagination vivid enough to have enabled him to embellish his tale. He was cautious and exact and he would have made a compelling witness at any trial. After he left us, I said as much to Holmes.

"I agree. Now we must – holloa!" The door was flung open and a man burst in. He was perhaps thirty years of age, middle-sized with a beaky nose, thick curly fair hair and a moustache. There were dark rings beneath his eyes and his cheeks were flushed with temper.

"Mr Sherlock Holmes?"

My friend bowed. "Allow me to introduce Dr Watson," he said in his suavest tone. "And you, I presume, are Mr John Abergavenny?"

"I am familiar with your legendary powers of deduction," the lawyer said tersely, "and in other circumstances I might be glad to pick your brains. What is wholly unclear to me today, however, is why you have come to these offices to listen to tittle-tattle from a member of staff who is old enough to know better. I can only assume that for reasons wholly unknown to me, your express purpose is to destroy my reputation so as to enable Mr Dowling to expel me from this practice."

"I can assure you that I have no reason whatsoever to believe that my client's motives are in any wise dishonourable. He simply seeks the truth."

"So you admit that Dowling is your client! He has engaged your services behind my back to spy on me! By God, sir, this is intolerable!"

He took a step forward and for a moment I believed that he was about to strike my friend. I tensed and so did Holmes, but then Abergavenny paused and uttered a hollow laugh.

"You will have to forgive me, gentlemen. For a moment I was about to cast legal caution to the wind." He gave Holmes a hard look. "I remembered in the nick of time my professional training – and also the fact that you once fought with McMurdo. Besides, fisticuffs will solve nothing. I would simply say this to you – a few errors at work, even an instance of professional negligence, none of these matters justifies the campaign of persecution to which I am currently being subjected. There is nothing worthy of your talents here, Mr Holmes. Good day, gentlemen."

With that, he turned on his heel and left the room. For a little while the two of us sat there in silence, Holmes stroking his jaw reflectively.

"What do you make of that?" I demanded at last.

"I recognize the symptoms of over-work," my friend said softly. "Curiouser and curiouser."

The door opened again, this time to admit Matthew Dowling. His face had crumpled in dismay.

"Mr Holmes, I think I may have achieved the worst of all worlds. John Abergavenny has just given me verbal notice to terminate our partnership with immediate effect. He said that since I preferred to believe gossip to his word of honour, the bond of trust between us had been irreparably damaged. He said he would finish the relationship between us himself rather than wait for me to do so on spurious grounds."

"Did he tell you where he was bound?"

Dowling shook his head. "He has rooms above the tailor in Lamb's Conduit Street, but I suspect that his first recourse may be to a den of infamy. I dread the thought that he might take some precipitate action at a time when he is clearly very disturbed."

He took a deep breath and made a visible effort to collect his thoughts. "Thank you for your time, Mr Holmes. This unfortunate outcome is not your fault. You will, of course, let me have a note of your fees in early course."

"You regard my investigation as concluded?"

"With respect, I do not see what else you can do."

"Does it not intrigue you that, for no obvious reason, your partner's behaviour should have changed so suddenly and in such a deleterious fashion?"

"It dismays me, but I do not know what else I can do. I cannot see rhyme or reason in it."

"Precisely. I still have the distinct impression that in this case, all the cards are yet to be put on the table. I would like to speak to the court usher you mentioned and also to your partner's brother, Hugh. Would you be willing to write me a note of introduction to the man Stewart?"

Dowling readily agreed to Holmes's request, although he was plainly unconvinced that any good would come of further enquiries. We walked directly to the Law Courts in the Strand

and were able after a short wait to see Stewart and hear about his encounter with Abergavenny at Blackfriars Bridge.

"Do you believe he meant to kill himself?" Holmes asked bluntly.

"I hesitate to say as much," said Stewart with care. He was a desiccated fellow, as dry and dusty as a tome of Blackstone's law reports. "I can add nothing more to the conversation I had with Mr Dowling, save to make the obvious point that I would not have troubled him with an account of the incident had I not thought it a matter which needed to be drawn to his attention as senior partner of an eminently respectable firm."

We could glean nothing more from him and made our way at once to the Temple. Holmes had expressed surprise when Dowling said we might be likeliest to find Hugh Abergavenny at his old chambers in King's Bench Walk. "I understood that he had long since ceased to practise at the Bar?"

"That is correct, but he told me he has continued to haunt the place where he first made his reputation. 'The legal world is a source of the best stories in the world,' he said, 'If one knows where to look. I found many of my neatest plots within the four walls of my old pupil master's room'."

The clerk's office was awash with papers and pink ribbon and I wondered how many of the briefs to counsel spread casually upon the floor contained material suitable for adaptation into tales of villainy and derring-do. Dowling's guess proved to be accurate and within a couple of minutes a boy was directing us in to a small room at the back of the building.

Hugh Abergavenny had the same beaky nose and build as his brother, but his hair was darker and thinning. I estimated that he was perhaps ten years older than John. He stood up behind a small roll-top desk on which lay a manuscript and came forward to greet us. It was clear from his expression that he was startled by our arrival, but there was no denying the handsomeness of his greeting as he stretched out his hand in welcome. I noticed that his cuffs were frayed, confirmation if it were needed that these days he regarded himself as a writer rather than an advocate.

"Mr Sherlock Holmes! This is a rare honour. I have long devoured your exploits and admired the facility with which Dr Watson here writes them up for publication."

"With some embellishment, I should make clear," Holmes said amiably. "I cannot deny that at times my colleague exaggerates my achievements in the interest of telling a good story."

"As a novelist, I cannot imagine a worthier aim or a better fault."

Holmes indicated the papers on the desk. "Your current work-in-progress?"

Abergavenny hesitated for a moment before a slow grin spread across his face. "Your legendary powers do not let you down, Mr Holmes. Yes, this is my latest novel. I put it into the hands of my literary agent this very week."

"Splendid!" I cried. "I am one of your most faithful readers and it is far too long since you published *The Hangman's Cellar*. I must confess that I have been hoping that your next book would continue the adventures of your character Alec Salisbury."

The author smiled but shook his head. "I am afraid that Alec was getting a little long in the tooth, which is why I felt the need to try something different. You are too polite to say that my last novel did not set your pulse racing, but the critics were not so diplomatic. The reason for my silence since then is that I have been endeavouring to come up with a story that would keep them, as well as my publishers, happy. It is difficult for a man to judge his own work, but I think I can promise that neither they nor you will be disappointed by *The Accusing Skeleton*."

"I am delighted to hear it," I said, unable to resist a covetous look at the sheets on the desk. "May I say also, that if by some chance you were willing to let me have an early opportunity to satisfy my hunger for your work, I would be forever in your debt."

He laughed rather nervously and said, "Well, like most authors I am rather superstitious and it is not my normal practice to show my work to third parties until it has finally been accepted for publication. Your words are very kind, though, and I am not immune to compliments, especially from such a quarter. I would be willing to loan you the first chapter for, say, twenty four hours if you wish to see whether it whets your appetite."

"You are most generous!" I said as he gathered a dozen sheets together and passed them to me.

"It is a pleasure to have such a celebrated reader. I await your verdict with bated breath. In the meantime, gentlemen, to what do I owe the privilege of this visit?"

As Holmes outlined the sequence of events that had brought us to the chambers, the smile faded from Hugh Abergavenny's face. He kept shaking his head and when he heard of the incident on Blackfriars Bridge he muttered, "Oh no." By the time Holmes had recounted our brief meeting with John at the office in Essex Street, it was clear that Hugh was deeply moved.

"It is as I feared," he said. "His mental state is severely disturbed."

"I wondered," I said, "about the part that drink may have played in your brother's apparent breakdown."

"You are an acute observer, Dr Watson. I have often suspected that modesty has prevented you from revealing in your narratives the extent to which you have yourself developed a detective's flair." Hugh cast his eyes down for a moment. "John has always had a weakness for alcohol. It can change him into a different person, aggressive, irrational and despondent by turns. His appalling behaviour whilst drunk was the main cause of the estrangement between us, a breach which I have lately been striving to repair. I had heard good reports of him in recent times and they led me to hope that he had turned the corner after accepting the offer of partnership in a sound practice. Sadly, it seems that my optimism was premature."

He shook his head. "Gentlemen, on any other day I would value the chance to spend a few hours in your company and perhaps to persuade you to discuss some of your unrecorded cases. Who knows? Possibly I could seek to dress them up in the guise of fiction. However, my immediate priorities lie elsewhere. I must try to find John, even if it means trawling through every drinking den in London, and see if I can make him see reason. I owe our late mother nothing less. When I have more news, I shall let Maxwell Dowling and your good selves know. Perhaps I could call at Baker Street tomorrow and see for myself the famous consulting room."

"You will be most welcome," I said warmly. "By then, I shall have read your manuscript. It really is good of you to afford me the opportunity in advance of publication."

Holmes was quiet throughout our journey home and once we had arrived, he sank into a meditative trance. I sensed that he was disturbed by the day's events, but knew better than to trouble him with questions or idle conversation. After dealing with certain correspondence, I decided to amuse myself by turning to the first chapter of Hugh Abergavenny's novel and devoured it within minutes.

"By Jove, Holmes, this is splendid stuff!" Such was my pleasure in the tale that I could not help disturbing his reverie. "It is almost unbearable that I cannot continue reading. The description of the hero's visit to a warehouse in the East End and what he finds there – but no, I must not spoil the story. You must read it for yourself."

Holmes opened his eyes and said languidly, "I am afraid I do not count myself amongst Hugh Abergavenny's devoted admirers. His early books were lively enough, but compared to Collins or even

Conway, he seems to favour contrivance ahead of the creation of plausible characters. The later stories are so dependent upon coincidence as to make it impossible to suspend disbelief. As for his hero, I fear that Alec Salisbury makes even Lecoq appear to be a master detective."

"You need not worry," I said, rather stiffly. "As we were told, Salisbury does not appear in this book. It really is rather fine, Holmes. Don't allow your prejudices to cause you to ignore it."

"You are the one who should have taken up the law," my friend remarked. "You are a persuasive spokesman. Very well, pass me the chapter."

He read the first pages of the book in silence and then, before I could ask his reaction, lapsed back into his dream-like state. Suddenly he sat bolt upright.

"I have been obtuse, Watson! Quick, we need to call on the younger Abergavenny at once!"

"But Holmes, what can we hope to achieve that his brother cannot?"

His strong-set features were twisted with pain. "We must strive to prevent a terrible crime. Yet I fear that already we may be too late."

"I don't understand," I said. "What crime are you talking about?"

"The murder", he said bitterly, "of John Abergavenny."

We hailed a cab and asked the driver to take us to the tailor's shop in Lamb's Conduit Street. When we reached our destination, I saw that a small crowd of onlookers had gathered outside the door beside the entrance to the shop. As we dismounted, two familiar figures emerged from the doorway.

"As I feared," my friend muttered under his breath. "We have been out-foxed."

"Mr Holmes!" cried Inspector Lestrade of Scotland Yard. "Were your ears burning? We have just been talking about you."

He indicated Matthew Dowling, who stood by his side. The old solicitor's face was grey and drawn.

"How is John Abergavenny?" demanded my friend.

"He was taken to hospital less than a quarter of an hour ago. He is in a coma."

"Not dead, then?" A flame of hope flickered in the eyes of Sherlock Holmes.

"Not expected to live, though," said Lestrade. "Seems that after marching out of his office, he came home and took a massive overdose of chloral hydrate. There's a half-empty jar of the stuff on his sideboard."

Holmes's shoulders sagged and so did mine. We both knew the power of the notorious sedative. Many East End publicans, to my knowledge, still kept a jar of chloral hydrate underneath their counter so that they could slip one or two knock-out drops into the drink of any customer who started spoiling for a fight. A highly effective remedy for trouble-makers, perhaps, but if administered in excess it was lethal.

"Apparently the fellow's been behaving oddly," Lestrade continued. "Mr Dowling here and his brother have explained to me his peculiar actions of the last few days."

"Hugh Abergavenny is present also?"

"Not now," said Dowling. "He arrived here a few minutes after I did. I had become increasingly concerned about John's safety after he left Essex Street. Finally I plucked up the courage to come out here. I wanted to talk to John, to make him see sense. I could see a light in John's room, but my knocking was not answered. Ultimately I prevailed upon the tailor, who lives in the back basement, to let me use the spare key. I rushed upstairs and found John in a dreadful state. It was clear that he was very sick. I immediately made arrangements for him to be taken to hospital and contacted the police. No sooner had I done that than Hugh turned up. He explained that he'd been searching for John, going round the drinking dens in which he might be found. When he had no luck, he came here. Like me, he was hoping that reason might prevail. The pity is that we were too late. I suggested to Hugh that his place was by John's side at the hospital, but we both fear that the omens are bleak."

Suddenly Holmes clapped a hand to his brow. "Lestrade, has anyone touched the jar of chloral hydrate?"

"Why, no," the detective replied. "There was no immediate need."

"Mr Dowling?"

"I did not, sir. The contents are plainly marked. I fear that John knew what he was doing."

"Not John," Holmes said harshly. "Hugh."

"I don't understand, Mr Holmes. What do you mean?"

"I mean," said my friend, "that your partner was poisoned by his brother. Quick, Lestrade, let us go upstairs. The question now is whether we can prove our case."

It was late the following night before my friend and I had the opportunity to talk at length about the case over a whisky-and-soda at Baker Street. By then John Abergavenny had died, a victim of cardiac and respiratory collapse, without having regained consciousness and his brother had been arrested on a charge of fratricide.

"My interest in the case", Holmes said, "was aroused by the differences in the way John Abergavenny reacted when his senior partner put complaints to him. He quickly acknowledged his acts of carelessness. It was plain that he was over-tiring himself. That might have been because he went out drinking every night, but it seemed entirely out of character for him to do so. Besides, there was a possible alternative explanation. Perhaps he was continuing to work on his fiction late into the night after a full day's legal work, keeping it a secret because of Dowling's disapproval and a natural lack of confidence in his own literary talents. I also entertained a degree of scepticism about the incidents reported by both Bevington and Stewart – which John vehemently denied. Yet why should the witnesses lie? The contradictions intrigued me. When I mentioned the case to you originally, I drew an analogy with Stevenson's romance and from the outset the business seemed to me to possess certain of the features of a cheap thriller. An apparently respectable man leading a double life, dipping his toe in the world of vice. It is a perennial theme."

He took another sip from his glass. "I had only to meet Bevington and Stewart to be sure that they were not lying. On the contrary, they seemed unimpeachable. So – either John was behaving as wildly as they described, or someone was impersonating him. I noticed at once that Hugh resembled him in build and features. True, he did not have a moustache, was balding and his hair was different in colour. But any actor worth his salt could easily change all that."

"But Hugh was a writer, not an actor," I objected.

"He had been a court advocate," Holmes said impatiently, "and few men are better suited to playing a part than barristers. They have the advantage of professional training coupled with constant practice. I once said to you, Watson, that when a doctor goes wrong he is the first of criminals, but I should have added the rider that a practitioner of the law comes a close second." He gave a grim chuckle. "I hope I was not unduly prejudiced because I had found his writing slick and meretricious. It puzzled me that, as little better than a hack wordsmith, he had not published a book for some time. With that in mind, I regarded his explanation for haunting his old chambers as less than convincing."

I raised my eyebrows. "Surely he was wise to be seeking out fresh stories?"

"If that was so, why had he been silent for so long? I wondered if he was suffering from simple inability to write. It is a curse which, I believe, afflicts many authors. I had rather the impression of a man living on past glories, a pathetic shadow of his former self, hanging around the legal world where he had scored his early successes. A sad man, too, no doubt overtaken by younger men who had not been distracted from their careers by the lure of appearing in print. Did you notice that his cuffs were threadbare?"

"I thought it a Bohemian touch, appropriate enough in a man who had given up his wig for the pen."

"That is no doubt what he hoped people would think," Holmes said dismissively. "He seemed alarmed to see us, which further fuelled my suspicions. Yet he was no fool. How careful he was to portray himself as a man on the brink of renewed success. I could not guess why he would wish harm to his brother – who had, according to Dowling, always envied him. I was concerned for John, but failed to realize that his life was in imminent danger. As soon as he knew of my involvement, Hugh decided that the time had come to perfect his plan."

"The cold-blooded devil," I said with a shiver.

"The legal world is small and enclosed. He must have known Bevington and Stewart or known of them and he successfully used them as his dupes. He was intent on creating the impression that his brother was on the downward slope and contemplating suicide. His own visit to Dowling ensured that the calumny seemed credible. Yet in his haste he made a crucial mistake. After he left us, he called on his brother – who had returned home to cool his temper after quitting Essex Street – and pretended to sympathize with him about Dowling's behaviour in calling on my assistance. They had a drink together. When a chance came, he slipped a murderous dose of chloral hydrate into his brother's glass. But in his haste to be away before the poison took effect he forgot to wipe the jar containing the sedative."

"Leaving his fingerprints on it, then!" I exclaimed.

"As Lestrade has now established, I am glad to say. Do you recall that as recently as last December, Lord Belper's committee of enquiry recommended that Edward Henry's method of identification of criminals by fingerprints be adopted in place of anthropometry and dactylography? The details are in my scrapbook, if you care to consult it. The decision is an excellent one, by the way. Henry is a sound man and he has been kind enough to acknowledge the assistance of a monograph of my own in compiling his textbook for police on the science of fingerprinting. Hugh Abergavenny was back in King's Bench Walk before it occurred to him that it would be prudent to clean the jar. Thankfully, by the time he returned to his brother's rooms, Dowling was on the scene and Hugh had no opportunity to make good his mistake without arousing suspicion."

"How did you hit upon the truth?"

"By reading the manuscript. The first chapter of the new book was written too beautifully and boasts a plot too original for it to have been the work of a man who could never aspire beyond the pot-boiler. I realized at once that Hugh Abergavenny had lied when he claimed it as his own. It must have been the story which his brother had lent him for an opinion. Hugh told John it was worthless at the same time as he was covertly transcribing it in his own hand."

Holmes sighed. "I shall always regret my inability to save John Abergavenny, Watson. There is only the crumb of consolation that his novel will serve as a fitting memorial to him."

"It is a kind of justice," I said.

My friend's sallow cheeks flushed. "And I sincerely trust that Hugh Abergavenny, too, will receive his just deserts when his case comes to trial.

It was a sentiment that I echoed, but the murderer contrived to cheat the law. Five days before his trial, Hugh Abergavenny hanged himself in his prison cell. It emerged that he, rather than his younger brother, had a long history of nervous trouble and he had once before attempted to take his own life, when the last book he managed to complete was rejected by every publisher in London.

THE LEGACY OF RACHEL HOWELLS

Michael Doyle

PREFACE

Another very singular case came within my own observation. It was sent to me by an eminent London publisher. This gentleman had in his employment a head of department whose name we shall take as Musgrave. He was a hard-working person, with no special feature in his character. Mr Musgrave died, and several years after his death a letter was received addressed to him, in the care of his employers. It bore the postmark of a tourist resort in the west of Canada, and had the note "Confl films" upon the outside of the envelope, with the words "Report Sy" in one corner.

The publishers naturally opened the envelope as they had no note of the dead man's relatives. Inside were two blank sheets of paper. The letter, I may add, was registered. The publisher, being unable to make anything of this, sent it on to me, and I submitted the blank sheets to every possible chemical and heat test, with no result whatever. Beyond the fact that the writing appeared to be that of a woman there is nothing to add to this account. The matter was, and remains, an insoluble mystery. How the correspondent could have something so secret to say to Mr Musgrave and yet not be aware that this person had been dead for several years is very hard to understand – or why blank sheets should be so carefully registered through the mail. I may add that I did not trust the sheets to my own chemical tests, but had the best expert advice without getting any result. Considered as a case it was a failure – and a very tantalizing one.

Sir Arthur Conan Doyle
"Some personalia about Sherlock Holmes"
The Strand Magazine, December, 1917

Over the years in which I have been associated with Mr Sherlock Holmes many players have appeared on our little stage at 221b Baker Street. The appearance of each was, of course, closely scrutinized by Mr Holmes and myself but once the spotlight has shifted these actors have all too often exited through the wings, never to return. I have often wondered what has become of these clients, and those associated with them in the cases which I have recorded – and in the hundreds which still await the attention of a competent biographer.

To this pattern there have been several exceptions. Professor Moriarty is a constant presence: his influence, if not the man himself, is likely to continue; the dark side of human nature will, it seems, be always with us. His colleague Colonel Moran, spectator of the Reichenbach drama, has appeared more than once on our stage as have Inspector Lestrade, his colleagues at Scotland Yard, our dear Mrs Hudson, our page boy Billy, my wife Mary and some few others. Of the majority however we have heard no more. For Sherlock Holmes, whose interest wanes rapidly with the solving of each problem, this is of little moment: friendship, like any other emotion, is to him distractive and to be avoided. To me however the passing of these ephemerae is a matter of regret; I am glad therefore for this opportunity to lay before the public a case which returns to the limelight a woman whose intelligence – and avarice – Sherlock Holmes had grievously underrated when he first had occasion to be involved in an investigation in which her wicked hand had played a part. This intriguing affair has not yet been brought to a conclusion. Tracing the final threads, and the identification and arrest of the murderer, whom neither Holmes nor I have yet met face to face, appear likely to provide a bonus: a visit to the Americas, and to the splendid young country of Canada. I have every hope of being accompanied, if the activities of the London criminal permit, by Sherlock Holmes himself.

With or without Holmes – for I make bold to say that the final steps can, if necessary, be entrusted to me – this excursion will bring home guilt to the person in question; until then however it cannot be positively asserted. The reader will forgive me if I obey the dictates of discretion by declining to specify the exact date on which these anticipatory words are penned.

It was in the spring of 1901, while Holmes and I were investigating the disappearance of the Priory School student and the murder of his bicycling German master in the north of England, that we learned of the death of Reginald Musgrave. The newspaper's account was terse: Sir Reginald, member of parliament for Hurlstone, West Sussex and squire of its Manor House and estates, had been tragically killed in a shooting mishap on Monday May 13th. A verdict of accidental death had been returned at the inquest; a memorial service was to be held at the village church and the estates were to be maintained by the deceased's next of kin, his cousin Nathaniel Musgrave.

"Is it not an irony," said Holmes, his distress obvious as we surveyed this brief announcement, "that we learn of the death of Musgrave, who inherited his estates from his father but died a bachelor, just as we make clear that the Holdernesse family has one son too many? The sibling Saltire is lured away, like young Copperfield to Dover, on the promise of a maternal affection which is not to be found at home, by a treacherous elder brother whose only aim is his destruction. Which is the better, to father two sons and such a misery or, like Musgrave, none at all?"

"That must be decided by each man for himself, Holmes. Opportunity travels always with risk as its companion."

"Just so, Watson, but I regret that Musgrave's sudden end has denied him the chance of an heir," replied Holmes thoughtfully "and also the pleasure of taking his own son through the family ritual. And what means 'shooting mishap'? One would expect from the press less reticence and more clarity. The coroner however has evidently found nothing amiss so, unless the fates decree that I am consulted in the matter, nothing appears to be done save to bid a silent *ave atque vale* to my erstwhile university friend and early client."

The fates were so to decree but, perversely, they stayed their hand for nearly two months; it was then their sister Atropos they sent. She came to us in the thin disguise of our landlady, bearing the morning's tray of correspondence and requests for appointments, medical for me, criminal and otherwise for Holmes. Her rap at our door, thus effected, was so gentle, and her tap so faint, that we were unaware she had entered our chamber. She gave no warning of the remarkable train of events, of the brazen attempt at an audacious new crime – and delayed retribution for a hideous old one – that would ensue; nor was I prepared for the demonstrations of my friend's amazing powers of observation, deduction and inference, of the quick workings of his intellect and of his astonishing ability to create and test hypotheses until the truth was revealed as clearly as are the pure golden tailings and nuggets in the pan of the prospector.

Thus it was that ten days ago Sherlock Holmes and I were visited by the eminent London publisher Garrison Bolt. He wished, he had said in his letter requesting the appointment, to consult Holmes about a matter arising from his business. On the grounds that this might involve my role of chronicler Holmes had asked me, despite a period of considerable activity in my medical practice, to be present. The shrewd, scholarly face of the bookman was known to us, although we had not met for some years. It was with the house of Bolt that I had negotiated publication of my account of one of our earliest cases. I remembered very well the hard bargain he had struck and admit to harbouring some resentment as a result, a resentment heightened by the contrasting generosity of the public, whose approval of my later efforts stood in such sharp contrast to Mr Bolt's parsimony. Despite the numerous reprints of my work, from which Mr Bolt's firm reaped a considerable income, nary a penny was paid over the modest sum agreed, a circumstance which directed me to other, more generous publishers. But a bargain is a bargain and neither Holmes nor I had ever allowed ourselves the indulgence of bearing any grudge or ill will towards Garrison Bolt save that, on the occasions when he had requested my contribution of short introductions to later editions, my dislike of his business ethics always caused me to respond with a positive "No!". We greeted him cordially as he entered our Baker Street rooms and seated him as comfortably as our quarters permitted.

"I am delighted to see you again, Mr Holmes – Dr Watson," said our visitor, settling himself into an armchair.

"And we, you", replied my friend cheerfully. "It was only last evening that we were speculating on the effects, beneficial or otherwise, of the new *Literary Supplement* on the fortunes of publishing houses such as yours, and on those who, like Dr Watson, supply the grist for your mills."

"It certainly introduces a new element into the novelist's equation," commented Garrison Bolt, with a wry smile, "the effects of which will be felt throughout the world. Indeed, there is an international aspect to this singular and tantalizing matter that has come up in our offices, which I believe will be of interest to you." Holmes and I leaned forward. Both paused, as though seeking the words that would best secure our attention. "It appears to me that the matter already does relate to you!"

"How so?" asked Holmes, laying aside his pipe.

"I have had in my employment, head of one of our departments, a Mr Musgrave," the publisher explained. "Some years ago he died."

"How?"

"Of natural causes."

"What type of man was he?"

"A hard-working person, of a religious bent but with no other special feature in his character. I have had no occasion to think of Newman Musgrave since – until a month ago, when we received a letter addressed to him care of ourselves. I have it with me now." Garrison Bolt handed an envelope to Sherlock Holmes. It appeared thus:

"As you see, the letter has been addressed not to Newman, but to Norman, Musgrave. We have had no other Musgraves in our employ so I feel sure that the letter was intended for Newman. It has been registered, carries Canadian postage and has the note 'CONFL FILMS' upon the outside of the envelope, with the words 'REPORT SY' in the top left hand corner, in the position where the sender's return address is usually given. No such return address, or any indication as to the sender, however, appears. The postman, after some demur, agreed to leave the envelope with us.

"As we had no note of the dead man's relatives we naturally opened it. To our surprise we found inside only these two blank pieces of paper." He handed these to me. I passed them to Holmes, who glanced at them cursorily and returned them to our visitor.

"Thinking that the sheets might have some connection with 'films', or perhaps 'confidential films'", he continued, "and not trusting them only to my own examinations, I employed the best expert advice I could secure by submitting them to Scotland Yard for analysis by every possible chemical and heat test – all without any result."

"Tut, man," cried Holmes, glancing at the envelope. "You surely received the letter at least a month ago. Have you not been tardy in submitting it for testing?"

"I fear so, sir. I had not read any emergency into the matter. It was only when the police laboratory failed me that I realized that if the mystery was to be solved more specialized advice was needed. It was then that I thought of you, Mr Holmes. Like all

Londoners I am aware of your extraordinary ability to solve the insoluble, and to bring light into darkness. You will recall that our house had the pleasure of publishing one of Dr Watson's first accounts of a *tour de force* in your astonishing career. I was struck, too, by the postmark 'Baskerville' on the envelope, mindful that the name is associated with another of your recent adventures. The name of my employee, Musgrave, of course is to be found in yet another of Dr Watson's accounts."

I interjected, "How the correspondent could have something so secret to say to Mr Musgrave and yet not be aware that this person had been dead for several years is very hard to understand – or why blank sheets should be so carefully registered through the mail."

"Quite so. To a man like me the matter is an insoluble mystery." He turned to Holmes. "Well, Mr Holmes, you are not a man like me, and there is my hope! May I leave this conundrum in your hands? I cannot see that even you will be able to find the key to it, and the matter may perhaps be of no importance but I, for one, find it intriguing."

"And so do I!" responded Holmes cheerfully. "I will turn my mind to it – aided, I hope, by Dr Watson. The part of suppliant biographer is not his only role in this agency. You will hear from us as soon as we are ready to report."

Our visitor thanked us and left. Holmes picked up the envelope and its enigmatic contents and examined them with his lens.

"There are points about this little problem which promise to make it unique – but an insoluble mystery? What think you, doctor?"

"I would not admit as much without first making some effort," I replied. "We have the Baskerville postmark and the reference to Musgrave to go on. Of Musgrave I know only what you told me years ago; as to Baskerville I suggest we contact Sir Henry without delay. He spent some years in Canada before he inherited his Dartmoor estate; he may well be able to throw some light on this letter and its origins."

"Right, Watson! We do have these two starting points. And we may have more! Let us leave Baskerville and Musgrave for the moment, and first see what the power of reason, applied to this billet-doux, will reveal. You opined, and Garrison Bolt agreed with you, that it is very hard to understand how the correspondent could have something so secret to say to Mr Musgrave and yet not be aware that he had been dead for several years. With respect, you make two assumptions – you advance two hypotheses – which enjoy the support of no data. Why should we assume that the correspondent is ignorant of Newman Musgrave's death? We know no such thing. It is quite possible that he is well aware of it but has had some good reason for not writing until now. Some recent event may have removed the impediment. I do not say that this is probable; only that it is possible. As to your first surmise, there is no certainty that this transmission was intended for Newman Musgrave at all. Indeed, as I turn my mind to it, the less likely does that premise become.

"Second, you find it hard to understand why blank sheets should be carefully registered through the mail. There you are certainly right. Such a mailing is absurd. If the message – for a message it must be – is not contained inside the envelope it follows that it must be found upon it."

"On the envelope itself?"

"Yes!"

"That is logical," I admitted, after a moment's consideration, "but why do you question that the message, however it is constituted, is intended for Newman Musgrave? If not for him, for whom?"

"For us!"

"For you and me?"

"Yes! Consider. The letter was brought to us by Garrison Bolt, an established publisher with whom you have done business, and are known to have done business. His name and address appear in every copy of your original work. As my brother Mycroft has remarked, your tales are to be found everywhere. It should not be surprising if the sender of this message from Canada has access to them; in fact, she clearly has."

"She?"

"The writing is in a woman's hand. The emotional characteristics – the swirling M's and E's, and the ambivalent C's in particular – are unmistakable. She, yes, she, is clearly aware of the reputation our agency enjoys. What more natural than that the publisher should refer her enigmatic communiqué to us? Bolt, provided he gave her letter his attention, must surely equate 'Baskerville' and 'Musgrave' to 'Sherlock Holmes'. She could be sure that he would. Indeed, to make certain of his attention she has sent it by registered post."

"You mean that she has deliberately addressed the envelope to a man she knows does not exist?" I asked.

"So I read it. This message is, and always was, intended for us, Watson!"

"Astonishing!" said I. "But what of the Baskerville postmark? Of the Canadian stamps? And what of my suggestion that we contact Sir Henry? Does it have merit?"

"I fear not," said Holmes.

"May I ask why?"

"Well, your suggestion is that he may be able to throw some light on the matter. But what light can he possibly throw?" Holmes paused. He gazed first at the ceiling, as though in concentration, then at me, in a manner reminiscent of my old school master when explaining a complicated matter to his class. "As you say, he once lived in Canada. So do some five million others. And how could this postmark possibly connect with him? Sir Henry's post office is not at Baskerville, but at Grimpen. You and I have used it frequently, as our Canadian reader of your tales is clearly aware. The seat of the Baskerville family for centuries has been in Devon, not Canada. There is, to the best of my knowledge, no town or village of Baskerville in Canada. No! Sir Henry is not involved here."

"But if the postmark is not genuine," said I, "it must be bogus!"

"Your reasoning does you credit, doctor," said Holmes with an encouraging chuckle. "You are an island of common sense in a bewildering sea of uncertainty!" He took up his lens and examined the postmark with intensity. "See here!" he exclaimed. "See that S in 'Baskerville'? What do you make of it?" He handed the lens to me.

"It is smudged and indistinct," said I. "It appears to have been tampered with."

"Exactly! The letter has been substituted for another. It appears first to have been the letter R."

I peered through the lens again. "Yes – R," I agreed.

"So we have not *Baskerville* but *Barkerville.* Is there such a place? Make a long arm for our Gazetteer if you please, Watson. Thank you. Now ... Baskerville. No. Nothing. But here! 'Barkerville'," he read, "and in the west of Canada too! 'In British Columbia; part of the Cariboo Gold Fields; the site of a major gold strike in 1862, second in importance only to the recent Yukon strike of 1898; a colourful frontier gambling town; an attraction to visitors; a tourist resort.'"

"But what could be the sender's object in tampering with the postmark?"

"To ensure that the envelope, with its striking allusions to Baskerville and Musgrave, would be brought to me. In this she has succeeded. Our correspondent in British Columbia has gone to extraordinary lengths to ensure delivery of this message to us, Watson."

"But why did she not communicate with you directly?" I asked.

"Why not, indeed!" Holmes leaned back in his chair, placed his forefingers together, with Garrison Bolt's envelope between them, closed his eyes and continued. "Two minds are better than one, Watson. Let us reconsider what we have deduced: This envelope is a message. Its contents are irrelevant. Its sender is an intelligent, imaginative, resourceful and determined woman. She lives in, or within travelling distance of, Barkerville in the west of Canada. She has deliberately sent it to a man she knows to be dead. She has sent it in such a manner, by registering it, by misspelling the dead man's first name as Norman, and by altering the postmark to 'Baskerville' to ensure – nay, to guarantee – that it reaches the hands not of the defunct addressee but of ourselves. She has deferred posting the letter until the occurrence of some event which has removed the reason for her not doing so before."

"Excellent!" said I.

"Have we reached the limits of what reason and energy can supply?"

"I fear that we have."

"Surely you do us an injustice. We have further avenues to explore. Do you provide the energy, Watson, and I the reason. Be good enough to make inquiries through the post office as to the origin, and if possible the sender, of this envelope. Records are kept of registered post. Now that we have ascertained the true location from which the letter was dispatched the task may not be an impossible one, especially since the postmaster who registered this envelope in Barkerville is left-handed, and therefore identifiable."

"Holmes!"

"Well, surely it is self-evident?"

"How?"

"Observe the two circular cancellation stamps. They are produced by a metal strike which, grasped by a right-handed man, naturally produces an imprint tilted to the left. These are tilted to the right."

"But is this single instance conclusive?"

"Corroboration is afforded by the registration stamp. The R, unlike the cancellations, which are upside down, is not inverted. The envelope faced the sender, not the postmaster, when handed over the counter and was turned round for the act of registration. You observe that the R stamp also tilts to the right. Cancellation and registration were therefore both effected by a left hander, and both by the postmaster. *Voilà tout!* The steps in this reasoning are so elementary as to be facile, but the induction itself may prove of the utmost importance. Why? Because this postmaster has faced the letter's sender across his counter. He may, even now, be able to recall and identity her."

"Holmes," I ejaculated, after a moment, "this is yet another of those occasions when I feel an overwhelming urge to rise in embarrassment and to knock my head against our ceiling in sheer frustration!"

"Worry not, friend Watson," replied Holmes with a smile. "Levity is not your forté! Do you gravitate to the post office and let us see what the high principles of deduction, allied to some common sense research, can produce."

"I will do so at once," I replied, laughing, as I turned to the door.

"Thank you. You are as a crutch to a cripple. Please, my dear fellow, indulge my infirmity by handing me my briar pipe and some shag tobacco before you go. This little problem requires thought."

I was able to report to Holmes within three hours. One of the staff of the Baker Street Post Office, an avid admirer of Holmes and his methods, gladly and enthusiastically threw himself into the task of helping us. Despite approaching closing time he transmitted without a moment's delay over the spans of the Atlantic Ocean and the vastness of the Americas to far away Barkerville. The eight hours time difference he explained ensured that our message would arrive at the Barkerville office as it opened its doors for the day's work. He even promised to wait for the reply. The Canadians, despite the unusual nature of our urgently-worded enquiry, checked their records immediately; the letter to Musgrave had indeed been dispatched from their office and, they reported, duly appeared in their ledger in its proper place. The entry however, they were embarrassed to inform us, had been tampered with: the name and address of the sender had been obliterated. Their postmaster, William Topping – and yes, they confirmed, he was left-handed and he was on duty that day – denied any knowledge of the erasure or of the sender of the message. It had been done cunningly and deliberately, he said, by some mischiefmaker, taking advantage of the distractions of a busy office. There was no question of the ledger's having been out of the station's possession – a serious breach of regulations – but it was not unusual for it to lie open on the counter. Neither Mr Topping nor his aides could recall any particular registrants, female or otherwise, on that day. The illicit erasure, they regretted, left them with no means of identifying or locating the sender. As I returned to Baker Street I reflected that Holmes was faced with an adversary armed with more than mere cunning; that an astute mind of high calibre was challenging, perhaps even threatening, us from the Americas.

"She must have tampered with the postmark at the same time, Holmes," said I, as I reported this unwelcome news. "She has taken as much care in falsifying it as in concealing her identity."

"Indeed! And she still leaves us with two puzzles: *why* does she wish to communicate with me, and *what* is her message?"

"The first I can fathom," said I. "From your account of the adventure of the Musgrave Ritual it seems that these Musgraves are not an over-bright lot. It seems clear that she intends to communicate with the family by an intermediary who is familiar with the events that arose from the ritual and intelligent enough to divine her message's true import. You qualify on both counts, Holmes."

"You may be right, Watson. I believe that you are right. It follows then that this mysterious sender knows the Musgrave family well. We progress! It now remains only to read her message." He picked up the envelope and studied it again with minutest attention. Laying down his pipe he picked up a pencil and opened his notebook.

"Bah!" He exclaimed. "Trysor, the Welsh name for treasure, can be extracted from 'Report Sy', but what of that? We have no indication whatsoever that the message's sender is a Welsh woman, or that treasure is involved. To the contrary, our correspondent is evidently a resident of Canada and our bullion mere blank paper. I get nowhere. What make you of REPORT SY', Watson?"

"SY is an identifying code perhaps?" I suggested. "Or an abbreviation for Sydney, in Australia? Or for 'symbol'?"

Holmes deliberated. "All three are possibilities. Let us consider a fourth: SYSTEM. 'Confidential Films' or if there has been a slip of the writer's pen, 'Confidential Files', implies some form of orderly arrangement. 'SYSTEM' would answer to both. Dare we take it as a working hypothesis and see where it leads us?"

"You are probably correct," I responded. "The word does suggest itself."

"Very well. REPORT SYSTEM it is, until further data proves otherwise. Now, what of 'CONFL FILMS'?"

It was my turn to scribble. "COFFINS!" I cried. "The word 'coffins' can be extracted from it, Holmes!"

"Good for you, Watson! 'Coffins' sounds promising; the word has a pleasing ring. That leaves us with MLL. It is evidently a Roman date. M of course is 1000 and L is 50. 1000 AD plus two 50s." He thought for a moment. "But the Romans never wrote LL to express 100. Its symbol was C. So our second L is suspect.

It is ambiguous. It is 'extra'. What date – or what message – is this sender trying to convey to us? 1050? 1100? Some date in between? What significance could such a date have on an envelope intended for us but addressed to Norman, or Newman, Musgrave?"

"I can think of none," I confessed.

Holmes rose to his feet. "I have it, Watson! I believe I have it!" His face glowed with excitement. "Reginald Musgrave, that devoted custodian of his ancient feudal keep, told me years ago that his estate's ancient oak tree was probably *in situ* at the time of the Norman Conquest. The Norman Conquest, Watson! 1066, as we were taught at school, when the feudal system was at its height. *This* is the explanation for the deliberate change of name from Newman to Norman! It is another of the sender's tricks. She grows more interesting hourly! She is directing us to that labyrinth of catacombs, crypts and ancient dungeons of which I told you before. Yes, my boy, the solution to this pretty puzzle lies in the ancient coffins of the Musgraves' manor at Hurlstone!"

I felt my blood quicken with excitement. "You have reasoned it out marvellously," said I.

"Well, if you will be kind enough to select an early train tomorrow to western Sussex I will send a telegram at once to Nathaniel Musgrave, the new squire, to tell him of our arrival. I have no doubt that he will be glad to see us. It will be a pleasure to introduce him to you, Watson."

"I look forward to it," said I heartily. "Reginald Musgrave was a man in whose family story, and your part in it, I found great interest. That fresh developments are now expected adds special appeal. The game is evidently afoot once more!"

"Indeed it is, old friend, and a 'grave' one it may prove to be," said Holmes with a chuckle. He was, as always, in good spirits when his brain was grappling with an intellectual challenge. At seven the next morning a first class smoker from Waterloo found us bound for Hurlstone. We arrived at the pleasant country station to find a two-wheeler waiting. The driver greeted us cheerfully.

"Mr Sherlock Holmes? Dr Watson? I am from Hurlstone, sirs, sent by Mister Nathaniel to meet you. I trust you had a good journey?"

"Thank you, yes."

Holmes glanced at me, then addressed the man again.

"Sir Reginald and I were friends for a good many years. Tell me, how did this tragedy happen?"

"An inexperienced house guest at a shooting party was the cause of it, sir. He was following Sir Reginald out of a copse to meet the beaters and failed to unload his gun while climbing over a fence. The triggers were caught by brambles. Sir Reginald took the full charge of both barrels in the back. We thank the Good Lord that the master did not suffer. It was all done in a flash."

"A tragedy indeed," responded Holmes, after a pause.

"Yes, sir. His death was a great loss. He had many friends in the district – very many. It was standing room only in St Mary's at the memorial service. He represented our district right well in Westminster, too."

On arrival at Hurlstone we were greeted warmly by Nathaniel Musgrave, a pleasant, courtly young man of aristocratic mien. Expressing our regrets at the calamity, we were ushered into the new wing of his ancient manor.

"Hurlstone appears to generate mysteries," remarked Holmes, as he seated himself in a proffered arm chair in Musgrave's study. "On my previous visit, as you know, I was summoned by your cousin to look into the disappearance of two members of your staff. I come now bringing my own puzzle: it developed yesterday in London in connection with a Mr Newman, or Norman, Musgrave, who died several years ago and who may, or may not, be related to you."

"Ah! Yes! Newman! He worked in a publishing company, did he not? He has certainly been to Hurlstone. I never met him but I know a little of him. He was a relative, but a distant one. He was an amiable churchgoer, living quietly and dedicating his spare time to the service of Rome. This prevented his taking more than a cursory interest in our estate, or indeed in the family. I am afraid we rather lost touch with him over the years. What problem has he produced?"

Holmes explained the matter, concisely summarizing Garrison Bolt's visit, the extraordinary letter and the chain of reasoning which had led him to this return visit to Hurlstone. Nathaniel Musgrave examined the envelope carefully.

"I have no correspondents in the west of Canada," he said. "I know no one there. I can make nothing of the letter other than to applaud your extraordinary deductions. You were clearly intended to bring the letter to Hurlstone, but what we are meant to do with it is utterly beyond me. Frankly I am amazed that you have deduced so much. My cousin told me of your extra-ordinary powers, Mr Holmes, and I can see that he was not exaggerating. As you know," he continued, "we have the crown which you so dramatically identified for us. We have had it fully restored. Perhaps you would like to see it. Incidentally, we have learned that it graced the brows of the Tudor, as well as the Stuart, kings. It was reportedly used at every coronation from that of Henry VIII until the dispersion of the regalia following Charles I's trial and execution in January of 1649, when it was, I understand, broken into pieces by Master Cromwell and his not-so-merry men. We have always kept the linen bag in which the Crown was retrieved from the mere, too. It seemed a sacrilege to separate them after nearly two hundred and fifty years together in solitary confinement in Brunton's strongbox, as we call it."

Holmes looked sharply at Musgrave, an expression of extreme alertness and concentration on his face. He paused before speaking again. "What do you infer, Mr Musgrave, from this reference to 'coffins', and a date of 1050, or 1100?" he asked. "It is clearly a directive we are meant to follow."

"There at least I see no difficulty," said the young heir. "The old part of the building, like the rest of the estate, does indeed date back to feudal times. It has always been one of the duties of the incumbent at Hurlstone to preserve the original burial sites of those who lived here before us. Some are merely marked by rude stone markers with the ancient engravings obliterated by nine hundred years of wind and storm but others, mostly wooden caskets and stone sarcophagi, have been sheltered from the elements. Those of the Norman period you mention are situated in an ancient catacomb abutting, as it happens, on the very cellar in which you and my cousin found the body of our unfortunate butler."

Holmes rubbed his hands in satisfaction. "Let us lose no time in examining these coffins. Our unknown correspondent has gone to considerable lengths to see that we do and I know of no reason why we should not oblige her. By the way, Mr Musgrave," he added, "are the Hurlstone relics, graves and coffins arranged in any particular order, or system? Do the phrases 'control system' or 'control sy' have any meaning for you?"

"The words mean nothing to me," replied Musgrave, "but yes, the graves are sited in chronological order. I suppose that is the way of graves. In any case it could not be otherwise at Hurlstone. Many of the stone cases are very heavy. It would be no easy matter to move them."

The entrance to the catacombs was a sloping tunnel. Its moss-covered flagstones provided firm footing as we entered from the daylight but became treacherously slippery as we descended. The dank, fungus-covered walls dripped with moisture – a reminder of the nearby Hurlstone mere. Our host carried a flare, by whose light we picked our way down the ancient ramp of the ossuary. The odour of nitrates was unmistakable. In many places the old wooden coffins had rotted and collapsed; skeletal remains of ancient Musgraves were glimpsed as we descended – mute but eloquent testimony to our host's ancient lineage. Nathaniel Musgrave halted at a small group of crumbling stone containers, one of which had a lid, slightly ajar.

"These are the coffins of the Norman period;" said he, "most of their occupants were recorded in the Domesday Book."

"Please excuse my lack of ceremony, Mr Musgrave," said Holmes, stepping forward. "I mean no disrespect but something of immediate significance, in addition to the remains of your ancestors may, I believe, be found inside these coffins. Help me to slide this lid further, will you, Watson?"

Musgrave and I turned our shoulders to the task Holmes watched closely, then thrust his arm into the half-opened casket and withdrew from its depths a linen bag, tied at the throat with twine. He regarded it thoughtfully for some moments before speaking.

"You paid me a compliment today, Mr Musgrave, when you alluded to the deductive powers I had the pleasure of bringing to the aid of Sir Reginald. These same powers will, I believe, now enable me in turn to surprise you! Before we open this bag it would please me to tell you precisely what we shall find inside it."

I could not help laughing at this preposterous suggestion. "It seems to me," I managed, with some difficulty, to articulate, "that only a psychic, or a thief who has had access to this chamber, could make such a prediction. Since I know that you are neither, I take the liberty of doubting you! There is no way in this world in which you could possibly foretell such a thing!"

"I must second Dr Watson's opinion," said Nathaniel Musgrave, also grinning broadly. "It is not possible."

"Very well," said Holmes. "I take up your gage!" He paused and continued, measuring his words in the manner of an orator addressing his audience: "In this bag you will find, certainly tamished, probably discoloured, possibly damaged but nevertheless recognizable, an orb – a ball of gold – and a sceptre. Unless the corrosion of three centuries prevents it, a smaller orb, surmounted by a cross on which rests a dove, will attach to the sceptre. When I add that the great orb is itself surmounted by a cross and that its weight is one pound, five and a quarter ounces, you will have no difficulty in verifying my prediction."

And so, to our amazement, it proved! One by one Nathaniel Musgrave withdrew the contents from the bag and placed them on the lid of the sarcophagus. The pieces were indeed horribly stained but they glittered nevertheless in the light cast by Musgrave's flare. "Rubbish they appear but rubbish I know they are not!" cried Musgrave. "They are just as you say, Mr Holmes. Whatever can they be? You astonish me!".

Sherlock Holmes bowed low in humorous acknowledgement, a look of immense satisfaction on his face.

"By Jove!" cried Musgrave. "This linen bag is identical to the one in which we recovered the crown from the lake, when you solved the puzzle of our Ritual."

"You are certain of that?" said Holmes. "Your cousin showed me the bag at the time, but I did not, as I now regret, make any special examination of it."

"Yes, I am certain. What can it mean?"

Holmes did not reply at once. He sat on the coffin, deep in thought. It was only when our host's flare sputtered out, leaving us in darkness, that he spoke again. "Musgrave," he said, "you mentioned that these catacombs abut the cellar in which we found Brunton's body. Where precisely is that cellar?"

"Within ten paces of this spot!" replied Musgrave, relighting his flare; "Up these stone steps and through that archway!" Thus we found ourselves at the site of the old Hurlstone tragedy. The stone slab that had snuffed out Brunton's life had been replaced, no doubt for reasons of safety, by a wooden trap door but, as Holmes commented, little else had changed. As before, on a barrel stood a large lantern, evidently still functional for Musgrave lit it at once. Wood was still stacked around the walls. Holmes was even able to show us two of the dented billets that Brunton and the girl Howells had used to raise the flagstone from the sepulchre. He had, he remarked, put them to one side, years ago.

On my first visit," said Holmes, "I sat here for twenty minutes, thinking over the meaning of what we had found. I must now do so again. We have much data to consider. May I suggest that you, Watson, and you Musgrave, take these historic relics to a place of safety in the house while I remain here. My pipe and tobacco will suffice for company."

I followed Musgrave as he led the way up a winding stone staircase to the daylight above. In half an hour we rejoined Holmes. He rose and stood before us, his hands on his coat lapels, his eyes alive with excitement.

"Musgrave, I have news which I fear will not please you, following as it does so hard on our discovery of . . ."

"Of what?" cried Musgrave. "What precisely *are* these rusted relics?"

"Reunited with the crown you already have, they are nothing less than the ancient Crown Jewels of England!"

Musgrave and I stared at Holmes in amazement.

"The Crown Jewels?"

"Just so. However, the fact is that others have rights to this new treasure and, hard though it may be to comprehend, they have already established an effective claim to it. They have done so moreover in a manner which will be hard to dispute or deny."

"But that is impossible!" cried Musgrave. "We only discovered the trove an hour ago. We three alone know of it! How can anyone else possibly be aware of it, let alone have registered a claim to it? And by what agency could such a claim have been made?"

Holmes smiled ruefully. "I fear that I am myself the agent!"

"You?"

"Yes, I."

"Mr Holmes, I must ask you to explain yourself. You are a friend of my family. You have helped us immeasurably in the past. My cousin admired, respected and trusted you. It is inconceivable that you would deliberately act against our family's interest on behalf of others. I will not – can not – do not – believe it!"

"My dear Musgrave, what you say is true. Of course I would never knowingly do anything against your interest," Holmes assured him. "The fact is that I have been duped."

"By whom?"

"By one with a mind of astonishing power; by a daring and imaginative schemer possessed of a considerable flair and ingenuity which is the more startling for being unexpected."

"Who is this Titan?"

"*Your family's former second housemaid!*"

"What? Impossible!"

"I assure you no. The person who has effectively lodged a valid claim against this priceless treasure is Rachel Howells: the same Howells whose unexplained disappearance at the time of Brunton's murder – for murder it was – created such a furore."

"But if she is a murderess, Holmes," I exclaimed, "she must be arrested. No criminal can be allowed to benefit from his crime."

"There is a difficulty," replied Holmes. "Rachel Howells has, by using us as her instruments, effectively lodged her claim. She knows however from Watson's account that there are legal obstacles. She cannot have expected to surmount them unaided. She has certainly enlisted confidants as her agents. It is to these that the crown jewels of the Tudors and Stuarts must be released. Rachel Howells undoubtedly expects to reclaim them; what arrangements she has made to that end I have as yet no way of knowing. I think it unlikely however that these surrogates yet know that they have laid, let alone established, good claim to the Crown Jewels of England; nor, I suspect, are they aware that they have a murderess in their midst."

"But where are these confederates?" cried Musgrave.

"In North America, the origin of this extraordinary letter."

"In Canada? In British Columbia?"

"It is not unlikely."

"But who are they? The Scowrers? The Mafia? The Red Circle?"

"That is what I must still discover. Now, Musgrave," said Holmes, laughing, "you are overwhelming me with your questions. Besides, you are leading me into Watson's deplorable habit of explaining matters backwards. Would it not be better if we repaired to your quarters, where I shall be happy to clarify the matter? Agreed? Come then, lead on!"

It was a remarkable gathering as we sat in comfortable arm chairs in Musgrave's rooms. On a table before us lay the newly discovered great orb and sceptre of the kings of England, steeped in centuries of history. Beside them Nathaniel Musgrave had placed the refurbished Hurlstone crown – golden, jewel-encrusted and magnificent. Beside these objects lay the two linen bags in which they had been found. Holmes explained:

"Before I could form a hypothesis capable of explaining the extraordinary message which directed us to these treasures, it was first necessary to assemble my data. My starting point was these two linen bags. They are, as you rightly told us, Musgrave, identical. The first, which has been kept with the crown since its recovery years ago from the mere, shows some signs of deterioration; the other little if any. On my last visit, when the existence of only one bag was known, I paid little attention to it, ascribing its damaged condition to its sojourn in the crypt of your cellar while ten generations of your ancestors lived out their lives above. *But of course I was mistaken.* I should have realized that centuries of corrosion by worms and fungi, sufficient to have eaten through the walls of the wooden strongbox, would have utterly destroyed a simple linen bag. The deterioration of the bag had of course been caused only by its comparatively short immersion in your lake. But these bags are otherwise identical and in similar condition. It must follow that the crown jewels were placed in them not at the time of Charles's trial and execution but comparatively recently."

"At the time the first bag was tossed into the mere?" I suggested.

"Precisely," said Holmes. "And who was the last person we know to have handled the crown and its bag?"

"Brunton!"

"Yes, the butler Brunton and his accomplice, the person to whom he passed up the treasure – handed it up from the crypt that was to be his coffin. But wait, we have not yet exhausted the resources of applied deduction! If the bags were not in the crypt when Brunton discovered the strongbox – and we have now established that they were not – they can only have been taken there by Brunton himself. We can be sure that it was Brunton who lowered himself into the crypt, while Rachel Howells waited above. Brunton, with the treasure at last within his grasp, was of course intent on examining it; he neither needed nor wanted a witness. It is unlikely that Howells, even if invited to descend, would have been prepared to enter the crypt herself, knowing that only a simple prop, a billet of wood, prevented the stone slab from crashing down, with none above to hear her cries. With an accomplice she trusted, her avarice might have overcome her fear; with a man who had already proved faithless, never. It was Brunton then who entered the crypt; Brunton who opened the strongbox; Brunton who discovered the treasure and Brunton who filled the bags."

"Bags?" said I. "Plural?"

"Yes, bags. One was retrieved years ago from the mere, the other by us today from your catacombs, Musgrave. Brunton we know never left the crypt alive. The two bags could therefore have escaped the crypt in only one way: both were handed up by Brunton to his accomplice."

"And that could only be Rachel Howells!"

"Just so," said Holmes. Musgrave and I remained silent, our eyes riveted on Sherlock Holmes as he continued: "We can now reconstruct the precise sequence of events. Brunton, redoubling his efforts following his dismissal on a week's notice by your cousin, discovers the site of the cache within two days. His problem is to retrieve the treasure he believes to lie below. He confers with the angry, and astute, Rachel Howells, who strikes a bargain: she is to share equally in the treasure as the price for her help – and her silence. She it is who provides the two linen sacks, one for each half share of the trove. Brunton takes them down into the crypt, fills one with half the treasure and hands it up to Howells. "*The sceptre and the orb for you; the crown for me, Rachel! Fair enough, my dear?*" I can almost hear the words. "What does Howells do then?" he continued. "Aware of the need for haste, she hastily stashes her bag in the nearby hiding place she has selected earlier: the sarcophagus from which we have retrieved it today. While doing so, she quickly examines the bag's contents. Despite Brunton's assurances she may well conclude that the discoloured old pieces of metal are worthless. I seem to hear her screaming imprecations down at Brunton, crouched below. Brunton, reaching up to raise himself from the dungeon, places his bag on the stone shelf beside the wooden billet. And then – murder!"

"You always suspected it!"

"Yes, Watson. Murder. No other hypothesis fits. Consider. Her means, and her opportunity, are all too close to hand. Of motives she has no lack! Revenge – for Brunton has recently wronged her – as I suggested before, perhaps much more than we know: passionate Celtic women do not take kindly to being thrown over for gamekeepers' daughters; anger – for Brunton has undoubtedly promised her that a great treasure awaits them at the bottom of the pit as a price for her help in raising the flagstone; and avarice, for Brunton's protestations that the trinkets are of immense value may – just may – be true.

"So she, the second bag lying at her feet, murders him: murders him by dashing away the wooden billet. The heavy slab crashes down. Her faithless lover is imprisoned in the tomb. *In pace requiescat avidus!*"

Musgrave and I had listened in fascination as Holmes's words vividly brought this ghastly tragedy to life. I took a deep breath to escape the spell he had cast.

"But this can only be a hypothesis!" I heard myself cry in protest.

"It is more than that," said Holmes. "Consider the significance of the second bag. A British jury might possibly have acquitted Howells for lack of evidence had she been brought to trial at the time of Brunton's death: the butler had been found dead in the crypt; the Stuart crown in the mere. There was no evidence connecting Howells directly to either. She had in any event disappeared. But now the second bag has been found and Howells's neck is in jeopardy for she, and only she, can have received it from Brunton's hand. Brunton never left that crypt alive. It was Howells, a jury will reason, who threw the one sack into the mere – her footsteps, leading to the edge of the lake, proclaim as much – after first secreting the other in its hiding place, a few steps from where she stood. This is no hypothesis, Watson. It is proof. This second linen bag places a hempen rope around the neck of Rachel Howells."

"I am sure you are right," said Nathaniel Musgrave, his eyes still fixed on Sherlock Holmes. "The facts are indisputable. They admit of no other explanation. Murder was done in our Hurlstone cellar that day: our butler the victim; our housemaid his executioner."

Holmes continued. "Aghast at what she has done, she snatches up Brunton's bag and flees to her room, her ears ringing with the sounds of muffled screams and the drumming of frenzied hands from the cellar. In the haven of her room she makes her plans for flight. What can she do with the bags, the evidence of her dreadful crime? Their discovery in her possession means the gallows. She decides to leave hers in its feudal hiding place. She spends the next two days in secreting her few belongings near the gate leading from the Hurlstone estate to the world beyond. On her final night she retires to bed as usual then, quietly, to avoid waking the night nurse, she leaves the house and walks to the lake – carefully leaving tracks to the water's edge to establish the possibility of her death by drowning as an explanation for her disappearance – flings Brunton's treasure into the mere and takes the gravel path leading from the grounds."

"How do you know she took the path?" I asked.

"Because her footsteps took her to the edge of the mere next to the gravel path. It was at their junction that her trail ended. The mere was dragged the next day so thoroughly that the linen bag was detected and brought to the surface. But they found no body! No Rachel Howells! She had not entered the lake, therefore she had taken the path. It was always my opinion," he went on, "that she had carried herself and the memory of her crime to some land beyond the sea, an opinion I now find justified. She left your grounds, Musgrave, walked to the village, thence, taking every care to remain inconspicuous, by coach to Portsmouth."

"But would a second housemaid be capable of devising such an undertaking?" Musgrave inquired.

"It was a formidable plan, but the Welsh have many characteristics besides passion and fire," replied Holmes. "Among them are courage, cunning, and intelligence. Your cousin had a high opinion of Rachel Howells. He told me so. Remember, too, she was engaged to Richard Brunton, a man of first rate education and intelligence. It is most unlikely that he would have allied himself to a simpleton.

"It now appears that the land she chose," he continued, "was North America. Her transatlantic vessel's first port of call was probably Halifax in Nova Scotia, or perhaps Boston in New England. From there she has made her way west, settling in the wilderness gold-mining town of Barkerville – an appropriate haven for an avaricious murderess with crown jewels on her mind. No doubt she changed her name and has supported herself there under her new identity."

"You think it is Rachel Howells who has sent you this letter from Canada, then?"

"It can be no other."

"The woman must be arrested, Holmes. She is a murderess! We know her abode. Why should we hesitate?"

"No, Watson, we cannot arrest her until we have identified her with certainty as the sender of this enigmatic letter which has, thanks to our dutiful playing of the role she has written for us, both revealed the treasure and laid claim to it. Consider: the murderess hid the second bag in the coffin. The sender of this letter, and she alone, knows that the bag was hidden there and has directed us to it. To bring home guilt to Rachel Howells we must identify her not only as Hurlstone's second housemaid, and Brunton's accomplice, but also as the sender of the letter."

"But how dared she send the message and risk detection?" asked Musgrave.

"Let us put ourselves once again in her place. She has learned long ago from Watson's published account of the affair of the Musgrave Ritual that Brunton had told her no less than the truth: that the contents of the bags are indeed of immense value. Watson's narrative has told her also that her share of the treasure remained undetected when Brunton's bag was recovered from the mere. She ponders how she can lay her hands on her fortune, as she no doubt considers it. How does she reason? How can she secure the treasure but avoid the scaffold? Watson's account has told her of the legal difficulties and expense encountered by the Hurlstone estate in retaining the crown. Revelation of her own treasure will kindle a similar investigation. To reveal her knowledge of its existence is to put a noose around her neck. At the cost of her life she must not be identified as the treasure's finder. She needs an untermediary, an agent capable of dealing with the authorities and of meeting the expense necessary to retrieve the trove. She therefore finds a surrogate – or surrogates. In their name she lays claim to the treasure, relying on them to provide her with both a share of the proceeds and continuing anonymity.

"But she cannot act! Reginald Musgrave, she knows, can identify her by sight. She cannot risk claiming her fortune, even indirectly through her agents, while the possibility remains that he might, during the negotiations for its return, meet her in broad daylight.

"She learns of Sir Reginald's death in the shooting accident. The promptness with which she acts – within ten days; that's quick work, you know – argues against her having learned of it from the *Hurlstone Village Chronicle*, which she may possibly receive regularly. Musgrave's death may have been timely reported in the Canadian newspapers but more likely a Sussex crony has sent her a wire. She immediately makes her move by laying claim to the riches in the name of her confederates.

"Our envelope, Watson, *must* identify her surrogates! Its senders have, by directing us to the hideaway in the Norman catacombs of Hurlstone, effectively laid claim to the crown jewels of the ancient Stuarts. The finders of treasure have important rights, which are recognized in courts everywhere." He turned to Nathaniel

Musgrave. "I believe, Mr Musgrave, that your family's rights vis-à-vis those of other claimants were in any case abandoned when your cousin signed a waiver of any further title when he established your claim to the Hurlstone crown. Yes? Then it is so: the right to our discovery today resides in the sender of this message – and that can only be the confederate, or confederates, of Rachel Howells. It is they, not we, who are the true finders. Knowing what we do, you and I, Watson, have no choice but to attest to that. You, Musgrave, will be wise to consider your position with care. These surrogates will undoubtedly approach you as negotiators but they may not be unreasonable."

Holmes withdrew the mystery epistle from his breast pocket and examined it again carefully. "So it is REPORT SYSTEM – together with our extra L – that we have available to us. What in the name of the devil can we infer from them?"

It was then that Sherlock Holmes looked up at me with a startled expression. He had evidently seen something on the envelope which we had missed.

"Watson, do you perchance have friends in the west of Canada?"

"None that I know of," said I, "save Sir Henry Baskerville, but we have already eliminated him from the equation. Why do you ask?"

"Because just as one inference often suggests another, one logo-gram can suggest another. But wait! I am not sure . . ." He scribbled furiously in his notebook. "REPORT SYSTEM L rearranges to . . ."

I looked over Holmes's shoulder.

". . . to STORMY PETRELS!" he cried in triumph. Musgrave and I stared at Holmes in astonishment. I checked his scribbled notes. It was just as he said. Holmes went on, speaking rapidly, as one whose brain races ahead of his power to communicate: "What or who can these 'stormy petrels' be? It is a phrase that I have applied to you, Watson! And to myself! Could it be that this is a reference to us? That it is yet another of those devices which this extraordinary woman has used to manipulate us? No. It cannot be so. The envelope is addressed not to 'Watson' but to 'Musgrave'. And the words appear on the top left hand corner, the space for the sender's name. 'Stormy Petrels' is therefore not a reference to us, Watson – it is the name of the surrogates themselves – the instruments of Rachel Howells!

"Their very name tells us who and what they are: students of my methods and readers of your tales. *Rachel Howells is clearly telling us so.* We are dealing here not with enemies but with friends!" He paused and shook his head in comic disbelief. "What a coup-de-maître it is! I once had occasion to chide you, Watson, in connection with the

Vermissa Valley murders in America I think, for suggesting that the recreant Porlock might possibly have enclosed both cipher and key in the same envelope. In that instance we were able to decipher the message by recourse to Whitaker's *Almanack*. Here we have no such advantage. The sender of *this* envelope has outdone even Porlock: she has combined not only the cipher and its key but the addresser of the message – her surrogates – and its true addressees, myself and the estate of Hurlstone, not in, but actually on, the envelope – leaving the contents blank! There is brilliance here, Watson – scheming, calculated brilliance!"

Musgrave and I were at a loss for words. He appeared as stupefied as I.

"Clearly, we must make contact with these 'stormy petrels'," said Holmes to me, briskly breaking the silence. "We must seek them in their haunts. Our enquiries must be made in Canada."

"We know," I interjected, "that at least one of them is a lady of Welsh origin, fiery, passionate and excitable.!"

"Yes, indeed," Holmes replied, his eyes atwinkle. "Well, Watson, what say you to a visit to the Pacific coast? Could your practice spare you for some weeks?"

"I have no doubt I can arrange it," said I, "but what will be our aim? To identify and arrest Howells?"

"As I read it, Rachel Howells is at present waiting anxiously in British Columbia for news of our discovery of the royal orb and sceptre, to which she has, using this flock of petrels as her unwitting agents, effectively laid claim. When she hears of it she will act. She will persuade the group to demand delivery of the treasure, probably by authorizing her to make the arrangements on their behalf. The claim of these petrels cannot be denied but it is within our power to thwart Howells herself."

"How?"

"By delaying announcement of our finding of the treasure until we can cause her arrest. You, I and Musgrave here are the only persons who know of it Musgrave, you will, I think, find it in your interests to fall in with our plans; this will give us time to visit and confront these people. Our information will startle them: that they have claim to the crown jewels of England – and a murderess in their midst! Courtesy, no less than common sense and common justice, demands delivery of such a message in person."

"It will be most dramatic," said I. "But what of the murderess herself? Shall we arrest her in front of her comrades?"

Holmes thought for a moment. "She must be given every opportunity to state her position. She may possibly give us facts of which we are unaware. But then we must act decisively."

"She will not be the first murderess we have apprehended," I observed, "nor will it be the first time we have acted as both judge and jury."

"No, indeed! And here I foresee no difficulty. I will take with me to Canada a copy of the Hurlstone's village news sheet giving details of her disappearance. It carries an excellent likeness of Howells. Identifying the lady, despite the passage of some twenty years, should be a simple matter."

"With Howells removed to a barred cell," said I, "these stormy petrels will be free to pursue their claim to the Hurlstone jewels directly with Nathanial Musgrave. That seems appropriate."

"I agree," interjected the master of Hurlstone.

"Quite so, and I feel inclined to render them every assistance," said Holmes. "A group of your readers in the New World deserves our support, Watson!"

"And so say all of us!" I replied heartily. "Perhaps we should take with us your book on international law – *De Jure inter Gentes*, as I recall. It might prove useful in effecting delivery of the jewels to these Canadians."

"From what little I know of British Columbia *The Origins of Tree Worship* might be a volume of more interest to them," suggested Holmes, his expression one of high good humour.

"At the risk of re-creating that space on my bookshelf," I replied, laughing, "we can safely donate our copy!"

"You know, Watson," said Holmes the following morning on our return to Baker Street, "in reading your accounts of some of the adventures we have shared over the years I have felt that, on occasion, I have behaved towards you in a cavalier fashion. It is easy to commit the crime of taking good friends for granted and I fear I am guilty of it."

"I have never taken the least offence," I assured him, not altogether truthfully. "There have been times, it is true, when I have been oppressed with a sense of the slowness of my wits compared to yours, but I can hardly blame you for that!"

"Well, you have other qualities, doctor. Do not underrate yourself; it is as much an offence as its reverse. Wisdom and common sense have a higher value than mere quick wits. To me you are a brother-in-arms. Besides, this proposed visit to British Columbia gives me an opportunity to show some long overdue appreciation. I of course insist that the expedition shall be at my expense," he continued. "The new Holdernesse fund is more than able to meet the cost. I can think of no finer way of putting it to use!" Holmes lit a cigarette and we sat in silence, wrapped in our own thoughts, as befits good friends who anticipate the pleasures of a new adventure.

"Holmes," I interrupted, as the thought struck me, "you have not yet explained how you were able to predict precisely what we would find when we opened the second linen bag in the Hurlstone tomb. How you did so is more than I can fathom. You also explained that our discovery of the orb and sceptre completed the reunion of the ancient jewels with their Stuart Crown. But how did – or indeed how do – you know this? In my account of the Musgrave Ritual I reported, I believe accurately, your comment that there could be little doubt that the diadem once encircled the brows of the Royal Stuarts. You now clearly have no such doubts."

Sherlock Holmes smiled. "I am glad," he said, "that you have raised these points, Watson, for we are dealing here with history itself. It is fitting that your account should close with that degree of certainty that leaves no room for dispute or conjecture, Proof you ask for and – if you will accompany me as dangerously far into the outside world as the nether regions of West Central, proof you shall have!"

Half an hour later we stood at the entrance to the National Portrait Gallery in St Martin's Place.

"Follow me, Watson!"

We ascended the stairways to the upper floor, where Holmes led the way to a spacious, high, rectangular gallery. Turning into it, he led me to the foot of a life-size portrait depicting a young man, magnificently apparelled, the whiteness of his face, lace collar and buff thigh-boots in sharp contrast to the sombre tones of his livery, standing next a table draped with deep crimson velvet. On it lay a magnificent crown and its regalia. The caption made me gasp: *Portrait of Charles I by Daniel Mytens* it read. *The Tudor Imperial Crown of State and the State Sceptre and Orb can be seen in the picture.*

"Holmes!" I exclaimed. "The crown! The jewels! They are the very ones! These are indeed the Hurlstone treasures!"

"Yes," he replied, "they are. And this portrait was painted from life! We can take pride in having restored to the light this ancient finery which has lain in a dungeon crypt for centuries. As to my prediction of the bag's contents," he continued, as though turning to a subject of more interest, "the explanation is a simple one. I had the advantage of having seen this portrait before."

"How so?"

"As part of an official group assembled to satisfy the authorities of the rightful claim of the Musgraves to the Hurlstone Crown. Reginald Musgrave was here, too. It was his solicitor, I recall, who pointed out that our discovery of the crown provided clear evidence of the success of the Stuart sympathizers in thwarting Cromwell's edict ordering the destruction of the regalia following the execution of Charles. I was thus able to astonish you, and the current custodian of Hurlstone, with my prognosis that, the crown having been found in the first linen bag, it was likely that the orb and sceptre were in the second. It was the existence of that second bag that gave me the key. The instant I drew it from the open coffin the whole sequence of events that followed Brunton's death became clear to me. I had no need to open it."

"That was quick thinking indeed, Holmes," I marvelled.

"Well, perhaps I had yet a further advantage. As you know I have always felt that we had not heard the last of Rachel Howells. My mind was, I suspect, ready to accept a hypothesis into which she would fit. Incidentally, Watson," he continued, changing the subject yet again, "King Charles's head was still firm on his shoulders when this portrait was struck off. Perhaps it is as well that with the jewels in the Hurlstone crypt we did not find also the several Royal cranium that the crown once encircled."

"That would have been a sensation indeed!" I responded.

"A sensation, yes, but it might have resulted in others accompanying us on our transatlantic adventure: the eccentric Mr Dick, and Boz himself, were ever fascinated by the events of Charles's execution! They would certainly wish to see the conclusion of this business. And very good company their shades might prove! However the appearance of Watson and Holmes accompanied by two ethereal companions might prove an experience for which these worthy Canadians are not yet prepared! By the way, Watson," he added as we turned to leave, "should you decide to write an account of this somewhat cerebral affair, you might consider giving Mr Garrison Bolt an opportunity to participate. I do not believe you will find him as churlish as on the last occasion – or that he will relegate your account to delayed publication at a cut rate price in a Christmas annual!"

THE ADVENTURE OF
THE BULGARIAN DIPLOMAT

Zakaria Erzinçlioglu

1901 also saw the cases of "The Priory School" and "Thor Bridge", whilst 1902 introduced us to "Shoscombe Old Place", "The Three Garridebs" and "The Illustrious Client". The year 1903 brings us to one of those great puzzles. "The Blanched Soldier" is a case recounted by Holmes himself, not Watson. Holmes was clearly in a begrudging mood when he wrote the case notes because he was rather vindictive about Watson having deserted him for a wife. It would seem that sometime towards the end of 1902 or early 1903 Watson married again, and Holmes felt rebuffed and neglected. In truth, however, Watson had not neglected Holmes. He was there all the time. Holmes just chose to write him completely out of the story of "The Blanched Soldier" by way of rather childish spite occasioned by Watson's marriage some years later when Holmes wrote up the notes.

During the course of the case Holmes mentioned that he had an urgent commission for the Sultan of Turkey that had to be dealt with. Thanks to the researches of Dr Zakaria Erzinçlioglu, the eminent pathologist, who had access to certain papers in his home country, it has been possible to bring together the full facts of "The Adventure of the Bulgarian Diplomat", and vindicate Watson's position once and for all. Holmes may have had one of the greatest brains we have ever witnessed, but at times he could be a cantankerous and awkward individual.

By the early years of the new century the extraordinary powers of Mr Sherlock Holmes had been put to many a severe test and his successes had brought him fame throughout the continent of Europe. Although many of those cases gave my friend great opportunities to demonstrate those deductive methods of reasoning by which he achieved such remarkable successes, yet no case involved a greater array of bizarre personalities and in none would the consequences, in the event of my friend's failure,

have been more horrific than in the case I am about to lay before
the public for the first time. For reasons that will become clear
to the reader of this narrative, it is only now possible to reveal
the full facts of what must be considered one of the crowning
points of my friend's career.

It was on a cold and bitter evening in January, 1903, that
my friend Mr Sherlock Holmes and I returned from a bracing
walk to the rooms at Baker Street. We ascended the staircase in
silence, for we were both frozen to the marrow, and a moment
later were glad to find ourselves standing in front of a roaring
fire in Holmes's large and untidy room. We stood rubbing our
hands before the grate and soon the warm blood was coursing
through our veins. Holmes took one of his empty pipes and
placed it between his teeth, then flung himself into the basket
chair and picked up a large envelope that had been lying open
on the table at his elbow. He removed the large, folded sheet of
paper from its envelope and, spreading it out on his knee, began
to read it quietly to himself with a frown of concentration on his
face. As he did so, I could not help studying the envelope, which
Holmes had replaced upon the table. It was of a cream colour
and uncommonly large, but its most extraordinary feature was the
design emblazoned across it. This was like a large and extremely
intricate treble clef mark in gold, the body of the mark being
made up of fine lines running back and forth along its length.

"Well, Watson," said Holmes, who had been watching me
furtively. "What do you make of it?"

"I must say it is a most unusual envelope, Holmes, but I confess
that I can infer nothing of interest from it," I replied.

Holmes rose from his seat and handed me the letter. "It arrived
by special courier this morning. You know my methods, Watson.
Apply them."

I took the letter in one hand and the envelope in the other
and started my examination. First, I looked closely at the envelope
with its singular design. Following my friend's methods I took
up his magnifying lens from the table and examined the design
minutely. I then sniffed at the envelope, as I have seen Holmes
do on occasion. I then unfolded the letter and read aloud the
contents:

Dear Mr Holmes,

I am commanded by my Sovereign to request your advice
on a matter of extreme sensitivity. It is impossible for me to
enter into the details of the problem in this letter, nor is it
advisable for me to identify myself in writing. I will take the

liberty of calling at your rooms this evening at 8 o'clock to acquaint you with the case. Your esteemed brother Mycroft is already fully conversant with the relevant facts.

"A case from a royal client!" I cried, "My dear Holmes, I congratulate you." Holmes waved a deprecating hand. "Pray continue with your examination," he said.

I sat down and turned the letter over and over in my hands, examining it from every angle. I cudgelled my brains in an attempt to come to some inference about the significance of the letter or the character of the writer, but, try as I may, I could not arrive at any profound conclusion upon the subject. Nevertheless, I was determined to show Holmes that I was not totally devoid of ideas on the matter.

"It would seem clear from the high quality of the paper and the envelope," I said, with some importance, "and from the fact that he is writing on behalf of his sovereign that your correspondent is a man of high position. I would also say that he is a foreigner, judging by the peculiar symbol on the envelope and by the fact that he refers to 'my Sovereign'. An Englishman would have written 'the King'. Also, the use of the word 'esteemed' in such a context strikes me as being distinctly un-English. I can find no further clues to the identity of the man."

Sherlock Holmes sat silently with his elbows on the arms of the chair and his chin resting on his clasped hands, eyeing me closely. At length he spoke.

"Quite right, Watson, quite right. The man is a foreigner of distinction and I will confess that I have not been able to arrive at many much deeper conclusions myself."

I felt a glow of satisfaction as he rose and crossed to the mantelpiece, where he rested his elbow and turned to face me.

"Indeed, Watson, apart from the obvious facts that the author is an old – I might say, *very* old – Turkish nobleman, who does not smoke, who has only recently arrived in this country, who is very highly educated, even by the general standards of modern diplomats, who is particularly well trusted by the Sultan of Turkey and who is of exceptionally robust health for a man of his age, there is little else that I can deduce. When I add that he has a smudge of ink on the little finger of his right hand, that he spent some considerable time composing his short letter, that he has a beard, that his hair is of an almost pure white, that he is a man of austere, almost Spartan, habits and that he is an old soldier who has seen action in many military campaigns, I will admit that my limited stock of knowledge about our correspondent is exhausted."

"I must say that your stock of knowledge is better described as exhaustive," I said with some asperity, for I was nettled by this display of omniscience, "since I do not admit that such a wealth of information can be considered limited by any accurate observer."

"Excellent, Watson!" he replied with a chuckle, "Touché! A most opposite response!" He came over to where I sat, took up the letter and envelope and seated himself again in the basket chair. Somewhat mollified, I asked him how he arrived at his remarkable conclusions about the letter-writer through a mere examination of the letter and envelope.

"That the man is a Turk and a nobleman is evident from the fact that the envelope bears the sign of the Tugra, which is the personal emblem of the Sultan of Turkey," said Holmes, "No commoner or foreigner could possibly have been entrusted with such stationery. That he is a very old man can be deduced from the nature of his handwriting. He does not smoke because, being a Turk, if he had been a smoker he would have smoked Turkish tobacco, which has a distinctive aroma that would have clung, however faintly, to his writing materials. I have an especially sensitive nose and yet I can detect no hint of a tobacco aroma on either the letter or the envelope. He is very highly educated because he wrote the letter in English in his own hand; if the letter had been written by a scribe the writing would undoubtedly have been that of a much younger man. In general, modern diplomats speak and write French for diplomatic purposes. This man wrote his letter in English – and quite acceptable English at that, Watson – which shows that he speaks at least two languages other than his own, since, being a diplomat, it is certain that he speaks French – he would not have gone far in his career if he didn't. He has only recently arrived in this country because, as we have seen, he has written his letter on the Sultan's own stationery and not on the usual stationery of the Turkish Embassy, which would have identified itself as such. It seems clear that our man is on a special mission from Turkey and is acting in an almost independent capacity from the officials at the embassy. Had he been in this country for some time he would hardly have written on special letter-paper from the embassy in Belgravia, which is where the courier came from. Also, the fact that he effectively states that he is on a mission for the Sultan means that he has just arrived, since he is unlikely to lie idle for any length of time before conducting the Sultan's business.

"As to his being a particularly trustworthy courtier, this is manifest from his age. The urgent tone of the letter tells us that the matter is of some importance and yet the Sultan did not choose a younger and more energetic man for the task. The fact that he sent an aged man across Europe must mean that he is particularly reliable and trustworthy. He is of exceptionally robust health because, not only was he capable of making such a journey at his age with apparent ease, but also because he is venturing out on a night like this soon after his arrival in this country. The ink-stained finger I infer from the very slight smudge on the letter 'y' in 'liberty', which can only have been made by the little finger of the right hand when the writer crossed the 't'. A number of hairs were caught in the fold of the paper, which suggests that the man had a beard at which he must have tugged while writing, which in turn suggests that he took some time over the composition of the letter, possibly because he was uncertain about how much he wanted to commit to paper. The hairs are of an almost pure white. Have I convinced you, Watson?"

"Your deductions are certainly very plausible," I replied cautiously, "but what about the Spartan habits and the military career?"

"It is well-known that upper-class Turks, and, indeed, the members of the ruling classes of our continental neighbours, are in the habit of anointing themselves with fragrant perfumes. You know what these foreigners are like, Watson! However, my sensitive nose was unable to detect any such fragrance on the envelope or enclosure. That, taken together with our man's robust old age and the fact that he does not smoke, suggests that he is of Spartan habits. At least, the probability lies in that direction. As for the military career, you will perceive this smaller design to one side of the main emblem on the envelope. This is the military version of the Tugra, which is used by the Sultan only when dealing with his most senior generals. Will it pass, Watson?"

I had opened my mouth to reply, when the sound of horses' hooves was heard in the street outside. Holmes sat up. "It is almost eight o'clock, Watson, and our visitor has arrived." He rose and crossed to the window, when I heard the door downstairs open and close. A slow, deliberate tread could be heard on the stairs. It is a curious thing, but I was suddenly filled with a sense of foreboding, such as I had never before experienced during any of Holmes' cases. The exotic source of the problem, the hint of international intrigue and the distance travelled by our, as yet nameless, visitor for the purpose of meeting my friend, all conspired to give me an irrational feeling of unease. I stood up, facing the door, uncertain what to expect, in spite of Holmes's confident conclusions regarding the appearance and character of our Turkish client.

There was a knock at the door. "Come in," said Sherlock Holmes.

Many persons of singular appearance and bizarre background have passed through the door of the room in Baker Street. And yet the apparition that now entered was by far the most grotesque of all those who came to seek the advice of Mr Sherlock Holmes; whatever I had expected, it was not the figure that now stood before us. I venture to say that even Holmes himself was taken by surprise, although he showed no sign of it. For the visitor who came from so far afield resembled nothing more than a mediaeval monk. His 'habit' was of good quality cloth, but there was no belt or rope round the waist, and the man's head and face were completely obscured under a huge cowl. Incongruously, the right hand held a black cane. A moment later the effect was abruptly transformed, when our visitor lifted his hands and threw back his hood over his shoulders, revealing the ruddy face of an old man with a luxurious white beard and moustache, neither of which bore any trace of the yellowing that comes from years of smoking. He was a man of at least eighty years old, yet still hale and hearty, of average height and build and on his head he wore a round astrakhan hat, which he now removed.

"Mr Sherlock Holmes?" he said, looking at my friend, "Permit me to introduce myself; I am Orman Pasha, personal emissary of His Imperial Majesty the Sultan and formerly Commander of the Ottoman Armies in Europe." He came across the room and shook hands with Holmes.

"This is my friend, Dr Watson, who has assisted me in many of my cases," said Holmes.

"Ah, Dr Watson, the chronicler," said our guest, with a smile, as he shook hands with me.

"Pray remove your cloak and have a seat beside the fire," said Holmes. The old man took off his extraordinary cloak-habit and I was astonished to find that he was wearing full dress uniform, complete with golden epaulets and a maximum of gold lace per square inch on his chest. He sat down slowly on the chair indicated by Holmes and turned his gaze upon us. Beholding this old man, with his shrewd but kindly eyes, all feelings of unease left me, but my curiosity as to the purpose of his visit increased.

"Orman Pasha," began Holmes, "your letter reveals nothing about the nature of your mission. Perhaps you could begin by furnishing us with the details of the case, before telling me how

I can be of service to your sovereign." The old Turk was silent for a few moments, before he began his narrative.

"You will be aware that the political situation in the Balkans, ever since the war between my country and Greece in 1897, has been in turmoil. Several of our Balkan neighbours have fomented trouble in our cities, most especially the agents of the Bulgarian Government. Three months ago, a Bulgarian emissary, one Anton Simeonov, arrived in London in order to seek support from the British Government in the matter of Bulgarian claims upon Turkish territory in the province of Rumelia on the grounds that it has a large Bulgarian minority. The British Government gave him no encouragement in the matter, but the Russians have given him their full support and are themselves pressing the British Government to support his country's claim. My own Government has rejected all Bulgarian claims. Four weeks ago Simeonov narrowly escaped death, when he was attacked in the street by a masked man with revolver, as Simeonov was on his way home from the Bulgarian Consulate in the evening. The shot missed its target and Simeonov fled to safety. The incident, however, was seized upon by the Czar's Ministers, who have sent a note to the Turkish Government, accusing Turkey of employing assassins to murder Simeonov and claiming that this was an act of war against the Slavonic peoples, whom the Russian Government sees as being under its protection.

"At that point my sovereign lord the Sultan commanded me to come to England to enter into negotiations with representatives of those countries that have an interest in the matter, as well as the British Government, which is acting as mediator. Since my arrival from Constantinople two days ago, however, matters have taken a more menacing turn, for Simeonov was found murdered last night in Royston Manor, the home of Lord Eversden, the Foreign Secretary. It is only through the intense efforts of the British Government that the Czar has been prevailed upon not to declare was against Turkey. My Government denies any involvement in the matter. Nevertheless, if this mystery is not resolved immediately and the true villain not brought to justice, there can be little doubt that Turkey and Russia will be at war before the week is out, and that other countries in Europe will join on either side. I am here to ask for your help in solving this problem so that a catastrophic war may be avoided."

I whistled; the very idea of a war engulfing the whole of Europe was unthinkable. I looked at Holmes, who appeared totally/unmoved by our guest's disturbing narrative. "Pray tell us about the circumstances surrounding the late Mr Simeonov's death," he said.

Our guest resumed his narrative. "It took place, as I have said, in the home of Lord Eversden, Royston Manor, near Stoke Morden in Surrey. Lord Eversden has a great interest in Balkan affairs and he had invited a number of diplomats concerned with the current dispute to dinner at his house yesterday evening, with the purpose of discussing the matter in a relaxed and informal setting. Those invited were Count Balinsky, the Russian Ambassador; Mr George Leonticles, the Greek Consul; Mr Anton Simeonov; Baron Nopchka, the Austro-Hungarian Ambassador; Colonel Yusufoglu, the Turkish Military Attaché; and myself. All Lord Eversden's guests were to stay the night, and the atmosphere after dinner was, as far as was possible under the circumstances, quite agreeable. We had dispersed after the meal, some having gone to the smoking room, others to the library, while I had accompanied Lord Eversden to his study, where he was showing me a number of rare Persian manuscripts, an interest we have in common. At about half past nine o'clock, we were horrified to hear the loud report of a revolver being fired, followed by a dreadful cry of agony. The sound came from the upstairs corridor and Eversden and I rushed out of the study and up the stairs as fast as we could. Lying on the floor, just outside his bedroom, was Simeonov with a bullet hole through his chest. He was not dead and was gasping for breath, while Yusufoglu knelt beside him. Standing a few feet away was Leonticles, the Greek, with an ashen face, looking down at the dying man. Lord Eversden and I both knelt down on the floor, since it was clear that Simeonov was trying to say something. I said: "Who shot you?" He gasped for a few moments then, pointing at Yusufoglu, said, quite clearly: "The salon . . . the salon", then fell back and breathed his last. When I stood up I was aware that Count Balinsky and Baron Nopchka had arrived and were staring aghast at the corpse on the floor. A number of servants had also collected, and stood frozen into inaction, awaiting their master's orders. Lord Eversden instructed one of them to telephone the Bulgarian Legation and dismissed the others.

"Yusufoglu and Baron Nopchka removed the body to the deceased's bedroom, while the rest of us stood outside. Count Balinsky was as white as a sheet and was clearly trying hard to control his emotions. As soon as Yusufoglu emerged from the bedroom, Balinsky strode up to him and said, "This is your doing, you murderer!" Then turning to me, he said, "You and your country will pay for this! You have massacred enough people of my race and you will pay! You *will* pay!" He was quite out of control and, as if this was not enough, Yusufoglu, who is a man of a rather brooding temperament, shouted back: "I am not a murderer, you know the truth, ask yourself who is the murderer!" He took a step forward, but I placed a restraining hand on his arm and Balinsky, who was shaking with rage, also made a move towards Yusufoglu, but Lord Eversden stepped forward and planted himself between them. "I beg you to calm down, Count," he said in a firm voice, then, turning to Yusufoglu, he said, "Colonel, please!" Balinsky pushed his way rudely past Eversden and went swiftly down the staircase.

"The most puzzling thing about this mystery, Mr Holmes, is that a revolver was found lying beside the body."

"Surely, that is not difficult to explain, since the murderer must have dropped it as he fled from the scene," interrupted Holmes.

"The revolver had not been fired, Mr Holmes," said Orman Pasha, "and no other revolver was discovered."

Holmes rubbed his hands. "Pray continue your most interesting narrative."

"Two hours later the officials from the Legation arrived and the body was removed. Baron Nopchka pointed out that, since the matter was of great diplomatic sensitivity, the investigation would have to be handled very discreetly. It was then that I told the assembled company of my instructions from the Sultan and there was general agreement that you should be invited to look into the case. An Inspector Lestrade of Scotland Yard was summoned and was asked to work discreetly and to offer you every assistance if you agreed to accept the case. I regret to say that his initial investigations revealed nothing.

"There is little that remains to be told. This evening I attended a meeting with the Foreign Secretary in Whitehall, a meeting at which Count Balinsky and Baron Nopchka were also present. The Count's contribution was a series of threats of war; he had contacted his Government by telegraph and reported to the meeting that the mood in St Petersburg is that war is imminent. I contacted the Porte by telegraph and I am informed that the Turkish Armies in Rumelia and the Caucasus have been put on a state of readiness. I have given you the full details of the matter, Mr Holmes, and it now only remains for me to ask whether you would agree to investigate the problem and discover the true perpetrator of this crime."

Sherlock Holmes sat silently in his chair for a while, his elbows resting on the arms of the chair and his finger tips together, just touching his chin. He appeared to be looking at the wall beyond our visitor. Suddenly, he stood up and, looking down at our visitor, he said abruptly, "I very much regret that I can offer you no assistance in this matter."

I was aghast. Apart from my disbelief at Holmes's rejection of the oppressive and weighty problem that had been brought before us, I was taken aback to see our aged friend rebuffed in such a brusque manner. "Holmes," I said, "What can this mean? Surely, you are not going to refuse to act in a matter of this kind? Think of the consequences – do you wish the world to be plunged into a horrific war, when it is in your hands to prevent it?" Holmes said nothing, but continued to look down at our guest with a face devoid of expression.

Orman Pasha sat with a frown of disappointment on his face and said nothing for some moments. At length he spoke. "Mr Holmes," he said, "I fail to understand –".

"Come, come, my dear Pasha," said Holmes, firmly, "you understand only too well. I fear you have not told me the whole truth in this matter."

"Mr Holmes!" The Pasha rose to his feet in indignation.

"Oh, I have no doubt that you have told me all the facts relating to the case as far as they are known to you," said Holmes, "but I regret to say that you have not been fully open with me concerning your motives in asking me to investigate this matter. I cannot accept the case unless I am taken fully into your confidence."

There was a silence, during which the Pasha stood looking at Holmes with a frown of displeasure on his face, while Holmes remained as impassive and as immovable as ever. At last, the Pasha spoke.

"Perhaps, you will explain what you mean, Mr Holmes," he said.

"By all means," replied my friend, "will you tell me the name of the young man you are trying to protect, or shall I?"

Orman Pasha stared at Holmes in disbelief. Slowly, he resumed his seat and soon his expression changed to one of wry amusement.

"In spite of everything I have heard about you, Mr Holmes, I still managed to underestimate you," said Orman Pasha, "Your brother warned me that you have an uncanny ability to arrive at the truth. It encourages me a great deal. What you say is the truth; I am under instructions from the Sultan, not only to do my utmost to resolve this dangerous political crisis and to prevent a war, but to safeguard the reputation of Prince Murat, the Sultan's nephew. But how could you possibly have known?"

Sherlock Holmes sat down on the edge of his seat and leaned forward towards the Pasha. "Two clues, both furnished by Your Excellency, revealed the truth to me. First, you told me that this Simeonov was attacked in the street about four weeks ago, which is shortly after the time young Prince Murat arrived in this country for an unofficial visit, as everyone knows from reading the papers. It became immediately apparent to me that you were concerned that no one should suggest any link between the two events, especially since the Prince has repeatedly made known his views concerning the Bulgarian question. Secondly, the very fact that the Sultan instructed you to seek my advice and did not put his faith in the regular police force suggests that he was anxious that if the truth be found out – and be found to be unpalatable – my discretion could be relied upon to keep the matter quiet until the Prince be removed from this country and, hopefully, be dealt with suitably in Constantinople. Am I correct?"

The Pasha was listening with an expression of mingled amusement and respect on his face as Holmes was speaking.

"Well done, Mr Holmes," he said, when Holmes had finished, "His Imperial Majesty, had he been present here, would have approved. He is well acquainted with your achievements and, indeed, is an enthusiast like yourself, having made a detailed study of the structure of the wood of the different kinds of tree that abound on his estates."

Holmes sat back in his seat. "His Majesty would seem to a most interesting man; I shall make a point of sending him a copy of my monograph upon the use of wooden objects as murder weapons," he said. "However, to return to the matter in hand, where was the Prince at the time of the murder?"

"He was residing in Buckingham Palace as a guest of the King. There is no question of his involvement in this affair."

"I have no doubt of it, but, if I am to act with the minimum of hindrance I must ask Your Excellency to prevail upon the Prince to leave England at once and return to Constantinople."

"I will do as you ask, Mr Holmes. The departure of the Prince would take a great weight off my mind."

He rose from his seat. "Will you accept the case, Mr Holmes?" he asked.

"I will gladly do all I can to assist in this matter," replied my friend, "but I will need an address at which I may contact you."

"The Turkish Embassy in Belgrave Square will find me," replied the Pasha and, after donning his hat and cloak, he departed. When the horses' hooves had died away in the street outside, I asked Holmes what he intended to do.

"I will have an early night, Watson," he said, "there will be much to do tomorrow."

The dawn of the new day saw us having an early breakfast, after which we took a cab for Victoria station, where we boarded the first train to the village of Stoke Morden. As the train rattled towards its destination, Holmes, after watching the scenery fly past for a time, suddenly turned to me and said; "What do you make of the dying man's last words, Watson?"

"He referred to a salon and pointed at the Turkish Military Attaché," I said, "On the face of it, it would suggest that he was accusing him of the murder, but I confess I cannot see the significance of his reference to a salon. Could it be that he and the Turk had agreed to meet in a particular salon to discuss some dispute, but that the Turk decided to take matters into his own hands and shoot Simeonov without taking the trouble to discuss the matter first? It seems far-fetched, but I can think of no more plausible explanation."

"And yet, Watson, other plausible explanations may be offered," replied Holmes, "It may be, for example, that he was directing those present to some incriminating evidence to be found in a salon that may be known to one of them. I will admit, however, that I do not find such an explanation compelling."

"There is also the most singular altercation that immediately followed the man's death, when the Count and the Military Attaché accused one another of murder," I said.

"Is that how you interpreted it?"

"Yes, what other interpretation could possibly be made?"

"Consider what was actually said," replied Holmes, "The Count shouted 'This is your doing, you murderer' at the Military Attaché, but the Military Attaché did not, in fact, make a counter-accusation, but said, 'I am not a murderer, you know the truth, ask yourself who is the murderer.' He did not say 'I am not a murderer, *you* are the murderer'; his actual reply would suggest that he did *not* believe that the Count was the murderer, for if he did he would, presumably, have said so quite openly, since there seems to be little love lost between the two of them."

"In that case his reply seems further to suggest that both he and the Count know the identity of the murderer," I said.

"That is, of course possible," said Holmes, cryptically, and was silent for the rest of the journey.

When we arrived at Stoke Morden, Holmes hailed a cab and asked our driver to take us to Royston Manor, the home of Lord Eversden. After a frosty drive beneath an iron-grey sky, we arrived at the ivy-covered Manor that was the scene of the terrible murder, the commission of which seemed to threaten the peace of the world. We rang the ancient bell and an aged, somewhat lugubrious butler opened the door. Holmes presented his card and asked to see Lord Eversden. We were shown into a large drawing room, where we awaited the arrival of his lordship. Holmes and I stood looking out of window at the bleak winter scene and at the rooks circling and cawing above the trees. Suddenly, the drawing room door was flung open and two men, apparently in the middle of an involved argument, entered together. One was a man of above average height, with a fine, domed bald head and a silver moustache, while the other was a large and corpulent man, whom I instantly recognized.

"Sherlock," cried the large man as soon as he saw my friend, "we were expecting you." It was Holmes's brother Mycroft, the wizard of Whitehall. Holmes was clearly delighted, if not surprised, to see his brother, who introduced us to the tall man, who was Lord Eversden, the distinguished Foreign Secretary.

When we had all sat down, Lord Eversden looked at Holmes and said: "Your brother has told me that Orman Pasha has been to consult you regarding the tragedy that has taken place in my house. It is no exaggeration to say that this matter is fraught with danger, as I believe Orman Pasha, who is highly regarded in British Government circles, has informed you. We welcome your involvement and I wish to assure you that my house and staff are at your disposal."

"Thank you, my lord," replied Holmes, "I should like to begin by making an examination of the house."

We all followed Holmes up the staircase and Lord Eversden showed us the spot in which the body had been found. Holmes knelt to the ground and examined the carpet minutely, then asked, "Which way was the body lying? Were the feet pointing towards or away from the staircase?"

"They were pointing towards the staircase," replied Lord Eversden, "and his head was lying just next to the small side table by the entrance to the room."

Holmes stood up. "Now, my lord," he said," can you recollect where everyone was standing when you and Orman Pasha arrived here?"

Lord Eversden thought for a moment. "Colonel Yusufoglu was kneeling beside Simeonov between him and the bedroom door. Mr Leonticles was standing some feet away beyond Simeonov's head."

"In other words, he was standing where Simeonov could not see him?" asked Holmes.

"No, Simeonov would not have been able to see Leonticles from where he was lying," replied Lord Eversden, "Count Balinsky and Baron Nopchka arrived after the Pasha and I did, and they stood looking over our shoulders at the dreadful sight."

"Thank you, Lord Eversden, your comments are most illuminating," said Holmes, "Now I would like to examine Mr Simeonov's bedroom."

We entered the bedroom and Holmes made straight for the window. "Was the window closed when you came upstairs?" he asked Lord Eversden.

"As far as I can recollect, although I did not enter the room, but I could see the window from the corridor. Only Nopchka and the Colonel went in, carrying Simeonov's body."

Holmes opened the wardrobe, which proved to be empty, then dropped to the floor and looked under the bed. He reached with his arm under the bed and pulled out a small and very old Gladstone bag.

"Did this belong to Simeonov?" he asked.

"Yes, it was all the luggage he had," replied Lord Eversden.

Holmes placed the bag on the bed and opened it. It appeared to contain nothing but clothes and the usual paraphernalia of a visiting guest. Suddenly Holmes looked up at the window and froze. The expression on his face was so startling, that we all followed his gaze, but I, for one, could see nothing out of the ordinary.

"What is it, Sherlock," cried Mycroft, "what was there outside the window?"

Holmes quickly recovered his composure. "Nothing," he said, "Just a sudden movement, probably a bird." He closed the bag and replaced it under the bed. We next went to the bedrooms of all the other guests, but there was nothing to be gleaned from those either.

After an examination of the outside of the house and of the grounds, where Holmes searched in vain for any signs of footprints, we returned to the drawing room, where we all sat down, except for Holmes, who remained standing beside the fireplace.

"Lord Eversden," he began, "it is my desire to meet the diplomats who were your guests two days ago, but, before I do so, I would like to have an assessment of their characters and backgrounds by yourself and my brother. To begin with, Orman Pasha. Of course, I have already made his acquaintance and he struck me as an able and honest man. You both know him better; do you accept my conclusion?"

Lord Eversden spoke first: "Yes, he is a thoroughly decent and honourable man. I have known him for thirty-seven years." Mycroft was nodding. "He is without doubt one of the most distinguished of Turkish diplomats. HMG has always had excellent dealings with him; he is known to be incorruptible."

"And Colonel Yusufoglu, the Military Attaché?" asked Holmes.

"Ah, he is a hard man to know," said Mycroft, "a rather dark, brooding fellow, who strikes me as being quite capable of nursing a grudge." He turned to Lord Eversden, who added: "I do not know the man well, but I will confess that I took an instant dislike to him."

"What is known of his background?"

"He was on the staff of the Turkish Governor of Thessaly,' replied Mycroft, the fount of political knowledge, "which is effectively a part of Greece that is still under Turkish rule, or so the Greeks would claim. The Governor, Hassan Pasha, dealt with a firm, but fair hand with the riots that broke out there last year and earned the gratitude of the Greeks, which is something out of the ordinary in Græco-Turkish relations. Yusufoglu was his deputy and he, too, earned a reputation for fair dealing when members of the various rioting factions were brought to justice. He took up his post in the Turkish Embassy in London only six months ago."

"And Count Balinsky – what kind of man is he?" asked Holmes.

"A man of very definite and set beliefs and of a violent temper, as you will have gathered from Orman Pasha's account," said Lord Eversden, "A dangerous man and not one to be trifled with. He is a strong believer in Pan-Slavism and has a deep-seated hatred and mistrust of the Turks. As for Baron Nopchka, he is a benign, if not very imaginative, nobleman, belonging to one of Austria-Hungary's oldest families. He is a close confidante of the Emperor. A liberal by temperament, he supported greater parliamentary representation for the Slavonic peoples of the Austro-Hungarian Empire, but is secretly highly suspicious of the political activities of the Slavs in his country."

"Which leaves us with Mr George Leonticles, the Greek Consul," said Mycroft, "He, like Yusufoglu, has not been long in his post. He held a number of Greek Government positions in Greece before he came to England. Rumour has it that he was involved in certain political activities that earned him the Greek king's displeasure. He is a man of a somewhat nervous disposition and keeps himself largely to himself."

"One final question; what was Mr Simeonov's London address?"

Mycroft drew out a small notebook from his pocket. "Number. 6, Harrington Mews, W1," he said, "but I fear that the Bulgarian Legation is unlikely to furnish you with permission to visit the place. Since the British Government's refusal to support his Government's claims, the Bulgarian authorities have been quite uncooperative."

Holmes and I returned to London during the early afternoon. On the way I ventured to say to my friend: "Holmes, you have not so far commented on the singular presence of the loaded, but unfired, revolver beside Simeonov's body. I have been giving the matter some thought and can only conclude that the revolver was Simeonov's and that he tried to protect himself from his murderer by pulling out his own revolver when he realized that he was about to be shot. Do you agree?"

"The facts will bear that interpretation, I suppose," replied Holmes, as the train arrived at Victoria station.

"Do any other interpretations occur to you?" I retorted.

"Yes, Watson," replied Holmes, with a light in his eyes and leapt off the train. We hailed a cab and Holmes asked the driver to take us to the Russian Embassy. On arrival, Holmes, handing his card to the usher, asked to see the Ambassador. A few moments later, we were shown into Count Balinsky's sumptuous room.

Count Balinsky remained seated when we entered and regarded us coldly and with tight lips as we stood before his desk. He wore an expression of barely controlled anger and was turning Holmes' card over and over between his fingers. He was a lean man, with a pale face and eyes that burned like fire. He was clean-shaven, except for a pencil moustache that pointed abruptly upwards at the edges.

"You are the agent of the Turk, are you not?" he said coldly.

"I have been requested to look into the mystery of the late Mr Anton Simeonov's murder by His Excellency Orman Pasha," replied Holmes.

"And you come to me for help?" he asked in tones of great astonishment.

"I came to ask whether you can shed any light on this tragic affair," said Holmes.

"I can shed a great deal of light, Mr Holmes," replied the Count, menacingly, "That Turkish colonel did it. I told him so quite openly in everyone's presence."

"What evidence do you have for this?" asked Holmes.

"Evidence?" asked the Count, with an expression of bitter

amusement on his face, as though the request for evidence was of questionable taste. "Who else had a motive? Why should any of the other guests, other than the Sultan's envoy, have wished to kill Simeonov? Orman Pasha was with Lord Eversden when the murder was committed, so that leaves Yusufoglu."

"Someone else could have murdered him in order to incriminate Yusufoglu," said Holmes, quietly, looking straight into the Count's eyes, "It is even possible that Simeonov was murdered in order to foment trouble between your country and Turkey."

The Count's eyes narrowed and his lips tightened. Suddenly, he stood up. "Thank you, Mr Holmes," he said, in a white rage, "This interview is concluded."

After our unceremonious ejection from the Russian Embassy, we took another cab, this time to the embassy of Austria-Hungary. When we arrived there, we received a totally different kind of reception, for Baron Nopchka was very much a gentleman. He was of medium height and robust build and had fair hair, paling into silver at the temples. His patient expression, good-humoured eyes and elegant blond moustache all combined to give the impression of an honest middle-European nobleman; it was not difficult to imagine him wearing his Tyrolean hat and shooting wild boar at a hunting lodge in the Vienna woods. He rose as we entered his room and shook hands with us, saying how pleased he was to learn that my able friend had agreed to investigate the tragedy.

"Baron Nopchka," began Holmes, after we sat down, "it is my desire to arrive at a conclusion about this tragedy without delay. You will forgive me, therefore, if I ask you whether you have any suspicions as to who committed the murder."

The Baron's eyebrows rose. "That is not a very diplomatic question," he replied, with a wry smile, "but, under the extraordinary circumstances in which we find ourselves, I must admit that it is a fair one. Nevertheless, I cannot say that I have any ideas on the matter, but I can only express my devout hope that Colonel Yusufoglu is not the murderer, since the consequences are unthinkable. And yet Balinsky is convinced that it is he."

"Where were you and Count Balinsky when you heard the shot that killed Simeonov?"

"I was in the smoking room and Balinsky, I believe, was in the library. At least, when I rushed out into the hall, I saw Balinsky outside the library door. We then ran up the stairs together."

"You say that Count Balinsky was outside the library door; was he standing there, or did he appear to be running out of the library?"

"No, he was just standing there," said the Baron, with a frown, as if some new thought had just struck him.

"Was there any indication of the direction in which he was walking before you rushed out of the smoking room?"

"No," said the Baron again, still frowning, "he was standing still, with his back to the library door."

"Was the library door open or closed?"

"Closed."

There was a silence, then Holmes spoke. "Do you know where Mr George Leonticles was when the shot was fired?"

"No, I only saw him when I reached the upper landing. He was standing a few feet beyond where Simeonov lay, looking quite white."

"In your opinion, would you say that he was capable of murder?"

"It is possible, of course, but he is such a mild-mannered man that I frankly cannot see him committing murder. He was quite shaken by the incident."

"If he had killed Simeonov, he would have had good cause to appear shaken."

"Yes, I expect he would."

"You carried the body into the bedroom with Colonel Yusufoglu; did you notice whether the colonel was armed?"

"I certainly did not see any weapon. He was not wearing a jacket at the time and, after we placed the body on the bed we went downstairs together and he remained within my sight for at least the next hour."

"Are you convinced of his innocence then?"

The Baron said nothing, but his frown returned. He shifted in his chair. "Mr Holmes," he said at length, "there is something else I feel I ought to tell you. I have shied away from so doing because I do not know the meaning of what I witnessed and I feared that my account would only confuse matters and possibly incriminate innocent individuals. However, from what I have heard of you and, moreover, now that I have met you in person, I am convinced that I can rely upon you utterly to arrive at the truth in this tangled affair." Holmes bowed his head solemnly to the Baron.

"Shortly after I and the other guests arrived at Royston Manor, I went into the library to examine some of Lord Eversden's books. (Books are a great passion of mine, Mr Holmes.) As I entered, which I did quietly in order not to disturb other readers, I heard the voices of Mr Leonticles and Colonel Yusufoglu, the Turkish Military Attaché. Leonticles was saying, "We have no choice, we must act now, we will not have a better chance." Whereupon

Yusufoglu replied: "No, no, not yet, not here. It would be safer —"
At that moment Count Balinsky walked noisily into the room and
their conversation ended abruptly. As I said, Mr Holmes, I do not
know what this means and I leave it in your capable hands."

I looked at Holmes and was thrilled to see on his face that
tense expression of exhilaration that indicated that he was hot
on the scent. He rose and bowed to our gentlemanly host.

"Baron Nopchka," he said with barely suppressed excitement,
"your observations were invaluable."

The Baron's honest face looked both bewildered and encour-
aged by Holmes' comments. He said: "Have you arrived at some
conclusion about the case Mr Holmes? Good news or bad?"

"I have not yet quite concluded my investigations and, in any
case, I am bound to report first to Orman Pasha, who commissioned me to look into the matter," said Holmes, "However, I
will say to you, Baron, that there is cause for optimism."

We took our leave from the embassy, leaving a considerably puzzled, but to a great extent relieved, Austro-Hungarian
nobleman behind us.

We arrived late at Baker Street, with Holmes in an excellent
mood. A telegram awaited Holmes; he tore it open and read
it aloud: "Prince on way to Constantinople. O.P." "Excellent!"
cried Holmes, "Our Turkish friend is playing the game."

We consumed a magnificent dinner prepared by Mrs Hudson,
during which Holmes refused to speak about the case. When we
finished and were sitting by the fire, Holmes smoking his most
malodorous pipe, he looked at me with shining eyes and said:
"Watson, I intend to commit a felony tonight. Do you still have
your service revolver and your jemmy?" I was thrilled; it was
some considerable time since Holmes and I had one of those
adventures that temporarily placed us on the wrong side of the
law. "Holmes," I said, earnestly, "I'm your man; just give me half
an hour to collect them from my rooms."

It was approaching midnight when Holmes and I arrived at
Harrington Mews. We made our way stealthily to Number 6 and,
as we approached, Holmes whispered in my ear: "Do you have your
jemmy to hand Watson." I nodded, and we stole up to the door like
burglars. I was about to put my jemmy into action, when I gasped:
"Holmes, the door is already open!" Holmes stood still.

"Interesting, Watson, interesting," said Holmes in a whisper,
"the night may yet yield many surprises." We entered the house
noiselessly. Holmes made his way swiftly but quietly to the study. As
we reached the door, we could see light coming through the crack

at the bottom. There was a sound as of someone shuffling papers in the room. We stood stock still and listened, when suddenly the shuffling stopped and the gas light was turned off.

"Now, Watson!" said Holmes and we rushed into the room, only to see a dark shadow leap out of the open window and into the yard at the back. "After him, Watson!", shouted Holmes. I rushed to the window and jumped out; I could see my quarry making for the railings, hopping on one leg as though he had injured a foot in his fall. I sped towards him, but tripped over some wood and fell heavily over. When I got to my feet the intruder had gone. I hobbled painfully to the railings, but there was no sign of him to be seen. I returned crestfallen to Holmes.

"It matters little, Watson," he said, when I told him of my failure, "we will make the gentleman's acquaintance in the morning." During my absence Holmes had not been idle, but had gone through the papers on the desk and in the drawers. He was now holding a small scrap of paper up to the light. 'There is devilry here, Watson!" he said, his face set and hard, "but it is now time to return to our beds, for there is much to do on the morrow." With that, we made our back to Baker Street and, in my case at least, a night of fitful and troubled sleep.

I awoke the next morning to find Holmes shaking me by the shoulder.

"Wake up Watson! The game is afoot!"

"What o'clock is it, Holmes?" I asked, drowsily.

"Seven, Watson, and breakfast is ready."

I rose, washed and went in to breakfast. Holmes had already had his and was eager to go, so I gobbled my toast and swallowed my tea as quickly as I could and, before many minutes had passed, we were on our way to an address Holmes had given to the driver of our cab.

By contrast with the previous night, Holmes appeared preoccupied rather than excited. I asked: "Have you arrived at a conclusion, Holmes?"

"You know the way I work, Watson, my conclusions will be given when I am ready."

We travelled in silence to our destination, which turned out to be the small building that housed the Greek Consulate. We entered the building and asked to see the Consul, Mr Leonticles, and were immediately admitted to the Consul's office.

Mr George Leonticles, the Greek Consul, was a short man with jet-black hair, a pale face and a fastidious pointed goatee beard and waxed moustache. He was suave and courteous in his manner, but seemed ill at ease. He rose stiffly and invited us to sit down.

"How may I help you, gentlemen?", he asked.

"Mr Leonticles, my name is Sherlock Holmes and I have been commissioned to look into the murder of the late Mr Simeonov," replied Holmes, "It would materially aid me in my investigation if you would answer a few questions relating to that mystery."

Mr Leonticles smoothed his beard and moustache before replying. "I would be happy to offer any assistance, Mr Holmes, but I regret to say that I know little that would be of interest to you."

"Nevertheless, you may well be able to help clarify a few points," said Holmes, "for example, could you tell me where you were when you heard the shot that killed Mr Simeonov?"

"I was in my room."

"Your room is two doors down from Simeonov's, and yet when Lord Eversden and Orman Pasha arrived, they found Colonel Yusufoglu kneeling beside the body, while you stood some distance away. Why did you not rush to his assistance?"

"Yusufoglu's room was between mine and Simeonov's and he was able to reach him first," replied Leonticles, beads of perspiration beginning to appear on his forehead.

"Was the colonel in his room when the shot was fired?" asked Holmes.

"I think so. When I came out into the corridor he was already there, kneeling beside Simeonov."

"Mr Leonticles," asked Sherlock Holmes, bluntly, "did Colonel Yusufoglu kill Mr Simeonov?"

"No!"

"You seem remarkably sure of that. How can you know that he did not kill Simeonov?"

"Colonel Yusufoglu is not capable of murder. I have – I am sure he did not kill him."

"And yet Count Balinsky seems certain that the colonel is the murderer."

"Count Balinsky is mistaken," said the Consul firmly.

"Thank you, Mr Leonticles," said Holmes, suddenly, and rose to leave the room. As we reached the door, Holmes stopped to examine a small Greek statuette on a table beside the window.

"I have a great interest in the art of the Ancient Greeks. Is this not a reproduction of Aphrodite?" he asked the Consul, with a charming smile upon his face.

"No, no," replied our host, "coming round his desk, limping slightly as he came, and pointing to another sculpture on a table on the other side of the room, "this is Aphrodite." "Of course," said Holmes. "Thank you again, Mr Leonticles, we will take no more of your valuable time."

"We progress, Watson," said Holmes, as we sat in the cab on our way to Belgrave Square, "You noticed his limp?"

I had, indeed, noticed it. "Very similar to mine, Holmes, after I tripped over the pile of wood at Harrington Mews," I said, "Why did you not confront him with it?"

"There was no need," replied Holmes, "he knew it."

"But might he not flee the country, now that he knows you suspect him of breaking into the Bulgarian's house?" I asked.

"No, Watson," replied Holmes, with a smile, "I think not."

We arrived at the Turkish Embassy and were admitted by a porter who reminded me of the genie from Aladdin's lamp. He wore red boots with upturned toes, black baggy trousers and a green and highly ornate tunic. He accepted Holmes's card without a word and went to deliver it to Orman Pasha. A few minutes later, a sombre fellow in a suit and a fez came and escorted us to the Pasha's room.

This time Orman Pasha was not in full dress uniform, but was wearing a black frock-coat. He rose from behind his desk and greeted us warmly.

"Mr Holmes," he said, as he motioned us to sit down, "dare I hope that you have good news to tell?"

"We are approaching a solution to the mystery, Orman Pasha," said Holmes, "but there are some loose ends that remain. I am hopeful that a disaster may yet be averted."

"I am greatly relieved to hear it, Mr Holmes," replied the Pasha.

"I do, however, have a few questions to ask you, after which I would like to meet Colonel Yusufoglu," said Holmes, sitting back in his chair. "Orman Pasha, if, as we shall for the moment assume, the Bulgarian emissary was not murdered by your Government's agents, who else would have a motive for killing him?"

The Pasha thought for a moment. "Of the people present at Lord Eversden's dinner, I cannot think of anyone who might have a motive. They are all people in prominent diplomatic positions and I cannot see what any of them would gain from doing such a thing."

"Do you not think then that the reasonable conclusion to be drawn is that one of your Government's agents did, in fact, commit the murder? Colonel Yusufoglu was kneeling beside Simeonov; Simeonov appeared to accuse him with his dying words; Count Balinsky is convinced of his guilt. No other evidence seems to suggest the guilt of any other man. Must not the conclusion be that the colonel is guilty?"

The Pasha looked at Holmes with an expression of mingled amusement and impatience. "Mr Holmes," he said, "why do you suggest such a thing when you are already convinced that it is not true?"

"Why does Your Excellency conclude that I do not accept this as the truth?"

"Because you have already told me that you have high hopes of averting disaster, Mr Holmes. If you did, indeed, believe in Yusufoglu's guilt, you would not have said that."

Holmes smiled his tight, secret smile. "Guilt is a matter of definition. We must not forget that, in any murder, the murderer's motive is of at least equal importance to his identity."

The Pasha's brow darkened. "I fear, Mr Holmes, that, whatever the motive, it will make little difference in this case if Yusufoglu is the murderer. Do you wish to speak with him now?"

Holmes nodded and the Pasha rang a bell. The sombre individual entered the room and was given a few brief instructions in Turkish, whereupon he left, to return a few minutes later with a tall, broad-shouldered man – Colonel Yusufoglu. He was a dark-complexioned giant, with fierce black eyes and a thick black moustache. I will admit that he struck me as a morose fellow, who might well commit murder if the need arose.

The Pasha introduced us and Holmes and I shook hands with him. He sat down, eying us suspiciously.

"Colonel," began Holmes, "I hope you will excuse me if I speak openly and bluntly, because of what is at stake in this matter. You are, no doubt, aware that you are seen as being the prime suspect for the murder of Anton Simeonov. What have you to say in your defence?"

"I did not murder the Bulgarian," replied the colonel stolidly.

"Then who did?"

"I had been given to understand that it was your task to find that out."

"Nevertheless, I would be interested in your views on the matter."

"I did not witness the killing, how could I know who killed the man?"

"What did you mean when you said to Count Balinsky that he knew the truth?"

"I meant that he must know that I had every reason not to commit the murder. Even he must be aware that such an act would precipitate the events we were all anxious to avoid."

"Why did you say 'Ask yourself who is the murderer'?"

The Military Attaché shifted uneasily. "I was inviting him to think more clearly." I noticed that Orman Pasha was looking at the colonel with a worried expression on his face, as though he found his answers to Holmes's questions weak and unconvincing.

Holmes leapt to his feet. "Thank you, colonel, you have told me everything I need to know."

The colonel rose from his seat, looking at Holmes with an expression half angry and half fearful. He turned and said something in Turkish to Orman Pasha, who nodded. The colonel turned and looked at Holmes with smouldering black eyes, then abruptly left the room.

"Orman Pasha," said Holmes, when the colonel had gone, "does any member of your staff speak Bulgarian?"

"I speak Bulgarian myself, Mr Holmes," replied the Pasha, with an expression of mild astonishment on his face.

"Good, then perhaps you would be good enough to tell me whether this English sentence is a correct translation of the Bulgarian sentence above it." He handed our host a small piece of paper. The Pasha took it and I was disturbed to see the old man start violently.

"What is the meaning of this, Mr Holmes," said the Pasha, "What are you telling me?"

"I am telling you that this case is much more complicated than we thought at the outset. I take it the translation is accurate?"

"It is accurate, Mr Holmes," said the Pasha, shaking his head in puzzlement and disbelief.

On our way back to Baker Street, Holmes stopped at a post office to send a telegram. He then went to pay a visit to his brother Mycroft at the Diogenes Club and I made my way to Baker Street alone. When he finally arrived, Holmes walked over to the mantelpiece and, to my horror, he stood contemplating the syringe that enabled him to indulge his only weakness.

"Holmes, my dear fellow," I said, "you have arrived at your final conclusion in this case."

"Yes, Watson, I have arrived at my final conclusion."

We had a quiet dinner, as usual prepared by the excellent Mrs Hudson. After the meal, Holmes stood up. "Tomorrow morning we will go Stoke Morden to save the world," he said. "Better have an early night, Watson." He disappeared into his bedroom, while I went to mine in a sombre mood.

Holmes was quite himself again the following morning. We had breakfast and were soon on our way to Victoria Station. When we eventually arrived at Royston Manor, I noticed that a number of fine carriages drawn by magnificent horses were moving off the broad gravel pathway that led to the house. We were admitted by the old butler and were shown into the drawing room, where, to my astonishment, I found that all the *dramatis personae* of the recent tragedy were present. Lord Eversden was seated in his armchair, with Orman Pasha on the settee beside him. Baron Nopchka sat at the other end of the settee, while Mr Leonticles and Colonel Yusufoglu were sitting on armchairs opposite the settee. Count Balinsky, as though disdaining the company of others, sat somewhat apart, near the window. Mycroft Holmes was sitting on an upright chair in front of a table behind the settee.

As we entered, Lord Eversden rose and came across to greet us.

"I received your telegram, Mr Holmes," he said. "As you can see, they are all here. Inspector Lestrade will be arriving in about one hour's time." He motioned us to sit down, which I did on an upright chair near Baron Nopchka. Holmes declined the invitation and remained standing.

"My lords and gentlemen," began Holmes, "I am happy to be able to report that I have unravelled the mystery that has recently cast a shadow over international relations. Regrettably, it is unlikely that we will be able to bring the culprit to justice, since we are dealing with a very clever criminal. My investigations allow me to conclude that an armed burgler managed to gain entry to the house. He made his way stealthily upstairs, where he was surprised by Mr Anton Simeonov. Before Mr Simeonov was able to raise the alarm, the burglar drew his revolver and shot him, just as the victim was about to defend himself by drawing out his own weapon. The murderer was then able to conceal himself behind the large armchair in the corridor and stayed there when you all arrived at the scene. When you all left the corridor, he made his escape through one of the windows, through which he jumped. He then cleverly concealed his tracks and made off. It is highly unlikely that he will ever be apprehended."

We all stared at Holmes. Lord Eversden said: "But this is not credible, Mr Holmes. There is nothing to suggest that such a thing happened." He turned a troubled look to Mycroft, who, alone in the gathered audience, was nodding, with an amused smile of understanding on his face.

Count Balinsky snorted derisively: "Do you think my Government will accept such a story, such a transparent fabrication?" He rose to his feet. "Excuse me, Lord Eversden, but I am obliged to telegraph the Czar's cabinet." He took a step or two across the room, with a smile of malicious satisfaction on his face, when Holmes took a long stride and barred his way.

"My dear Count," he said severely, "I strongly advise you to sit down. The story I have given you may be preferable to your Government – and to you – than the alternative I am able to offer." The Count glared at Holmes, but slowly his expression changed to one of hunted suspicion. Holmes returned to the spot at which he had been standing, while the Count remained standing for a few moments. The whole room was tense. Slowly, the Count resumed his seat.

"The difficulty with this case was the absence of a motive, other than the obvious one in the case of an assassination by agents of the Turkish Government," said Holmes. "The foolishness of such an undertaking, especially under the present political atmosphere, suggested that murder by a Turkish agent was extremely unlikely. Such a crime could not possibly have served the aims of the Turkish Government – in fact, quite the reverse – so I dismissed it as a real possibility from the outset. However, this does not mean that the murder could not have been committed by a Turkish person for non-political reasons. This, too, seemed unlikely, since such a person committing such a crime would be perfectly aware of the political interpretation that some people would put upon it.

"Therefore, my working hypothesis was that the crime was not committed by either of the Turkish guests. Orman Pasha, in any case, was not under suspicion, since he was with Lord Eversden at the time. But Colonel Yusufoglu was found kneeling beside Simeonov and Count Balinsky accused him of the murder. On the other hand, the colonel appeared to be unarmed but, had he been the murderer, he would not have had time to dispose of the weapon, unless he shot Simeonov, rushed away to dispose of the weapon and then, perversely, returned to place himself in the incriminating position of kneeling beside the man he had shot.

"The other confusing aspect of this case is that I had started with the assumption that Simeonov's murderer and the man who assaulted him some weeks ago were one and the same. At least, it seemed reasonable to assume that the two events were related. My investigations revealed to me that they were not and *that* was the clue that solved the mystery."

Holmes turned to Lord Eversden. "Someone in this room killed Simeonov, but he is no murderer. The only murderer among your guests was Simeonov himself!"

Except for Mycroft, we all gasped with astonishment. Count Balinsky sat forward in his chair and his expression looked more hunted than ever. Leonticles looked paler than usual. Colonel Yusufoglu covered his face with his hands.

"Yes," said Holmes, looking in turn at the Greek Consul, the Turkish Colonel and the Russian Count. "You know the truth of this. When Colonel Yusufoglu said that Count Balinsky knew the truth, he was speaking the truth, was he not Count?"

"You dare to accuse a member of the Czar's Government of killing –" he began, rising to his feet.

"Control yourself, Count," said Holmes, harshly. "No one has accused you of killing Simeonov. Your crime is far more diabolical." The Count opened his mouth to reply, but all eyes turned towards him, and no sound came from his throat. He sat down, his face working.

"When the colonel said that Count Balinsky knew the truth, he meant that he knew that Simeonov was a murderer. Count Balinsky understood this very well, but preferred to pretend he did not, for reasons that will become clear presently. In fact, Simeonov was shot as he was about to commit another murder. His intended victim was ready for him and the tables were turned. The revolver lying on the ground was the one with which Simeonov intended to commit murder, not one that he drew out to defend himself.

"When I examined Simeonov's belongings, I discovered a small box containing what appeared to be greeting cards. So they were – of a kind. I hope I will be forgiven for distracting attention by pretending to see something through the window, but it was necessary for me to extract them without being seen to do so. Each card had the letters VMRO on it." Holmes drew one out of his pocket and held it up. The letters were very large and were easily visible across the room. Holmes turned to Count Balinsky: "You recognize these symbols of the notorious Balkan anarchist organization with no name, do you not, Count? I imagine everyone else in this room does as well. However, only three people here present knew about Simeonov's murderous past and of his membership of that organization. When Watson and I broke into Simeonov's house, I discovered three other cards, each with the letters IMRO printed on it. IMRO is a rival anarchist organization, bitterly opposed to the first. One card had the following written on it in Bulgarian: "Death is near. You have been warned." My translation was kindly confirmed by Orman Pasha when I showed it to him yesterday. The card also bore the December date on which Simeonov was assaulted in the street. His would-be assassin on that occasion was a member of the opposing criminal group.

"Understanding this helped me to understand the rest. Baron

Nopchka overheard Mr Leonticles urging Colonel Yusufoglu to act, but the colonel was urging restraint. The Baron was worried by this because he thought that Mr Leonticles may have been referring to a planned murder of Simeonov, but he was wrong. Mr Leonticles wished to expose Simeonov for the criminal he was, whereas the colonel was probably urging Mr Leonticles to wait until they were at a meeting in London, where the building would be guarded by policemen, making it difficult for Simeonov to escape once he was identified. Count Balinsky barged noisily into the room while the colonel was speaking, but it is my belief that he had overheard enough of the conversation to understand its significance. He then told Simeonov what he had heard and Simeonov determined to take matters into his own hands.

"It was Mr Leonticles who recognized Simeonov. He was in Thessaly when Colonel Yusufoglu was serving there as the Governor's Deputy and they were both involved in quelling the riots instigated by VMRO. As soon as he recognized Simeonov as one of the criminals who were condemned to death, but later escaped, he told Colonel Yusufoglu.

"We come now to the question of why Count Balinsky told Simeonov of Mr Leonticles' recognition of him. The Count is, as we all know, determined to start another Russo-Turkish war, from which he believes Russia would benefit. The Count was well aware that, if he told Simeonov that Leonticles knew of his past, Simeonov would try to silence him. If a Greek is murdered during this meeting, suspicion would immediately fall upon the Turks. If Simeonov was killed, suspicion would still fall upon the Turks. Either way, he could use the event as an excuse to foment trouble and urge the Czar to declare war against the Sultan. His plan could not fail. He waited downstairs outside the library so that he would be able to rush upstairs when someone else appeared – in the event it was Baron Nopchka – in order to ensure himself an alibi."

"Mr Leonticles was armed with a revolver, when he heard Simeonov creeping up behind him. He shot him first and ran to the other end of the corridor to hide the weapon temporarily behind the large armchair in the corner. I have no doubt that he disposed of it efficiently later. The colonel heard the shot and rushed out of his room; he may have seen Mr Leonticles hiding the weapon, but he then went to the dying man, perhaps to hear what he had to say. When I interviewed the colonel yesterday he as good as told me that he knew Mr Leonticles killed Simeonov. I asked him whether he knew who murdered Simeonov and he did not say 'No', but replied: 'I did not witness the killing, how can I know who killed him?' His avoidance of the word 'murder' was also revealing."

Holmes turned to George Leonticles, the Greek Consul. "Have I given a passable account?" he asked.

The Consul remained silent, with a strained face, for a few moments. "Yes, Mr Holmes, you have. But you have not explained the meaning of the dying man's last words, although I am sure you understand that, too."

Yes," said Holmes, "I understand the meaning of his last words. A dying man fighting for breath cannot easily say a word of many syllables. The capital of Thessaly is Salonika and the riots there became known as the Salonika Incident. I think Simeonov recognized Colonel Yusufoglu as he was dying and was trying to tell him that he remembered him from the days of the Salonika Incident."

A heavy silence descended upon the room. Presently, Lord Eversden spoke, addressing the gathered company in general: "Tomorrow I will seek an audience with His Majesty the King, with the purpose of requesting His Majesty's approval for a diplomatic deportation order to be prepared. I will also ask His Majesty to invite the Czar's Government to appoint an Ambassador to the Court of St James, that post being currently vacant." Count Balinsky sat perfectly still, although the fire still burnt in his eyes.

There was a soft knock on the door and the lugubrious butler entered. "My lord," he said, "a person from Scotland Yard has just arrived. His name is Inspector Lestrade."

"Thank you, Jenkins," said Lord Eversden, "ask him to wait a few moments." The butler withdrew, lugubriously.

Holmes looked at Lord Eversden. "I am now obliged to make my conclusions known to the police. Which account am I to give them?"

Lord Eversden turned to Orman Pasha, who shook his head and said: "It is abundantly clear that a burglar broke in." He rose, came across the room and shook Holmes warmly by the hand. "Mr Holmes, thank you. What we owe you is beyond evaluation."

Holmes and I returned to Baker Street in the evening. Holmes started ascending the stairs, but I went to have a few words with Mrs Hudson. When I joined Holmes upstairs, I found him sitting in his chair with an air of dejection and despondency about him. He was looking at the syringe on the mantelpiece.

"An interesting case, Watson. I wonder whether the world will ever come to its senses. This Balkan crisis nearly plunged the whole world into misery; I trust no such crisis will arise again in our lifetime."

"I trust not, Holmes," I said, as Mrs Hudson entered with a tray, which she placed on the table and left. Holmes sniffed the air and said: "Hello, what's this, Watson?"

"Turkish coffee, Holmes. One of Orman Pasha's attendants gave it to me as we were leaving Royston Manor. He said that the Pasha asked him to say that it was a better stimulant than many others."

Holmes smiled to himself as he sipped the coffee. "Excellent, Watson," he said.

THE ENIGMA OF
THE WARWICKSHIRE VORTEX

F. Gwynplaine MacIntyre

According to Watson's accounts, Holmes investigated just three more cases in 1903 – "The Mazarin Stone", "The Three Gables" and "The Creeping Man". After the last case he decided to retire. He probably did this on the occasion of his fiftieth birthday. He settled in a small house on the South Downs near Eastbourne and spent his time beekeeping, on which he wrote a treatise, the Practical Handbook of Bee Culture, *and bringing together all of his own papers to produce the definitive volume* The Whole Art of Detection.

He was very strict about his retirement, refusing to venture back to his old practice. Nonetheless, a mind as active as Holmes's would never be at rest. He recorded an investigation of his own, "The Lion's Mane" in 1907, but it is rather surprising that he did not record the culmination of a case that had puzzled him for thirty years. This was the remarkable one of James Phillimore, who stepped back into his house to collect his umbrella and was never seen again. Holmes investigated the case early in his career but had been unable to resolve it. The mercurial interests of F. Gwynplaine MacIntyre have caused him to undertake research into a number of areas, none of which were Holmesian, but a stroke of luck while researching the development of the cinema in New York brought the conclusion of the case to light. Many others have attempted to resolve this enigmatic case but here, at last, is the answer.

STRANGE DISAPPEARANCE OF LOCAL BUSINESSMAN

A peculiar and unexplained incident is reported from Leamington. On the Wednesday morning, two bankers of this community made a visit to Number 13a, Tavistock-street, the residence of Mr James Phillimore, age 33, who desired to accompany these gentlemen to their place of business for the purpose of discussing a financial transaction.

Stepping into the street, Mr Phillimore glanced momentarily upwards, and – although the weather has been fair this past fortnight – he remarked to his companions: "It looks like rain. Let me get my umbrella." Whereupon he stepped back into his own house, closing the front door but leaving it unlocked, whilst his colleagues remained on the doorstep.

A moment later, the two gentlemen overheard Mr Phillimore shouting from within: "*Help me! I can't –*" His words were terminated in mid-sentence. Mr Phillimore's two callers straight away entered the house's antechamber, where a most peculiar sight awaited them.

The floorboards in the centre of the foyer were *scorched*, in a pattern forming *a circle roughly six feet in diameter*: as if some unknown vortex had visited this portion of the room, and no other. Mr Phillimore's muddy footprints could be clearly seen, in a trail leading directly to the perimeter of this circle. *The rear half of a footprint* protruded from the outer edge of the circle: the front half of Mr Phillimore's right foot had evidently entered the circular mystery, yet *it left no imprint within.*

An umbrella-stand stood unmolested in a corner of the vestibule, well away from the circle. The ferrule of Mr Phillimore's umbrella, with several inches of the shaft, was found on the floor at the outer edge of the circular enigma. The missing portion of the umbrella – which presumably had accompanied Mr Phillimore into the circular zone – had been neatly *sheared off.*

Both of the witnesses to this astonishing occurrence are prominent bankers of Leamington Spa, whose veracity and sobriety are above reproach.

The house has now been thoroughly searched by the local police, and there is no evidence of sink-holes nor of any hidden chambers. At this reporting, no trace of Mr Phillimore has been found.

Extract from *The South Warwickshire Advertiser*
for Thursday, 26 August 1875

My friend Sherlock Holmes had recounted the Phillimore case to me in only the briefest terms, for he was disinclined to discuss his rare failures. I knew only that the incident had occurred very early in his detective career, shortly after the *Gloria Scott* affair. Mr Phillimore of Leamington Spa, Warwickshire, had vanished quite as if the Earth itself had swallowed him up, and he might never reappear unless the Earth itself should open and regurgitate him.

On the afternoon of 18 April 1906, I was examining a patient in my London surgery when word arrived that a great earthquake had lain waste to the mighty city of San Francisco. By nightfall the grim toll was confirmed: several hundreds were injured or dead, and many thousands were homeless. For the next thirty hours, the transatlantic cable relayed further news: the coal-gas lines beneath the San Francisco streets had ruptured in the earthquake, in consequence of which the entire city was now engulfed by fires that raged unchecked. In the safety of my Harley Street surgery, I resolved myself to make a modest contribution to any public subscriptions which might be set up in London to aid the San Franciscan victims.

Scarcely a fortnight later, a telegram bearing a familiar return address in the Sussex Downs was delivered to my rooms. The message consisted of only three words: "COME AT ONCE" and the signature "HOLMES". No further text was necessary.

I made haste to Victoria station and purchased a first-class return for the down train to Brighton. After an unusually long wait for my train's arrival, the railway journey passed quickly enough. At the Brighton cab-rank, a coachman conveyed me to the gateposts of my destination.

The house of Mr Sherlock Holmes was outwardly like any bachelor's domicile, but the gardens surrounding it provoked astonishment. The house was flanked and garrisoned on all sides by long thin wooden cabinets which – upon closer inspection – were in fact *bee-hives*, oozing the pale beeswax and darker secretions of their insect inhabitants. The constant buzzing was a thousandfold Babel. As I strode up the front path amid an escort of inquisitive bees, I glimpsed the face of my friend and summoner at a nearby window. Before I even had time to make use of the boot-scraper beside the doorstep, I was ushered within. The bees, fortunately, elected to remain outside. A moment later I was cross-legged on a haircord settee, in the parlour of my good friend Sherlock Holmes.

"Delighted you came, Watson." He passed forth his cigar-case, and I accepted a black *perfecto*. Whilst I cut this and lit it, Holmes resumed: "You must pardon my bees. One of the hives has just today produced a new queen, and she has been kept busy murdering all of the dormant queens."

"I had not known that bees could be persuaded to live in wooden cabinets," I said.

Holmes selected a Havana *panatela*, and lit his cigar without cutting it. "The bees live in a nearby hollow oak. Those cabinets are my own creation, inspired by the devices of an American beekeeper, the Reverend Langstroth. Each honeycomb occupies its own cabinet, and may be removed without disturbing the other combs." Without warning, my friend changed the subject abruptly:

"Watson, I regret that you were obliged to wait so long for your train at Victoria station."

"You were aware of the delay, then?" I asked him.

"Not at all," said Sherlock Holmes. "As soon as you entered my house, I observed that your train was delayed."

I smiled indulgently. "You must have memorized *Bradshaw's Railway Guide*, and you inferred the tardiness of my train from the hour of my arrival."

"I never memorize idle data, Watson. My mind is a workroom, not a storage room." Holmes pointed his long fore-finger towards my feet. "Your shoes, I observe, are freshly polished. Owing to the urgency of my telegram, you would not have chosen to delay your departure from London by devoting time to such trifles. You must have been unwillingly detained at the railway terminus, and – during the enforced wait – you availed yourself of the bootblacks who ply their trade along the Belgrave wall of Victoria station."

"Remarkable, Holmes! What you say is the truth."

"Furthermore," my friend continued, "there is one particular bootblack in the Belgrave Road whose brown boot-cream is of a distinctive *russet* colour, not available commercially. I believe that he makes up the mixture himself, from an original receipt. Your footgear, Watson, bears the mark of that tradesman."

Once again I was astonished. "But surely, Holmes, you did not summon me here to discuss bootblacks," I ventured.

"Indeed not." Holmes went to the fireplace, and retrieved a folded document from the mantelshelf. "You are doubtless aware of the recent holocaust in San Francisco."

I nodded sadly. "Yes, the earthquake and the subsequent fires. A dreadful accident."

"*Accident* is hardly the word, Watson. Precisely *one day* after the San Francisco earthquake, my good friend Pierre Curie – the distinguished French scientist – was struck and killed by a horse-cart in Paris. *That* misfortune was an accident. This San Francisco affair is something rather worse: our planet Earth has burst open at the seams."

I nodded once more. "In spite of scientific progress, men are still at the mercy of Nature."

There was a dark look in his eyes as Sherlock Holmes spoke: "It is not Nature which preys upon men, Watson. The predator who threatens humanity is man himself." Holmes sat down and unfolded the document in his hands. "I have received a despatch from two American gentlemen: Mr Henry Evans, the president of the Continental Insurance Company; and Mr James D. Phelan, a former mayor of San Francisco. These men have pledged themselves to the cause of resurrecting their dead city, and of seeing San Francisco rise from the ashes."

"Strange that a *former* mayor, rather than the current officeholder, should undertake such a mission," I remarked.

"The current mayor is part of the problem, Watson." Sherlock Holmes glanced at the document before him. "Mr Phelan informs me that, during his own term as mayor of San Francisco, municipal funds were allocated for the wages and training of police officers and firemen, as well as funds for the purchase and maintenance of fire-engines and pump-waggons, and for horses to convey them."

"A prudent investment, surely," I said.

"Perhaps not," Holmes's frown deepened. "Mayor Phelan's letter goes on to state that the present mayor of San Francisco – one Eugene Schmitz by name – is the agent of a ring of thieves and grafters who have systematically looted the city's coffers and enriched themselves by several *millions* of stolen dollars. Due to the absence of funds, the police force and fire department of San Francisco are mere skeleton crews: ill-trained, and obliged to fulfil their duties with defective equipment. In consequence, when the earthquake struck, the death-toll was far higher than it might have been. Doctor, it may interest you to know that the recent San Francisco earthquake, and the ensuing conflagrations, have claimed *seven hundred* human lives."

"*Good heavens!*" I exclaimed.

"Indeed. But if Mr Phelan is to be believed – and I believe him, Watson – more than 300 of those deaths, as well as 20 million dollars' worth of property damage, are the direct result of Mayor Schmitz's embezzlements. Had the city's funds been allocated to their rightful needs, those people never would have died."

"A tragedy, surely. But what has this to do with you, Holmes?"

My friend refolded Mr Phelan's epistle and pocketed it. "The Continental Insurance Company, and several other assurance firms as well, are now threatened with bankruptcy as a result of the torrent of policy claims emanating from San Francisco. Mr Evans and his colleagues intend to make good on all claims, but they are resentful at bearing the costs for this tragedy whilst the thieves who caused it go free. Mayor Schmitz and his corrupt associates are to blame, yet no evidence of their guilt can be established."

We smoked in silence for a moment, and then Holmes spoke again: "Evidently my reputation has travelled all the way to California, Watson. This letter is the result. Mr Phelan and Mr Evans, joined by a syndicate of insurance brokers, have offered me *carte blanche* if I will but journey to San Francisco and place myself at their disposal. These men wish to engage my

services in a matter of deduction and investigation. They desire me
to find solid *proof,* such as will stand up in any American court, of
the malfeasances of Schmitz and his henchmen."

"And do you intend to accept this commission, Holmes?" I
asked him.

"My dear Watson, I already have. American politics are a dark
labyrinth which I have never entered before, and the challenge
intrigues me." Holmes arose and stretched himself. "One more
thing, Watson. The hospitals and emergency wards of San Francisco
are filled to bursting with the injured and the dying; there are not
enough doctors in that broken city to attend to them all. Your
medical talents would be welcome in this crisis. And I may have
need of your assistance during my own investigations. Shall I notify
Continental Insurance to advance me the funds for *two* steamship
tickets to America?"

The question was altogether unexpected. I hesitated for the
briefest of moments while I considered how to inform my wife,
then extended my hand. Sherlock Holmes clasped it in both of
his own.

"Capital, Watson! We shall be occupied for two months at the
very least. Inform your Harley Street patients to make other
arrangements in your absence. As for my bees: until we return
I can only hope that their new queen will rule wisely."

And so our adventure began. We sailed from Southampton on
12 May bound for New York City aboard a steamship aptly
christened the *New York.* During the voyage, Sherlock Holmes
kept his remarkable brain occupied with the game of observing
our fellow passengers and deducing their origins, vocations and
personalities from the clues offered by their physical appearances
and behaviours.

We arrived in New York City's harbour on the morning of 19 May.
There was still the wide continent of North America to be traversed,
but Mayor Phelan had arranged for us to be granted passage on
any of the US Army's relief trains bringing provisions and medical
aid from New York to the refugee camps outside San Francisco.
After clearing the New York customs house, health station, and
currency exchange, Holmes and I secured a four-wheeler and
made haste with our luggage north and east through Manhattan
to the Pennsylvania station – for Holmes was determined to begin
the long transcontinental railway journey as soon as possible.

By noon we reached the New York Central terminus, where
Holmes was much distrait to be told that the next relief train
did not embark until tomorrow morning. "There's nothing for

it, Watson," he said. "We are obliged to spend a night in this metropolis. Let us quarter ourselves in an hotel, and then we shall see what diversions the island of Manhattan can offer us."

I took charge of the transfer of our bags to the Herald Square Hotel, on the south side of West Thirty-Fourth Street, whilst Holmes sent a telegram to Continental Insurance's main office. "I have cabled Mr Evans with the news that I shall be aboard tomorrow's train," Holmes informed me after I had dealt with the hotel's guest-register, "and I have told him that I am bringing with me the greatest field surgeon of my acquaintance."

"You flatter me, Holmes."

"I think not. Come, Watson! For this afternoon and evening, at least, let us seek such pleasure as this city affords, knowing that tomorrow morning our unpleasant task begins. In the telegraph office I overheard that Maude Adams is appearing in *Peter Pan* at the Empire Theatre in West Forty-Sixth Street. Let us spend tonight in Neverland, and give no thoughts to pain or San Francisco."

Sherlock Holmes and I proceeded northwards, up the wide Manhattan thoroughfare known as Broadway. Just south of West Thirty-Seventh Street, at Number 1367, Broadway, my attention was arrested by a brownstone building papered with gaudy posters. This proved to be the Edisonia Amusement Hall, and the posters outside advised us that, for five cents' admission, we might view an exhibition of Thomas Edison's miraculous invention, the Vitascope.

"I have heard of this machine, but never seen it in operation," I remarked to Holmes, with more than a hint of eagerness in my voice. "Mr Edison's Vitascope has gone one better than the magic-lantern: his invention can project images that actually *move!*"

"'Invention', indeed!" Holmes remarked with an audible sniff. "Edison has no more invented the Vitascope than I have invented the wheel. Watson, the first kinetographic camera and projector were devised by Louis Le Prince, a Frenchman who dwelt in Yorkshire. I myself attended a demonstration of his apparatus in Leeds in 1888. But come: since you are clearly so keen to witness this Vitascope, let us pay the admission and enter."

The amusement hall's afternoon programme was well attended, but Holmes and I were able to secure two seats in the pit-stalls, conveniently adjoining the centre aisle. The stage of the amusement hall was bare, except for a large white rectangular screen that seemed to afford no great promise of entertainment. The performance had not yet begun, and in the theatre seats all round us the audience were abuzz with a myriad of conversations. "I am no longer homesick for my bees." Holmes murmured to me, amid the general huzzbuzz. "It appears that we may converse freely without breaching etiquette, since everyone else in this place is talking anyway. Watson, I can never sit through a moving-picture exhibition without thinking of the strange case of James Phillimore."

For a moment the name meant nothing whatever to me, but then the penny dropped: "Wasn't he the man who vanished from his own house in Warwickshire?"

"The same." In the red plush seat beside me, Holmes sighed wearily. "One of my earliest failures, Watson. Following his vanishment in 1875, neither I nor anyone else ever clapped eyes on Mr James Phillimore again."

"Surely a man who vanished in 1875 could have nothing to do with moving-pictures," I proposed, "for they had not yet been invented."

Sherlock Holmes nodded. "Watson, I have told you that the kinetograph was invented in England by Louis Le Prince. In 1890, during a visit to his native France, Monsieur Le Prince consented to demonstrate his device at the Paris Opera House. In September of that year, he boarded a train at Dijon, taking his camera and projector into a first-class compartment. When the train reached Paris, Watson, that compartment was empty. Despite an exhaustive investigation, neither Le Prince nor his motion-picture apparatus were ever seen again."

"Astonishing!" I remarked.

"I had read of the case at the time, and offered my services to the French authorities," Holmes went on. "The Sûreté declined my offer. Still, to this day I can never view a kinetograph without thinking of its inventor's curious fate, and when I think of Le Prince's vanishment I am naturally put in mind of James Phillimore."

"Was Phillimore a friend of yours, Holmes?"

"I never met him," said my companion. "Phillimore's peculiar disappearance in 1875 aroused much attention at the time, and I journeyed to Leamington Spa to join the search for him. Among the furnishings in Phillimore's house in Tavistock Street was found a cabinet study of a man in his early thirties; his two banking colleagues identified this photograph as a likeness of James Phillimore. I obtained a copy of the portrait, and committed it to memory. Watson, for twenty years after his vanishment – even when my wanderings brought me to the gates of Lhassa and Khartoum – I never was able to pass through a crowd without searching amongst its constituents for the face of James Phillimore. But now, after thirty-one years, I am resigned that he has vanished forever."

At that moment the house lights dimmed, and the theatre audience fell silent. A man stepped forth upon the stage, and introduced himself to us as Mr Edwin Stanton Porter of the Edison

Film Company. He assured us that the Vitascope possessed a full palette of diversions – comedies, dramas, nature studies – and that all of these would be on offer at this afternoon's performance.

"I particularly wish to draw your attention to the closing item on the bill," said Mr Porter to his wrapt audience. "This very morning, a Vitascope photographer set up his apparatus in the streets of Manhattan. He has captured true-life scenes of New York City, taken in natural sunlight. Ladies and gentlemen, the photographic record of those events has already been developed and shipped to this theatre, barely four hours after they occurred." An excited murmur went round the auditorium at this point. Mr Porter continued: "It is hoped that, in future, the Edison Film Company will devise a means by which any newsworthy event anywhere on the globe can be captured by Mr Edison's wonderful Vitascope, and projected onto screens throughout the planet instantaneously."

In his seat beside me, Sherlock Holmes muttered something. Now Mr Porter left the stage, and of a sudden we were plunged into utter darkness.

Without warning, *a railway engine* burst onto the stage, rushing headlong towards the audience. There was a general panic, followed by gasps and applause as the realization came that this oncoming juggernaut was a kinetographic image in one of Mr Edison's Vitascope films. I confess that I had risen halfway from my seat, in flight from the illusion, before Holmes's grip on my arm restrained me. "Calm yourself, Doctor. It is only a toy."

I regained my seat, and the programme resumed. The next Vitascope was a *tableau vivant* of several plump ladies striking poses in Grecian robes. This was followed by a display of ocean waves. Next came an extract from the opera *Faust* – an opera, that is, without music or voices, for I was disappointed to observe that these Vitascope life-studies were devoid of sound and colour. The actors were obliged to perform their roles in dumb-show. Still, they were remarkable – and their silence lent them an air of dignity that speaking actors often lack.

"'Pon my word, Watson," Holmes whispered beside me. "This thing is no mere toy. It is marvellous! Long after the actors on that screen have died, their images will still walk and gesticulate for generations yet unborn!"

Now there commenced a low comedy titled *Why Mrs Jones Got a Divorce*, followed by an even lower melodrama called *Ching Lin Foo Outdone*. Beside me in the darkness, Holmes writhed in his seat.

"The greatest educational tool ever devised, and this man Edison squanders it on knockabout farces," Holmes remarked in disgust.

Now the picture changed again, to a play titled *The Dream of a*

Rarebit Fiend. On the screen before us, a man wearing a frock-coat was seated at a table, consuming his dinner of Welsh rarebit. The picture faded momentarily, and at once this same man was in his bedroom, attired in a nightshirt and a peaked nightcap. The transformation was instantaneous, and I did not see how it was done. The nightshirted man clambered into his bed, drew up the counterpane, and went to sleep with remarkable alacrity.

Suddenly the bed rose from its moorings and flew out the window, with its occupant – now awake and terrified – clinging fast to the headboard. The bed flew over the rooftops towards the spire of a church that was surmounted by a weathervane which seemed rather larger than necessary. Here the animated bed ejected its passenger, and flew onwards without him. All about me in the dark of the music-hall, the audience roared with laughter whilst the poor fellow in the nightshirt dangled helplessly from the weathervane, kicking and bellowing. The last scene – with no intervening transition – showed him safe in his bedroom again, wakening from a nightmare. Solemnly raising his right hand and gazing heavenward, whilst moving his lips in dumb-show, the fellow vowed a silent oath: presumably against eating Welsh rarebit at bedtime.

"Watson, this is really quite enough," Sherlock Holmes remarked beside me, amidst the raucous merriment of the audience surrounding us. "Surely, in Manhattan's vasty deeps, we might find entertainment more refined than this. Let us elsewhere ourselves."

The image on the screen had changed once more. Now it depicted an urban crossroads, quite unremarkable excepting that the trams, broughams, and other conveyances – in the American manner – were moving on the wrong side of the street. Upon the screen, men and women were proceeding in their usual fashions and varying gaits, entering at the one side and exeunting at the other. A newsboy hawked his gazettes between two hoardings underneath a street-lamp, and although this object was unlit – the *tableau* taking place in full daylight – I was surprised to observe that the street-lamp was outfitted for electrical current, not gaslight. Two signs depending from the lamp-post apprised us that this crossroads was the intersection of "BROADWAY" and "W. 58TH STREET". In the background, a clock-dial set into the face of a distant tower gave the time as ten-seventeen. Evidently, this newest Vitascope film was neither farce nor tragedy, but merely an impromptu vignette of Manhattanites in their native environs . . . and as such, no especial drama was about to unfold.

"You are right, Holmes," I whispered to my friend. "I have beheld my fill. Let us away to the Empire Theatre, and pay tribute to Miss Adams."

During the while I said these words, the images, on the screen continued their silent processions. As I spoke, yet one more figure made his entrance within the background of the *tableau* before us. He was a man of above the middle height, thirtyish, with neatly trimmed moustaches. He was well-shod, in expensive cordovans, and clutching in his left hand a furled umbrella. But something about him was out of the common: his pin-striped suit was of a cut which had passed out of fashion some thirty years ago, and he sported side-whiskers in the style called dundrearies, which have long been out of vogue. Suddenly I felt a sharp pain in my wrist: the finger-tips of Sherlock Holmes were pressing into my flesh, as Holmes's body went rigid.

"*Watson!*" he shouted, so loudly that every person in the theatre might have heard him. "That man on the screen! *He is James Phillimore!*"

From the dark rows behind us, someone shouted for Holmes to keep still.

I felt a chill run up my spine as I beheld the flickering Vitascope image. James Phillmore had vanished thirty-one years ago, yet the newcomer on the kinetographic screen looked barely thirty years of age. "You must be mistaken, Holmes," I whispered, so as not to disturb the audience. "If Phillimore is still alive, he is in his sixties now."

"I tell you, Watson, *he is the very man!*" Holmes stood erect, and pointed his long arm towards the screen. "That man is James Phillimore to the life, and *he has not aged a single day since he vanished!*"

I think that every head in the audience must have turned towards us at that moment, and every tongue – in harsh American accents – shouted at us to be quiet. Therefore I was certain that no one save Holmes and myself observed what happened next upon the Vitascope's screen.

As if responding to Sherlock Holmes's voice, the man on the screen abruptly turned and looked *directly toward us.* His eyes widened in delight, and his mouth split into a broad grin. His lips moved silently, in unheard speech.

Holmes leaped forth from his seat. "Down in front!" bellowed some person behind us.

I have said that the man in the picture stood within its background. No longer. Looking directly at Sherlock Holmes, the silent image of James Phillimore strode boldly to the foreground of the image. With a brief sidelong glance before resuming his gaze in Holmes's direction, he traversed West Fifty-Eighth Street, stepped onto the kerb of the near side, and placed his well-shod feet firmly atop the pavement whilst he raised his umbrella, and pointed it squarely at Holmes. Now I too leaped out of my chair.

The other *simulacra* within the Vitascope screen took no notice of James Phillimore, but continued their own exits and entrances at both sides of the rectangular image. At the centre of the screen, the left hand of James Phillimore silently aimed his umbrella into the audience: directly towards the head of Sherlock Holmes. At the same time, Phillimore raised his right hand to his brow in a sardonic salute.

At that instant, *James Phillimore vanished!*

There was no question of a trap-door beneath him. With my own eyes, I had seen Mr James Phillimore *disappear into thin air.* On the Vitascope screen, the people and conveyances of West Fifty-Eighth Street maintained their kinetographic cavalcade, utterly oblivious to the fact that a man had vanished from their midst.

"Quickly, Watson!" In a trice, Sherlock Holmes bounded into the theatre's gangway and made a dash for the nearest exit. And once again, as so often in the past, I found myself following at his heels, in pursuit of our quarry.

"James Phillimore is in Manhattan, Watson, for that kinetograph was photographed *today!*" Holmes declared as we pelted through the lobby of the Edisonia Amusement Hall. "I have promised the officers of the Continental Insurance Company that I shall be aboard tomorrow's train to San Francisco, and I am honour-bound to keep that pledge. Therefore we have a trifle less than sixteen hours in which to find a man who has eluded me for thirty-one years. Watson, come! *The game is afoot!*"

We raced out of the theatre, emerging into Broadway. My friend made haste to flag down a passing hansom. Holmes instructed the cabman to convey us to Broadway and Fifty-Eighth, the scene of Phillimore's latest disappearance. The cabman whisked up his reins, and a moment later the pursuit of Phillimore had begun.

"There must be some mistake, surely," I said to my companion, as we settled into the seat and our hansom proceeded northwards through difficult traffic. "How can you be certain that the Vitascope we saw was photographed today?"

"It was obvious, Watson. You saw the newsboy in the image? The caption scrawled across his hoardings duplicated the headline in today's New York *Herald.*"

I still was utterly astounded at having seen a man *vanish.* "But are you certain that the man on the screen was really James Phillimore? We are in Manhattan, Holmes: perhaps this fellow was an American who bears a chance resemblance to Phillimore."

Sherlock Holmes shook his head. He had withdrawn a jotting-book from his pocket, and was busily sketching within this as he spoke. "Depend upon it, Watson: that man on the Vitascope screen was an Englishman."

"How can you be certain, Holmes?"

"No man can hide his heritage, Watson. I can tell an American from an Englishman by the arrangement of his boot-laces: the man we saw just now was British . . . or else he has an English valet to tie his shoes for him. And did you observe the salute that Phillimore gave as he vanished?" Holmes duplicated it now – cocking his right elbow, Holmes's hand went to his forehead: the upper edges of his finger-tips went flat against his brow, whilst his thumb pointed downwards. "*That* is how a soldier in the British army salutes . . . as you know full well from your own campaign in Afghanistan." Now Holmes saluted again; once more the hand went to his brow, but this time his fingers were parallel to the ground, and his thumb pointed rearwards. "*This* is the American military salute, Watson: it is also the salute of our own Royal Navy. When I investigated Phillimore's background in 1875, I found no record of military service. Yet he must have been a boy once, and boys play at being soldiers. They learn their drill from observing *real* soldiers, and copying them."

Holmes was right: the man in the Vitascope had displayed a *British* salute.

"Furthermore," Holmes went on, sketching furiously in his jotter as our cab progressed, "did you remark, Watson, that the man on the screen briefly glanced to one side?"

"Of course." I nodded. "As he stepped off the kerb into the road, he glanced sideways to see if there was oncoming traffic."

"Quite so, Watson. But he glanced to the *right.* That is as we do in England. In American roads, and European ones, a pedestrian glances first to the *left.* An Englishman acquires the foreign habit when he has spent some time outside our Empire. But the man on the screen, Watson, turned the wrong way: he is accustomed to British thoroughfares, and has only recently arrived in the United States."

Of a sudden, I shuddered once more. "The fact remains, Holmes, that we saw a man vanish *into thin air.*"

"We saw nothing of the kind, Watson. Are you aware of the French illusionist Georges Méliès? He works his conjuror's tricks inside a kinetoscope. Our quarry Phillimore knows the same dodge."

"I don't understand."

"Did it seem to you, Watson, that Phillimore's eyes on the Vitascope screen were looking directly at *us* in the orchestra-stalls? I thought the same thing . . . for a moment. But such a thing is impossible. When we observe a moving-picture, we see only what the camera saw. Phillimore did not see us, did not salute us. He was looking directly into the lens of the *camera*, whilst saluting the cameraman . . . and through the camera's borrowed gaze we fancied that he looked at *us*."

"But, Holmes! We saw him *vanish* . . . like a phantasm!"

"Watson, no. A kinetographic camera records movements not only through *space*, but through *time*. I think I know why Phillimore saluted: to distract the cameraman's attention towards his right arm, and *away* from his left."

"His left hand carried an umbrella," I recalled.

"Quite so, Watson. And did you mark what he did with it? Just before he disappeared, Phillimore seemed to aim the shaft of his umbrella directly towards us. In fact, he extended it towards the *camera*."

"And then he vanished, Holmes!"

"No. He merely cut out a fragment of *time*. That is, he thrust the tip of his umbrella into the camera's mechanism – thereby jamming it – then withdrew his umbrella and walked away. The cameraman required precisely four minutes to unjam the mechanism."

"How the deuce can you know how long . . ."

"When our quarry vanished, Watson, did you not observe a sudden lurch within the image on the Vitascope screen?"

I shook my head. "I saw only James Phillimore . . . and then the place where he *wasn't*."

"Ah! But just before he vanished, the clock on the tower behind him read ten seventeen. And then, at the precise instant *after* he vanished, the clock abruptly jumped to ten twenty-one. The newsboy's posture shifted instantaneously from one position to quite a different one. All the other people and vehicles in the *tableau* vanished as well . . . and were replaced by others. Georges Méliès learned the same trick by accident, Watson. He was photographing traffic in Paris when the mechanism of his camera jammed. The traffic kept moving whilst Méliès endeavoured to restart his apparatus. Afterwards, when Méliès developed his film and projected it, he was astonished to see a Parisian omnibus abruptly transform itself into a hearse."

By now we had reached West Fifty-Eighth Street; Holmes paid the cabman, and we alighted. I had never been here before, yet I recognized the place: the buildings, the newsboy underneath the street-lamp, even the clock-dial on the distant tower were just as I had marked them on the Vitascope screen . . . except with colours added to Mr Edison's photographic palette of greys. As our cab departed, I remarked to Holmes: "Then the man in the Vitascope film cannot be James Phillimore at all, Holmes."

My friend's jaw tightened. "No, Watson. He is Phillimore to the life. In every particular, the man whom we saw is identical to his cabinet photograph. I committed the portrait to memory in 1875, Watson. I shall never forget those dundrearies! Our quarry is even wearing *the same suit*: pin-stripe, of a cut and design favoured by tailors in Savile Row some thirty years ago. I interviewed the two Leamington bankers who were present when Phillimore vanished: they assured me that the suit he wore in his portrait is the one that Phillimore was wearing on the morning when he vanished."

"Very few suitings last for thirty-one years," I remarked.

"And very few men can vanish for three decades and return without growing a day older," Holmes replied. "Yet our quarry is just such a man."

The day was warm, yet I felt suddenly cold. "Holmes, is it possible that James Phillimore has slipped sidelong in Time? I recall the original case: there was evidence of some sort of circular *vortex* in Phillimore's house. Can a man fall through a hole in Warwickshire in 1875, and emerge in Manhattan in 1906? It would explain why Phillimore has not aged, and why his suit has not become more worn."

We were standing outside a greystone edifice at Number 1789, Broadway. A brass plate near the entrance informed us that this was the home of something called "THE COSMOPOLITAN. A HEARST PUBLICATION". Sherlock Holmes tapped his fore-finger alongside his nose, as if taking me into a confidence. "Ignore the newsboy, Watson, and humour me in a *charade.*"

Holmes strode purposefully to the exact spot where the Vitascope apparatus had stood. "This is a good place to start, Watson," said my friend in a loud voice, "if we intend to collect the reward."

I did not take his meaning, but I played along: "Yes! Certainly! A good deal of money is at stake."

Sherlock Holmes now took out a tape-measure, and began making precise measurements of the kerb and the pavement, all the while muttering about a large reward. He seemed wholly unaware of the newsboy, who was observing Holmes's every movement with the keenest attention. When he was unable to contain his curiosity any longer, the urchin spoke in thick American tones: "*Wutcha lookin' fer, cul?*"

"Go away, lad," said Holmes. "Can't you see that we're busy? The

officers of the Edison Film Company have engaged us to investigate
a serious incident of vandalism, and . . ."

"I know wutcher aftuh," said the boy conspiratorially. His mouth
was crammed full of some glutinous substance which he chewed
furiously whilst he spoke, thus obscuring his diction all the
more. "You're lookin' for the jasper who jiggered that camera,
ain'tcher?"

Holmes looked up from his measurements. "The Edison Film
Company have offered a substantial reward for information
leading to the arrest of the man who damaged one of their
kinetographic . . ."

"*How much?*" said the boy. "That reward, I mean."

"We have no intention of paying good money for idle rumours,"
said Holmes. "Since you clearly did not witness the incident . . ."

"I seen him!" boasted the newsboy. "I seen the whole thing!" Now
he began to re-enact the whole affair, in broad movements, taking
by turns the roles of James Phillimore, the Edison cameraman, and
even the camera itself. "There was one o' them camera fellers here,
takin' pitchers. A dude came along, swingin' his umbreller, see? He
looked like the kind of a guy who would make trouble just fer the
sport of it. Sure enough, I seen him poke his umbrelly into that
camera there. He pulled it out again, and then he walked away
laughin'. The umbrella weren't damaged, but the camera started
racketin' loud enough to wake yer dead granny. The cameraman
started cussin', and he had to stop the camera. I seen him fiddle
it fer a coupla minutes, and then he started it up again." The boy's
face split into a broad grin. "Do I get the reward?"

"Not unless you can tell me the culprit's name and address," said
Sherlock Holmes, pocketing his tape-measure and drawing forth
his jotting-book. Somehow a five-dollar banknote had gone astray
from Holmes's note-case and was now protruding – by accident,
surely – from the leaves of his jotter. "If you can offer us some
useful information . . ."

"*That's them!*" said the boy, stabbing a grimy finger towards the
book as Holmes opened it.

I looked over his shoulder, and was amused to see what my friend
had been sketching so industriously during our cab-journey. In the
pages of his jotting-book, Holmes had drawn two large portraits
that I recognized as likenesses of our adversaries from bygone
adventures: Professor Moriarty and Colonel Moran. Between
these two, scarcely more than an afterthought, was a small
and hastily scribbled rendition of James Phillimore. Yet the
newsboy now ignored the large conspicuous drawings of Moriarty
and Moran, and pointed unerringly at the tiny likeness of

Phillimore. "That's them!" he said triumphantly. "That's *both* o' them!"

For once, Sherlock Holmes seemed confused . . . but he regained his composure swiftly enough to withdraw the jotting-book an instant before the freckled urchin tried to snatch the banknote within. "*Both* of them, you say?" asked Holmes.

The newsboy nodded. "You heard me, boss. That guy wit' the umbreller: after he wrecked the camera, I seen him walk into that buildin' over there." The newsboy nodded towards the offices of the *Cosmopolitan.* "The cameraman left, an' I kept peddlin' my papers, see? Then, mebbe half an hour later, the umbrella man comes out again. Only this time there's *two* of him."

Holmes and I exchanged glances. "Can it be that there are *two* James Phillimores?" I wondered aloud.

"There were, 'coz I seen 'em," the newsboy replied. "Like they could o' been twins . . . an' that there's a pitcher o' both o' them." The boy tapped his hand against the jotting-book, leaving ink-stained finger-prints upon the drawing of James Phillimore. "Same suit, same hat, same lip-spinach, the works. Only difference was, one twin had an umbreller and one twin didn't." As he spoke, the newsboy's fingers gravitated towards the stray banknote, but Holmes kept this just out of reach.

"And did you see where he . . . where *they* went, lad?" Holmes enquired.

The newsboy's eyes gleamed greedily. "What's it worth t'yuh?" he asked.

"Five dollars," said Holmes. "But I want the *truth*, mind!" He brandished the sketch of James Phillimore again. "Where did this man go?"

"There was *two* of him, I tol' yuh . . . so y'ought to pay *double*," said the newsboy.

Holmes sighed, and pressed two fivers into the newsboy's eager hands. "Now, then!"

"I seen 'em get into a cab," the boy reported. "Just b'fore the door closed, I heard one o' the twins – the one 'thout an umbreller – tell the driver to take 'em both to Madison Square."

Thus it chanced that, five minutes later, Sherlock Holmes and I were in another cab hastening towards Madison Square: a place unknown to us, yet which the cab-driver assured us he knew intimately.

"'Pon my word, Watson," Holmes declared, as our cab went south on Broadway, "but this mystery gets stranger every moment. Thirty-one years ago, James Phillimore stepped through a doorway and ceased to exist. This morning he returned from the void: not a day older, and none the worse for his absence. And now it seems that he has become *identical twins.*"

"Do you suppose the newsboy told the truth, Holmes?" I pondered. "He might have lied to us, just to claim a reward."

"I think not, Watson." Once more Holmes produced his jotter, revealing the thumb-nail portrait of James Phillimore flanked either side by the two colossi of Moriarty and Moran. "A liar posing as an eyewitness would have claimed to recognize the first likeness he saw. Our newspaper johnny went right past the two largest and most obvious portraits in my impromptu rogues' gallery – he did not recognize them, Watson – and he seized upon the smaller study that he *did* recognize: our quarry James Phillimore . . . who now appears to have borrowed a trick from the *amœba* and split himself into identical twins."

The southward traffic along Broadway was more congenial than its northbound counterpart had been, and soon we turned eastward and arrived at the crossroads of Madison Avenue and East Twenty-Seventh Street. Here awaited us a green quadrangle of parkland which, of a certainty, must be Madison Square. I paid the cabman, and I had no sooner alighted on the kerb than the hand of Sherlock Holmes was at my shoulder: "Watson! *Look!*"

I turned, and looked . . . and thought I must be seeing double.

At the far end of the park stood two identical men. Both were dressed in pin-striped suiting, of an outmoded cut. Both wore moustaches and dundreary whiskers.

Both of them were James Phillimore.

In swift movements of his lithe muscular limbs, Sherlock Holmes crossed the quad. In consequence of my Jezail wound, I was unable to keep pace with him. Thus I was still several yards from our quarry when Holmes approached them and asked: "Have I the honour of addressing Mr James Phillimore and Mr James Phillimore?"

Both men laughed in unison. "You have that honour, sir," said one, in British tones.

"You have indeed," said his twin, in an American accent.

Now I came huffapuffing up to join them, and I made a strange discovery. The two James Phillimores were not identical. One of them – the Englishman – was in his early thirties: of a certainty, the same man whose likeness we had witnessed in the Vitascope. But the American was in his sixties. He was also, I saw now, some three inches shorter than his British confederate, and slightly fuller of physique. The American's eyes were light blue, whilst the Englishman's eyes had irises of a queer pale hue which I can only describe as *horn*-coloured. His face was long and lantern-jawed, whereas the American's face was nearer square-shaped. The strong resemblance of the two men was due to the fact that they were dressed in matching outfits, and their faces sported identical side-whiskers and similar moustaches of chestnut-coloured hair.

Remembering Holmes's words, I glanced at both men's shoes. Neither one's footwear matched the other man's, nor did their boot-laces. The eyelets of the older man's shoes were laced criss-cross, in what I gather to be the American manner. The younger man's boots were laced straight across the instep, in the familiar British form.

"Might as well take these off, don't you think?" asked the Englishman. He reached up to his face, and plucked off his own whiskers ... leaving only a few stray wisps of crepe hair still stuck in place with spirit-gum.

The American laughed. "Yes, I was getting hot in these." He snatched away his own set of side-whiskers. His moustaches remained in place, and they appeared to be the genuine articles. But now, in the bright sunlight of Madison Square, I noticed a faint chestnut-coloured stain along the edges of his collar: the American's hair was naturally *white*, and he had dyed it brown in order to match the colouring of his British companion.

And yet, even without their disguises, there was a certain kindred quality in these two editions of James Phillimore, a look of keen intelligence within the countenance of both men ... which suggested that – despite their outer discrepancies – these two men might indeed be identical twins of the *mind*.

The southwest corner of Madison Square's quadrangle was truncated, creating a space in which a row of park benches were secluded from the traffic of nursemaids and perambulators. My friend beckoned the three of us to join him there. "I am Sherlock Holmes, and this is my associate Dr Watson," he announced to the counterfeit twins. "Please have the goodness to reveal your true names, and the reason for this peculiar hoax."

The American bowed before seating himself. "Might as well tell it all, since no harm's done. My name is Ambrose Bierce, and I am the Washington correspondent for Mr Hearst's *Cosmopolitan*. Perhaps you've read my column 'The Passing Show'?"

"I have not." Holmes transferred his attentions to the younger man. "And you, sir?"

The lantern-jawed Englishman smiled. "My name is Aleister Crowley."

"Ambrose and Aleister." Holmes sniffed. "Two unusual names, with the same initial. What is the connexion between you two, pray?"

The two culprits exchanged shamefaced glances. "We may as

well spill the works," the American ventured to his cohort, with a grin. "It's too good a joke to keep to ourselves."

"Very well," said the long-faced Englishman. He turned to confront Sherlock Holmes, and began to explain: "My name at birth was *Edward* Crowley, *Junior.*"

"Named after your father," I murmured, but Crowley shot a glance of the most withering scorn in my direction as soon as I said this.

"Named for my mother's *husband,*" he corrected me. "At the time of my birth, my mother Emily Bishop Crowley resided at number 30, Clarendon Square, in Leamington, Warwickshire. I was born there on 12 October, 1875."

"Shortly after the disappearance of James Phillimore," said Sherlock Holmes, nodding sagely. "Come, what else?"

"As to *my* birth," ventured Ambrose Bierce, "that calamity occurred in Ohio, in 1842. Nine siblings preceded me. For some reason, it amused my father to afflict all his offspring with names employing the initial letter 'A'. Our *dramatis personæ*, in the order of appearance, reads as follows: Abigail, Amelia, Ann, Addison, Aurelius, Augustus, Almeda, Andrew, Albert . . . and Ambrose."

"What has this to do with James Phillimore, then?" asked Holmes.

"I was just coming to that," said Ambrose Bierce. "In my thirtieth year, in the company of a wife whom I never loved, I emigrated to England and became a writer for Tom Hood's *Fun* magazine and *The Lantern.* My wife and I lived at first in London, but during the spring of 1874 we set up housekeeping at Number 20 South Parade, in . . ."

". . . in Leamington, Warwickshire," Holmes finished for him. "Watson, I recall the general topography of Leamington Spa from my sojourn there in 1875. Clarendon Square and the South Parade are scarcely a mile apart. Directly between them is Tavistock Street . . . and the house from which James Phillimore performed his disappearance. Which was indeed a *performance* . . . was it not, Mr Bierce?"

Ambrose Bierce nodded sadly. "I shall say nothing against the character of Mrs Crowley, except to observe that – like myself – she was trapped in a loveless marriage. Suffice it to report that she and I . . . *consoled* each other during the spring and summer of 1875."

I began to see where this was leading. There was a physical resemblance between Bierce and Crowley that transcended their identical costumes. And if Ambrose Bierce had known Emily Crowley some eight or ten months before the birth of her son Aleister, then it was quite possible that . . .

"The house in Tavistock Street, Bierce," said Sherlock Holmes impatiently. "Was this the scene of your trysts?"

Bierce nodded once more. "Leased by me from the estate-agents. A false identity was advisable, of course . . ."

"And so you took the name James Phillimore?"

"I did." said Bierce. "Edward Crowley was a strait-laced man who considered all forms of entertainment to be highly immoral. He avoided restaurants, theatres, and music-halls . . . and forbade his wife to visit such emporia. My own wife Mollie was of similar demeanour. On the other hand, Mr James Phillimore *and his female companion* – do I make myself clear, sir? – gave much custom to Leamington's pleasure-palaces. At some point during this period, Emily Crowley found herself with child."

Bierce paused a moment, then resumed: "In May of 1875, my wife departed for California . . . taking our two infant sons with her. Tom Hood – my literary sponsor in England – had died a few months previously. By late August, Mrs Crowley's expectant condition was approaching its climax, and – as she had no intention of leaving her husband – I felt it politic to return to America."

This time it was my turn to serve as questioner: "But what about Mr Phillimore's strange disappearance?" I asked. "The signs of the peculiar vortex . . ."

Ambrose Bierce threw his head back and laughed. "I have always been intrigued by the idea that there might be holes in the universe – *vacua*, if you will – capable of swallowing a man whole, so that he vanishes without a trace. I have written several stories on the subject. I have already decided that – when my time comes to call it quits – I shall vanish into one of the holes in the universe, and leave no mortal remains. So when it came time for me to abandon my Tavistock residence – and my Phillimore identity – I fancied that it might be amusing to stage-manage such a vanishment. And then to watch the results from a distance, in the safety of my own *persona*."

Sherlock Holmes shifted his posture on the bench. "Now I understand a detail which has baffled me these thirty years", he nodded. "The weather in Warwickshire was *fair* for two weeks before Phillimore vanished, with no rain at all. Yet Phillimore somehow tracked mud into his own house, even though he stepped outside for only a moment. Had I not been so untrained in the art of detection in those early days, I should have noticed that the muddy trail within the house had no corresponding source in the gutters without. Now I comprehend: the muddy footprints in the antechamber were set there in advance, *moulded from clay*."

With a smile, Ambrose Bierce acknowledged his handiwork.

"Brilliant, wasn't it? All the various details – the footprints leading to nowhere, the scorched floorboards, the decapitated umbrella, even the two impeccable witnesses brought to the scene by a pretext – all the details were part of my scheme, sir."

"And yet you vanished *into thin air . . .*" I began.

"Not at all, sir. 'Twas simplicity itself. When I came out the house's front door to greet my callers from the bank, the foyer was already bedecked with the tokens of my abduction. I went back in through the front door as James Phillimore, took a moment to call out for help while I donned a cobbler's smock and yanked off my false whiskers . . . and then I slipped out the back way, like any respectable tradesman."

Aleister Crowley chuckled. "Because James Phillimore was heard to *cry for help*, the witnesses assumed that he disappeared *against his will.* It never occurred to anyone that he'd done a bunk voluntarily."

Sherlock Holmes arose from the park bench and – with great solemnity – bowed to Ambrose Bierce, then reseated himself. "Come now, sir!" said my companion to Bierce. "I confess that you foxed me. Now for the rest of the tale, if you please: why, after so many years, has James Phillimore resurfaced of a sudden?"

This time it was Bierce's turn to chuckle. "Although I left England shortly before the birth of Emily Crowley's only child, I corresponded with her secretly. She kept me apprised of her son's progress. In 1897 – following the death of Edward Crowley, Senior – I took the liberty of writing to his heir, and revealing my role in his past. I also mentioned my family's tradition of forenames beginning with the letter A."

Crowley nodded. "That was the year in which I changed my forename to *Aleister.*"

"We have maintained our correspondence ever since," Bierce revealed. "In the meanwhile, my tasks as a journalist have obliged me to travel throughout the United States without ever returning to Europe. Young Crowley here has journeyed to Russia and Tibet, but never until now has he visited America. My wife died in April of last year, and my two sons that I had off her have been dead these past five years: one of them a suicide. I am therefore alone, which means that I am in bad company. I live in Washington at present, but I make frequent trips to New York City to call upon my employer Mr Hearst. When Aleister Crowley wrote to me a few months ago from his home in Scotland, informing me of his intention to visit New York, I decided that we should meet at last."

"But why bring James Phillimore back from the dead?" queried Sherlock Holmes.

"That was part of the joke," answered Aleister Crowley, placing his hand upon Bierce's shoulder fondly. "I have always had a taste for bizarre jests. My mother's husband was entirely devoid of humour, yet Ambrose Bierce's wit is keenly similar to my own: I should like to believe that I have inherited this from him. Several years ago, Father Ambrose – as I choose to call him – sent me a cabinet photo of himself in his James Phillimore disguise, with a letter recounting the hoax in all its delicious details. When I agreed to call upon Mr Bierce at the *Cosmopolitan* offices, I decided to amuse myself by visiting him in the guise of James Phillimore. I had the costume made up in London before my departure."

"Clearly my own sense of humour and Aleister Crowley's run on similar lines," said Ambrose Bierce. "For we both hatched the same notion independently, and I too decided to resurrect James Phillimore for our meeting. I still had the suit handy in camphor-balls, so I let it out a bit and bought some stage-whiskers to match the ones I wore thirty years ago. Say, all the boys in Hearst's office busted out laughing fit to kill when I walked in there dressed like Prince Albert. Then, when young Aleister here came traipsing into the room *in the same get-up* . . ."

"I can imagine the hilarity," said Sherlock Holmes, without smiling. He rose again from the bench, beckoning me to join him whilst he strode towards the cab-rank at the southern edge of Madison Square. "Watson, come! We still have time to see Maude Adams give her evening performance at the Empire." Turning back, my friend doffed his hat to the pair of erstwhile Phillimores. "*Adieu*, gentlemen," said Sherlock Holmes. "I suggest that James Phillimore's latest vanishing-act should be his farewell performance. Since Doctor Watson and I are on our way to San Francisco – where the list of recent deaths is a prodigious one – I can easily arrange for James Phillimore's name to be inserted among the rolls of the dead. Let us keep him that way. Farewell!"

THE CASE OF
THE LAST BATTLE

L. B. Greenwood

*After the last case and that of "The Lion's Mane" Holmes kept himself
to himself for several years until the ominous rumblings of war brought
him into government service in the episode recorded by Watson in "His
Last Bow". That was the last published case of Sherlock Holmes,
set in 1914. There have been many who have written apocryphal
cases of Holmes's wartime adventures and continuing cases into the
1920s, but I believe almost all of these are apocryphal. But there was
one last case, the details of which remained hidden in the archives
of the War Office until Canadian author and Sherlockian, Beth
Greenwood, unearthed them. Here, at last, is the very final case of
Sherlock Holmes.*

"He's dead, sir."

"I know that, Jackson," I snapped.

Quite unpardonably, but I was still wet with the boy's blood, and
his death was only the last of so many. For this was early November
of 1918, I was the sole doctor in the field dressing station, and if
any few acres in all history had been as tortured as those around
Ypres, I have never heard of it.

A mug of something hot and brewed – front-line coffee could
seldom be told from tea – was poked into my hand. "Thanks,
Jackson. Sorry about the temper."

"'S all right, sir. Wot 'bout them in the corner? They're quiet
enough now, but . . ."

Stiff-legged with exhaustion, I staggered over to the five mounds of
blankets. No cots could be spared for the merely sick, no matter how
desperate their condition, nor could we hope that any ambulance
would have room for several days. Not after such an attack as had
all too recently once again blasted this segment.

Of course we had dealt with illness from the earliest days of
the war. (In fact, my first medical task for the army had been
to inform a furious major that he had contracted measles.) The

present sickness, however, was one that I hadn't seen until a month or so ago, since when an increasing number of cases from both sides had been brought to my station.

The cause seemed to be some kind of respiratory infection, with a high fever, furiously aching limbs, and all too often an agitated delirium. For a small dressing station over-run by wounded, attended by one elderly doctor whose only assistant had until a year ago been a butcher's apprentice at Smithfield, the sufferers made very disruptive patients, poor fellows.

So, sometime during the previous night, I had injected the present five victims with morphine. One I now found had died, two were still deeply unconscious, three were beginning to stir, with amazingly cool skin and regular breathing. This was far better than I had expected: mortality of fifty per cent or more had been common. I told Jackson to soften some hardtack in boiled water – we had nothing better to offer – and to start sponging them off, with now at least some hope of their remaining clean.

I was leaning wearily against a tent pole, sipping the cooling concoction in my mug, when from behind me seemed to come that never forgotten voice, in words as few and peremptory as always. "Watson, I need you."

I'm hallucinating, I thought, not much surprised: I couldn't remember when I had either slept or eaten. I knew that since the early days of the war Holmes had been immersed in something most secret, and I had heard whispers of his having been occasionally glimpsed in the very private drawing rooms of the mighty of several countries. Wherever he was this night, he would not be in a bloody dressing station on the Western front.

Yet the steel grip that had descended on my shoulders was real enough, and so was the asperity with which I was being shaken. "Pull yourself together, doctor. You're wanted."

An embossed silver flask had been raised to my lips.

I pushed it away. "Right now, Holmes, that would finish me. And as for being wanted, I believe I am. Far more so than a man with my white hair should be –"

I stopped because I had been unceremoniously turned so that I could see a spotless whitecoated figure, with a stethoscope in his pocket and a large glistening black bag in his hand, already moving among my sick and wounded. He glanced over at me with grave young eyes and nodded.

"Dr Ostenborough, Watson," Holmes waved a perfunctory introduction. "I know you too well to think that you would leave without a replacement, and he begged for the opportunity. Now *come*."

"Ostenborough," I repeated stupidly as Holmes pulled me firmly out of the tent. "Wasn't he with the palace?"

"One of the King's personal medics, yes. Which should give you some idea of the seriousness of what we're facing."

Waiting for us was a British sergeant at the wheel of an old French taxi!

"She's a right proper bitch," the sergeant told me cheerfully, "dunno when I've driv worse, but she'll go, sir, she'll go."

"I have been getting around by rather unconventional means," Holmes explained with some of his old light air, "and took what was available. In with you, Watson, and take a pull at this." He again handed me the silver flask. "There's nothing we can do until we reach the chancellory. No, no explanations now."

The brandy was like a liquid memory of luxuries that had never been common in my life. "Did both flask and contents come from the palace too?"

"The monks of France made the brandy, the late Czar sent some bottles from the White Palace to his royal cousin of England, the flask is Bavarian and was given me by Prince Max."

"So even the Chancellor of Germany is behind you, Holmes."

"*He* is, yes. I cannot say the same for all his countrymen. Drink up, Watson, and catch up on some sleep. I fear you will need it before our present mission is over."

My last sight was of Holmes's familiar lean figure (Had he lost weight? Probably. Who had not?) settled deep in the corner beside me, his head on his chest, his hands locked on his knees. We could have been just pulling out of Paddington.

Was that world still there, somewhere, the world for which we were fighting?

I remember only fragments of Holmes's and my journey. I know that we lurched along for some time, more than once getting stuck and being freed by soldiers who were already as mud-coated as the road, and then transferred to first one train, then to another. Somewhere I foggily became aware that my old medical bag was resting between my feet – trust Holmes to remember to bring it – and was comforted by its familiarity.

I came to myself as we climbed on board yet another train, to discover that we were in a decidedly elegant car. Holmes flung open a corner door to reveal the nearly forgotten wonders of a spacious bathroom, with a spruce attendant carefully arranging a complete set of gentleman's attire.

I emerged a new man, and sat down with Holmes to the kind of breakfast that haunts the dreams of every hungry Englishman.

"These clothes," I questioned while rapidly spooning up melon balls in orange juice. "They're a perfect fit."

"So they should be," Holmes replied austerely, "I was most specific. All right, Watson, eat and listen. You know the military situation. The last German attempt has failed, our counterstroke has stalled —"

"Once more American forces arrive," I began, only to be interrupted in my turn.

"Exactly, and the Germans know that as well as the Allies. The only realistic question now is the terms of peace. Prince Max agreed to become chancellor for precisely that purpose, and there seemed some hope that he could succeed."

"If ever a man could be trusted by all sides," I agreed, "it is Prince Max."

"With the secret approval of both London and Paris, he has been in covert communication with the President of the United States."

"At last!" I cried, over a mouthful of fresh roll.

"Contain your jubilation, doctor, for Prince Max sent his inquiry about what would be necessary to end the war without the knowledge of the Kaiser, and his Most Foolish Majesty is now adamantly refusing to accept the necessity. Even more worrying, General Ludendorf has regained his nerve and is urging another attack, in which scheme he has the support of the more fanatical officers."

"Suicidal!" I exclaimed. "Murderous!"

"All of that, and yet unfortunately still possible. The Kaiser has once more taken to his private train and is busily rattling about well behind the lines, well away from anyone who would press unwelcome truths upon him. And Prince Max has fallen ill: he is now quite incapable of trying to trace and corner Germany's official leader."

I groaned. "Is the illness serious?"

"I fear so. Even yesterday, when I last saw him, the prince was . . . not himself. The trouble is that we have so little time. By now the prince will have received the American president's reply, a message that must be answered very soon, or the hounds of war will bay once more."

He was looking at me with a grave significance that I couldn't pretend not to understand. "The prince will certainly have doctors, Holmes. Surely the best that Germany has to offer, and that is saying much."

"Medically, no doubt. Politically and militarily, however, they belong to the Kaiser and to General Ludendorf, all determined to chase the chimera of victory yet once more."

"Even so, Holmes, I doubt that the prince would accept my poor services. Why should he?"

"Because you're English, doctor, and my friend," Holmes replied with unanswerable finality.

We arrived in Berlin in the early hours of the morning, and were met by a chauffeured limousine with curtained windows, Several times I peered out, always to see clusters of people, men and women, drifting restlessly around; some soldiers were also on the streets, even a few officers, but they were doing nothing except to mingle with the strangely moving crowds. I glanced often at Holmes, but he neither looked out nor spoke.

At the Chancellory we were escorted directly to Prince Max's quarters. As we climbed those marble steps and passed through those ornate halls, however, more than one officer turned pointedly away: obviously Holmes had spoken truth and we were not welcome to all here.

As we waited in the anteroom of the prince's suite, the door to the inner chambers was thrown open by a plain black-clothed figure, with short grey hair and honest peasant face now taut with worry, scowling ferociously at a departing visitor. This was a gentleman of aquiline features, in evening dress, who bowed to Holmes with a deference that was openly mocking.

"Good morning, Mr Holmes," he said in perfect English. "I fear you will find that the prince is no longer capable of attending to business matters. Good day, Hans, be sure to take good care of your master." He smiled unctuously as Hans stiffened with fury, and swaggered away.

"Who was that, Holmes?" I asked, puzzled. "I'm sure I've never seen him before, yet he seems familiar."

"No doubt because Count Hoffenstein resembles his cousin, Von Bork, whom you . . . met, shall we say, some years ago."

I had indeed, having been with Holmes when he trapped that master spy in his own house on the Dover hills.

"*Bad*," Hans's angry interjection showed both his deep concern and bitter frustration. "I keep all others away, but he, this Count, he come anyway. Bother my master. He . . . lost, Herr Doktor, lost like child. You help, please, please, Herr Doktor."

I was already hastening into the inner room, with Holmes close behind me. That poor Hans had cause for worry was obvious from the first glance.

Prince Max stood by his desk in a shifting sea of paper – letters, envelopes, memos, notepads. His hands were full, the desk top was covered, every drawer was open, the carpet littered.

The prince looked up at us with a flushed and despairing face. "I cannot find it!" he cried, his chest heaving. "I had it, I had it in my hands only moments ago, but it has gone! Where is it? Where?" He flung his arms wide, and paper flew like confetti.

"Your Highness, this is Doctor Watson. He –"

"I had it moments ago, Mr Holmes! Moments! Yet now it has gone!"

"Have you had the paper since Count Hoffenstein left, Your Highness?"

Awareness flickered briefly in the prince's strained face. "I had just taken it out of my pocket when Hans announced him, and I ..." He turned his wild eyes on me. "I have always kept it in my inside pocket, always from the first, and when the new message came ... I must ... I must ... *Where is it?*"

He was shaking from head to foot, panting for breath.

"Your Highness," I said firmly, grasping his arm, "you should be in bed."

"No, no, doctor, I cannot. Not until I have found it. I cannot otherwise answer, you understand ... No, no, no!"

Between the three of us we finally managed to get the poor prince into bed, and, with Hans on one side and I on the other, to keep him under the covers until exhaustion at last claimed him. The respite, I knew, would be brief.

Meanwhile Holmes had quickly gone through the prince's outer clothing, removed a small ring of keys from a buttoned pocket, and returned to the office. When I joined him, he was sitting at the desk, on which now lay neat piles of papers, staring thoughtfully at one page, which had been ruled off into regular squares, all filled with letters.

"Your verdict was correct, Holmes," I said. "The prince is very sick and I'm afraid worsening."

Holmes looked at me with distant eyes in which awareness of my presence only slowly dawned. "Do you know the cause?"

"Some kind of influenza, I think," I replied. "It's spreading fast among the troops on both sides of the front."

"The outcome?"

"Some survive, though few when they're as close to pneumonia as the prince."

"Pneumonia," Holmes repeated grimly. "So at best he'll be incapacitated for days. Can you do nothing to hasten recovery? Time is so precious, Watson, even hours may make the difference between whether hundreds – thousands – live or die."

"I have had some small success with injections of morphine," I said. "I have nothing else."

"Then by all means try the injections, doctor. I had hoped that the prince might come to himself long enough to remember something – anything – that would help me with this, but . . ." He handed me the following.

I stared at the meaningless rows of consonants in bewilderment. "*This* is the latest message from the President of the United States?"

Holmes nodded. "I believe so. Certainly it is on American paper, was stored in a locked inner drawer of the prince's desk, and is obviously in code."

"Then what had the prince lost? Or was that merely a delusion of his illness?"

"Far from it, doctor. What he had lost – to be precise, what Count Hoffenstein carried away with him – is the key to this and all such communications from the American president. The prince kept it, as he said, in an inner pocket, and had no doubt just taken it out

P	M	B	F	D	R	C	S	T	C	N
R	W	N	T	D	H	S	T	V	S	N
C	Y	C	R	S	S	S	G	N	R	R
F	N	T	W	H	D	R	L	S	L	B
D	R	T	G	T	H	C	T	K	F	M
R	M	T	N	H	N	N	T	T	P	H
R	S	M	C	P	N	T	T	R	N	P
N	L	T	Y	N	V	W	T	N	L	T
B	N	C	C	D	N	F	C	G	V	H
D	J	K	N	L	M	L	N	P	B	Q
R	S	R	T	T	V	Y	W	X	W	W

in order to read this message with its aid when the count forced his way past Hans and entered.

"Whether or not the count knew that the prince had, moments before, received this page from the president I do not know, though I should think it highly likely. Certainly he used the prince's near delirium to remove the paper from wherever the prince had hastily shoved it – child's play for a man like the count."

I looked again at the page I held, with no more enlightenment than before. "What on earth would the key to this be like?"

"A page of lightly transparent paper of the same size and shape and with the same squares ruled on it, but with the random letters that are added as mere disguise blacked out. By placing that page over this, one can see at once the letters that form the true message."

"There are no vowels," I pointed out.

"Not necessary." Holmes scribbled on a notepad and handed it to me. "Can you read that?"

He had written HLMSNDWTSN. "Holmes and Watson," I said.

"Precisely."

I stared back at the page of filled squares. "Without the key is it hopeless?"

"I won't concede that, doctor. It is only the pressure of time that worries me. At least we do start with some advantages."

"I can see none, Holmes, absolutely none."

Holmes tapped the top left and bottom right of the page. "We know that this is a personal message from the American president to the German chancellor. Since the first two letters here are PM and the last WW, surely it is probable that these stand for Prince Max and Woodrow Wilson."

"That is not much."

"There are other assumptions that we can, I think, safely make. For instance, since the prince is fluent in English and the president not in German, almost surely the language used is English. Also, though the two are naturally of the highest political status, they are amateurs in the employment of codes. Therefore the device selected is apt to be simple.

"Further, even sending such pages as this between them is becoming increasingly difficult to arrange safely: Count Hoffenstein will not be the only spy on the watch along the route. Therefore the same code will most probably have been meant for all their covert communications, meaning that ample space will have been allowed. You will note that the last three lines of the squares on this page have the consonants interspersed in regular alphabetical order, from B to X. That almost surely indicates that the message is contained in only the first eight lines.

"We're not beaten yet, doctor. Not while we both have work to do."

With that I certainly agreed, though heaving a deep sigh at our chances of success. I returned to the prince, who was struggling to get out of bed, and administered a small dose of morphine.

Though this quickly quietened him, he still had periods in which his whole body jerked, his eyes fluttered uneasily, and he would cry out thickly, "Where . . . where . . . where . . ." as long as he could find breath. These symptoms ceased after the second injection, but his breathing became increasingly strained, his face even more flushed, his skin burning. He was, for good or ill, nearing the crisis of his illness.

Hans was invaluable during these hours, doing unquestioningly whatever I bade. Even when, all else seeming to be failing, I turned to that simple nursery remedy of alternating hot and cold fomentations high on the chest and low on the back, for an hour at a time.

When not actively engaged in such tasks, Hans stretched out at the foot of his master's bed, alert to the smallest move or sound. I dozed in a chair by the fire; if my waking thoughts were on my patient, those in my moments of haze were filled with an endless parade of consonants.

Concede that the secret message began with "Prince Max," yet what words or words was hidden within BFDRCSTCN that completed the first line? Certainly nowhere in the message had I been able to decipher either the Kaiser's name or title, and yet I would have expected that Queen Victoria's deluded grandson would be a major topic of such a message.

For, as long as he refused to accept the reality of Germany's sure defeat, and as long as the officer corps retained their steadfast devotion to their oath of loyalty (how praiseworthy a trait had only the man and the cause been worthy!), the war would continue, for weeks, even months. Literally buckets of blood would pour forth in every dressing station across the front, and that would be only from those who survived long enough to be brought to such medical oases.

Sometime toward evening I went back into the office to tell Holmes of the prince's continuing struggle: like the world, he was in but not yet through the darkest hour. I found Holmes still seated at the desk, still frowning down at that page of lettered squares, and above him swirled the blue smoke of his pipe. I returned to the bedside.

Near evening, following more hot and cold fomentations, the

prince's breathing eased. Could I hope that he would shortly rouse enough to be able, even briefly, to assist Holmes? Dare I try to force my patient to that point? I decided the risk was not worth it: the prince was too ill, my faith in my friend too great. Instead I administered another dose of morphine.

As the second dawn brought a trace of blue to the sky's blackness, Hans woke me, tears of joy streaking his old face, and led me to the prince's bedside. The drugged coma had faded into genuine slumber, the chest rose and fell naturally, the cracked lips were tinged with a normal pink. The Chancellor would recover.

I hastened to tell Holmes the good news, and found the office and the adjacent rooms all deserted. The guard in the antechamber told me that "the other English Herr" had gone out hours ago.

Did that auger well or not? Who could say?

In a couple of hours the prince awoke with that weak and unquestioning acceptance of everything that marks the early recovery from serious illness. I wanted to order a bowl of gruel for him, but Hans would have none of it: his master hated gruel and should have hot bread and milk, made as only Hans could make it, with honey.

"And coffee, please," the prince murmured, a clasp of the hand showing his gratitude for his old servant's devotion.

I willingly agreed, and was myself devouring sandwiches when Holmes walked in unannounced.

"I am pleased to see you better, Your Highness," he said to Prince Max with his customary calm. "May I put on the wireless? An announcement from the palace is expected momentarily."

We waited motionless, all four, as the moments that seemed like hours passed. Then the music – one of the more sombre selections of Bach, as I recall – was abruptly cut off, and in hushed tones a man's voice stated that the Chancellor, Prince Max of Baden, had just issued a statement: His Most Gracious Majesty Kaiser Wilhelm II had abdicated, and all the royal princes agreed to renounce the throne in the cause of peace.

Prince Max and Holmes exchanged a long and ultimately understanding gaze. At last with a little sigh the prince said, "So His Majesty wouldn't see you, either. Even at the last."

"What can you expect", I said, with the bitterness of four years, "from a man who has never been in battle and who yet would sport a huge golden helmet?"

The prince gave a small smile. "Spoken like a true Englishman, Dr Watson. I am greatly relieved at what you have done, Mr Holmes, for I fear that I could not have. Necessary though I can see that it was."

"I think you would have done so, Your Highness, if you had seen the growing turmoil in the streets and also read the message from President Wilson."

Slow and painful memory grew in the prince's tired eyes. "I had asked what the terms would be for the end of the war and had just had his reply – I remember that, though I had had no time to decipher the message when the count arrived. You found the key to the code, then, Mr Holmes? Where was it?"

"I fear in Count Hoffenstein's pocket, Your Highness."

The prince passed a weak hand across his face. "Somehow I am not surprised. We have never been intimate, yet he shook my hand so heartily before leaving! No doubt in order to remove the key that I had pushed under the blotter on my desk. However did you manage to read the message, Mr Holmes?"

"With more effort than it should have taken, Your Highness. The trick in making out such a code, you understand, is to run through all possible combinations of the letters, adding vowels as required, until words are formed.

"All I could see at first was *score*, shortly extended to *fourscore*. I couldn't imagine President Wilson using such arcane language, yet I could make nothing else out from the first letters. Then I realized that the squares unneeded for the message had not been filled at random, as is usual, but with words that, while not part of the communication to Your Highness, yet meant much to the President of the United States. What would such a man at such a time quote that begins with *fourscore*?"

"'Fourscore and seven years ago,'" Prince Max promptly began, "'our fathers brought forth on this continent a new nation –'"

"'Conceived in liberty,'" Holmes finished.

"The start of the Gettysburg address!" I exclaimed.

"I could have told you that and saved much time and trouble," the prince observed sadly, "if I had been able."

"That could not be helped, Your Highness. When the consonants of the address are taken out, what remains are those that form the president's message, his reply to your question as to what would be needed to end the war. 'Abdication without succession. Renewed Allied attack imminent. Prompt reply vital.'"

"'Prompt reply'!" the prince breathed, "and I was delirious! Mr Holmes, very many owe you great thanks. Did you have any difficulty in convincing the chief of our wireless services that your order came from me?"

"Oh, I have friends everywhere," Holmes replied vaguely. "Also I had taken the liberty of using Your Highness' stationery."

And, I was sure, of forging the prince's handwriting with mastery skill.

"The last time I called on the Kaiser," Prince Max observed sadly, "he sent out word that he couldn't see me as it was already seven o'clock and he was late in dressing for dinner. It was then five minutes past midnight. I fear it has been five minutes past midnight for my poor country for a long time, Mr Holmes. What is the date?"

"The tenth of November, Your Highness. All should be concluded tomorrow."

"Hans, champagne." We raised our glasses. "To the eleventh of November," Prince Max said with tears in his eyes. "May the world never forget."

That is why I pen these lines, so that the part that Sherlock Holmes played in those final days may be known to all. *May the world never forget.*

After this case Holmes retired again to his cottage in Sussex. Watson paid him the occasional visit but they were both now in their seventies and travelling became tiresome. By 1926 Watson had finished compiling the last of his notes. The final published story, "Shoscombe Old Place" appeared in the March 1927 Strand Magazine. *Watson died soon after, but Holmes's remarkable constitution kept him active well into the 1930s. It is somewhat bizarre that no death certificate exists for Sherlock Holmes, but I do know that his cottage in Sussex was sold in August 1939, just before the outbreak of the Second World War. Holmes was, by then, about eighty-six and is unlikely to have been involved in any further war-time investigations, but the fact that his death is not recorded in the United Kingdom is suggestive that, just before the outbreak of War, he emigrated. Where to and why I do not know. No doubt he had decided it was time for one last great adventure.*

APPENDIX 1:
A COMPLETE CHRONOLOGY
OF SHERLOCK HOLMES CASES

There have been many attempts at producing a definitive chronology of Sherlock Holmes's career, and whilst they may agree on some things many also beg to differ. This list is probably no different in that respect, but it is what I believe to be the position so far as I know it.

The list covers all known cases in which Holmes was involved, and attempts to date them as accurately as possible. The stories in bold print are the sixty stories in the original Doyle canon. Those in italics are the unrecorded cases noted by Watson. Where these cases have been written up by others their authorship is noted. Those in normal roman print are new (i.e. apocryphal) cases, not mentioned by Watson, but subsequently identified by others as found amongst Watson's papers. This last list is not exclusive, as I have deliberately left out those cases which concentrate on other characters (e.g. Irene Adler, Billy the Page, Inspector Lestrade, Moriarty or Mrs Hudson) or which are very evident spoofs and not to be taken seriously, such as involvement with fictional characters created by others, like Dracula or Fu Manchu. There are also many minor pastiches that weren't worth listing plus, I am sure, many others of which I don't have copies.

The stories included in this anthology are shown in small capitals.

1853/4   Sherlock Holmes born. In "His Last Bow" (a case which began in 1912) Holmes is described as "a man of sixty". No location is given in the canon.

1872   Likely date at which Holmes goes to college. No college is mentioned in the canon although research suggests that Trinity College, Dublin and Oxford are the most likely.

1873/4   Likely date of "**The Gloria Scott**" (Holmes talks of his "two years at college"). This was the case that Holmes states first turned his attention to the idea of detection as a profession. Also the dating of "THE AFFRAY AT THE KILDARE STREET CLUB" and "THE BOTHERSOME BUSINESS OF THE DUTCH NATIVITY."

1875   Holmes became aware of the puzzle of "*the disappearance of James Phillimore*" though the case was not concluded until 1906. Note also the apocryphal cases written as "The Highgate Miracle" by John Dickson Carr and set in December 1893, though this date is clearly wrong, and "The Case of the Vanishing Head-Waiter" by June Thomson.

1877   Holmes settles in rooms in Montague Street, London, spending most of his time studying various branches of science. "Now and again" cases came his way. He does not mention the first two but the third was "**The Musgrave Ritual**", likely to have happened in 1878.

1878/80   Holmes investigates many cases, only a few of which are referred to. These include "*The Tarleton Murders*", "*Vamberry, the Wine Merchant*" [written up by A. Lloyd Taylor]; "*The Adventure of the Old Russian Woman*" [written up as "The Case of the Old Russian Woman" by June Thomson], "*The Singular Affair of the Aluminium Crutch*" [written up by several writers including H. Bedford-Jones], and "*Ricoletti of the club-foot and his abominable wife*". Other stories may be set at this time, especially those listed in "The Adventure of the Sussex Vampire" where Holmes's comments suggest that Watson was not aware of the cases. These include "*Victor Lynch the Forger*", "*Venomous Lizard or Gila*", "*Vanderbilt and the Yeggman*" [written up as "The Case of the Itinerant Yeggman" by June Thomson but dated June 1895 and to which she adds a sequel, "The Case of the Maplestead Magpie"] and "*Vigor, the Hammersmith Wonder*" [written up as "The Case of the Hammersmith Wonder" by June Thomson but set in the early days with Watson; it is also incorporated in "The Case of the Paradol Chamber" by Alan Wilson]. In "The Speckled Band" Holmes is reminded of the case of "*Mrs Farintosh and the Opal Tiara*" which was "before your time Watson". Also to this period may be the cases referred to in "The Empty House", especially "*Mathews, who knocked out my left canine in the waiting-room at Charing Cross*", since Holmes needs to explain it to Watson, and perhaps also "*Merridew of Abominable Memory*". Mortimer

Mabley, referred to in "The Three Gables" was also one of Holmes's earliest clients.

1880   July. The setting of "The Adventure of the Stalwart Companions" by H. Paul Jeffers in which Holmes and Theodore Roosevelt are involved in a US murder. This case has some possibilities but I regard it as highly apocryphal.

1881   January. Holmes and Watson meet. In the first few weeks at 221b Baker Street Watson observes various visitors, whose cases are not discussed. These include "*a young girl, fashionably dressed*", a "*Jewish peddler*", "*a slipshod elderly woman*", "*an old white-haired gentleman*" and "*a railway porter*". There were also several visits by the police, especially by Lestrade, and Holmes later refers to helping him with "*a forgery case*".
March. **"A Study in Scarlet"**.
October. **"The Resident Patient"**.

1882   February. **"The Beryl Coronet"**. Despite the argument by some commentators that no snow fell in London in February that year, this is clearly an early case because Watson is still a little surprised that Holmes urged him to accompany him. This month is almost certainly the setting for "Sherlock Holmes and the Case of Sabina Hall" by L.B. Greenwood.
Winter. "The Devil's Tunnel" by John Taylor.

1883   March. "Sherlock Holmes and the Somerset Hunt" by Rosemary Michaud.
April. **"The Speckled Band"**.
Summer. Uncertain date but likely time for "The Wandering Corpse" by John Taylor.

1884   The Missing Year. It is possible that this was the year of the cases known as "*The Delicate Case of the King of Scandinavia*" and "*The Service of Lord Backwater*".

1885   January. "THE CASE OF THE INCUMBENT INVALID" based on "*the dreadful business of the Abernetty family*".
April/May. **"The Copper Beeches"**. Although set by many commentators in April 1890, this is clearly an earlier case into which Watson slipped references to later cases for the purposes of his introductory argument.

1886   April. **"The Yellow Face"**. This is the earliest case to make reference to Holmes's cocaine habit, though Watson had clearly known about it for some while.
This year probably saw other cases alluded to by Watson including "*The Woman at Margate*", "THE DARLINGTON

SUBSTITUTION SCANDAL", "*The Arnsworth Castle Business*" [written up as "The Adventure of the Red Widow" by Adrian Conan Doyle], "VITTORIA, THE CIRCUS BELLE" and "THE ADVENTURE OF THE SUSPECT SERVANT."

1887 In "The Five Orange Pips" Watson refers to a long series of cases in 1887 including "*The Paradol Chamber*" [written up as "The Case of the Paradol Chamber" by Alan Wilson who linked it with Vigor the Hammersmith Wonder; and also by June Thomson who set it in November 1887 just after Watson's marriage]; "THE ADVENTURE OF THE AMATEUR MENDICANT SOCIETY" [also written up as "*The Case of the Amateur Mendicants*" by June Thomson set in June 1887 and under the same title by Ken Greenwald, set in November 1887]; "*the loss of the British bark* Sophy Anderson", "*the singular adventures of the Grice Patersons in the island of Uffa*" (included here as "THE ADVENTURE OF THE SILVER BUCKLE") and "*the Camberwell poisoning case*" [recorded as "The Adventure of the Gold Hunter" by Adrian Conan Doyle and John Dickson Carr, and as "*The Case of the Camberwell Poisoning*" by June Thomson where it is set in Spring 1887 but confusingly after Watson's marriage, and as "*The Case of the Camberwell Poisoners*" by Ken Greenwald set in October 1887]. Also during this year was the "*death of Mrs Stewart of Lauder*" in which Holmes suspected Colonel Moran to be involved. In "The Norwood Builder" Holmes reminds Watson of the case of "*the terrible murderer, Bert Stevens*" who wanted Holmes to get him off. 1887 was probably also the year of the "*Tankerville Club scandal*" where Major Prendergast was accused of cheating at cards; it may also have been the year of "*The Bishopgate Jewel Case*" which Holmes later used as an example in his lectures; and quite likely the year when Holmes and Watson captured "*Archie Stamford, the forger*" an episode referred to in "The Solitary Cyclist".

January. "**Charles Augustus Milverton**". Although included in *The Return of Sherlock Holmes*, this story has all the feel of a pre-Hiatus story. Watson needs introducing as a "friend", meaning his work was not well known at that time, but he was sufficiently close to Holmes to be referred to as a "partner" and for Holmes to state that "we have shared this same room for some years". Watson introduces the story by saying "it is years since the incidents . . . took place."

Spring. "*The Netherland-Sumatra Company*" and "*The*

Colossal Schemes of Baron Maupertuis", cases which led to Holmes's ill-health [written up as "The Case of the Maupertuis Scandal" by June Thomson]. It may be to this period that "The Horror of Hanging Wood" by John Taylor belongs and one of the best known cases, *"The Giant Rat of Sumatra"*, for which the world is not yet prepared [written up as "The Case of the Sumatran Rat" by June Thomson who sets it after 1888 as Mycroft is referred to; and as "The Giant Rat of Sumatra" by Richard L. Boyer who sets it in September 1894].

April. **"The Reigate Squires"**.

August. "The Secret of Shoreswood Hall" by Denis O. Smith.

September. "THE ADVENTURE OF THE SILVER BUCKLE".

October. **"Silver Blaze"**. Although usually ascribed to October 1888 I prefer the earlier dating and must assume the reference to already published cases is wrong.

1888   By this time (as noted in "The Speckled Band") Watson had made notes of over seventy of Holmes's cases since they met in 1881. (It is possible the reference to "the last eight years" dates from the date "The Speckled Band" was written for publication, which was late 1891, so the seventy cases may relate to mid 1884–mid 1891.)

January. **"The Valley of Fear"**.

February. "THE CASE OF THE SPORTING SQUIRE" (also known as "*Morgan the Poisoner*").

Spring. Likely date for "The Adventure of the Unique Hamlet" by Vincent Starrett.

Summer (July/August). The unrecorded "*Manor House Case*" followed by **"The Greek Interpreter"**, the first reported case in which Watson meets Holmes's brother Mycroft.

August. **"The Cardboard Box"**. The case also refers to "*the bogus laundry affair*" which Holmes had also worked on with Lestrade and which probably happened not long before.

September. **"The Sign of Four"** in which Watson meets Mary Morstan whom he marries a few months later, and settles down again to local practice as a GP; "*The Little Problem of the Grosvenor Square Furniture Van*"; and **"The Noble Bachelor"**.

Autumn. Throughout the months of August–November Holmes was probably consulted on the Jack the Ripper case but this was one series of murders that Watson did not write up and probably explains some of the confusion in dates around this period. Michael Dibdin did explore the case in "The Last Sherlock Holmes Story", which includes Moriarty, but is entirely apocryphal. October. **"The Hound of the Baskervilles"**. Despite attempts to redate this to 1899 or 1900, Watson is clearly recounting an earlier tale. Although he dates it after his marriage it would seem to have happened prior to his marriage, and 1888 is the likeliest date to at least keep within a rough five-year time span from 1884 – the date on Mortimer's stick. It may also seem strange that Watson is happy to drop everything and visit Dartmoor when in the stages of arranging his marriage and without any reference to his fiancée, but as we find elsewhere Mary Morstan was a very flexible and obliging wife who didn't seem to worry about these things, and for the purpose of the story Watson decided to leave out reference to all of this. At the time of Baskerville's death Holmes was involved in the case of "*the Vatican cameos.*" At the start of the Baskerville case Holmes states he is involved in a "*blackmail case*" which could besmirch "one of the most revered names in England" [written up as "The Adventure of the Two Women" by Adrian Conan Doyle but set in September 1886].

November. "*Colonel Upwood and the card scandal of the Nonpareil Club*" [written up as "The Adventure of the Abbas Ruby" by Adrian Conan Doyle though set in November 1886] and "*Mme Montpensier and Mlle Carère*" [written up as "The Adventure of the Black Baronet" by Adrian Conan Doyle but set in October 1889].

1888/89   After Watson's marriage and before he is next involved in a case ("A Scandal in Bohemia") Holmes is involved in several cases including "*the Trepoff Murder*" in Odessa [this is dated to November 1887 in "The Adventure of the Seven Clocks" by Adrian Conan Doyle and John Dickson Carr], "*the singular tragedy of the Atkinson Brothers at Trincomalee*" (presented here as "THE VANISHING OF THE ATKINSONS") and the "*delicate mission with the Dutch royal family*".

1889   March. **"A Scandal in Bohemia"**. Despite the internal dating of March 1888 this is clearly set after Watson's marriage. This is the case which deals with Irene Adler.
March/June. **"A Case of Identity"**. At this time Holmes reports he has some ten or twelve minor cases in

hand. He had also just helped clear up *"The Dundas Separation Case"*. The case refers back to Holmes tracing the *"husband of Mrs Etherege"* which probably happened a year or two earlier.

June. "THE ADVENTURE OF THE FALLEN STAR", "The Stockbroker's Clerk", "The Man With the Twisted Lip" and probably "The Engineer's Thumb". Either now or earlier was also the case of *"Colonel Warburton's Madness"* mentioned in "The Engineer's Thumb" [written up as "The Adventure of the Sealed Room" by Adrian Conan Doyle and dated April 1888 though erroneously set after Watson's marriage; and as "The Case of the Colonel's Madness" by June Thomson set in July 1890]. Ken Greenwald sets "The Case of the Baconian Cipher" in the same month.

July. *"The Adventure of the Second Stain"* [written up as "The Adventure of the Green Empress" by F.P. Cillié and set in July 1888]; "The Adventure of the Naval Treaty" and *"The Adventure of the Tired Captain"* [written up under that title by Alan Wilson].

August. "The Crooked Man."

September. "The Five Orange Pips". Despite internal inference that this story is set in 1887 it is clearly after Watson's marriage, and after "The Sign of Four". At this time Holmes commented that he had been beaten four times, thrice by men and once by a woman.

November. "The Case of the Exalted Client" by June Thomson, and "The Adventure of the Megatherium Thefts" by S.C. Roberts.

December. "The Blue Carbuncle".

1890   Spring. "The Strange Case of the Tongue-Tied Tenor" by Carol Buggé.

June. "The Boscombe Valley Mystery".

June/July. "The Adventure of the Purple Hand" by Denis O. Smith.

Autumn. "Sherlock Holmes and the Thistle of Scotland" by L.B. Greenwood.

September. Possible date for "The Adventure of the First-Class Carriage" by Ronald Knox.

October. "The Red-Headed League".

November. "The Dying Detective". The same date is chosen for "The Problem of the Purple Maculas" by James C. Iraldi.

1891   April/May. "The Final Problem" leading to Holmes

and Moriarty plunging over the Reichenbach Falls on 4 May.

1891/4   The Great Hiatus during which period Holmes travelled extensively, mostly in disguise. He states he spent two years in Tibet (under the alias of the Norwegian Sigerson – written up as "Murder Beyond the Mountains" by Ken Greenwald), then travelled to Persia, Mecca, Khartoum, returning to France where he undertook scientific experiments. This period is also covered by Nicholas Meyer in "The Canary Trainer" (a title suggestive of the 1895 case but not the same) which brings Holmes and the Phantom of the Opera together.

1894   February. **"The Empty House"** (not April as recorded in the story). The story refers to Watson's own "sad bereavement" following the recent death of his wife.

March. **"The Second Stain"**. A different case to others with this title. Despite reference to Autumn this episode clearly happened earlier in the year. The episode must have been early enough in the month to allow for a further case, involving the arrest of Colonel Carruthers (about which we otherwise know nothing) and for Holmes to get bored for lack of cases before the onset of **"Wisteria Lodge"**. The story's reference to 1892 is clearly wrong. This must be the same case as "The Papers of ex-President Murillo" referred to in "The Norwood Builder".

Summer. *"the shocking affair of the Dutch steamship* Friesland, *which so nearly cost us both our lives"* [written up as "The Case of the *Friesland* Outrage" by June Thomson set in November 1894].

August. **"The Norwood Builder"**.

September. "THE ADVENTURE OF THE DORSET STREET LODGER".

October. "THE MYSTERY OF THE ADDLETON CURSE" (based on *"the Addleton tragedy and the singular contents of the ancient British barrow"* [also written up as "The Adventure of Foulkes Rath" by Adrian Conan Doyle set in 1894; and as "The Case of the Addleton Tragedy" by June Thomson set in November 1894]; "THE ADVENTURE OF THE PARISIAN GENTLEMAN" (based on the case of *"Huret, the Boulevard assassin"*) and "THE ADVENTURE OF THE INERTIAL ADJUSTOR".

November. "THE ADVENTURE OF THE TOUCH OF GOD" (based on the case of *"the terrible death of Crosby the*

Banker"); "**The Golden Pince-Nez**" and "The Sunleys of Canterbury" by Miles Elward.

From 1894–1901 Watson records that Holmes was "very busy", with hundreds of private cases plus frequently being consulted on many major public cases. In "The Golden Pince-Nez" he refers to three volumes of his notes about the cases, which include "*the repulsive story of the red leech*", and "*the Smith-Mortimer succession case*" [written up as "The Case of the Smith-Mortimer Succession" by June Thomson set in September 1894].

1895 Watson highlights 1895 as a year when Holmes was on top form. Cases included "*the sudden death of Cardinal Tosca*" to "*Wilson, the notorious canary-trainer*" [written up as "The Adventure of the Deptford Horror" by Adrian Conan Doyle and set in June 1895; as "The Case of the Notorious Canary-Trainer" by June Thomson set in January 1895; and as "The Adventure of the Notorious Canary Trainer" by Ken Greenwald though this is set in Summer 1908] both of which happened in the first half of the year.

March. "THE ADVENTURE OF THE PERSECUTED PAINTER"; "**The Three Students**".

April. "**The Solitary Cyclist**". Watson undertook the initial investigation of this case because Holmes was busy with the case of the "*persecution of John Vincent Harden the tobacco millionaire*" [a case later written up as "Sherlock Holmes and the Devil's Grail" by Barrie Roberts; and as "The Case of the Millionaire's Persecution" by June Thomson]. This month is also cited for "The Adventure of the Marked Man" by Stuart Palmer and "Sherlock Holmes and the Mysterious Friend of Oscar Wilde" by Russell A. Brown.

May. "Prisoner of the Devil" by Michael Hardwick.

July. "**The Adventure of Black Peter**". About this same time occurred "The Ball of Twine" by Miles Elward.

September. "*The Case of the Harley Street Specialist*" (written up by June Thomson: it recounts Holmes's dramatic introduction to Dr Moore Agar referred to in "The Devil's Foot"). The same month is the timing for "The Case of the Featherstone Policeman" by Tony Lumb (despite the erroneous internal dating of 1893) and "The Hentzau Affair" by David Stuart Davies.

October. "The Case of the Man Who Was Wanted" [*aka* "The Adventure of the Sheffield Banker"] by Arthur

Whitaker, a story once believed to be by Doyle but clearly apocryphal. It contains many inconsistencies including a reference to Watson's wife still being alive. If that is true this story may fit better into October 1889.

November. "**The Bruce-Partington Plans**". This case also refers to Brooks and Woodhouse, two of some fifty criminals who would wish to see Holmes dead.

December. "THE ADVENTURE OF THE GRACE CHALICE" based on the case of Henry Staunton.

1896   Spring. At some early part of this year Holmes helped Mr Fairdale Hobbs, a small matter later referred to in "The Red Circle".

Summer. "**The Disappearance of Lady Frances Carfax**". At the time of this case Holmes was involved with the problem of "*old Abrahams in mortal fear of his life*" an episode later written up as "The Case of the Shopkeeper's Terror" by June Thomson.

October. "**The Veiled Lodger**". This case also refers to the case of "*the politician, the lighthouse, and the trained cormorant*" which could have happened at any time up to Holmes's retirement [W.R. Duncan Macmillan wrote this up as "Holmes in Scotland" and dated it August 1899 or 1900; June Thomson wrote it up as "The Case of the Abandoned Lighthouse" and set it in July 1903]. "THE ADVENTURE OF THE SUFFERING RULER".

November. "**The Sussex Vampire.**" Ken Greenwald set "The Adventure of the Headless Monk" in the same month. This month would also encompass the little episode of "The Field Bazaar" and the second case of "THE REPULSIVE STORY OF THE RED LEECH".

Winter. "The Case of the Demon Barber" by Ken Greenwald.

1897   January. "**The Abbey Grange**".

February. "**The Red Circle**" and "THE ADVENTURE OF THE FAITHFUL RETAINER."

March. "**The Devil's Foot**" which follows from Holmes's health suffering due to pressure of work.

July. "**The Dancing Men**".

December. "**The Missing Three-Quarter**". This is also the likely date for "The Silent Night Before Christmas" by Gene DeWeese, set at Christmas.

1898   April. "A Trifling Affair" by H.R.F. Keating.

May. "The Egyptian Hall Adventure" [aka "The Randolph Case"] by Val Andrews.

July/August. "**The Retired Colourman**". This case ran into the case of "*the two Coptic Patriarchs*".

1899   December. "The Adventure of the Iron Box" by Ken Greenwald.

1900   February. "THE CASE OF THE SUICIDAL LAWYER" based on "*The Abergavenny Murders*" which is noted as coming up for trial at the start of "The Priory School".
May. "**The Six Napoleons**", followed immediately by "*The Conk-Singleton Forgery Case*".
September. "The Out-of-Date Murder" by Ken Greenwald.

1901   April. "THE LEGACY OF RACHEL HOWELLS."
May. "*The Case of the Ferrers Documents*" [written up as "The Adventure of the Dark Angels" by Adrian Conan Doyle] and "**The Priory School**".
October. "**The Problem of Thor Bridge**", a case which followed a month of trivialities and stagnation. This case refers to earlier cases which are undated but which probably happened during the 1890s and include "*The Disappearance of the cutter Alicia*", and the fate of "*Isadora Persano*" with its worm unknown to science [written up as "The Case of the Remarkable Worm" by June Thomson set some time after Watson's first marriage].

1902   Spring. "Sherlock Holmes and the Arabian Princess" by John North [Val Andrews].
May. "**Shoscombe Old Place**".
June. "**The Three Garridebs**". In this same month Holmes refused a knighthood "for services which may perhaps some day be described." After this case Watson moved out of Baker Street and set up practice again.
July. "The Revenge of the Hound" by Michael Hardwick.
September. "**The Illustrious Client**".

1903   January. "**The Blanched Soldier**". In this story told by Holmes himself, not Watson, Holmes refers to Watson having "deserted" him for a wife. Whilst Watson had indeed remarried, he had far from deserted Holmes and was involved in the case for the "*Sultan of Turkey*" presented here as "THE ADVENTURE OF THE BULGARIAN DIPLOMAT".
June. "**The Mazarin Stone**" and "**The Three Gables**". Sometime around now would also be the case of "The Phantom Organ" by John Taylor.
September. "**The Creeping Man**".
October. Holmes retires to a house on the Sussex Downs and spends his time beekeeping. In "Exit Sherlock

Holmes", Robert Lee Hall suggests the retirement was prompted by the reappearance of Moriarty.

1906   April. "The Brighton Pavilion Mystery" by Val Andrews, which is entirely apocryphal. At this time Holmes was with Watson in America and resolving "THE ENIGMA OF THE WARWICKSHIRE VORTEX."

1907   July. "The Lion's Mane".

1909   March. "The Adventure of the Second Generation" by Ken Greenwald in which Holmes meets the daughter of Irene Adler.

1914   August. "His Last Bow", a case which began in 1912.

1918   November. "THE CASE OF THE LAST BATTLE."

1920s   The passing of Holmes and Watson is not noted and some writers continue their adventures into the thirties and forties. These are all apocryphal. Watson was a year or two older than Holmes so both had entered their 70s by the mid-20s. Watson died soon after publication of *The Case-Book of Sherlock Holmes* in 1927. The final date of Holmes's death is not known. One touching story of these last years is "How a Hermit was Disturbed in His Retirement" [*aka* "The Adventure of Hillerman Hall"] by Julian Symon where Holmes is visited by a very young Miss Marple.

APPENDIX II: THE TALES OF SHERLOCK HOLMES

Part 1. The Original Canon

The following lists all of Sir Arthur Conan Doyle's original stories in order of book publication, with original publication sources in both Britain and the United States.

A Study in Scarlet. *Beeton's Christmas Annual,* 1887; London, Ward Lock, 1887; Philadelphia, Lippincott, 1890.

The Sign of Four. *Lippincott's Monthly Magazine,* February 1890; London, Spencer Blackett, 1890; Philadelphia, Lippincott, 1893.

The Adventures of Sherlock Holmes. London, Newnes, 1892; New York, Harper, 1892. Contains:

"A Scandal in Bohemia", *The Strand,* July 1891.

"The Red-Headed League", *The Strand,* August 1891.

"A Case of Identity", *The Strand,* September 1891.

"The Boscombe Valley Mystery", *The Strand,* October 1891.

"The Five Orange Pips", *The Strand,* November 1891.

"The Man With the Twisted Lip", *The Strand,* December 1891.

"The Adventure of the Blue Carbuncle", *The Strand,* January 1892.

"The Adventure of the Speckled Band", *The Strand,* February 1892.

"The Adventure of the Engineer's Thumb", *The Strand,* March 1892.

"The Adventure of the Noble Bachelor", *The Strand,* April 1892.

"The Adventure of the Beryl Coronet", *The Strand,* May 1892.

"The Adventure of the Copper Beeches", *The Strand,* June 1892.

The Memoirs of Sherlock Holmes. London, Newnes, 1894; New York, Harper, 1894. Contains:

"Silver Blaze", *The Strand,* December 1892; *Harper's Weekly,* 25 February 1893.

"The Yellow Face", *The Strand,* February 1893; *Harper's Weekly,* 11

February 1893.

"The Stock-broker's Clerk", *The Strand*, March 1893; *Harper's Weekly*, 11 March 1893.

"The 'Gloria Scott'", *The Strand*, April 1893; *Harper's Weekly*, 15 April 1893.

"The Musgrave Ritual", *The Strand*, May 1893; *Harper's Weekly*, 13 May 1893.

"The Reigate Squires", *The Strand*, June 1893; as "The Reigate Puzzle", *Harper's Weekly*, 17 June 1893.

"The Crooked Man", *The Strand*, July 1893; *Harper's Weekly*, 8 July 1893.

"The Resident Patient", *The Strand*, August 1893; *Harper's Weekly*, 12 August 1893.

"The Greek Interpreter", *The Strand*, September 1893; *Harper's Weekly*, 16 September 1893.

"The Naval Treaty", *The Strand*, October 1893; *Harper's Weekly*, 14–21 October 1893.

"The Final Problem", *The Strand*, December 1893; *McClure's*, December 1893.

The Hound of the Baskervilles. *The Strand*, August 1901–April 1902; London, Newnes, 1902; *The Strand* [New York], September 1901–May 1902; New York, McClure Phillips, 1902.

The Return of Sherlock Holmes. London, Newnes, 1905; New York, McClure, 1905. Contains:

"The Adventure of the Empty House", *Collier's*, 26 September 1903; *The Strand*, October 1903.

"The Adventure of the Norwood Builder", *Collier's*, 31 October 1903; *The Strand*, November 1903.

"The Adventure of the Dancing Men", *The Strand*, December 1903; *Collier's*, 5 December 1903.

"The Adventure of the Solitary Cyclist", *Collier's*, 26 December 1903; *The Strand*, January 1904.

"The Adventure of the Priory School", *Collier's*, 30 January 1904; *The Strand*, February 1904.

"The Adventure of Black Peter", *Collier's*, 20 February 1904; *The Strand*, March 1904.

"The Adventure of Charles Augustus Milverton", *Collier's*, 26 March 1904; *The Strand*, April 1904.

"The Adventure of the Six Napoleons", *Collier's*, 30 April 1904; *The Strand*, May 1904.

"The Adventure of the Three Students", *The Strand*, June 1904; *Collier's*, 24 September 1904.

"The Adventure of the Golden Pince-Nez", *The Strand*, July 1904; *Collier's*, 29 October 1904.

"The Adventure of the Missing Three-Quarter", *The Strand*,
August 1904; *Collier's*, 26 November 1904.

"The Adventure of the Abbey Grange", *The Strand*, September
1904; *Collier's*, 31 December 1904.

"The Adventure of the Second Stain", *The Strand*, December
1904; *Collier's*, 28 January 1905.

The Valley of Fear. *The Strand*, September 1914-May 1915; London:
Smith, Elder, 1915; *The Philadelphia Press*, 6 September-22
November 1914; New York, Doran, 1915.

His Last Bow. London, John Murray, 1917; New York, Doran, 1917.
Contains:

"The Adventure of Wisteria Lodge", as "The Singular Experience
of Mr J. Scott Eccles", *Collier's*, 15 August 1908; *The Strand*,
September-October 1908.

"The Adventure of the Cardboard Box", *The Strand*, January
1893; *Harper's Weekly*, 14 January 1893.

"The Adventure of the Red Circle", *The Strand*, March–April
1911; *The Strand* [New York], April–May 1911.

"The Adventure of the Bruce–Partington Plans", *The Strand*,
December 1908; *Collier's*, 12 December 1908.

"The Adventure of the Dying Detective", *Collier's*, 22 November
1913; *The Strand*, December 1913.

"The Disappearance of Lady Frances Carfax", *The Strand*, December 1911; *The American Magazine*, December 1911.

"The Adventure of the Devil's Foot", *The Strand*, December 1910;
The Strand [New York], January–February 1911.

"His Last Bow: The War Service of Sherlock Holmes", *The Strand*,
September 1917; *Collier's*, 22 September 1917.

The Case Book of Sherlock Holmes. London, John Murray, 1927;
New York, Doran, 1927. Contains:

"The Adventure of the Illustrious Client", *Collier's*, 8 November
1924; *The Strand*, February–March 1925.

"The Adventure of the Blanched Soldier", *Liberty*, 16 October
1926; *The Strand*, November 1926.

"The Adventure of the Mazarin Stone", *The Strand*, October 1921;
Hearst's International, November 1921.

"The Adventure of the Three Gables", *Liberty*, 18 September
1926; *The Strand*, October 1926.

"The Adventure of the Sussex Vampire", *The Strand*, January
1924; *Hearst's International*, January 1924.

"The Adventure of the Three Garridebs", *Collier's*, 25 October
1924; *The Strand*, January 1925.

"The Problem of Thor Bridge", *The Strand*, February 1922; *Hearst's
International*, February 1922.

"The Adventure of the Creeping Man", *The Strand*, March 1923;
Hearst's International, March 1923.

"The Adventure of the Lion's Mane", *Liberty*, 27 November 1926;
The Strand, December 1926.

"The Adventure of the Veiled Lodger", *Liberty*, 22 January 1927;
The Strand, February 1927.

"The Adventure of Shoscombe Old Place", *Liberty*, 5 March 1927;
The Strand, April 1927.

"The Adventure of the Retired Colourman", *Liberty*, 18 December
1926; *The Strand*, January 1927.

Part 2. The Apocryphal Tales

The following is a selective list of stories, novels and "biographies"
featuring Sherlock Holmes written by others than Sir Arthur Conan
Doyle. The list is not complete, as that would fill a book in itself, but
it focuses on those stories which are faithful to the life and career of
Sherlock Holmes and do not attempt to distort the facts. It excludes
all science-fiction and fantasy-based adventures and for the most
part those incorporating characters from other works of fiction.
Most of the cases are apocryphal but are included for completeness.
It excludes those stories written about other characters who feature
in the Holmes stories but where Holmes is not central to the story,
such as the very fine Irene Adler books by Carole Nelson Douglas.
The items are listed in author order; books are in italics, short-story
titles are in quotes. I have added occasional notes where the title is
not self-explanatory.

Altamont, Brett Spencer and Altamont, Dorian David. *Draco,
Draconis*. Florence, Italy, MySher Altamont Publishing, 1996.
A beautifully produced novel set in 1895 and introducing the
young nephew of Moriarty.

Andrews, Val. *The Beekeeper, The Fair, The Fowlhaven Werewolf, The Last
Reunion* and *The Carriage Clock*, all New York, Magico Press, 1983.
Five booklets suggesting incidents in Holmes's retirement.

Andrews, Val. *Sherlock Holmes and the Egyptian Hall Adventure*.
Romford, Ian Henry, 1989. Set in 1898 where Holmes investigates Maskelyn's theatre of mystery. Although almost certainly
apocryphal this story has much to commend it.

Andrews, Val. *Sherlock Holmes and the Brighton Pavilion Mystery*.
Romford, Ian Henry, 1989. Set in 1906. Andrews has also
written *Sherlock Holmes and the Greyfriars School Mystery* (London,
privately published, 1993), a wholly apocryphal but rather fun
spoof which brings together Holmes and Billy Bunter in the
year 1912.

Andrews, Val. *Sherlock Holmes and the Houdini Birthright.* London, Breese Books, 1995. Set in 1922 and entirely apocryphal but a tempting combination of Holmes and Houdini. *For further books by Val Andrews see under John North.*

Baring-Gould, W.S. *Sherlock Holmes*, New York: Clakson N. Potter, 1962. A purported biography of Holmes which is great fun and occasionally hits on the truth.

Barr, Stephen. "The Procurator of Justice", *Ellery Queen's Mystery Magazine*, February 1950. One of the many apocryphal attempts to explain the disappearance of James Phillimore.

Barrie, James M. "The Adventure of the Two Collaborators". A humorous spoof, written for Arthur Conan Doyle personally in 1893 and not intended for publication, but which so amused Conan Doyle that he called it "the best of all the numerous parodies" and printed it in his own autobiography, *Memoirs and Adventures*, London, Hodder & Stoughton, 1924.

Bedford-Jones, H. "The Affair of the Aluminium Crutch", *Palm Springs News*, January 16-February 20, 1936. A reasonably faithful attempt to recreate one of the early pre-Watson cases.

Biggle, Jr., Lloyd. *The Quallsford Inheritance*, New York, St. Martin's Press, 1986; and *The Glendower Conspiracy*, Tulsa, Council Oak Books, 1990. Two cases related by Edward Porter Jones, a former Baker Street Irregular, the first set in 1900, the second in 1904. Excellent stories, though the authenticity is suspect.

Boyer, Richard L. *The Giant Rat of Sumatra*, New York: Warner Books, 1976; London: W.H. Allen, 1977. One of the most highly regarded pastiches.

Brooks, Clive. *Sherlock Holmes Revisited*, London: Hallmark Books, 1990. Seven stories based on the following unrecorded cases cited by Watson: "The Abergavenny Adventure", "The Alicia Cutter", "The Aluminium Crutch", "The Red Leech", "The Conk-Singleton Affair", "The Disappearance of James Phillimore" and "The Problem of the Peculiar Pipes".

Brooks, Clive. *Sherlock Holmes Revisited, Volume Two*. Southampton, Spy Glass Books, 1990. Five further cases based on unrecorded episodes mentioned by Watson: "The Friesland Case", "The Politician, Lighthouse and Trained Cormorant", "The Abernetty Affair", "The Case of the Canary Trainer" and "The Adventure of the Amateur Mendicants".

Brown, Russell A. *Sherlock Holmes and the Mysterious Friend of Oscar Wilde*, New York, St. Martin's Press, 1988. Set in 1895.

Chujoy, Anatole. "The Adventure of the Tainted Worm", *Baker Street Journal*, July 1955. A faithful attempt to recreate the story of Isodora Persano and the remarkable worm.

Cillié, François P. "The Adventure of the Second Stain", *Sunday Times* of South Africa, 3 December 1967; also reprinted as "The Adventure of the Green Empress".

Clarke, Benjamin. "Sunshine, Sunshine", *Baker Street Journal Christmas Annual* #5, 1960. Another of the many apocryphal attempts to explain the disappearance of James Phillimore.

Collins, Randall. *The Case of the Philosophers' Ring*, New York, Crown, 1978; London, Harvester, 1980. A self-evident apocryphal novel with little regard for Holmesian data, but an interesting philosophical novel which pits Holmes's wits against those of Aleister Crowley.

Conan Doyle, Adrian and Carr, John Dickson. *The Exploits of Sherlock Holmes*, London: John Murray, 1954; New York, Random House, 1954. A collection of twelve stories based on the unrecorded cases referred to by Watson. Some have the air of authenticity but most are apocryphal. The stories are (all prefixed "The Adventure of . . .") "The Seven Clocks", "The Gold Hunter", "The Wax Gamblers", "The Highgate Miracle", "The Black Baronet", "The Sealed Room", "Foulkes Rath", "The Abbas Ruby", "The Two Women", "The Dark Angels", "The Deptford Horror" and "The Red Widow".

Davies, David Stuart. *Sherlock Holmes and the Hentzau Affair*. Romford, Ian Henry, 1991. Apocryphal novel set in 1895. Holmes in Ruritania.

Davies, David Stuart. *The Tangled Skein*. Romford, Ian Henry, 1992. Almost certainly a genuine case though the date of 1888 following on from the Baskerville case must be wrong.

DeWeese, Gene. "The Silent Night Before Christmas", *Ellery Queen's Mystery Magazine*, January 1996. A faithfully rendered story set in the first Christmas after Holmes's return from the grave.

Dibdin, Michael. *The Last Sherlock Holmes Story*. London, Jonathan Cape, 1978; New York, Pantheon, 1978. A totally apocryphal novel which brings Holmes and Moriarty together in the murders of Jack the Ripper.

Elward, Miles. *Sherlock Holmes in Canterbury*. Canterbury, Wynne Howard, 1995. Three stories set in Kent which should be apocryphal but have a considerable authenticity.

Fisher, Charles. *Some Unaccountable Exploits of Sherlock Holmes*, Philadelphia: Sons of the Copper Beeches, 1956. Seven very short and rather frivolous accounts, originally written for the *Philadelphia Record* in 1939–1940.

Gardner, John. *The Return of Moriarty*, London: Weidenfeld & Nicolson, 1974; New York, Putnam's, 1974; and *The Revenge of Moriarty*, London: Weidenfeld & Nicolson, 1975; New York,

Putnam's, 1976. Very evident apocrypha, but extremely good stories.

Green, Richard Lancelyn (editor). *The Uncollected Sherlock Holmes*, London, Penguin Books, 1983. An anthology of seventeen pastiches, parodies and associated ephemera by Conan Doyle.

Green, Richard Lancelyn (editor). *The Further Adventures of Sherlock Holmes*, London, Penguin Books, 1985. An anthology of eleven excellent pastiches, some of them faithful reconstructions of cases. The stories are (all prefixed "The Adventure of . . .") ". . . the First-Class Carriage", Ronald A. Knox (*The Strand*, February 1947); ". . . the Sheffield Banker", Arthur Whitaker; ". . . the Unique *Hamlet*" by Vincent Starrett; ". . . the Marked Man" by Stuart Palmer (*Ellery Queen's*, July 1944); ". . . the Megatherium Thefts", S.C. Roberts; ". . . the Trained Cormorant" W.R. Duncan Macmillan (originally "Holmes in Scotland", *Blackwood's Magazine*, September 1953); ". . . Arnsworth Castle", Adrian Conan Doyle; ". . . the Tired Captain", Alan Wilson; ". . . the Green Empress", F.P. Cillié; ". . . the Purple Hand", D.O. Smith, and ". . . Hillerman Hall", Julian Symons.

Greenberg, Martin H., and Waugh, Carol-Lynn (editors). *The New Adventures of Sherlock Holmes*. New York, Carroll & Graf, 1987. Anthology of fifteen original stories: "The Adventure of the Unique Holmes" by Jon L. Breen, "The Adventure of the Persistent Marksman" by Lillian de la Torre, "Dr and Mrs Watson at Home" by Loren D. Estleman, "Moriarty and the Real Underworld" by John Gardner, "The Two Footmen" by Michael Gilbert, "The Adventure of the Gowanus Abduction" by Joyce Harrington, "Sherlock Holmes and 'the Woman'" by Michael Harrison, "The Return of the Speckled Band" by Edward D. Hoch, "Sherlock Holmes and the Muffin" by Dorothy B. Hughes, "The Shadows on the Lawn" by Barry Jones, "The Final Toast" by Stuart Kaminsky, "The Doctor's Case" by Stephen King, "The Curious Computer" by Peter Lovesey, "The Infernal Machine" by John Lutz, "The Phantom Chamber" by Gary Alan Ruse and "The House That Jack Built" by Edward Wellen.

Greenberg, Martin H., Lellenberg, Jon L. and Waugh, Carol-Lynn (editors). *Holmes for the Holidays*. New York, Berkley, 1996. An anthology of fourteen new stories each set at Christmas. Stories are "The Adventure of the Canine Ventriloquist" by Jon L. Breen, "The Adventure of the Christmas Ghosts" by Bill Crider, "The Adventure of the Christmas Tree" by William L. DeAndrea, "The Thief of Twelfth Night" by Carole Nelson Douglas, "The Adventure of the Three Ghosts" by Loren D. Estleman, "The Italian Sherlock Holmes" by Reginald Hill, "The Christmas

Client" by Edward D. Hoch, "A Scandal in Winter" by Gillian Linscott, "The Adventure in Border Country" by Gwen Moffat, "The Sleuth of Christmas Past" by Barbara Paul, "The Watch Night Bell" by Anne Perry, "The Yuletide Affair" by John Stoessel, "The Adventure of the Angel's Trumpet" by Carolyn Wheat and "The Adventure of the Man Who Never Laughed" by J.N. Williamson. All are well written, but most are apocryphal.

Greenwald, Ken (adapter). *The Lost Adventures of Sherlock Holmes*, New York, Mallard Press, 1989. Thirteen stories adapted from the original 1945 US radio series scripted by Dennis Green and Anthony Boucher and starring Basil Rathbone and Nigel Bruce. The stories are of dubious authenticity but are good fun. They are: "The Adventure of the Second Generation", "The April Fool's Adventure", "The Case of the Amateur Mendicants", "The Adventure of the Out-of-Date Murder", "The Case of the Demon Barber", "Murder Beyond the Mountains", "The Case of the Uneasy Easy Chair", "The Case of the Baconian Cipher", "The Adventure of the Headless Monk", "The Case of the Camberwell Poisoners", "The Adventure of the Iron Box", "The Adventure of the Notorious Canary Trainer" and "The Case of the Girl with the Gazelle".

Greenwood, L.B. *Sherlock Holmes and the Raleigh Legacy*, New York, Atheneum, 1986; Bristol, Chivers, 1988. An early case set in 1881 with a ring of authenticity.

Greenwood, L.B. *Sherlock Holmes and the Case of Sabina Hall*, New York, Simon & Schuster, 1988. Set in 1882 where Holmes follows up a request from an old college friend.

Greenwood, L.B. *Sherlock Holmes and the Thistle of Scotland*, New York, Simon & Schuster, 1989. Set in 1890 where Holmes investigates the theft of a legendary Scottish jewel.

Haining, Peter (editor). *The Final Adventures of Sherlock Holmes*, London, W.H. Allen, 1981. An anthology of fifteen items by Conan Doyle with Holmesian associations.

Hall, Robert Lee. *Exit Sherlock Holmes*, London, John Murray, 1977; New York, Scribner's, 1977. Moriarty returns to London in 1903 which forces Holmes into retirement.

Hardwick, Michael, *Prisoner of the Devil*, London and New York, Proteus Publishing, 1979. Holmes takes on the Dreyfus case.

Hardwick, Michael, *Sherlock Holmes, My Life and Crimes*, London, Harvill Press, 1984; New York, Doubleday, 1984. A purported autobiography of Holmes.

Hardwick, Michael. *The Revenge of the Hound*, New York, Villard Books, 1987.

Iraldi, James C. *The Problem of the Purple Maculas*, Culver City, Luther

Norris, 1968. A serious attempt to recreate the case of Henry Staunton.

Jeffers, H. Paul. *The Adventure of the Stalwart Companions*, London, Cassell, 1978; New York, Harper & Row, 1978. Set in July 1880. Holmes and Roosevelt team up to investigate a crime in New York. The book is apocryphal but is remarkably convincing.

Kaye, Marvin (editor). *The Game is Afoot*, New York, St Martin's Press, 1994. An anthology of fifty "parodies, pastiches and ponderings", very few of which are authentic.

Kaye, Marvin (editor). *Resurrected Holmes*, New York, St Martin's Press, 1996. A gimmick-based book where Watson's unchronicled cases are apparently written up by such celebrities as H.G. Wells, Somerset Maugham, Ernest Hemingway, Edgar Rice Burroughs, Lord Dunsany and even H.P. Lovecraft. The real perpetrators of this anthology are John Gregory Betancourt, Carol Buggé, Peter Cannon, William L. DeAndrea, Craig Shaw Gardner, Edward D. Hoch, Marvin Kaye, Morgan Llywelyn, Richard A. Lupoff, Terry McGarry, Mike Resnick, Roberta Rogow, Darrell Schweitzer, Henry Slesar and Paula Volsky. Although most of the stories are apocryphal at least one is based on apparently authentic notes.

King, Laurie R. *The Beekeeper's Apprentice*, New York, St Martin's, 1994 and *A Monstrous Regiment of Women*, New York, St Martin's, 1995. Set after Holmes's retirement, in 1914 and 1920 respectively, these are the investigations of Mary Russell who becomes Holmes's protegée.

Kurland, Michael. *The Infernal Device*, New York: Signet Books, 1978; London, New English Library, 1979. Set in 1885, it brings Holmes and Moriarty together against a common enemy.

Kurland, Michael. *Death by Gaslight*, New York, Signet Books, 1982.

Lloyd-Taylor, A. "The Wine Merchant", *Sherlock Holmes Journal*, Winter 1959. A faithful attempt to recreate one of the early cases.

Lumb, Tony. *Sherlock Holmes and the Featherstone Policeman*, Featherstone, Yorkshire, Briton Press, 1993; and *Sherlock Holmes and the White Lady of Featherstone*, Featherstone, Yorkshire, Briton Press, 1995. Two totally apocryphal cases set in 1893 and 1904 and involving Holmes in two local historical incidents.

Meyer, Nicholas. *The Seven Per-Cent Solution*. New York, Dutton, 1974; London, Hodder & Stoughton, 1975. A totally apocryphal novel in which Holmes and Sigmund Freud collaborate.

Meyer, Nicholas. *The West-End Horror*. New York, Dutton, 1976; London, Hodder & Stoughton, 1976. Holmes investigates murders in London's theatreland.

Meyer, Nicholas. *The Canary Trainer*. New York, Norton, 1993. An apocryphal novel set after Holmes's feigned death in 1891. He becomes involved in Paris with the Phantom of the Opera. See also Siciliano's *The Angel of the Opera.*

Michaud, Rosemary. *Sherlock Holmes and the Somerset Hunt,* Romford, Ian Henry, 1993. An early tale set in 1883 and quite possible an authentic case.

North, John. *Sherlock Holmes and the Arabian Princess,* Romford, Ian Henry, 1990; and *Sherlock Holmes and the German Nanny,* Romford, Ian Henry, 1990.

Pearsall, Ronald. *Sherlock Holmes Investigates the Murder in Euston Square.* Newton Abbot, David & Charles, 1989. Set in 1879 the novel presents a series of reports of a murder and then lets Holmes loose on the case. Whilst it has all the appearance of an authentic case, the author's tendency to spoof spoils the overall effect.

Queen, Ellery. *The Misadventures of Sherlock Holmes,* Boston, Little, Brown, 1944. The earliest anthology of pastiches and parodies, most of them apocryphal but including a few tantalizing items.

Resnick, Mike and Greenberg, Martin H. (editors). *Sherlock Holmes in Orbit,* New York, DAW Books, 1995. An anthology of twenty-six all new Holmes stories, most of them with a science-fiction or fantasy base and all apocryphal. It includes the excellent story "The Case of the Detective's Smile" by Mark Bourne which is so delightful that it ought to be true.

Roberts, Barrie. *Sherlock Holmes and the Railway Maniac.* London, Constable, 1994; *Sherlock Holmes and the Devil's Grail,* London, Constable, 1995; and *Sherlock Holmes and the Man from Hell,* London, Constable, 1997. Three potentially authentic novels though the author himself states he cannot vouch for certain.

Roberts S.C. "The Death of Cardinal Tosca", *Sherlock Holmes Journal,* June 1953. A purportedly authentic recreation of one of the unrecorded cases. Roberts also wrote *The Strange Case of the Megatherium Thefts,* Cambridge, privately printed, 1945, which is reprinted in Green's *The Further Adventures of Sherlock Holmes.*

Rosenkjar, Pat. "The Adventure of the Persecuted Millionaire", *Studies in Scarlet,* December 1965; and "The Little Affair of the Vatican Cameos", *Baker Street Pages,* August–September 1965. Fairly faithful attempts to recreate two unrecorded cases.

Siciliano, Sam. *The Angel of the Opera,* New York: Otto Penzler Books, 1994. An entirely apocryphal but highly enjoyable novel in which Holmes encounters the Phantom of the Opera. See also Meyer's *The Canary Trainer.*

Smith, Denis O. *The Adventure of the Purple Hand,* private, 1982; *The Adventure of the Unseen Traveller,* Newport Pagnell, Diogenes,

1983; *The Adventure of the Zodiac Plate*, Diogenes, 1984; *The Secret of Shoreswood Hall*, Diogenes, 1985 and *The Adventure of the Christmas Visitor*, Diogenes, 1985. Faithful accounts of unrecorded cases that suggest a strong air of authenticity.

Starrett, Vincent. *The Unique Hamlet*, Chicago, private, 1920. A recognized classic with all the hall marks of an authentic case. This is reprinted in Ellery Queen's *Misadventures of Sherlock Holmes* and in Starrett's own *The Private Life of Sherlock Holmes* (University of Chicago Press, 1960).

Symons, Julian. "How a Hermit was Disturbed in his Retirement" in *The Great Detectives*, London, Orbis, 1981; New York, Abrams, 1981; also reprinted as "The Adventure of Hillerman Hall". Wherein an aged Holmes is visited by a young Miss Marple. Obviously apocryphal, but delightful none the less.

Taylor, John. *The Unopened Casebook of Sherlock Holmes*, London, BBC Books, 1993. Six apocryphal stories adapted by the author from his BBC radio series. "The Wandering Corpse", "The Battersea Worm", "The Paddington Witch,", "The Phantom Organ", "The Devil's Tunnel" and "The Horror of Hanging Wood".

Thomson, June. *The Secret Files of Sherlock Holmes*, London: Constable, 1990. Seven stories based on the unchronicled cases, all prefixed "The Case of . . .": "The Vanishing Head-Waiter", "The Amateur Mendicants", "The Remarkable Worm". "The Exalted Client", "The Notorious Canary Trainer", "The Itinerant Yeggman" and "The Abandoned Lighthouse". This and the next two volumes contain some of the best Sherlockian pastiches and have the ring of authenticity, though several are clearly apocryphal.

Thomson, June. *The Secret Chronicles of Sherlock Holmes*, London: Constable, 1992. Seven more stories: "The Paradol Chamber", "The Hammersmith Wonder", "The Maplestead Magpie", "The Harley Street Specialist", "The Old Russian Woman", "The Camberwell Poisoning" and "The Sumatran Rat".

Thomson, June. *The Secret Journals of Sherlock Holmes*, London: Constable, 1993. Seven further cases: "The Millionaire's Persecution", "The Colonel's Madness", "The Addleton Tragedy", "The Friesland Outrage", "The Shopkeeper's Terror", "The Smith-Mortimer Succession" and "The Maupertuis Scandal".

Thomson, June. *Holmes and Watson*. London, Constable, 1995. A well considered biography of the duo based solely on the writings of Watson.

Whitaker, Arthur. "The Case of the Man Who Was Wanted", *Cosmpolitan*, August 1948; also reprinted as "The Adventure of the Sheffield Banker". A story once mistakenly believed to have been by Conan Doyle but which is clearly apocryphal.

Williamson, J.N. (editor). *The Illustrious Client's Case-Book* (edited with H.B. Williams), Indianapolis, Illustrious Clients, 1948, and *The Illustrious Client's Second Case-Book*, Indianapolis, Illustrious Clients, 1949. A collection of pastiches of spurious authenticity. Include recreations of "The Terrible Death of Crosby the Banker" and "The Adventure of the Politician, the Lighthouse, and the Trained Cormorant."

Wilson, Alan. "The Adventure of the Tired Captain", *Sherlock Holmes Journal*, Winter 1958–Spring 1959; and "The Adventure of the Paradol Chamber", *Sherlock Holmes Journal*, Spring–Winter 1961. Two faithful and possibly authentic recreations of unrecorded cases.

Wolfe, Sebastian (editor). *The Misadventures of Sherlock Holmes*, London, Xanadu, 1989. Anthology of fourteen apocryphal pastiches, parodies and spoofs. All are reprints except "The Affair of the Midnight Midget" by Ardath Mayhar.

THE CONTRIBUTORS

Stephen Baxter, *"The Adventure of the Inertial Adjustor"*. Since his first novel, *Raft*, in 1991, Stephen Baxter (b. 1957) has established himself in the front rank of British writers of science fiction. His related novels include *Timelike Infinity, Flux, Ring* and the collection *Vacuum Diagrams*. One of his most popular books was *The Time Ships*, a sequel to H.G. Wells's *The Time Machine* and it is Baxter's interest in Wells that resulted in his story in this collection, which is a fully fledged murder mystery and not science fiction.

John Betancourt, *"The Adventure of the Amateur Mendicant Society"*. John Betancourt (b. 1963) is an American author and publisher whose Wildside Press is dedicated to producing quality books of fantasy and supernatural fiction. His own books have been mostly science fiction or fantasy, though *Rememory* contained a strong mystery element. Other novels include *Rogue Pirate, The Blind Archer* and *Johnny Zed*, plus the story collection *Slab's Tavern and Other Uncanny Tales*. He is currently working on a series of fantastic adventure novels featuring the Greek hero Hercules, starting with *The Wrath of Poseidon*.

Eric Brown, *"The Vanishing of the Atkinsons"*. Brown (b. 1960) is best known for his science fiction, much of which has appeared in the British magazine *Interzone*. Several of his best stories have been collected as *The Time-Lapsed Man* and *Blue Shifting*. His novels include *Meridian Days* and *Engineman*.

Simon Clark, *"The Adventure of the Fallen Star"*. Clark (b. 1958) has rapidly established himself as a writer of serious horror novels, the books exploring much deeper aspects of the human psyche than the titles – *Nailed by the Heart, Blood Crazy, Darker* and *King Blood* – convey. Born and bred in Yorkshire where he still lives with his wife and two children, Clark worked for several years in local government before becoming a full-time writer in 1993.

Basil Copper, *"The Adventure of the Persecuted Painter"*. Copper (b. 1924) is a prolific writer of thrillers and supernatural fiction. He is as popular amongst devotees of hard-boiled American detective fiction, with his long-running Mike Faraday series of novels, as he is amongst the gothic-horror brigade with his excellent brooding novels *Necropolis* and *The Black Death*. Closer to Holmes, Copper continued the adventures of Solar Pons started by August Derleth in 1929 in emulation of Sherlock Holmes. Copper's Pons is, if anything, even closer to the character of Holmes, perhaps because Copper has a deeper affinity with the fogbound streets of Victorian London. His Pons collections are *The Dossier of Solar Pons*, *The Further Adventures of Solar Pons*, *The Secret Files of Solar Pons*, *Some Uncollected Cases of Solar Pons*, *The Exploits of Solar Pons* and *The Recollections of Solar Pons*.

Peter Crowther, *"The Adventure of the Touch of God"*. Crowther (b. 1949) is a prolific British writer and editor who hails from Yorkshire, the home of many contributors to this volume. He made a name with his series of anthologies based on superstitions which began with the award-winning *Narrow Houses*, and he has also produced an anthology of stories about angels, *Heaven Sent*. His recent work includes the well-received novel *Escardy Gap*, written with James Lovegrove, and the anthologies *Destination Unknown* and *Tales in Time*. His first story collection, *The Longest Single Note*, is in the works.

David Stuart Davies, *"The Darlington Substitution Scandal"*. Davies is a noted Sherlockian, co-founder and Co-President of The Northern Musgraves Sherlock Holmes Society and editor of its journal the *Sherlock Holmes Gazette*. He has written two Sherlock Holmes novels, *The Tangled Skein* and *Sherlock Holmes and the Hentzau Affair*, plus the assiduously researched survey *Holmes of the Movies*, and his biography of Jeremy Brett, *Bending the Willow*.

Michael Doyle, *"The Legacy of Rachel Howells"*. To answer the obvious question, Michael Doyle (b. 1930) is not related to Sir Arthur, at least not so far as he's been able to trace, though there does seem to be a family resemblance. Although born and educated in England, Doyle settled in Canada in 1956 and has Canadian nationality. He is by profession an export trade consultant and is recognized as one of the world authorities on international trade and letters of credit. He shares Conan Doyle's interest in boxing and has even written a monograph called *A Study in Sparring* about Sherlock Holmes, the Prize Ring and the Corbett-Fitzsimmons fight.

Martin Edwards, *"The Case of the Suicidal Lawyer"*. Martin Edwards (b. 1955) is a practicing solicitor and has used his experience as the background for his series of novels about Liverpool solicitor and amateur detective Harry Devlin. The series began with *All the Lonely People* and there's been a novel a year ever since. Edwards has also edited the crime anthology *Northern Blood* and others in a regionally related series.

Zakaria Erzinçlioglu, *"The Adventure of the Bulgarian Diplomat".* Dr Erzinçlioglu is a practising forensic scientist. He has been working on criminal cases (mostly murder) for over twenty years, investigating over five hundred in Britain and abroad. He was formerly Senior Research Associate at Cambridge University and, subsequently, Director of the Forensic Science Research Centre at Durham University. He is now an Honorary Lecturer at London University. He is working on *Evidence*, a book which looks at the interpretation of evidence in criminal trials and historical events.

L. B. Greenwood, *"Five Minutes Past Midnight".* Lillian Beth Greenwood (b. 1932) is a Canadian writer who lives not too far from Michael Doyle and Barbara Roden. Her first novel, *The Street Sparrows*, is a historical set in the Victorian era – she describes it as a female version of Oliver Twist. She has also written three Sherlock Holmes novels listed in the appendix, and is a member of the Vancouver Holmes organization known as the Stormy Petrels.

Lois H. Gresh, *"The Adventure of the Parisian Gentleman"* with Robert Weinberg. Gresh works in the computer industry as a programmer and systems analyst and has written hundreds of technical manuals and related texts. She is the proprietor of Technohell, Inc., which designs and codes corporate websites, software and systems. Oh what fun Holmes would have had with the Internet! She has sold many short science fiction and horror stories and her first novel, *The Termination Node*, written with Weinberg, is in the works. It's the first of a series of near-future computer technothrillers.

Claire Griffen, *"The Case of the Incumbent Invalid".* Claire Griffen is a new writer who has previously appeared in *Classical Whodunnits* and the magazine *Boggle*. She is Australian, and spent several years as an actress and dramatist before turning to writing fantasy and mystery stories. She wrote a Sherlock Holmes play in 1986 which saw several performances with an Adelaide theatre repertory company.

Edward D. Hoch, *"Vittoria, the Circus Belle".* Edward Hoch (b. 1930) is a phenomenally prolific American short-story writer with over seven hundred to his credit. He has created many fascinating detectives, including Captain Leopold, Dr Sam Hawthorne, Nick Velvet, Ben Snow and Simon Ark. His stories appear regularly in *Ellery Queen's Mystery Magazine* and *Alfred Hitchcock's Mystery Magazine* but only a few have made it into individual story collections. Well worth tracking down is his Captain Leopold volume, *Leopold's Way*, his Simon Ark series, *The Judges of Hades, City of Brass* and *The Quests of Simon Ark*, the Nick Velvet books *The Spy and the Thief* and *The Thefts of Nick Velvet*, whilst a few of his Sam Hawthorne stories have been collected as *Diagnosis: Impossible*. His more general mystery fiction will be found in *The Night My Friend*. Hoch has written several Sherlock Holmes stories including "The Return of the Speckled Band" in *The New Adventures of Sherlock Holmes*, "The Manor House Case" in *Resurrected Holmes* and "The Christmas Client" in *Holmes for the Holidays*.

Roger Johnson, *"The Adventure of the Grace Chalice"*. Johnson (b. 1947) is a noted Sherlock Holmes afficianado and writer of ghost stories. It was through Sherlock Holmes that Roger met his wife, Jean. He was the founder of the Newsletter of the Sherlock Holmes Society and writes regularly on matters Sherlockian. A small private press produced his first collection of ghost stories, *Deep Things Out of Darkness* in 1987, and a more extensive volume, *A Ghostly Crew*, is under production.

H.R.F. Keating, *"The Adventure of the Suffering Ruler"*. Keating (b. 1926) is the renowned author of the novels featuring Inspector Ghote of the Bombay CID, which began with *The Perfect Murder* in 1964 and is still going strong. He was won many awards and has compiled the invaluable reference works of the crime and mystery fiction field *Whodunit?*, *Agatha Christie: First Lady of Crime* and *Crime Writers: Reflections on Crime Fiction*. He has also written *Sherlock Holmes: the Man and His World* and two Holmes pastiches, this story and "A Trifling Affair".

David Langford, *"The Repulsive Story of the Red Leech"*. Langford (b. 1953) is a popular writer of science fiction, not averse to the occasional spoof. His first book-length work, *An Account of a Meeting with Denizens of Another World, 1871*, issued under the alias of William Robert Loosley fooled many people into believing it was a genuine Victorian account of a close encounter with aliens. His science-fiction novels include *The Space Eater* and *Earthdoom!* (with John Grant) plus the clever satire on the scientific establishment *The Leaky Establishment,* drawn from Langford's own direct experiences.

F. Gwynplaine MacIntyre, *"The Enigma of the Warwickshire Vortex"*. F. Gwynplaine MacIntyre – Froggy to his friends – is a Scottish-born, Australian-raised, American-resident author who is a fund of knowledge on a wide range of esoterica, as his story reveals. He is the author of the excellent Victorian science-fiction novel *The Woman Between the Worlds,* as well as several pseudonymous novels and many stories for the science-fiction magazines.

Michael Moorcock, *"The Adventure of the Dorset Street Lodger"*. Moorcock (b. 1939) scarcely needs an introduction. He was one of the prime movers in the reshaping of science fiction in the mid-sixties, with his editorship of *New Worlds* and his Jerry Cornelius series of stories, and is one of the most popular writers of heroic fantasy with his many series featuring the various incarnations of the Eternal Champion, the most famous being Elric of Melniboné. Moorcock has long been fascinated with the end of the Victorian era and a number of books, most notably the Oswald Bastable series, sought to recreate an alternate Victorian world, whilst his Dancers at the End of Time sequence, also reflected that *fin-de-siècle* mood. It was clearly only a matter of time before Moorcock turned his creative energies to Sherlock Holmes, and I'm delighted he did.

Amy Myers, *"The Adventure of the Faithful Retainer"*. Amy Myers is best known for her books featuring the master-chef with the remarkable deductive powers, Auguste Didier who first appeared in *Murder in Pug's Parlour* in 1987 and has built up a dedicated following. The stories are contemporary with Sherlock Holmes and there is little doubt that the two would have been acquainted

Barrie Roberts, *"The Mystery of the Addleton Curse"*. Roberts (b. 1939) is a criminal lawyer who lives in the West Midlands but was born and raised in Hampshire. He is a criminal lawyer, although he has also worked as a journalist, computer programmer and lecturer, most recently lecturing on ghosts and unsolved mysteries. He is a tireless Sherlockian having developed his own chronology of the cases into which he has woven three novels to date, *Sherlock Holmes and the Railway Maniac, Sherlock Holmes and the Devil's Grail and Sherlock Holmes and the Man from Hell.*

Barbara Roden, *"The Adventure of the Suspect Servant"*. Barbara Roden (b. 1963) is a Canadian enthusiast of the ghost and mystery story who helped found the first Canadian Holmes society west of the Rocky Mountains, the Stormy Petrels of British Columbia, in 1987. With her husband, Christopher Roden, she is joint organizer of the Arthur Conan Doyle Society. They also operate the specialist ghost-story press Ash-Tree Press and the Calabash Press devoted to books about Sherlock Holmes. "The Adventure of the Suspect Servant" won a pastiche contest sponsored by the Bootmakers of Toronto in 1989 but is published here in a slightly revised form for the first time.

Denis O. Smith, "*The Adventure of the Silver Buckle*". Smith (b. 1948) is a dedicated Sherlockian scholar who has produced a number of Holmesian pastiches starting with *The Adventure of the Purple Hand*, issued from his own Diogenes Publications. All are listed in Appendix II and have been reissued by Calabash Press with a new story as *The Chronicles of Sherlock Holmes*. He also has a passion for old maps and Victorian railways, both of which are germane to Holmes's adventures. Although a Yorkshireman by birth he now lives in Norfolk with his wife and three daughters.

Guy N. Smith, "*The Case of the Sporting Squire*". Smith (b. 1939) was both a bank clerk and a gamekeeper before he settled down to full-time writing in 1975. He is probably still best remembered for his early gruesome horror novels such as *The Sucking Pit, The Slime Beast* and the best-selling *Night of the Crabs*, and though most of his sixty or more books are horror fiction, he has produced other material including westerns and, rather surprisingly, film novelizations of *Snow White and the Seven Dwarfs, Sleeping Beauty* and *Song of the South*, as well as books for children under the alias Jonathan Guy. He began his writing career selling mystery and horror short stories to the *London Mystery Magazine* and has long been a devotee of Sherlock Holmes.

Peter Tremayne, "*The Affray at the Kildare Street Club*". Peter Tremayne (b. 1943) is the pseudonym of Celtic scholar and historian Peter Berresford Ellis who, under his own name, has written many books tracing the history and myth of the Celts, including *The Celtic Empire, Celt and Saxon* and *Celt and Greek*. In the fiction field he established an early reputation for his books of horror and fantasy, particularly his Dracula series collected in the omnibus *Dracula Lives!*, and his Lan-Kern series based on Cornish mythology, which began with *The Fires of Lan-Kern*. He is now, perhaps, best known for his series of historical mysteries featuring the seventh-century Irish Advocate, Sister Fidelma, in the books

Absolution by Murder, Shroud for an Archbishop, Suffer Little Children, The Subtle Serpent and *The Spider's Web*.

Robert Weinberg, "*The Adventure of the Parisian Gentleman*" with Lois H. Gresh. Weinberg (b. 1946) is an American bookdealer, collector and author who has written a number of novels of fantastic fiction. He has produced several featuring occult detective Alex Werner, starting with *The Devil's Auction*, plus a sequence of humorous fantasy novels which began with *A Logical Magician*.

Derek Wilson, "*The Bothersome Business of the Dutch Nativity*". Derek Wilson has written over thirty books of history, biography and fiction, including the acclaimed family biographies, *Rothschild: A Story of Wealth and Power* and *The Astors 1763–1922: Landscape with Millionaires*. He also also written two fascinating books on the circumnavigation of the globe, *The World Encompassed – Drake's Voyage 1577–1580* and *The Circumnavigators*. In the world of mystery fiction he has created the character of Tim Lacy, international art connoisseur and investigator whose cases have been chronicled in *The Triarchs, The Dresden Text* and *The Hellfire Papers*.